"Ross is a powerful and enduring creative genius."
—*Affaire de Coeur*

"One of the best storytellers the genre
has produced."
—Amazon.com

HOMEPLACE

"Like cherished silver, *Homeplace* just shines."

—*Romantic Times*

"You can really go home again and there's no better guide for the journey than *Homeplace* and JoAnn Ross. . . ."

—CompuServe Romance Reviews

FAR HARBOR

"[E]nchanting and warmhearted. The lives of these special people are played out beautifully on the pages of this touching and exceptional novel."

—*Romantic Times*

"A powerfully moving story of intense emotional depth, satisfying on every level. You won't want to leave this family."

—CompuServe Romance Reviews

"This story is a wonderful relationship drama in which JoAnn Ross splendidly describes love the second time around."

—Harriet Klausner

Books by JoAnn Ross

Homeplace
Far Harbor
Fair Haven
Legends Lake
Blue Bayou
River Road
Magnolia Moon
Out of the Mist
Out of the Blue
Out of the Storm
Blaze

Available from POCKET BOOKS

JoAnn Ross

Homeplace
and
Far Harbor

POCKET BOOKS
New York London Toronto Sydney

POCKET BOOKS, a division of Simon & Schuster, Inc.
1230 Avenue of the Americas, New York, NY 10020

Homeplace copyright © 1999 by JoAnn Ross
Far Harbor copyright © 2000 by The Ross Family Trust
created 10/23/97

ISBN-13: 978-1-4165-1715-3
ISBN-10:   1-4165-1715-4

This Pocket Books trade paperback edition November 2005

10 9 8 7 6 5 4 3 2 1

POCKET and colophon are registered trademarks of Simon & Schuster, Inc.

For information regarding special discounts for bulk purchases, please contact Simon & Schuster Special Sales at 1-800-456-6798 or business@simonandschuster.com

Homeplace and *Far Harbor* were previously published individually by Pocket Books.

Manufactured in the United States of America

HOMEPLACE

During the writing of *Homeplace*, I've had reason to be grateful for a number of special people: Caroline Tolley, for her keen eye and thoughtful editorial advice; Lauren McKenna, who smooths the way and is a joy to work with; Damaris Rowland, the wisest, most supportive agent in the business; as well as the terrific members of RWA—Online.

Also—my son, Patrick; his wife, Lisa; their wonder daughter, Marisa; and the newest family miracle, Parker Ryan Ross, who handled early obstacles with a great deal more aplomb than his elders.

And, once again, and always, to Jay, the grand love of my life.

❦ 1 ❧

Coldwater Cove, Washington

It was a damn three-ring circus. And Olympic County sheriff Jack O'Halloran had gotten stuck with the job of ringmaster. Despite the cold spring drizzle, the hillside was covered with people, many carrying cameras. Some bolder, or more curious, individuals pressed as close as they could to the white police barricades. Kids were running all over the place, laughing, shrieking, chasing one another, having themselves a dandy time. The mood couldn't have been any more electric if a bunch of TV stars had suddenly shown up on Washington's Olympic Peninsula to tape an episode of *NYPD Blue*.

Ignoring the rain dripping off the brim of his hat, Jack scowled at the vans bearing the names and logos of television stations from as far away as Spokane. Which wasn't all that surprising. After all, Coldwater Cove had always been a peaceful town. So peaceful, in fact, it didn't even have its own police department, the city fathers choosing instead to pay for protection from the county force. Crime consisted mainly of the routine Saturday night drunk and disorderly, jaywalking, calls about barking dogs, and last month a customer had walked off with the ballpoint pen from Neil Olson's You-Pump-It Gas 'N Save. It definitely wasn't every day three teenage girls barricaded themselves in their group home and refused to come out.

Meanwhile, Dr. Ida Lindstrom, their court-appointed guardian and owner of the landmark Victorian house, had apparently set off this mini–crime wave when she'd been taken to the hospital after falling off a kitchen stool. Although the information was sketchy, from what Jack could determine, when a probation officer had arrived to haul the unsupervised kids back to the juvenile detention center, Ida had held an inflammatory press conference from her hospital bed, adding fuel to an already dangerously volatile situation by instructing the girls to "batten down the hatches."

Having grown up in Coldwater Cove, Jack knew Ida to be a good, hardworking woman. Salt of the earth, a pillar of the community, and unrelentingly generous. During her days as the town's only general practitioner, she'd delivered scores of babies—including him. Since lumbering was a dangerous business, she'd also probably set more broken arms than any doctor in the state, and whenever she lost a patient—whether from illness, accident, or merely old age—she never missed a funeral.

She'd inevitably show up at the family's home after the internment with a meatloaf. Not one person in Coldwater Cove had ever had the heart to tell her that her customary donation to the potluck funeral supper was as hard as a brick and about as tasty as sawdust. Ida Lindstrom had many talents, but cooking wasn't one of them. Six months ago, when they'd buried Big John O'Halloran, Jack's father who'd dropped dead of a heart attack while hiking a glacier on nearby Mount Olympus, Jack's mother had surreptitiously put the heavy hunk of mystery meat and unidentifiable spices out on the back porch for the dogs. Who wouldn't eat it, either.

Jack admired the way Ida had taken to opening her home to at-risk teenagers at a time when so many of her contemporaries were traveling around the country in motor homes, enjoying their retirement and spending their children's inheritances. But the plan, agreed to by the court, the probation officer, and Ida herself, dammit, had been for the retired doctor to provide the kids with a stable environment, teach them responsibility and coax them back onto the straight and narrow. Not turn them into Junior revolutionaries

"I still think we ought to break down the damn door," a gung ho state police officer insisted for the third time in the past hour. Jack suspected the proposed frontal attack stemmed from an eagerness to try out the armored assault vehicle the state had recently acquired at a surplus government military auction.

"You've been watching too many old Jimmy Cagney movies on the *Late Show*," Jack said. "It's overkill. They're only juveniles."

Juveniles whose cockamamie misbehavior was proving a major pain in the ass. The standoff was entering its sixth hour, television vans were parked all the way down the hill, the satellite systems on their roofs pointed upward, as if trying to receive messages from outer space. Jack figured he was a shoe-in to be the lead story on the six o'clock news all over the Pacific Northwest. Hell, if he didn't get the girls out pretty soon, they may even make the national morning programs. And while Eleanor O'Halloran would undoubtedly be tickled pink to see her only son on television, the idea didn't suit Jack at all.

"They're not just your run of the mill juveniles," the lantern-jawed officer reminded him unnecessarily. "They're juvenile delinquents."

"Minor league ones. The most any of them are guilty of is truancy and shoplifting. Want to guess how a bunch of grown men wearing combat gear staging a military assault on three little girls would play on TV?"

"Crime's crime," another cop from neighboring Jefferson County grumbled. Although the standoff wasn't occurring in his jurisdiction, that hadn't stopped him from dropping by for a look-see.

He wasn't alone; Kitsap, Island, Clallam, and King counties were also well represented. Even the Quinault and Skokomish reservations had sent uniformed men to offer backup and gain experience in hostage situations. Not that this was exactly a hostage situation, since the girls were all alone in the house. The assembled cops were having themselves a grand old time. Jack was not.

"He's right," another cop agreed. "You may not consider shoplifting a punishable offense in your county, Sheriff, but in my jurisdiction, we view teenage malfeasance as a slippery slope to more serious crimes."

"Got a point there," Jack agreed dryly. "One day a kid's swiping a tube of Mango orange lip gloss from a Payless Drugstore and the next day she's toting an Uzi and holding up the Puget Sound National Bank."

He took the cellular phone from its dashboard holder and dialed the Lindstrom house again. The first time he'd called, the oldest girl, Shawna, had informed him that Ida had instructed her not to speak to him. Then promptly hung up. From that point on, all he'd gotten was a busy signal, suggesting they'd taken the phone off the hook. And dammit, apparently still hadn't put it back on.

"There's always tear gas," one of the Olympic County deputies suggested.

"In case you've forgotten, one of those girls is pregnant. I'm not willing to risk harming any unborn babies."

"So what do you propose to do?" a grim-faced man asked. His belted tan raincoat with the snazzy Banana Republic epaulets on the shoulders made him stand out from the local crowd clad in parkas and Gore-Tex jackets. He'd introduced himself as being from Olympia, an assistant to the governor. Unsurprisingly, the state's chief executive was concerned about the public relations aspect of this situation.

Jack shrugged and thought of his six-year-old daughter. He imagined how he'd want the cops to respond if Amy took it into her head to barricade herself in their house.

"They aren't going anywhere." They'd also refused to speak to anyone but Ida. Deciding the contrary old woman would only get them more stirred up, he'd instructed the hospital to remove the phone from her room. "The way I see it, the best thing to do is wait them out. For however long it takes."

No one argued. But the grumbles from the assembled lawmen told Jack that he was all alone, out on an increasingly risky limb.

New York City

The mob began to gather early. The senior citizens chanted slogans and marched in circles, holding their placards high. One of their leaders bellowed through a bullhorn, reminding them that this was a war. They all cheered. Some waved their signs, others their fists.

By the time Raine Cantrell walked out of the federal courthouse a little before noon, the protesters were primed for battle. Anxious for blood.

"I think I've just discovered how it feels to go diving for sharks without the metal cage," she murmured.

She'd been warned there'd be a demonstration, but given the demographics of the plaintiffs in the class action lawsuit, she hadn't expected such an unruly mob. The cacophonous chants echoed off nearby buildings; catcalls and belligerent shouts rang out over the blare of car horns.

The street was jammed with illegally parked vans bearing the insignias of all three major networks, along with CNN and various local television stations; thick black cables snaked across the sidewalk and the crowd of reporters, photographers and cameramen jockeyed for position.

"Christ. Every reporter for every half-assed paper and television station in the country must have shown up for this circus," her client, Rex Murdock, muttered.

During the months they'd worked together preparing a defense, the CEO and principal stockholder of Odessa Oil Company had revealed himself to be a man accustomed to controlling everything and everyone around him. He was brash, rough-mannered, impatient as hell, and handsome, in a rough-hewn way. All the women at Choate, Plimpton, Wells & Sullivan would inevitably cease work whenever he strode through the offices, the wedged heels of his lizard skin cowboy boots tapping a purposeful tattoo on the Italian-marble flooring. Even sixty-four-year-old Harriet Farraday, who'd worked as comptroller at the law firm since the Stone Age and had a dozen grandchildren, had taken notice.

"Why, he's a man's man, dear," Harriet had explained one day when Raine had questioned the effect her client had on seemingly the entire female staff. "You don't find many of those anymore in these so-called enlightened years." She'd made a little sound of disgust as she looked around the office. "Especially around here."

"You'd think the bastards would have better stories to chase than this half-baked, bush-league case," that man's man was grumbling now.

"Perhaps we should go back into the building and try leaving by the rear door," a second-year associate attorney from the firm's investment division suggested. His face was pale, his anxiety, evident. Raine wondered if he was rethinking his decision to enter the glamorous world of big-city corporate law. She also decided that as bright as he admittedly was, he wouldn't pass Harriet's male litmus test.

Raine's legal team was made up of a clutch of associate attorneys, a paralegal whose job it was to hand over briefs with the precision and speed of a transplant-team surgical nurse, and various dark-suited minions who'd been at her client's beck and call during the past three weeks of the trial.

Standing between them and the elderly crowd was a reassuring wall of blue. The police were grasping riot sticks she suspected none wanted to use. After all, video of burly cops beating up Grandpa and Grandma headlining the nightly news would definitely undermine the mayor's effort to refurbish the city's image.

"Slinking out the back way would make it look as if we were ashamed of our case," she said.

Okay, she may have made a slight miscalculation regarding the emotional impact of what, had it not been for the millions of dollars involved, should have been a routine contract case. But her Grandmother Ida had taught Raine that nothing could be solved by sticking your tail between your legs and running away from a problem. "Perhaps I should stop long enough to answer some questions."

"No offense, Raine. But I'm not real sure that'll calm them down," Murdock warned.

"They're definitely in a feeding frenzy. But avoiding the issue won't make it go away. We may have won in court, but believe me, Rex, the media's going to play this as a David-and-Goliath story. And from the average person's point of view, you're going to be cast as a malicious, greedy giant."

"Remind me once again why I should care?"

A low burn began to simmer just below her ribcage. Raine ignored it. "Do the two little words *Exxon Valdez* ring a bell?"

His scowl deepened.

"I'll just try to defuse the situation a bit," she said, taking his nonreply as begrudging consent. "Before it gets totally out of hand.

"Hell, you've handled this case damn well so far." He did not add, as Raine suspected he might once have—*for a woman.* "Might as well let you ride it out to the whistle."

Raine realized this was a major concession on his part. A wildcatter who'd struck it rich back when the gushing black gold could put a man on easy street for life, Rex Murdock did not surrender the reins easily. In fact, there'd been more than one occasion in court when she'd seriously wished the bar association guidelines allowed attorneys to muzzle their clients.

They'd reached the police barricade. *Show time.* Raine willed herself to calm as she faced down the crowd. The motor drives of the still cameras whirred, sounding like the wings of birds fighting against the wind that was ruffling her chin-length brown hair.

It was a cold day that gave lie to the fact that according to the calendar, spring had sprung; atop the building the flags snapped loudly in the wind and the taste of impending rain rode the brisk air. Foolishly believing the wake-up forecast predicting sunny skies, Raine had gone to work in a lightweight charcoal gray suit and white silk blouse that allowed the wind to cut through her like a knife.

"Ms. Cantrell!" A sleek blond woman sensibly clad in a black trench coat shoved a microphone past one of the cops. Raine recognized her as an attorney turned legal correspondent for CNN. She also occasionally showed up on *Nightline*. "What is your response to those who say your client is snatching bread from the mouths of the elderly?"

Raine looked straight into the camera lens. "I would simply reiterate what the court has decreed. The plaintiffs' claim was rejected because my client adhered to United States law by properly informing all employees, upon the signing of their employment agreement, that the company reserved the right to alter or terminate their retirement benefit package at any time."

As her response was answered by a roaring tidal wave of boos, Raine's attention drifted momentarily to an elderly woman sitting in an electric wheelchair. The woman was dressed in a navy blue fleece warm-up suit and high-topped sneakers bearing a red swoosh. Her white hair had been permed into puffs resembling cotton balls and her apple cheeks were ruddy from the cold. A black helium-filled balloon bearing the message *Shame* in bold red letters floated upward from a white string tied to the back of the chair.

Strangely, as Raine looked down at the elderly protestor, the white curls appeared to turn to salt-and-pepper gray, and the apple-round face morphed to a narrow, more chiseled one that was strikingly familiar. Impossibly, Raine could have sworn she was looking down at her grandmother.

She blinked, relieved when the unsettling hallucination vanished. It was not the first such incident she'd had in the past few months. But they seemed to be getting more vivid, and decidedly more personal.

"Excuse me?" she asked a reporter whom she belatedly realized had been speaking to her.

"Jeff Martin, *Wall Street Journal*." The intense young man wearing wire-framed glasses impatiently reintroduced himself. "Would your client care to comment on the Gray Panthers' latest press release claiming that by cutting off access to health care for retirees and their spouses who are not yet qualified for Medicare, the defendant—and you, by association—are risking the lives of our nation's grandparents?"

This question was followed by a roar from the crowd. When the fanciful vision of Ida Lindstrom's disapproving face wavered in front of her eyes again, Raine shook her head to clear it. Then forced her uncharacteristically wandering mind back to the reporter's question.

"No offense intended to the Gray Panthers, but not only is that accusation an overstatement of the facts of the case, it's blatantly false, Mr. Martin. My client"—she purposefully avoided using the reporter's negative term *defendant*—"offers one of the most generous retirement packages in the industry."

The boos intensified. Protesters shouted out rude suggestions as to what Odessa Oil—Rex Murdock in particular—could do with its retirement package.

"But Odessa Oil also has a responsibility to its stockholders, many of whom are those same retirees." Determined to make her point, Raine doggedly continued, fighting back a drumming headache as she raised her voice to be heard over the crowd. "The decrease in crude-oil prices worldwide has left

the company with no option but to discontinue free
health-care benefits to those who opt for early retirement. As a federal court has determined today they
are well within their rights to do."

The boos reached the decibel of the jackhammer
that had begun pounding away inside her head. The
placards were waving like pom poms at a football
game. Someone in the crowd threw an egg that
broke at Raine's feet, spattering her black suede Italian pumps with bright yellow yolk and gelatinous
white. The attack drew enthusiastic applause from
the coalition of protesters even as two of the cops
waded into the crowd to find the assailant.

"You've given it your best shot, Raine. But these
folks are flat-out nuts." Murdock had to yell in
Raine's ear to be heard. "We're like Crockett and
Bowie at the Battle of the Alamo. Let's get the hell
out of here."

The icy wind picked up. The adrenaline rush of
her courtroom victory had begun to wear off. Fearing that the next egg—or something even more dangerous—might hurt more than her shoes, Raine was
ready to call it a day.

With two of New York City's finest clearing a path,
Raine and the others began making their way to the
black stretch limousine double-parked in the street
beside an *Eyewitness News* van. They were pursued
by the pack of reporters who shouted out questions
like bullets from automatic rifles. Without waiting
for the uniformed driver to get out of the car, one
of the minions rushed to open the back door.

The limo, boasting two televisions, a fully stocked
bar, and wide leather seats, was the height of comfort. The first time she'd ridden in the lush womb

on wheels, Raine had felt exactly like Cinderella on her way to the ball. Today, although she'd never considered herself even a remotely fanciful woman, Raine imagined she could actually hear her grandmother's voice.

"Never forget girls," she'd instructed Raine and her sister on more than one occasion while they'd been growing up under her Victorian slate roof, "it's a lot easier for a camel to get into heaven than a rich man."

The saying was only one in her grandmother's seemingly endless repertoire of malapropisms. The last time Raine had heard it had been six years ago, the weekend she'd graduated from law school, when she and her grandmother had shared a grilled-portabello-mushroom-and-feta-cheese pizza at Harvard Law's Harkbox Café.

She glanced out the tinted back window at the protesters, watching them grow smaller and smaller. While the men rehashed the trial, Raine wondered why she didn't feel like joining in the conversation.

She should be jubilant. After all, she was the one who'd brought Odessa Oil into the firm in the first place, which had bolstered her reputation as a rainmaker. Today's verdict should put her on the fast track for partner in one of the largest, most prestigious law firms in the country. It was precisely what she'd been working toward for years, ever since she'd grabbed hold of the brass ring that had landed her a summer intern job at Choate, Plimpton, Wells & Sullivan. It was her personal Holy Grail and it was finally in sight.

She was intelligent, articulate, a former member of the oldest, most respected law review in the coun-

try, and currently a successful litigator who'd put
the tiny northwestern town of Coldwater Cove,
Washington behind her. She was a winner in a city
that lionized victory. She had a three-thousand-dol-
lar-a-month apartment furnished in sleek Italian
leather, brass, and marble, and since the firm paid
the tab for hired cars to drive their attorneys home
at the end of the admittedly long workdays, she
hadn't stepped foot on the subway since her arrival
in New York.

Life was nearly perfect. So what the hell was
wrong with her?

Raine rubbed her cheeks to soothe tensed facial
muscles and sat up straighter in an attempt to untangle the knots in her back muscles. When the simmering flames began burning beneath her ribcage,
she took out the ever ready roll of antacids and
popped two into her mouth.

She'd become more and more restless these past
weeks. And, although each night she'd fall into bed,
physically and mentally exhausted, she'd been unable to sleep. She'd conveniently blamed it on the
gallons of coffee she'd drunk while preparing for the
trial, but if she were to be perfectly honest, her uncharacteristic distraction and anxiety, laced with a
vague feeling of discontent, had been stirring inside
her even before she'd begun preparing Odessa Oil's
appeal.

As she chewed on the chalky tablets, which were
advertised to taste like mint but didn't, Raine decided that her only problem was that she'd been
working too hard for too long. After all, one-
hundred-hour workweeks were common for those
trudging along the yellow brick road to partnership.

Especially litigators, who tended to do the lion's share of the firm's traveling.

At first, after escaping the grinding poverty of law school, she'd been excited by the prospect of seeing the country at the firm's—or, more precisely, the clients'—expense. She'd looked forward to the frequent-flier perks attorneys at smaller firms could only dream about: being met at the airport gate by a uniformed driver holding a sign bearing her name, automatic hotel upgrades, and first-class airline tickets.

In reality, most of the time the only part of the country she was able to see was from thirty-thousand feet in the air. During visits to clients' cities, she tended to spend her entire time in airports, hotels, and office conference rooms and jet lag had become a way of life.

But life was filled with trade offs, Raine reminded herself with a stiff mental shake as the limousine wove its way through the snarl of midtown traffic. And unlike so many others, hers came with a six-figure salary, health, life, and disability insurance, a 401(k) plan, bar association dues, and in the event she were ever crazy enough to try to juggle a demanding career and motherhood, paid parental leave.

She just needed a breather, she assured herself as she felt the familiar steel bands tighten around her head. She reached into her briefcase, took out a bottle of aspirin and swallowed two of them dry as she'd learned to do over the past months. On afterthought, she swallowed a third.

A short break to recharge her batteries would be just what the doctor ordered, she considered, picking up her thoughts where she'd left off. Perhaps it was time to take that long-overdue vacation she'd been planning—and putting off—for years. The one where she'd spend several sun-drenched days lounging beside a sparkling blue tropical lagoon while handsome hunks delivered mai tais and rubbed coconut oil all over her body.

This time the image that floated into Raine's mind was not one of her grandmother, but of herself, clad in a floaty, off-the-shoulder sundress emblazoned with tropical flowers. Not that she owned such a romantic dress, but this was, after all, a fantasy, so Raine wasn't about to quibble. She was strolling hand in hand with a drop-dead gorgeous man on a romantic, moonlit beach.

Music drifted on the perfumed night air as he lowered his head to kiss her. His mouth was a mere whisper away from hers when the rude blare of a siren shattered the blissful fantasy.

This time she was really going to do it, Raine vowed as a fire engine roared past the limo. While the others continued to gloat, she took out her Day-Timer and made a note to call a travel agent.

As soon as she cleared her calendar. Sometime in the next decade, she amended as she skimmed the pages filled with notations and appointments. If she was lucky.

2

Coldwater Cove

The continual drizzle finally drove the reporters back into their vans and the cops into their units. The sky over Puget Sound was as dark as a wet wool blanket and fog curled thickly around Ida Lindstrom's house. Jack telephoned the girls again, as he'd been doing every thirty minutes. When the only answer was a busy tone, he figured the damn phone was still off the hook.

It was nearly supper time. Concerned that they might be getting hungry—who knew how much food they had in the house?—Jack had decided to try to talk them into answering the door again when the cellular phone inside his Suburban trilled. Hoping it was Shawna Brown, who appeared to be the spokesperson for the trio, he scooped it up on the second ring.

"O'Halloran."

The silence on the other end told him what he already knew—that his tone had been too brusque. He dragged his hand down his face and tried again. "This is Sheriff O'Halloran. Is this Shawna?"

"No," the young female voice answered after another hesitant pause. "It's me, Daddy. Amy," she added as if he had another daughter he might possibly confuse her with.

A jolt of parental concern struck like lightning. "What's wrong, honey?" She'd gone over to his mother's house after school as she did every day. Having called earlier to explain his situation, he knew his mother wouldn't be letting Amy call unless it was important. "Where's your Gramma?"

"She's in the kitchen. Making cookies." Another pause that tested his patience. "The kind with the M&Ms in them."

"I see." He looked out the rain-streaked windshield at the house. The lights that had been turned on inside were blurred by the filmy curtain of fog and mist. He kept his voice mild, even as concern was replaced with mild exasperation. "Is there some special reason you're calling, Amy?"

"Yes."

Jack told himself that he should know better than to ask a six-year-old a *yes* or *no* question. "Can you tell me what it is?"

"I was calling about Puffy."

"Puffy?"

"My Nano Kitty." Unlike her father, Amy didn't attempt to conceal her exasperation. "The one you said you'd take care of for me," she reminded him.

Since the electronic pet had been banned from the first-grade classroom yesterday, Jack had agreed to keep it in his pocket. He'd also promised to tend to it while Amy was at school. If he'd known ahead of time just what that entailed, he might not have been so willing.

"Puffy's doing just fine, darlin'."

"Have you been feeding him?"

"You bet." If today was any example, the damn virtual cat ate more often than any real cat.

"Did you play with him?"

"Yep. We played chase the mouse not more than ten minutes ago." According to the instructions, a neglected Nano Kitty was a sad kitty; a sad kitty could become ill, requiring even more attention, including regular doses of virtual-kitty antibiotics.

"Oh. Good." Her obvious relief made him feel guilty for having considered, on more than one occasion today, tossing the damn gizmo into Admiralty Bay. "I was worried you might forget and accidentally let Puffy die."

"I promise, Amy, I won't let Puffy die." Since he hadn't been able to make that same promise when her mother had been diagnosed with ovarian cancer four years ago, Jack had every intention of keeping his word now. Even if his surrogate parenting of an electronic kitten was proving a source of vast amusement for his fellow cops.

"Okay." That matter seemingly settled, she turned to another. "Uh . . . I was wondering, Daddy . . ."

Yes, Amy?" He managed, just barely, to keep from grinding his teeth.

"Well, I was wondering . . . if I could maybe watch one of the tapes. Not the whole thing. Just a little bit."

He suspected she wasn't referring to *Pocohantas* or *The Little Mermaid*, but rather one of the videotapes Peg had made when she'd accepted the fact— long before he had—that she was going to die. What had begun as a simple love letter to the child she'd be leaving behind had evolved into a legacy of maternal comfort and advice.

The tapes—an amazing one-hundred-and-six hours of them—were tucked away in Peg's cedar hope chest with other personal memorabilia as a legacy for the daughter she would never see grow to womanhood.

"I was thinking maybe Gramma and I could drive over to our house after we finished baking the cookies. Just for a little while," she cajoled prettily when he didn't immediately answer.

"You know the rules, honey. You and I always watch the tapes together."

It had been what Peg, concerned about her daughter's possibly fragile emotional state, had wanted. And Jack was not about to let her down.

He couldn't count how many times during the past two years he'd wanted to tell his first and only love about some new event in Amy's life—like when she'd lost her first tooth and had left cookies and chocolate milk out for the tooth fairy, or last December when she'd played the part of a reed piper in her kindergarten's performance of *The Nutcracker Suite* and had insisted on keeping her stage makeup on while the two of them had celebrated afterwards with Ingrid Johansson's blueberry waffles at the Timberline Café.

Her first report card; her first sleepover, which he'd discovered was ill-named since the four little six-year-old girls certainly hadn't done much sleeping—so many firsts Jack knew Peg would have given anything to share.

"But Daddy—"

"Don't whine, Amy," he said automatically. It was

a new stage she'd entered into, not nearly as appealing as the previous ones and he hoped it would be short-lived. "I'll tell you what. Why don't you practice reading your new Dr. Seuss book, and I promise we'll go out for burgers, then watch a tape together tomorrow night."

"Okay," she agreed with an instant acceptance he sure would enjoy receiving from the teens inside Ida's house. "I'll go read it to Gramma while she bakes the cookies."

"Good idea," Jack agreed. "Hey, Amy . . . whose little girl are you?"

She giggled as she always did whenever he asked that question. "Yours, Daddy," she answered on cue.

"Love you, Pumpkin."

"I love you, too, Daddy." She gave a smacking kissing sound.

Jack gave one back, then hung up and dialed the house again, only to receive another busy signal. Next he called Papa Joe's Pizza Emporium and ordered two pepperoni-and-mushroom pizzas—a large for the girls and a medium for himself. He didn't know what they'd prefer, but figured since they were still refusing to talk with him, they could damn well eat whatever he ordered.

Then, frustrated, and fearing he wasn't going to make it to his mother's house in time to pick up his daughter, take her home and tuck her into bed, he went back out in the slanting, icy rain that was now falling like needles and strode toward Ida's front door.

New York City

The victory celebration took place high above the city, in a mahogany-paneled conference room overlooking Central Park. The mood was unrestrained, bordering on jubilant, as the cream of the legal profession celebrated yet another battlefield victory.

Champagne flowed, Waterford decanters of Scotch and brandy had been brought out, and even Oliver Choate, senior partner and founder of Choate, Plimpton, Wells & Sullivan, who usually remained ensconced upstairs in his executive suite, had joined the revelry.

"To the little lady of the hour." Murdock lifted the glass of Jack Daniel's the firm had begun stocking when he'd first become a client. "The toughest—and prettiest—litigator in the business," he boomed out. "The sharp as barbwire lady who managed to save our collective hairy asses."

"You have such a way with words, Rex," Raine murmured, earning a laugh from the others.

"Well, now, darlin', that's why I pay you the big bucks to do the talkin' for me."

More laughs. More corks popped, more brandy poured, more martinis shaken.

It was Oliver Choate's turn to toast. "To Raine. Choate, Plimpton, Wells and Sullivan's Wonder Woman."

"I'm hardly Wonder Woman," she demurred. "It was, despite the dollars involved, an uncomplicated case." Since much of litigation consisted of smoke and mirrors, Raine had become adept at setting up smoke screens to protect the firm's clients. But the *Retirees v. Odessa Oil* suit had been a text book ex-

ample of the Golden Rule taught in her second-year
Law and Economics class: He who has the most
gold rules.

"You're right," Murdock agreed. "Wonder Woman's not quite right. Linda Carter looked real cute
in that skimpy red, white, and blue outfit, but she
didn't have your ball-busting, take-no-prisoners attitude." He skimmed a look over her, from the top of
her head down to her egg-stained Bruno Magli
pumps. "I know. That spunky gal on the TV show
set back in olden times. The one with the big—"

"Breastplate," Oliver cut Murdock off before he
could use the *T* word they all knew he'd intended.
"And the *gal* you're referring to is Xena," he said,
revealing himself to be a man of surprisingly eclectic
tastes. "Warrior Princess."

"You got it," Murdock agreed.

Oliver lifted his glass again. "To our very own
Warrior Princess."

The others followed. Even, Raine noticed, Stephen
Wells, managing partner of the firm, which was
mildly surprising since she and Stephen had
bumped heads on more than one occasion. Raine
had been at the firm less than a week when she'd
realized that Wells was one of those stuffy dinosaurs
who, if given the choice, would have never permitted
women to enter these hallowed legal halls.

But that was before today. Before she'd proven
that she could do anything any of the male attorneys
could do. And she'd done it wearing high heels.
Breathing in the heavy ether of admiration, Raine
took a sip of the champagne. In contrast to the rain
that had begun to fall, it tasted like sunshine on

her tongue. Outside the floor-to-ceiling windows the entire city appeared to have been laid at her feet.

It was a moment to be savored. To tie up in pretty ribbons and tuck away in her memory, like the prom photographs and dried corsage petals her sister Savannah had Scotch-taped into floral-covered scrapbooks back in high school. Raine had never gone to a prom. The closest she'd come to teenage romance was the snowy December night her junior year of high school right after she'd gotten her braces off when she and Warren Templeton, a worldly senior and president of her debate team, had been parked out by Lake Quinault. It was the memorable night Raine had learned how to French-kiss.

Cigars were pulled out of a Honduran-mahogany humidor and passed around. Smoke filled the room as the conversation shifted from a rehash of the court case that had taken months of twenty-hour-days to prepare and a mere three weeks to present, to where to eat lunch. They were arguing over which steakhouse to go to—the mood was unanimously carnivoristic—when Raine's secretary stuck his head in the door.

"I'm sorry to interrupt, but you have a phone call, Raine."

"Tell whoever it is that Raine's off the clock until tomorrow morning," Stephen Wells instructed curtly, not giving Raine a chance to respond.

"The caller says it's an emergency."

"Who is it, Brian?" Raine asked.

"She refused to give her name." Having worked long enough at the firm not to be intimidated by the managing partner's irritation, Brian Collins ignored Wells's scowl. Raine suspected that being the only one who understood the Byzantine filing system he'd set up didn't hurt, either. "But the area code on the caller ID is from Washington."

"Perhaps it's the President," James Sullivan suggested.

"Calling to offer Raine the Attorney General's job," Rex said.

More laughter.

Raine found nothing humorous in this news. Especially since she suspected the call was coming from Washington State, and not the nation's capitol.

"I'll take it in my office." As her headache spiked again, she put her glass down on the table. Promising to return as soon as possible, she escaped the smoke-filled office. The heels of her pumps sank into the plush pewter carpeting as she made her way down the curving staircase to her office.

"I smell like a damn pool hall," she muttered. "The only problem with winning is it gives the partners an excuse to pull out the stink sticks."

"It's a guy thing," her secretary said. "You may be able to hold your own on the playing field with the big boys, Raine, but there are some things you'll just never understand."

"I prefer to think of myself—and all women who are sensible enough not to want dog breath and smelly hair—as a superior life form."

"You probably are. But I'll bet you don't have nearly as much fun. By the way, your caller is a kid. She sounds like a teenager, perhaps sixteen, seventeen. She wouldn't tell me what the problem was. All she'd say was that it was an emergency and she had instructions to call you. I didn't think you'd want me to share that with the others upstairs."

"No." A chill skittered up Raine's spine. Her grandmother wasn't a young woman. If anything had happened to her . . . "Thank you, Brian." Raine managed a vague smile for the young man who kept her life so well organized.

She went into her office, sank down in the swivel leather chair she'd splurged part of her end-of-the-year bonus on, and took a deep breath as she looked down at the blinking orange light. Then, spurred by apprehension, she pressed the button. "Hello. This is Raine Cantrell."

"Raine?" The voice on the other end of the phone sounded young and extremely nervous. But not hysterical, Raine decided with a modicum of relief. "This is Shawna Brown. I'm one of your grandmother's girls—"

"I know. She told me all about you." Raine couldn't remember which of the teenagers Shawna was, but decided it wasn't germane to the point. "Is my grandmother all right?"

"Well, that's not an easy question to answer."

"Why don't you try, dear?" Nerves made her want to snap at the girl; years of courtroom experience allowed her to keep her voice calm.

"Well, she says she's fine and dandy, but the doctors, they don't seem so sure. So they're making her stay in the hospital for tests, but—"

"Hospital?" Forgetting everything she'd ever learned about questioning a witness, Raine abruptly cut the girl off. "My grandmother's in the hospital? What happened?"

Visions of Ida Lindstrom driving her ancient Jeep off the twisting wooded road into town flashed through Raine's mind, followed on close order by the possibilities of a stroke or heart attack.

Her grandmother had always seemed as strong as one of the towering Douglas firs surrounding the Washington peninsula town. But then again, Raine reminded herself, it had been more than five years since she'd been back to Coldwater Cove. Some quick calculation revealed that somehow, while she hadn't been paying attention, her grandmother had edged into her late seventies.

"It's probably nothin' real serious," Shawna hastened to assure Raine. "She just had herself a little dizzy spell this morning when she climbed up on a kitchen stool to get the cornstarch. She was going to make a boysenberry pie.

"I've told her not to get up on that rickety old stool, that if she wants something on the top shelf of the cupboard, I'll get it down for her. She's so short, it's a real stretch for her to reach. I don't know why she even keeps things up that high, but you know your grandma. Told me she'd set things up that way when she first came to Coldwater Cove from Portland after her divorce, and didn't see any reason to change."

Just when Raine was about to scream, the girl stopped for a breath. "But I guess you already know that story."

"Yes. I do. So, if you could just get back to this morning, I'd certainly appreciate it."

"Oh . . . Sure. Well, I was out bringing the clothes in off the line because it was looking like it might rain, you know how iffy the weather is this time of year and—"

"Shawna." Having spent years learning to organize

her thoughts, Raine was growing more and more frustrated by the way the teenager's explanation kept wandering off the subject. "Why don't you please just tell me what exactly happened to Ida? Without any embellishments."

There was a pause. Then Shawna said, "I'm sorry I'm not tellin' this good enough for you."

There was no mistaking the hurt feelings in the girl's tone. *Nothing like badgering your own witness.* "And I apologize for sounding impatient," Raine immediately backpedaled. "I'm just trying to find out what happened."

"Mama Ida fell off the stool and, like, hit her head on the floor."

"I see." And she did, all too clearly. Raine's heart clenched as she imagined her grandmother—all four-feet, eleven inches, ninety-eight pounds of her—sprawled on the kitchen floor. "Did she knock herself unconscious?"

"She says no. But we called 911, anyway. Which really riled Mama Ida up, but Renee was scared. And so was I."

"Renee's another one of the girls?"

"Yeah. She's my sister. We ended up in the system after our mama and daddy died in a car wreck over by Moclips. For a while we were put in different homes, which is why Renee started running away. To be with me." She paused as if trying to decide how much to reveal. "I wanted to take care of us, but I'm underage, and after I got busted at a kegger on the beach, the judge said I wasn't responsible enough, so we had to stay in foster care. But things got better after we moved in with Mama Ida."

"I'm glad to hear that." Nice little boarding school

her grandmother was running, Raine thought acidly. Whatever happened to sponsoring a Brownie troop, where your biggest concern was the annual cookie sale? "So, you called 911. And the paramedics came?"

"Yeah. Though she was spittin' like a wet cat, they took her off to the hospital in Port Angeles. Which was when all the trouble started."

Raine pressed her fingers against her temple, where the jackhammer had been replaced by a maniac who'd begun pounding away with a mallet. The fire that had died down a bit during the conference-room celebration flared again in her chest. Higher. Hotter. "I'm almost afraid to ask."

"Our probation officer—that's Ms. Kelly, who Mama Ida always calls Old Fussbudget—was at the hospital checking on some guy who robbed a 7-Eleven a few years back. He'd been in a bar fight and was gettin' a cut on his head stitched up when your grandmother was brought into the emergency room.

"Ms. Kelly called the house, and Renee, who's too young to know any better, admitted we were here all alone. So, Ms. Kelly right away called Mrs. Petersen. She works for the county. In social services. She's found Renee foster homes the other times she's run away. Gwen, too."

"Gwen?"

"She's the pregnant one."

The thought of three delinquents alone in her grandmother's antique-filled home was not the most encouraging thing Raine had heard today. "I don't understand. You said it happened this morning."

"Yeah."

"Why isn't my mother handling things?"

"Oh, Lilith's on the coast with her friends, preparing for some sort of return-of-the-sun celebration, or something. It's like one of the coven's most important gatherings."

"Coven? My mother's a witch, now?" Despite her ongoing concern for her grandmother, Raine couldn't help being sidetracked by this little news flash.

"Not exactly. At least I don't think so. I mean, I haven't seen her waving a magic wand or boiling up toads and lizards in the Dutch oven or anything. It's Mama Ida who's always callin' it a coven. Mostly it's just some of your mama's New Age stuff. She's a pagan now," Shawna added matter-of-factly.

"I see." Raine poured a glass of water from the carafe on her desk and took a long drink, hoping it would put out the inferno blazing in her gut. It didn't.

"I don't care if the sun's coming back, sucked into a black hole, or explodes, Shawna. I want you to call my mother right now and have her get back to Coldwater Cove."

Not that Lilith would prove that much help. During her lifetime, Raine's mother had been a flower child, a war protester, an actress usually cast as the soon-to-be-dead bimbo in a handful of low-budget horror films, as well as a rock singer with a pretty but frail voice who'd managed to stay in the music business because of her looks. Which were stunning. Unfortunately, she could be selfish, like beautiful women often are, and in Raine's opinion, habitually behaved like a foolish, willful schoolgirl, mindless of the consequences of her actions. But at least she should be capable of preventing the kids from stealing the silver before Raine could get back home.

"I tried calling the lodge where they were supposed to be staying, but the lady who answered the phone said they all left to go camping out in the woods. She said Lilith said something about a ceremonial bonfire. But maybe the sheriff's sent someone out—"

"The sheriff? How exactly did he get involved in all this?"

"Oh. That happened after we locked ourselves in the house."

"You did what?" Raine jumped to her feet. At the same time she reached into the drawer for her plastic bottle of Maalox. "Why on earth would you do that?"

"Because Mama Ida told us to batten down the hatches and barricade the doors. She quoted something—you know how she does that all the time, right?—about free fighters and defenders of old homes and old names."

"And old splendors," Raine murmured. "It's from *Cyrano de Bergerac*." But, like everything else her grandmother quoted, it always came out twisted.

"Oh. That's the guy with the big nose, right? Mama Ida brought home the video last month. Gwen thinks Steve Martin's really funny. For an old guy, that is. Ever since then, she's been thinking of maybe naming her baby Steve. If it's a boy, I mean. Renee is voting for Leo. After Leonardo DiCaprio? I kinda like Denzel."

"They're all lovely names," Raine said. She ground her teeth, making a mental apology to Ida, who'd paid for years of expensive orthodontia. "Now, if we could get back to why my grandmother told you to barricade yourselves in the house—"

"Oh, sure. That's easy. She said there was no way she was letting any government bureaucrat take us away from our home just because we didn't, like, have a responsible adult present in the house."

"I see." Personally, Raine thought that they'd be in the same fix if her mother *had* been home. No one, in her memory, had ever used the words "responsible adult" to describe Lilith Lindstrom Cantrell Townsend. "And I suppose it was when you wouldn't open the door that the social worker called Sheriff O'Halloran?"

"Yeah. Along with half the police in the state, it looks like," Shawna said. "They're all outside. The TV stations are out there, too." She paused. "Mama Ida also told us that we weren't to bother you. And I've always tried to do what she says, but there are a lot of men with guns in the driveway.

"And I don't want to scare Renee or Gwen, but I think you'd better get here as quick as you can. Before they send in a SWAT team to break down the door or something."

Her knees grew weak. Raine sank back down into her chair and tried to ignore the movie hostage scenes flashing through her mind. The rain streaking down the window blurred the view of the tulips and spring green trees in the nearby park.

"I'll be there as soon as I can. Meanwhile, do you have a phone number for the sheriff?"

"I can look it up. He's called the house a couple times, but after I saw Mama Ida's news conference on the television—"

"My grandmother gave a news conference from her hospital bed?"

As she twisted open the cap and chugged the Maalox, Raine told herself that she shouldn't be surprised. Her grandmother was a lifelong firebrand. Ida had even gone to jail back in the fifties for setting up a mobile vasectomy clinic in the parking lot of the annual Sawdust Festival and offering two-for-one bonus pricing during the three-day event.

"Yeah. She looked real good, too," Shawna said. "For a lady her age. Though I don't think the sheriff is real happy about her callin' him a storm trooper . . . Gwen taped it so she could watch it when she got home.

"Anyway, Mama Ida told us—on the TV—not to talk to anyone until she managed to escape the jackasses at the hospital. Those were her words, not mine," Shawna added, as it afraid Raine might not approve of the vulgarity. "So I took the phone off the hook."

After assuring Shawna that she'd take care of matters with the sheriff, Raine asked Brian to book her on the first flight to Seattle's Sea-Tac Airport. From there she could rent a car and take a ferry to Coldwater Cove. Fortunately, she always kept a suitcase packed with essentials in her office, which would prevent having to waste time by going to her apartment to pack.

She was anxious to call the hospital to check on her grandmother's condition, but along with marshaling her thoughts before speaking, law school had taught her to prioritize.

Raine vaguely recalled Sheriff John O'Halloran to be an intelligent, easygoing man who continued to

generate enough good will in the county to get
elected year after year. She couldn't imagine him
attacking a house inhabited by three unarmed,
frightened teenage girls.

Still, it didn't take Clarence Darrow to realize that
the most critical item on the agenda was to prevent
any one of the other cops Shawna had mentioned
from deciding to play Rambo.

Olympic National Park, Washington

Cooper Ryan had received three calls in as many
hours regarding the strange goings-on near Heart of
the Hills. The third call, and the one that had captured his attention, had begun the same as the others—an illegal campfire, discordant music, and eerie
chanting. However, a new wrinkle had been added:
several women were reported to be gallivanting
around the forest, as naked as jaybirds.

Ascribing to a live-and-let-live philosophy, normally Coop wouldn't have been all that bothered by
the reports. However, a Boy Scout troop was scheduled for a nature hike through that area tomorrow
and he doubted that their parents would be thrilled
if the usual environmental ranger talk was replaced
by an up-close-and-personal demonstration of the
differences between boys and girls.

Coop drove out to the trailhead nearest the site of
the reports and began hiking through the old-growth
rainforest. They couldn't be far, he determined when
the scent of burning wood and silvery flute music
drifted through the fog-shrouded tops of towering
fir and hemlock trees. Mist rose off a cushioned forest floor that was a mosaic of countless shades of

green. Starflowers were just beginning to blossom amidst the interwoven ferns and mosses, bright harbingers of summer. Except for the distant music, the occasional chirp of a bird, and the sound of water running over rocks, the ancient old-growth forest was as silent as a cathedral.

When he reached the edge of a clearing, he saw them: a dozen women, all as naked as the day they were born. Hands linked, they'd directed their attention toward a woman who stood atop a pyramid of stone between twin fires. Her hands reached skyward, her voluptuous body outlined by the light of dancing flames. Long waves, topped with the woven band of red and white flowers that encircled her head, streamed down her bare back like molten silver. Despite the fact that her hair was no longer a rich, tawny blond, Coop instantly recognized her.

She was half chanting, half singing, while a heavyset young woman with her hair braided in colorful ribbons sat cross-legged in front of the stones, playing a flute.

"Ancient ones, trees of ancient Earth. Older than time can tell. Grant me the power at your command to charge my magic spell."

Coop wasn't all that surprised to discover Lilith Lindstrom had grown up to be some sort of witch. After all, she'd never really fit into the hard-working community of loggers and fishermen. Flighty, harebrained, and frivolous had been a few of the descriptions he'd heard over the years. Jealous wives or worried mothers of sons were more likely to call her dangerous.

Coop, however, had always thought her magnificent. And as elusive as quicksilver, as out of reach

as the moon. Deciding that she wasn't really going
to escape, not dressed—or undressed—the way she
was, he folded his arms, leaned back against the gigantic trunk of a red-barked Western cedar and
waited for the show—which included several provocative references to fertility—to come to a
conclusion.

When it did, Coop began to slowly clap his hands.
Heads swivelled toward him and female faces drew
into tight, disapproving scowls. All except Lilith's.

"Cooper!" Bestowing a smile as warm as a thousand suns upon him, she stepped down from the
stones and ran toward him. "What a lovely
surprise."

With her usual impulsiveness, she flung herself
into his arms and touched her smiling mouth to his.
The kiss was light and brief. But it still sent a jolt
straight to his groin.

"Imagine seeing you here," she said when he'd
lowered her back to the mossy ground. "Do you
know, I was thinking about you just last month. It
must have been a foreshadowing. When did you get
back to Washington?"

"A couple weeks ago." Around them, the other
women were wrapping themselves in capes or pulling on sweats. If Lilith felt at all ill at ease about her
nudity, she was sure hiding it well, Coop thought.

"I wish I'd known. I would have thrown you a
huge blowout of a welcome-home party."

"I'm not going anywhere."

"Well, then there's still time." Seeming pleased
with that prospect, she nodded. "What brings you
out here?"

"I work here. In the park."

"Oh. Well, isn't that a coincidence? You being out here, and us running into one another—"

"It isn't exactly a coincidence. I received some complaints."

"Complaints?" She lifted a brow and combed a hand absently through her hair, causing it to drift over her breasts. Her still-magnificent naked breasts. "Whatever for?"

"To begin with, there's the little matter of an illegal fire."

"It's Beltane. We couldn't possibly celebrate without our fires. In the olden days the druids passed cattle through the flames to ensure prosperity. Since that seemed a bit impractical, we reluctantly decided to forego that portion of the ceremony."

Practical had never been a word Coop would have used to describe Lilith Lindstrom. And it sure wasn't now. "It's still not in a prescribed campground, he pointed out.

"Well, of course it isn't, darling. If you've received complaints about us celebrating our festival all the way out here in the middle of nowhere, can you imagine what would have happened if we'd held it in a designated campground?"

"Look, I'm willing, for old times sake, to overlook the illegal campsite and the nudity, but the fires are another matter. You're going to have to put them out."

She lifted her chin, changing from some ethereal woodland sprite back into the headstrong young girl who'd once driven him to distraction. "Not until we've concluded our celebration."

"Dammit, Lilith—"

"You can curse all you like, Cooper, but we are not

extinguishing those fires until tomorrow morning. I still have to draw down the moon tonight, after all."

"You can draw down the entire Milky Way for all I care, but the fires have got to be extinguished, and you all have to move to a designated campsite. And I want you dressed. Now." He feared if he told her about the Boy Scouts, she'd refuse to put her clothes on just to aggravate him further.

"Gracious, that's a great many orders." Her midnight blue eyes sparked with barely restrained temper. "I remember you having such wonderful potential, Cooper. What a shame you've turned out to be a narrow-minded dictator. And a governmental one at that."

Refusing to rise to the bait, Cooper pulled a narrow notebook out of his jacket pocket, scribbled a few lines, ripped the ticket from the book and held it out to her.

"What's that?"

"It's a citation. For the fires." Because she'd gotten under his skin, he flicked a quick gaze over her from the top of her head down to her crimson-lacquered toenails. "Though I may be a narrow-minded dictator, I decided to give you a pass on the lewd behavior."

"Lewd?" She plucked the ticket from his hand, tore it in half and dropped the pieces at his feet. "I happen to know for a fact that I'm not the first person to enjoy these woods sans clothing." Her pointed gaze reminded him that he should damn well know that, too. "Obviously, you've also turned into a puritan. Which is even worse than a dictator."

"I'm just doing my job." Because he was really

starting to get pissed, he scribbled out another ticket
and shoved it toward her.

"And what a nasty, small-minded job it is, too."
Lilith tore this one into four pieces and tossed them
to the ground along with the others.

"Dammit, if you'd just agree to put the fires out
and put some clothes on—"

"Not until we're finished with our ceremony."

He furiously scribbled a third. "This is your last
chance, sweetheart. Tear this up and I'm going to
have to take you in."

"I am very disappointed in you, Cooper." That
stated, she grabbed the entire citation book from his
hands, ripped the pages into confetti, then flung
them into his face.

"Goddammit, that's it." Coop pulled the set of
handcuffs from the back of his belt.

"What do you think you're doing?"

"What does it look like? I'm taking you in." He
snapped the cuffs around her wrists, receiving a perverse pleasure at the sound of the metal clicking
shut. After tossing his khaki jacket over her shoulders, he turned toward the others.

"I would advise you all to extinguish those fires.
Now. We're a little short on holding cells down at
park headquarters, but if you don't cooperate, I'm
sure I can manage to squeeze you all in for a day
or so. Until I can get the paperwork processed."

Without their leader, the coven, or whatever the
hell it was, crumbled. Coop watched with satisfaction as the flute player retrieved a bucket of water
and threw it onto the fire, which caused the flames
to hiss and sputter. The others followed suit.

"Where the hell are your clothes?" he asked Lilith.

"That's my business." She looked amazingly cool for a naked woman whose wrists were handcuffed behind her back.

"Since I'm going to be booking you into my jail cell, I figure it's just become *my* business."

They were standing toe to toe, nose to nose. Coop reluctantly gave her credit for not flinching at either his tone or his glare.

"You're too uptight, Cooper," Lilith said with a toss of her silver head. "I happen to embrace nudity. It is, after all, our natural state." She skimmed a disapproving look over him. "You certainly weren't born wearing that uniform. Which, by the way, is not at all flattering. And the color is wrong for your eyes."

He hated that he cared what Lilith whatever-the-hell-last-name-she-was-going-by-these-days thought about him. Hated the fact that he had to resist the urge to suck in his gut, which while not as hard as it had been in the days they rolled around on a blanket in these very same woods, wasn't bad for a guy who was about to hit fifty.

"You can tout the universal appeal of nudity all you want, but if that squall that's out over the Pacific hits, you'll be embracing frostbite," he said.

"I happen to have it on good authority we're scheduled to have mostly clear skies with some high cirrus clouds, and a possibility for scattered showers come evening."

"See that in your crystal ball, did you?"

"Actually, it was the forecast on the Weather Channel."

"Well, don't look now, sweetheart, but I think your forecast is wrong. Because those black anvils gathering overhead sure as hell look like they mean business."

"So? Even if it does rain, the human body is waterproof."

Coop felt his jaw lock and realized he was clenching his teeth. He stabbed a finger toward a twenty-something young woman now dressed in a Seattle Seahawks sweatshirt, leggings, and sneakers. "If you don't want to be next, go into whatever tent belongs to this throwback to the sixties and fetch her some clothes."

"Go get my pack, Annie, please," Lilith said when the young woman hesitated. "Before Dudley Doright here decides to put us all in shackles."

The Seahawks fan ran to a nearby tent, returning with a dark blue backpack decorated with silver stars. Coop stuffed it under his arm and began dragging his prisoner down the trail.

"You're a bully, Cooper Ryan," Lilith said scathingly. "A horrible, rude, misogynist bully."

"Sticks and stones, darlin'." Now that he'd restored order, Coop was actually beginning to enjoy himself. He couldn't remember another time when he'd had the upper hand where this woman was concerned.

"I can't believe this is happening."

"I warned you about the consequences."

"Oh, I understand all about consequences. After all, I have been arrested before." Coop recalled those days all too well. While he'd been slogging through a goddamn jungle, trying to stay alive, she'd been throwing red paint on army recruiters and sleeping with long-haired, pot-smoking, hippie draft dodgers. "I know the drill," she continued. "What I cannot believe is that you would actually arrest a woman who gave you her virginity the night of high school graduation."

They'd both been virgins. But since Coop hadn't admitted to that back then, he saw no reason to set the record straight now.

They were still about two hundred yards from the trailhead when the dark sky overhead opened up, dumping buckets of icy rain that hit like needles down on them.

"It figures," Coop ground out as he ran toward the truck, dragging her along with him. "It just goddamn figures!"

Lilith Lindstrom had always been trouble with a capital *T*. Nothing had changed there. She was also still a knockout. Coop figured that having the woman rumored to have been the inspiration for the Stones' *Ruby Tuesday* back in his life again was proof positive that Fate had one helluva skewed sense of humor.

❧ 3 ❧

The Delta jet was streaking westward, managing to stay just ahead of the setting sun. Raine sat in seat 3A in first class, a yellow legal pad on the laptop table, making a list of things that would need to be taken care of once she reached Washington.

Obviously, a visit to her grandmother was high on the list. The doctor she'd spoken with on her cellular phone while waiting at the gate for her flight had informed her that Ida appeared to have suffered merely a fleeting case of vertigo. If the additional tests failed to reveal any serious underlying condition, Raine's grandmother would probably be discharged and allowed to return home tomorrow afternoon.

Although that didn't give her much time, Raine had every intention of getting those three delinquents out of the house before then. She understood all too well her grandmother's strong sense of social responsibility, but if she'd begun endangering her health, it was time for someone to put a foot down. And from Lilith's latest disappearing act, it was more than obvious Raine couldn't count on her mother for any show of responsibility. So, what else was new?

That left it up to her to set things straight. Fortunately, Raine thought, she was up to the job. Hadn't one of the wealthiest, most powerful men in America called her a warrior? If she couldn't handle one elderly woman and three teenagers, then she might as well resign from the bar.

One piece of good news she'd discovered was that it turned out Shawna and Renee had an aunt no one had known about. Child protective services was currently conducting an investigation, but according to the caseworker Raine had spoken with, the woman and her navy husband should be receiving custody of both girls within days. Which left only the pregnant Gwen to deal with.

She debated calling her grandmother from the plane, then decided that there was no point in risking a confrontation. Although the doctor's diagnosis had been encouraging, she didn't want to get Ida wound up and risk something far more serious than vertigo. Although her grandmother would probably never admit it, even to herself, Ida Lindstrom was, after all, a senior citizen. Not unlike the ones who'd been demonstrating against her client earlier. Had it only been two hours ago? The recent courtroom victory seemed as if it had happened in another lifetime.

Sighing, she took the phone from the back of the seat in front of her, swiped her platinum AMEX card, and dialed the number she'd already memorized.

"Well, hello, Ms. Cantrell," the now familiar deep

voice drawled. "What a surprise to hear from you. Again."

All right, so she'd called twenty minutes ago from over Ohio. Since when was it a crime to be concerned about a possible life-threatening situation taking place in the very home where she'd grown up?

"I was checking to see if there were any further developments.

"Well now, that depends." He dragged the subsequent pause out, as if he'd guessed how such delays irritated her.

"Depends on what?"

"Whether or not you think finding out Renee's a vegetarian is a development."

Renee was Shawna's runaway sister, Raine recalled. "I fail to see how that has any relevance in this case."

"She didn't like the pizza."

"Pizza?"

"The one I had delivered. Mushroom and pepperoni."

"That was a good ploy," she allowed. "Feeding them to create a bond." Raine had seen much the same tactic used on an episode of *Homicide* last season.

"Actually, it wasn't a ploy. I was starving and figured they might be hungry, too."

"Well. Then it was a very thoughtful gesture." Raine wondered how many New York cops would bother to think of such a thing. Then again, she decided, standoff situations in the big city were probably a great deal different than in Coldwater Cove.

"It wasn't that big a deal." She could hear the

shrug in his voice. "Shawna—she's the one you spoke with," he reminded Raine, as if she could have forgotten such a call—"was willing to pick up the phone long enough to call and tell me that the kid was refusing to eat it."

"Couldn't Renee just take the damn pepperoni off?"

"Now, you know, that's pretty much what I suggested." Raine heard the renewed humor in his tone and wondered if it was meant to be at her expense. "Turns out she's one of those absolutely pure sprout eaters who won't touch cheese, either."

Although she'd pulled every legal string she could from across the country, Raine still feared for the girls' safety. Her earlier reassurance regarding the sheriff's ability to pull this off without bloodshed had evaporated when she'd discovered, during their first conversation, that it wasn't Big John O'Halloran outside her grandmother's house, but his son, Jack, infamous high school make-out artist and jock extraordinaire.

Jack O'Halloran had been legend around Olympic County for both his athletic achievements and the stunts that kept him in judicial hot water and were particularly inappropriate for the son of the county's chief lawman. He'd been the quarterback of the Cold-water Cove Loggers High School football team, state all-star pitcher for the baseball team, and his senior year had been voted student-body president by the widest margin in the school's history.

He'd subsequently had the office taken away from him six weeks later during homecoming weekend when he'd led a raid to kidnap the mascot of a rival school. The members of the Fighting Beavers varsity football team had not found the ransom note's instructions—that they parade down Coldwater Cove's main street wearing only their jockstraps and helmets—all that humorous. Neither had school authorities.

From what Raine could remember of his antics, the term *hell-raiser* could have been coined with Jack O'Halloran in mind. He drank too much, drove too fast, and just about every female in the county between the ages of eight and eighty had found him irresistible. Including, dammit, she thought now, her. Not that he'd ever noticed her, four years behind him, skinny as a lodgepole pine, with bark brown hair as straight as rainwater and a mouthful of braces. The idea that such a man could actually grow up to be sheriff was incredible.

Putting aside an adolescent feminine pique she was vaguely surprised to discover lurking inside of her, Raine returned to business.

"I'm assuming that you were informed I've filed a TRO to stop the police from using violence against my grandmother's wards."

While she'd been on the way to the airport, Oliver Choate had telephoned a friendly judge he played golf with every Wednesday morning. That judge, in turn, called another in Washington State, who hadn't hesitated issuing the temporary restraining order.

"Yeah." For a man who'd been handed a court order, Sheriff O'Halloran sounded less than impressed. "Wally called a little bit ago with the news."

"Wally?" Not at all encouraged by the familiarity in the lawman's tone, Raine reminded herself that the legal good-old-boys club was not limited to New York City.

"Wally Cunningham. Judge Wallace Cunningham," Jack elaborated. "You might remember him. He played a little baseball before a torn rotator cuff had him taking up the law."

Damn. Wally Cunningham had been Jack O'Halloran's catcher on the Loggers baseball team. Raine vaguely remembered hearing he'd gone on to play Triple-A ball in Tacoma.

"That's all very interesting," she replied, her courtroom-cool tone suggesting otherwise. "But I'm more interested in whether the injunction was issued."

"Oh, sure. Wally and I had ourselves a pretty good laugh over it."

The easy, masculine dismissal in his tone had Raine grinding her teeth for the second time today. "I fail to see how either you or *Wally*"—her use of the judge's first name was tightly edged with sarcasm—"could find any humor in the potential use of force against three teenage girls."

"What we found humorous is the idea that anyone would think I'd stoop to using force against three teenagers in the first place. . . . Although," he added, as if on afterthought, "I can't deny being tempted on more than one occasion today to take my hand to those kids' backsides."

"If you so much as touch a single hair on those children's heads, Sheriff, I'll have you hauled in front of the bench on charges of police brutality."

"Threat noted, Ms. Cantrell." His tone suggested weariness with both their conversation and the situation in general. "Now, if you don't mind, the pizza guy's back with the veggie special and I have a dinner to deliver."

Before Raine could object, he ended the call.

Jack climbed out of the Suburban and, despite his continuing aggravation, grinned at the pizza delivery man.

"Things must be pretty rough down at the law offices, if you're taking on extra work delivering fast food," he drawled. "What's the matter, run out of ambulances to chase?"

Dan O'Halloran grinned as he handed his cousin the red-and-white box. "Why should I bother to go to all that trouble, when all I have to do is hang around here and wait for you to tromp all over those little girls' civil rights. Then sue the county for millions."

"Good luck. If my salary's any indication of Olympic County's assets, you'd be lucky to get peanuts." Jack lifted the lid, assuring himself that both meat and cheese had been left off the pizza, which appeared to consist of crust, red sauce, mushrooms, onions, and green peppers. He hoped to hell this would satisfy the finicky vegetarian delinquent. "So, I guess Mom called you?"

"Your mom, my mom, along with half the folks in town. But by then I'd already caught the promo on the early news when I dropped into Papa Joe's to pick up my dinner. I gotta tell you, Cuz, you didn't look half bad. I was thinking that if Hollywood got hold of this story, they might even want to build a new cop series around you. How does Jack O'Halloran, Hunk Cop with a Heart, sound?"

"Like you've been smoking the kind of funny cigarettes you can't buy in machines. . . . Jesus, and here I thought taking over Pop's office would be a walk in the park after being a city cop. Right now I think I'd rather be taking my chances with one of your everyday drug dealers wielding a Street Sweeper."

He began walking up to the front porch, his cousin and best friend, Daniel Webster O'Halloran falling in step beside him.

"I also heard that Wally signed a TRO to keep you from storming the house with a SWAT team." The humor in Dan's voice echoed that of the judge when Wally had called with the news of the temporary restraining order.

"Yeah. One of Ida's pit bull granddaughters has gotten her teeth into this and won't let go."

"That'd be Raine."

"Yeah." He climbed the steps to the porch, placed the pizza on the white wicker table and rang the bell. There was no answer, but out of the corner of his eye he saw the lace curtain on the front window move just a little.

"Veggie pizza for one!" he called out. Then waited. And waited some more. Realizing that they weren't about to open the door while he was standing there, he cursed and turned back toward the truck. "So, what do you know about her?"

"Not much. I took her half sister, Savannah, out once in high school." Dan's lips curved into a smile at the memory. "God, she was one gorgeous female. Masses of wild red hair that smelled like strawberries, curves that would make a *Playboy* centerfold look like Olive Oyl, and wraparound legs that went all the way up to her neck."

Since Dan was four years behind him, Jack hadn't

known Savannah. He also had no memory of the granddaughter that had been driving him nuts all day. "Only one date? What happened? Did she dump you?"

"Nah. She didn't get the chance. I just never called her again after that first date."

"Why not?" She definitely sounded like Dan's type. Actually, Jack considered, if looks counted for anything—and they sure had back in those hormone-driven teenage days—Savannah sounded pretty much like any guy's type.

Dan's grin was quick and abashed. "Because she flat out scared me to death."

They shared a laugh over that. "Sounds like I've got the wrong sister in my life. Can you remember anything about Raine?"

For a man who'd always enjoyed women, Jack had had about his fill of females today. Ida and the kids were damn aggravating, but the lady lawyer, with her constant phone calls, writs, injunctions, restraining orders, and sundry other legal threats, was turning out to be a herculean pain in the ass.

"Well, thinking back on it, we were on the debate team together my senior year. I remember her as being skinny, with braces and a chip on her shoulder as big as a Western cedar."

"The braces are undoubtedly gone by now. But if the phone conversations are any indication, I'd say the chip is still there. Larger than ever."

"Guess that means she still hasn't gotten her dad's attention."

Since Raine Cantrell's mother, Lilith, had been providing Coldwater Cove with gossip for years,

Jack recalled that Ida's granddaughters each had a different father. "And her dad would be . . . ?"

"Owen Cantrell." When that didn't seem to ring a bell, Dan elaborated. "He was the lawyer for the Sacramento Six."

"Is that supposed to mean something?"

"They were counterculture revolutionaries back in the 60s. Along the lines of the Chicago Seven, but they didn't get as much press. They were accused of firebombing a selective service office in Sacramento and conspiring to blow up others all over the West. Cantrell pulled a lot of magic legal rabbits out of his hat and got them acquitted. The case study was required reading in my criminal law class."

"Were they guilty?"

"I told you—"

"Yeah, yeah, I know," Jack interjected impatiently. "A jury let them off. But did they do it?"

"From what I've read of the testimony, yeah. But Cantrell was brilliant in revealing some of the government's heavy-handed tactics. So, the guys walked and he went on to become a hired big gun of the legal profession. In fact, I read in this morning's paper that he's heading up the team representing that TV sitcom star. You know, the one arrested the other day for stalking his ex-girlfriend, then slashing her throat."

"Cantrell sounds like a dandy guy," Jack muttered. "So his daughter is trying to live up to his lofty legal reputation?"

"You have to remember that I haven't seen her for years. And I'm no shrink. But yeah, at least back in high school, I'd say that was definitely the case."

"Terrific." Jack's curse was rich and ripe. That was

all he needed messing in this: a mouthy woman with an Oedipus complex waving her fancy Harvard law degree in his face. As the door to the house opened and an arm, clad in a pink sleeve reached out and snatched the pizza from the porch table, Jack wondered if his father had ever had days like this.

Finally, her long journey almost over, Raine was standing at the railing of the ferry *Walla Walla* that was making its way across Elliott Bay. The stiff wind, carrying with it the pungent bite of green fir and the softer scent of pending rain, cut through her suit and tore at her hair. But needing to clear her head after her long flight, and to prepare for battle with that small-town sheriff who'd been the bane of her existence these past hours, Raine resisted the lure of the ferry's warm interior.

Although night would have already fallen back in New York, here on the West Coast the sun was just beginning to set, turning the choppy waters a shimmering copper. Behind the white boat, the glass towers of the Seattle skyline faded into the distance. On the top deck, two suit-clad businessmen—obviously commuters—were taking advantage of the stiff breeze to fly kites that soared like colorful dragons overhead. On any other occasion, Raine would have enjoyed the carefree sight. But not today.

Perhaps it was the emotional roller coaster she'd spent the day riding, but her feelings were veering back and forth like an out-of-control pendulum. Visions, like isolated snapshots, flashed through her mind: a vague memory of a little girl holding tight to her mother's hand as they crossed these very same waters, excited at this new adventure, but se-

cretly worried that they might be swallowed up by
a huge killer whale, just like Pinocchio.

Another memory, from two years later, sponging
Savannah's face with a wet paper towel after her
younger sister, seasick from choppy waters, had
thrown up the hot dog, barbecue potato chips, and
Dr. Pepper Lilith had fed them for dinner.

And then there'd been that painful day when she
was a beanpole-skinny thirteen-year-old, desperately
wishing for some magic word that would make her
invisible while her glamorous mother leaned against
the railing, her hair flying out like a shimmering
banner in the crisp sea breeze as she flirted with a
trio of lovesick sailors who were drooling over Lilith
like three chocoholics raptly gazing upon a giant
Hershey bar.

During those childhood years, part of Raine had
looked forward to coming back to Coldwater Cove.
It was, after all, the closest thing she'd ever known
to home, the only place she felt safe. Secure. But
always, deep inside the most secret places in her
mind and heart lurked the fear that this would be
the time Lilith would leave them at their grandmother Ida's house and never return.

A young, obviously pregnant woman came out
onto the deck with a little girl who was about the
age Raine had been the first time she'd taken this
ferry ride. As the woman pointed out the kites
brightening the pewter sky and mother and daughter laughed together, obviously enjoying each other's
company, Raine experienced a sharp feeling of loss
for a childhood she'd never known.

Less than twenty minutes after leaving Seattle, she
caught her first glimpse of Coldwater Cove in the

distance. The turreted, gingerbread Victorian buildings perched atop the green bluff overlooking Admiralty Bay were backlit by the setting sun in a way
that made them look as if they were on fire. A
slanted gray curtain between the water and the town
suggested rain. A suggestion that was borne out
when a random drop carried on the salt-tinged wind
hit her face. Then another. Then more, finally driving Raine inside.

As the ferry approached the pier, she sipped from
a foam cup of espresso that provided a much needed
burst of caffeine and watched a brown pelican skim
along the coastline in search of fish, the ungainly,
awkward looking bird surprisingly graceful in flight.
More pelicans perched on wooden pilings. When the
docking call sounded, Raine tossed off the last of
the espresso, left the glassed-in observation deck and
took the metal stairs to her rental car.

She'd no sooner driven off the ferry when she
found herself immediately engulfed in the wet, gray
curtain she'd seen from the railing. Rain sheeted the
windshield as she made her way through town,
headed to her grandmother's home. She hit the
search button on the car's radio, stopping when she
landed on what seemed to be a news station. She
listened to the weather forecast, which predicted
rain.

"Now there's a newsflash," she muttered, turning
the wipers to high as raindrops hit the glass in front
of her like bullets, obscuring her view.

The Pacific Northwest hadn't gotten these towering green trees that rose into the silvery mist like
shaggy arrows, or the seemingly endless supply of
crystal creeks and tumbling waterfalls, without re-

ceiving a lot of precipitation. Most residents considered the tradeoff worthwhile.

Coldwater Cove, originally founded a century ago by a Swedish lumberjack, remained a town of Nordic cleanliness, where shop owners still swept the sidewalks each morning and the streets were as clean as a Swedish kitchen. There was one theater, and churches outnumbered taverns three to one. The crack of Little League bats could be heard on Saturday mornings, the chime of church bells on Sunday.

She paused at the only stoplight in town where a wide, grassy town square at the end of Harbor Street served as the centerpiece of the town. A fountain bubbled at one end of the green; a horseshoe pit claimed the other. A clock tower, made of a red brick that had weathered to a dusty pink over the century, could be seen for miles. Raine wondered if each of the four sides of the clock still told a different time, and suspected, given the way the town seemed frozen in time, they probably did.

"We've just received an update concerning the ongoing crisis in Coldwater Cove," the male voice announced as she continued through town. "Stay tuned for the latest development following this word from Timberland Bank, neighbors serving the Puget Sound community for fifty years."

Raine dove forward and began twisting the dial. Having no doubt what the crisis referred to, she didn't have the patience to listen to a commercial pitching debt-consolidation loans.

After skimming through various country, jazz, religious, rock, and oldies stations, she gave up and returned to *K-SOUND—More News, Less Chitchat.*

"How about less commercials?" she suggested acidly as the bank commercial segued into one for a franchise fish restaurant, then a break for station identification. Then, finally! The news update she'd been waiting for.

"This is Patrick Christopher, with an update on the crisis in Coldwater Cove. Sources tell us that fire trucks from neighboring Port Townsend and Port Angeles have been dispatched to the Lindstrom residence. Although the weather has grounded K-SOUND's *Eye in the Sky*, we have our pilot, Captain Jim, in the newsroom, monitoring the situation. . . . Jim, what are you hearing from your sources?"

"Well, Patrick, there have been several confirmed reports of smoke coming from inside the house. We've been told that whatever fire may have been started seems to be under control at this time. Although that hasn't been confirmed by either Sheriff O'Halloran or any involved fire personnel."

"A fire?" Raine echoed, her blood going even colder than the rain lashing against the car.

"What about the three delinquent girls, Jim? Have you received any word regarding them?"

"Something's coming in now, Patrick. If you'll just wait a minute . . ." There was a moment of dead air. "Yes, the sheriff has reported that all three girls escaped the house unharmed."

Raine let out a long breath she hadn't even been aware of holding.

"Any word regarding a possible cause of the fire, Captain Jim?"

"Nothing's been confirmed as yet. But speculation seems to be that the police may have grown tired of waiting for the girls to surrender their standoff and shot an incendiary device into the house to smoke them out."

"A bomb?" Raine shouted at the radio. "He bombed three teenage girls?" The sheriff was going to pay for this, she vowed. She was going to keep the hick Lone Ranger wannabe in court until doomsday.

"Thank you, Captain Jim," the voice on the radio was saying. "Of course we'll keep you informed on further word regarding this potentially dangerous situation. Meanwhile, this is Patrick Christopher, K-SOUND Radio, returning to our weekly *Focus on State Government* with moderator Jane Kendall, in progress."

By the time she reached her grandmother's house, Raine was fuming, scheming the legal revenge that would not only cost the sheriff his job and whatever good reputation he may have inherited from his father, but everything he owned. Everything he might ever own. She was Xena, Warrior Princess. And she wasn't going to put away her weapons and cease fighting until she had Sheriff Jack O'Halloran's ass nailed to the courthouse door.

The bubble lights on top of the fire trucks were flashing through the mist, creating a surrealistic red glow as Raine plowed straight through the yellow police tape and pulled up behind a state police cruiser.

Fortunately, Raine noticed, the house was still standing, with no outward sign of fire damage. Normally, the sight of the weathered gray gingerbread house with its wide front porch and fish scale–roofed tower would have given her a sense of homecoming. Today, however, her mind was on other things.

She threw open the driver's door, then heedless of the rain, little caring that the heels of her suede pumps were sinking into the mud, she marched toward the group of uniformed men gathered together beside a black Chevy Suburban bearing the Olympic County insignia.

She stopped in front of them, dragged a handful of wet hair out of her eyes, then splayed her hands on the hips of her soon-to-be-ruined Donna Karan suit. "So which one of you cowboys is Sheriff Jack O'Halloran?"

Conversation came to an abrupt halt. All eyes shifted toward her before returning to the rangy man who seemed absurdly tall, standing literally head and shoulders above the others.

"That'd be me." Rainwater dripped off the brim of his—wouldn't you just know it? she thought scathingly—black Stetson. He was wearing a black Gore-Tex jacket that carried the same insignia as his ridiculously macho truck. "And you must be Ms. Raine Cantrell. The New York lawyer who's kept our county judicial system so busy the past few hours."

His half smile was obviously feigned, his gunmetal gray eyes offering not an iota of welcome. The tinge of sarcasm in his baritone voice frayed Raine's last nerve.

"If I weren't an officer of the court, I'd hit you for what you did to those girls." Her voice was tight with anger.

He gave her a bland look. "Since *I'm* an officer of

the court, if you were to hit me, I suppose I'd have no choice but to haul you in for assaulting an officer." He shrugged. "Looks as if we're at a stalemate, Counselor."

Raine thought about that. But not for long. "Not exactly. There's still the little matter of you bombing a house with three innocent teenagers in it, *Sheriff*." She heaped the same amount of sarcasm on his title as he'd used on hers.

"A bomb?" His dark brows crashed down toward his nose. A nose that looked as if it had been broken at some time in the past. "As an *officer of the court*"—there it was again, Raine thought, that damn sarcasm—"you, of all people should understand the power of an accusation. I didn't do any such thing."

"And I assume that fire just started by itself?"

"No." He skimmed a look over her. Then turned away. She was about to demand to know where he was going, to insist he not walk away while she was talking to him, when he opened the front door of the truck and retrieved a school bus yellow rubberized poncho. "And it wasn't really a fire. Just a lot of smoke. When the storm knocked out the power lines, the heat went out. Of course, since they were refusing to talk with me, I had no way of knowing that. Until they got cold and decided to light a fire in your grandmother's old wood stove. Unfortunately, no one ever mentioned the advisability of opening the damper first."

She caught the rain gear he'd tossed toward her with a murmured, reluctant "thank you," yanked it over her head, then followed his gaze to the back seat of the truck, where the three girls seemed none the worse for their experience.

"And now that we've settled that, Counselor," he said wearily, "I think I'll leave the logistics of straightening out this mess to you and the juvenile-court system. Because it's been a long day and my patience is hanging by a very thin thread."

"I have a Swiss Army knife in my bag," she said with a blatantly false smile. "Would you care to borrow the scissors?"

He rubbed his jaw and gave her an appraising look. "You know, I didn't see the family resemblance at first. But now I do. Your grandmother's a smart ass, too."

Before she could think up a scathing response to that remark, they were interrupted by a woman wearing a belted tan raincoat, clear-plastic rain boots over sensible shoes, and a frown. She was carrying a clipboard.

"Ms. Cantrell?" she asked.

"I'm Raine Cantrell," Raine confirmed.

"I'm Marianne Kelly. I'm a probation officer for Olympic County."

Old Fussbudget, Raine remembered. "It's a pleasure to meet you, Ms. Kelly," she lied. "I only wish it could have been under more pleasant circumstances."

"Yes. Well." It was the probation officer's turn to glance toward the truck where the teenagers were watching the proceedings with glum expressions. "It's getting late and I need to ensure that my probationers are settled for the night. If there isn't an adult available to take responsibility for them, I'm going to have to transfer them to a juvenile-detention facility."

Raine could just imagine her grandmother's reaction if she stood idly by and allowed that to happen. "Isn't that a little harsh, Ms. Kelly?" she asked mildly. "Under the circumstances? After all, they're just young girls."

"Perhaps you haven't been kept apprised of the situation, Ms. Cantrell. These *girls* created a crisis today—"

"There wasn't any crisis," Jack interjected. "That was just the stupid word the media came up with to boost ratings for the six-o'clock news."

A nerve twitched at the corner of the probation officer's left eyelid. "That may be your view of matters, Sheriff, but the fact remains that their behavior was highly unacceptable for probationers. And they cost the county a great deal of money."

He shrugged. "I get paid a straight salary, Ms. Kelly. Which doesn't make allowances for overtime. The most I can see that they cost the county was the price of a couple of pizzas, and if it'll keep them out of the pokey, I'll spring for them myself."

"That's a matter you'll have to take up with the county treasurer," the woman said briskly. "My concern is what to do with these delinquents."

"Girls," Jack corrected.

"Girls," Raine said at the same time.

They exchanged a look.

"What about my mother?" Raine asked, directing her question at the sheriff. "Has Lilith been found?"

"Yep. But I don't think she's going to prove a solution to this problem."

"Why not?"

"Because she's currently incarcerated."

"*What?*" It had been a long day for Raine, too. She decided that Sheriff O'Halloran's patience wasn't the only one hanging by a very thin thread. "You arrested my mother?"

"Not me. Cooper Ryan. He's a park service cop. Seems your mother was breaking a few fire regulations."

Talk about your small worlds. Raine remembered Lilith once expressing regret that she'd let her high school sweetheart get away. Coming from her mother, who'd never been one to admit to errors in judgement, that was definitely saying something.

"Well." Her mind, dulled by the long day and a touch of jet lag, went into overdrive, attempting to come up with a solution. She looked over at the Suburban again, viewed the expectant expressions on all three girl's faces, and knew that what they were expecting was to be thrown back into the system.

"Would the court find me an acceptable temporary adult guardian?"

"I believe that would be satisfactory," Ms. Kelly said after a moment's hesitation. "Until the hearing."

"When will that be?"

"The juvenile-court calendar's extremely crowded at the moment, but since this is a special case requiring immediate attention, I could probably find a judge to hear the case in say, three days?"

Three days. It wasn't that long, Raine assured herself as she took the clipboard Marianne Kelly was now holding out to her. It was more than enough time to get Lilith out of jail, Ida out of the hospital, the two sisters off to their aunt's custody, and determine whether the pregnant shoplifter posed a risk to her grandmother.

Ignoring Jack O'Halloran's challenging grin, Raine signed her name at the bottom of all three guardianship forms.

4

"Well, that makes it official. They're all yours." From Marianne Kelly's grim expression, Raine did not find the words at all encouraging.

That matter settled to her satisfaction, Old Fussbudget marched back to a tan sedan. Both Jack and Raine watched her go.

"That was a nice thing to do," he said finally.

Somehow, the compliment, laced with obvious surprise, irritated her more than his earlier sarcasm. "It wasn't as if I had any choice." Her words were clipped, designed to forestall any further conversation on the subject. "Now, where did you say I could find my mother?"

"I didn't." Just when she was certain she was going to grind her molars to dust, he added, "But she's at the ranger station on Hurricane Ridge."

"I didn't realize they had jail cells in federal parks."

He shrugged again, drawing her gaze to his shoulders, which were wide enough to gain him a position on the Giants' offensive line back in New York.

Not that she could ever picture Jack O'Halloran living in New York City. He was absolutely country, from the tip of that black Stetson down to the pointy toes of his—what else?—cowboy boots.

The fact that she was even the slightest bit intrigued by the steely, Clint Eastwood glint that occasionally appeared in his narrowed gray eyes only proved how exhausted she was.

"Unfortunately, bad guys show up from time to time even in federal parks," he said. "Although mostly it's just drunk and disorderly, that sort of thing."

"And breaking fire regulations."

A wry twitch that hinted at a smile tugged at one corner of his mouth, momentarily drawing her attention to a faint scar bisecting his top lip. "That, too. Coop said something about teaching her a lesson."

"If he can pull that off, he's a miracle worker." Along with flaunting rules and regulations, Lilith had a knack for ignoring the little morality lessons most people learned from life. "But there's no way I'm going to allow him to keep her locked up in a cell all night."

"It's not like she's doing hard time."

"I realize that," Raine said stiffly.

It was the principle of the thing. After all, she used her education every day to defend individuals far less deserving than Lilith. If she couldn't help her own mother, she might as well have stayed in Coldwater Cove, married some logger or cowboy cop like Jack O'Halloran right out of high school, and had a passel of kids. She wondered about her chances of getting a writ of *habeas corpus* to get her mother out tonight.

"But surely disobeying fire regulations is a misdemeanor. Besides"—she glared up at the rain which continued to pelt down on the hood of the borrowed poncho—"we're obviously not in fire season yet."

"True. And if it were just the fires, Coop might have been willing to give her a pass." He rubbed a square, clefted jaw that suggested a stubborn streak. "Not that I'd claim to know his mind, but as a fellow cop, I'd have to guess that it was the lewd and lascivious behavior, along with indecent exposure and assault and battery, that landed your mother in the pokey."

"Lewd and lascivious behavior? Indecent exposure?"

Forget *habeas corpus*. Raine was forced to consider her chances of insisting on a competency hearing for her mother. If past behavior were taken into account, she doubted it would be all that hard to win a finding of *non compos mentis*. Although her mother might not be certifiably insane, anyone who took the time to have a serious discussion with Lilith for more than five minutes could easily judge her incompetent to stand trial.

"And assault and battery," he reminded her.

"Damn." Raine rubbed the back of her neck, where strands of hair clung like seaweed. "I don't suppose you'd happen to know whom, exactly, she's accused of committing this battery on?"

"Actually, I do. It was Coop."

Her heart sank all the way down to the toes of her sloshy, egg-stained pumps. "My mother assaulted the arresting officer?"

"Well, it was more like a slap, to hear Coop tell it. But I suppose, technically, he could hit her with a resisting arrest charge, too."

Even worse. She just didn't need this. Not now. She'd been running on caffeine and adrenaline for weeks. Now that the buzz from the espresso she'd drunk on the ferry was beginning to wear off, she could feel the physical and mental letdown sneaking up behind her.

"You know," he suggested mildly, "the park jail isn't exactly Folsom Prison. It won't hurt her to spend a night there. And it just might give her time to think about behavior and consequences."

Raine's answering laugh was flat and humorless. "It's obvious you don't know my mother." She looked back at the Suburban. "Since there's no way I'm going to risk leaving those girls alone in my grandmother's house, I suppose I'll just have to take them to Hurricane Ridge with me."

He swore under his breath. "You are definitely Ida's granddaughter." Seemingly mindless of the rain, he yanked off his hat and raked his fingers through his thick dark hair. "Neither of you women know the meaning of the word *quit.*"

Raine tossed up her chin, bracing herself for another skirmish. "Oh, I know the meaning all right. I just don't believe in it."

He jammed the hat back down on his head. Then closed his eyes and pinched the bridge of his crooked nose. Then sighed heavily. And cursed again. It was, Raine considered, the most emotion the man had shown thus far.

"That road to Hurricane Ridge is tricky enough in

the daylight in dry weather. If you insist on bailing your mother out tonight, I'll drive you up there."

He seemed torn between aggravation and pity. It was the pity that Raine hated.

"That's not necessary." Unwilling to surrender to his unblinking cop stare, which she had no doubt had earned him a dandy confession rate during interrogations, she straightened both her back and her resolve. "I'm perfectly capable of taking care of my own family, Sheriff. Legally and personally."

"You're dead on your feet," he countered. "No offense intended, Counselor, but you kind of remind me of one of the walking zombies in all those horror flicks I used to like as a kid.

"And although I've no doubt that you're a real go-getter back in New York City"—he drawled the name of her adopted city with an unmistakable lack of respect—"this just happens to be *my* county. And there's no way I'm going to spend the rest of tonight out in this damn rain picking up the pieces after you drive off that cliff. Because as bad as you look right now, you'd look a helluva lot worse dead."

His granite face tightened into harsh angles and dangerous planes; his expression turned as uncompromising as the jagged, snow-spined Olympic mountains jutting up behind him.

It was at that moment, as he looked down at her, arms folded across his chest, that Raine knew for certain what she'd already begun to suspect. Jack O'Halloran's outwardly easygoing facade and good-old-boy behavior concealed a granite will that might actually prove more unyielding than her own. Oh yes, she thought grimly, Choate, Plimpton, Wells &

Sullivan's comptroller, Harriet Farraday, would definitely approve of this man.

"Well." She stared up at him. "No one can accuse you of mincing words, Sheriff."

When he didn't say anything, just stood there, his brows and his mouth both drawn into an unrelentingly unyielding line, Raine experienced a renewed spark of competition.

"You realize, of course, that you have no legal authority to keep me from driving anywhere in this county I wish to go."

"I wouldn't bet the farm on that one."

Proving to be just one unpleasant surprise after another, he turned on a booted heel, strode over to her rental car, and while Raine watched in stunned shock, this man wearing the badge of authority—a sheriff who'd taken an oath to uphold the law!—took a huge black flashlight from his wide belt and smashed the car's left taillight.

All her verbal skills abandoned Raine. She was still sputtering in protest when he returned to where her feet seemed to have been nailed to the driveway.

"Although you may be a little rusty on Washington State law, having spent all that time back east, even in New York City, it's undoubtedly illegal to drive without two working taillights. Especially at night.

"You move that car five feet out of this driveway, Counselor, and I'm going to have to pull you over. And, perhaps, just for good measure, I'll impound the car. As evidence."

Coldwater Cove may not be the big city, but it had always been a civilized little town. At least it had been when she'd last visited, three years ago. Of course back then, this man's father had been sheriff.

"Surely you don't think you're going to get away with that?" Raine hated the way her fractured voice sounded like a stranger's. Her elocution had always been one of her best courtroom weapons.

"I can sure as hell give it the old college try. If push comes to shove, I'll throw myself on the mercy of the court."

The trace of renewed amusement in his voice reminded her that the court in question just happened to be presided over by his old high school baseball team catcher, Wally Cunningham. *Hell.*

Knowing when she'd been out maneuvered, Raine tried to remind herself that the key was to keep her eye on the prize. How many times had she had to remind clients of that little truism? So long as you remembered what you wanted to achieve, the road to that end could take any number of unexpected twists and turns along the way.

And Jack O'Halloran was definitely the most unexpected and unwelcome detour on a very exasperating trip.

Unable to throw in the towel without having the last word, Raine glared up at him. "If breaking my taillight was your idea of upholding the law in your county, Sheriff, I'd love to know how you got elected. What did you do? Threaten to drag out the truncheons and rubber hoses to anyone who didn't vote for you?" The scowl was replaced with a blatantly false smile. "Or did you simply stuff the ballot boxes?"

"Neither one."

If he was at all wounded by her sarcasm, he didn't

show it. His grin was one she remembered well from high school days. The dangerous, cocky-as-hell grin that had undoubtedly coaxed more than one buxom cheerleader into the back seat of his Batmobile black Trans Am.

"I simply relied on my devastating good looks and legendary superhero crime-fighting abilities. Oh, and of course my natural O'Halloran male charm," he tacked on with an exaggerated display of that alleged charm.

The man really was impossible. "I suppose being the son of the former sheriff didn't hurt either." Her tone was as dry as a legal brief.

"No." The grin faded at the mention of his father. Shutters came down over his eyes. "I suppose it didn't." He rubbed a broad hand down his face, and when he took it away, Raine realized that he was as weary as she was.

Which wasn't all that surprising, she supposed, given the fact that the day undoubtedly hadn't been a picnic for him, either. The sensible thing to do would be to just bury the hatchet and get on with springing Lilith from jail so they could all get to sleep.

"Since I don't want to explain to Hertz why my car was impounded, I suppose I have no choice but to let you drive me to Hurricane Ridge."

"With such a graceful acceptance, how could I possibly refuse?"

Raine ignored his sarcasm. "But first I need to call the hospital and check on Ida."

"You can call from the truck. So, now that we've settled that, let's get moving, Harvard. Your mother isn't getting any younger. And neither am I."

Raine wasn't all that surprised that he knew where she'd gone to school. After all, Ida had always enjoyed bragging about her granddaughters accomplishments. Although he certainly didn't seem at all impressed by her Ivy League credentials.

When he put his fingers around her waist and lifted her into the bucket seat of the Suburban, she had the uncomfortable feeling that she was being taken into custody. Because she wasn't honestly certain she could have made it up there in her snug skirt and high heels, Raine didn't object.

A call to the hospital revealed that since the doctors had decided her grandmother's fall was merely a passing case of vertigo compounded by a rickety stool, Ida could be released in the morning. Her concern eased, Raine turned toward the three teenagers who were sitting as stiff and silent as stumps in the back seat of the Suburban, as if afraid they'd be thrown back into juvenile hall if they breathed a single word.

"Well, I suppose, since we're going to be spending the next three days together, we should get acquainted. As you've undoubtedly figured out, I'm Raine." She attempted a smile that didn't quite work.

Still acting as spokesperson, Shawna introduced herself. Then the others. As she greeted them all, accepted their uncensored gratitude, and lied a little by professing to be pleased to meet them, Raine reluctantly decided that none of them looked all that dangerous.

Shawna was already a beauty. With her long swan's neck and high cheekbones, she reminded Raine a bit of Tyra Banks. Her face was framed with a mass of beaded braids, her earlobes each adorned with three gold hoops.

Sixteen-year-old Gwen, with her wide eyes and freckled face surrounded by carrot-hued curls, resembled a pregnant Orphan Annie. Or, Raine thought, taking in the red-and-white boat-necked polka-dot top she was wearing over black leggings, Lucille Ball, just before she'd given birth to Little Rickie.

Renee—Shawna's vegetarian runaway sister, Raine remembered—would have looked like any other thirteen-year-old girl poised on the threshold of womanhood. Had it not been for the terrified look in her Bambi brown eyes.

"Are we going to jail?" Gwen asked, casting a nervous glance toward Jack. Raine watched her place a hand on her bulging stomach in unconscious protection of her child. "I don't want to have my baby in jail!"

Her high tone wavered toward hysterical, making Raine hope that the stress of the day—a day that already seemed forty-eight hours long—wouldn't have the teenager going into labor anytime soon. At least if such an unfortunate event were to happen, having Jack O'Halloran along might prove useful. Weren't all cops trained to deliver babies?

"Of course you're not going to have your baby in jail," Raine assured her, not honestly knowing anything of the kind. If looks were any indication, the child appeared ready to give birth to a ten-pound basketball at any moment. "By the way, when are you due?"

"In two and a half weeks."

"Oh, well then," Raine said airily, "you've plenty

of time. After all, first babies are always late." She was certain she'd heard that somewhere.

"But he's already dropped."

"Mama Ida said that's normal with a first baby," Shawna reminded the younger girl. "It's called lightening, remember?"

"As if," Gwen scoffed. "I still think that's a dumb thing to call it, because the baby hasn't gotten any bit lighter," she complained. "And I sure won't mind if he decides to come early, though I don't want him born in any jail cell."

"You don't have any reason to worry about that," Raine said again. "Because none of you are going to jail."

"Then where is the sheriff taking us?" Renee asked, speaking up for the first time.

"It's Lilith who's in jail. Sheriff O'Halloran was kind enough to offer to drive us to Hurricane Ridge to bail her out."

"Lilith's in jail?" Renee's eyes got even wider.

"I'm afraid so." Raine sighed. Although she should have grown used to her mother's antics by now, it wasn't always easy playing grown-up to Lilith's adolescent rebellions. "Apparently she got in a little trouble in the park, and—"

"I told her that she'd never get away with it," Shawna broke in knowingly. "I warned her that the rangers would spot those fires, and as soon as they did, they'd catch her prancing around naked."

"You knew what she was planning to do?" Raine asked.

"Oh, sure. Like I said, it was part of an old druid ritual. Or Celtic, or something like that. Anyway, she invited me to come with her, but Mama Ida put her foot down."

"Good for Ida."

"To tell the truth, Mama Ida didn't have to object all that hard," Shawna said with a grin. "Taking off my clothes and dancing around in the woods would be like, totally pathetic. Not that Lilith is pathetic," she said quickly, as if belatedly realizing she'd just insulted their savior's mother. "I didn't mean it that way."

"I know what you meant. And you certainly showed more sense than Lilith."

"That wouldn't be difficult," Jack, who'd remained quiet during the conversation, murmured.

Although she might criticize her mother, Raine was not about to let anyone else. Especially a man who'd broken her taillight. Vowing to make him pay for any extra damage charges Hertz might add onto her credit card, she turned toward him.

"What did you say?"

Before he could answer, he was distracted by a sudden sound that seemed to be coming from his shirt. One that didn't resemble any beeper she'd ever heard.

"Damn." He pulled off the road and cut the engine. As Raine watched in amazement, he pulled a small plastic device from his shirt pocket. "Wouldn't you just know it," he growled. "The damn thing took a shi—" He glanced back toward the girls. "Needs the litter box cleaned out," he amended.

"Is that what I think it is?" Raine asked. His hand dwarfed the green plastic egg-shaped gadget.

"It depends on what you think it is. If your guess

is a damn electronic cat, you'd be right on the money."

"I see." Actually, she didn't see anything, but Raine was perverse enough to enjoy his obvious discomfort at the situation. "Do you often take your toys to work with you, Sheriff?"

"It's not mine. It's my daughter's." With a deftness that seemed at odds with such powerful hands, he pressed a button on the front of the toy. "She's not allowed to have it at school, so I promised her I'd keep the damn thing alive for her."

"That's very admirable," Raine said grudgingly. "Especially since most men would undoubtedly leave any virtual-cat-box emptying to their wives."

"I probably would, too." The problem taken care of, at least for now, he jammed the Nano Kitty back into his pocket. "If I had a wife." He twisted the key in the ignition, bringing the huge engine back to life. "She died."

"I'm sorry." Raine was truly sorry his wife had died. She was even sorrier she'd brought it up.

He shrugged as he pulled back onto the road. "It's been two years. I've come to accept it." His soft, weary sigh was barely audible, but Raine heard it. "Most of the time, anyway. It's harder on Amy."

"Amy's your daughter," she guessed.

"Yeah."

Although her mother hadn't died, Raine knew, more than most, how difficult it was for a girl to grow up without a mother. How it felt to be abandoned by the one person in the world who wasn't supposed to ever leave you. "How old is she?"

"Six." This time it was a smile she heard in his voice. "Going on thirty."

"Ah, one of those children my mother would refer to as an old soul."

"Or just a kid who's just had to grow up a little faster than most. Peg got sick when she was still a toddler."

Raine did some quick mental mathematics. If his daughter was six and he'd been widowed two years, obviously his wife hadn't died quickly. Sympathy stirred, but suspecting that Jack O'Halloran was a man who preferred to keep his feelings to himself, she allowed the unexpectedly personal conversation to wind down.

As her thoughts drifted back to her reason for being in this truck with him—Lilith in trouble yet again—Raine felt just about as glum as Sheriff O'Halloran looked.

As he drove up the steep and winding road to the Hurricane Ridge ranger station, Jack mentally horsewhipped himself. What the hell had gotten into him? Spouting off about Peg that way?

It was the forced intimacy, he decided. This situation—two people driving through a dark and foggy night, with the rain hitting the roof of the truck—would tend to encourage conversation. Especially after they'd both suffered an exhausting day. It wasn't anything personal.

That idea had him feeling better for about two minutes. Until he slanted a sideways glance toward his passenger who seemed to have fallen asleep. The flourescent green glow from the dashboard lights illuminated features that, while a bit too strong for conventional beauty, were still damn easy on the eyes. Her nose could have been considered aristocratic were it not for the fact that it tilted up, just a bit, at the end. Her mouth was a tad too stubborn for his taste, but he remembered the way it had softened when she'd asked about Amy and decided it had possibilities.

He watched her lips part to expel a faint, shuddering breath. In sleep, her features softened appealingly. Too appealingly, he considered, forcing his mind to focus on all the unnecessary grief she'd caused him today as she'd wielded the power of the law like a cudgel. No, he decided, more like a dueling foil, flourished with the cool efficiency of those rapiers in the old Errol Flynn flicks that still showed up on late-night cable from time to time.

Efficient she might admittedly be. But cool? Although some might look at her severely tailored suit and cinnamon brown hair and believe that, he'd seen glimpses of another woman. A woman who wasn't nearly as self-controlled as the lady attorney would like people to believe. The passion surrounding her as she'd stood up for those three girls she didn't even know, had flared like a newborn sun. After the unsatisfying phone conversations they'd shared before her arrival in Coldwater Cove, Jack had been surprised by the display of white-hot energy. And, dammit, interested.

As he set his jaw and glared out into the dark night, he reminded himself that even if he was in the market for a woman—which he wasn't—a skinny, mouthy New York lawyer with an attitude the size of Puget Sound and chips the size of Mount Rainier on both shoulders wasn't his type.

Even as he reminded himself of that, her perfume bloomed in the heat of the car. Unlike the sweet floral scent Peg had favored, this was spicy and complex and caused a disturbing churning deep inside him.

During the last months of Peg's life, intimacy had been one of hearts and minds rather than of shared bodies. Even in the beginning, before physical lovemaking had become impossibly painful for her, Jack had understood that his wife had needed reassurance that she was still attractive. That he still wanted her. Which, of course he had. But whenever he'd tried to prove that to her, he hadn't been able to stop from treating her like spun glass, delicate enough to shatter at the slightest touch.

On such occasions he'd pull back, foregoing the earthy passion that characterized their precancer lovemaking. His touch turned more gentle—almost tentative—his kisses gifted rather than plundered, and on more than one occasion when she'd cried out in what he desperately feared might be pain, his body had betrayed him, deflating like a three-day-old balloon.

She had, of course, assured him that she understood, that it didn't matter. But as he'd lain beside her, feeling like the world's greatest failure, Jack had known that deep down inside, it did.

After she died, the responsibilities of juggling single fatherhood with the demands of the seventeen thousand residents of Olympic County, who expected him to keep their streets and homes safe, had blotted out all desire for sex.

Until now. When it was returning with a vengeance,

As if sensing his unbidden, unwelcome hunger,

Raine opened her eyes just in time to catch him looking at her lips.

Feeling a lot like he had back in junior high, when his mother had caught him sneaking a look at his first *Playboy* centerfold, Jack dragged his gaze back up to hers.

Her eyes were soft, nearly unfocused as they met his, leaving him to wonder if he was imagining the sudden spark of feminine awareness in those gold-hued depths. What would she do, he wondered, if he pulled off the road, yanked her out of that leather bucket seat and plundered her wide, lush lips with his own?

Damn. He didn't need this, Jack reminded himself as he pulled into the nearly deserted parking lot. Not now. And definitely not with her.

5

After instructing all three girls to remain in the truck, Raine braced herself for dealing with her mother. Which, even in the best of times, had never been easy.

"Darling!" Lilith burst into the room in a whirl-wind of her usual energy and flung her arms around Raine's neck. "I knew you'd come rescue your poor abused mother!"

Raine didn't think her mother looked all that abused. In fact, except for that ugly orange jump-suit, she looked as stunning as ever. Even more so with the edgy emotion glittering in the midnight blue depths of her eyes. Lilith Lindstrom was a daz-zling creature of the moment, a wild child, even at fifty.

"You know I wouldn't let you spend the night in jail."

Raine slipped free of this woman who'd given birth to her, this woman whom she'd never under-stood. Although on some abstract basis, Raine could think of Lilith as her mother, it had been years since she'd thought of her as *mother*. And never, not even in the secret privacy of her own mind, had she ever thought of this radiant, ethereal creature as *mom*.

"You're such a good girl." Lilith's voice was light and sweet and young. Then, as her bright eyes took another, longer look at her eldest daughter, the smile faded and horizontal lines formed in a porcelain-smooth forehead. "Although I'd hoped that living in New York would have taught you a bit more about style. Wherever did you get that unattractive rainwear?"

"You're not exactly a fashion plate yourself." Raine's tone was a great deal drier than the weather. "Shawna told me about the nude dancing. But didn't you take some clothes with you?"

"Well, of course I did, darling. Surely you don't think that I'd drive nude on the highway?"

"Quite honestly, Lilith, I never quite know what to expect."

"Join the club," the man who'd released Lilith from the cell, muttered.

Cooper Ryan was yet another surprise in a day—and now night—of surprises. Raine knew that a fifty-year-old man certainly wasn't old, especially these days when the baby boomer generation seemed determined to continue to shatter stereotypes. But she certainly hadn't been prepared for him to be quite so—well, stunning.

Unlike Jack O'Halloran, whose rugged features appeared to have been harshly hewn from granite with an axe, her mother's jailer was as classically beautiful as a Renaissance statue. Lines fanning out from riveting blue eyes added character, rather than age, and his dark blond hair was streaked at the temples with silver that somehow added to his patrician appearance. Although she did not consider herself a fanciful woman, Raine had no trouble at all picturing this man strolling down from the heights of Mount Olympus to dabble with the mortals.

No wonder Lilith had fallen in love with this man. The pertinent question, Raine considered, was how on earth she'd walked away.

"Was it absolutely necessary to force my mother to wear prison garb?"

Unfortunately, Cooper Ryan proved to be yet another Coldwater Cove male she couldn't intimidate. He met her censorious gaze with a level one of his own. "Why don't you ask your mother that question?"

Raine turned back to Lilith, who was now perched on the corner of the cluttered oak desk, legs crossed, appearing more like an empress granting an audience to a roomful of needy peasants than someone who'd been arrested.

"Well?" she invited.

"It's quite simple." As Lilith tossed her head, Raine considered grimly that *nothing* about this woman had ever been simple. "I'm making a statement."

"I see." Raine was aware of the sheriff's faint, annoying chuckle, but refused to look at him.

"I'm a political prisoner. That being the case, I may as well dress the part."

Oh, good Lord. Would this damn day never end?

"You're not a political prisoner, Lilith." Raine bit the words off with exaggerated patience. Another day like this one and she'd have to begin buying antacids by the case. "You were arrested for setting fires outside of a designated campground."

"It's Beltane. The fires were necessary. And, as I've already explained to Cooper, surely he couldn't expect me to conduct a nude ceremony in a public campground with unbelievers." Lilith shot a blistering look toward the Greek god who was leaning against the wall, arms folded across his chest.

"I don't suppose you could have conducted the ceremony with clothes on?"

"Don't be silly, darling. Clothing inhibits magic. Everyone knows that."

"Try telling that to David Copperfield."

"David Copperfield, as talented as he admittedly is, is merely an illusionist." Lilith lifted her chin. "I'm speaking of real magic, Raine, dear. As ancient as Earth itself."

"Well, we certainly wouldn't want to inhibit that."

Raine momentarily wished that her mother was back in her Greenpeace save-the-dolphins mode. Until she recalled an incident concerning a motorboat and a Japanese tuna-fishing fleet that had nearly caused an international incident.

"But I believe the unofficial report also mentions assault and battery. On a police officer. Not to mention that little charge of resisting arrest."

"Oh, pooh." Lilith waved the accusation away as if it were little more than a pesky moth. "The only reason Cooper arrested me was to get back at me for not marrying him."

"If today's performance was any example of what you've turned out to be, I ought to be on my knees, thanking God that we didn't get hitched." From Cooper Ryan's gritty tone, Raine guessed that Lilith's barb had hit its mark. "Because we wouldn't have made it to our first month's anniversary."

"You're undoubtedly right." Lilith's answering smile was dazzling. It was also blatantly false. "Since there's no way I could have possibly lived with an ultraconservative right-wing bully."

"And there's no way I would have lived with a witch," he countered with a flare of heat that nearly took Raine's breath away. And it hadn't even been directed at her.

She couldn't resist slanting a quick glance toward Jack, whose expression told her that for once, they were in agreement. Cooper Ryan and Lilith Lindstrom had left a great deal unsettled between them. Including a surfeit of sexual chemistry that almost had Raine on the verge of an estrogen meltdown herself.

Although there were times, such as now, when she was forced to view her mother as a sexual being, Raine had never liked the feeling.

"I can see you two have a great deal of catching up to do," Jack said. "If you'd like us to leave you alone—"

"No!" Both Cooper and Lilith spoke as one, at precisely the same time. They stared at each other for a long moment. Then, finally, he gave her a weary go-ahead gesture.

"After the horrid day I've suffered, I just want to go home," Lilith said, trying for an air of martyrdom that fell decidedly short of the mark.

"You're welcome to her." Coop addressed his words to Raine. "And if you promise to keep her under control, I'll drop the charges."

"You certainly will not, Cooper Ryan," Lilith spoke up before Raine could answer. She tossed her head with renewed spirit. "I fully intend to see you in court. Where your tyrannical behavior can become public record."

He shrugged, seeming to decide that further discussion wasn't worth the effort. "Whatever. I'm sick and tired of arguing."

"As am I." She eyed him with what appeared to be honest regret. "I am horribly disappointed at how you turned out, Cooper. Why, you may as well have become a Republican."

"As it happens, I *am* a Republican."

"Oh, dear heavens. That's so tragic. I have half a mind to stage an intervention."

"If your behavior today was any indication, sweetheart, half a mind might be overstating your qualifications."

Lilith surprised Raine by laughing at that. Then slid off the desk in a litho, graceful movement and glided over to where he was still standing in the doorway.

"All the boys in Coldwater Cove used to throw themselves at my feet. And while such groveling was admittedly flattering, absolute adoration can get horrendously boring. But you always were a challenge, Cooper." She placed her hand against the chest of his khaki uniform shirt. "I'd almost forgotten how stimulating fighting with you can be."

"Dammit, Lilith—," he warned.

"Yes, darling?" She went up on her toes and pressed her lips against his grimly set ones.

Although the kiss was brief, if the fevered crimson color rising from his collar was any indication, it packed one helluva punch. Even as accustomed as she was to her mother's outrageous behavior, Raine found herself worrying what Jack O'Halloran might be thinking.

She sneaked another glance his way, instantly realizing her mistake when their eyes met again and a jagged bolt of lightninglike desire shot through her body, all the way to her toes. The only thing that kept her from melting into a puddle right here on the ranger station floor was her impression that the sheriff was every bit as disconcerted as she was by the flare of sexual heat.

The drive home blurred in Raine's mind. She vaguely remembered leaving the park headquarters with her mother and Jack and, wanting to put a little distance between herself and the sheriff, insisting Lilith sit up front while she took the third back seat for herself.

Lilith grudgingly admitted that Cooper had informed her about the standoff and Ida's hospitalization and had even checked several times for updates on both conditions.

"That was very considerate of him," Raine suggested.

Lilith shrugged. "He and Mother always got along. I used to think the only reason she wanted me to marry him was so he could become the son she'd always wanted."

Raine had no intention of getting into a discussion about her mother's love life. "Well, whatever the reason, it was still nice."

Her mother didn't answer. Silence settled over the interior of the truck. The girls appeared understandably wiped out by their eventful day and even Lilith proved uncharacteristically subdued as they drove back through the rainy, foggy night to Coldwater

Cove, stopping once at the Port Angeles McDonald's for Gwen to use the restroom. Then they were back on the road.

The distance between Raine and Jack precluded conversation. But they didn't need to talk for her to sense that they were both thinking about that unbidden, stunning moment of awareness.

Unlike her mother, who could still cause grown men to walk into walls, Raine had never been the type of woman to inspire hunger in any man. She'd never wanted to be that type of woman. To her mind, lust involved surrender—of control, willpower, of self. And surrender was simply not in her vocabulary. It never had been, and as far as she was concerned, it never would be.

When she leaned her head against the truck window and closed her eyes, she recalled a dream she'd had sometime during her teens. She and Savannah had been riding in a convertible driven by her mother down a steep, winding mountain road in the rain. The top was down and they were getting soaked. They were speeding around the switchbacks, the car taking on more and more speed, until it was racing downhill out of control.

"Take the wheel, Raine!" her mother, who was now inexplicably in the backseat, called out to her.

"I can't," she'd shouted over the squeal of the tires. The convertible was going faster and faster; the rain was falling harder and harder. "I'm not sixteen, yet."

"Neither am I," Lilith had shouted back without missing a beat.

Shaking off the memory, Raine sighed. The gray fog formed a seemingly impenetrable wall outside the rain-chilled glass, that had her once more wishing for that sun-drenched beach. The romantic vision she'd experienced in the limo fluttered enticingly back into her mind. Although this time the phantom lover was no anonymous stranger. This time his all too recognizable gray eyes were silvered by the moonlight.

Raine was gazing up at him like a besotted teenager, mesmerized by the lips that were inexorably lowering toward hers, when suddenly she was no longer standing with her lover on a moon-spangled beach, but all alone, knee-deep in quicksand.

No! She squeezed her eyes tight. This was ridiculous! She was not, by nature, an overly imaginative woman. She was an attorney, for heaven's sake, trained by Socratic method at what was arguably the finest law school in the country. Perhaps even the entire world. Intelligent women who'd spent years studying the strategies of legal thought and argument did not suffer from hallucinations.

As Jack turned off the road onto the long driveway leading up the hill to her grandmother's house, Raine worried that the stress of the past months may have finally gotten to her. Wondering if this is what a nervous breakdown felt like, she decided she really needed to take that vacation. Three days, she reminded herself. Surely she could stay sane that long.

Since he hadn't wanted to drag a sleeping Amy out into the rain, Jack had reluctantly agreed to let her spend the night at his mother's. But only after assuring her that he'd be by first thing in the morning so they could have breakfast together before he drove her to school.

As he entered the kitchen of the ramshackle old farmhouse Peg had begged him to buy before her death, he felt an unexpected surge of anger at his wife. One he hadn't experienced for months. How dare she desert him? Hadn't she understood that he didn't know a damn thing about bringing up a little girl?

Oh, sure, he thought, as he pulled a bottle of Rainier beer from the refrigerator and twisted the cap off with more force than necessary, he'd learned a lot in the past two years. But it wasn't the same as Amy having a mother, dammit.

Peg should have stayed here where she belonged. With her daughter. With him.

And that, he thought as he threw his body onto the family room sofa, was the crux of the problem. He took a long pull from the dark brown bottle, momentarily wishing the beer was something stronger. A lot stronger.

"You're not thinking about Amy."

His words seemed to echo in the empty house. The falling-down house he'd tried to tell Peg was larger than they'd ever need. But she'd proven surprisingly assertive those last months of her life, insisting that after all those years living in a Seattle townhouse, they needed a "real home." When he'd realized that she wasn't about to give in, he'd reluctantly acquiesced, even though they both knew that she'd never live to see it properly renovated.

"It's yourself you're feeling so fucking sorry for." The gloom he'd thought he'd put behind him settled over his shoulders. The roof had found a new place to leak; rain was tapping an annoying rhythm on the hand-pegged wooden floor. "Shit, nothing like a goddamn pity party to cap off a less than spectacular day."

He pushed himself to his feet, unlocked the small cedar chest and chose a videotape at random from the stacks Peg had created. He shoved the tape into the VCR, moved the wastepaper basket he kept for such purposes beneath this new leak, then flopped back onto the couch.

It was one of the tapes Peg had made outdoors, on the rugged coastline strewn with piles of driftwood she'd claimed always made her think of Sasquatch playing a game of pick-up-sticks. She was laughing, with her gentle eyes and her generous mouth, as she related the legend of Big Foot, that huge, hairy Pacific Northwest version of the Abominable Snowman, to her daughter, who'd someday be watching this tape.

Groaning, Jack shut his eyes against the pain. Then, unable to resist, reluctantly opened them again and watched his wife as she strolled down the beach, pausing to point out the wonders found in tide pools. She could have been any mother taking a lazy summer day to share her world with her child. She could have had all the time in the world. But sometimes pictures lied, Jack thought. And appearances could definitely be deceiving.

In the background the rising tide roared, gulls and cormorants wheeled over the towering offshore sea stacks and although he couldn't hear it on the tape, Jack remembered the sough of the wind in the fir trees atop the cliff. That same wind that was ruffling the fiery auburn bob beneath Peg's Seattle Mariners baseball cap.

The hair was a dazzling flourescent red color

never seen in nature, too bright to be real, which it wasn't. Claiming wigs were too hot, but unwilling to go out in public looking like, as she'd put it, "a transvestite Yul Brynner," she'd sewn strands from a cheap vinyl wig into the cap. And somehow, on her, it had looked just right.

Jack found himself reluctantly smiling back at his wife. Just as he knew she'd intended when she'd begun the ambitious legacy in the first place. As if Mother Nature couldn't remain immune to such a warm heart, the sun swept from behind a low-hanging pewter cloud and lit the gunmetal sea to shimmering sapphire.

A dizzying tumble of images appeared on the screen, disjointed scenes of sky and surf that had Jack remembering dropping the camera. For a long time the unblinking camcorder eye stared at the gray sand. A crab scuttled sideways into view, then disappeared again. Iridescent bubbles sparkled, then winked out like fallen stars. The frothy white foam seemed to be growing closer with each succeeding wave that washed onto shore.

"Jack!" Her voice was breathless. With laughter, and, he remembered, lingering passion from the kiss they shared after he dropped the camera. "It's going to get wet!"

There was a disorienting image of Peg's slender hands scooping it from the sand. Her gold wedding band gleamed, reminding Jack of the until-death-do-us-part promise that had seemed so far away on that sun-blessed Saturday afternoon they'd exchanged vows.

"We should get that on tape," she was saying.

He grumbled in the background.

"No, it'll be perfect," she coaxed prettily, turning the camera on him, catching him in midscowl. "Let's show our daughter what a blissfully perfect kiss looks like."

In the end, of course, she'd won. After steadying the camera atop a stack of bleached logs, she held out her arms to him. And, as always, he found it impossible to resist.

The staged kiss wasn't all that long. Neither was it as hot as the earlier, unplanned one had been. But it was sweet enough to make his eyes burn as he relived it in heart-wrenching detail.

Then, without warning, memories of kissing Peg battled with unbidden images of taking Raine Cantrell on the rough wet sand, like Burt Lancaster rolling around in the surf with Deborah Kerr in *From Here to Eternity* that had been broadcast on The Movie Channel the other night.

It didn't matter that he didn't particularly even like the New York lawyer who'd riled up hormones he'd almost forgotten were lurking inside him. The fantasy had caused a painful stirring in his loins and Jack didn't need to look down to know that although his mind might not want anything more to do with Ida's mouthy granddaughter, another, more vital part of his body was literally throbbing with the need to bury itself inside her.

"Goddammit!"

He pushed himself up from the sofa, jerked the tape from the VCR and locked it away in the chest again. Then went upstairs and stripped off his clothes, tossing them uncaringly onto the floor since there was no longer anyone around to complain. Jack's last thought, as he drifted off to sleep, was a strict command to both his mind and body to forget about Raine Cantrell.

When he awoke the next morning stiff, sore, and painfully horny, Jack reminded himself that a man couldn't hold himself responsible for his dreams. But that didn't make him feel any better as he showered, the stinging, ice-cold needles of water designed to chill any lingering desire.

❧6❧

Raine awoke to the clear, sweet song of a morning bird. Momentarily disoriented, she lay in the tester bed, looking up at the dancing dots of water-brightened light on the white plaster ceiling. It was when her gaze shifted to the square of sunshine on the bedcover that she remembered where she was. The familiar quilt was a living history of her family. Raine remembered her grandmother pointing out the pieces of her own mother's blue-serge church going dress stitched next to the red-and-black-checked flannel shirt Raine's great-grandfather John had worn while logging.

There was a pink square from the dress Ida had worn to her first day at school, two dotted Swiss triangles from the dress she'd worn to receive her medical degree, and a piece of lace, once white, now aged to the hue of old parchment, that had been cut from her wedding dress. Raine thought it ironic that although her grandparents' marriage had ended in divorce, the memory lived on, along with others, the fabric of so many lives sewn into this brightly colored family quilt.

Pushing herself out of bed, she made her way into the adjoining bathroom, which seemed smaller than she remembered it, brushed her teeth, ran her fingers through her hair, and decided to put the coffee on before her shower. Before going downstairs, she paused to look out the bedroom window.

Last night's rain had moved eastward toward Seattle, leaving the air as clear as crystal and from her window, located at the very top of the house's tower, Raine had an eagle's-eye view of the jagged, snow-capped peaks of the Olympic Mountains in one direction, the town and bay in the other. In the distance, a white ferry chugged from the dock toward Seattle. Three small skiffs—one with an eye-catching red sail—skimmed over morning-still water like butterflies over rippled blue silk.

Closer to home, Raine could see Coldwater Cove waking up. Kathleen Walker, pharmacist and the third generation of Walkers to run the Walker Drug Emporium, was on the sidewalk outside her red-brick, brass-plaqued storefront, unfurling blue-and-white awnings. The Orca Theater's marquee announced a Mel Gibson festival while across the street, the smoke coming from the chimney of the Gray Gull Smorgasbord & Grill revealed that Oley Swensen had begun smoking ribs for the lunch and dinner crowds. Although some might not consider barbecue a traditional Scandinavian dish, faithful customers swore Oley made the best ribs on the peninsula.

Directly below her window, a flock of shiny black starlings strutted across the dew-bright lawn like an army laying claim to conquered territory. In the center of the lawn, a pair of nuthatches splashed in a white stone birdbath surrounded by daffodils; the scattered water from their energetic wing flapping sparkled like diamonds.

The house was quiet, suggesting the others were still sleeping off the effects of yesterday's events. Raine tiptoed down the staircase, avoiding the stair that had always creaked like a rusty hinge.

The country kitchen was blinding yellow—like the inside of a lemon. It had always been this way, at least as long as Raine could remember. The paint strip Ida kept in the kitchen junk drawer referred to it as *buttercup*, but it had always reminded Raine of sunshine. Winter on the peninsula could, at times, turn unrelentingly gray and wet; the color was an uplifting antidote for the gloom.

Although Ida's cooking talents were marginal at best, the kitchen had always been the heart of the house, the room where new days were greeted with fishing reports broadcast on the old tabletop radio and broken hearts were soothed over cups of hot chocolate made with Quick from the yellow can that had been a mainstay in the pantry for as long as Raine could remember. Her own kitchen back in New York was closet-size, certainly not big enough for people to gather, not that she had any time for entertaining.

She spooned some dark ground coffee from a Starbucks stoneware jar she found on the counter into the white paper filter of the coffee maker, and poured in water. While she waited for the water to drip through the machine, Raine sat down at the pine table in front of the window, intending to make a list of all the things she needed to do today.

It seemed so strange not to be rushing off for

work. Drumming her fingers impatiently on the tabletop, she glanced up at the copper-teapot clock. It was still too early to show up at the hospital. Last night she'd been informed that Ida couldn't be released until after morning rounds, which began around nine.

"Perhaps I'll just check in," she decided out loud as she compared the silence of the kitchen—disturbed only by the soft hum of the refrigerator—with the beehive of activity of her office. Undoubtedly a host of phone calls had been piling up.

Conveniently ignoring the fact that Brian ran their little corner of Choate, Plimpton, Wells & Sullivan with the efficiency of the joint chiefs preparing for an invasion, Raine called her office.

"You haven't even been away for twenty-four hours yet, Raine," Brian reminded her, amusement evident in his voice after she expressed concern about the work she'd left behind. "Don't worry, I'm certainly capable of holding down the fort."

"I know." What had she thought? That Choate, Plimpton, Wells & Sullivan couldn't survive three days without her? "Thank you, Brian. I don't know what I'd do without you."

After laughing at his assertion that he didn't know what she'd do without him, either, Raine hung up, feeling vaguely dissatisfied by the brief conversation. While she was grateful that things hadn't fallen apart without her, deep down inside, part of her wished that they also weren't going so smoothly.

"What did you expect? You've been gone less than twenty-four hours. No one's indispensable," she muttered into the stillness. "Not even a Warrior Princess."

Since the coffee seemed to be taking forever to drip through the filter of Ida's jazzy new coffee maker, Raine had just decided to use the time to go back upstairs and take a shower when something outside the window caught her attention. Grabbing a corduroy barn jacket from the hook beside the kitchen door, she marched outdoors.

"What do you think you're doing?" she demanded of the man hunkered down behind her car.

"Taking care of your taillight," he answered with bland innocence. He held up some broken pieces of red plastic as evidence. "I've just about got it replaced."

"That's not necessary."

"Sure it is." He tightened a couple of final screws. "Since I'm the one who broke it in the first place."

"Surely the rental agency has people to take care of things like that."

"They probably do. But if you tried to drive with that taillight, I'd have had to write you up a citation, which would involve you having to stop by the magistrate's office—"

"That'd be Wally."

"Got it in one." His smile suggested that she'd just given the correct answer for Double Jeopardy. "Anyway, while you can undoubtedly afford the fine, I figure we both have better ways to spend our time."

"I don't suppose you could just overlook it? For today?"

He rubbed his chin and appeared to be giving her question serious consideration. "Surely you wouldn't be trying to talk a law enforcement officer out of doing his sworn duty?"

"Not at all. I was merely suggesting that you must

have more serious crimes to handle than worrying about my taillight."

"Not really." He shrugged. "This is a pretty peaceful county."

"Except for the occasional standoff situation."

"There is that." Jack stood up. "Nice pajamas."

Irked by the laughter in his voice, Raine pulled the edges of the jacket together over the top of the men's styled pajamas where black lambs gamboled on a background of red flannel. "I suppose you'd prefer it if I'd come waltzing out here in some black lace nightgown from Frederick's of Hollywood?"

"Now, that's a real nice offer, and I sure wouldn't want to discourage you, if you've ever a mind to greet me some morning in a getup like that," he said. "But I've always been partial to black sheep. Being oort of a black sheep, myself."

"Since you brought it up, I have to admit I was surprised when I realized that you'd taken over your father's job. I always figured you'd end up on the other side of the bars."

He laughed at that. "My folks figured the same thing. Especially my dad."

"So, what happened to turn you around?"

"The same thing that happens to most black sheep, if they're lucky. The love of a good woman."

She studied him and decided he was serious. "Some women might consider that an outdated, chauvinist statement," she said finally.

"Some women might be right. But that doesn't stop it from being the truth."

Before she could decide how to answer that, the Nano Kitty beeped. She watched him press the buttons, handling whatever electronic-cat emergency

had occurred this time. Although it didn't make any
sense at all, as she compared Jack's behavior with
that of her own absent father, who'd never acknowl-
edged her existence, Raine found herself almost en-
vying Amy O'Halloran.

"Got that taken care of," he said with satisfaction
as he stuffed the flourescent green egg back into his
shirt pocket. "When it gets sick, you have to make
sure it gets its antibiotics on time," he explained.
"Otherwise, you run the risk of it getting worse.
Maybe even becoming catatonic."

She couldn't quite hold back the smile. "That's
terrible."

Instead of defending his foolish pun, Jack gave
Raine a slow, appraising study that warmed his eyes
and her blood. "You know, Counselor," he said, "you
really do have a nice smile." He tugged on the ends
of hair curving around her jaw. "You should use it
more often."

Before she could determine how that outwardly
casual touch had affected her, he was headed back
toward the Suburban. "See you in court."

Raine blinked away a new, distressing hallucination she'd become momentarily lost in. One that had
her standing in the fog, the motors of a 1940s pro-
peller plane droning behind her. She was looking up
at Jack O'Halloran, who'd inexplicably changed last
night's parka for a trench coat, and was desperately
wishing he'd tell her that the fate of the world didn't
mean a hill of beans when compared to a man and
a woman's happiness.

Just when she'd been about to beg him to let her
stay in Casablanca with him, the familiar word
brought her hurling back into the 1990s.

"Court?"

"For the juvenile hearing. Old Fussbudget will undoubtedly call me to testify in the kids' case."

"How did you know the girls call her Old Fussbudget?"

"Hell, everyone in the county calls her that. But as annoying as the woman can admittedly be, she's got a reputation for fairness. I don't think Ida'll have too much of a problem keeping Gwen. And the girls, for the time being."

He touched his fingers to the brim of his hat. Then climbed into the truck and drove away.

The coffee was finally done when she returned to the kitchen. Raine tossed the broken pieces of plastic taillight into the wastebasket beneath the sink, quickly downed two cups while standing at the kitchen window, then went upstairs to get dressed to go to the hospital for her confrontation with Ida.

"I'm not hearing a word of it." The elderly woman was sitting on the top of her bed, dressed and obviously more than ready to escape the institutional confines of the hospital. The scent of talc floated over that of disinfectant and illness. Her salt-and-pepper hair was pinned up, looking like an untidy bird's nest atop her head, but her crimson lipstick was intact. "Those poor girls have been moved around enough, Raine."

She folded her arms across the front of a sweatshirt which read: *I can only please one person per day. Today is not your day. Tomorrow's not looking all that good either.* "Old Fussbudget assures me that Renee and Shawna's aunt and uncle will make good parents, but I'm not going to let anyone take Gwen away."

"Did it ever occur to you that your shenanigans yesterday—telling them to bar the door and not talk to anyone, for heaven's sake—didn't exactly endear you to the authorities? You didn't just hurt your guardianship chances, Gram. You caused some pretty serious black marks on those girls' juvenile records."

"Nothing would have happened if that Old Fussbudget hadn't gone and called the sheriff," Ida grumbled.

"Well, she did. Which made things really serious."

"Lucky for me I've got a good lawyer."

"I suppose it slipped your mind that I'm not licensed in Washington?"

"Would you believe me if I said it did?" Ida hedged.

"Not in a New York minute."

"Well, then, I suppose there's no point in lying. Of course I realize you're not licensed in the state, Raine, darling, which, by the way, I've never been able to understand, since it is your home, after all—"

"My home is in Manhattan."

"Don't be silly. Manhattan is where people work. Not where they live. And while I understand your desire and your need to be independent, Raine, I think you're overdoing things a bit by moving all the way across the country and living with . . . with . . . ," she searched for just the right word, ". . . Easterners."

"Some of them can be quite pleasant. When they're not eating their young," Raine said, her tone as dry as a legal brief. "And you're not going to sidetrack me, again, Gram. My point is that I can't possibly be your attorney because I'm not licensed in this state."

"Don't be such a stickler for details, that's only a technicality. Besides, how will it look, you turning your own aged grandmother away when you're willing to work for those thieving oil company scoundrels?"

"That's unfair. A court declared that Odessa Oil didn't steal from anyone."

"Try telling that to those poor pensioners your filthy rich client left without insurance."

"I'm not going to argue the case with you, Gram," Raine huffed on a frustrated breath. "Besides, since when did you care what people think?"

"I don't. But I have to admit that I wasn't real thrilled to turn on the television and see my own flesh and blood turn traitor to an entire class of senior citizens."

The muscles in the back of Raine's neck knotted and the familiar iron band around her forehead tightened. "The case was open and shut. Those retirees who'd filed suit didn't have a legal leg to stand on."

"How about a moral leg?"

"I'm not paid to be Mother Teresa. I'm a litigator. I get paid a great deal of money to fight my clients' battles."

Which left her living in the most adversarial environment possible, Raine thought, but did not say. While the battle eventually ended for a client, she moved from case to case, remaining in a constant state of conflict.

"Ha." Ida speared her with still-bright dark eyes

that reminded Raine of a curious magpie. "As Orson
Welles said in *Citizen Kane,* "It's not difficult to make
a lot of money, if money is all you want."

Despite her rising frustration, it crossed Raine's
mind that this was undoubtedly one of the few times
Ida had actually gotten a quote right. Unfortunately,
she'd tossed it into the argument like a verbal
grenade.

"It's not just the money, Gram. I like my job. I
love it," she claimed with a bit more force than
necessary.

"Does it make you happy?"

"Happy?" Raine was momentarily stumped. Having achieved a level of success that most young attorneys could only dream of, she was certainly
supposed to be happy. Wasn't she?

"Of course I'm happy," she answered briskly. "But
we shouldn't be wasting time talking about me.
Since you're the one with the guardianship hearing
scheduled for tomorrow morning."

"So you *are* taking my case?"

Feeling as if she was juggling flaming torches
while walking a tightrope blindfolded, Raine ignored
the escalating headache and prepared for the argument her grandmother was bound to launch. "It's
not that simple. Now, I don't want you to fly off the
handle—"

"When have I ever done that?"

"Well, there have been a few occasions—"

"Don't be foolish." The elderly woman broke in
again. "I've always been the epitome of gracious
manners. Ask anyone in Coldwater Cove."

There was no way Raine was going to touch that
outrageous assertion. The truth was, her grand-

mother had a knack for stirring up more than her share of hornet's nests. A firebrand Ida Lindstrom had been born, and a firebrand she'd obviously die.

"How old are you?" Raine asked suddenly.

"What the dickens does my age have to do with the price of tin in China?"

"It's tea."

"What?"

"It's tea in China. Not tin."

"Really?" Ida frowned. "They don't have tin in China?"

"I'm sure they must." Raine wished she hadn't allowed herself to get off track. "I was referring to the old adage. Which mentions tea. And to get back to your question, the court may well feel that your age has a great deal to do with your ability to care for three troublesome teenage girls."

"Pooh," Ida scoffed. "They're not at all troublesome. In fact, they've been a marvelous help around the house. And it's nice to have some companionship. It's no fun being alone. Especially at my age."

Raine was not going to let Ida make her feel guilty about not returning home to Coldwater Cove after graduating from law school. "You're not exactly alone. Lilith's back home again."

"I love my daughter dearly. But believe me, having Lilith living under my roof is not exactly all that peaceful."

Since there was no way Raine could argue with that, she didn't even try. "What's she doing home again anyway?"

"Finding herself. At least that's how she explained it when she showed up on the doorstep without any warning last month. If you want to know the truth,

I believe it has more to do with the fact that she nearly lost her shirt in some business down in Arizona. The way she tells it, she was getting tired of her singing life on the road, so she went into business with a friend conducting vortex tours. But the woman turned out not to be much of a friend, since she embezzled most of their assets."

"Surely Lilith filed charges."

"Actually she didn't. You know your mother. She believes that insisting on retribution causes bad karma and the embezzler will have to work toward redemption in her next life."

"We can only hope," Raine said dryly. "Now, getting back to your case, I really can't legally represent you. But I suppose there's nothing to prevent me from addressing the court as your granddaughter."

"Who just happens to be a hotshot lawyer. Even if you do sometimes lack judgment when choosing your clients." The bird's nest atop her head wobbled and threatened to tip over as Ida nodded with obvious satisfaction. "That should clinch a win for our side."

"I'm still not certain it's for the best."

"Gwen's a good girl, Raine. She deserves a chance to prove it."

"Not if the stress of dealing with a delinquent teenager puts your health at risk."

"I'm as healthy as a mule."

And as stubborn as one, Raine thought. "You nearly fainted yesterday."

"I was merely lightheaded for a moment."

Raine gave her grandmother another long, judicial perusal. She seemed so much smaller, so much more birdlike, than Raine remembered from her last trip home. Almost frail. Yet the determination in those intense dark eyes was, indeed, that of a woman at least half her age.

"You never did tell me how old you were."

"Didn't anyone ever tell you it's not polite to ask a lady her age?"

"You're not a *lady*. You're my client. Sort of," Raine qualified yet again. "So, how about it? I should know, in case the presiding judge brings it up."

"Let's just put it this way, darling . . . if you were counting in dog years, I'd probably be dead."

It was Raine's turn to fold her arms. "That's no answer. If you want me to represent you, you're going to have to do everything I say."

"Absolutely," Ida said with a conviction Raine didn't believe for a moment.

"So, for starters, once more, how about telling me how old you are?" Ida wasn't the only stubborn female in the family.

Her grandmother rubbed her chin, drawing Raine's attention to her hands. Once they'd been long and slender and strong, capable of delivering hundreds of Coldwater Cove's babies. Now the knuckles were swollen with arthritis, proving, Raine thought sadly, that life didn't stand still just because you might want it to.

"That's a bit hard to say," the elderly woman said slyly. "Since I seem to forget more often these days."

"Terrific. I'll simply claim early Alzheimer's. That should definitely gain you custody."

"Well," Ida huffed at Raine's sarcasm, "I see you still have a smart mouth."

"I suppose I do. But I also happen to be proud of

it. Since I inherited it from my grandmother, whom I love and admire more than anyone I've ever known."

Ida's bright eyes glistened at Raine's assertion. "Now you've done it." She pressed a finger beneath her eye to catch the single tear that had escaped beneath sparse lower lashes. "Gone and made me choke up."

"Too bad. Because I *do* love you, which is why I'm still not certain that those girls staying with you is a good idea."

"I'm not letting them go without a fight, Raine. No matter how much you try to soft-soap me."

"I wasn't trying—"

"Of course you were." Ida cackled with obvious satisfaction. "You're right about being a warrior, Raine. Maybe even more than me, which is saying something. And I know you'll use any weapon in your arsenal it takes to win. Which is why I need you standing up for me in that courtroom. I may be old, but I'm no fool. Without you, we'd be up a creek without a paddlewheel. But I know you can make the judge see the light at the end of the tunnel."

Raine sighed. It was emotional blackmail, pure and simple. "Talking about using weapons—"

"I'll use whatever it takes," Ida vowed.

"I can't promise anything." Knowing the futility of arguing any further, Raine threw in the towel. "But I'll do my best."

"That's all I've ever expected, dear." That little matter taken care of, she slid off the bed and pulled on a pair of beaded moccasins that looked nearly as old as she was.

"And for the record," Ida said as they walked out

of the room, "I don't have Alzheimer's. In fact, my mind is as tarp as a shack."

Terrific. Raine groaned inwardly and wondered how, exactly, she was going to keep her grandmother from testifying. Although everyone who knew her could attest that Ida Lindstrom had been the queen of malapropisms long before her hair had turned gray, a judge might just take a different view.

7

"So," Ida said as they were driving along the winding evergreen-lined road back to the house. "Have you spoken with your mother this morning?"

"She was still asleep when I left the house."

"I'm not surprised. After last night's antics."

Raine shot her a surprised look. "You know about that?"

"Coldwater Cove is a small town. A story as juicy as that one is bound to get around pretty fast. So, is it true what they're saying about Cooper?"

"What are they saying?"

"That he's as hooked on the girl as he ever was?"

"I wouldn't know about that. But there was definitely something there. Some spark." Hot enough to set the entire forest ablaze, Raine thought but did not say.

"Interesting." The shaggy green trees shot by the window as Ida thought about that. "He was always good for her. The boy had a quieting effect on your mother that none of the rest of us could manage."

"She didn't seem very quieted last night." And

nothing about Cooper Ryan had been at all boylike. He'd practically radiated testosterone.

"We can always hope," Ida said. "It would be nice to see Lilith settle down with a good man like Cooper Ryan."

Since she personally thought that about as likely to happen as her mother sprouting gossamer wings and flying to the moon, Raine merely murmured something that could have been an agreement.

After they returned home, Raine called a meeting. When Ida started to come into the sunroom along with them, Raine insisted she wanted to speak with the girls alone.

"It's my hearing, too," the elderly woman grumbled.

"True. But I don't want you coaching the girls on what to say. The worst thing that could happen for our case would be for them to get caught lying on the witness stand."

Ida stiffened her back, pulling herself up to her full four feet, eleven inches. "It's a fine kettle of cossacks when a woman's own granddaughter accuses her of advising children to tell falsehoods in a court of law."

"I was merely suggesting that you'd encourage them to be creative in their answers. I thought we agreed that if I was going to represent you, I'd be the one calling the shots."

"You really are a hard woman, Raine Cantrell."

"I'm also a damn good attorney."

They stared at each other for a long, drawn-out minute, both women aware that this was a deciding moment in not only the case, but their future relationship.

"I've got some laundry to do," Ida muttered finally. "Best get to it." Thus conceding defeat, she marched out of the kitchen.

Raine sighed. Mission accomplished, but at what cost? She knew that Ida was accustomed to ruling the roost. She also felt a bit guilty in forcing an old woman, especially one she loved, to back down that way. Reminding herself that the ends justified the means, especially when dealing with courtroom battles, Raine put her personal concerns aside.

The sunroom, on the first floor of the tower, looked a bit like a gazebo that had been glassed in. The pine plank floors had been painted a bright summer-sky blue and a profusion of bluebells, daylilies, and peonies bloomed on the cushions of the white wicker chairs and sofa. Clay pots filled with multicolor displays of ruffled tulips, trumpet-shaped daffodils, narcissus, and hyacinths had been placed about the room. The colorful blooms perfumed the air.

"All right," she said, "the first thing I'm going to need to present your case is a bit of background. I realize it might not be easy to talk about, and if you'd like to have these conversations one at a time—"

"No," Shawna broke in. "We don't have any secrets from one another. Like Mama Ida always says, we're all family."

Raine experienced a little tinge of jealousy at the idea of her grandmother considering these strangers to be members of her family. She tamped it down.

What kind of person could be jealous of three homeless children?

She turned to the others. "Gwen, Renee, do you agree with this?"

Both girls nodded.

"All right, then." Raine sat down in the wicker rocker, her yellow legal pad on her lap, pen poised. "Shawna, let's begin with you. How long have you been in the juvenile justice system?"

"Mama and Daddy died last September. So, that'd make it almost nine months. I was never in trouble before that party, but since we didn't have any relatives to take us in, we just got turned over to county."

"But you do have an aunt."

"She and my mama hadn't talked to each other for a lot of years. They'd had a fight back after Renee was born, then Aunt Jean got married to some guy in the navy and started traveling all over. She says she wrote to Mama last fall, and again at Christmas, but the post office sent the letters back, since we weren't living at that address anymore. Then, when her husband got reassigned back here to Washington, she decided to look Mama up and set things straight." She sighed and her lips turned down in a frown. "But it was too late. When she found out Mama and Daddy were dead, she petitioned for custody. We were all set to move in with her next week. Until the ruckus."

"I see."

"Do you think the judge will stop us from going to live with Auntie Jean now?" Renee asked in a trembling voice.

"No. I don't think that'll be a problem," Raine re-

assured the thirteen-year-old. "Considering the miti-
gating circumstances." She turned to Gwen. "How
about you?"

"I'm pregnant."

"Unfortunately, lots of girls get pregnant, but they
don't end up in the juvenile system."

"Okay. I'm pregnant and I shoplift."

Raine made a note on her pad. "Is that all?"

"Isn't that enough?"

"I don't know. I suppose it depends on what you've
shoplifted. And how often."

"A bunch of stuff. A lot of times." The teenager
thrust out her chin, challenging Raine.

"You sound almost proud of that."

"I'm not proud. It's just the facts. You asked what
got me put in juvie. Well, there's your answer."

And not exactly an encouraging one, either, Raine
considered. "When was the last time you were
caught?"

"About five months ago."

"Before you came to live with Ida?"

"Yeah."

"So, are you saying you haven't shoplifted since
you arrived here?"

"I wouldn't dare. Mama Ida'd probably take a
switch to me."

"I'm not certain switching is exactly my grandmother's style," Raine said. "But I do agree that she
can be a strict disciplinarian."

"She's the only person who ever cared about me
enough to get on my case for my own good. Most
of the other places I've lived, the folks just tended
to knock me around for no reason. Or because they
got off on it."

Hearing this had Raine feeling even more guilty about her random flash of jealousy. "How many places have you lived? And were these foster homes?"

"Yeah. And there've been too many to count. I landed in my first home when I was still a baby and my mama got arrested for dealing pot. After she did her time, she got me back. Then she landed back in jail for prostitution. And after that, she was in rehab, but she's never stayed straight. I guess I've been in foster care most of my life."

Sixteen years. The idea was abominable. "I'm sorry."

"It wasn't your fault," Gwen said. "Besides, some of them weren't so bad. And a couple were even pretty nice. But none of them ever made me feel like I belonged to a real family."

Until here.

"Until Mama Ida," the girl confirmed.

A thought occurred to Raine. "These episodes of shoplifting wouldn't happen to be whenever you were about to be moved again, would they?"

"Mama Ida's right. You're real smart." The tinge of acid in Gwen's tone kept Raine from taking the remark as a compliment.

"So, I'm right?"

"Yeah. So what now, you gonna send me to a shrink?"

"That's not my place." Raine wondered if Gwen had ever received counseling.

"Yeah," she said when Raine asked her. "When I was a kid. The guy said I was acting out because of separation anxiety." She folded her arms over her stomach in an unconscious gesture of self-protection

and directed her gaze out the wall of glass toward
the rolling emerald lawn and beyond that, Admiralty
Bay. In her bright green trapeze top and capri pants
Raine thought she looked a bit like a pregnant Laura
Petrie today. "Big deal."

"It would be to me, if I hadn't had a place to call
my own. A place I'd feel safe," Raine said calmly.
"Actually, I admire you for handling things as well
as you have. Shoplifting, as serious as it is, is a very
minor offense considering some of the trouble you
could have gotten into."

Raine couldn't help comparing the young girl's upbringing with her own. Although her mother had
been anything but reliable, at least whenever her life
had become too unstable, Lilith had always shipped
her daughters back to Ida, who provided not only
the necessary shelter, but a haven.

As her eyes drifted to the driveway, a distant
memory flashed back, as clear as if it had happened
yesterday. Raine recalled the creak of the stairs in
the predawn silence, the squeak of the kitchen door,
the crunch of gravel underfoot. Looking out her bedroom window, she'd seen her mother walking
toward her car, suitcase in hand.

Raine remembered tearing down the stairs and
running out of the house in her nightgown, begging
her mother, who'd gotten a tour gig opening for The
Grateful Dead, not to leave. The commotion roused
Ida, who came downstairs, then held a hysterical
Raine tight as her mother drove away.

A shadow moved across Raine's heart, like a cloud
moving in front of the sun. She shook off the sudden
chill and dragged her mind back to the problem at
hand.

"All right, I think we can finesse the shoplifting," she decided. "Especially since the psychologist's report should already be in your file. Do you have any plans for the future?"

"I always wanted to be a doctor. Like Mama Ida." The sixteen-year-old dropped her gaze to her hands, which rested on the shelf of her stomach. She was squeezing them together so tightly the knuckles had turned white. "But I guess now, with the baby and all . . ." Her voice drifted off, her shoulders drooped.

"So you're going to try to keep the baby?" Raine asked carefully.

"I don't know." Gwen sighed. "At first I was going to get an abortion, because that's what the guy who knocked me up wanted, so he borrowed the money from his cousin and we went to this clinic in Seattle where nobody knew us. Since I was pretty nervous, I wanted Randy—he was my boyfriend—to stay with me, but he doesn't like blood and gore and yucky stuff. He won't even watch *ER*. So, he waited at the Denny's next door."

"Creep," Shawna muttered.

"Yeah, well, I knew it wouldn't do any good to argue with him, so I just, you know, filled out the forms. Then the nurse took me into this cubicle, and told me to take off all my clothes and put on this paper gown, and someone would come get me when it was time.

"I sat on the bench and tried to read a magazine someone had left behind, but I couldn't concentrate. The curtain was still closed, but I could sorta see through the cracks, and every so often they'd call out a name and I'd see a girl going by my cubicle, and I'd wonder about her story. How she ended up there.

"Which got me thinking about my boyfriend. I hadn't wanted to go all the way in the first place. I kept telling him that I wasn't ready, but then one night he told me that I couldn't expect him to be satisfied just making out. That if I really loved him, I'd show him. By having sex with him. So I did. So I wouldn't lose him, you know?"

"I can understand why you might feel that way," Raine said mildly. "But if he truly cared for you, he wouldn't have given you that ultimatum."

"I sorta figured that out while I was sitting there. I mean here I was, dressed in this stupid blue paper gown, waiting to have my baby sucked out of me, and he was next door eatin' his way through a Grand Slam breakfast. It was like he got all the fun and I was stuck with the trouble."

"I'd say that's a fairly accurate assessment of the situation."

"So I was already thinking that maybe this was a mistake. But then the nurse called my name, and I told myself it was too late. That my boyfriend had already paid the money, so I'd have to go through with it."

Since the girl obviously hadn't gotten an abortion, Raine remained silent and waited for the end of the story.

"But then I walked into this room that was like something from *The X-Files*. The only furniture was a chair and a table with stirrups. And beside the table was a tray with all sorts of instruments that looked like stuff from some torture chamber."

Her eyes welled up. "I looked at all that stuff and

just freaked. Then ran out of the room, back to my cubicle, threw on my clothes and got out of that place."

When the tears that had been threatening spilled, the teenager scrubbed them away with the back of her hands, reminding Raine more of a little girl who'd just had her bright red birthday balloon burst on her than a young woman who was weeks away from becoming a mother.

She drew in a deep, gulping breath. "I threw up on the sidewalk outside. My boyfriend saw me out the window and he got really mad and told me that if I was gonna have the baby, I was going to do it by myself."

"He's still financially responsible," the lawyer in Raine felt duty-bound to point out. "In fact, there are laws—"

"I know. Old Fussbudget told me all about them. But he got a bunch of his friends to say they slept with me, so we have to wait until the baby's born for a blood test. Not that it's going to do any good proving it's his," she said, looking far older—and more defeated—than her sixteen years. "Because he'll figure out some way not to pay."

She drew in a ragged breath. "Anyway, if I keep the baby, at least something good will come out of all this bad. And I'll have someone to love me."

Raine wondered how many thousands of unwed teenage mothers believed exactly the same thing. "How did you end up here?"

"I was hanging out in Seattle and panhandling on the ferry. I asked Mama Ida for some change, and she gave me a long lecture about how dangerous it was to be living on the street. And how I owed my baby more. Then she brought me home."

Home. Family. It could not escape Raine's notice that these two themes kept popping up. "Well, we'll do our best to keep you here," she promised.

Only yesterday Raine had been responsible for the financial future of a multibillion-dollar petroleum company. Yet somehow, that hadn't felt nearly as weighty as the responsibility Ida had placed on her—the future of this troubled girl who was obviously desperate for the stability of a loving, protective family. Which, it appeared, she and Ida had already created.

"There's one thing I want to make clear." Raine's voice and her eyes turned firm. "If I have any indication you're making life harder on my grandmother, I'll do everything in my power to get you moved to a new foster home."

"Mama Ida says that we've all been a real help to her," Gwen said. "We've taken over most of the cleaning and cooking."

"That was wise," Raine murmured. "Taking over the cooking."

"It was kinda for self-defense," Shawna spoke up. "And Gwen's been a whiz in the garden."

"I've always liked flowers," Gwen revealed shyly. "But I never lived anywhere long enough to grow a garden."

"You must be responsible for all these." Raine gestured toward the cheerful displays.

Gwen ducked her head. "I ordered the bulbs out of a catalog."

"They're lovely. In fact, I think I'll take a few pictures, showing all you've done."

"Do you think that will cause the judge to let me stay?" Gwen asked, openly dubious.

"I don't know," Raine admitted. She'd never lied to a client and she wasn't about to begin now. "But it's one more weapon in our arsenal."

"So Gwen has a chance?" This from Shawna.

"About a fifty-fifty one. But I'm going to do my best to raise those odds."

"You'll win," Renee said. "Mama Ida says that you're the best lawyer there is. That you never lose."

With that positive endorsement, a weight as heavy as a truckload of bricks landed smack on Raine's shoulders. When she saw Gwen's wretched, unconfident expression, it got even heavier.

This was turning out to be one helluva week, Jack thought, two days after the standoff as he pulled the Suburban up in front of Linda's Beads and Baubles, a small boutique located in the outlet mall a few miles outside of town. And now, after a less than spectacular day, it looked as if he and Raine Cantrell were due for another skirmish.

Timing, Jack reminded himself as he hauled himself out of the truck, was everything. He clicked the lock shut with a beep of the remote, and headed for the store.

Sure enough, the first thing he saw when he entered was one of Ida's girls, slumped in a chair while a tall red-haired woman stood guard over her. The store smelled like flowers, reminding him of the fragrant potpourri Peg had scattered around the house in pretty crystal dishes shaped like seashells. New Age music drifted from hidden speakers on the scented air.

It was a decidedly female atmosphere, which had
him feeling like a bull elk on the loose in a crystal
shop as he wove his way through the racks of bright
silk scarves, summer straw hats, and sparkly
jewelry.

"What's up?" he asked, already suspecting the answer. He'd run a records check on all three girls
during the standoff and had discovered that this one
had particularly sticky fingers.

"I caught her leaving the store with a pair of earrings." Linda Hanson held out a pair of dangling
gold earrings set with colorful stones Jack couldn't
identify.

"Had she actually left the premises?"

"Well, not exactly." The boutique owner's mouth
pulled into a tight frown. He and Linda had graduated from high school the same year and Jack remembered how back in her cheerleader days, those
cherry-tinted lips had been a lot friendlier. "After all,
if I'd let her get away, I might not have caught up
with her."

"So, she was technically inside the store?"

"Technically." Linda's frown reached her eyes and
made horizontal lines in her forehead as she followed his train of thought. "If you want to split
hairs. But I've been in the retail business long
enough to recognize a shoplifter when I see one.
And this kid had every intention of stealing those
earrings."

"That may be, but a court just might see it a little
differently." Irritated at the way she was complicating his life yet again, Jack speared the delinquent
with his sternest look. "Is she right? Were you going
to steal those earrings?"

Gwen shrugged. "I could have been."

"You realize I'll have to report this to your juvenile probation officer."

"Geez. Now there's a surprise." Her mouth pulled even tighter than the boutique owner's.

Shit. "Let's go."

"Where?"

"I should just haul you down to juvie, hand you over to social services authorities, and suggest they throw away the key until you turn eighteen."

"Might as well," Gwen countered. "Since I'm gonna end up back there anyway."

"Well, it just so happens that this is your lucky day, kid. Because I'm going to give you a break and take you back to Ida's."

He motioned her to her feet, grateful when she obeyed, placed a hand on her elbow, and began shepherding her out the way he'd come.

"Aren't you going to put handcuffs on her?" Linda asked, openly miffed that her case wasn't being treated seriously enough to suit her.

"I usually save the shackles for the serial killers and bank robbers."

"You don't have to use that tone with me, Jack O'Halloran. After all, you and I go back a long way."

Jack wasn't surprised that her voice indicated a past intimacy. They'd dated for a brief, carefree time, back when he was playing high school football and she'd been waving her green and white pom-poms.

"Sorry," he said, reminding himself that public servants weren't supposed to resort to sarcasm, no matter how provoked. "But I think I can handle one teenager."

"That's not what I heard. I heard this one and the other delinquents—" her scornful tone made them sound like mad dog killers—"had you over a barrel the other day."

"You heard wrong. And now that we've stopped this crime wave, I'd better get back to work. No telling how many miscreants are out there planning to bring mayhem to our peaceful little town."

As he led Gwen out the door, he couldn't miss the girl's chuckle. "Something funny?"

"I guess you put Miss High and Mighty in her place."

"Miss High and Mighty just happens to be the mayor's daughter. His *only* daughter. Not to mention being the youngest of five kids, the other four being boys, which makes her just about as spoiled as any pretty girl can be.

"Now, I don't see any point in putting you in a cell just because you're acting stupid because you're afraid you're going to be sent away again," he said as he opened the door and helped her up into the passenger seat. "But if you felt moved to return to a life of crime, you definitely picked the wrong store. If you were trying to get taken out of Ida's home and thrown back into the system, you might have succeeded. And you sure didn't help my day any."

She turned away and pretended vast interest in the towering trees flashing by the truck window as they drove back toward Coldwater Cove.

"I don't suppose I could talk you into not telling Mama Ida about this?" she asked finally.

"Sorry. If she's going to stand up and vouch for you in court, she's entitled to know what you've been up to."

Another silence. Then, "I know I'm fat right now. But before I got pregnant, a lot of boys thought I was pretty."

He slanted her a glance, afraid he knew just where this conversation was heading and hoping like hell he was wrong. "A lot of boys are right."

"Lots of them wanted to sleep with me. Even after I got pregnant. But I said no."

"Smart girl."

"And pretty," she reminded him.

"That, too." His fingers tightened on the steering wheel as he waited for the inevitable. Jack decided to try to sidetrack her before things got really sticky. "When you grow up, you'll probably be a heartbreaker."

"I'm almost grown up now," she reminded him. "So, maybe we could work out a kind of deal? You could forget this ever happened, and I could give you something—"

"Dammit, that's it." He jerked the wheel, pulled off the road onto the gravel shoulder, and cut the engine. "You listen to me, and you listen good, kid, because I'm not going to repeat myself. Understand?"

Biting her lip, Gwen nodded.

"I asked if you understood." His sharp tone could have cut diamonds. "When a law enforcement officer asks you a question, you damn well better answer."

"Yes, sir!" she snapped back, with a flare of spirit he suspected had kept her alive and reasonably sane during a lifetime bereft of any security or affection. "Sheriff."

She'd spat his title from between tight lips. Not

wanting to break her spirit, but needing her to understand exactly who was boss, Jack nodded his approval. "That's better. Now, a smart girl like you should realize that prostitution is a one-way ticket straight to the gutter."

"It wouldn't be prostitution, because I wasn't asking for any money. Besides, you're a lot nicer than the other guys I know."

"Which definitely suggests you need to find new friends," Jack said dryly. "As for not asking for any money, it doesn't matter. What you were suggesting was wrong, kid. Legally and morally. And damn dangerous, because some guys might actually take you up on it."

"But not you."

"No. Not me. Not in this lifetime. No way. No how."

"Well, I guess you made yourself real clear." She turned and began staring out the passenger window again, but not before Jack witnessed the sheen of tears that matched the strangled, frail voice.

Once again he was given an insight he could have done without. *Christ*. And here he'd fooled himself into believing that life was only nasty in the big city.

"Look at me, Gwen."

Apparently having learned her lesson, she obeyed, giving him a view of a face even more miserable than the one he'd seen when he'd put her into the back seat of the Suburban last night.

"Whatever happened to you in any of those foster homes, whatever anyone did to you, whatever you thought you had to do, it wasn't your fault." He wanted to touch her, just a soothing hand to her shoulder, but feared that a male touch right now was the last thing she needed. "Do you understand?"

She bit her lip and nodded. Then, remembering his instructions to answer his questions, managed a weak, "Y-y-yes."

But her bleak, dark eyes said otherwise. Jack cursed again, mentally this time. "Is he the one who got you pregnant?"

"No." She sniffled. "It was his son. Randy was my boyfriend for a while. Until he knocked me up. But it could've been his father. If I hadn't gotten away in time."

"Did you ever tell anyone at social services??

"Are you kidding? Hell, no. Not that there was all that much too tell." She sniffled. "It was the last home I was in, before Ida's. The guy kept trying to cop a feel whenever his wife wasn't looking. He always pretended it was just an accident, but I knew better.

"Then one day, when she was working late and I was fixing dinner, he caught me alone in the kitchen and said that he'd found out I was putting out for his son. And then he said that if I was that hot to trot, I oughta try a real man." She bit her lip and closed her eyes for a moment. "He pushed me up against the refrigerator, shoved his tongue down my throat and put his hand up my skirt."

"Son of a bitch."

"He sure was that, all right. But I took the butcher knife I'd been using to cut the chicken and threatened to cut off his balls."

"I imagine that had some effect."

"Yeah. He let go of me real quick and afterwards, he pretended that he'd just been kidding and that if

I knew what was good for me, I'd better keep my mouth shut. Which I was going to do anyway, because I knew that when it came down to my word against his, Old Fussbudget would believe him. Because he's a deacon at his church and he and his wife are always taking in stray kids. Back when I was staying there, he got an award for being foster parent of the year."

"Yet another example of how screwed up bureaucracies can get."

She gave him a long look, appearing encouraged by the fact that Jack seemed to believe her. "But the next day his wife's diamond ring went missing," she continued. "When it was found in the bottom of the hamper in my room, they yanked me outta that home and plunked me back into juvie." She shrugged. "When I found out I was pregnant, Randy wanted me to get an abortion. When I didn't, he told his dad about the baby. That's when his dad said he'd teach me a lesson I'd never forget."

She took in a deep breath. "So I ran away and was living on the street. Until Mama Ida took me in."

Unfortunately, during his time in Seattle, Jack had heard similar sordid stories. But he'd never gotten used to them.

"Okay, here's what we're going to do. First thing on the agenda is to get tomorrow's hearing out of the way. Then we're going to take care of that creep once and for all."

Any color that had returned immediately drained from her face again. "You're not going to tell anyone about this?"

"You bet I am."

"But it'll only be my word against his." Jack could

see the scared child beneath the street-hardened exterior.

"We'll work to get corroborating testimony." His tone and his expression were meant to reassure. "You undoubtedly weren't the first girl he tried to rape."

"But—"

"You've got to trust me, Gwen."

"Maybe I do. A little. I guess." Jack thought she sounded surprised by that. "But all that stuff happened before I came to Mama Ida's. I don't want to stir things up again."

"I can understand that. But I'm also willing to bet that you don't want any other girl to suffer what you did. Or maybe even worse. We have to make sure the county doesn't put any more kids in that dangerous situation."

This time the silence was long and strained. Jack could practically hear the wheels turning around in her head.

"I hate the idea of any other girl having to put up with that shit," she said finally. "Because most of them probably wouldn't be as tough as me, so no telling what he might do to them." She heaved a deep, resigned sigh. "Okay. I'll do it."

"Good girl." This time he went ahead, followed his instincts and patted her knee in a purely paternalistic gesture. "It's going to be all right. *You're* going to be all right."

"You don't know that."

"Sure I do." He twisted the key, bringing the engine to life again.

They'd gone about a mile when she asked, "How?"

"Because someone I knew went through the same

thing when she was growing up. Unfortunately, she wasn't as quick with the knife as you were. But she got past it. And so will you."

Gwen appeared to think about that for another long silent time. "Was she my age?"

"Not when it happened. But she was just a couple years older than you when she started dealing with all those feelings she'd kept bottled up. After she told me about it."

Despite Peg's tearful protests, he'd wanted to track down the bastard who'd raped a thirteen-year-old girl and kill him with his bare hands. Fortunately, he'd avoided prison when it turned out the guy had died in a hunting accident two years earlier. Jack's only regret at the time was that pervert's death hadn't been long and excruciatingly painful.

"She must have trusted you a lot."

"I guess she must have." Even as he felt that familiar, bittersweet tug on his heart, Jack managed to slant the teenager a faint smile. "Since she married me."

❧8❧

The minute she opened the front door, Raine knew that the sheriff had not come to the house on any social call. She drew back to study Gwen, who was standing a bit behind him. Guilt shadowed the teenager's eyes.

"Let me guess. Your fingers got a little sticky again."

The girl shrugged. If her downcast face were any longer, she'd be in danger of stepping on it. "I didn't mean to. It just happened."

"No," Raine corrected firmly. Frustration made her voice sharp. "It didn't just happen, Gwen. You made the choice to steal." She turned toward Jack. "What did she take?" *Oh, please*, Raine thought, *let it be something small.*

"A pair of earrings. The tag said ten dollars, which keeps it from being a felony," he said, answering her unspoken prayer. "And proving once again that God does indeed watch out over fools and kids, she got caught before she took them out of the store. Which doesn't officially make her guilty of anything. But it's sure not going to help your grandmother's custodial case any."

Raine had already figured that out for herself. "I suppose you have to make a report?"

"Yeah." She reluctantly gave him points for looking nearly as chagrined as she felt. "The call from the dispatcher was already logged. Also, the shop owner is the mayor's daughter. I couldn't sweep this one under the rug, even if I wanted to. So, the thing we've got to decide now is what we're going to do about it."

"We?" Brows knit, Raine shot him a suspicious look. Life in the city, along with her litigious occupation, tended to make her unwilling to trust anything. Especially something as seemingly out of nature as she and Sheriff Jack O'Halloran being on the same side of any issue. "It appears you've already done your job, Sheriff. When you took Gwen into custody."

"I didn't take her into custody, dammit. I brought her home. There's a huge difference. And believe it or not, Counselor, my goal in life is not to put every teenager in Coldwater Cove behind bars. The thing is, the kid's going to need representation at her probation hearing tomorrow morning—"

"So soon?"

"Olympic County's known for its rocket docket. As you've undoubtedly noticed, Coldwater Cove isn't exactly the big city. We don't get a lot of crime, which means the court calendar isn't as jammed up as you're undoubtedly accustomed to. Gwen's case will be one of the first on tomorrow's docket."

"Damn. You're right. She needs an attorney."

Gwen turned toward her. "Why can't you be my

lawyer?" Her eyes turned harder than any sixteen-year-old's should be. "Or maybe you'd just as soon have me in jail so I'd be out of your grandmother's house."

"Of course Raine doesn't want you out of my house. And don't worry, darling, none of us will allow you to go to jail." A familiar voice entered the conversation.

Biting back a curse, Raine turned toward her grandmother. Today's sweatshirt announced her to be *Director of Everyone's Life*. Raine thought that to be about the most accurate statement she'd ever read. "I thought you'd agreed to stay in bed."

The elderly woman's initial response to that was a grunt and a steely gaze. "You and the doctor agreed. I don't remember being a party to such a pact. Besides, when I looked out the bedroom window and saw the sheriff's truck, I figured I'd better come see what was up." She shook her head as she shifted her gaze to her young charge. "I thought we'd agreed that filching things was an inappropriate way of dealing with stress, Gwen, dear."

The girl's expression got even glummer. "I forgot."

"Well, I suppose, that's excusable, under the circumstances," Ida agreed with a consoling smile that frustrated Raine all the more. Surely her grandmother didn't believe such a blatant lie? "This has been a trying time for all of us. So, the best we can do is deal with it. And move on." She turned to Raine. "Of course you'll represent Gwen."

"Dammit, Gram," Raine flared, irritated by the way she was being steamrollered again. "I've told you time and time again today, I'm not licensed in Washington."

"But you're standing up for me."

"As your granddaughter," Raine reminded her firmly. "I'll only be speaking to the court as a family member."

"Gwen's a member of this family."

"Not legally."

It was Ida's turn to shake her head in disgust. "As much trouble as your mother gave me, there are times, dear, and this is definitely one of them, when I do find myself wishing you'd inherited a bit more of her free-spiritedness."

Raine lifted her chin. "I wouldn't be where I was today if I had." Her voice remained calm, belying the inner turmoil she so often experienced when compared with her glamorous, flighty mother.

"I'm not certain where you are is exactly where you should be," Ida grumbled.

"Not that I want to interfere in a family discussion," Jack interrupted mildly, "but may I make a suggestion?"

"What?" Raine and Ida asked in unison.

"What about my cousin Dan?"

Raine blinked. "What about him?"

"He's an attorney. With a private practice. I could give him a call."

"I don't know," Raine vacillated uncharacteristically.

There was always the chance that the country lawyer could do more harm than good. She recalled Daniel Webster O'Halloran from the high school debating team. He'd certainly seemed intelligent, despite his unfortunate habit of making out on bus trips to various competitions around the state. While he might not have been the hellion his cousin was back then, the sheriff's cousin certainly hadn't lacked for female companionship, either.

"Dan's not some hick ambulance chaser," Jack said, as if reading her mind.

"I didn't say he was." But that was precisely what she'd been worried about.

"Daniel wrote up my will," Ida volunteered. "Seemed like a real smart boy."

"Writing a will isn't exactly on a par with providing a criminal defense," Raine pointed out dryly. "Or dealing with a custody case. No offense intended," she said to Jack.

"None taken." He shrugged again. "Since it was my cousin you insulted this time. But if it eases your mind any, before he returned home to hang out his shingle, Dan was a federal prosecutor in San Francisco. I figure he should be able to handle a simple case of juvenile shoplifting."

"Well." Embarrassed at having been caught in an act of negative stereotyping, Raine vaguely wished they could begin this conversation over again.

"I think you ought to call him," Ida volunteered. "After all, dear, one should never look a gifted horse in the mouth."

"He does sound like a solution to our problem," Raine allowed. "But do you think he'd be willing to take our case?" she asked Jack.

"Sure. Just let me give him a call."

Five minutes later, after sending Gwen upstairs to her room to think about the consequences of what she'd done, Raine was with Ida in the kitchen, listening to one side of a telephone conversation that didn't begin all that encouragingly.

"I didn't realize you were out of town," Jack was saying.

Her spirits sinking even lower, Raine was forced to watch him listen to his cousin on the other end of the line, his occasional "uh huhs" and nods giving her not a single clue as to the direction the conversation was taking. "Just a sec," he said finally. "I'll ask her."

He covered the mouthpiece of the kitchen wall phone and turned toward her. "He's in Anacortes running down a deadbeat dad for a client. But he says it's just a matter of waiting for the guy to show up at his favorite bar after work. So, he could meet with us later this evening, if that's okay with you."

"That sounds fine." Evening meetings were a way of life in Raine's legal world.

"Terrific." He returned to the conversation. "She says that's fine. So, how about meeting at my place when you get back to town. Say around eight? Okay. See you then." He hung up, seeming satisfied with both the situation and himself.

"Your place?" Raine inquired coolly. "What's the matter with meeting here? Or at your cousin's office?"

"Because he wants me at the meeting for background."

"*Your* office, then."

"Your grandmother's problems have already cost me one evening with my daughter this week. I figure if we get together at my place after I put her to bed, I can kill two birds with one stone."

That was admirable, Raine admitted reluctantly. If any of the men she'd worked with at Choate, Plimpton, Wells & Sullivan had shared similar feelings, none of them had ever dared state them out loud.

"I suppose, since you put it that way . . ."

"Then we're set. In fact, if you're willing to settle for spaghetti, you can eat supper with Amy and me."

Mental warning sirens sounded. Raine folded her arms. "Are you accustomed to cooking dinner for people whose cases you're working on, Sheriff?"

"Not as a rule. Since most of the people I meet in my line of work aren't the kind I'd want to spend all that much personal time with."

"I've never believed in mixing business and pleasure."

"Now why doesn't that surprise me? And for the record, Harvard, I'm not planning to seduce you with pasta and a jug of red wine, then jump your bones the minute you let your guard down. The only reason I suggested you join us for dinner is that the farm's a bit of a drive out of town—"

"You live on a farm?" Raine was distracted by that idea. There was no way she could picture this man wearing denim overalls and tilling soil. Not that he didn't look strong enough to haul around plows, or bales of hay, or whatever farmers did all day. Farming just seemed too tame.

"A Christmas tree farm," he divulged. "And since it's off the beaten track, it can be difficult to find if you're not familiar with the back roads, which is why you'd be better off making the drive in the daylight."

"I grew up here," she reminded him. "I'm certain I can manage."

Another shrug drew her gaze to his shoulders, which seemed even wider than they had last night.

Even as she assured herself that she wasn't the slightest bit interested, Raine couldn't but help notice how strong and hard his chest appeared beneath that knife edge-creased uniform shirt.

"Well," Ida said, rubbing her hands together with obvious satisfaction as he sketched them a map to the farm on a notepad he'd pulled from his pocket, "now that we've got that settled, how about joining us for lunch, Jack? I was planning to rustle up some tofu chili and cold meatloaf sandwiches."

"Thanks anyway, ma'am," he said quickly. Too quickly, Raine thought. Obviously, he'd had occasion to sample her grandmother's infamous meatloaf. "But I'd best be getting back to the office. A lot of paperwork piled up during yesterday's little drama."

With that excuse hanging in the air, he escaped out the door. Watching him leave, and thinking about the upcoming lunch, Raine was tempted to follow.

"Such a nice young man," Ida enthused as they watched him walk across the driveway with a long, masculine ground-eating stride that Raine found reluctantly pleasing. "Did you know he's a widower, Raine?"

"He mentioned that." Instead of the traditional khaki uniform trousers, he was wearing a pair of Wrangler jeans. As he climbed into the truck, the denim pulled snug, causing Raine's mouth to go a little dry. "And, although I know you can't resist meddling in other people's lives—"

"I never meddle," Raine's grandmother protested on a huff of breath.

"Of course you do. But any ideas you might have

concerning Sheriff O'Halloran and me would be a waste of time."

"Ideas?" Ida feigned innocence.

"Matchmaking ideas."

"Oh, fiddlesticks," Ida scoffed. "That thought hadn't even occurred to me." She waited just a beat, then added, "But if a woman were interested in finding herself a man, she could certainly do a great deal worse than Jack O'Halloran."

"That's a matter of opinion. Besides, my life is already full enough. I'm not in the market for a man."

"Don't be silly," Lilith, who chose that moment to enter the sunny kitchen, stated. "Every woman's in the market for a man, whether she admits it or not."

"I'm not."

Lilith gave her elder daughter a long, silent appraisal. "If that's true, darling," she decided finally, "you're in even worse shape than I'd feared."

Not wanting to get into an argument with her mother, Raine managed, just barely, to hold her tongue.

Jack was irritated as hell at himself. It wasn't bad enough that he'd shaved twice today, when he found himself actually watching out the window for Raine, he knew he was in deep, deep trouble.

"She's still got ten minutes," his cousin, who'd arrived a half hour earlier advised.

"I wasn't keeping track."

"Of course you weren't." Barely repressed laughter thickened Dan's deep voice. "You just figured it'd be good exercise to wear a path in that rug."

"She could be lost."

"True enough. But from what you've told me, I'd guess that the lady travels with a cell phone. If she has any problem, she'll undoubtedly call."

"She might not have the number."

"So, she calls 911."

His cousin's grin was wicked and all too knowing. "You know, you can be every bit as much of a pain as you were when you were a snot-nosed kid," Jack muttered.

"And you're as much of a control freak as ever. When are you going to get it through that thick Irish head that even you can't control everything and everyone around you?"

"Believe me, I've already learned that. The hard way."

"Shit." Dan scrubbed a hand down his face. "I'm sorry, Jack. I wasn't thinking."

"It's okay. For the record, you're probably right." He glanced up at the grandfather clock again. The pendulum was still swinging, its slow back-and-forth arc revealing that it hadn't really stopped. "Although controlling Raine Cantrell would undoubtedly be like trying to capture mercury. Frustrating and ultimately impossible."

"So, the chips are still there?"

"Only about the size of Mount Olympus. But then again, every once in a while there are flashes of . . ."

His voice drifted off as he saw the headlights coming up the long driveway. If he'd been annoyed with himself earlier, he was downright disgusted at the sharp rise of anticipation he felt.

"Of what?"

"Huh?" As he watched her climb out of the driver's seat, Jack wondered why he hadn't noticed how long her legs were. An image wavered tantalizingly into his mind—a provocative picture of those long slender legs wrapped around his hips.

"You were mentioning flashes?"

He shook off the jolt of pure lust and reminded himself that he'd given up tumbling into the sack with every female who caused a spike in his hormones a very long time ago.

"I just get the impression that she's not as tough as she tries to come off."

She was wearing the same slacks and sweater she'd had on earlier when he'd taken Gwen to the house and as he watched her approach the house with a smooth, feminine sway of hips, Jack considered, once again, that Raine Cantrell was a lot softer than the tough big-city lawyer image she'd put on.

When he imagined burying himself in that soft female warmth, he decided he'd definitely been too long without a woman. Perhaps he ought to pay a visit to Jenny Winger. He and the former Miss Teen Olympic County had shared some good times back in high school. Now that Jenny had recently shed her second husband, she'd gone out of her way to make it clear that she wouldn't mind picking up where they'd left off so many years ago.

Reminding himself yet again that playing with fire only resulted in burned fingers, Jack assured himself that the only reason he was hurrying to the door was to keep her from ringing the bell and waking up Amy, who'd finally, after three readings of *Where the Wild Things Are*, fallen asleep.

"I see you found the house okay," he said as he opened the huge hand-carved oak door. He nearly groaned out loud at the pitiful opening line.

"Your instructions were very clear." It had begun to rain again, just a soft mist that sparkled in her hair like scattered diamonds. The spreading yellow glow of the porch light brought out red glints in that sparkling hair Jack hadn't noticed before. She was wearing those black-framed glasses again. Jack was surprised to discover that he was a sucker for a female in glasses.

"I'm glad." He was grinning down at her like some besotted kid. It was definitely past time he got laid. Jack made a mental note to give the newly footloose and still-sexy Jenny a call.

She glanced past him. "Are you going to let me see the inside?"

Shit. "Sorry." Damning the heat he felt rising from his collar, he stepped aside, letting her into the house.

"Oh, it's lovely," she breathed with what he took for honest appreciation. She glanced around at the cozy foyer, with its oak coatrack, oak floor, and cream wallpaper edged with a border of perfectly formed evergreens. "I like the way that border brings the farm indoors. I wish I'd taken your advice to come during daylight so I could see the trees."

"Perhaps some other time," he heard himself saying.

She gave him a brief look. "Perhaps," she agreed.

He led her into the living room, unreasonably pleased when she oohed and aahed over the cedar paneling and rustic beamed ceiling. At first he'd been dead set against Peg selling off her life insurance policy to get the down payment for the house and Christmas tree farm they couldn't quite afford.

But when, during those final, horrific months,

she'd gotten such delight out of refurbishing the place, he'd decided going into debt was definitely worth it, if it brought his wife pleasure at a time when so much of her life was filled with pain.

After she'd died—having managed to complete the tiny foyer, the living room, and gotten started on the kitchen—he'd given no further thought to the house. Amy, after all, was too young to care about such decorating details as carpet and paint samples, and his mother, if she did disapprove of the state of the rest of his home, was wise enough not to say so.

"I would have thought your tastes would run toward modern art, brass, and Italian leather," he said.

"Actually, you've just described my apartment." She ran her fingertips down the cedar wall that gleamed in the lamplight like burnished copper. "But this is more cozy."

Raine turned her attention toward the man standing beside a tall stone fireplace that looked large enough for some past homesteader family to have cooked in. Even if she hadn't recognized him, she would have taken him for an O'Halloran. His hair was more of a sun-bleached sandy brown than his cousin's, his eyes a morning-glory blue rather than gray, and his handsome face more smoothly sculpted, but there was no mistaking that square chin and the sublime self-confidence that radiated from every male pore.

"Hello, Daniel."

He smiled with his mouth and his eyes and held out his hand. "Hi, Raine. And, it's Dan."

When his long fingers closed around hers, Raine was more than a little distressed that she didn't feel that sensual tug that his cousin could instill with just a look. She'd been hoping that her uncharacteristic response to Jack O'Halloran had merely been the result of her celibate lifestyle.

"It's great to see you again," Dan said with genuine warmth. "I wish it could have been under more pleasant circumstances. You're looking terrific, by the way."

"Thank you. It's nice to see you, as well." That was the absolute truth. She knew it was ridiculous, but Raine was grateful for a chaperone, of sorts. Dan O'Halloran's presence would ensure that she wouldn't go completely over the bend and act out any of the crazy, sensual fantasies she'd been having about Coldwater Cove's sheriff. "So you became a lawyer."

"Yep. Though I'm not a high-powered corporate one like you. I run a family practice. And speaking of family, how's Ida?"

"She gave us all quite a scare, but the doctors say she's fine. Thank heavens."

"That's good to hear. She's a super lady."

"Even though she can be one gigantic pain in the ass from time to time," Jack muttered.

Raine turned back toward him. "I should be offended by that."

He lifted a dark brow. "But?"

"But it's hard to get up on my high horse when you're right."

They all had a little laugh over that. Then, after Jack had served a coffee that Raine found surprisingly tasty, they settled down to business.

An hour later, she'd been forced to reexamine her

feelings about Daniel Webster O'Halloran. "You're very good."

"You sound surprised." His smile held not a hint of annoyance at the idea she'd obviously misjudged him.

"I suppose I am." She ran her fingers up and down the barrel of her pen. "I have to admit that when Jack first mentioned you, I thought that since Coldwater Cove is such a small town—"

"I'd not only have a small practice, but a small, provincial mind, as well."

"Yes." There was no point in denying it. "And I'm sorry. As a litigator who spends a great many hours studying jury prospects, I should know better than to prejudge anyone."

He shrugged shoulders that were as wide as his cousin's. Another O'Halloran trait, she thought as her gaze slid to Jack, who looked even more substantial than usual in his black fisherman's sweater and dark jeans. And, dammit, more appealing.

"You don't have to apologize, Raine." Dan's easy voice drew her attention back to their conversation. "There was a time when I would have felt the same way. Which is why, after I graduated Stanford law, I stayed in the Bay Area. San Francisco might not be New York, but it sure seemed like Oz to a kid from Coldwater Cove."

Dan O'Halloran was not only intelligent, he was a genuinely nice man. The type of man any sensible woman would find appealing. Unfortunately, from her reaction to his more annoying cousin, Raine was discovering that she wasn't nearly as sensible as she'd thought.

"Jack said you worked in the prosecutor's office?"

"Yeah."

They passed a few pleasant minutes sharing war stories and lawyer jokes. For the first time since she'd arrived in Coldwater Cove, Raine relaxed and began to enjoy herself. Of course, she thought, Dan was a lot easier to talk with than his cousin.

"So," Dan wrapped up another story, "After we'd determined that my client had been unconscious when she was pulled from the car, I asked her what had happened next. 'Mr. Abernathy gave me artificial insemination,' she answered. 'You know, mouth to mouth.'"

Raine laughed at that. Jack, she noticed, did not. In fact, now that she thought about it, he'd barely said two words since they finished talking about Gwen's case.

"I guess I'd better get going." Dan stood up. "I still have a brief to write before I hit the sack."

Raine rose as well. Jack stayed sprawled on the overstuffed green-and-cream-dotted-chintz covered sofa. "Well, I certainly appreciate you helping out with this." She extended her hand to Dan. "I'm feeling much more positive about Gwen's case."

"You should." His fingers curled around hers. "Actually, there wasn't much reason to be too concerned in the first place." He glanced over at his cousin, who merely gave him a bland look in return. "I'm surprised Jack didn't tell you."

"Tell me what?"

"That we've got an in with the judge."

"Let me guess. Judge Wally will be hearing Gwen's case."

His eyes twinkled, his lips curved upward in another one of those woman-melting smiles that while appealing, failed to move Raine on any primal level. "None other. You know the old adage: A good lawyer knows the law. A great lawyer knows the judge."

He flashed a grin toward Jack. "Don't bother seeing me out, cuz. I know the way."

Jack's response to that was a grunt.

With that Dan was gone, leaving Raine and Jack alone.

"Well," she said. "I suppose I'd better be leaving as well."

"I suppose so."

His tone was gruff and he sounded definitely irritated. "Are you going to tell me what I did?"

"I don't have any idea what you mean."

"Don't you?" They were standing toe to toe, her looking up at him, him looking down at her. "I may have misjudged your cousin, but I can certainly tell when someone's ticked off. So, do you want to tell me what I did to offend you? Or are you going to just continue to sulk?"

"Sulk? I never sulk."

"Well, for a man who never sulks, you're certainly doing a pretty good imitation of it, Sheriff."

"You realize, that most women wouldn't be so quick to insult a man."

"I'm not most women."

"No. You're definitely not." He tucked her hair behind her ear, then slowly trailed his thumb around her jaw. "You and Dan sure seemed to hit it off."

The edge was back in his voice. *Could he possibly be jealous?* "He's a nice man. And we have a lot in common."

"Yeah. You both have incredible opportunities to screw up other people's lives."

"That's a rather unattractive accusation."

"You can't deny that you're always looking for the angle. The loophole. Any way of putting the facts together that'll make your case persuasive to the court or jury. Even if the truth gets lost in the process."

"I hadn't realized you'd attended law school, Sheriff."

"I didn't. But if you spend enough time in court-rooms you catch on pretty quick. Don't they teach you to argue both sides of a case in law school?"

"Well, of course, but the law is incredibly complex. Arguing both sides teaches the implications of using one rule, as opposed to another."

"Whatever, the way I see it, law schools are designed to turn out lawyers uncommitted to any ultimate personal values. The kind who can indulge in intellectual and moral acrobatics in the courtroom because clients want contentious, razor-toothed sharks who'll perform whatever distasteful deeds it takes to win. Lawyers willing to prostitute their legal skills and beliefs to represent clients they might have, at one time, before their heads got all screwed up with power games and courtroom battles, found repugnant."

Those were the most words he'd strung together since she'd met him. They were also decidedly un-flattering. "Why don't you say what you really think, Sheriff?"

"Are you saying I'm wrong?"

She paused, giving the matter honest consideration. "I suppose that in some ways, your description might apply to some litigators I know. But it certainly doesn't fit me. And surely you don't believe your cousin's unethical?"

"Of course not. But Dan's the exception."

"Not the only one."

He skimmed a look over her face. "Point taken."

"Besides," she continued, "law doesn't come wrapped in neat, tidy little packages. Just because I can see shades of gray along with the black and white—"

"Now see, that's where you and I are different, Harvard. Because I tend to stick to the black-and-white view. Good guys and bad guys. We cops like to keep things simple."

"That may be true for some cops. But not you. You're more complex."

He lifted a brow. "Think so?"

"I know so. Despite all the trouble they've caused you, you treated those girls with kid gloves."

"Unfortunately, the courts and citizen review groups tend to frown on police brutality these days."

"That's not the reason. You didn't think of them as just delinquents, you thought of them as individual kids with problems. You saw the grays, Sheriff. Whether you want to admit it or not."

He appeared to think about that for a moment. Then, as his gaze settled on her mouth, Raine drew in a breath.

"Well, whatever our individual take on jurisprudence, Dan's definitely right about one thing."

"What's that?" Once again the atmosphere between them had become intensely charged. Raine imagined she could feel the electricity humming beneath her skin.

"About it being late. You probably should be getting home as well."

"I suppose you're right." From the way he was still looking at her, like a man looks at a woman he wants, she suspected it was not his first choice either. When she felt herself responding to that hot gaze, like a woman responds to a man she *wants* to want her, Raine tried to remind herself that giving into these feelings would not be at all wise.

A light mist that was not quite rain had begun to fall. All too aware of the man walking her out to her car, Raine barely noticed it. A foghorn tolled out in the foggy bay; somewhere a dog let out a long, sad howl.

"Aaron Olson's beagle-terrier mix," Jack murmured.

"What?"

"The dog. The night shift usually logs about three complaints a month about the mutt."

"Oh." Raine was amazed either of them could hear anything over the hammering of her heart. "Well," she said, trying for a briskly professional tone that failed miserably, "I suppose I'll see you at the courthouse tomorrow, then."

"I suppose so."

When she would have opened the driver's door, Jack curled his fingers around her shoulder and turned her back toward him. "No. Not yet." He skimmed a thumb around her uplifted jaw.

Unable to help herself, Raine shuddered in response.

"You shivered."

"I did not."

"Liar." Without taking his eyes from hers, he

slipped his hand beneath the back of her sweater, splaying his fingers on flesh that felt as if it was burning up. "You did it again."

"If I did, it's only because I'm cold." She lied again.

"Perhaps we can do something about that."

"Jack . . ." The sighed word was more invitation than complaint. She found herself leaning toward him, felt her lips part in anticipation.

Before Raine could remind herself, yet again, that this was *not* a good idea, Jack lowered his mouth to hers.

9

Prepared for power, Raine was surprised by the gentleness of what was more promise than proper kiss, as the entire world narrowed down to the drugging feel of Jack O'Halloran's lips against hers. It was as if he was the first man to kiss her, the first man she'd ever *wanted* to kiss her.

As Jack deepened the kiss, degree by intoxicating degree, Raine felt a golden heat flow through her, making her feel as if she'd swallowed the sun. They could have stood there in the cool night mist, Jack kissing Raine, her kissing him back for a minute, an hour, or an eternity.

Desire uncurled inside her and as she found herself wanting more, Raine struggled to remember that she'd never been the type of woman who indulged in one-night stands or brief sexual flings. She was only going to be here in Coldwater Cove one more day. Which definitely precluded giving into temptation where this man was concerned.

As if possessing the power to read her mind, Jack slowly lifted his head, breaking the exquisite contact. "There you go. Thinking again." He smoothed the lines in her forehead with a fingertip. "Trying to figure all the angles."

"I can't help it." Until meeting Jack O'Halloran, Raine had never regretted being so analytical. "I'm a lawyer. That's what I do."

"Not now." When she would have dragged her hand through her damp hair, he caught it and kissed her fingertips, one at a time. "Not with me."

Raine felt as if she were melting. "This is impossible," she complained weakly.

Was it so wrong to want order in her life? Rules? Structure? Until a few days ago, Raine wouldn't have even had been asking herself this question. And now, distressingly, she couldn't come up with a quick or easy answer.

"You're probably right," he surprised her by agreeing. "But that hasn't stopped me from thinking about it since you first plowed into my crime scene."

"You didn't like me."

"Can you blame me? You'd been going out of your way to make my job—and my life—harder on a day that was already rough enough. You were, Harvard, pretty much a pain in the ass, which was only one of the reasons why I didn't want to get involved with you. Hell, I'm not sure I do now."

Raine felt a prick of wounded feminine pride and tried to remind herself that she had been thinking exactly the same thing. "That's not very complimentary."

"You want compliments?" He leaned closer, bent his head again.

"I didn't say that." She backed up a step. "I was merely making an observation."

"You know," he said conversationally, "when I was a kid I used to like to walk along the coast and look for flotsam from old shipwrecks. I had a pretty good collection of Japanese glass floats, some bleached boards—one with the part of a ship's name on it— and when I was sixteen, I unearthed part of a ship's figurehead from a pile of driftwood that had washed up on shore near Cape Disappointment.

"It was just her head and shoulders, but I took her home and hung her up on my wall. Late at night, I'd lie in bed and think of all the sea tales about how, when a ship was about to go down, the sailors would hear singing in the wind. Of course it would turn out to be the song of mermaids, luring them to their doom."

His eyes turned weary, his voice resigned. "That's pretty much how I felt about you the other night while we were driving up to Hurricane Ridge."

Over the years, Raine had been described as opinionated, stubborn, argumentative, and, on one memorable occasion, a rebuffed would-be suitor had accused her of being encased in enough ice to cover Jupiter. The one thing no man had ever accused her of being was a *siren*. That description fit Lilith. Not her. She'd spent her entire life molding herself into a woman who was the polar opposite of her glamourous, seductive mother.

She drew in a breath, expelled it. "I can't decide whether to be insulted or flattered."

"Why don't you sleep on it?" When he touched his mouth to the palm of the hand he was still holding, on some distant level Raine was vaguely amazed that her skin didn't sizzle.

Then, when he ruffled her hair in a friendly, casual gesture, Raine decided that as devastating as those kisses had been, Jack O'Halloran was even more dangerous when he was being friendly.

She'd have to stay on her guard tomorrow, she reminded herself as she drove back through the deserted streets, her headlights shimmering on the wet asphalt. Her carefully planned life was on track. She knew where she was going and exactly how to get there. She'd worked hard from childhood to become the cool, logical, dispassionate woman she was; she was on the verge of achieving everything she wanted. Sheriff Jack O'Halloran, as sexy as he might admittedly be, was simply a complication she couldn't afford.

Without warning, she was spinning back in time, metamorphosing into a too tall, too skinny, too serious girl with heavy glasses, freckles across her nose and a mouth full of metal braces that would have foiled the most intrepid teenage boy from kissing her. Not that many had been inclined to try. Which had been just fine with her. At least that's what she'd always told herself. Until Jack O'Halloran's kiss had tilted her world on its axis.

Dammit, what was the point in being so strong and confident in the rest of her life, if she was going to melt whenever she got within kissing distance of this man? What had happened to Xena? Where was the intrepid, take-no-prisoners female warrior princess when you needed her?

Raine asked herself that question all the way back to Ida's house. Unfortunately, when she pulled into the driveway, she was no closer to figuring out the answer than she'd been when she'd escaped the surprisingly charming old farmhouse and a man who, if she let him, could disrupt her life.

By the time she climbed between the sheets that smelled of the Mrs. Stewart's bluing that Ida had always added to the wash, Raine was forced to admit that somehow, when she hadn't been paying attention, Sheriff Jack O'Halloran had already become a major distraction.

Go to sleep, she instructed herself firmly. *You've got to be sharp in court tomorrow morning. Forget him.*

Much, much later, as she lay on her back, looking up at the swirls in the white plaster ceiling while a soft predawn silver-and-rose light slipped beneath the window shade, Raine realized that forgetting Coldwater Cove's sheriff was a great deal easier said than done.

After a restless night, Raine met everyone downstairs. She was relieved that the girls had followed her instructions to dress as demurely as possible. Dressed in a stiffly starched black-and-white jumper, Gwen resembled a cross between a pregnant Flying Nun and Mary Poppins.

"You look lovely," she reassured the girl, who was worried that her obvious pregnancy might hurt their cause.

Raine then turned toward her grandmother who was dressed in a vintage cranberry-hued Jackie Kennedy–style suit that smelled vaguely of mothballs. A pillbox hat in the same color perched atop the upswept gray bun like an egret's nest crowning a Sitka spruce snag. "You look pretty snazzy, too."

"I had to get this out of the attic." Ida ran her

hand down the skirt, smoothing nonexistent wrinkles. Raine noticed that her hands were trembling. She couldn't recall ever seeing her grandmother this nervous. "Don't have much need to dress up in Coldwater Cove."

"Well, isn't it fortunate it's back in style," Raine said with a reassuring smile her grandmother didn't return.

"Did you call the school?" Gwen asked suddenly.

"The school?"

"To tell them we're not coming. I don't want to get an unexcused absence on my permanent record."

Not wanting to upset the girls before their court date, Raine refrained from pointing out that holding law enforcement officers from several counties at bay for hours undoubtedly hadn't done much for Gwen's permanent record.

"Gwen's in the running for valedictorian," Shawna revealed.

"Really?" Raine had just picked up the phone to dial the number of the school that her grandmother had written at one time on the small slate board above the wall phone.

"You don't have to look so surprised," Gwen complained. "I said I wanted to be a doctor."

"That's true. But I also seem to recall something about living on the street and panhandling on the ferry."

"Oh, that. I didn't drop out for very long. Mama Ida got me a tutor and since I was ahead of my class anyway, it didn't take me all that long to catch up."

"Well." Raine gave her a long look, seeing the girl through new eyes. This entire misadventure was turning out to be just one surprise after another.

"I'm very impressed." She wondered how, if Gwen decided to keep this baby, she thought she'd be able to keep her grades up while dealing with the demands of a newborn.

The principal passed along the word that everyone at the school was pulling for Gwen to do well in her hearing today. Obviously, Raine thought as she hung up, she'd been guilty of stereotyping yet again.

"Well, that's taken care of." She glanced around. "Where's Lilith?"

"Here I am," a silvery voice trilled from the doorway. Raine turned and viewed her mother, dressed in a flowing silk skirt, matching tunic, and ballet slippers with ribbons that laced up her still-shapely calves. The hue—a watercolor swirl of color blending through shades of blue from turquoise to cobalt—was an attractive foil for her silver hair and made her eyes appear even bluer. While not at all businesslike, Lilith's attire would do, Raine decided. Except for one thing.

"The crystals have to go." Lilith had obviously gone for broke. Pink and violet amethysts, a smoky quartz interspersed with green tourmaline, amber, and other stones Raine couldn't recognize hung from her earlobes, adorned her neck, wrists, and, Raine noticed with a glance back down at the ballet slippers, even her ankles.

"Oh, I couldn't possibly go to court without them, darling." Lilith lifted a hand, which sported a milky crystal the size of Vermont, to the sparkling gems at her throat. "They're vital for focusing my inner energy."

Raine tried not to roll her eyes. "I don't care. I

refuse to allow you to enter that courtroom looking like Carlsbad Caverns."

Lilith's ruby lips turned downward in a pouty moue. "That's not a very nice thing to say to your mother, Raine."

"That's exactly the point. I'm not your daughter today. We can't admit it to the court, but I'm acting as Gram's attorney. The deal was that everyone was to do exactly what I say."

Lilith tilted her head and studied Raine silently. "Well," she said on a little huff of breath, "far be it from me to impede our defense." With that, she flounced from the room, returning moments later without the rocks.

"I'm not taking these off, Raine," she warned as she saw Raine taking in the earrings that had replaced the crystals. The onyx beads on the right earlobe nearly brushed her shoulder while an embossed shining silver replica of a Buddhist prayer wheel hung from the left. "They're shamanistic. You may not believe in a power higher than you, but the way I see it, Ida and these poor girls are going to need all the help they can get."

"All right." They were due in court in fifteen minutes; there was simply no time to argue any further. "But if you're called to testify, I don't want you saying a single word about psychic energy, chakras, shamans, vortexes, or any of that other New Age nonsense."

"I would have expected a daughter of mine to have a more open mind," Lilith complained.

Not even wanting to get into a discussion about mothers and daughters, Raine merely shook her head, picked up her briefcase, and turned her mind to what it did best—honing her upcoming legal argument.

If Raine was nervous about the importance of this court appearance, she was downright appalled by the way her heart skipped a few vital beats when she viewed Jack O'Halloran standing outside the courtroom, talking with his cousin.

Raine and Dan exchanged a greeting. When he turned away for a brief talk with the group regarding their testimony, Raine had no choice but to acknowledge Jack.

"Good morning, Sheriff." It took an effort, but she managed to keep her tone professionally brisk even as her heart continued to go pittypat in a most unprofessional way.

"Counselor." He smiled charmingly. "Sleep well?"

"Absolutely," she lied.

"It's the fresh air," he said. "Makes you sleep like a baby." Gray eyes skimmed over her in a thoroughly masculine perusal. "Nice suit." He pushed away from the wall and moved a little closer. "Woman with a suit like that could probably conquer the world."

He took two more steps forward. Raine took one back. "It's good for taking on the road. The material is three-seasonal, and the color goes with anything."

"Mmmm." He was still looking at her in that silent, thoughtful way. "Gray flannel always makes me think of that old movie," he said. "With Gregory Peck."

"I don't think I know it." He was close. Too close for comfort. Definitely too close for courthouse propriety.

"*The Man in the Gray Flannel Suit.* Great flick from the fifties and one of Peck's best. It's sort of a morality play with a business plot. You should see it some time."

"I'll make a point of it," she said coolly. "What do you think you're doing?" she hissed when he rubbed her flannel lapel between his thumb and index finger.

"Yep, great flick," he repeated distractedly, making Raine wonder if he'd even heard her question or simply, in his own hardheaded way, was choosing to ignore it. "Flannel and silk." The gray in his eyes deepened as he took another unnervingly long perusal of her tailored white silk blouse. Didn't the man ever blink? "That's quite an intriguing contrast."

Reminding herself of all her late-night resolutions, she slapped his hand away. "Are you hitting on me, again, Sheriff?"

"Hitting on you?" he repeated, as if trying the words out might provide a clue to whatever was happening here. "No. I don't think so."

She heard the slight rasp of his thumb against the cloth of her lapel again and reminded herself of the way he'd placed one of his large hands on Gwen's shoulder yesterday. That gesture hadn't been the slightest bit seductive, leading her to believe that Jack O'Halloran was merely a toucher. She was not.

"Next time I hit on you, Harvard, you won't have to ask. You'll know." His smile charmed yet again, but his dark, intense eyes made her mouth go dry.

Raine was trying to think of something, anything to say to that provocative challenge when she felt a tap on her shoulder.

"What is it?" she ground out as she spun around.

Dan held up both hands. "I just thought we ought to be getting into the courtroom."

"That's a grand idea." She stalked off, causing the rest of the family to nearly run to keep up.

The two men watched her walk away, her high heels contributing to a sexy swing of her hips beneath the gray flannel skirt.

"She may still have the chips on her shoulders," Dan murmured. "But damn, the woman does have dynamite legs."

"You won't get any argument from me on that," Jack agreed.

Dan slanted a look toward his cousin. "If a man was looking for a woman—"

"Which I'm not."

"Don't you think this grieving widower act has gone on long enough?"

"It's not an act."

"Hell, I know that." Dan swiped a frustrated hand through his hair. "But it's not natural, Jack. Peg's been gone, what, two years now?"

"Twenty-two months," Jack said tightly. He'd been sitting beside her hospital bed that morning, holding her slender hand in both of his when she'd finally slipped away from him. "But, since I've recently come to the conclusion that you may have a point, you might as well know that I'm thinking of asking Jenny Winger out to dinner."

"Christ, you can't be serious. She may be gorgeous, in a big hair, big teeth sort of way, but all Jenny ever talks about is her glorious reign as Miss Teen Olympic County."

"So?" Jack shrugged. "I'm not looking for conversation."

"It's not going to work, you know," a new voice entered the conversation. Both men glanced over at Cooper Ryan, who'd obviously arrived at the courtroom in time to hear the exchange.

"What's not going to work?" Jack asked.

"Trying to hide from your feelings for one woman by spending time with another."

"That's not what I'm doing."

"Isn't it?" both Cooper and Dan said together. They exchanged knowing grins.

"Believe me," Cooper advised, "I've been where you are, Jack, and I can tell you that you're headed down a rocky road. But it can also be one helluva trip."

"So why aren't you taking it with Lilith? Since it was more than a little obvious the other night that you two left a lot unsettled."

Cooper rubbed his jaw as he watched the covey of females disappear into the courtroom. "True enough. But I have every intention of settling those issues once and for all."

"Brave man," Dan murmured. "As charming as the lady is, I imagine she'd be a handful."

"She can be that," Cooper agreed. "And more. But the way I figure it, nothing worth having comes easy. You know, though I'd hate to think that looking back is a sign of impending old age, it's damn true what they say about the things you regret being things you didn't do. I let youthful pride rule my behavior back when we were kids."

His square jaw firmed. "As she recently reminded me during that little ruckus up on Hurricane Ridge,

I was the first man in Lilith Lindstrom's life. And it doesn't matter how many guys she's known since then, or how many last names she's acquired. Because I have every intention of being the last."

Jack and Dan wished the older man luck. As they entered the courtroom of his longtime friend, Jack decided that if the sparks he'd witnessed between Cooper Ryan and Lilith Lindstrom the other night were any indication, people in Coldwater Cove weren't going to have to wait until the Fourth of July for a display of fireworks.

He may have left his ball playing days behind him, but Judge Wallace Cunningham looked like a jock. His face was darkly tanned, his brown hair had been streaked by the sun, and beneath the black robe Raine could tell that his shoulders were nearly as broad as his old teammate's.

Surprisingly, he also seemed to have a quick legal mind, rapidly cutting through the courtroom legalese to get to the bottom line.

"Well, young woman," he boomed, looking down at Gwen, who was currently standing before him. Her face was ashen and from her seat behind the railing, Raine watched the girl twisting her hands together behind her back. "While I suspect that you had every intention of leaving the store"—he glanced down at the casework his bailiff had provided—"Linda's Beads and Baubles, with those earrings, it's my guess that you also planned to get caught.

"After all, it's always easier to be the one to cut your losses, rather than wait around and have the rug pulled out from under you. Isn't it?"

"Yessir," Gwen said in a low, miserable voice that

had Raine reaching out to take her mother's hand on one side, Ida's on the other. "Your Honor," the teenager corrected quickly, obviously recalling Raine's earlier instruction.

Dan had put forth a sound defense, yet even though she doubted she could have done better, Raine worried it might not be enough. While juvenile criminal law was not her area of expertise, there had been times over the past years when she was required to appear in court to defend the rebellious offspring of one of the firm's wealthier clients.

It hadn't taken her long to discover that in big cities, with their overburdened jails, judges tended to overlook lesser juvenile offenses. While small towns, on the other hand, tended to apply the weight of the law more heavily, to send a message to other kids who might be tempted off the straight and narrow.

Raine had been relieved when Jack, looking like an outrageously macho model for a law enforcement recruiting poster in his stiffly starched uniform with the five-sided star pinned to his broad chest, managed to help their case even as he stuck to the facts. While technically Gwen hadn't been guilty of shoplifting, circumstantial evidence—like those earrings in her pocket—didn't look good. Especially for a kid who was already on probation for a series of similar charges.

"I played a little ball back when I was younger," Judge Wally was telling Gwen. "So, I know, just a bit, how it feels to be yanked from place to place. I wasn't exactly pro-quality," he confided. "I was a step too slow to make it into the Big Leagues, so I spent most of my less-than-brilliant career being traded throughout the minors—Tacoma, Springfield, Albuquerque.

"It got to be a drag, so I accepted reality and finally threw in the towel after three years when I was about to be traded to Midland, Texas. Of course that's nothing compared to the instability you've experienced."

He rubbed his chin thoughtfully. "As sorry as I am about what you've gone through over the years, I don't think I'd be sending the right message to the other kids in the county if I give you a pass on this." That earned a soft moan from Gwen and a gasp from Ida. The other girls looked on the verge of bursting into tears.

"However," Judge Wally continued, "I can't see how moving you to a juvenile detention facility would be beneficial. So, here's what we're going to do." He leaned back and began swiveling his tall black leather chair. "After your baby's born, I'm sentencing you to three months community service, the details of which you'll work out with Ms. Kelly." He nodded toward Old Fussbudget, who was seated nearby, her rigid spine making it look as if someone had put a steel rod up the back of her navy blue suit jacket. "I'm also requiring weekly counseling sessions during this time. Again, the details to be handled by your probation officer."

He leaned forward, his friendly expression turning judicially stern. "If you land back here in my courtroom, or any other of my colleague's courtrooms, I will immediately revoke these conditions and you'll find yourself down on your knees scrubbing toilets in juvie so fast your head will spin. Is that clear, young lady?"

"Yessir. Your Honor." Gwen's frail voice was choked with tears; whether from fear or relief, Raine couldn't tell.

"Fine." That matter settled, he turned to his bailiff. "So, what's the next case, Marian?"

Back in the hallway, hugs were exchanged and more than a few surreptitious tears shed. Apparently swinging on hormones, Gwen was both weeping and laughing.

"Thank you," Raine said as she shook hands with Dan. "You were terrific."

"It wasn't that big a deal."

"Not to you, perhaps. But to Gwen and my grandmother, it was more important than any Supreme Court case."

Raine had been surprised at how stressful it had proven to be to be forced to sit and watch and hope. Law school hadn't taught her the tumultuous range of emotions you suffered through as you watched a virtual stranger fight your battle for you. It was as if Dan had held their entire lives in his hands.

Raine wondered if this was how her clients felt, then decided probably not. Her cases dealt with business law and there was certainly a great deal more to life than business. When that stunning revelation struck like a blow from behind, Raine decided she was really going to have to give the idea more thought. Later, when things settled down.

"Something wrong?"

Still focused on the idea that there may actually be a world outside her legal circles, Raine realized her mind had been drifting again. A dangerous thing for it to be indulging in right before she was due to argue Ida's guardianship case.

"Not really," she said, trying to dismiss that sudden flash of insight. "I was just thinking of something."

"It must have not been all that pleasant."

"It was just a little . . . ," she searched for the word, ". . . surprising."

"That's what I love about the law," Dan said with a winning smile that was a near duplicate of his cousin's. "It's chock full of surprises." He glanced over at the little group who were headed down the hall toward the Pepsi machine, the girls trailing behind Ida like a trio of downy ducklings. "I wish I could stick around for Ida's case, but this deposition in Forks has been scheduled for a month, and—"

"Don't worry." Raine assured herself that after saving Odessa Oil millions of dollars in profits, a simple guardianship argument should be a snap. "I can handle it."

"I've not a single doubt of that." He flashed her another of those warm and winning grins that unfortunately didn't strum a single feminine chord. "Take care, Counselor. Maybe we'll bump into each other in a courtroom one of these days."

Since she was going to be returning to Manhattan on the red-eye tonight, the possibility of that was slim to none. But Raine politely agreed, thanked him again, then sat down on a bench in the hallway to go over her argument one final time.

Unfortunately, their luck didn't hold. Raine knew they were in trouble the minute they'd entered the courtroom when Lilith drew in a sharp breath.

"Oh, no."

"What?" Raine whispered, not wanting to disrupt

the proceedings going on at the front of the courtroom.

"I know the judge."

Raine thought back to the old joke Dan had tossed at her last night about a good lawyer knowing the law, but a great lawyer knowing the judge. Unfortunately, if the bleak expression on her mother's face was anything to go on, they weren't going to experience the same advantage they'd enjoyed with Judge Wally.

"And?" she asked, her sharper-than-usual tone inviting elaboration.

"We went to school together. In fact, we used to be best friends."

"Used to be?"

"Well, it's a little difficult to explain."

"Try." It was more order than request.

"It's complicated." Lilith shrugged her silk-clad shoulders. "But Barbara accused me of stealing Jimmy Young away from her."

Raine assured herself that a thirty-two-year-old teenage dispute over a boyfriend certainly wouldn't affect their case. Not after all these years. The woman in question had graduated from law school. Not only had she been well-versed in the tenets of justice, she'd achieved the honored black robe of judicial prudence. Besides, from her name—Barbara Patterson-Young—it appeared that the judge and the faithless Jimmy Young had managed to patch things up.

Unfortunately, even as Raine was giving herself that little pep talk, Judge Patterson-Young glanced up. Her gaze unerringly zeroed straight in on Lilith like a heat-seeking missile. The hatred in those hazel eyes was unmistakable.

"Great," Raine muttered as they sat down on one of the back benches. "This is just great. She hasn't forgotten you."

"Barbara always was one to hold a grudge. But I didn't exactly steal Jimmy, Raine. She'd already left him to go off to college in Hawaii."

She might not have dated all that much in high school, but even Raine understood that in the world of teenage romance, the going-away-to-college excuse was a mere technicality. The guilty look in her mother's not-so-vivid eyes told her that Lilith knew it too.

"I thought Cooper Ryan was your high school boyfriend," Raine hissed.

"This was later. After Cooper was drafted."

Terrific. The love of her life was about to be shipped off to Vietnam and Lilith was stateside, blithely stealing the boyfriend of a girl who'd grow up to be the judge who'd hear the most important case in Ida Lindstrom's life.

"This is just goddamn great," she muttered again as she retrieved the aspirin bottle from her briefcase.

The judge had returned her attention to the case in front of her. But Raine could feel her antipathy linger like heat lightning hovering on a nearby horizon.

❦ 10 ❧

Raine had barely gotten into her opening statement, when BANG!—the judge pounded her gavel, silencing her in midsentence.

"If you're going to keep using those big words, Counselor," Judge Patterson-Young said with heavy sarcasm, "I'll be forced to move this case to the city. Where they indulge in that type of legal gobbledegook."

Raine felt her blood rise, but suspecting the judge would just love to slap her with a contempt charge, she relentlessly schooled herself to calm.

Her argument hadn't been wrapped in legal jargon. Even so, Raine took extra care to keep it short, sweet, and simple. She'd also arranged for Ida's neighbors, her doctor, and the pastor of the Lutheran church Ida had attended for more than half a century to speak on her grandmother's behalf. Even Jack testified that at no time during the standoff had the girls posed a threat to themselves or others.

But as each of Coldwater Cove's sterling citizens

provided glowing testimony to Dr. Ida Lindstrom's stamina, her lifetime of community service, and her generous heart, Raine knew she could have had a choir of gilt-winged angels take that witness stand and it wouldn't make a bit of difference. Because the judge had made up her mind the moment Lilith entered the courtroom.

"It is the court's opinion," Judge Patterson-Young stated after all that testimony, "that Dr. Lindstrom, her admirable reputation for being a caregiver not withstanding, is not capable of handling three teen-age girls. Especially ones who have been in trouble with the law.

"On the other hand, since two of the girls are already scheduled to move out of Dr. Lindstrom's home, I'm not inclined to take the third from what just may be one of the few stable environments she's known. Especially since she's due to deliver any day. However, if the teenager is to remain in the Lindstrom home, I'll require the presence of a responsible adult. A younger one than Dr. Lindstrom."

Ida tugged on Raine's sleeve. "You should remind that girl that age discrimination is against the law," she hissed.

"Let me handle this." Raine put a firm hand on her grandmother's shoulder to keep her from leaping up to protest.

"If the court pleases," she said carefully, "there *is* another adult living in the home."

"Good try, Counselor." If a snake could smile, Raine thought, it would look exactly like Judge Barbara Patterson-Young. "But I doubt if there's a judge in this county who'd be inclined to declare Lilith Lindstrom Cantrell Townsend"—she spat out the lengthy name as if it had a bad aftertaste—"to be a responsible adult."

Raine privately agreed. As Lilith's daughter and Ida's sort-of attorney, she felt obliged to answer the unflattering charge against her mother. "May I ask on what the court is basing that opinion?"

The cold, reptilian smile disappeared, replaced by a warning glare. "It's not your place to ask the questions, Counselor."

"I understand that, Your Honor. But if the court is judging my mother by some past behavior—"

"That's enough!"

BANG! The gavel slammed down again, making Raine decide the judge had missed her calling. The unpleasant woman would have made a terrific hanging judge back in the days of the Wild West.

"Any further argument from you, Ms. Cantrell, and I'll be forced to hold you in contempt."

"If it pleases the court," Raine spoke carefully, reminding herself that she wouldn't be able to do anyone any good if she landed behind bars in Sheriff O'Halloran's Olympic County jail, "I'm not here in the capacity of Dr. Lindstrom's attorney today. I'm merely a concerned family member, speaking on my grandmother's behalf."

"You went to law school, didn't you?"

"Yes, but—"

"Harvard, right?"

"That's right."

"And you passed the bar?"

"Yes, Your Honor." Raine suspected she knew where the judge was headed with this line of questioning.

"And you became licensed to practice?"

"In New York, yes."

The judge ignored the pointed qualification. "Well, in my book that makes you Dr. Lindstrom's attorney. Unless," she tacked on evilly, "you'd prefer to have your grandmother address the court herself?"

"No, your honor. I don't believe that's necessary in this case."

"You're right." The judge surprised Raine by agreeing on something. "Because it wouldn't change my ruling. I'm allowing the girls to stay in Dr. Lindstrom's home—"

She was interrupted by Gwen's and Renee's jubilant screams. They began jumping up and down and hugging each other.

BANG! The gavel crashed down again. "There will be no disruptions in my courtroom!"

Oh, yes, Raine confirmed, refusing to cringe even though the sharp sound felt like an ax blade to her aching head. Definitely a hanging judge. She had no problem picturing Barbara Patterson-Young smiling with grim satisfaction as a Stetson-wearing sheriff— who looked discomfortingly like Jack O'Halloran— put a thick rope around Lilith's neck.

The room instantly went silent. The girls obediently sat down again. "That's better." The judge nodded. "I'm setting a one-month trial period, during which time Dr. Lindstrom will be given an opportunity to prove herself up to the task of guardianship. I am also requiring that an adult other than Dr. Lindstrom's daughter reside in the home during this time."

As everyone turned to look directly at her, Raine had a sinking feeling she knew what adult they all had in mind.

"Your Honor," she protested, once again feeling as if she were walking across a legal minefield, "I can't possibly leave my law practice for a month."

"Fine. Then the three probationers in question are returned to Ms. Kelly's control. "

Ida was on her feet in a flash. "You can't do that! Why, in case you've forgotten, Babs Patterson, I just happen to be the doctor who treated your chicken pox when you were five."

BANG!

On a roll, Ida ignored the sharp warning crack of the gavel. "I also got rid of your acne when you came crying to me that no boy would ask you out, and don't forget that I was the one who wrote your first prescription for birth control pills when you came home for Christmas vacation your freshman year of college and wanted to sleep with Edna Young's boy Jimmy."

BANG! BANG!

"Gram!" Raine grabbed hold of Ida's shoulder once again and forced her grandmother back down onto the bench. "Shut up."

"It's not fair, Raine," Ida protested, her voice ringing out over the laughter and buzz of excited conversation in the courtroom. "The only reason she's doing this is to get back at your mother for having sex with her boyfriend the minute her back was turned."

BANG! BANG! BANG!

Raine slapped a hand over her grandmother's mouth. "I apologize, Your Honor. It's just that Dr. Lindstrom feels very strongly about this issue."

"I understand that, Counselor." Scarlet flags were waving in the judge's cheeks. Raine figured they were sunk. "And it's only because of my longtime affection for your grandmother that I'm going to overlook her outburst. This time," she tacked on, shooting Ida another icy warning glare. Ida, uncowed, set her chin and glared back.

"However," the judge continued, "there's no room for emotion in the law. The fact that your grandmother obviously cares about these teenagers has no effect on my ruling."

She couldn't do it, even if she wanted to. Three days was one thing, Raine thought. There was absolutely no way she could stay away from her caseload for an entire month.

"May I make a suggestion to the court?"

Judge Patterson-Young sighed dramatically, then waved her manicured hand in a go-ahead gesture.

"May I suggest that I stay at the house for the next fifteen days." With no court appearances scheduled during that time, by utilizing the phone, fax, and e-mail, she and the always efficient Brian should be able to manage. "After which time my sister, whom I'm certain the court will find exceptionally responsible, will take another fifteen days."

Raine knew Savannah wouldn't hesitate to help their grandmother. Oh, she might have a bit of trouble getting away from her job as chef at that *chichi* Malibu resort hotel, but since her husband was resort manager, surely he wouldn't protest his wife taking a brief leave of absence for a family emergency. Even if she suspected that he may have sensed that the family in question did not consider him the right man for Savannah. Personally Raine had always privately thought him too slick. Too smooth. Too untrustworthy.

"The court will agree with that schedule," the judge said. "On the condition your sister proves herself to be a suitable guardian."

"Thank you, Your Honor." Raine didn't bother to hide her relief.

"Thirty days. And if there's a single instance of trouble during that time, Counselor, all bets are off."

BANG! With a final, swift rap of the wooden gavel, Judge Barbara Patterson-Young signaled the guardianship hearing concluded.

"You won't have that much to do," Raine assured her sister when she phoned her after they'd all returned home. "Since the court just wants a warm, responsible body in the house until Gram proves she's up to handling things."

"The day Gram runs into something she can't handle will be the day the world comes to an end. Do you ever wonder what we would have done without her?"

"I try not to. Which is why I decided not to fight her too hard on this one. It's more than obvious that Gwen needs her. But I think Gram needs Gwen, too. I get the feeling that she misses having family around." Which was why, Raine understood, Ida had created her little flock in the first place.

"Actually, your timing couldn't be better," Savannah said. "Since I just quit my job yesterday afternoon."

"You quit? But I thought you loved working at the resort."

"I do. I did," she corrected. "But that changed."

"I'm sorry." Raine decided not to press. Savannah would fill her in on the details when she was ready.

"What does Kevin think about this change?" she asked, wondering if her sister could possibly be pregnant. Although she couldn't picture Savannah's husband as a doting father, Raine nevertheless liked the idea of being an aunt.

"Other than the fact that he has to find a new chef just before the summer tourist season really takes off, I doubt he much cares." She paused. "I've left him, Raine."

"Oh, Savannah." Raine was standing by the kitchen window, watching a pair of red-breasted robins playing musical branches in the huge monkey puzzle tree that dominated the front lawn. "I'm sorry. I'd sensed the two of you were having problems when you came to New York last fall. But I was hoping you could work things out."

"I'd hoped the same thing. But I've come to the unhappy conclusion that the resort business was the only thing we had in common. We certainly had a different view of marriage."

"Oh?"

"I thought monogamy was a given. Kevin thought he should be allowed to date. I, naturally, disagreed. When I caught him playing hide the torpedo with a female lawyer from the hotel's legal division, I decided that I'd come to the end of my rope."

"You should have put it around his neck and tossed him off the nearest pier," Raine declared heatedly. "He's a fool. And a bastard."

"That's pretty much what I told him after he admitted to what he referred to as his little indiscretion. Since this wasn't the first time he's wandered,

I threatened to hack off said little indiscretion with a rusty cleaver."

"I didn't know." Raine hated thinking that her sister had been suffering through such pain alone.

"That's because I didn't want you to. I didn't want anyone to know. I realize now that I shouldn't have hung in there for so many years, but I was trying so damn hard not to follow in Lilith's footsteps. If that makes any sense."

"Absolutely." Hadn't she spent her entire life trying to avoid the same thing?

"It was also embarrassing to admit that the perfect marriage I'd always dreamed about wasn't so perfect after all."

Raine knew all too well how Savannah had always longed for a perfect, *Leave It to Beaver* family life. Being more realistic, or perhaps more cynical than her sister, Raine had preferred to devote herself to her work, rather than depend on any man for her happiness.

Savannah sighed. "So, I moved into the Beverly Wilshire, arranged to have my calls forwarded from the resort, unless they were from the rat, and ordered a bottle of ridiculously expensive champagne to celebrate my freedom. After which I proceeded to get drunk, which took my mind off the horny, unfaithful little prick for a while. Until I woke up this morning with the mother of all hangovers. Then you called."

"I really am so sorry, Savannah. This is a horrible time to ask any favors of you."

"Don't be silly, the timing couldn't be better. I'm still so furious—and, dammit, hurt—I could use a little distance and distraction to prevent me from following through on the cleaver threat."

If nothing else, Raine decided that Ida and the girls would definitely prove a distraction.

"Not that I'd ever recommend violence, but if you were to take matters into your own hands, so to speak, I just happen to know a good lawyer who'd take your case *pro bono.*"

Raine heard a throaty sound and was unable to decide whether it was a choked off laugh or a sob. "God, I miss you," Savannah said on a rush of shaky breath. "And Ida. And even Lilith, believe it or not. In fact, when I woke up this morning, I thought about going home to lick my wounds, but I didn't want to look as if I was running home to Gram at the first sign of trouble."

"That's what the family is for."

Savannah laughed again, this time with more humor. "Right. And I'll bet Coldwater Cove would be the first place you'd think of hiding out if your life crumbled beneath your feet."

"Probably not," Raine admitted.

She wanted to say something reassuring. But when words failed her, Raine assured herself that there would be time for tears and hugs later. When they didn't have all these miles between them.

"And you don't have to stick to that two weeks schedule," Savannah said. "I should be able to tie up loose ends and get up there in a few days. Then I'll take over."

"Just try to make it before we run out of frozen dinners to nuke and Gram decides to start cooking," Raine instructed.

After Raine hung up, she sat for a while, thinking

how Savannah might be a perfectionist when it came to her work, but had always been ruled by her heart. She also had the unfortunate tendency to think the best of people until she was proven wrong.

Which was why, Raine considered with a flash of hot fury, her sister hadn't picked up on the warning signals that the rest of the family had when they'd first met the groom after Savannah's sudden elopement to Monte Carlo.

During their high school years, Savannah had been the flame that drew eyes as she'd laughed and flirted and had every boy in the school falling a little bit in love with her. Her natural sexuality had left Raine feeling a bit of an observer to a play in which she'd never be the star.

Not that she'd minded. Savannah having inherited Lilith's lush feminine appeal was nothing more than a quirk of fate, a fortunate accident of genetics. To envy such beauty would be like the cool silver moon resenting the brighter, bolder sun for rising in a blaze of glory each morning. Besides, they'd each carved out individual identities early on in life.

She was, of course, the "smart, sassy one," while Savannah, everyone would agree, was "the pretty, sweet one."

But even as they followed their individual dreams down different paths, deep down inside, where it really counted, despite having different fathers, she and Savannah were sisters of the heart. When one was hurting, the other felt the pain and when they spoke, they spoke with the same voice.

Family matters taken care of, at least as well as they could be for now, Raine called her office. Brian quickly caught her up on what was happening with

her cases, then transferred her to the managing
partner.

"I must say, Raine," Stephen Wells complained,
"I'm less than pleased to hear that you're not returning any time soon."

"It's only a few days. Fifteen at the most. Fortunately, I don't have any court dates scheduled, so as
long as I have my laptop and can access the firm's
mainframe, I can work anywhere."

In fact, if she wanted to, she could essentially set
up her office on some faraway beach. When that
all too appealing idea brought up her now familiar
tropical fantasy starring Jack O'Halloran, she
dragged her mind back to the droning voice on the
other end of the phone.

"I understand, Stephen. Yes, it's a bit of an incon-
venience, but it's nothing that can't be worked out."

More complaints, along with a pointed comment
about the upcoming decision to be made on the new
partnerships that caused the temper Raine usually
kept on a taut leash to spike. If he thought he could
make her abandon her grandmother by threatening
to pass her over for promotion, he definitely had
another think coming!

She swallowed hard to force down her annoyance.
"I promise nothing will fall between the cracks."
With effort, Raine kept the irritation from her voice.
"And really, Stephen, when you come right down to
it, my taking a few days to deal with a family emergency is not nearly as disruptive as if I'd taken a
vacation. A long-overdue vacation," she stressed. "As
I'm certain many attorneys would do after obtaining
an important victory like the Odessa Oil appeals
decision."

For a moment, she could hear only the *tick tick tick* of the kitchen clock. "All right," he finally said. "We'll consider this a vacation, then. And I'll assure the other partners that you'll be back at your desk no later than fifteen days from now."

His point made, rather ungraciously, Raine thought, considering the money she'd brought into the firm's coffers just this month alone, Stephen Wells brought the conversation to an abrupt close.

❧ 11 ❧

Worries filled Raine's mind, circling around and around like fallen leaves caught in a whirlpool. She worried about her work, which, despite her brave words to Stephen Wells, she knew would pile up during her absence. She worried about Ida, who while as bossy and mule-headed as ever, was obviously growing older.

As they all were, Raine thought as she crawled out of bed, pulled on a robe and a pair of thick green-and-orange-striped ski socks that she'd left behind when she'd gone to law school. But Ida wore her years more heavily.

She worried that Gwen would prove too much for her grandmother to take care of on her own. Especially if she decided to keep her baby. She worried what would happen to the teenage mother and child if that proved the case. And, finally, she couldn't stop worrying about Savannah.

What many people, who made the mistake of concentrating only on her stunning looks, missed was that Savannah Townsend had a deep-seated domestic streak. As a child she'd spent hours at her Easy-Bake oven, turning out tiny cakes and cookies for the teas she'd serve with a flourish and an eye for detail far beyond her years. The miniature plates were scrubbed and decorated sand dollars she'd collected on the beach, the paper cups always sported hand-painted motifs, and Martha Stewart would have envied the ideal simplicity of Savannah's seasonal centerpieces.

While Raine had spent hours role-playing with their scores of Barbie dolls—always opting for the career look, even as a secret part of her had been drawn to the glam gowns—Savannah had tended more toward baby dolls she could bathe and rock and pretend to feed.

"A natural born mother," Ida had often said whenever Savannah brought home yet another wounded dog or cat. She'd once rescued a hawk whose wing had been broken by some older boys throwing stones. The ungrateful bird had viciously ripped the skin on Savannah's index finger during the rescue operation, but just the memory of the sight of the hawk soaring off the cliff after its recovery was enough to give Raine goosebumps.

As she went downstairs, planning to get some air on the front porch, Raine thought about the miscarriage Savannah had suffered last summer. When her sister had visited her in New York last fall, they'd spent hours talking about her sister's lifelong desire for a large family. Now Raine considered that perhaps it was fortunate she hadn't had any children. Being a single mother like Lilith would obviously be difficult.

No. Not like Lilith, Raine amended as she went

out onto the porch. The screen door opened with a rusty creak. Her sister would never abandon her children.

And speaking of her mother . . . Raine was surprised to find Lilith sitting alone in the dark on the swing. "Looks as if I'm not the only one who can't sleep," she said.

"It's been a busy past few days." A red glow brightened the dark as Lilith drew in on a cigarette.

"That's putting it mildly." Raine chose a wicker chair. "At least Shawna's case went well."

"That was something." Lilith took another longer drag on the cigarette, then exhaled a cloud of smoke that hung between them like an acrid curtain. "I still can't believe that we were unlucky enough to get Bloody Babs Patterson for a judge.

"Bloody Babs?"

"She always was horrendously vicious whenever she felt crossed. Most of the girls were terrified of her, which is why they always voted her onto the pep squad and prom committees, even when they didn't want to."

If the judge hadn't turned out to be a major problem, Raine might have laughed at Lilith's pique. It had been thirty-two years, yet from the way her mother spoke about Judge Barbara Patterson-Young, it could have been yesterday.

"Well, she definitely found a way to get the upper hand today."

"That's true." Lilith stabbed her cigarette out in the empty cup she'd been using for an ashtray. "Did you see Cooper?"

"No. Was he in the courtroom?"

"He was sitting in the back. He came in while Babs was drilling you on your credentials. And left right about the time Mother shot off her mouth."

Raine couldn't help chuckling, just a little, at the memory. "I thought I was going to have to sit on her."

"She'd have bit your ass if you'd tried," Lilith said. "It *was* funny, though. I don't think I'll ever forget Bab's face when Mother brought up the birth control pills."

"She reminded me of St. Helens, about to blow its top again."

"Didn't she?" Lilith laughed softly. Then sighed again. "Of course, to be fair, I realize now that I never should have gone out with Jimmy. They'd just had a little spat over her deciding to go to school in Hawaii instead of Washington State, like she'd originally planned."

"Sounds as if they made up the first time she came home," Raine said mildly. "If Gram's right about the pills."

"Oh, she's right. Mother has always had a steel-trap mind."

"Perhaps not so much anymore."

Lilith glanced over at Raine. "Sometimes it's still hard for me to imagine that little girl I brought into the world as an attorney. From what Ida says, you're quite an important one, too."

"Not that important. And we all grow up."

"True. We're also all getting older." Lilith drew her knees up to her chest and rested her chin on them. "Lord, that's a damn depressing thought."

"Don't worry, Lilith." Raine couldn't quite keep the

veiled sarcasm from her tone. It was so typical that her mother would find a way to put herself in the center of the situation. "You'll never get old."

"Grow up, you mean," Lilith said.

"I suppose that's a matter of semantics."

"No." Silver hair flashed like a comet in the dark as Lilith shook her head. "You're extremely skilled in the use of words, Raine. You were avoiding the truth because you didn't want to hurt my feelings. But I notice you didn't argue when Bloody Babs ruled that I wasn't competent to care for the girls."

"She didn't exactly say you were incompetent—"

"She said I was not a responsible adult." Showing a flash of her usual spark, Lilith lifted her chin, just a little. "And with your silence, you agreed."

"I couldn't lie. Not in a court room. Not with Gwen's future at stake."

"Are you saying that you honestly don't believe I could take care of her? For four short weeks?"

"Honestly?" Tired of tap dancing around the issue, Raine decided not to mince words. "No. I do not believe you'd be a stable influence on Gwen. Even allowing that we haven't seen much of each other the past few years, Lilith, after that little New Age musical you performed in the forest, the one you invited Shawna to participate in"—she reminded her mother pointedly—"I don't see how anyone could consider you a decent role model."

"The last time I looked, the constitution granted all Americans freedom of religion."

"True. But I don't recall anything about the founding fathers writing in a clause granting the freedom to dance nude in a public park."

"We weren't in public, not really . . ."

"Dammit, Lilith!" Raine was on her feet now. "Would you just drop it? You were wrong. Your behavior was outrageous. And irresponsible, since people take their children into Olympic National Park, which makes it very, very public."

"There's nothing wrong with the human body."

"True. Until you decide to flaunt it in front of a bunch of Boy Scouts."

Lilith looked up at her in surprise. "There weren't any Boy Scouts anywhere around where we'd camped."

"Not yet. But Jack told me an entire troop of them were scheduled for a nature hike the next day."

"Really?" She tilted her head and pursed her lips as she thought that over. "I wonder why Cooper didn't mention that little fact while he was slapping the shackles on me."

"They were handcuffs, Lilith. Not shackles. Besides, he only resorted to using them after you slapped him. And to answer your question, he didn't tell you about the scouts because he was afraid once you heard about them, you'd refuse to get dressed."

"Did he actually tell you that?"

"He told Jack. Sheriff O'Halloran," Raine corrected quickly. "The sheriff told me." The less-than-pleasant subject had come up last night while they'd been planning for Gwen's hearing.

"I see." Lilith's gaze turned to look out over the rolling, dark-shadowed lawn. "It appears Cooper doesn't think very much of me."

"Would you if you were in his shoes? After what you did?"

"I admitted going out with Jimmy was a mistake, but—"

"We're not talking about some stupid, damn teen-age tryst," Raine said through clenched teeth. "I was referring to the way you resisted arrest."

"That's ridiculous. All I did was tear up his stu-pid ticket."

"Three times. Along with his citation book."

"Well, there was that," Lilith reluctantly agreed. She allowed a faint smile at the memory. "I hate to admit this, but I was a little embarrassed when he came in the courtroom today."

Stop the presses, Raine thought. Lilith Lindstrom may actually have regrets about her behavior. Since there was nothing reasonably safe she could say to that, she didn't respond.

"Maybe even a bit ashamed," Lilith went on to confess. The silence lingered between them, so pal-pable Raine imagined she could reach out and touch it. "But it was still wrong of Babs to imply that I wouldn't be a proper caretaker. After all," she said with a flare of pique, "I have two daughters of my own—"

"Whom you continually abandoned like a mother cat dumping a litter of kittens." Continued exhaus-tion, plus the events of the past few days, caused Raine to respond more harshly than was her nature. She regretted the words the moment she heard them come out of her mouth. Almost.

"That's not fair." Moisture glistened in Lilith's ex-pressive eyes. "I didn't abandon you. Leaving you girls with your grandmother, whenever things got too difficult for me to handle on my own, whenever my life got disrupted, was my way of providing you with a stable home."

Raine's barked laugh held not an iota of humor. "That was your idea of stability?"

"It was the best I could do, at the time," Lilith responded defensively. "You don't know how it was for me. Ida divorced my father when I was five years old—"

"He was a gambler. He stole money from her and he hit her."

"I never saw him lift a hand to Mother, but if she says it happened, it undoubtedly did. The thing is, Raine, I never got over losing him. Which is why, I suppose, I've spent so much of my life needing men to find me attractive. To want me."

"I really don't think we should go down this road," Raine warned.

"Oh, *I* think we should. Because it's important. . . . It's not easy for me to admit this, Raine. But I've been thinking a great deal about you and your sister lately, and I've come to the conclusion that in your own way, you're the most like me."

"That's preposterous!" Raine shook her head, stunned by her mother's outrageous suggestion. "We're nothing alike."

"Oh, I think you're a great deal more like me than you care to admit," Lilith said mildly. "I saw you on television the other day. You photograph very well, by the way."

"Gee, thanks. That really puts my mind at ease."

"You don't have to be sarcastic. I was merely making an observation. You have the Lindstrom bones. They'll serve you well as you grow older.

"But despite having my features, you looked amazingly like Owen, when he held his press conference on the federal-courthouse steps after he'd gotten the Sacramento Six acquitted.

"I was pregnant with you at the time. He wasn't at all happy about that, but since he was considering a possible political future, he agreed to get married. I'd known it was merely a marriage of convenience—his convenience," she clarified with an edge to her voice. "But I honestly believed that I could get him to love me. In time."

"Which you didn't have."

"No. The day we got back from Tijuana, he moved out of our apartment and we never spent another night together."

Her parents ill-fated marriage was definitely not one of Raine's favorite topics. But there was one part of Lilith's story that had captured her attention. "I reminded you of my father?"

Lilith lit another cigarette and took her time in answering. "Unfortunately, yes."

"Unfortunately?" She couldn't help herself. Lilith had Raine wondering if, just perhaps, her father had seen her on television, speaking with the press. And if he had, whether he'd been even a little bit proud of her.

"Your father is not a nice man, Raine, dear. Oh, he's admittedly intelligent and charismatic, but he's also totally egocentric—"

"And a brilliant attorney," Raine broke in, thinking that Lilith calling Owen Cantrell egocentric was definitely a case of the pot calling the kettle black.

"True. He's both brilliant and ruthless. I do believe that all those lawyer-shark jokes were coined with Owen in mind. It was that part of him I saw in you.

That's when I knew for certain that what I've been suspecting all these years was true."

"Which was?" Raine inquired icily.

"In the same way I've spent my life trying to prove to an absent father that I was appealing enough to love, you're trying to prove yourself to *your* father by becoming even more heartless than he is."

After Jack's comments about lawyers, this accusation hit particularly hard. "That's a ridiculous assumption. It's also patently wrong."

"You were on the wrong side of that retirement issue, darling. You took the shark's side. If you're not careful, you could end up just like Owen, turning your back on morality and taking on any high-profile case that will win you big bucks and a reputation as a top hired gun. I fear that if you keep going down the path you're on, Raine, someday you may well find yourself defending someone like your father's current client. A horrible, abusive bully that everyone knows is a cold-blooded killer."

Raine was so angry she could barely push the words past the painful lump in her throat. "Not that it's pertinent to this discussion, but that same constitution that gives you the right to worship the sun or moon or a damn oak tree, if you want, also declares every defendant innocent until proven guilty."

"Are you saying that if you'd been asked, you would have defended that murderer?"

"No." Despite her claim of a defendant's right to innocence, the very idea of defending that *particular* defendant was unthinkable. "But—"

"Yet you were willing to take on Odessa Oil as a client."

"Odessa didn't kill anyone."

"Not yet," Lilith countered. "But without health-care—"

"I am not going to discuss this!" Raine's shout caused a startled bird to fly out of the monkey puzzle tree into the night sky on a whirl of wings. Preferring to leave the scene making to her mother, she immediately lowered her voice. "You have no right telling me what to do with my life."

"I'm your mother."

"No." Raine shook her head emphatically. Hot, furious moisture was welling up behind her lids but she refused to give in to tears. "You abandoned any maternal rights years ago, Lilith. When you abandoned your daughters."

Even as she saw her mother flinch, Raine didn't retract her harsh words. Or apologize.

Instead, she went back into the house on unreasonably shaky legs, managing, just barely, to keep from slamming the screen door behind her.

By the following morning, Raine felt horrendously guilty for her uncharacteristic outburst. The fact that she'd believed most of what she'd said was no excuse for having lashed out and hurt Lilith. Especially since the behavior that had caused so much pain was in the past.

Lilith opened her bedroom door at Raine's first knock. Her quick response, and the shadows beneath her eyes revealed that Raine hadn't been the only one who'd found sleep difficult after their argument.

Not that the fatigue diminished her beauty. Actually, Raine considered, it made her mother appear even more delicate, like spun glass. She'd obviously gotten Lilith out of bed, yet somehow her mother had avoided the crease marks that usually marred Raine's cheeks upon awakening, and every silver hair was in place. She was wearing a blue silk night-gown and matching robe that matched her eyes and made Raine, in her dancing-sheep pajamas, feel like a street urchin.

A long-ago memory flooded back. That of a little girl, no more than seven years old, sneaking into her mother's lingerie drawers, drawn by the brightly hued silk and satin and lace confections. Raine had loved the colors that reminded her of the shimmer of rainbows, loved the slick, but oh, so soft feel of them against her fingertips and cheeks as she'd lifted them to her face, breathing in the exotic scent of Shalimar that she'd always identified with her mother.

One time, when she sensed Lilith was about ready to take her daughters back to Coldwater Cove again, Raine had stolen a scarlet, lace-trimmed slip from the drawer and hidden it away in her suitcase. For months, as she'd lain alone in her bed in the room she shared with her sister at their grandmother's house, she slept with that silk slip, feeling as if in some way, she was sleeping with her mother.

"Would you like to come in?" Lilith asked.

"No. I haven't checked in with my office yet." Raine felt a distant pain and realized that she was digging her fingernails into her palms. "I just wanted to apologize for what I said last night."

"Oh, that's not necessary." Lilith gracefully waved the words of contrition away.

"Yes, it is." Raine took a deep breath that was meant to calm. It didn't. "You were right, Lilith. No matter how I feel about certain past aspects of our relationship, you're still my mother. I had no right to speak so disrespectfully to you."

"Well." Lilith was silent for a moment, seeming to take that in as she studied her elder daughter's grimly set face. "Thank you, darling. I appreciate your thoughtfulness."

They stood there, a few inches apart on opposite sides of the door jamb. There was an aura of expectancy in the air, as if both knew that such a circumstance demanded a hug, but each was unable to make the first move. Then Lilith lifted a hand to brush some tousled hair off Raine's face.

"As it happens, I promised your grandmother I'd take Shawna shopping for a graduation dress this morning. Ida wanted it to be a going-away gift. Perhaps we could go together. Maybe even have lunch afterwards. Sort of a girl's day on the town."

Raine fought against the flood of yearning that single, casual maternal touch seemed to trigger. She wanted to refuse Lilith's invitation, but found the words difficult.

"If you'd rather not, I'll understand," Lilith said when Raine didn't immediately respond.

Raine watched her mother fussing with the silk tie of the robe, twisting it in her hands and realized with surprise that Lilith was actually nervous. "It sounds like fun," she said, falling back on politeness as she tried to analyze her feelings.

"Doesn't it?" Lilith agreed.

As she left her mother's bedroom, Raine assured herself that the moisture that had seemed to glisten in Lilith's blue eyes had only been a trick of the morning light. Even stranger was the way she inexplicably felt like crying herself.

Short of traveling to Seattle, the Dancing Deer Dress Shoppe was the best—and only place—to buy women's clothing in Coldwater Cove. The store had been established by sisters Doris and Dottie Anderson, nee Jensen, identical twins who'd been married to Coldwater Cove's only other pair of twins, Harold and Halden Anderson, for nearly fifty years. For all those years the two women had lived next door to one another, worked side by side, worn their snowy hair exactly the same way, and even dressed alike, although Doris, who was elder by ten minutes, favored earth tones while Dottie, displaying an independent flair, usually chose scarlet.

"How wonderful that you've come home again," Dottie greeted Raine as the others began searching through a display of pastel prom and graduation dresses.

"I imagine Ida's on cloud nine," Doris agreed. "You and your sister are just about all she talks about. One of Savannah's recipes was featured in the *L.A. Times*, Raine just won a multimillion-dollar case," she quoted Ida. "You both certainly did your grandmother proud, that's for certain."

"Not just your grandmother," Dottie said before Raine could respond. "We're all proud of you."

"Thank you," Raine murmured. In the city, she lived in a world of anonymity. Like *Beauty and the Beast*'s castle, her life was made easier by the performance of a host of invisible servants. Her garbage was taken away, her apartment cleaned, her mail and groceries delivered. But here in Coldwater Cove, everyone not only knew each other's business, but their life histories, as well.

"We saw you on television," Doris said. "You photograph very well, dear, doesn't she, Sister?"

"You looked beautiful," Dottie agreed. "But a bit subdued. I thought I'd read that it was always preferable to wear bright colors on television."

"I didn't dress for the television cameras," Raine said mildly.

"Well, I suppose you have a point. Although it's still possible to look feminine and professional at the same time. Have you ever watched *Melrose Place?* Or *Ally McBeal?*"

"Ally McBeal is a fictional lawyer."

"Well, that may be," Dottie allowed as she fluffed her cotton-candy hair. "But that girl certainly does know how to catch a male eye with those short skirts."

"Perhaps Raine has more important things on her mind than attracting men," Doris suggested dryly.

"Well, I can't imagine what." Dottie tilted her head like a curious bird. "After all, dear, you're not getting any younger, and I know how dearly Ida is yearning for some great-grandchildren to bounce on her knee.

Why she talks about it all the time, doesn't she, Sister?"

"She's mentioned it," Doris confirmed. "Ida misses both you and Savannah, dear. Now, I realize that it isn't really any of our business—"

"None at all," Dottie broke in. "But of course that never stopped Doris from handing out advice."

"Sister," Doris complained, "it was my turn to speak."

"I realize that, Sister," Dottie said. "But I'm sure Raine didn't come here today for a lecture."

"I had no intention of lecturing her," Doris said stiffly. "I was merely intending to point out how good it's been for Ida, taking in those three poor misguided girls."

"It's given her a new lease on life, that's for certain," Dottie agreed. She leaned forward and placed a plump hand on Raine's arm. "I have to admit that I did worry in the beginning that one of them might sneak into her bedroom in the middle of the night and kill her while she was sleeping."

"If the girls were killers they wouldn't be in a group home, Sister," Doris snapped. "They'd be locked up somewhere."

"You can't always tell," Dottie insisted. "Why, just last week, I was watching that Jerry Springer show and he was interviewing this handsome young man who, to look at him, you would have easily taken for a choirboy. In fact, he reminded me a little bit of Daniel O'Halloran, at least around the eyes. But of course, Daniel is older than he was. . . ."

"I assume there's a point to this?" Doris ground out.

"Of course. As I was saying, before I was interrupted," she said, shooting a censorious look at her sister, "you never would have suspected that the young man on the show was anything but a model citizen. But it turned out he's in prison for strangling women. Then, after they're dead, he sautés their hearts in a Napa Valley chardonnay with a touch of olive oil and pesto, while wearing his victims' clothing, if you can believe such a dreadful thing."

"Sister!" Doris's expression revealed her shock. "You're forgetting your manners! Didn't Mother teach us that some subjects are not meant to be discussed in public?" She shook her head in frustration as she turned back toward Raine. "Don't pay any attention to Dottie, Raine, dear. Ever since she started watching those daytime television shows, her conversation has become absolutely scandalous."

Dottie lifted both pink chins. "It's important to know what's going on in the world. Unlike some of us who are content to only pay attention to the goings-on here in Coldwater Cove."

"I doubt that cross-dressing, cannibalistic serial killers are all that common even outside our small hamlet," Doris argued. "In fact, I would imagine that you don't hear about them all that often even in the big city. Do you, Raine?"

It was all Raine could do to keep her lips from giving into the smile that was tickling at the corners of her mouth. "Not as a rule."

Doris turned back to her twin and folded her arms over the front of her olive green shirtwaist dress. "See? I told you those horrid shows are not reflective of real life. The outrageous stories are probably even made up."

"Oh, I can't believe they'd allow people to lie on television," Dottie replied vaguely. "But I'm getting off track. My initial point was that at first many of us were concerned for Ida when she took those girls in. However, I, for one, have decided to give them the benefit of the doubt."

"Still," she amended as her intense blue eyes drifted toward the little family group across the room, "I'm afraid their shenanigans the other day didn't exactly help their cause any."

"That was unfortunate," Raine agreed.

"Oh, well," Dottie said with a flare of her unsinkable optimism, "at least the standoff brought you home, Raine. So, I've no doubt that your grandmother must think all that pesky trouble was worth it. Speaking of that standoff, what did you think of the sheriff?"

Since the Anderson sisters were the closest thing Coldwater Cove had to town criers, Raine decided not to share her initial impression that he was too sexy for comfort. "He seems like a fair man."

"Oh, he is. But I wasn't talking about that. I was referring to his looks. Didn't you find him absolutely dashing?"

"I didn't really notice."

"Oh, darling, if that's truly the case, then you have been working too hard. Every single woman in town has been chasing after that man since he was widowed. I suspect that quite a few of the married ones wouldn't mind him putting his cowboy boots beside their beds, either. While just the other day I was in the market and I saw Marianne Wagner—you remember her, Raine, she's Peter and Elizabeth Garrison's youngest daughter—flirting with our sheriff over the broccoli.

"Of course I can understand how she'd be lonely, especially now that her husband had to take that timber job down in Oregon, but still, with three children to take care of, you'd think she'd be too busy to find time to pick up men in the market, not that he seemed all that interested."

"Sister!" Doris spat out. "Really, that's enough. Raine didn't come here to gossip about the sheriff. She came here to shop. So, we should just let her get to it." With that, she literally dragged her talkative sister away.

The others had already disappeared into the dressing rooms when Lilith approached with a silk dress awash with tropical flowers.

"Look, darling. Isn't this lovely?"

"Gorgeous," Raine agreed, easily picturing her mother in the vastly romantic dress.

"I'm so pleased you think so. Since I want to buy it for you."

"That's not necessary."

"It is to me." The earnest look in Lilith's eyes brought back last night's argument.

"It's not suitable for the city," Raine said in a weak attempt to resist her mother's silent appeal.

"You're not in the city now, darling."

"True. But I can't imagine needing a dress like that here in Coldwater Cove, either."

"You never know." Ignoring Raine's frown, Lilith held it up against her body. "Perhaps you'll be invited out to dinner."

Raine tried to imagine wearing the ultraromantic

dress to Oley's for barbecue and couldn't. "I didn't come home to date."

"Well, of course you didn't, dear. But it's such a lovely dress."

"It's beautiful," Gwen, who'd suddenly appeared, cajoled. "Try it on, Raine, please?"

It wasn't her style. Raine thought of all the neat little dress-for-success suits hanging in her closet. She'd never owned a dress like this in her life.

"It wouldn't hurt to try it on," Lilith said. "Unless, of course," she added slyly, "you're afraid."

"Why on earth would I be afraid of a dress?"

"I have no idea." Lilith shrugged. "Perhaps because you're afraid that you'll discover a sexy, tempestuous female lurking beneath that grim, serious legal facade you present to the world?"

It was more challenge than insult. Even knowing that her mother was pushing buttons, Raine couldn't quite resist taking her up on it.

She snatched the dress from Lilith's manicured hand. "It's not my size. It's too small."

"I don't think so." Lilith skimmed an appraising look over Raine. "Give it a try, and if you need a larger size, I'll go get one. . . . Meanwhile, I'm going to see how Shawna's coming along."

It wasn't her style, Raine repeated to herself as she stripped off her slacks and sweater. Besides, her mother was wrong. There wasn't a single tempestuous bone in her body. She was intelligent, reasonable, and cool headed. She preferred classic styles and colors—like a little basic-black dress worn with a single strand of very good pearls. The kind of dress that could go from the office out to dinner.

As she pulled the dress over her head, Raine overlooked the fact that it had been a very long time since any man had asked her out to dinner. Even longer since she'd accepted.

The dress slid over her like a silk waterfall. Raine refused to be enticed. Until she looked into the mirror and viewed the stranger who was looking straight back at her.

"Raine?" Lilith called out to her. "How does it fit?"

"I think it's a little snug." The bodice bared her shoulders and the silk hugged her curves like a lover's caress on the way down her body to swirl around her calves. It felt cool and carefree and, dammit, sexy.

Raine reminded herself that she'd never *wanted* to be sexy. That was her mother's role. While there were, admittedly days that she found her own life less than perfect, there was no way she'd want to trade places with Lilith. Not in a million years.

"Come out and let's see."

"That's not necessary—"

"Oh, Raine, don't be such a party pooper," Lilith complained as she pulled open the curtain. "Oh, darling, it's perfect."

"For you, perhaps. But it's not me." Was it her imagination, or did the brightly hued hibiscus blossoms bring out red highlights in her hair she'd never noticed?

"Of course it is. If you hadn't spent most of your life working overtime, pretending to be someone, and something you're not, you'd realize that."

"I'm not pretending." Raine turned sideways and skimmed her palm over a silk-covered hip. It really was stunning. "Not really."

"Then what would you call it?"

"Surviving."

Their eyes met. Another of those thick, uncomfortable silences settled over them. Raine viewed the hurt in her mother's expertly made-up eyes and felt a tinge of guilt for having put it there.

"Oh, Shawna, that's gorgeous!" they heard Renee exclaim. "Lilith, Raine, come see how beautiful Shawna is! She looks just like a supermodel!"

The tense mood was broken. Grateful for the interruption, Raine escaped the dressing room. And her mother.

"Oh, that is truly lovely." she breathed as she took in the seventeen-year-old standing in front of the three-way mirror just outside the dressing rooms. The white lace top, held up by slender satin ribbons, skimmed the waistband of a short tight skirt trimmed at the hem with more lace. The girl's coltish legs looked a mile long.

"Do you really think so?" the teenager asked, holding her arms out to her sides.

"It's perfect," Lilith and Raine said together. Unaccustomed to agreeing about anything, they exchanged a brief, surprised look. "Absolutely perfect," Lilith insisted.

Shawna grinned. "I love your dress, too," she said to Raine.

"It's not my dress," Raine said.

"You're not going to get it?" Renee and Shawna asked in unison. They both stared at her in disbelief. Gwen, Raine noticed, looked absolutely crestfallen.

"No. It's just not my style, it's too small, and—"

"Oh, look, girls," Lilith trilled, overrunning Raine's planned rejection of the dress that was proving too tempting for comfort. "It's the sheriff."

Terrific. This was all she needed. Raine briefly closed her eyes, then turned toward the door where he was holding the hand of the most beautiful child she had ever seen. The little girl could have been a princess who'd stepped right out of the pages of a fairy tale book.

Her heart-shaped face was the color of cream tinged with an underlying peach hue, like one of the antique roses in Ida's backyard garden. Her petal pink mouth formed a perfect cupid's bow; long, pale, sun-gilded hair the color of a palomino's tail rippled down her back.

"I'm so glad to see you, Sheriff," Lilith greeted him with one of her practiced smiles that somehow didn't cause a single crinkle at the corner of her eyes. "You left the courthouse so quickly yesterday, I didn't have an opportunity to thank you for your expert testimony in Shawna's case. Why, I do believe you saved the day for us all." She glanced over to Raine, who was edging back toward the dressing rooms. "Didn't he, Raine?"

"It meant a lot to our case," Raine agreed. Unnerved by the flare of obvious male interest she viewed in his gaze, but realizing that escape now was impossible, she turned her attention toward his daughter. "Hello. I'm Raine. And you must be Amy."

"That's right." Emerald green eyes fringed by a double row of long, curly lashes smiled up at Raine. "How did you know?"

"Your daddy told me about you. When he was taking care of your Nano Kitty."

"Puffy," Amy said with a nod of her gilt head. "He's a lot of fun, but I'd rather have a real one."

She slanted a sly look upward at her father, who laughed.

"Keep trying, kiddo," he said. "You'll wear me down one of these days."

"He's very stubborn," Amy confided in Raine.

Six going on thirty, Raine remembered Jack saying. He'd been right. "I've discovered that for myself," she agreed.

"We're here to buy underpants," Amy announced. "My old ones are too small. Gramma says I'm shooting up like a beanpole, huh, Daddy?"

"That's what she said, all right," Jack agreed.

"Daddy brought some home last week, but they were little-kid ones. They had Barney on them." She wrinkled her nose in childish displeasure. "But I'm too old for Barney, so we brought them back. To exchange."

That settled, Amy turned her attention to Shawna. "You look really pretty in that dress. Like when Brandy played Cinderella on TV. Do those earrings hurt?" she asked as she took in the trio of gold hoops adorning each earlobe.

"Nah," the older girl said.

"I really really want to get my ears pierced. But Daddy says I'm too young."

"I was just a baby when I got my first holes," Shawna revealed. "I can't even remember getting them."

"Really?" Amy looked up at her father. "Did you hear that, Daddy?"

"I heard. But it doesn't make any difference because my mind is made up, my feet are set in concrete, and the subject is not even up for discussion until you're at least twelve."

"I told you he was stubborn," Amy said to Raine on a huge, dramatic sigh that had Raine smiling.

"I've got a belly-button ring, too," Shawna announced.

"Really?" Amy's eyes widened. "Can I see it?"

"Sure." As Shawna lifted the lacy top, Amy slipped free of her father's hand and moved closer to investigate.

"Christ," Jack muttered under his breath as he watched the avid discussion going on a few feet away, "that's just what I need, to have her wanting to get holes punched into her body. Next she'll be wanting a tattoo."

"I doubt that. She's a stunningly beautiful little girl," Raine said as the group of girls discussed the pros and cons of body piercing. Even as she told herself that she wasn't interested in any personal way, she couldn't help wondering how closely Amy took after her mother. "You're definitely right about her being mature for her age."

"I know. It's bad enough to discover that she's already outgrowing kid underwear."

"Perhaps she merely doesn't appreciate purple dinosaurs," Raine suggested.

"She made that more than clear." He dragged his hand through his dark hair. "What I know about raising a daughter could fit on the head of a pin. I think the safest thing to do is to just lock her in a closet until she's thirty-five."

Although he looked honestly distressed, Raine laughed at the idea of this teenage Lothario growing up to be the father of a daughter who was bound to attract a new generation of sex-crazed boys. "It appears you're doing just fine."

"Thanks. But I'm keeping that closet idea as an option for when she becomes a teenager and wants to start dating." His gaze intensified a bit as he studied her. Then he reached out, took off the darkframed glasses she was wearing again today and traced the smudged lines beneath her eyes. "You're carrying a lot of luggage here, Harvard."

"I have a lot on my mind." She plucked the glasses from his hand and shoved them back onto her face. They weren't much protection from that steady, searching cop stare, but they were better than nothing.

"Now that I'll believe."

"Daddy," Amy called to him. "I'm going to help Shawna pick out some earrings to go with her new dress, okay?"

He glanced back over at the family group again. "I'll keep an eye on her," Lilith answered his unspoken question.

"Thanks," he answered. "Go ahead, Pumpkin," he said to Amy. "We're not in that much of a hurry."

Amy took off, holding Lilith's hand as she practically skipped across the store to where the jewelry displays had been set up. Jack watched her for a moment, sighed again as envisioning his little girl growing up before his eyes, then turned back to Raine.

"That's one dynamite dress."

"I was just trying it on. Lilith insisted. In her own way," Raine said dryly, "my mother can be every bit as stubborn as Ida. If you don't stand up to her, you'll suddenly find yourself being run over by a velvet bulldozer. "

"I've always gotten a kick out of Lilith. But I can

understand how she could become a bit tiring on a day to day basis," he allowed. "Sounds as if the two of you are having problems."

"Is it that obvious?"

"When I walked in this place, the tension between you was downright palpable."

"Only to someone who's looking," she pointed out.

"True enough."

"It's my fault," she admitted on a sigh. "Both of us had trouble sleeping last night, so we ended up outside talking. Naturally we started discussing both of the court appearances, and one thing led to another, and well"—she shrugged her shoulders, her face as miserable as he'd seen it—"I was overly harsh and said some things I shouldn't have."

Obviously a man comfortable with touching, he rubbed at the lines etching their way into her forehead. "Things you didn't mean?"

"No." She briefly closed her eyes, allowing herself to enjoy the soothing touch. "They were true. But also hurtful."

"Mothers and daughters argue. Even grown daughters."

She opened her eyes again. "Lilith and I have never argued before." She didn't add that she'd always been too afraid to rock an already leaky boat.

He lifted a brow. "Never?"

"Never."

"Well, if that's really the case, it sounds as if this tiff was long overdue. Did it ever occur to you to just lay your cards on the table and tell your mother how you felt?"

"Is that what you'd do?"

"Absolutely. I'm not into playing games. Partly because they're a waste of time and partly because I'm not very good at them."

"Neither am I," Raine found herself admitting. "One of the reasons I've never spoken up before is because there really isn't any point. Accusing Lilith of being Lilith is a lot like scolding a butterfly for being flighty."

"Nevertheless, you can't deny that the situation has you tense." His thumbs skimmed a path from her temples, down her face, to her jaw. "Too tense." He brushed a light caress in the silky hollow between lips and chin.

Raine backed away. "You really shouldn't touch me like that."

"I like touching you."

"Doris and Dottie Anderson just happen to be the biggest gossips in Coldwater Cove," she reminded him. "If you keep it up, it'll be all over town by nightfall that we're lovers."

"Would that be so bad?"

"That it would be all over town?"

"No." Because she was finding his touch impossibly alluring, Raine was relieved when he dipped his hands into his pockets. "That we were lovers."

She felt the color flood into her cheeks. "You shouldn't be talking to me like that, either.

"You started it." When she lifted a brow, he said, "When you put on that dress."

"I certainly didn't put it on for you."

"Perhaps not. But you'd make me the most grateful man in Coldwater Cove if you'd go ahead and buy it."

It was at that moment that Raine belatedly recognized the dress Lilith had challenged her to try on. It was the one in her tropical hallucination. The very same one she was wearing on that moon-spangled beach when a man—this man—kissed her. Heaven help her, the unbidden romantic fantasies had been unsettling enough before they'd somehow become intertwined with her real life.

"I don't want this," she complained.

"What makes you think I do?"

"*You're* the one who keeps looking at me that way. Talking to me that way." She drew in a ragged breath that had the silk pulling against her breasts and caused heat to flash in his eyes. "Touching me."

"I can't help it. I like looking at you, Harvard. I like talking with you. I especially like touching you. In fact, since you brought it up, I suppose this is where I warn you that I'd like to do a whole lot more of it."

She held out a hand like a traffic cop. "You're hitting on me again."

"Absolutely."

Electricity was arcing around them once again. Raine felt as if a thunderstorm was hovering on the horizon, about to hit with a vengeance at any moment, while they were standing at ground zero. Her nerves strung nearly to the breaking point, she nearly wept with relief when a small bundle of gold hair and tanned arms and legs came hurtling into Jack, shattering the expectant, intimate mood.

❧ 13 ❧

"Daddy!" Amy said, "I just had the most wonderful, scintillating idea.

She'd always been a talkative child, constantly picking up new words like other kids might pick up pretty sea shells on the beach, which gave her a vocabulary beyond her age. *Scintillating* seemed to be her new word this week, gleaned from the remake of *The Parent Trap* they'd watched on video the other night.

"Did you, now?" Jack scooped her into his arms.

"Yes. I was telling everybody about the farm, and Renee said she's never seen a Christmas tree growing out in the woods, so I invited them to our planting party. That's okay, right?"

"I think it sounds like a dandy idea. The more hands the better."

"Planting party?" Raine asked.

"Every spring we plant new trees to make up for the ones we harvested the previous Christmas season. Peg started inviting friends and family and Amy and I've continued the tradition."

"It's bunches and bunches of fun," Amy said. "Isn't it, Daddy?"

"Bunches," Jack agreed with a smile for his daughter.

"That's why Mommy wanted the farm in the first place," Amy divulged with childish candor. "So whenever we felt bad because she died, Daddy and I could watch the new trees grow and think about the future. Instead of the sad times."

"I see." Raine risked a glance at Jack, who gave her a chagrined kids-what-can-you-do-with-them? look in return. "That's a lovely idea."

"Trees take a very long time to grow," Amy said matter-of-factly. "Daddy says I'll be a big kid, in high school even, before we can cut the ones we planted last year." Her expression revealed that to her six-year-old mind, that waiting time may as well be forever.

"That should be fun, though," Raine said. "You can invite all your teenage friends to the party."

Amy chewed on her thumbnail as she considered that suggestion. "Big kids like parties. I saw that on an *After School Special* at Gramma's. So, I guess it'll be fun, too."

"Bunches and bunches." Raine smiled.

"That's a pretty dress," Amy said suddenly.

"Thank you."

"You're pretty, too. Are you married?"

Raine exchanged another brief look with Jack. "No."

"Neither is my daddy, anymore."

Jack rubbed the bridge of his nose at that heavy-handed announcement. His mother and cousin weren't the only ones who thought he should be moving on with his life. His daughter had, in the past few months, become relentless in her campaign for a new mother.

If she'd had her way, he'd be married to her teacher, or Kelli Cheney, a pretty blond nurse in the doctor's office, or Marilyn Foster, a single mom who tended bar at the Log Cabin nights and picked up much-needed extra cash working mornings and afternoons as the school crossing guard.

"Lilith said Dr. Lindstrom wouldn't mind if Shawna, Renee, and Gwen came," Amy was saying when Jack dragged his mind back to the potentially hazardous conversation. He was tempted to remind her that she shouldn't call adults by their first names, then realized he didn't know which last name Lilith was going by these days.

"I'm sure she wouldn't," Raine said with another warm smile. "I'm also positive they'd love it."

"Oh, they would. But you have to come along, too."

"Me?" Her smile deflated like a hot-air balloon that had just sprung a leak.

"As the court ordered, darling," Lilith, who'd joined them, reminded Raine pointedly. "I'm sure, if she were asked, Judge Babs would insist that you accompany the girls on any outing. To make certain they don't get into any more trouble."

Jack was enjoying the way Amy and Lilith had essentially boxed Raine into a corner. "A little physical work outside in the fresh air will probably be good for the girls," he pointed out. "Gwen should probably take it easy, though."

"Definitely." Raine's mind was scrambling for a way out.

"Then you'll come?" If his daughter's wide eyes had been brown rather than green, she would have looked like a cocker spaniel, begging its owner to come out and play. Jack had had that look aimed at him enough times to know how difficult it was to resist.

Raine shrugged, as if knowing when she was licked. "Okay. I'll come."

"Oh, goodie!" Amy clapped her hands. "Hey everybody," she called out as Jack lowered her back to the floor. "Raine says you can all come to our planting party."

She ran back to the girls, followed by Lilith, who had obviously decided that her work was done.

"Well." Raine breathed out a frustrated breath. "Obviously subtlety is not my mother's strong point."

Jack laughed at that, finding himself actually looking forward to the weekend. "Nor my daughter's. I'm sorry if Amy embarrassed you. If it's any consolation, it isn't exactly personal. She's been on a campaign to get her old man married for months." He gave her his best grin, the one he hadn't tried out for nearly two years. "I guess she's getting tired of my spaghetti."

Raine smiled at that, as he'd intended her to.

Damn, the woman was downright gorgeous when she smiled. She had him feeling things he hadn't for a very long time. Thinking things that he probably shouldn't.

"It'll be fun." Because he couldn't be this close to her without touching, Jack skimmed his fingertips up her face. "Put some sun in that city pallor." When she batted at his hand, he caught hold of hers and linked their fingers together.

"You really have to stop this touching, Sheriff,"
she insisted, returning to that cool-as-frost courtroom voice that instead of annoying or intimidating
him, only made Jack want to kiss the breath out
of her.

"Now that you're on my daughter's candidate list,
you may as well drop the *sheriff* and call me Jack,"
he reminded her mildly. "I'm just checking."

"Checking what?"

"If they fit. They do." He touched palm to palm,
ignoring the fact that his hand dwarfed her smaller,
whiter ones. "I thought they might." His smile was
slow, arrogant, and designed to seduce.

"That's definitely hitting." She tugged her hand
free, spun around on her heel and made a beeline
toward the dressing rooms. Jack watched the sexy
sway of her hips beneath that flowered silk and resisted, just barely, the urge to tackle her.

"Hey, Harvard," he called.

"What now?" She turned half toward him, her fists
planted on her hips in a way that pulled the material
even tighter.

Amused, and more interested than he should be,
Jack grinned. "The party's informal—old jeans and
T-shirts. But buy the dress anyway. It's definitely
you."

"It's definitely you," Raine mimicked later. After
finally finishing their shopping, they'd had lunch at
the Timberline Café, and were now headed back to
the house. "The nerve of some people."

"Did you say something, darling?" Lilith asked
with a feigned innocence that Raine didn't buy for
a minute.

"Nothing that can be repeated in front of children," she answered through gritted teeth.

"You're angry at me again."

"Angry? Why should I be angry?" Raine asked with a calm she was a very long way from feeling.

"I have no idea. But you definitely seem upset about something."

"How about the way you practically threw me at Jack O'Halloran?"

"I didn't do any such thing."

Raine shot her an accusatory glare. "Didn't you?"

"Not at all," Lilith lied blithely. "However, to be perfectly honest, darling, I think the tree-planting outing could do you a world of good. Living in the city has you looking much too pale."

"I wish people would quit saying I look pale, because I'm not. I'm merely fair skinned." Raine frowned as she remembered Jack O'Halloran's cocky grin. It had been slow, arrogant, and undeniably charming. "As for that that dress . . ."

"It's stunning," Lilith filled in when Raine's voice dropped off.

"It's not my style," Raine insisted yet again.

"Of course not, dear," Lilith agreed.

Neither one of them mentioned that the dress in question was currently covered in a green-and-white-striped plastic bag, hanging on a hook behind the driver's seat,

"Now, a chat about"—Peg wiggled her nose—"boys."

Jack was sitting with Amy, watching one of the tapes. Peg's hair had begun to grow in when she'd taped this one; he remembered how surprised and pleased she'd been when she'd discovered that the debilitating chemo that had almost killed her had left her with curls.

"One of these days," Peg was saying, "if you haven't already, you're going to meet a boy you really like. Probably at school, which is where I met your father, although we were older than you. If you're lucky, he'll like you, too.

"Now the problem is," she said, leaning back in the wing chair and steepling her slender fingers, "boys aren't as mature as we girls. They get nervous when they realize that they're starting to like us. Most of the time that has them acting a little goofy." She turned and seemed to be grinning at someone offscreen. Jack knew that someone had been himself. "Okay, a lot goofy."

"Put it on pause, Daddy," Amy said suddenly. Jack did as instructed, freezing his wife's image onto the screen.

"What's the matter, Pumpkin?"

"Is that true? Do boys act goofy? Did you?"

"Absolutely." Jack smiled at the memory that was so clear it could have been yesterday. "I offered to carry your mother's library books back to her dorm."

"But you were so busy staring at her, thinking how pretty she was, that you tripped over a sprinkler head and dropped them in the fountain. And they got all wet." Amy had heard this story before.

"Soaking wet. They ballooned up to about ten times their original size."

"Then you paid the library fine so Mommy wouldn't have to."

"It was my fault." He'd gotten a second job busing

tables at a sorority to pay the bill for the ruined books. "It was only right that I take responsibility."

"Then you fell in love. And got married. And adopted me."

"That's exactly how it happened," he agreed. "Except you forgot the part about how we loved you to pieces."

"I know that. . . . Okay." Amy nodded, satisfied. "You can start it again, Daddy."

It was not the first time they'd watched this particular tape. In fact, it had become such a favorite over the past month, that Jack figured he could probably say the words right along with Peg. As his wife went on to talk about boys chasing girls on the school ground, and how, in the third grade, Jimmy Hazlett had washed her face in the snow, and then, that same day, had given her a lace-trimmed valentine with a puffy red satin heart, Jack's mind wandered, as it had been doing far too often these past three days, to Raine Cantrell.

There's no future in this, pal; a nagging voice in the back of his mind pointed out what he'd already decided.

Having given the matter a great deal of thought, he'd come to the conclusion that the kind of men the lady usually went out with were undoubtedly sophisticated, cultured guys who'd take her to the ballet and the opera. Guys who could whisper sweet nothings in at least one foreign language. Guys who, if not at the pinnacle of their profession, would at least be on the fast track up to that lofty peak.

She's city, you're country. You arrest the bad guys and put them in jail; she gets them out. She's French champagne, you're whatever beer's on sale. It would never work out.

On that point, both Jack and his internal voice agreed. But he wasn't interested in forever. He'd gone into his marriage with Peg with that goal, only to discover that real life wasn't anything like the fairy tales Amy loved to have him read at bedtime.

In fairy tales, the beautiful princess never got ovarian cancer; the princess's hair stayed long and shiny and strong enough for the prince to climb up, and when she did die, or go to sleep for a hundred years, she could always be awakened by the prince's kiss and they both lived happily ever after. Whenever the princess's life was threatened, the prince would come charging in on a white steed, armor gleaming in the sun, and save the day.

Which just went to show what a flop he was as a knight in shining armor, Jack thought grimly.

The following day, while Amy was at school, Jack called in to dispatch that he was turning his radio off for the rest of the afternoon. Then he drove out of town, up into the mountains.

The meadow was ablaze in wildflowers, just as it had been when he'd first made love to Peg on a blue-and-black plaid blanket beneath a buttery spring sun. As it had been, years later, when he'd scattered the ashes of the woman he'd thought he was going to grow old with in this very same spot.

He sat on a flat rock which offered a breath-stealing view of green forests and water. Clouds formed overhead, blocking out the sun.

"I don't know what to do," he admitted out loud. "Ever since you"—he couldn't say the word *died*, not in this place that held so many bittersweet memories—"went away," he said instead, "I've been so busy trying to stay sane and take care of our daughter and fill Dad's shoes, that I haven't had any time to even think about a woman."

He plucked some spring green grass from beside the rock. It was not the first time he'd come up here to talk with his wife. In the beginning he'd cried, sobbing like a baby, releasing tears that he hadn't dared shed in front of his friends, his parents, his daughter. Especially his daughter. Later, after he couldn't cry anymore, the anger had come out and he'd stomped over the alpine meadow, screaming at the top of his lungs. The only witnesses to his anguish were the marmots and a red-tailed hawk that lived in a nearby tree.

Finally, he'd moved past the pain and the anger to a point where he could come here to find comfort—even a strange sort of companionship—when he got too lonely. Jack knew that some people might think him nuts for talking this way to his dead wife. He didn't care.

"Then Ida's damn granddaughter came roaring into town with all guns blazing," he said.

He couldn't help smiling at the memory of her, marching through the rain and mire on that long-legged stride. Even soaked to the skin, she'd reminded him of some amazing female warrior princess. Like the one Amy liked to watch on TV. Xena, he recalled after a moment's thought.

"She can be a real pain in the ass. But there's another side to her. A gentler, caring side that I think she's tried real hard to bury over the years.

Which, if you'd ever met her mother, you'd probably understand."

Peg had always been much more forgiving of human failings than he was. Then again, until she'd gotten sick, she'd taught kindergarten, which had sheltered her from the daily examples of man's inhumanity to man that he'd witnessed on Seattle's mean streets.

"Of course there's no future in it. She's only going to be here for a couple more weeks, then she'll go back to her fancy, high-rise office in New York."

If what Dan had told him about Raine's win for Odessa Oil was even half-true, she was a power player in a city that defined high stakes. He had no trouble picturing her in a corner-window office that looked out over the city and made the cars on the street below look like Hot Wheels toys.

"Get this—she's a lawyer." He shook his head. Despite his affection for his cousin, Jack was having trouble getting past this one. "At first I thought it was just hormones. Which wasn't any big deal. . . . But I'm beginning to think it's more than that. And that scares the hell out of me."

Peg didn't answer, of course. But when he felt a soft breeze against his cheek, Jack was reminded of yet another tape she'd left behind. One she'd given to his mother for safekeeping until after she'd gone.

He'd first viewed what turned out to be her final goodbye in the early hours of the morning the day after her memorial service. Or at least he'd tried to watch it. It had taken three attempts before he was able to get all the way through it.

"Darling Jack," she'd soothed, her soft voice and her liquid blue eyes filled with warm comfort. "I know how horrible you must be feeling now. But I don't want you mourning me. Because I'm not gone. Not really."

That was when he'd turned off the VCR the first time. If she wasn't really gone, then why the hell wasn't she upstairs in their bed where she belonged?

"I'll always be in your heart, Jack," the farewell had continued when he'd tried again a week or so later. "In our daughter's heart. I'll be with the both of you always, for all eternity. I'll watch over you while you honor your oath to keep our friends and neighbors safe. I'll be with you on the sunniest summer days and the darkest winter nights.

"When you hear the breeze in the treetops, it will be my breath whispering your name, and whenever you feel a soft rain cooling your skin, it'll be my spirit passing by."

This was where he'd stopped on that second attempt. Then proceeded to drink himself into temporary oblivion.

Finally, nearly six months after he'd kissed his wife for the last time, he'd worked up the courage to watch the tape to the end.

"I know you love me, Jack. As I love you. Truly, madly, deeply. Forever. But sometimes forever on earth isn't as long as we'd hoped and it would break my heart to think of you alone, mourning my death instead of celebrating the wonderful life we had together and the blessings that brought us our darling daughter."

Jack heard a moan and realized it had been torn from his own throat. He felt the moisture on his cheeks, looked up, and while the gunmetal gray sky was getting increasingly lower, it hadn't yet begun to rain.

"Now I know this will make you angry, Jack," Peg said, in that sweet, cajoling way that he'd always found impossible to resist. "But I want you to marry again. Partly for Amy's sake, so she'll have more of a mother than this mountain of video tapes I've created can provide. She needs a real Mommy, Jack. A living, breathing one who can make Jell-O when she has a tummy ache and help soothe teenage broken hearts.

"A mother who'll someday watch you walk her down the aisle to begin a new life with a young man, who if she's very, very lucky, will love her the way you always loved me."

Her voice choked up at this point. Her blue eyes shimmered with tears. She bit her lip, drew in a ragged breath and combed her graceful fingers through her short blond cap of curls.

"I'm sorry," she murmured. "I just need a minute." She drew in another breath. This one more shallow than the first. Then, demonstrating the same strength of will he'd witnessed during the two years she'd valiantly fought off death, she forged on to the end.

"But I also want you to get married again for yourself. Because you have such an amazing capacity for caring, Jack, it would be a sin not to open your heart to someone else. Someone who needs you as much as you need her. Someone who loves you the way you will her.

"Now, I know how your mind works." She'd sniffled away the tears that had threatened earlier, now sounding more like the Peg who could keep a class of two dozen rambunctious five-year-olds in line. "I know how you feel about honor and loyalty, but you mustn't ever feel guilty about loving again, or even think you're abandoning me or my memory."

Her voice and her eyes gentled again. Offering re-assurance. "Because I believe, with every fiber of my being, that someday, darling Jack, we'll meet again in a beautiful place where love is infinite and there will be plenty for all of us to share."

Alone on the mountain, in the meadow they'd laughingly once claimed as their own, Jack closed his eyes and pictured the way her wedding band had gleamed in the sun slanting through the hospice window as she'd touched her fingertips first to her lips and then to the camera lens.

Fade to black.

The sky overhead opened up and the rain that had been threatening began to fall. But as he sat there, remembering, Jack didn't notice.

⤜14⤙

Raine had come to expect the unexpected from Lilith. But it appeared her mother had found a new way to drive her crazy.

For as long as she could remember, her mother had glowed with an internal light. But after Ida's guardianship hearing—and their argument—it was if that inner light had been snuffed out by an icy wind. Lilith became uncharacteristically subdued. She seldom spoke, and when she did it was in a listless voice lacking its customary music. She'd twisted her flowing silver hair into a decidedly unglamourous knot at the nape of her neck and exchanged her rainbow of colorful silks for clothing that could have come from Raine's own closet. Everything was now charcoal gray, bark brown, or black.

When Raine entered the kitchen a week after the hearing and found her mother clad in black slacks and a matching cotton shirt, it crossed her mind that in this new camouflage clothing Lilith could blend in quite well on the streets of Manhattan.

Even more surprising was the sight of her dropping cookie dough onto a greased aluminum sheet.

"Hello, darling." Lilith smiled a bit uncertainly. "I hope you like chocolate chip cookies."

"Of course I do." Raine tried to remember a previous time she'd seen her mother engaged in any domestic activity and came up blank. Obviously Lilith had been working for some time; there were spatters on the cupboard doors, the counter was covered with flour, and there were enough mixing bowls, measuring cups, and assorted utensils piled up in the sink to create an eight-course dinner.

"I decided baking cookies to welcome Savannah home this evening would be a nice, maternal thing to do." Atypical worry lines bracketed her mouth. "I do hope she likes chocolate chip. Perhaps I should have made oatmeal instead. I forgot to buy raisins when I was at the store, but I could always go back, and—"

"Don't worry. Everyone loves chocolate chip," Raine assured her, feeling strangely as if she'd walked through some unseen psychic curtain and landed in *The Twilight Zone*. That was the only excuse she could think of for Lilith Lindstrom Cantrell Townsend wearing an apron. "Savannah's going to be pleased you went to the trouble." *And surprised as hell.*

"I also bought some pancake mix while I was at the market. I thought they might be a nice change from cold cereal tomorrow morning."

"Sounds great." If it wasn't *The Twilight Zone*, she must have somehow entered a parallel universe, Raine decided.

"I couldn't make up my mind whether to buy the

buttermilk or the blueberry." Lilith wiped her hands distractedly on the front of the apron. "So I bought both."

"Good idea." Or perhaps, Raine considered, some aliens had landed in Coldwater Cove, snatched her mother up to the Mother Ship for some sort of strange medical experiments and left a Stepford Wife in her place.

"Of course, I realize that Savannah would never, in a million years, use a mix," Lilith continued as she returned to filling the cookie sheet with mounds of dough. They were eerily the same size, precisely the way a programed Stepford Wife might form them. "But I hoped that . . . Oh, no!"

Smoke was billowing from around the edges of the oven door. While Lilith twisted her hands together and made little wailing sounds, Raine grabbed the quilted oven mitt from the counter, opened the oven, pulled out the cookie sheet, and dropped it into the sink.

"Oh no." Lilith repeated bleakly, staring in abject dismay at the rounded black mounds. "They're burned."

More like cremated, Raine thought but did not say. "They are a bit crisp," she agreed carefully.

"They're ruined!" Her mother's pansy blue eyes were swimming with moisture.

"It's no big deal. You can just bake more."

"I'll ruin them, too." The tears that had been threatening began to fall, streaming down Lilith's face in wet, mascara-darkened trails. "I'm such a mess. I can't do anything right!"

"We're only talking cookies." The smoke alarm began to blare; Raine opened a window.

"I was thinking about what you said the other night, about how selfish I'd been, and decided that you were right. I truly didn't mean to cause you pain, Raine, but obviously I did. So I decided that I was going to turn over a new leaf and try to make things up to you and Savannah." The tears began to flow faster. "But those damn burned cookies are a metaphor for my entire life."

This display of dramatics was the most emotion her mother had shown in days. It was also surprisingly welcome. "If that's the truth, then we're in trouble," Raine said soothingly. "Because, with the exception of Savannah, none of the Lindstrom women have ever been able to cook."

"We've always had better things to do," Ida, drawn by the smoke and the alarm to the kitchen, pronounced from the doorway. "More important things than spending our lives in an apron and standing in front of a hot stove."

"That's just the point," Lilith wailed. "I've never done anything even the slightest bit important with my life." She sank onto one of the ladderback chairs, buried her face in her hands, and wept copiously.

Raine exchanged a distressed look with Ida, who shrugged. "Nonsense," the elderly woman said. "Don't go talking such foolishness, Lilith. Your singing has obviously given a lot of people pleasure."

"They only put up with me because I still look good in short skirts and leather and they're waiting for the star performer."

"Now, you know that's not true. You've always had a lovely voice.

"And you were a good actress," Raine said encouragingly.

"I was a terrible actress."

"Well, you weren't exactly Bette Davis or Kate Hepburn," Ida allowed. "But I'll bet there wasn't anybody in the horror movie business who could scream louder than you. Or who looked better in a wet nightgown."

Raine knew things were serious when her mother didn't agree with the nightgown assessment.

"And you've given birth to two exceptional young women," Ida continued. "That in itself is an accomplishment."

Lilith lifted her head. "Even an alley cat can give birth," she said, reminding Raine uncomfortably of the words she'd flung at her mother in anger. "That doesn't mean that she's capable of taking care of her kittens."

"You did the best you could at the time," Ida said briskly. "That's all any of us can do."

The words seemed to have a settling effect. Lilith's weeping trailed off to ragged, gulping sobs, and the flood of tears began to subside.

"What a mess." Her bleak eyes looked around the kitchen. Her shoulders slumped. No longer a Stepford Wife, she looked like a dejected fifty-year-old woman who'd just discovered that real life wasn't always fun. "I'd better start cleaning up before Savannah arrives." She pushed herself out of the chair, tipped the blackened mounds into the wastebasket and returned the cookie sheet to the sink. When she turned on the tap, water sizzled on the still-hot aluminum.

The sight of her mother with her rubber-gloved hands in soapsuds was even stranger than Lilith baking. Raine was about to suggest she take over when Gwen and Renee came into the room.

"Wow," Renee said.

"I know." Lilith's voice threatened renewed tears. "It's a mess." Soapy water sloshed over the rim of the sink onto the pine floor, which, like the counter, was dusted with flour. The resulting mixture resembled library paste.

"Why don't you let us help?" Gwen grabbed a dishrag. "I'll clean up while Renee finishes baking the cookies."

"It's my mess." More water sloshed onto the floor as Lilith energetically scrubbed at a Pyrex mixing bowl. "I'm going to clean it up."

Realizing that her mother's efforts were only making things worse, Raine decided to attempt to distract her.

"You know," she suggested, "as much as Savannah's going to enjoy those cookies, I'll bet she'd love some fresh flowers in the bedroom. None of us have the marvelous eye for color and design you do, Mother."

Lilith spun toward her, billowy soapsuds dripping unnoticed from the yellow rubber gloves. "What did you call me?"

Raine was as surprised to have said the word out loud as Lilith was to have heard it. "Mother." Strangely, it sounded almost right. "Does that bother you?"

"Oh, no, darling! Of course not!" There was a renewed flood of tears as Lilith threw her arms around Raine. "It sounds wonderful. Does this mean you've forgiven me?"

Her T-shirt was getting soaked by dishwater and

tears. "There's nothing to forgive," Raine said, not quite truthfully. Grateful to have the old Lilith back, she was nevertheless discomfited by the emotional display. "Now, why don't you let the girls finish up and go take care of those flowers?"

"That's a grand idea." Lilith released Raine from the tight embrace. "I think hyacinths might be nice. Or sweetpeas." She nodded. "Definitely sweetpeas." She peeled off the gloves, untied the apron, and threw it uncaringly onto one of the kitchen chairs, seeming not to notice when it slid onto the gummy floor. "They're perfect for spring."

"Well," Ida said, after Lilith left the room with renewed purpose in both her step and her eyes, "I never thought I'd say it, but it's a relief to have the old Lilith back with us."

The others murmured heartfelt agreement.

"You know," Ida mused, "she did have a good idea, making those cookies for Savannah. Family coming home is cause for a celebration. I believe, since we're being so domestic, I'll make my meatloaf."

As Raine exchanged a fatalistic look with the girls, she hoped Savannah stopped for dinner before she arrived in Coldwater Cove.

Savannah Townsend's late-night arrival in Coldwater Cove might just as well have been accompanied by a flourish of trumpets. Looking at her younger sister, if she hadn't known better, Raine would have thought nothing had gone wrong in her life. Indeed, she resembled Alexander the Great entering Babylon for the first time—strong, bold, invincible.

"It's about time you came back home where you belonged," Ida said with her usual bluntness.

"It's good to be here," Savannah agreed as she hugged her grandmother.

"Of course it is. Everyone knows that home is where the hearth is."

Savannah laughed. "Now I know I'm home." She bestowed a smile on her mother. "Lilith, I swear you look younger every day."

"It's the clean life your grandmother makes me lead whenever I come back to Coldwater Cove." More laughter, hugs were exchanged.

After embracing Raine, Savannah leaned back and observed her sister more closely. "You've lost weight."

"Not that much."

"You've also got circles beneath your eyes and you're too pale. If I didn't know better, I'd think that you were the one getting a divorce."

"I've been busy." Raine was getting tired of people's negative comments on her looks. She also couldn't help marveling at the way her sister could have her marriage collapse, give up a job she'd worked like hell to achieve, move out of her home, drive for three long days, and still arrive looking like some supermodel in a white jumpsuit trimmed in gold braid that didn't have a single wrinkle or stain. There were times, and this was definitely one of them, that Raine was forced to wonder if Savannah sprayed herself with Teflon before leaving the house each morning. "I just finished a big case."

"I know. I saw you on television. That took a lot of guts."

"Making myself a target for egg throwers?"

"No. Taking Odessa Oil's side in the first place."

"They're a client."

"They're also an oil company."

Raine glanced at the sporty red BMW illuminated by the spreading glow of the porch light. "Try running those snazzy wheels on tap water and you may just develop a different view of oil companies."

"Touché," Savannah said with a dazzling smile that was a twin to Lilith's. "I also realize that you don't always have a choice which of your firm's clients you represent, so—"

"Actually, I'm the one who brought Odessa to Choate, Plimpton, Wells & Sullivan in the first place. The revenues it's already generated have about guaranteed my partnership."

"Well, isn't that wonderful. You must be on cloud nine."

Ever loyal, Savannah gave Raine another big hug and the subject was dropped. But as they went into the house, Raine couldn't help thinking how her sister's take on the case echoed that of seemingly everyone around her.

As they gathered around the table while the girls slept upstairs, it occurred to Raine that this was almost like old times. Except in the past, Lilith had seldom been part of the family group.

"I knew that Kevin was trouble the first time I met him," Lilith said heatedly. "He was too slick and too smooth for my taste."

"Heaven knows, your track record with men is terrific," Ida said beneath her breath.

"I heard that." Lilith tossed her head. Raine had been relieved this afternoon when her mother had finally pulled her hair loose of that ugly bun she'd been wearing it in these past days. "That's exactly how I recognized that he was wrong for our Savannah. Because he reminded me of exactly the type of man I've always tended to get involved with. Smooth and charming and handsome as sin."

"Ha!" Ida scoffed. "That kind of charm is the oily kind that you can wash off in the shower with a bar of Lava soap. As for him being handsome, I suppose he wasn't all that hard on the eyes," she admitted grudgingly. "But to be perfectly honest, Savannah, dear, I always felt that *his* eyes were a bit too close together. And did any of the rest of you ever notice that he squinted?"

"That was because of his contacts," Savannah said. "He had dry eyes."

Ida was not to be deterred. "They were squinty. Just the type of eyes a man who'd run around on his wife would have. So, I suppose the gal's some bikini-clad beach bunny bimbette half his age?"

"Bimbette?" Despite the seriousness of the topic, Savannah exchanged an amused look with Raine. "Where on earth did you pick up that one?"

"I have lunch with Dottie Anderson in the back office of the Dancing Deer once a month," Ida said. "We watch television while we eat. Last month we watched a show where new mothers confronted the bimbette babysitters who were sleeping with their husbands. Well, needless to say, things got wild. I'll tell you, there's more violence on some of those shows than on the wrestling programs."

"You watch wrestling?" Raine asked.

"At times. No matter what people say about it being staged, it's great entertainment. Gwen and I like to make popcorn and root for Hulk Hogan." Ida jutted out her Lindstrom chin. "Do you have any problem with that?"

"None at all," Raine said quickly. "I was just surprised."

"It's important to try new things. Getting old is kind of like being a salmon. . . . If you don't keep moving forward you die."

"It's a shark that has to keep moving," Raine murmured.

"Whatever." Ida turned back to her younger granddaughter, "So is she a bimbette?"

"Actually, she's an attorney from the resort's legal department. One of those hard-edged, ice-water-in-the-veins, career Amazons with brass balls." The moment she heard the words come out of her mouth, Savannah cringed. "I'm sorry, Raine. I certainly didn't mean to imply that *you* were anything like that."

Raine managed a smile. "I know." But she was a lot like that. And everyone in the kitchen knew it. Cream puffs did not become Xena, Warrior Princess.

"I'll bet she keeps them in her fancy briefcase," Ida decided.

"Keeps what, Mother?" Lilith asked.

"Her brass balls."

They shared a laugh at that.

Savannah sighed and poured more wine from the bottle Lilith had placed in the middle of the table. "When I first moved out, Kevin insisted he didn't want a divorce. But now he's playing hardball."

She combed her fingers through her long auburn hair. The California sun had brightened the red curls with gold streaks. Looking at all that lush hair, the

Malibu tan, and bright emerald eyes, Raine thought that Savannah resembled some glorious goddess created by a master alchemist, rather than a mortal woman.

"He called me on my car phone about the time I crossed the California-Oregon border to warn me that the company considered any recipes I created while I'd worked there to be the resort's intellectual property."

Lilith lifted a beringed hand to her throat. "Surely you're not serious, darling?"

"That's what he's claiming."

"We can take care of that," Raine assured her briskly. "We'll get you a good lawyer and make the squinty-eyed, cheating bastard regret that he ever messed with a Lindstrom woman." Sometimes being a take-no-prisoner warrior woman could be a good thing.

When they'd been young, she and Savannah had shared M&Ms, popsicles, chicken pox, Barbie dolls, and the absence of a beautiful, but flawed mother. Later, they fought over bathroom time and hair dryers, even as they shared teenage confidences, secrets, and dreams. Now, during this trying time, Raine vowed to stand by her sister, just as Savannah would have stood by her, with the solidarity of the March sisters.

"I'd hoped we could end things civilly." Savannah rubbed her temples, momentarily letting down her guard long enough for Raine to see the incredible stress her sister was feeling. "But since I also refuse to cave in and let Kevin keep making money off my creations, I guess that's going to be impossible."

"Well, of course it is, dear." Lilith leaned forward

to pat her daughter's knee before refilling her own glass. "If God had intended for us to be friends with our ex-husbands, She wouldn't have made them such bastards in the first place."

Ida retrieved a second bottle of wine from the refrigerator. "He'll get his comeuppance," she predicted. "Everyone knows that time wounds all heels."

As the full, white moon outside the window sailed across a star-studded jet night sky, and both the chardonnay and the conversation continued to flow, Raine couldn't help thinking how good it felt to be home.

After another restless night spent chasing sleep, the first thing Raine noticed the next morning was that Savannah's bed was empty. Which was a bit surprising since Raine doubted that her sister had gotten all that much sleep.

It had been sometime after midnight when Raine had realized that the weeping ghost woman in her dream wasn't a ghost at all, but her sister, crying softly in the adjoining bathroom.

She'd slipped soundlessly out of bed and stood outside the door for a long, hesitant time, torn between trying to offer comfort and allowing her sister privacy. She'd even lifted her hand to knock, then, at the last moment, turned away and returned to bed.

It was a full twenty minutes more before Savannah returned to bed. Once again, Raine considered saying something. Anything. She might be a whiz at coming up with exactly the right words to sway a judge or jury, but personal matters were another story. Try as she might, she couldn't think of a single thing to say that might ease Savannah's obviously wounded heart. So, she'd kept silent.

But more than once during the long night, Raine was all too aware of her sister, lying awake in the next bed, only a few feet away, and wished that she could be, just for this one instance, as open and uninhibited as Lilith.

Thinking back on her sisterly failure now, Raine sighed and looked around the pretty little room. The curtains were white priscillas, the lace hand-tatted in a floral pattern. More flowers bloomed on the cream-colored wallpaper, reminding Raine of the day Ida had taken her young granddaughters shopping. Raine had wanted a muted white on white stripe, while Savannah, unsurprisingly, had opted for blindingly red poppies. The delicate purple violets had been a compromise. One that, in time, they'd both come to appreciate.

When she'd first returned to Coldwater Cove, after the clamor of the city, Raine had found the silence of the rural little town unnerving. But over the past days, she'd gradually come to realize that it wasn't silent at all. The window was halfway open, allowing her to hear the sweet morning song of birds, the rhythmic clang of a buoy out in the bay, and a *click click click* she could almost, but not quite recognize.

She went over to the window and looked out just in time to see the neighbor's eight-year-old son ride by on his bicycle, playing cards clipped to the spokes. Raine smiled, remembering having done the same thing so many years ago. Unfortunately, that was the week Ida had hosted her bridge club luncheon. Needless to say, her grandmother had not been pleased to discover the face cards missing.

The town was alive with signs of seasonal renewal: the watercolor colors of the flower beds in Pioneer Park could have washed off an Impressionist painting, and the blossoming fruit trees lining Harbor Street looked like giant pink-and-white lollipops. Looking out over the quaint town that resembled a Charles Wysocki painting of spring in New England, Raine thought that if there was a prettier place on the planet, she certainly hadn't seen it. If she were ever to choose somewhere other than New York to live, she could do far worse than come home to Coldwater Cove.

Not that she wanted to, Raine reminded herself. Turning one's back on the fast life and a lucrative urban law practice might be fine for Daniel O'Halloran, but not for her.

With that thought firmly etched in her mind, she took a quick shower, dried her hair, and went downstairs to the kitchen that smelled cheerily of just-brewed coffee. Her sister's head was inside the refrigerator door.

"Good morning," Raine greeted her.

"Good morning." Savannah turned around. Her smile was as warm as ever, but smudges beneath her eyes hinted at a sleepless night. "Gram's already out and about by the way. She said something about running by a friend's to pick up some plant cuttings that Gwen was all excited about planting out back. She took the girls with her."

"I assume Lilith's still sleeping?" So much for her mother's plan to make pancakes. Raine couldn't quite keep the note of censure from her voice.

"We were up late. Besides, you know Lilith and her beauty sleep."

"I know it certainly seems to have worked. Other than her hair, I don't think she looks any different than she did when we were kids."

"She may look the same, but she seemed less flamboyant than usual last night."

Raine sighed and poured some coffee from the carafe into an earthenware mug handpainted with sunflowers. "That's my fault. I got angry after the hearing and accused her of being selfish and irresponsible."

"Of course she is," Savannah said easily. "So, what else is new? Your problem is, Sister dear, that you've always expected her to suddenly turn into Mrs. Cleaver. Which isn't going to happen in this lifetime. . . . You've got your choice between French toast or an omelet."

"An omelet sounds great." Raine couldn't argue with Savannah's perception of their mother. But you don't have to go to the trouble."

"It's no trouble." She took a carton of eggs and a wedge of cheese out of the refrigerator. "Normally, I'd be cooking for a lot larger crowd than just family. Especially on the weekend."

"It's not fair," Raine muttered. She took a sip of coffee and tasted cinnamon. "Having to give up a job you love because your husband was unfaithful."

"I can always get another one." Savannah began breaking eggs into a bright blue bowl.

"But you shouldn't have to. You lost more than your marriage, Savannah. You lost your livelihood, a generous benefit plan, profit sharing. Not to mention that without you in the kitchen, the resort undoubtedly wouldn't have earned nearly the profits, which makes you a valuable corporate asset. You know, you could always sue to keep your job. Since the company would undoubtedly settle just to avoid the negative publicity, the case wouldn't even come to court."

Savannah laughed at that. "Spoken like a born lawyer. I'm not going to fight Kevin to stay at a place where I'd have to work with him everyday."

"I imagine that would be hard." Since her sister didn't seem eager to pursue legal measures, Raine didn't mention that they could undoubtedly force the company to transfer the cheating rat to another resort. Preferably somewhere far away, like Timbuktu. Or Mars. When she found herself comparing her sister's rat of a husband with Jack, Raine decided there was no comparison.

"It would certainly be difficult to resist throwing all my pots and pans at his head." Savannah whisked the eggs with a bit more force than necessary.

"How are you doing? Really?" Raine asked carefully, remembering last night's weeping.

"As well as can be expected. Actually, my pride is a lot more wounded than my heart. I mean, it's not as if his sleeping around came as any great surprise." She sighed as she sprinkled crushed dill into the eggs. "Our marriage has been rocky for a long time. I think the only thing keeping us together, other than my determination not to repeat our mother's mistakes, was inertia."

She began grating the cheese into the egg-and-dill mixture. "I knew if I left him that it'd cost me my job at Las Casitas. But since I haven't exactly been happy there, either—"

"You haven't?" This was one more surprise in a week of surprises. "I thought you loved your work."

"I love cooking for people." Savannah smiled back over her shoulder. "But the resort was so large and impersonal that it wasn't what I'd imagined back when I went off to Paris for cooking school." She opened a cupboard and found a shiny, copper-bottomed omelet pan that looked as if it had never been used. Given Ida's lack of domestic skills, Raine suspected it hadn't. "I've always had a fantasy of something more intimate."

"Like our teas."

Savannah flashed another of those smiles that was a twin of their glamorous mother's. "Exactly." Butter sizzled fragrantly in the pan, making Raine's mouth water. "The past year I've been thinking of leaving the resort and opening up a small inn. Perhaps a bed-and-breakfast. I even looked for a building, but of course the real estate prices in Los Angeles were beyond my budget."

She tilted the eggs from the bowl into the pan with a twist of the wrist. "So, on the drive home, it occurred to me that I should just look around here."

"In Coldwater Cove?"

"Sure. The last couple times I've been back, I've been amazed at the amount of tourist business the town's been getting during the summer, now that the Pacific Northwest's become such a popular vacation spot. I was looking at the real estate ads in the paper before you came down and did some quick number crunching and I think, once Kevin and I divide up our assets, I should be able to swing buying a fixer-upper."

Life was getting stranger and stranger. Raine was becoming more and more convinced that she'd tumbled down a rabbit hole and instead of landing in Coldwater Cove, had ended up in Wonderland.

"Do you even know *how* to renovate a house?"

"No. But I figure I can learn. The same way I learned to cook. The same way you learned to be a lawyer."

"Your point," Raine allowed, watching with admiration as her sister deftly flipped the omelet onto a plate. "I'd just never pictured you living in Coldwater Cove."

"We're not all cut out for big-city life." Savannah cut the omelet, slid the halves onto two pottery plates, placed the plates on the table and refilled both their coffee cups. "I'm almost afraid to mention it, but if those dark circles under your eyes are any indication, it doesn't look as if you are, either."

"It's been a rough few months," Raine hedged. Not eager to have to defend herself yet again, she took a bite of omelet and nearly wept. "This is delicious." It was also so light and fluffy it could have floated off the plate.

Savannah shrugged. "An omelet's easy."

"For you, maybe. Newsflash, baby sister, more Americans eat a Pop Tart or Egg McMuffin for breakfast than dill-and-cheese omelets."

"All the more reason they'll want to stay at my inn," Savannah pointed out. "As flattered as I admittedly am by your appreciation of my culinary skills, I believe we were discussing your life?"

"There's nothing to discuss. At least it doesn't make me cry at night." Not yet, anyway.

"You heard." Savannah didn't look all that surprised.

"I heard." Raine put down her fork with a sigh

that was directed inward, reached out and linked their fingers together atop the table. "I was a rotten sister not to try to do something about it."

"There's nothing you could have done." Savannah looked down at their joined hands. "I was just so angry. Angry at Kevin. But angrier at myself. For avoiding the truth all these years." Her smile was less brilliant and more than a little chagrined. "But I suppose I shouldn't be surprised. Since you and I are both queens of denial."

Raine's first thought was that perhaps that description fit Savannah, who tended to look at life through rose-colored lenses, but she'd always been unflinchingly honest with herself. When that idea caused a little twinge somewhere deep in the far recesses of her mind, Raine's second thought was that she didn't want to think about this.

"This conversation is getting depressing," she said. "Why don't you tell me what kind of house you have in mind?"

Savannah did not need a second invitation. As she shared her rosy, if a bit overly optimistic, plans for her future, her face lit up with enthusiasm. Raine felt a quick, unexpected stab of envy.

Which was, of course, ridiculous. In spite of the good face her sister was trying to put on it, Savannah's life had just crumbled down around her. While Raine's own, on the other hand, was right on course. After all the years of personal sacrifice, of long hours, take-out meals eaten at her desk, and restless nights anticipating or rerunning trials in her dreams, partnership was finally in sight.

When she finally achieved that long-sought-after objective, she could afford to kick back and relax a little. She could begin eating more healthily and return to the running that had burned off the excess tension during her law school days. Perhaps she'd even take up meditation. Heaven knows, Brian swore by the practice, claiming it soothed both his mind and body.

Of course she currently didn't have the twenty minutes to spare each morning and evening Brian spent chanting his mantra or whatever one did while meditating. But she would soon. Once she made partner.

"Enough about me," Savannah said, drawing Raine's attention back to their conversation. "Gram's told me you're about to make partner. Which didn't surprise me, since when he was reporting your oil story, Peter Jennings actually referred to you as the up-and-coming attorney of choice for the high-powered corporate world. I think it's wonderful and I couldn't be more proud of you. But what I really want to know about is your personal life."

"What personal life?" Raine's laugh lacked humor.

"Well, to cut it down to one word—men. Since my love life's turned to mud, why don't you cheer me up by telling me that you're having a mad, passionate affair with some eccentric, bearded SoHo-artist type who adorns your hot naked flesh with edible body paint, then spends all night licking it off."

This time Raine's laugh was genuine. "A bearded artist type?"

"It's always an artist in the movies."

"That proves it. You've definitely been living in LaLa Land too long."

"Well, you may be right about that," Savannah allowed with a little laugh of her own. "But you're dodging the question."

"I don't have time to think about men. At least not in that way."

Raine didn't dare admit that since arriving back home, she'd been thinking about one man *that way*. Too much for comfort.

15

Now that her sister had arrived, Raine could return to New York. After helping Savannah with the breakfast dishes, then spending an hour on the phone with Brian and another two hours catching up on e-mail and some brief-writing that needed to be done, she went upstairs to begin packing.

As she went to open the drawer, her attention was drawn to a photograph atop the bureau. She remembered the day as if it were yesterday. It had been the summer of her eleventh year and she and her mother and sister had spent a rare, carefree day at the beach. She held the photo up to her face, pulled her hair back, tried to see any part of her mother in the reflection looking back at her from the mirror, and with the exception of a possible faint resemblance around the eyes couldn't see anything that declared her to be Lilith's daughter.

Driven by feelings that had been simmering on the surface since she'd first arrived home, Raine put the photo back, then went into the closet beneath the eaves and took down the box she'd hidden beneath another box of blankets. She placed the box on the bed, opened the lid, and pulled out a scrapbook. The yellowed newspaper clippings were as crisp as dried autumn leaves. As she ran her fingertips over one, the edges that had come loose from the Scotch tape crumbled beneath her touch.

Sighing, she returned to the mirror and held the book up, this time comparing her reflection with a photo of her father that she'd cut out of *Newsweek* so many years ago. Again, nothing. She could have been a changeling.

Which was just fine with her, since she preferred to think of herself as her own woman. A self-made woman who was intelligent and self-confident. A woman capable of fighting her own battles. A woman who didn't need anyone.

Liar.

Raine thought back on those hurtful words Lilith had thrown at her the other night, the accusation that her entire life had been nothing but an attempt to gain her famous father's attention. That wasn't true. Oh, perhaps it had been in the beginning, but most of the time Raine was resigned to the idea that she and Owen Cantrell would never have any sort of father-daughter relationship.

She stared into the mirror, looking hard and deep, now searching for Xena. But the Warrior Princess appeared to have abandoned her.

"Just like Lilith," she murmured, beginning to understand that her personal armor had first been donned to protect a child against feelings of anger, confusion, and fear. And it had done its job well, for so many years. But now it was beginning to unravel and Raine realized that if she wanted to finally heal her relationship with her mother, she was going to have to discard it entirely.

That idea was more terrifying than any court case she'd ever presented. Even more frightening than facing that mob on the federal courthouse steps last week. Feeling as if she were suffocating, Raine practically ran down the stairs, fleeing old ghosts and ancient hurts.

She didn't know how long she sat on the porch swing, vaguely aware, on some level, of the distant buzz of a lawnmower. As she breathed in the scent of newly mown grass, Raine reminded herself that in contrast to her flighty mother, she preferred an orderly life. Since she didn't like leaving things undone, it was time to try to resolve her rocky relationship with her mother.

Knowing that this could take time, Raine decided that if Stephen Wells wouldn't allow her to continue to work away from the office, at least until after Gwen's baby was born, she'd just take advantage of the firm's generous family leave policy.

Not that she knew anyone who actually ever had taken precious work time off for family. But there had to be a first time, Raine thought. Why not her?

Jack's mind kept wandering on the morning of the planting party, making it difficult to keep his mind on his daughter's conversation.

"Gramma made cakes for the party," she revealed as they cleared the table. "One's devil's food." She was carrying the plates over to the counter. When the stack tilted precariously, Jack managed to refrain from reaching out to take it away from her. "The other's carrot cake. With her special frosting."

"Your favorite."

"Even better than strawberry shortcake with whipped cream," Her youthful brow furrowed. "Do you think Raine will like it?"

"I can't imagine anyone not liking your grandmother's carrot cake."

"Yeah. It's really good. That's why she always wins the blue ribbon at the fair. Grandpa always said that Gramma is the best baker in the county."

"Your grandfather knew what he was talking about. Since he had the biggest sweet tooth in the county."

"I know. He always carried those M&Ms around in his pocket and let me have the red ones . . . . I wonder if Raine can make cakes."

"She's Ms. Cantrell to you, Pumpkin," Jack corrected, "I have no idea if she can bake or not." However, if he were to hazard a guess, he'd say no.

"I know you said I should always call adults by their last name, but when we were in the Dancing Deer, she told me I could call her Raine," Amy reminded him as they stacked the plates in the dishwasher. "Maybe you could ask her today."

Jack dragged himself back from a fantasy of licking fluffy clouds of whipped cream off Raine Cantrell's slender, but eminently appealing body. "Ask her what?"

"About if she knows how to bake."

"Maybe we should just mind our own business," he suggested on a mild tone that invited no further discussion. "How about bringing me your milk glass?"

"I don't see what the big deal is. It's just a question." Amy's frustrated sigh ruffled her pale gold bangs as she returned to the table. "Don't you always tell me that if I want to know something, I should just ask?"

Jack was extremely grateful that the citizens of Coldwater Cove were more inclined than his daughter to view him as a symbol of authority.

"Whether or not *Ms. Cantrell*"—he stressed again—"bakes is not only none of our business, it's beside the point. Since she's going back to New York soon."

"Maybe if she has a good enough time at the party, she'll decide to stay here. I'll bet she doesn't ever plant Christmas trees in New York." She put the glass in the top rack and gave him a guileless smile Jack didn't buy for a minute. His daughter was many delightful things. Subtle definitely wasn't one of them.

"They sell Christmas trees in the city."

"I know that. But if she stayed here, she could just cut one of ours. Or you could cut it for her."

"She's not staying in Coldwater Cove." Less than pleased by the memory of allowing himself to think along much the same lines somewhere just before dawn, he poured the detergent in the machine and slammed the door with more force than necessary. "Her job is in New York."

A job he realized was immensely important to her. It had only taken Dan a few calls to learn that Raine Cantrell was definitely on the fast track to partnership in an old, established practice Dan had described as a "white shoe" firm. How many people would be willing to turn their back on that? Especially to come home to Coldwater Cove, where her biggest case could involve a dispute over a parking spot?

How many people would be willing to turn their backs on a career that undoubtedly paid in the mid--six figures, for the type of practice where clients occasionally paid their bills with fresh-caught fish, poultry, or baked goods? Not many he'd guess. And not her.

"*Your* job used to be in Seattle," Amy reminded him. "But now we live here."

"That's us." He smoothed his hand over the top of her head. "It doesn't work that way for everyone, kiddo."

Jack had always vowed to keep his daughter out of his personal life, when and if he ever got around to having one. Unfortunately, it appeared he wasn't doing a very good job where Raine was concerned.

Maybe if we asked her to stay, she would."

"We're not going to ask. Because Ms. Cantrell's life is none of our business," he reminded her yet again.

"It is if you like her." She paused a beat, then looked up at him through a fringe of thick lashes. As impossible as it was, since she was still a child, she almost reminded him of the way Vivien Leigh had looked at Clark Gable when she'd put on drapes and gone to coax Rhett Butler into giving her the money to save Tara. "You do like Raine, don't you, Daddy?"

Wondering where on earth his six-year-old daughter had picked up such a blatantly female seductive look, it took Jack a stunned minute to answer. "Well, yeah. Sure I do, but—"

"I do, too," Amy said quickly, before he could add a qualifier. "I think she'd make a neat Mommy. And besides, you're not getting any younger, Daddy. If you don't stop being so particular, you'll be too old for anyone to marry you."

With that pronouncement hanging in the morning air, she swept out of the kitchen, leaving Jack more than a little bemused and feeling as if he were growing more ancient by the minute.

Although Shawna and Renee had moved to their aunt and uncle's home in Bremerton, there'd been no thought of going to the planting party without them. Raine had picked them up earlier, then taken them back to the house to join the others. She'd been relieved when they'd assured her that they were fitting into their new home just fine.

"Oh, look at that!" Gwen said as they drove past the acres of conical blue-green fir and spruce trees. "They look exactly like Christmas trees."

"Duh," Shawna responded with teenage disdain. "Maybe that's why they call it a Christmas tree farm."

"I knew that," Gwen said with a toss of her Orphan Annie curls. "I just never imagined that they'd look so . . . well, finished."

"They've been shaped," Raine revealed. "Even though the spruce and fir trees are trained to grow in more of a pyramid shape than pine trees, they still need to be trimmed at least once a year to shape them." Gwen was right in a way, though, she thought. The only thing missing were gilt angels smiling benevolently atop the trees and some lights and colored glass balls.

"How in the world do you know that?" Ida, sitting beside Raine in the front seat, shot her a curious

weathered jeans, plaid shirt, and spring-straw Stetson, was enough to make any woman suffer an estrogen meltdown.

With her heart thudding like a foolish schoolgirl's, she somehow managed to park the Jeep between a white Chevy pickup and a forest green Explorer. As the rest of the family clamored out of the Jeep, she stayed where she was, her gaze transfixed on his face. Although the day had dawned a bright one, Raine imagined she heard the rumble of thunder in the distance. And when his mouth curved in a welcoming smile, she felt as if a bolt of lightning had suddenly struck from out of the robin's egg blue sky.

Her own mouth went dry and her suddenly damp hands tightened on the steering wheel as if to tether her to the planet which had begun spinning out of control. She was vastly relieved when, after another suspended second, he merely touched his fingers to the brim of his hat and left the porch, joining the group of friends and family who'd shown up for the planting.

A surprising number of townspeople were present—including, Raine noticed with surprise, Judge Barbara Patterson-Young. She guessed that the slightly pudgy, bespectacled, balding man with the judge was Jimmy Young, whose brief teenage indiscretion so many years ago was still causing problems. The way he was going out of his way to avoid Lilith, who was decked out in teal cowboy boots, a teal-and-purple broomstick-pleated skirt, and a purple western-cut shirt adorned with silver studs, suggested that he'd heard about the confrontation in court. And was desperately trying to prevent Round Two.

The fact that so many people turned out gave testimony to the fact that Jack was as well-liked in Coldwater Cove as he'd been when he'd been a high school star jock.

He was also, Raine noted, obviously respected. Which didn't come as the surprise it might have her first night home, having already witnessed firsthand how fair-minded he could be. How kind. Watching him organize the work teams, she also couldn't help contrasting him with the men she was used to— brash, arrogant, domineering, win-at-any-cost males who brandished their control like Barbary Coast pirates brandishing cutlasses.

The sheriff was neither brash nor domineering. But without raising his voice, he had everyone doing exactly what he wanted them to. Willingly, even eagerly. For the first time she understood why he'd always been voted football team captain. Jack O'Halloran may have raised hell in his younger days, but he was a born leader. The type of male who could lead men on the gridiron, into battle, or even into fields of freshly tilled earth.

She was relieved when the information she'd gleaned about tree farms from her lengthy Internet search proved to be accurate. The work itself turned out to be relatively simple. Planting strings, with knots tied at five-foot intervals, marked off the fields.

"When the first tree in each row is planted straight," Jack explained to the first-timers, "subsequent trees will all be in straight rows, up and down, back and forth, and diagonally. It makes it a lot easier to mow between the rows." Then he'd grinned and seemed to be looking straight at her. "It also just looks prettier."

Raine smiled back and decided that while the detail-oriented part of her appreciated the exacting layout, another, more instinctive part of her agreed that the seemingly endless rows of deep green trees were indeed lovely.

They were divided into groups, Raine assigned to work with Lilith and Shawna, while Ida, Savannah, and Renee made up another team. The work went quickly as Raine used a short-handled spade to dig slits in the fragrant freshly turned soil, Lilith plunked in the transplanted seedlings which had spent their first two years in a greenhouse on the property, and Shawna tamped the soil down around it. It took Raine a few times to get a hole straight rather than digging at a slant, which would, Jack had warned, leave the tree roots too near the surface, allowing the roots to dry out too quickly and weaken the tree. But they soon developed a rhythm and were planting nearly as fast as they could walk.

From time to time, whenever they'd take a break while Renee ran back to get more transplants, Raine would glance around, watch the others working in the dark brown fields, and be reminded of the reproduction of *The Gleaners* she'd bought for her office wall. There was something about the painting that had both emotionally moved and relaxed her when she'd spotted it on the wall at the SoHo gallery. She was enjoying those same feelings now as she worked beneath the cloud-scudded sky, breathed in the pungent scent of fir and earth and the faint tinge of salt riding on the air.

Since so many people had turned out, it didn't take long to complete the planting. Which signaled the beginning of the party phase of the day. The mood was unabashedly festive. Meat, salmon, and oysters sizzled on barbecue grills, tables covered in red-and-white-checked paper cloths were groaning beneath bowls of colorful salads, casseroles, pots of vegetables, and myriad desserts. Fortunately, Savannah had provided the contribution for their family— a Tex-Mex shrimp salad with flavor that burst on the tongue, a chickpea burger topped with fennel-olive relish for Renee, and a plate of rich fudge brownies that disappeared almost as soon as the plate had been placed on the table.

Ida had brought along her infamous meatloaf in a casserole dish decorated with perky daisies. And while more than a few people, Jack included, put it on their paper plates, Raine noticed that no one was actually eating it. Not that she blamed them. But it did say something about the close-knit community that so many people went out of their way to avoid hurting an elderly lady's feelings.

"Are you going to keep your baby?" Amy, who was sitting across the table from Raine, asked Gwen.

"Amy, darling," Eleanor O'Halloran chided, "that's a very personal question. And none of your business."

When she'd first been introduced to Jack's mother shortly after arriving, Raine had found her to be a gracious, pleasant woman. Her smooth complexion, short blond hair and still-lithe figure that looked terrific in a pair of faded Wranglers suggested she must have been stunning in her youth. She was, in a less flamboyant way, Raine decided, every bit as

beautiful as Lilith. Having shared a casual conversation with her over grilled salmon and Savannah's
salad, she'd also proven to be intelligent, with a
lively wit.

"That's okay," Gwen answered with a shrug. "It's
not as if my being pregnant is a secret, or anything."
She glanced down at her bulging belly, which Raine
could have sworn had grown even larger in the past
days. "And I haven't decided yet." She sighed.
"Sometimes I really want to keep her, because it's
so hard to imagine giving her away to strangers after
having her inside me for so long.

"But other times I think I should give her up for
adoption, so she'll have a Mom and Dad who'll take
care of her better than I can."

She sighed again and looked out over the freshly
planted fields. But Raine suspected it was not the
bright green seedlings she was seeing, but some idyllic *Father Knows Best* family that only existed in
fiction.

"I went to some adoption agencies last month
with Lilith, and—"

"With Lilith?" Raine interrupted, exchanging a
glance with Savannah, who was sitting beside Gwen
and appeared equally surprised. "My mother went
with you to interview prospective adoption agencies?" If Raine had given any thought to the matter,
which she hadn't, she would have guessed that Ida
would have been the logical one to take on that
responsibility.

"Yeah. She's real easy to talk to," Gwen said. "A
lot easier than most adults and she doesn't tell me
what she thinks I should do. Like Mama Ida . . .
Not that I don't really appreciate Mama Ida's ad-

vice," she assured Raine quickly as a hectic blush stained her cheeks.

"Don't worry, Gwen," Savannah said with a reassuring smile. "Raine and I know firsthand how bossy Gram can be."

"Of course, the problem is she's usually right," Raine said.

"True." It was Savannah's turn to sigh. "She certainly never liked Kevin. That should have been my first clue as to what a rat he was." Her emerald eyes sparked with a hint of lingering anger. And determination. "But it's too lovely a day and we're having too good a time to think about him. . . . So, how did the interviews go?" she asked Gwen.

"Okay, I guess." Despite her positive assessment, the teenager's expression was gloomier than Raine had witnessed during her visit. "I was nervous, but Lilith asked some great questions. Ones I never would have thought of. At first I was surprised, but she said that since she'd been such a failure at being a mother, she could spot a bad one a mile away."

That remark brought Raine's mind back to her vow to attempt to bridge the gap between them. Working together today had been a good start, but eventually they were going to have to have a real talk. Soon, Raine vowed.

She glanced over at a neighboring table, where, a few seats down from Ida, who was engaged in a lively conversation with Dottie and Doris Anderson, her mother was sitting with Cooper Ryan. Not only were they not arguing, they seemed to be miles away in their own private world. The chemistry was more than obvious, even from this distance. But there was something else there, too, Raine considered. Something that appeared to be affection.

"It sounds as if they left you depressed," she suggested carefully, returning her mind to the conversation.

"Yeah. I guess they kind of did. Though most of the people were nice and the offices were real fancy with Oriental rugs and paintings and stuff. But that was part of the problem."

"The paintings?" Eleanor O'Halloran asked gently.

"No. I just kept feeling like they were places just for rich people, and I didn't really belong there. I'll bet if I wasn't having this baby they all want so bad, they wouldn't have even let me in the door in the first place."

"Oh, I'm sure that's not the case," Raine assured her.

"You didn't see them," Gwen argued. "Besides, you're probably used to all that fancy stuff, having an office in New York City and all, but it made me real uncomfortable. Like, though everyone was smiling, they were secretly afraid I was going to knock over a lamp or something. I kept thinking about my baby in a place like that, never being allowed to touch anything, always having to worry about being on her best behavior, and, though it's kinda hard to explain, it made me feel real bad."

Lilith paused as she passed the table. Raine was surprised to see her holding two glasses of lemonade. Her mother's usual role at functions like this was that of Scarlett O'Hara being waited on by the Tarleton twins.

"Gwen felt as if the agencies, and, by extension, their clients, were more concerned with buying a child to complete their perfect lives than the baby's happiness," she explained. "Isn't that right, dear?" Both her tone and her gaze were solicitous.

Gwen nodded. "Yeah. It felt as if I was selling my baby."

"I was adopted," Amy volunteered. "Wasn't I, Gramma?"

"You certainly were," Eleanor agreed with a warm smile. She gave the little girl a brief hug. "And there's not a day that goes by I'm not grateful for that."

"Me, too," Amy agreed, returning the hug. Then she turned back to Gwen. "Mommy and Daddy weren't poor. Not like those homeless kids Daddy took me to buy Christmas presents for last winter. But we weren't rich, either. Not even when Mommy was working. Before she got sick.

"Daddy says it's just the same as if I was their born child." Six-year-old eyes widened earnestly. "Even better. Because out of all the babies in the world, they chose me."

"That's very special," Savannah agreed quietly.

Remembering her sister's miscarriage last year, Raine understood the undertone of sadness she heard in Savannah's voice.

"Oh! I have the most wonderful, scintillating idea," Amy said suddenly. She leaped up from the table and went running back toward the house.

"You raised a wonderful son," Lilith said to Eleanor. "It's such a shame his daughter has to grow up without a mother's guiding hand."

"Isn't it?" Eleanor agreed.

Everyone was suddenly looking at Raine, who was madly trying to think of something, anything to say to deflect attention from herself, when she was saved by Amy's return.

"Here." She held up an orange egg, shaped like the green nano Kitty that had been driving Jack to such distraction. "It's a Nano Baby. Daddy just bought it for me yesterday, because I've been wanting one more than anything. But you can borrow it," she said to Gwen.

"I think it's more for little kids," Gwen demurred.

"But it'll be perfect," Amy insisted. "Because there are all sorts of things you have to do. Like, see that," she said, pointing out the digital droppings that suddenly appeared on the screen. "When you see those, or tiny little footprints, you have to clean the baby up."

She pressed a button, selected a cleaning icon, and wiped away the mess. "You also have to play with her. The game where you help her crawl is my favorite, and she has to get plenty of sleep, so when you hear her snoring, you have to turn out the lights. But you have to remember to turn them on again when the baby wakes up and then you have to feed her."

A serious frown furrowed the childish brow. "But not too many snacks, or she'll get sick and then you have to give her medicine. You also have to teach her to behave, but Daddy says that's not really important because newborn babies don't know about being good or bad.

"It's a lot like a real baby, but if you forget to take care of it, all that happens is that the game ends. Then you can start a new Nano Baby. Daddy says that's a lot easier than in real life, but this way you'll be able to practice. Maybe it'll help you decide if you can take care of a real baby by yourself."

"From the mouths of babes," Lilith murmured as Gwen, seeming intrigued, accepted the gift.

Raine didn't say anything. But it didn't escape her notice that for the first time in her life, she and her mother were in perfect agreement.

❧ 16 ❧

The day grew longer. The sun began casting long shadows across the back lawn and the acres of Christmas trees beyond. Gradually, some people wandered away, back to their homes, their lives. But most stayed, laughing and eating and enjoying the company and the evening. The yard was illuminated with glowing Japanese lanterns and warmed by the fragrant applewood fire Jack had started in an outdoor clay fireplace.

Sometime after sunset, to the obvious delight of his guests, he, Dan, and Cooper Ryan pulled out guitars and began playing a medley of country songs. When they segued from a rockabilly tune to a slow, romantic ballad about a lost love reclaimed, Raine watched the way Cooper seemed to be singing directly to Lilith. In turn, Lilith only had eyes for him. They could have been the only two people in Coldwater Cove. The only two in the world.

That idea caused a vision of being alone on a raft, in the middle of a storm-tossed ocean while the sky poured down icy water, to flash through Raine's mind. It faded quickly, leaving behind a profound sense of loneliness.

She belatedly realized someone was talking to her. "I'm sorry, Amy. My mind was drifting. What did you say?"

"I was wondering if you'd like to see my room," Amy, who was standing beside the redwood chair, invited. "Maybe you can watch a video with me, too. Daddy and I usually watch one together after supper, but he's out by the pond teaching my cousin John how to cast with his new fishing rod."

She was wearing a pair of red jeans, a T-shirt bearing a drawing of a Disney mermaid, and a pair of sneakers. She had a smudge of dirt on one cheek; a bit of chocolate from the homemade ice cream Eleanor O'Halloran had contributed to the party was smeared at one corner of her mouth. But neither detracted from the fact that she was going to grow up to be a beauty. Her thickly fringed eyes were wide and innocent, her smile, persuasive. Raine wondered how Jack managed to deny this golden child anything.

Raine bent down and tied one of Amy's loose sneaker laces. "I'd love to watch a video."

"Have you ever seen *The Little Mermaid?*"

"No, I missed that one."

"You'll like it a lot. It's the best." With that promise, Amy streaked off toward the house. A little bit in love, Raine followed.

"And Ariel and Prince Eric got married and they lived happily ever after," Amy announced as the tape ended. "That's my favorite story. Even better than

Pocohontas or *Snow White*. But they're good, too. Would you like to watch another tape?"

"If you'd like," Raine said, trying not to reveal she'd been more than a little discomfited by the fact that the television turned out to be in Jack's bedroom.

The first thing she'd noticed when Amy had practically dragged her into the room by the hand was the sterling-silver-framed photograph on the bedside table. Time had tarnished the silver a bit, but the smiles on the faces of the bride and groom hadn't faded in wattage a bit.

"That's Daddy," Amy said when she saw the direction of Raine's gaze. "And Mommy."

"I can see that."

"It was on the day they were married. They hadn't adopted me yet," she said matter-of-factly. "Isn't Daddy handsome?"

"He certainly is." Having grown accustomed to seeing him in jeans, Raine wouldn't have pictured him in a tux. But if she had, even her vivid imagination couldn't have made him look any better. "And your Mommy's pretty, too."

"She was sooo beautiful. Like a princess in a fairy tale." Amy slid off the bed, went over to the dresser, picked up a silver-backed hand mirror and studied her reflection. "Daddy says that even though I'm adopted, I'm going to grow up to look just like her. That I'll be beautiful, too."

"Your daddy's right. You're already a very pretty little girl."

"That's what Daddy says." Again, this was said with a complete lack of guile or pride, suggesting that Jack had done an excellent job building his daughter's ego. "Would you like to see a tape about when I was still a baby?"

"Sure."

"I'll be right back!" The little girl left the room and Raine could hear her flying down the stairs.

Feeling as if she were snooping into personal things that were none of her business, Raine couldn't resist the lure of the wedding photograph. She picked the frame up to study it closer.

Peg O'Halloran looked like a fairy princess, dressed in a froth of white satin and beaded lace that must have weighed almost as much as she did. Her train was beaded as well, her veil, topped by a band of white roses, was fingertip length, drawing a viewer's eye to the gold band she was wearing on her left hand. Her billowy cloud of long blond hair was so pale and so shiny it could only have been natural. She literally glowed with life.

Jack, on the other hand, looked poleaxed. But in an endearing way, Raine decided. The way he was staring down at his bride suggested that he couldn't quite believe his good fortune. It was obvious that they'd been so in love. So optimistic. So unaware of the tragedy that was lurking just around the corner.

"Here it is!" Amy announced, holding up the black videotape case. "It's one of my very favorites. But I don't remember that day because I was just a tiny baby."

She switched tapes, then crawled back up onto the queen-size sleigh bed beside Raine, whose instincts, which had kicked in of late, were already telling her this was a mistake.

That proved to be an understatement. As she sat there, in the bedroom Peg and Jack had shared, on the bed where they'd made love, watching one of the most intimate acts a man and woman can share— bringing their new infant home from the hospital— she felt like the worst kind of voyeur.

"See, that was my old room. Before we moved to this house." Amy's voice managed to penetrate the white noise filling Raine's head. "Mommy hung that wallpaper with the storks on it all by herself. Daddy painted the crib. They got it secondhand from one of Daddy's cousins, but they fixed it up so it was just like new."

Raine suspected Amy was parroting what her parents had told her about that day. That seemingly endless day. The joy was almost painful to watch, especially knowing how short-lived it would be. Amy, on the other hand, didn't seem at all distraught as she kept on a running commentary of every little thing that was happening on screen.

"And that's when Daddy gave me my bath. And splashed Mommy and got her blouse all wet. Then she splashed Daddy back. And we all laughed and laughed," Amy was saying when Raine became aware of a third person standing in the open doorway.

"Amy." Jack's voice was low, but intense. "I thought we had an agreement about you not watching those tapes alone."

"I'm not watching those tapes, Daddy." She turned to Raine. "He's talking about the tapes Mommy made me. So I'd always feel like she was here with me."

A painful lump had risen in her throat. Raine swallowed, then forced her words past it. "That was a very special thing for her to do."

"I know." The lamplight haloed Amy's blond hair as she nodded. "It's my legacy."

She looked back up at her father, who was now standing beside the bed, arms folded, the remote in his hand. He'd stopped the tape, Raine noticed when she saw the news footage of tonight's Seattle Mariners baseball game appear on the television screen in place of the seemingly perfect, picture-book family.

"Raine said I was pretty. Like Mommy. Then she said she wanted to see the tape of when I was a baby."

"After you asked her first, I'll bet."

"It wasn't one of Mommy's tapes," she stressed again, sounding perilously close to tears. "Besides, Raine liked it, didn't you?"

The distressed face looking up at her tugged at Raine's heartstrings. She gathered Jack's daughter to her and began rocking in an instinctive motion she hadn't even realized she knew how to do. "I thought it was a wonderful video. And I'm glad you shared it with me."

"Daddy and Gramma say I'm supposed to share." Her voice was muffled against Raine's sweater. Feeling somehow to blame, and more than a little helpless, Raine stroked her hair and looked up to Jack for guidance.

"Gwen's looking for you, Amy," he said gently. "She needs some help with the Nano Baby you gave her."

"Okay." Proving that recovery came fast for the young, she wiggled out of Raine's embrace, slid off the bed, gave her father's legs a quick hug, and took off down the hall. Moments later they could hear her footfalls on the stairs.

The mattress gave as Jack slumped down beside her. "I'm sorry." He put his arm around her in that way she was beginning to enjoy far too much.

"It's all right. She's right. She was a beautiful baby. She's a beautiful little girl, too."

"Modest, too," he said dryly.

"A strong ego is a good thing. I think you have a lot to do with that."

"Don't make me out to be something I'm not, Raine." His voice was tight, offering her as much of a warning as the foghorn tolling somewhere in the bay. "I'm just a regular guy. An ordinary guy who went through some tough times. There are people handling worse every day."

"You can protest all you want, Jack," Raine said. Slipping free of his light embrace, she stood up. "But I've gone through enough jury selections to know that the trick is to ignore what people say, and concentrate on what they do. And what you've done with your daughter is far from ordinary."

Because she found being alone with him in his bedroom too tempting for comfort, Raine brushed her lips against his, then left to rejoin the party.

Because he wanted more than that light, sweet kiss, Jack followed Raine, intending to steal more. Unfortunately, he was sidetracked by an aunt, who professed that she had met the nicest young woman at her widows survival group at church and since the lady in question and Jack had so much in common, she was certain they'd be perfect for one another.

Deciding that it would do no good to explain that

compatibility required more than the loss of a spouse, he dodged the matchmaking with the excuse that right now his work was keeping him too busy to enter into a relationship. Although it was obviously not the response she'd been seeking, he managed to get away before she could press her case.

It took a few minutes, but he found Raine in the driveway, leaning against Ida's Jeep, gazing up at the sky.

"I've forgotten how many stars there are," she murmured, seeming not all that surprised by his appearance. "You never see stars like this in the city."

"True. But we don't have the bright lights."

"No." She turned her gaze from the sky toward him. "I was listening to you play the guitar with Dan and Cooper after dinner. You're very good."

"I made a few bucks playing at some country bars while I was in college."

"So, is it true what they say about musicians and women?"

"I don't know. What do they say?"

"You know." She shrugged. "That you all have harems of groupies."

"I don't know about other guys. But I didn't." He half smiled at the bittersweet memory of Peg sitting at a front table, drinking cherry cokes while he did his best to entertain a bunch of hard-drinking cowboys who hadn't come there to listen to the music. "I've always been pretty much a one-woman-at-a-time kind of guy."

"That's nice. And unusual."

"Monogamy's not all that unusual," he said mildly. "Perhaps you've just run into some bad apples."

"Perhaps." Her tone sounded unconvinced.

"Which brings up something I've been meaning to ask you."

"What's that?"

"Is there a man in your life, Harvard? Some guy in a fifteen-hundred-dollar pinstriped suit and gold cufflinks waiting for you back in New York?"

"Would it matter if there was?"

"Would you like me to say it would?" he asked, moving still closer, encouraged when she didn't back away. "Do you want me to say that I'd back off and leave you alone if you belonged to some other man?"

"I'll never *belong* to any man."

"Objection sustained." He was close enough to touch. Nearly close enough to taste. "Let's not waste time on semantics, Counselor." When he reached up to touch her cheek, she stepped back. "I told you I wasn't into playing games, so I'm going to say this straight out."

Knowing he was pressing his advantage, but not feeling a bit guilty, since she'd already caused him more sleepless nights than any woman he'd ever encountered, Jack took another step, trapping her between Ida's Jeep and him.

"You've riled me up from the beginning. At first I figured that it was just sex. That'd I'd been too long without a woman and you came along and stirred up my juices."

"Charmingly put. Once again you flatter me, Sheriff."

"The flattery part comes later," he promised. "After I get this out of the way. Now, like I said, at first I thought it was only a case of runaway hormones. Which a woman like you could give any man, even one who hadn't been celibate for the past three years."

"Three?" She seemed surprised by that.

"I told you, I'm a one-woman man. There was no way I was going to fool around on my wife. Then she got sick. And I haven't wanted any other woman since she died. Until now."

He skimmed his fingers up her cheek into her hair. "Until you. I'm not going to apologize for wanting you, Raine. Especially since, unless every instinct I have has gone on the blink, I think you want me, too."

When she didn't argue, he bent his head and brushed his lips against her temple. "But the thing is, since I keep getting the feeling there's something else going on here. I figure we'd be cheating ourselves not to test it out."

A ghost of a smile hovered at the corners of her lips. "That's some seduction line."

"Is it working?"

"I don't know." She closed her eyes and took a deep breath that did intriguing things to her breasts beneath her T-shirt.

"How long has it been since you've been on a picnic?"

Her eyes flew open. "A picnic?"

"Yeah. A picnic. You know, where you go out into the woods, spread a tablecloth on the ground, sit on a blanket, and fight off ants while you share a loaf of bread and a jug of wine. The forecast calls for blue skies tomorrow. Come play with me."

"Surely you need to work."

"Since I'm sheriff, that makes me the boss. So I'll give myself the day off."

"How convenient."

"Isn't it?" He watched her sliding into her lawyer skin and found himself enjoying the anticipation of stripping it back off again with her clothes.

"If you're taking me out into the woods to have sex with me, you should know that it's not going to happen."

"Actually, I believe I mentioned taking you out into the wilderness to feed you," he said mildly. "Having sex would, admittedly be icing on the cake, speaking metaphorically." He wondered if she'd run away if he told her that he was beginning to think that when it did happen, they'd be making love rather than having sex. "But I'm willing to settle for a few hot kisses and some groping that's bound to leave us both hot and frustrated. If that's what you really want."

"A picnic sounds lovely." Her tone was cool, designed to deter a less-determined man. Jack had never backed down from a challenge and he wasn't about to start with her. "But without the groping," she insisted unsteadily as he rubbed his cheek against the silk of her hair.

"Fine. We'll settle for the kissing."

"That sounds an awful lot like just sex."

"Hey." He curled his fingers around the nape of her neck. "Sex isn't such a bad start. Besides, you can't deny that all this chemistry has been a distraction. For both of us." He nibbled on her lower lip, satisfied when he drew a soft, ragged moan from her throat. "Once we get the sex part out of the way, we can see if there's anything more going on here."

"What if there is?" She was tempted. Jack could taste it on her lips. See it in her soft-focused eyes as she tilted her head back to look up at him. "Something more than sex?"

Although he suspected that she'd throw herself off Mount Olympus before admitting it, she was afraid, Jack realized. He knew the feeling all too well.

"Then we'll jump off that bridge—together—when we get to it."

"You have to understand . . ." Her planned protest faded away as he began nuzzling at her fragrant neck. "I've never . . ." When he caught her earlobe in his teeth and tugged, she expelled a long, shuddering breath. "Oh, God." She put both hands against his chest and pushed. Not hard, but enough to put a little distance between them. "What I'm trying to say is, that I've never taken sex casually."

"Then you don't have to worry. Because believe me, sweetheart, there's nothing casual about the way I feel about you."

"Oh, God," she repeated, lifting her hands from the front of his shirt to drag them through her hair. "I think I've just run out of arguments."

"A lawyer without arguments." He caught her distressed face in his hand. "Now that's gotta be a first."

Deciding that he'd been patient long enough, he lowered his head, watching her lips part in anticipation. A soft, yielding sigh slipped from between her lips to his. The night air had turned cool, but her lips were warm and moist and generous. She welcomed his tongue with a breathless moan that burned through him like wildfire and when his teeth scraped at her bottom lip, she went up onto her toes and twined her arms around his neck and clung.

Her body strained against Jack's. Her hot, avid mouth was as urgent and impatient as his. The way she was moving her body against his was causing all the blood to rush from his head to his groin and with the last vestige of coherent thought he possessed, Jack realized that he'd miscalculated.

He hadn't intended for things to get so hot so quick. Nor had he intended to ache. Not just the physical ache that had him as hard as a damn boulder, but a deep, grinding ache that went all the way to the bone. Some deep primal urge had him wanting to drag her into the backseat of the Jeep, never mind that nearly half the town could stumble across them at any minute. He forced himself to break the exquisite contact.

"Oh, no." She was staring up at him, giving him the impression that she shared the disorientation that had him feeling as if someone had just informed him that the law of physics had been suspended, that down was now up, up down, and gravity no longer existed. "I was afraid of that."

He watched her take a deep, ragged breath and felt a renewed slap of lust. "Of what?"

"Of what just happened." She dragged a trembling hand through her hair. "Of how you'd make me feel."

"I'm admittedly out of practice, but if it was that bad, perhaps I'd better work on polishing my technique."

"No." She wrapped her arms around herself in an unconscious gesture of self-protection that made him want to hold her close, this time to soothe rather than arouse. With effort, Jack stayed where he was. "Your technique was fine." She sighed. "Better than fine," she admitted. "It was terrific. And that's the problem."

"We can try again," he suggested helpfully. "I'll try to do worse, if it'll make you feel any better."

"Dammit, Jack." This time she dragged both hands through her hair. "I'm serious." Even as her eyes brightened with a wet sheen, a reluctant smile tugged at the corners of her mouth. That lush, sweet mouth he could still taste.

"I know." Because he couldn't be this close to her without touching, he caught hold of one of those slender hands and brushed his thumb over her knuckles. "But perhaps you're overanalyzing things again, Raine. Didn't you ever just go with the flow?"

"No."

She looked so miserable, like a little girl who'd just had her dog die on her; Jack's heart went out to her. "It's getting late. Why don't I go get the rest of the family, and—"

"That's not necessary." She was looking past him, over his shoulder. Jack didn't need to turn around to know that they were no longer alone. The sound of female voices drifted on the night-cooled air. "Well," she drew in another breath. "I guess I'll be calling it a night. Thank you for the invitation. I had a lovely time. Please tell Amy I enjoyed watching *The Little Mermaid* with her. And seeing her baby video."

Her tone had turned so impersonal, she could have been asking a judge for a sidebar. Suspecting the ploy was more for the others' sake than his, he didn't call her on it.

"I'll tell her." Still tempted to touch, he stuck his hands deep into his pockets. "I'll see you tomorrow, then. How's ten sound?"

"Oh, do you have plans, darling?" Ida asked, proving that although she may be nearly eighty, her hearing was working just fine.

"We're going on a picnic," Jack said, before Raine could respond.

"Oh, what a wonderful idea," Lilith declared, obviously pleased by this idea. Then again, Jack thought, having watched Cooper and her, he suspected the lady had romance on the mind tonight.

The three girls concurred.

"I'll make a lunch," Savannah said.

"That's not necessary," Raine protested.

"Don't be silly. What's the point of having a Paris trained chef in the family if you don't take advantage of her?" Savannah was obviously as pleased with this development as her mother was. The wattage of her dazzling smile was enough to light up Coldwater Cove for a year.

When she'd shown up at the farm tonight, Jack had taken one look at the lushly built, red-haired goddess and understood all too well how his cousin had been scared spitless of her back in their high school days. The funny thing was, as gorgeous as Savannah Townsend admittedly was, and as genuinely nice as she seemed to be, she still couldn't cause his testosterone to spike the way her sister could.

As if realizing she was outnumbered, Raine surrendered the skirmish. "I have some work to do in the morning," she said to Jack. "Eleven would be better."

"Eleven it is."

That taken care of to everyone's satisfaction, with the possible exception of Raine, whose mind he had every intention of changing, Jack watched the family of females climb into the Jeep.

He stood in the driveway, watching the taillights as they disappeared down the long driveway out to the road, until they'd finally disappeared around a corner. Then whistled as he walked back to the house.

❧ 17 ❧

A silvery pink light was slipping around the edges of the window curtain. In a desperate attempt at control, Raine told herself that the only reason she'd woken up at dawn was that her internal clock had somehow reset itself back to New York time.

Liar. She was, Raine told herself as she tossed back the quilt, pitiful. It was expectation, pure and simple. No, she corrected as she stealthily slipped into her robe, trying not to wake her sleeping sister. Not simple at all.

Although she still had several hours before Jack showed up, Raine wasn't in the mood to start work. Instead, rather than take the time for real coffee, she nuked a mug of instant in the microwave and carried it out onto the front porch. Then stopped in her tracks when she viewed the Greek god leaning against the white porch railing.

"Good morning, Cooper." She wondered idly if he was coming or going then reminded herself that her mother's sex life was none of her business. "Can I get you some coffee? It's instant, but—"

"Thanks anyway. But I've got a thermos in the truck."

"Oh." She glanced past him at the park service pickup. Then up at her mother's bedroom window.

"We're going to drown some worms." His answer to her unasked question only gave birth to more.

"You're drowning worms?"

He grinned. "Fishing, Raine. Lilith and I are going out to see if we can catch some brook trout for Savannah. Seems she has this new recipe she's been wanting to try out."

"My mother's going fishing?" She looked up at the window again and wondered if she was still asleep. Surely this must be a dream. Or yet another hallucination.

He rubbed his chin. His grin widened. "Well, to tell the truth, she's probably going to spend most of the day sitting on a rock prettying up the scenery."

She sat down in the swing. "That's one of her strongest talents."

"Have you ever taken any martial arts?" he asked.

Raine blinked at the seemingly sudden change of subject. "No. I've been thinking about taking up yoga, though."

"Good idea. It's supposed to be great for relaxation." She was grateful when he didn't point out what everyone else had since her arrival home. That she looked as if she needed relaxation. "I've studied aikido since I was a kid."

"Oh. Is that like karate?"

"In a way. It's one of the martial arts that teaches self-defense without weapons. It teaches you to neutralize any attack by learning to blend with the opposing energy. Or redirect it. To put it simply, once you know the right techniques, you can be empowered by staying in your center."

Raine grasped his analogy immediately. "Lilith never attacks." That she would have been able to handle. After all, she was an expert on the battlefield. It was her own feelings that she'd never been able to quite vanquish.

"No, that's never been her style," he agreed mildly. "Another thing aikido teaches is the ability to sense openings in your opponent. When we're working on the mat, we learn to sense our practice partner's strengths and weaknesses and honor and blend with them, to create harmony."

Lilith and harmony were two words Raine never would have used in the same sentence.

When she didn't respond to that, Cooper seemed to sense her vulnerability. He also seemed to possess mind-reading ability. "Your mother didn't try to make your life tougher than perhaps it should have been, Raine," he said gently. "She was only a girl, a decade younger than you are now when she became a mother for the first time with no real support system of her own."

"She could have come home."

"True. But between that glossy exterior and a very warm heart, Lilith definitely possesses her share of the Lindstrom female pride. She hadn't wanted to admit to your grandmother that she'd failed."

"Time and time again."

"True. But she was only human, honey. Playing the cards she'd been dealt as best she knew how. Also, don't forget that she swallowed that pride every single time she brought you and Savannah back to Ida. Because she was trying, in her own, admittedly flawed way, to do right by her daughters."

His take on the situation left her feeling even more guilty than she had the morning after the blowup. Raine bit her bottom lip and looked out over the bay, which was draped in a light layer of white fog, like the angel hair she remembered Savannah draping over the limbs of the Christmas tree one year.

Like Jack, he was a man comfortable with silence. For a long time there was only the morning sound of the birds and the creak of the swing chain.

"Well, you've definitely given me something to think about," she said finally.

"I'm glad. For both your and Lilith's sake. Would you mind one more piece of unsolicited advice?"

"Of course not."

"When I first started my training, I was young and stubborn. My sensei didn't think I'd ever learn how to let go enough to follow the rhythm and the movement, rather than my expectations. It took me a very long time to discover that I got hurt a lot more when I'd think I knew what my practice partner's next move was. Because by planning for it, I allowed myself to become more vulnerable to a different move."

She took a sip of the cooling coffee. "Go with the flow, you mean."

"It's a bit more complicated than that. But yeah, it's the general idea."

She thought some more. About her mother. Herself. And, this man who seemed so comfortable on Ida's porch. Raine suspected he'd spent a great deal of time on this very same swing in the past.

"May I ask you something?"

"Anything," he said promptly.

"Are you going to be my new stepfather?"

"You bet." He smiled at her. With his mouth and his eyes and as she smiled back, Raine wondered if there was something in the air here on the peninsula that made the male population so self-confident.

She smiled back. "I'm glad."

At that moment the screen door opened and Lilith came out, dressed in a designer version of fishing chic. Her blouse was a washable silk the color of mountain streams, her jeans had obviously been custom-tailored to fit her lush curves like a glove, and the sneakers on her feet were snowy white, suggesting they were new. Her gold earrings resembled fishing lures and flowers the same color as her blouse bloomed on the baseball cap atop her head.

"Good morning," she greeted them. "Gracious Raine, darling, I was wondering who Cooper was speaking with. Whatever are you doing up so early?"

"It was a lovely morning. I thought I'd sit out here and enjoy it."

"You couldn't have found a better place. I know I always feel ever so much better whenever I come home." Her smile, as she looked over at Cooper, was overbrimming with private meaning. "Especially this time."

He smiled back and once again the air was so charged, Raine felt as if she couldn't breathe. Deciding that if Savannah was actually counting on these two returning home with any fish, she'd be disappointed, Raine rose from the swing.

"Have a good time, you two." She brushed a kiss against her mother's cheek and felt another little stab of guilt at the surprise and pleasure that sparked in Lilith's eyes. Raine couldn't recall the last time she'd initiated kissing her mother.

A week ago she never would have thought of going up on her toes to kiss Cooper's cheek as well, but as she did so, Raine decided that it felt eminently right. "Good luck," she murmured,

Then, feeling even more heady anticipation than she had when she'd first awakened, she took her cup and went back into the house, counting the hours until eleven o'clock.

The Suburban was not exactly designed for tight cornering, but Raine was not surprised by the way Jack maneuvered around the twisting switchbacks leading deep into the forest. He seemed to do everything well. When that thought caused a little spike in her heartbeat, she turned her attention to the scenery in an attempt to tamp down rampaging hormones.

The sky had turned a tarnished silver hue that hinted at a storm lying somewhere out to sea, while a pale sun latticed the landscape with a tapestry of green. The willows wore their bright spring coats of goldish green leaves, while bolder, red-green maple leaves unfolded from newly burst buds. Scattered amidst blushing meadows dotted with Indian paintbrush, bracken ferns were uncurling new, frothy, delicate pale fronds.

Growing more and more comfortable with each other, despite the sexual tension that still lingered as strong as ever, they allowed the silence to settle. For a long time the only sound was that of falling water, as crystal streams born in melting glaciers fed the roaring rivers that ran into the sea.

"Are you going to tell me where we're going?" Raine asked finally.

"A little place I know out by Lake Crescent."

Set dramatically amidst the majestic Olympic Mountains, the dazzling blue-green lake was considered by many to be the gem of the peninsula.

"Not the lodge?"

"No." He glanced over at her. "I thought we'd go someplace off by ourselves. Unless you'd like to go to the lodge."

Knowing that he had definitely not planned on sharing the stolen day with tourists, Raine appreciated him giving her a choice. "No. I get enough of people in the city. I'm starting to enjoy the peace and quiet."

"Better be careful," he said easily as he turned off onto another even narrower road that twisted like a snarled fishing line unreeling through the mountain passes in a series of sharp zigzags that defied compass reckoning. "This place can get in your blood if you let it. You might have a hard time getting away again."

"I'll admit that I'm seeing the town with new eyes. But I am going back to New York." She wondered which of them she was reminding—him or her.

"All the more reason to make the most of the time you have here."

They passed a waving green sea of meadow on which white Sitka valerium bobbed like whitecaps atop cresting waves. "You must spend a lot of time at this place, wherever it is." She'd been lost for the past half hour. "To be able to find it so easily."

"I haven't been here for years, so I may not. We may end up getting hopelessly lost and forced to live off the land. Which, I suppose, could turn out to be an adventure."

"Obviously we have different definitions of adventure."

"You just need to use your imagination."

"I was. I was imagining icy rain, hurricane gale winds, and mountain lions. Not to mention bears. So, if you don't mind, I think I'll pass on playing Grizzly Adams with you."

"You've got the wrong adventure story." He reached out, caught her hand and linked their fingers together. "It'd be more like Adam and Eve. Just you and I, Harvard, alone in a lush green Garden of Eden."

"I don't like snakes."

"Fine. Since it's our imaginary game, we won't have any."

"What about clothes?"

"Only if you insist."

"I do."

He sighed heavily. "I was afraid you were going to say that. Well, I suppose you can whip something up out of some leaves while I build our log cabin.

"You're going to build a cabin? With what?"

"My bare hands. And, of course, my handy-dandy Swiss Army knife."

"I didn't realize those came with a chain saw feature."

"Never underestimate the Swiss. Then, when I get it all constructed, you can make us a comfy bed out of pine needles."

"Two beds."

He shot her a sideways glance and another of

those boyish grins that Raine kept telling herself shouldn't affect her so strongly, but did. "Spoilsport."

He made a sharp left turn that, even with her seat belt fastened, almost had her sliding into his lap. They passed a herd of deer peacefully grazing in yet another meadow awash in color.

"Lucky for us these woods are filled with game, so we won't have to go hungry," he said.

Raine folded her arms. "I categorically refuse to eat Bambi."

"How about fish?"

She thought about that. "I suppose that would be preferable to starving."

"Absolutely. Then we don't have any problem. I'll catch some tasty salmon with the pointed stick I whittle with my knife then smoke them over a fire, just like I learned when I was a Boy Scout."

"You were a Boy Scout?"

"You don't have to sound all that surprised. As a matter of fact, I earned a merit badge in survivalist skills."

"I knew you were a hell-raiser. But I had no idea you were also training to be one of those antigovernment militia types." Her faint smile took the accusation from her tone.

"That was before those nutty guys who like to blow things up gave the term a bad name," he said mildly. "We learned all sorts of handy stuff. I'd almost made Eagle Scout when I got kicked out."

"Now that I believe. What did you do? Row across the lake in the middle of the night and lead a panty raid on the Girl Scout camp?"

"You can be a sharp-tongued woman, Harvard.

Fortunately for you, I like a woman with spunk.
And, as a matter of fact, I put a skunk in the counselor's tent."

"Once again I'm not surprised. What does strain
credulity is the idea of you actually growing up to
serve as the symbol of law and order in Olympic
County."

"Hey, the guy deserved it. There was this kid,
Kenny Woods, who was packing a few too many
pounds. The damn jock counselor wouldn't let up
on him. Not even after Kenny almost passed out
from heat exhaustion on a five-mile hike. Someone
had to do something."

"And that someone was you?"

"I was the one who was there at the time."

"What about other counselors? Parents? Camp
authorities?"

He laughed at that. "I would have thought all
those years in the city would have made you a real-
ist. In the undemocratic world of kids and counselors, the counselors reign supreme. Which means the
kid was on his own."

"So you took the law into your own hands."

"Yeah. And before you tell me that you can't con-
done that, as sheriff, I'll admit I don't recommend
the policy as a habit. But I'd do it again. In a New
York minute."

Raine thought about that. "I have to admire you
for sticking up for that boy. Even if I don't approve
of your solution."

"Hey, it worked. The guy was a pariah for days.
You can't imagine the cans of tomato juice he went
through trying to bathe out the eau de skunk.

"And getting back to our little survivalist game,

while I'm impressing you with my manly food-acquiring skills, you can play domestic by gathering up wild berries for our dessert."

"In the little basket I've woven from reeds while you've been spearing poor unsuspecting fish," she guessed.

"Nah. I figure you can gather them up in that skirt you insisted on sewing out of leaves."

"Giving you a look at my legs."

He let go of her hand and ruffled her hair. "I knew you were a perceptive woman."

Moments later, he pulled off into a secluded glen that could have served as a model for paradise. A crystal waterfall tumbled over moss-covered rocks into a sapphire blue pool at one end of the lush green chamber; in the far distance, the sun glinted off the waters of Lake Crescent.

"Oh!" Raine drew in a breath as she climbed out of the truck and surveyed the pristine scene. "It's lovely. Like a secret garden."

"Dan and I used to come here when we were kids to play Tarzan." He touched his canted nose. "I broke this when he dared me to ride the waterfall face first while we were searching for the jewels of Opar."

"You could have died. That was foolishly reckless." A wayward breeze fluttered her hair across her eyes. She brushed it away.

"Yeah." Another whispery gust blew the hair back; this time Jack pushed it away. His hand stayed on her cheek. "But I've always had a tendency for recklessness."

They both knew that he was no longer talking about some childhood accident. Electricity sparked

in the air like heat lightning and Raine found herself
holding her breath, waiting for the kiss she kept insisting she didn't want.

"I promised you lunch."

"Yes." If she were to make a list of needs and desires
right now, food wouldn't even make the top ten.

He gave her another of those long enigmatic looks
that gave Raine the uncomfortable feeling that he
could see inside her heart. Then he dropped his
hand and backed away. "I'd better get the basket out
of the truck."

Unable to respond, with her words clogged in her
throat, Raine merely nodded.

Savannah had outdone herself, preparing crudités
shaped like flowers, a grilled-chicken salad with goat
cheese and fresh raspberries, a loaf of crunchy,
homemade sourdough bread, a key lime cheesecake
so light it seemed to melt in Raine's mouth, and iced
tea sprigged with mint.

The conversation stayed light during lunch. As if
by mutual agreement, they stuck to family anecdotes
and career stories before somehow moving on to all
the places around the world they'd visited, or
wanted to.

"I've been planning to go to the islands," Raine
admitted.

"Which ones?"

She shrugged. "It doesn't really matter. Any one
with tropical breezes, lagoons as clear as aquama-
rines, and white sugar beaches. Oh, and a steel band
and mai tais would be nice, too."

"Maybe we should take a trip to one for our second date."

Even knowing he was kidding, Raine felt her

nerves tangle at his casual mention of a future when she hadn't allowed herself to think beyond today. Which, given her penchant for planning every last detail of her life just went to show how crazy the man made her.

"This isn't a date. Not really."

"Okay." He leaned back on his elbows and crossed his long legs at the ankles. "What would you call it, then?"

Good point. "I suppose"—she shrugged, trying to appear nonchalant—"two friends having lunch."

His smile was slow, seductive, and openly skeptical. Raine wasn't surprised he didn't believe her. She didn't believe her flimsy definition either. He looked at her again, hard and deep, then, apparently deciding not to push, reached out and snagged another piece of cheesecake. "Your sister's a dynamite cook."

"She's always had a magic touch in the kitchen." Raine couldn't decide whether or not to be relieved that he was backing away yet again, allowing—no, forcing—her to be the one to make the decision how serious this would get. "She's also the only woman in our family who can do more than boil water or nuke a frozen dinner in the microwave."

"There's always Ida's meatloaf."

They shared a laugh over that. Then sat in comfortable silence for a time. Clouds continued to gather over the mountaintops and the air was growing cooler, but Raine was in no hurry to leave. A bright blue jay fluttered down from an overhead branch, stole a bit of crumb crust that had dropped onto the blanket, and disappeared back into the trees again.

Raine realized, with some surprise, that she was

beginning to get used to the quiet. That first morning, alone in the kitchen, the lack of noise had made her edgy. Now, as she drank in a landscape created to soothe the soul, she reveled in the exquisite serenity. She also realized that it had been nearly a day since she'd worried about what was happening at work. Which had to be a record.

"Your mother looks as if she'd be a good cook," she said.

"Mom's real good, but she doesn't fix fancy stuff like Savannah. Dad was more of a meat-and-potatoes kind of guy."

There was no mistaking the warmth in his voice at the mention of his father. "You must miss him."

"A bunch. It's been six months and there are times when I walk into the office and am surprised not to see him sitting behind the desk. He always seemed larger than life to me, not just when I was a kid, but even after I'd grown up. It wasn't just because he was a big man, but because he was strong in a way that made people trust him."

"I'd imagine that would be important in his line of work, especially since it's an elected position."

"He won eight straight elections," Jack divulged. "The last two no one even bothered to run against him. I always figured that wasn't so much that a would-be opponent was afraid of losing, as much as the fact that no one in the county could think of a better man for the job."

"That's quite a legacy."

"You can say that again. And one that's not always easy to live up to."

"Actually, I think you're doing a very good job. If it hadn't been for you, I'm afraid to think what could have happened the night the girls locked themselves in the house."

His lips curved a bit. "Is that a compliment I hear coming from those delectable lips, Harvard?"

Delectable. Even as her nerves skittered at him bringing an intimacy back into the conversation, a lovely warmth flowed through Raine. She couldn't remember the last time a man had described her lips as delectable. Probably because none ever had.

She moved her shoulders, pretended vast interest in a chipmunk gathering berries at the edge of the blue pool, and avoided what she knew would be a teasing look. "I've always believed in giving credit where credit is due."

"Me too." He skimmed a hand down her hair. When his arm settled casually around her shoulder, she did not shrug it away. "Who would have thought a big city lawyer and a country sheriff would have anything in common?"

Because his touch was so inviting, his smile so seductive, because once again she was finding herself on a steep precipice that she was struggling not to fall over, Raine decided to turn the subject back to something safer.

"When I was in the eighth grade, my class took a tour of your dad's jail. Everyone else had a great time. I had nightmares of being locked away in one of those cells for weeks."

"He caught me playing chicken with log trucks in my Trans Am when I was sixteen," Jack divulged. "Locked me up for twenty-four horrible hours. Fortunately, the jail was empty that weekend, so I didn't have a roommate."

"He sounds strict."

"He was. But fair. He made sure I knew what the rules were, and the penalty for breaking them. Then nothing on God's green earth would get him to give in." He shook his head, but his expression was one of affection. "He was a man of his word. A man who could be trusted. . . .

"Another time, when I was eight, I got a bellyache while we were backpacking deep in the Olympics, in a wilderness area. I didn't say anything because I didn't want him to think he had a sissy for a son. But finally he noticed that I was sweating more than I should be, even for a kid who was carrying a twenty-five pound pack up a mountainside. He immediately dumped both our packs, put me on his back, and carried me out, ten miles to the trailhead where we'd parked the truck.

"The entire time he kept assuring me that I was going to be all right. And I believed him. Because he was my pop."

"What was wrong with you?"

"Appendicitis. They had me in the operating room five minutes after we got to the hospital. Afterwards, they told my dad that I was minutes away from having it burst."

"That was lucky. That he got you there when he did."

"Real lucky," he agreed. "The doc gave me the appendix. I kept it in a jar of formaldehyde in my room until I went off to college."

"You realize that's gross."

"Not to an eight-year-old boy. I kept it for a trophy, but also because it reminded me of one of the more eventful trips Pop and I took together."

Compared to these stories of his childhood, Raine

could have grown up on Jupiter. "It must have been wonderful," she murmured wistfully. "Knowing that you could always count on someone like that."

"Like I said, Pop was special. I always knew that, on some abstract level. It was only after Peg and I adopted Amy that I realized how he'd been the rock of the family, while Mom has always been the heart."

"I envy you such a strong family bond."

His arm tightened around her shoulder, pulling her a little closer. He skimmed his lips against the top of her head. "You have that, too. With Ida and Savannah. And Lilith."

She thought about that for a moment. "With Ida and Savannah. But Lilith . . ." Not wanting to ruin a lovely afternoon with negative thoughts about her mother, Raine's voice drifted off.

"You know, when I was still toddling around in diapers, my folks figured every boy should have a dog," he said conversationally. "So, they went to the animal shelter and adopted a springer spaniel–sheltie mix, figuring we could grow up together.

"That's sweet."

"I've always thought so. She was a dynamite dog. And loyal to a fault. She loved to go duck hunting with Dan and me, but we'd have to take her home at lunchtime, because the damn mutt would've kept diving into that icy water all day long. Partly because she loved fetching ducks. But mostly because she wanted, more than anything, to please me. She died when I was fifteen."

"I'm sorry."

"So was I. Even if she did live a helluva long time

for a dog. After a couple days, Dad took me down to the animal shelter and I suppose there were some pretty good candidates, but I was determined to get a dog exactly like Cleo."

"Cleo?"

"Because she had these dark lines around her eyes, kinda like Elizabeth Taylor when she played Cleopatra. . . . Hey"—he complained when she grinned—"I didn't name her. My mother did. If you'll recall, I was too young to be making such weighty decisions."

"Point taken."

"Okay. So, bein' a stubborn sort of kid, I kept trying to find a replacement for Cleo. It took six months, but I finally found a dead ringer. Right down to her crazy, brown nose with its black racing stripe down the center. I took her down to the beach to start training her for hunting season and must've thrown a hundred pieces of driftwood, but this new Cleo just sat there, looking up at me with a cockeyed adoring dog look, wagging her stub of a tail.

"After about a month, I finally got her to chase the damn sticks, but she never did figure out that she was supposed to bring them back. For a while I was so ticked off at the dog, I didn't even want to look at her. Because she didn't live up to my expectations."

Raine was silent for a moment, taking in the parable that was so similar to what Cooper had said earlier. "You think I'm too hard on Lilith."

"I think you're trying to make her into something she isn't," he said gently. "Because you've got some idealized beliefs about what a mother should be and anyone who doesn't live up to your high standard is bound to prove a failure in your eyes."

"That's not a very attractive picture." But painfully close to the truth, she secretly admitted. "If you truly believe I'm so judgmental, I can't imagine why you'd want anything to do with me."

"That's easy. You've got a great ass and the best legs I've ever seen on a female. And you taste pretty good, too."

Despite her discomfort with the topic, Raine smiled at that, just, as she suspected, he'd meant her to. "You realize, of course, that my mother would not be pleased to hear you compare her to a dog. Especially a mongrel."

"You're right. So, we'll just have to let that be our little secret." He pulled her closer. Then lowered his head, until his mouth was a whisper away from hers. "If you don't want this to happen, Raine, tell me now. Because while we're sharing secrets, I gotta tell you, sweetheart, I'm dying here."

His voice was rough. Pained. Thrilling. "Me, too," Raine whispered.

"Thank God." Jack's words exploded on a rush of air as he covered her lips with his and lowered her down to the blanket.

❦ 18 ❦

He wanted her. Really wanted her. The idea was as terrifying as it was thrilling. What if she couldn't satisfy him? Raine worried. What if she did something wrong and disappointed both of them? What if . . .

"Jack . . ." Her mind fogged, her voice drifted off and her body arched instinctively as he skimmed a hot kiss down her neck. "I think this is . . . Oh, God," she murmured when he touched the hollow of her throat with the tip of his tongue and sent her pulse hammering. "I have to tell you . . ." She could barely speak. Barely breathe. "It's been a long time since I've done this."

"Don't worry." He began unbuttoning her blouse while kissing his way back up to her mouth. "It's like riding a bicycle. It'll come back to you."

Her body arched when his hand closed over her breast. "It already has." Waves of pleasures flowed through her, as warm and liquid as a tropical sea. "More than I . . . Oh!" Raine gasped, then shuddered as he nipped at an erogenous zone on her neck she'd never even known she possessed. "More than I ever thought possible," she said on a quick rush of tangled breath. "But I'm not on the pill, and I don't have anything. . . ."

Her voice trailed as another wave, this time of embarrassment, threatened to engulf her. What was she thinking? To go so far without having given any thought to the consequences? She was behaving no more intelligently than poor, needy, lovesick Gwen had behaved with the faithless Randy. And look how that had turned out.

"Don't worry. I do." He lifted his hips just enough to dig into a pocket and pull out a handful of condoms.

From somewhere, a sense of humor she thought the intense world of corporate litigation had burned out of her years ago rose to ease what had proven to be an embarrassing moment. "Are you sure you brought enough?"

"For starters." As his mouth returned to hers, Raine could feel his smile against her lips.

She looked up at him, positive he was joking. "You're very sure of yourself, Sheriff." With good reason, she suspected as she watched the sexy glint flash in his midnight dark eyes.

"Nah. I'm just pretty damn sure of us, Counselor."

Her heart hitched. Then tumbled dangerously. She could lose it to this man, she realized in a blinding flash of realization. So easily. If she was smart, if she knew what was good for her, she'd back away now, even if she would go through life knowing she'd earned one of the most unflattering words used to describe a woman.

"May I ask one more question?"

His laugh was rough. "Could I stop you?"

Raine couldn't decide whether his gritty humor was directed at her, himself, or their situation. She knew she was talking too much, which could undoubtedly be blamed on nerves. But there was one more thing she needed to know.

"Did you ever bring . . ." she couldn't quite bring herself to say Jack's wife's name. Not when she was about to make love with him. Have sex, she corrected. "Bring anyone else here?"

His teasing grin faded and his expression was as sober as she'd ever seen it. "You're the only woman I've ever brought here, Raine. In fact, I'd forgotten it even existed. Until sometime in the middle of last night, when I was trying to think of a place I could get you alone and do this."

One hand tangled her hair as his mouth captured her tingling lips again, his kisses growing deeper. More drugging. The other was doing glorious things to her breasts that sent a sweet pleasure humming through her veins even as the caressing touch made her want more.

"And this." He pushed the cotton blouse aside and lightly bit her shoulder, then soothed the flesh with his tongue. Her breathing quickened as he unfastened her bra with a quick flick of the wrist and began torturing her unfettered breast with first his hands, then his mouth. Raine shivered as his teeth tugged on a taut nipple, causing sparks that shot straight down to that warm, moist place between her legs. Her head spun, her body craved. Desire rose so high and so hot it stunned.

"Please, Jack." Her fingers turned unusually

clumsy as she fumbled with the metal button on his jeans. "I need you." It was not an easy admission. Raine had never been one to give up control. She'd never wanted to surrender power. Until now. Until Jack.

"And I need you, too, sweetheart." He captured her hand and pulled it away, lifting it to his lips. When he began sucking on her fingers, one at a time, she felt a strong, corresponding pull deep inside her. "But it's been a while for me." His free hand opened her jeans, as she'd been planning to do to him, but with a great deal more finesse. "I don't want things to go too fast."

When he trailed a lazy fingertip down her stomach, through the nest of soft curls into the aching, dark warmth below, Raine heard a whimper and realized that it had come from between her own ravished lips.

"Fast would be okay," she managed as she bucked against his intimate touch. *Need* was too weak a word. She craved him. With every burning atom in her body. "In fact, fast would be fine."

He laughed at that, a deep, rich sound that rumbled through her. "Next time," he promised. "But I've been waiting too long for this not to at least try to make it last."

"Not that long." Desperate to touch, she pulled her hand free, ripped open his shirt and pressed first her palms, then her lips against the hard wall of his chest. His heart was pounding like a jackhammer, vivid proof that she was not the only one so harshly affected. His skin was hot and moist, and as she touched her tongue to it, Raine tasted a faint tang of salt. "I've only been home a few days."

"Ah, but I've been waiting for you longer than that." When he grabbed hold of her wrists and held her hands above her head, an edgy excitement crackled along her skin like flashfire.

"You couldn't have been," she managed to argue on a gasp as he touched his open mouth to that surprisingly sensitive spot at the base of her throat. "There was no way you'd know I'd be coming back to town."

"True enough." He continued his tender torture, skimming a trail of wet kisses down her rib cage. When he got to the waist of her jeans, he released her hands and slid them slowly down her legs, then followed the denim with his mouth in a slow, erotic journey that had her writhing on the blanket. "I didn't know you'd be coming. Hell, I didn't even know that I was waiting for you to come back. Until you showed up one rainy night and triggered something inside me I'd thought had died."

Lilith might endorse New Age beliefs, but Raine had never been one to accept the idea of fate. Or destiny. She'd never given credence to the idea of the Easter Bunny or the tooth fairy, and had stopped believing in Santa Claus when she was three years old and had gotten up on Christmas morning to discover that he hadn't shown up.

A week later, she was back at her grandmother's house, unwrapping gifts Ida assured her that Santa had delivered to Coldwater Cove by mistake. But Raine had known the truth. And that was the year trust had died.

But now, as she surrendered to Jack's murmured words, his tender touches, his devastating kisses, Raine wondered, through the rosy haze clouding her mind, if perhaps she'd been waiting for him, too. Without knowing she'd been waiting. Wanting him, without knowing she'd been wanting.

The idea was as thrilling as it was terrifying.

A sound that was half gasp, half sob was ripped from her throat as he licked his way back up her legs again, creating a sizzling pleasure-pain at the inside of her thighs. "Please," she moaned again. She'd never begged for anything in her life. But she was willing to now if that's what it took to end this exquisite torture.

"Not yet." He lifted his fingers to his mouth, touched his tongue to them, then slipped the wet tips beneath the elastic leg band of her panties. "Not nearly."

Hot, heavy moisture had soaked the cotton crotch. Raine tossed her head back and forth as he stripped the panties off and eased one of those treacherous fingers deep inside her. When his thumb parted the sensitive pink folds, she was certain she could feel her bones melt. When the rough pad of his seeking thumb stroked a swathe across the nub that was aching for his touch, sensation after sensation tore through her. Then, before she could catch her breath, he was lifting her to his mouth, feasting on her, claiming her, ravishing her.

Raine's eyes, which had been squeezed shut against the devastating assault on her senses flew open, wide with shock as she felt her body explode into a fireball, like a new sun being born.

She was boneless. Limp. Helpless. The entire forest could suddenly follow her up in flame and she wouldn't be able to move a muscle to save herself.

"That was," she gasped on a labored breath as he

held her in his arms while she tumbled back to earth. "Amazing."

"No." He touched his mouth to hers in a kiss that was surprisingly tender compared to his earlier hunger. "It's just the beginning."

As the afternoon lengthened and silver-edged clouds swept by overhead, Jack proved to be a man of his word as he drew out their lovemaking, treating her to a pleasure so sublime it nearly made her weep and a renewed passion so intense she feared it would make her shatter.

And when he finally took her over that final peak, Raine's last coherent thought was she felt as if she'd dived off the towering cliff above Neah Bay into a storm-tossed sea. Then risen from the waves again, exactly where she was fated to be. In his arms.

A light fog was skimming along the ground, like little gray ghosts as they drove in thoughtful silence back to town. He'd been afraid of this. While Jack had no idea what was going through Raine's mind at the moment, his own was rerunning every minute from that fateful moment he'd first seen her, wet and furious and sexy as hell. He hadn't lied when he'd told her that he'd wanted her from the beginning. Since he was, after all, human, he wasn't going to apologize for an all too human craving. The only problem was that he'd miscalculated.

He'd tried to tell himself that his only problem was he'd been celibate too long. And, although he wasn't the type of man to hop into the sack with the first available woman, he'd also tried assuring himself that Raine Cantrell wasn't the only attractive, intelligent, desirable woman in Coldwater Cove. Unfortunately, she was the only one he'd wanted.

Since they were, after all, both single, unattached adults, he'd decided there was no reason to deny themselves what they both wanted. He'd hoped that once he made love to Raine, once he satisfied the hunger that had tormented his daytime hours and haunted his sleep, he'd be satisfied. Ready to move on. Ready to let her move on.

But there had been a moment there, when he'd been deep inside her, just before his own climax, that his head had begun to swim and all the air seemed to have been sucked out of his lungs. It had felt as if he were drowning; and the crazy thing about it was that he couldn't even care.

This was ridiculous. Nothing could come of it; any relationship between them was a dead-end street. She lived in the fast lane a continent away; the life he'd made for himself and his daughter in Coldwater Cove was so laid back the lady lawyer would probably get more excitement from watching paint dry. She was rich—not Manhattan megamogul rich, but she sure as hell brought in a bigger paycheck than a civil servant. Jack figured she probably earned about three times what he did. That idea didn't really bother him, but it might her, since it could prove a bit difficult to explain to high-living friends that she'd married a small-town Western sheriff.

Marry? The idea hit with the force of a sledgehammer at the back of his head. Christ, talk about getting carried away just because of a couple hours of good sex. Okay, make that *great* sex. But it was still important to keep it in perspective. Raine may have spent a great deal of her childhood in Coldwater

Cove, but she'd moved on. She was city; he was country. She was Chateaubriand; he was ground chuck.

"Tomato, tomahto." He murmured the old song lyric as the fog lights cut through the mist rising from the damp pavement. A light sprinkle dotted the windshield, causing him to turn on the wipers.

She glanced over at him. "What did you say?"

He shrugged. "It's not important. I was just talking to myself."

"Oh."

Her voice invited elaboration he wasn't yet prepared to share. "I was thinking that it was too bad you had to run off so quick."

"I was thinking the same thing." she murmured. Since he'd already determined that Raine Cantrell was not a woman who was comfortable with touching, the foolishly romantic part of him that Jack thought had died was encouraged when she placed her hand gently, almost casually, on his thigh. "Talk about your rotten timing."

He covered her slender hand with his. "Hey, at least we'll always have Coldwater Cove."

Her laugh was light and warm and made him want to pull over to the side of the road and take her again in the back of the Suburban. "That's the difference between us. I'm always looking for the catch while you manage to find a bright side to everything."

"You make optimism sound like a flaw."

"I didn't mean it that way." Turning her hand beneath his, she linked their fingers together. "To tell the truth, I rather envy you your positive outlook on life. Especially after . . ." Her voice drifted off.

"Peg's death," he finished for her.

"It must have been difficult."

"It wasn't exactly a walk in the park."

"I imagine not." She paused again, as if choosing her words carefully. For a time the only sound was the intermittent *swish swish* of the windshield wipers. "If you don't want to talk about it—"

"I don't mind. I don't talk much about those days since the role of a grieving widower definitely isn't all that appealing. To me or anyone who has to put up with it. But after this afternoon, I'd say you're entitled to ask anything you want."

Her fingers tensed in his. She was silent and thoughtful in that way that he suspected would prove advantageous in a courtroom situation. She was a woman who used words carefully. Except, Jack thought with a very primitive male satisfaction, when she'd been bucking beneath him.

Sensing that she was curious, but uncomfortable with the topic, he decided to help her out. "It was bad. It took a very long time, and, though she fought like a trooper, I knew she was in a lot more pain than she ever let on."

"She was lucky to have you."

"Not always," he confessed. "In the beginning, during the initial treatment stage, we were a team. Granted, I hated having to stand on the sidelines while she fought the battle, and there were times when the role reversal was hard to take."

"But she knew you were in her corner. Supporting her, urging her on, putting your own pain aside to concentrate on reassuring her that everything would be okay. That she'd be okay."

"I'm not sure she always knew that. Not after we

ran out of options." Because that memory still hurt, he drew in a breath. "Peg accepted things even when I wanted her to keep fighting. There were still a lot of experimental treatments we could have tried. Granted, they hadn't proven effective in clinical trials, but it was damn well better than the alternative." At least that's what he'd argued at the time.

"But she put her foot down, insisting she wanted to be at home, with her family instead of in some Mexican or Swiss clinic. She said she wanted to enjoy her last months with her daughter and die in peace."

He released Raine's hand to drag his down his face. "From the first day I met her, she was unrelentingly easygoing, eager to do whatever she thought would make me happy. But then, just when it really mattered, she dug in her heels and refused to budge."

"That must have been difficult," Raine said.

Jack hated the pity he thought he heard in her voice. "I was furious that she was willing to give up; I yelled at her that if she loved me she'd keep on fighting." The guilt still hurt. Jack figured it always would. "What kind of man yells at his dying wife?"

"A human one," Raine suggested quietly. She caught hold of his hand again. "You're being too hard on yourself."

"Perhaps you're being too easy."

"No, I'm not." She lifted their joined hands and touched his knuckles to her lips. "There was a time in my life when I would have given away everything I owned, for even a little bit of that commitment you gave Peg."

Having figured out that she seldom said anything

she didn't mean, Jack immediately noticed her use of the past tense. "And now?"

Another pause. "And now," she said slowly, and a little regretfully, he thought, "I've learned not to count on anyone except myself."

"That's sad."

"No," she corrected, lowering their hands and releasing his. "It's safe."

"Safe can be a close cousin to boring," he said mildly. He reached out and put his arm around her shoulder. "And believe me, Harvard, you are anything but boring."

She smiled at that, as he'd intended. "I believe I'll take that as a compliment."

"Oh, I've got a lot more where that one came from."

Deciding that self-restraint was definitely overrated, he pulled off the highway again onto an unmarked logging skid road, cut the engine, unfastened their seatbelts, and hauled her onto his lap.

"Did I mention that your hair reminds me of silk?" He fisted his hand in the dark strands.

"I vaguely recall something along those lines."

He kissed her. Hard. "How about the fact that the color in your cheeks after I kiss you reminds me of strawberries on new snow?"

"Oh, I like that one." The smile was shining in her eyes again. "But maybe you ought to kiss me again. Just to be sure."

"Absolutely." Light, quick nibbles turned longer, deeper. "And your eyes." Her lids fluttered obediently shut as he dropped a kiss on each one. "Are like antique gold coins."

"They're hazel." She twined her fingers around his neck and arched her back, inviting his lips to continue their sensual quest.

After a few more deep, drugging kisses, he obliged, pleased when her pulse began to thrum wildly in the fragrant hollow of her throat.

As Jack worked his way down her body, fog thickened around the Suburban, sheltering them in a private, sensual world of their own making.

❦ 19 ❧

Raine had suspected that making love with Jack would complicate her life. It was more than just the sex, as wonderful as that was. Their earlier conversation, comparing her upbringing with his, had gotten her thinking about families and loyalty and commitment again.

She hated to admit it, even to herself, but suspected that he may have been right about Lilith. About so much of her unhappiness over the years having been because she'd been hoping for something that her mother had not been able to give. Granted, Lilith had not been a rock of stability, but as Cooper had pointed out, she'd at least admitted her own faults enough to take her daughters back to Coldwater Cove whenever her own life had spiraled out of control.

The problem was, Raine had always only thought of her mother as a flawed parent. Not a woman with dreams and hopes and disappointments of her own. And certainly never as a friend.

Yet with all her faults, despite her flaws, Lilith had

displayed an honest willingness to at least attempt to change during the time Raine had been back in Coldwater Cove. Some people might feel that fifty years old was a bit late to be deciding to grow up. But, Raine thought, better late than never.

These thoughts led uncomfortably to another. Over the past years, whenever Ida had complained that her eldest granddaughter didn't come home often enough, Raine had used work as an excuse. That had been partly true. But she also couldn't deny that she'd always felt more comfortable at work; it was one place where she felt in control. While family matters, on the other hand, tended to become emotionally sticky. Which was why she tried to ignore them.

Which brought her to the realization that in one small but important way, she was more like her mother than she'd tried to pretend all these years. Lilith had been infamous for thinking of herself first and last. Now Raine was forced to concede that she'd been guilty of exactly the same behavior.

She hadn't even known the names of the girls whom Ida obviously cared deeply about. It had been so long since she'd spent any time with her sister, she hadn't known how bad the trouble in Savannah's marriage had become. Just as her mother hadn't been there for her while she'd been growing up, Raine now was faced with the possibility that she'd developed her own form of abandonment. Her legal work, while important, was only that. Work. It shouldn't be her life. Should it?

She was also forced to consider that what she'd viewed all these years as independence, was, in a way, a form of solitude that had cut her off from her family ties, a symbolic cutting of the cord connecting the generations of females.

The father she'd never known may have been the role model for her success, but Lilith was the mile marker she used to measure her own personal travels.

Dammit, she wasn't used to this. This need to balance her own needs and desires with anyone else's. She wasn't any good at it. Especially when compared to Jack, who somehow managed to balance his duties as sheriff with his even more important responsibility to his daughter. Raine tried to picture any attorney she knew—including herself—pausing during an argument in court to keep a toy kitten alive for a little girl who'd already lost too many people she loved, and failed.

"I hope I'm not the cause of that frown." Jack's mild voice infiltrated her turmoiled thoughts.

"No. I was just thinking of something." The afternoon's peace and sublime pleasure began to fade away as if it had never been. Almost as if she'd imagined it.

"Want to talk about it?"

Raine believed in keeping her life neatly compartmentalized. There was her career. And everything else. The two tracks ran parallel, never crossing. Until three little girls had locked themselves in her grandmother's house, setting up a confrontation with this man. Accustomed to keeping her private thoughts strictly to herself, she found it difficult to share them now.

Her careless shrug was as fake as her smile. "It's not that important."

It was a lie and they both knew it. Jack didn't

immediately answer. Instead he slanted her one of those deep looks that made her once again think that he'd be a whiz at interrogation. She hadn't had much occasion to handle criminal work, but understood that cops, like attorneys, knew how to use silence to their advantage. Raine had always considered herself pretty good at this tactic. She was beginning to realize Jack just might possibly be even better.

"Your confession rate must have been the highest in the city," she muttered, switching her irritation at herself to him.

He turned his attention back to the wet, slick road. But that didn't stop his continued silence from making her even more edgy. Oh yes, any criminal unfortunate enough to end on the wrong side of the interrogation table with this man would undoubtedly soon find himself on a one-way trip up the river.

He glanced at her again, brow lifted. "That's what you were thinking about?"

"I was just picturing you in the box."

"The box?" His lips quirked.

"That's what it's called, right?" Feeling challenged, her voice turned as cool as the rain falling outside the truck. "Where you drill a suspect to win a confession?"

"Yeah. The box." She could hear the repressed laughter in his deep voice. "And if that's what you were thinking about, Harvard, I sure as hell must not have done a very good job of relaxing you this afternoon."

Just the mention of their shared lovemaking was all it took to cause a wave of desire that hit as quick and hard as a spring squall. Furious pride warred with an equally furious need inside Raine. Eventually pride won out.

"As I said, it's not that important."

He shrugged. "Whatever you say." His tone remained casual, but Raine wasn't fooled for a moment. She wasn't completely off the hook. And they both well knew it.

Jack and Raine had no sooner entered the house when a blood-curdling scream came from somewhere upstairs. A moment later Gwen came clattering down the stairs. She was wearing her *Lucy* maternity outfit, but there was absolutely nothing humorous about her appearance.

"What's wrong?" Ida, who'd rushed in from the front parlor, caught the trembling teenager by the upper arms. "What happened? Are you in labor?"

"No-o-o! I k-k-killed it!"

"What?" Savannah asked, as she joined them. From the white cotton chef's apron she was wearing over her jeans and T-shirt, Raine figured her sister had been saving them from another night of takeout or meatloaf.

"The baby."

"The baby?" Ida ran her hand over the teenager's swollen belly. "Are you cramping? Bleeding?"

"Not that baby!" Tears were streaming down Gwen's cheeks. "The N-N-Nano Baby. I was studying for my chemistry final and didn't hear it beeping and it s-s-starved to death!"

"Oh, darling." Ever the nurturer, Savannah gathered the tearful girl into her arms. "It's okay. It's just a toy."

"I know it's just a toy!" The teenager's words were muffled against Savannah's shoulders. "But don't you see?" When she lifted her head, her face was twisted in a very real agony that pulled painfully at Raine's heart. "It c-c-could have been a real baby."

"Oh, pooh," Ida scoffed. "You're a levelheaded young lady, Gwendolyn. And even if you weren't, your maternal instincts will kick in once you give birth. You'd never forget to feed your own child."

"That's not necessarily true," a new voice entered the conversation. Raine turned to see her mother standing in the arched doorway of the parlor, Cooper right behind her.

"This doesn't really have anything to do with you, Lilith," Ida said, her sharp tone declaring the matter settled.

"Perhaps not. But in a few days Gwen's going to have to make the most important decision of her life. And I think she deserves to hear more than the Pollyanna side of the story."

Lilith took a deep breath and briefly closed her eyes in a way that suggested she was garnering strength. Which, Raine figured, she undoubtedly was. Motherhood had never been Lilith's favorite subject. Especially since it had never been her forte.

"I was only a few years older than you when I had Raine, Gwen, dear," she said. "I hadn't intended to get pregnant, and while abortion was illegal in those days, everyone knew someone who could, I was assured, 'take care of the problem.' But while I suppose that would have been an easy solution, the practical solution, I was stunned by the depth of my feelings for the child I was carrying."

She turned to Ida. "Now I know, you'll say it's

impossible, but I knew, the moment after I'd made love with Raine's father, that I was pregnant."

"It *is* impossible," Ida muttered. "Owen Cantrell may have turned out to be some big-name hotshot attorney, but he doesn't have supersperm. It would have taken those guys a while to swim upstream. And even longer to penetrate an egg. So you weren't pregnant."

"Perhaps not physically. But emotionally, my heart somehow knew that Owen and I had made a baby. Of course there wasn't any way to tell whether I was carrying a girl or a boy in those days, but I knew I was going to have a daughter. I also knew that I loved her more than life itself."

"That's nice," Gwen sniffled.

"It's the truth." Lilith exchanged a glance with Raine. Her pansy blue eyes swam with moisture. Raine's own eyes stung. "The thing is, Gwen, darling, that as much as I was looking forward to being a mother, insisting on keeping Raine was selfish. Because I was incapable of taking care of a child. I was flighty, selfish, and there would be times that I'd be out having fun, like young girls will, and would actually forget I had a baby at home."

She wasn't surprised. Still, hearing her mother voice those words out loud made Raine flinch. Without a word, Jack reached out and took hold of her hand, linking their fingers together in the same intimate way he had when he'd so wondrously filled her earlier.

"You left Raine alone?" Gwen asked disbelievingly. "When she was a baby?"

"No. Of course she wasn't alone." Lilith shook her head. Then combed her fingers through the tousled silver strands. Raine couldn't help noting how her mother's hand was shaking. "Fortunately even I was never that irresponsible. And, thanks to Mother, Raine survived. But she might not have. Because, while I dearly loved both you girls to pieces"—she directed her words to Savannah and Raine—"my maternal instincts were, at best, lousy. At worst, nil."

"You weren't that bad," Ida insisted.

"Yes, I was," Lilith said, her voice low, but just as firm. "As you well remember."

"Well."

Raine could recall very few times when her grandmother had been at a loss for words. This was one of them. As the silence hovered, she saw Cooper slip a supportive arm around Lilith's waist in a move that appeared entirely natural.

"You're comparing oranges and orangutans," Ida said finally. "Because you and Gwendolyn are not at all alike. Gwen's a steady, studious girl and—"

"That's just the point," Gwen broke in again. Hectic red flags flew in her paper white cheeks. "I forgot to feed Amy's Nano Baby because I was studying so hard I didn't even hear it beeping."

"That's alright, kiddo," Jack assured her. "Amy won't mind."

"Maybe not. But I do." She bit her bottom lip. Tears filled her anguished eyes. "I've wanted to be a doctor ever since I was a little kid. I even wanted Doctor Barbie, when all the other girls were going crazy over Malibu Barbie. And maybe I'm being selfish, but how can I do that if I'm trying to take care of a baby while I'm still in high school?"

Not one person in the room could give her a good answer.

"Wanting to care for people isn't at all selfish,"
Raine tried. "But you're right. You still have another
year of high school, then college, then medical
school, which is even more difficult than law school.
And I know I never could have juggled a baby and
school. But some people do."

"Adults," Gwen suggested. "So." She took a deep
breath. "I guess I don't have any choice but to go
back to one of those adoption agencies and let one
of those rich people adopt my baby."

"Oh, darling." Lilith's eyes filled with empathetic
tears again. "I know how unhappy you were with
those prospective parents. Surely there's another
solution?"

She looked toward Raine, as if expecting her eldest daughter to pull one out of her legal bag of
tricks. Which, of course, was impossible. Raine suspected mothers-to-be had been forced to make such
decisions since the beginning of time. She doubted
it ever got any easier. Or less painful.

Another silence settled like thick, wet morning
fog.

"May I make a suggestion?" Savannah asked
hesitantly.

"Okay," Gwen said, looking more forlorn than
Raine had ever seen her. She looked even more depressed than she had that first night, when she'd
watched Raine sign Old Fussbudget's custody forms
from the backseat of Jack's Suburban.

"I have some friends who have been trying to
adopt a child for years, since Terri can't have any
herself, but the waiting lists for public agencies are
terribly long, and they can't afford private adoption.

"Not that they're poor," she hastened to add. "It's

just that they have all their liquid assets tied up in their business. It's a winery. And it's not that far away. In Sequim, as a matter of fact. They make a marvelous, reasonably priced selection of red wines. During the three years I've been buying wine from them for the resort, we've become friends, and I can certainly vouch that no two people could love a child more than Terri and Bill. Or take better care of one."

"A winery?" Gwen asked on a sniffle. She rubbed her nose with the back of her hand.

"One that's becoming more successful every year," Savannah said. "I've no doubt that someday they could be rich. But right now, they're merely comfortable."

"Comfortable's okay." Gwen sniffled again, then wiped her nose on the Kleenex Lilith silently handed her. "Do they live at the winery?"

"Right on the grounds, in a wonderful old turn-of-the-century home that they're restoring." Savannah's smile was warm and reminiscent. "The nursery was the first room they completed. It's been sitting empty for the past five years."

"Five years is a long time to wait for a baby." Gwen looked thoughtful. And, Raine thought she could see the worry lift. Just a bit.

"Yes," Savannah agreed quietly. "It is."

"Do you think they might want my baby?"

"I know they'd love it as if it were their own natural-born child. Perhaps even more," Savannah said, glancing over toward Jack in a way that suggested she was remembering Amy's declaration at the party.

Gwen blew her nose. A more normal color was

returning to her complexion. "Do you think I could meet them?"

"Absolutely. Whenever you like."

"Maybe you can call them now?"

"I'll do that. But I won't make the appointment until the weekend. That way you won't have to miss finals. And you'll have more time to think things over. To make certain this is really what you want to do.

"Not that agreeing to meet with Terri and Bill means that you'd be agreeing to let them adopt your baby," Savannah hastened to assure the teenager. "We'll just consider it a getting-acquainted meeting."

"Okay." Gwen's relief was more-than-a-little obvious. She turned to Lilith. "Will you come? To help ask the questions, like you did before?"

Although her eyes were still swimming, Lilith's smile only wobbled slightly. "Of course, darling. I'd love to."

Gwen turned to Raine. "Will you come, too?"

"Oh, Gwen, I'm afraid I can't draw up any papers—"

"No. Not as a lawyer. As family."

Family. Raine reminded herself of all the years she'd spent wishing for a traditional, Ozzie-and-Harriet family. What she'd belatedly discovered might not fit the two-parent, two-point-five-children model, but somehow, when she hadn't been looking, it appeared she'd landed smack into the middle of one.

"I'll be there. And I'll stay here until your baby's born."

While the others, including, Raine noticed, Cooper Ryan, followed Savannah back into the kitchen to be present for the important call, Raine wandered back out onto the front porch with Jack.

"That was a nice thing to do," he said.

"I didn't have a choice." It was a foolish thing, perhaps, but she was inordinately pleased by his compliment.

He cupped her face with his hand and gave her a long look. "That's not exactly true," he said eventually, "Between Savannah and Dan, Gwen's in good hands. Even before you factor in Ida's common sense and Lilith's empathy. I'm not the least bit surprised by your decision, but I'll bet dollars to dentures that you are, just a little."

Hearing him repeat one of Ida's malapropisms made her smile at the same time the light touch of his fingertips on her cheek caused a renewed rise of desire. Had it only been desire, Raine figured she could have handled it. After having experienced Jack's exquisite lovemaking, it would only be natural to want more. Any woman would. It was the realization that she needed him, needed him in ways that had nothing to do with sex, that had her shaken.

"Perhaps, just a little," she admitted in a voice she wished was stronger.

His fingertips skimmed up her cheek and into her hair. "You just need to spend a little more time getting in touch with your inner Raine."

His lips were smiling; his eyes were smoldering in a way that created a spike in her hormones. Since looking into those eyes had her wanting to pull him down onto the swing, Raine concentrated on his lips. Which proved a big mistake when she could recall their taste in exact, glorious detail.

"Perhaps I do." Her legs were turning as shaky as her voice. "Are you offering to help?"

"Absolutely." When his mouth covered hers, Raine could feel his smile broaden. As she twined her arms around his neck and went up on her toes to kiss him back, Raine's answering smile broke free.

∽20∽

"How would you like to have dinner at the farm?" Jack asked after the blissful kiss finally ended.

"I'd love to have dinner with you." After this afternoon, Raine saw no point in being coy. Besides, she wanted to spend as much time as she could with Jack before she went back to New York. "But what about Amy?"

"Well, that's kind of the thing." He rubbed his cheek. "I've pulled a couple nights I don't usually do the past couple weeks, and I'd just as soon not leave her alone again tonight. I was thinking that if you don't mind the drive and you're willing to trust my cooking, we could have dinner at the farm."

"I like spaghetti," she said, recalling an earlier invitation she'd turned down.

"Hey, I can cook more than that. In fact, I'm also a whiz at steaks, lasagna, and grilled salmon."

"Ah, yes. You mentioned something about grilled fish in your little survival fantasy."

"Our *lovemaking* fantasy," he corrected.

"Lovemaking? I don't remember anything about

that. In the fantasy I heard, you were sharpening sticks and building log cabins with your Swiss Army chain saw while I made beds and sewed skirts."

"The skirts were your idea," he reminded her. "And didn't I mention the lovemaking part?"

"No."

"Damn. And that's the best part." He looped his arms around her waist and pulled her toward him. "After dinner, I take that skirt off you, leaf by leaf—"

"Sounds a lot like peeling an artichoke."

He shook his head. "Anyone ever tell you that you can—at times—be a bit too literal?"

"I'm an attorney. It goes with the territory."

"With you, perhaps. Most lawyers I've met tend to be verbally creative types. Creative with the truth, anyway."

"Truth is a bit like beauty. It's in the eye of the beholder."

"Objection sustained." He drew her a little closer. "And speaking of beauty, I strip those banana leaves off you, one at a time—"

"Banana leaves? I thought this fantasy took place here on the peninsula."

"There you go, getting bogged down in details again. Besides, Coldwater Cove is in the Pacific Northwest's banana belt."

"A banana belt, like beauty and truth, is relative. We happen to be across the Strait of Juan de Fuca from Canada. That's not exactly the tropics. We grow Douglas firs here. Not bananas."

"Yeah, but you ever try to wear a skirt made out of prickly fir needles?"

Raine shook her head. "This is ridiculous. And irrelevant. Salmon sounds terrific. Lasagna is great. Heck, I'll even settle for a peanut butter sandwich."

"Peanut butter was one of my specialties even before I had a six-year-old." He lowered his head and kissed her. Lightly, quickly. The kiss caused Raine's heart to turn cartwheels even as it left her wanting more. Much, much more. "Is that the only reason you're taking me up on my invitation?"

On some level, she knew that at least waffling a bit would be prudent. But Raine couldn't lie. Not after their brief discussion of truth, not about this. Not when her heart was still spinning. And her body felt all tingly. She smiled faintly when she remembered reading that people who were about to be struck by lightning felt the same sort of beneath-the-skin sensation.

Too late. The little voice of reason she'd steadfastly ignored earlier managed to make itself heard in the far reaches of her mind. *You've already been struck.*

"No," she said, smiling up at Jack, wondering if he could read her foolish, reckless heart in her eyes and oddly not caring if he could. "I'm not going to feel guilty about taking time away from work, because I've earned it. But I will have to go back to New York as soon as Gwen's had her baby. Meanwhile"—she framed his face with her hands—"what time do you want me?"

"Anytime. All the time."

How was it that those few little words could send her heart into another series of somersaults? "I meant what time you wanted me at the farm."

"Anytime," he repeated. "You're the one having to do the driving, which I'm sorry about—"

"That's okay. The drive to the farm should be especially lovely this time of evening. I'll start out in about an hour. That way you can have some private time with your daughter."

"Sounds like a plan."

He kissed her again. Neither of them saw the family, standing at the front parlor window, barely concealed by the white lace curtains.

"I knew it," Ida crowed. "There'll be a summer wedding or I'll eat my shoes."

"Some kisses don't necessarily make a marriage," Savannah said.

"True," Lilith agreed. "But their auras are nearly blinding, they're so bright. It's obvious that Raine and the sheriff are destined to be with one another."

"You don't have to see auras or any of that other New Age folderol to see that they're in love," Ida said. "If that kiss got any hotter, they'd be setting the porch on fire."

"I don't think we should be watching," Gwen murmured.

"If you're that uncomfortable, dear, why don't you just go on upstairs," Lilith suggested.

"And miss this?" Gwen pressed her nose against the glass. "It'll be so neat."

"What darling?" Lilith asked absently.

"Raine and Jack getting married. It'll be fun having Amy for a sister. And boy, we could really use a man in this family."

"Women need men like fish need rollerskates," Ida stated her oft-repeated opinion firmly.

"Speak for yourself, Mother," Lilith drawled as she exchanged a warm smile with Cooper, who'd chosen to stay across the room. "I think Jack O'Halloran is

going to be a marvelous addition to our little
family."

Gwen murmured instantaneous agreement. Ida
didn't respond. But, uncharacteristically, she didn't
argue, either.

Jack had already put the lasagna in the oven by
the time Raine arrived at the farm. The rich aromas
of basil, oregano, and tomato sauce filled the air.

"If that tastes half as good as it smells," she said
as she shrugged out of the jacket she'd worn in def-
erence to the cool evening air, "you could quit the
cop job and go into the inn and restaurant business
with Savannah."

"Guests might get a little bit tired of four things
on the menu." Jack hung the jacket on the antique
coatrack.

"Five." She smiled. "Don't forget the peanut
butter."

"I think I'd better stick to the things I do well." He
skimmed an appreciative gaze over her. "You look so
lovely."

"Oh, you definitely do that well." Raine felt the
color rise in her cheeks again and thought that she
hadn't blushed as much in her entire life as she had
since returning home. "The sweater is Lilith's. I was
afraid cashmere might be a little much for a dinner
at home, but—"

"It's perfect." The soft ivory-hued sweater's neckline cut across her collarbone in a way that encouraged it to slide off a shoulder, as it was now. Drawn
by the fragrance, Jack skimmed first his fingertip,
then his lips over the bared skin that was gleaming
like porcelain in the spreading glow of the overhead

light fixture. "And, in case I get hungry while I'm waiting for the lasagna to heat up, I can always nibble on you."

"Surely you wouldn't want to set a bad example for Amy."

"That's something we need to talk about. I tried to call you and see if you wanted to cancel, but you'd already left the house and—"

"Cancel? Why would I want to do that?" She'd no sooner said the words when an unpalatable thought occurred to her. "If she doesn't want me to be here—"

"No." It was his turn to interrupt. "Of course she wants you. Hell, if you'd come planning to set up housekeeping, she'd be tickled pink. The problem is, she's sick."

"Oh, no." She experienced a sharp, unbidden need to run upstairs and check on the little girl herself. "I hope it's nothing serious. Has she seen a doctor?"

"No, it's not serious, and I called the doctor as soon as I picked her up at Mom's. It's just one of those stomach virus things that all the kids in her class apparently have come down with. It's not bad. But, it's not real pretty, either. In fact, if Hollywood decides to remake *The Exorcist*, Ariel'll be a shoe-in for the role of the pea soup kid."

"Oh, the poor thing." Something else he said belatedly sunk in. "Ariel?"

"She woke up this morning and informed all of us—me, my mom, her teacher, the other kids at school—that we're supposed to call her Ariel. I'm hoping this will be a short-lived stage."

Raine laughed. "When I was in the second grade, I changed my name to Jane."

"Well. That's, uh, very down to earth," he decided.

"Certainly more than Raine. You can't imagine the jokes I used to get—Raine, Raine, go away; come again another day." She shrugged. "Stuff like that."

"I can see how that might have been tough. So, when did you change it back?"

"When Lanny Davis told me that he thought Raine was prettier. You might remember him. He was three years older and delivered the paper every afternoon. He had a maroon mountain bike with jet striping, black hair, and a pouty scowl that seemed incredibly sexy when I was ten years old. He tended to wear white T-shirts, jeans, and a black motorcycle jacket. Even in the summer."

"Yeah, I remember him. Coldwater Cove's own James Dean."

"I suppose that was his appeal. Since girls tend to have a tendency for falling for bad boys."

"So I've heard, and your little story only confirms my decision that if I'm smart, I'll just lock Amy—"

"Ariel," Raine reminded him.

"Right. I'll just lock the little mermaid in the closet—preferably one located in a nunnery—and not let her out until she's at least thirty-five."

"That's a bit drastic," she said, enjoying the conversation. And him. "Besides, I'm not certain reaching adulthood is any guarantee of choosing the right man."

Since Dan's calls hadn't uncovered anything about a boyfriend, Jack suspected the shadow in her eyes had something to do with her sister. "Is Savannah home for good?"

"I don't know." The laughter had faded from her voice and her eyes. "She says so. I hate to see any marriage break up, yet in this case, I suppose it's for the best."

"Guess she got one of those bad boys by default."

"Yeah. She sure as hell did." Raine shook her head. And tossed the somber mood off. "Do you think it'd be okay if I went upstairs and said hi to Ariel?"

"She'd love to see you, but I have to warn you. She's not in the best of moods."

"I believe I can handle one ill, cranky six-year-old," Raine assured him.

She was nearly to the landing when Jack called out to her. "Hey, Harvard. What about you?"

"What about me, what?"

"Are you the type of woman who falls for bad boys?"

"The past couple years I haven't had any time to think about it. But since you brought it up, I think if I were looking for a man, he wouldn't be a bad boy, but a good man. He'd be strong enough to be sensitive, and confident enough not to be threatened by a woman. Oh yeah, and he'd be a wonderful lover."

"What about money?"

"What about it?"

"Would he have to be rich?"

"Of course not. Besides, we'll be too busy making love and celebrating all we have to pay any attention to what we might not have."

"Sounds as if tangling the sheets is pretty high on the list."

"Oh, it is." Raine shot him a blatantly flirtatious,

from beneath-the-lashes glance. "Because, as Ida always says"—her voice turned Marilyn Monroe breathy—"a hard man is good to find."

With a toss of her head, she resumed climbing the stairs, pleased by the way her behavior had caused that wicked gleam in his eyes. No wonder her mother was such a flirt, Raine thought. It was more fun than she could have ever imagined.

The child formerly known as Amy was propped up in bed with a trio of pillows. Mermaids and various forms of colorful sea life swam over her sheets and comforters and she was surrounded by enough stuffed animals to start her own plush zoo.

"I'm sick," she announced when Raine appeared in the doorway. She was wearing a pink nightgown that matched the bedclothes.

"I know. Your daddy told me." Raine crossed the room, pushed aside a purple polka-dot elephant dressed in a rainbow-hued tutu and a tiger with one ear missing, then sat on the edge of the narrow bed. "I'm so sorry." She pressed the back of her hand against a forehead that felt unnaturally warm.

"I have a fever." Her eyes were dull, her cheeks pink. "It's one hundred degrees. Daddy gave me some medicine, but then I threw up again, so he was afraid to give me any more for a while."

"Sounds as if your Daddy has everything under control."

"Oh, he always does. That's why he's sheriff." She pulled the Lion King from the pile and hugged it to her chest. "I threw up at school, too. In the cafeteria. Johnny McNeil said it was because the cafeteria ladies put dog food in the tacos. But the school nurse said it's just something that's going around.

"Daddy said I'll only feel bad for a few days. Then, when I get better, we can go to the aquarium in Seattle. That's my favorite place," she confided.

"That sounds like a very good favorite place for a little girl named Ariel."

"That's not my name any more." If the child's bottom lip sank any lower, it'd be resting on the bright comforter. "When I was Amy, I didn't get sick. Then I was Ariel for just one morning and I threw up. So I changed it back."

"Amy's a very pretty name." Raine brushed some damp flaxen hair from her forehead.

"I know." She sighed. A moment later, her eyes got saucer wide and her skin took on a faint green tinge.

Sensing what was about to come, Raine grabbed the copper-bottom Dutch oven Jack had placed on the white-enamel-painted bedside table and stuck it in front of Amy just in time.

Fortunately, after having been sick all day, there wasn't much left to come up, although the painful retching nearly broke Raine's heart.

"I hate that," Amy muttered as she flopped back against the pillow.

"I know." Touched, Raine smoothed her fingers across the forehead that she thought might feel a bit cooler. "I'll be right back with a cool cloth."

"Daddy brought me one." She waved a small hand toward the Winnie-the-Pooh and Tigger washcloth on the table. "But then it got hot. Like me."

"Well, sounds as if it's time for a new one." Raine washed out the pan in the bathroom across the hall, dampened the washcloth again with cool water, then returned to the bedroom where Amy, lying back against all those pillows again, was pulling off a fair impression of Camille.

"Thank you," she said in something perilously close to a whimper as Raine wiped the small face and placed the folded cloth on her forehead.

"You're welcome." Raine picked up the members of the menagerie that had fallen onto the pink carpeting during the excitement and rearranged them around the little girl again.

"The cloth feels good." Her eyes were closed, the gilt tipped lashes looking like gold dust against her fair cheeks.

"I'm glad." Raine perched on the edge of the bed again and began finger-combing the long, tousled curls.

A faint purring sound slipped from between the childish lips. "It's not true, is it?"

"What, darling?" Raine asked absently, as she struggled with an overwhelming urge to hold Jack's daughter close.

"About the dog food."

"No. I think Johnny McNeil must have an overactive imagination."

"I knew he was lying. I told him that if the cafeteria ladies put dog food in the tacos, Daddy would put them in jail."

"They certainly would be in trouble," Raine agreed carefully.

"I wish he'd put Johnny in jail." She breathed a frustrated sigh. "He's not very nice. Last week he got a Time Out for calling the teacher a bad name. . . . You're nice," she said, displaying a child's ability to switch topics on a dime.

"So are you."

The blue eyes opened, spearing Raine with a direct look. "Do you like aquariums?"

Raine knew where this was headed and was vaguely surprised that she wasn't bothered. "They're one of my favorite things."

"Mine, too. I like the saltwater fish best, because they're so pretty. Like jewels. But the sharks are neat, too." One hand was busying playing with an errant curl, the other absently stroking a stuffed red lobster. "Maybe you can go with Daddy and me when I get better."

Raine smiled, bent her head and kissed the feverish brow. "I'd like that. Bunches and bunches."

"Hey, Pumpkin," a deep voice called from the doorway. "I brought you a bowl of orange Jell-O, a glass of 7 Up, and some crackers. It's what my Mom always gave me when I was sick."

He looked a little weary, somewhat frazzled, and, Raine thought, absolutely wonderful.

"I threw up again," Amy informed him. "But Raine took care of me."

His expression as he looked over at her was apologetic. Raine shrugged it off. "We've been having a nice visit," she said mildly.

"Raine said the same thing you and the nurse did. That it wasn't dog food that made me sick. And guess what, Daddy?"

"What, sweetheart?"

"When I get better, Raine's coming to the aquarium with us. I asked her and she said yes. Isn't that the best thing?"

"Absolutely the very best," he agreed.

Jack's dark eyes met Raine's and held. The intimate look, while not overtly sexual, nevertheless possessed the power to send rivers of warmth flowing through her and had her thinking, for one wild, wonderfully irrational moment, that if the gods were to suddenly grant her the power to stop time, she might very well choose this moment.

❧ 21 ❧

Three days later, Raine was sitting on the swing, answering e-mail when Ida came out of the house.

"We've got to get going," she announced.

Raine glanced up. "Where?"

"To those friends of Savannah's who might be adopting Gwen's baby."

Wondering if she could have gotten so laid back since returning to Coldwater Cove that she might have lost track of what day of the week it was, Raine glanced down at her watch.

"The meeting's still another four days away."

"It was four days. Until Gwen asked Lilith to read her tarot cards. Apparently, according to your mother, the girl's going to give birth within the next forty-eight hours."

"Oh, for heaven's sake." Raine hit *save* in order not to lose the message she'd been composing. "You're a doctor. Didn't you explain to Gwen that those cards are merely superstition?"

"Of course I did. But she's insisting on going out

to that winery to meet the Stevensons before she goes into labor."

"Does she look as if she's about to go into labor?"

"It's impossible to tell." Her grandmother shrugged shoulders clad in a T-shirt that told the world *Where There's Smoke, There's Toast*. "I know Savannah and Dan wanted to give her more time to think it over, but since she's so determined, it's probably best to try to get the adoption issue settled before the baby's born."

Raine called Dan, who fortunately had a free morning and agreed to meet them at the Stevensons' winery in Sequim.

"Oh, it's so pretty," Gwen breathed at her first glimpse of her unborn child's possible future home. It's like out of a fairy tale book."

"I certainly wouldn't mind growing up here, if I were your little girl," Lilith told Gwen.

Savannah, Ida, and Raine all agreed that it was indeed one of the most scenic spots on the peninsula. Situated on the hilltop former summer estate of a Seattle lumber baron, Blue Mountain Winery overlooked a vast sweep of spring green vineyards set in dark soil that stretched nearly to the Strait of Juan de Fuca. The winery itself was located in a century-old stone-castle-like building, while the nineteenth-century house with its sharp spires revealed the original owner's roots in Germany's Rhine Valley.

Dazzling gardens curled through an emerald lawn; the waters of a duck pond glistened in the spring sunshine. The scent of lilacs perfumed air alive with birdsongs. Serving as a glorious backdrop for the scene were, as always, the snow-capped spines of the Olympic Mountains.

The current owners were refugees from California's Napa Valley, where, Terri offered with unmistakable pride, Bill had worked as a wine master. When she named the winery, even Raine, who certainly didn't have her sister's knowledge of such things, was impressed.

"A person should never go into the wine business to get rich," Bill Stevenson said. A soft-spoken man whose gentle brown eyes were a contrast to his wife's dancing blue ones, he'd spoken little during the tour of the winery, only interjecting the occasional technical explanation into Terri's enthusiastic spiel. "So much depends on the weather, and the soil, and wine drinkers' personal tastes."

"Which is why it's so wonderful that people like you are willing to put your love of wine before the demands of the accountants," Savannah said.

His smile was slow, a little shy, but Raine, who'd been watching the couple closely, had decided he was a kind and gentle man who'd undoubtedly make a wonderful father. "It's a little easier to take risks when you don't have all that much to lose." He looked out over the rolling green hills. "Unfortunately, in the larger wineries, the accountants tend to be winning."

"Are you saying your business could fail?" Gwen asked. She'd said little during the tour, but this, apparently concerned her. "And lose all this?"

"Of course we won't," Terri hastened to assure her. "We were fortunate enough to receive a nice inheritance from my great-grandmother. We used that, along with our savings to put a large enough down

payment on Blue Mountain that even if we do have
a few lean years we won't have to leave. This is our
home, Gwen. A home where we hope to be able to
raise children and someday sit on the lawn and
watch our grandchildren feeding pieces of bread to
the ducks on the pond."

"That sounds nice." Gwen's tone was wistful. Although she'd never considered herself a very fanciful
person until recently, Raine found herself wishing
that she possessed a magic wand she could use to
make the teenager's troubles disappear.

They'd gathered together on a little patio overlooking the duck pond, protected by a wide overhang
from the misty rain that had begun to fall. Raine
couldn't help noticing that Lilith had prepared Gwen
well. She was a font of questions, all of which the
Stevensons answered openly and honestly.

"What if there's something wrong with the baby?"
Gwen asked. "I've tried to take good care of myself.
I don't drink and I've never done drugs or smoked
any kind of cigarettes, regular ones or pot. Mama
Ida makes sure I eat right and exercise and get regular checkups, but all the books still say that things
can go wrong. Would you still want the baby if she
wasn't perfect?"

"Of course we would," Terri said.

"We have insurance that would cover any health
expenses, so that wouldn't be a concern," Bill added.

"And since a child would be the answer to all our
prayers, we'd love any one God might bless us with."
Terri's response was too heartfelt not to be sincere.

"What if she turns out to be gay? Would you kick
her out?"

Terri laughed a little at that. "Darling, I grew up

in San Francisco. Bill and I both have gay friends. There's no way we'd turn any child of ours away."

"Not even if she gets pregnant when she's a teenager?"

"Not even then."

Gwen valiantly blinked back tears. "It's too bad you don't want a teenager," she said with a forced, wobbly smile. "Then you could adopt me."

Even as they all shared a little laugh at that, Raine found the mood decidedly bittersweet. Then Terri sobered. "Bill and I have given a great deal of thought to this and have decided that we're proponents of open adoption. You're welcome to be part of your daughter's life, if you'd like."

"I don't know." Gwen bit her teeth into her lower lip, as if to stop it from quivering. "It might be too hard."

"Well, the final decision is up to you." Terri reached across the wrought-iron table and covered Gwen's hand with one tanned from days spent working in gardens and vineyards. "The amount of involvement in her life is up to you to choose."

A single tear escaped to trail down the teenager's cheek. Then another. She wiped them away with the backs of her hands, looking like a forlorn urchin. The funereal black dress she'd worn for this important occasion only made her face appear paler.

"What if I want her back?"

It was the Stevenson's turn to look concerned. They exchanged a look. "Of course you're given time to change your mind," Terri assured her.

"Do you think you might want to call the adoption off?" Bill asked in his quiet way.

Gwen swallowed visibly. Then turned her swimming gaze out over the strait where a cruise boat, with *Midnight Sun* painted in black script on gleaming white, was heading out to the sea.

"No." It was a ragged whisper. The teenager closed her eyes and took a long breath that had the rest of them taking one right along with her. "No," she said more firmly. "You can give her more than I ever could. You can keep her safe and she'll live in this nice house, and you'll be able to send her to college." She took another deep, obviously painful breath that caused Raine to bite her own lip.

"I know I'll always miss her, and probably feel bad on her birthday and on Mother's Day for a long time, but Lilith is right when she says that this isn't about me. It's about my baby. And what's right for her."

The tears were flowing openly now. Streaming not just down Gwen's cheeks, Terri's, Savannah's, and Raine's as well. Lilith, too, was weeping silently, Bill blew his nose, and as she pressed a Kleenex beneath her eyes, Raine noticed that even Ida's eyes were unnaturally bright.

"There's just one thing," Gwen said from the comforting protection of the arm Lilith had put around her shoulder.

"Anything," Terri said without hesitation.

"If she ever needs anything, like a blood transfusion, or a kidney, or a bone-marrow transplant, or anything like that you might not be able to give her, will you promise to call me first?"

"Absolutely," Terri and Bill promised together.

There were more tears. More hugs. Finally, the papers Dan had brought with him were signed and they left the winery headed back to Coldwater Cove.

"I think you did the right thing, Gwen," Raine said into the silence. "For both you and your baby."

"I know," the teenager sniffled as she huddled against the window in the back seat. "But it's still so hard."

"Of course it is," Ida said. She glanced into the rearview mirror. "Which is only partly why I'm proud to know you."

"Really?"

"You bet. You're definitely one of the bravest, most unselfish people I've ever met."

"That's a nice thing to say."

"It's the truth."

"Oh, look, darling." Lilith said suddenly. In the distance, rising from a silvery mist, a rainbow arced over the mountains. "It's a sign. From the Goddess that everything is going to turn out all right."

Gwen didn't answer. But as she cast a glance up into the rearview mirror, Raine thought the teenager looked a bit more hopeful about her future.

All too aware that they'd become a subject of speculation in Coldwater Cove, Raine hadn't hesitated to accept Jack's invitation to escape to Seattle so they could spend an entire night together.

"Don't be foolish," Ida said briskly when she suggested canceling in case Gwen went into labor. "First births take several hours. In the off chance she does have to go to the hospital, you'll have plenty of time to get there."

"If you're sure."

"Oh, for heaven's sake, darling," Lilith said. "I'll be the first to admit that I haven't exactly been a model of propriety over the years, but it is possible to carry duty too far."

"One of the reasons I stayed here was to be around when Gwen had her baby," Raine reminded her mother. But not the only reason. During the past days the tensions had eased between them as Raine tried to focus on the positive things about Lilith—her zest for living life to the fullest, her humor, her ability to always look for that silver lining no matter how dark the cloud—and not take the negative so personally. They were still at the baby-step stage. But in the past two weeks they'd made more progress than in the entire previous thirty years of Raine's life.

"Please, Raine," Gwen said. "I'd feel horribly guilty if you stayed home just for me."

Raine hesitated, even as she longed to accept their permission to go. "If you're sure."

"We're sure!" all three shouted at once just as Jack pulled into the driveway.

Feeling as free as Savannah's hawk when it soared into the sky, Raine picked up her overnight bag and ran out to meet him.

Four hours later, Raine was sitting across from Jack in the Lighthouse Restaurant, high atop the Seattle Windsor Palace hotel.

"God, you are gorgeous." He lifted a glass of the champagne he'd ordered in a silent toast. "Beauty, intelligence, and courage, all wrapped up in one package. The gods were definitely generous to you when they were handing out gifts, Harvard."

She'd never had a man talk to her the way Jack did. Never would she have believed any other man if he had. "While you obviously received the gift of blarney." She smiled at him over the rim of the crystal flute.

"It's not blarney if it's true." He leaned across the table and skimmed a fingertip beneath her eyes. "The shadows are gone. And you seem more relaxed."

"I am." It was the truth. She belatedly realized that she hadn't had a headache for days. "However, if you keep touching me that way, my nerves are going to get all tangled."

"No problem. We'll just go back downstairs to our room and untangle them again."

The memory of their predinner lovemaking caused that now-familiar warmth to flood into her cheeks, making Raine wonder why it was that she'd never blushed before knowing Jack. Because, she answered her own rhetorical question, she hadn't had all that much to blush about before Jack.

"You promised me crab cakes."

"True." He leaned back in his chair and lifted his own glass of champagne to his lips, the long-stemmed crystal flute looking even more flimsy in his large hand. "But you can't blame me for being distracted." Desire thickened his voice, causing a thrill to skim up her spine. "I suppose it would damage your hard-earned professional reputation if I were to drag you beneath the table and have my way with you."

"Is that what you feel like doing? Dragging me beneath the table?"

"For starters."

Raine had never flirted; had never known how to flirt. But she was discovering that Jack made it easy.

"I don't believe you'd actually do it." She stroked the stem of the champagne glass with her fingers in a blatantly seductive way that, from the way his eyes darkened, she knew wasn't lost on him.

"You don't?"

"No. Because you have your own sterling reputation to protect. Everyone knows that Dudley Doright would never ravish a woman in a public restaurant."

"Maybe Sweet Nell never tempted him the way you are me." He tossed back his wine. "How hungry are you?"

"Not very. Not now."

"How does ordering something up from room service later sound? Much, much later."

"It sounds glorious." She took the snowy damask napkin from her lap, placed it on the table, and stood up.

On his feet in a flash, Jack tossed some bills onto the table, placed his hand on her back in a proprietary way, and led her out of the restaurant.

"Have I thanked you for buying that dress?" he asked as the elevator doors closed behind them.

It was the flowered one she'd been trying on at The Dancing Deer when he'd brought his daughter to the store in order to exchange underwear. The one she'd sworn she was not going to buy. But had, with him in mind.

"Yes. But not in the last twenty minutes." Dizzy with an appetite that had nothing to do with any need for French food, Raine twined her arms around his neck and leaned against his hard body.

"Then I've definitely been remiss." When he lowered his mouth to within a breath from hers, Raine held on tighter, bracing herself for his kiss. But instead he began nibbling at her neck. "But don't worry, sweetheart. I have every intention of making it up to you."

The woman in her was turning weak and woozy. The lawyer couldn't resist a challenge. "I suppose I'll just have to take a wait-and-see attitude on that." Her voice, which had started out courtroom cool, skimmed up the scale when he nipped her ear.

"Lord, I never would have guessed that I'd find contrariness in a female such a turn-on." He switched targets and gave her chin a teasing nip. "As for waiting, now that you bring it up, it sounds like a pretty good idea. After all, I've already proven I can make you scream." His hand slipped between them and cupped her breast. "Perhaps this time I'll see if I can make you beg."

"I could have you on your knees." Her voice was half moan, half laugh.

"In a heartbeat." When his thumb brushed against a nipple, Raine heard the rasp of roughened skin against scarlet silk. "Especially since that was already in the game plan."

He released her breast to capture her chin between his fingers, holding her gaze to his. His eyes burned in his rugged face like two hot coals; a nerve jumped in his cheek. Raine had never seen him looking so dangerous. So uncivilized.

A need rose up inside her—so huge, so powerful, that it took her breath away. She drew in a deep gulp of air, and then his mouth was on hers, his kiss hot and greedy and wonderful. The thought that they were in a public elevator briefly flashed through her mind, but then he lifted her off her feet and pulled her even tighter against him and caution spun away. He was a hot, fully aroused male and dear heavens, how she wanted him.

"I need you." Teeth scraped as she gasped the admission out. "I've never needed any one like I need you."

His rough laugh vibrated against her lips as the elevator dinged. "Believe me, darlin', I know the feeling."

Behaving as if carrying women through hotels was a common occurrence, Jack nodded to the elderly couple dressed in formal wear who'd been waiting for the elevator. "Good evening," he said.

"Oh, God," Raine giggled as he strode down the hallway toward their room. That was another thing that had changed. She *never* giggled. "I think we shocked them."

"If that's all it takes, then it's a good thing they're not going to witness the rest of the night." He deftly managed to unlock the door with the key card while still holding her in his arms.

After carrying her over the threshold, he lowered her to the floor. Her high heels sank into the plush carpeting. He shrugged off his suit jacket and tossed it onto a nearby chair, then backed a few feet away.

"Don't move," he murmured huskily. "I just want to look at you." When he silently twirled a finger, Raine turned. After she'd gone full circle and faced him again, the heat in Jack's dark eyes made her a little wobbly in the impossibly impractical and outrageously sexy and dangerously spindly hibiscus red high heels Savannah had pressed on her before she'd left the house.

"That really is one dynamite dress," he said finally. "Too bad you're not going to get to wear it all that long." He drew her back into his arms. The zipper slid down, exposing her back to the air.

"Are you cold?" he asked when she shivered.

"No." She lifted her eyes to his. "Actually, I think I'm burning up."

His answering laugh skimmed beneath her heated flesh, stimulating nerve endings in erogenous zones she'd never known she possessed until she'd made love with Jack. "The trick," he said, as he pushed the silk off her shoulders, allowing it to skim down her body, "is not to put the fires out too soon."

The dress fell to the floor in a pool of crimson silk. Still in the unaccustomed heels, Raine managed to step out of it, relieved when she didn't destroy the sensual mood by toppling over. The heat in his gaze rose even higher when he viewed the strapless ivory lace teddy and thigh-high stockings, making Raine vastly grateful that she'd surrendered when her mother and sister had insisted on raiding their lingerie drawers.

She watched his Adam's apple bob viciously as he swallowed. "I see you pulled out the heavy artillery."

"It's not often I have an opportunity to have you at a disadvantage." Feminine instincts kicked in. "I decided I may as well make the most of it."

Removing his tie didn't go quite as smoothly as it had in all her fantasies, but Jack didn't seem to notice her slight clumsiness. She slipped her fingers under the buttons of his shirt and reveled in the warmth of his skin.

"Are you seducing me?"

"Absolutely." His shirt proved easier than the tie, and Raine loved the way he sucked in his stomach as her fingers skimmed over his flesh. "Is it working?"

When she reached his belt, Jack caught hold of her wrist and pressed her hand against the front of his dress slacks. "What do you think?"

He stirred against her palm, huge and full and ready. The knowledge that she was responsible for such a powerful male response caused another thrill of female power to rush through her.

"I think you're magnificent," she murmured as she unfastened his belt buckle. She pulled the belt through the loops, then tossed it aside. It landed on top of his discarded jacket, then slid to the carpeting. Neither Jack nor Raine noticed.

"You're going to have to take your shoes off," she instructed as she moved to the button at the top of his dress slacks. "To make this work."

"Had a lot of practice undressing men, have you?" he asked blandly as he nevertheless toed off the cordovan loafers she was extremely grateful he'd chosen to wear in place of the usual boots.

"Actually, there's not all that much to it," Raine responded blithely. "Unlike women's clothing, there aren't any hidden fasteners to get caught or delicate lace to tear. Just durable white cotton—"

"You haven't finished yet. You'd think all those years in the courtroom would have taught you not to leap to judgement."

"Ah, but a good attorney factors in previous evidence." Although it was a little tricky, she managed to lower the zipper without causing any dire damage, then began sliding the charcoal gray slacks down his legs. "See? Just as I said. White briefs."

"You mean *boring* white briefs."

"You could never be boring." Her sultry voice was part honey, part smoke.

Expectation pounded hot and heavy in Jack's blood, and when she pressed her open mouth against the placket of those ordinary Jockey briefs, he bit the inside of his cheek, afraid he'd explode before things even got started.

"Sweet Jesus." His fingers tangled in her hair, but when he would have pulled her away, she murmured a refusal and tightened her hands around his thighs. She was on her knees, looking up at him, her amber eyes as earnest as he'd ever seen them.

"Every time we've made love, you've been the one doing all the work."

"You haven't exactly been passive, sweetheart." Jack knew, when he was an old man, looking back on the golden moments of his life, the memory of this woman writhing on the backseat of the Suburban, short, utilitarian nails raking down his back, would remain as crystal clear as it was today.

"I know." The color he loved to watch bloomed on her cheeks. Then spread across her chest like a fever rash. "But you've always been the one to initiate things. Not that I'm complaining," she said quickly. "I just want you to feel as wonderful and as crazy as I do, when I surrender all my control to you."

Jack had known, from the beginning, how important control was to Raine. But for the first time, he truly understood the value of the gift she'd given him. How could he give her any less?

He held both hands out to his sides. "I'm all yours."

That proved to be an understatement as Raine quickly proved herself to be fully in command. Of his body, his senses, and his heart. As they lay on the bed, her hands were never still, fluttering over him with the light teasing touch of butterfly wings. Then, just when he least expected it, they turned stronger, searching out and exploiting hidden centers of passion so intense it skimmed the edge of pain.

His flesh turned hot and damp beneath her roving touch; his muscles tensed as her lips followed the flaming path her hands were burning into him. As his stomach muscles clenched, then quivered, he reached for her, but it felt as if he were caught in a dream; his arms were heavy, his movements, slow. Too slow to catch her as she moved over the mattress, over him.

Their room was situated high above Seattle, allowing privacy even though they hadn't taken time to close the drapes. Far below, city lights, sparkling like fallen stars, stretched out to the mysterious indigo darkness of Elliot Bay.

Through his dazed senses, Jack realized Raine was quickening the pace, her hands streaking faster, her mouth hotter, and more greedy. His breath clogged in his lungs, smoke clouded his mind. He couldn't speak. Couldn't think. There was nothing to do but to feel.

Bathed in silvery moondust that made her flesh gleam like pearls, she was straddling him, rocking against him, causing the last bit of blood to rush from his head to his groin. Desperate for the feel of flesh against flesh, to be deep inside her, he tore the frothy bit of ivory silk and lace away. His hands dug into her waist.

"Now." His voice was rough with a pent up need bordering on the violent.

Her eyes flashed, her moist lips were parted; her hair was damp, her body, hot. "Now," she agreed breathlessly.

Raine cried out as he pulled her down onto him at the same time he arched off the mattress, impaling her, claiming her.

She froze, her expression stunned. Jack's last thought, before she rode them both into the flames, was that the sight of Raine astride him, cast in molten silver by the streaming moonlight, was the sexiest thing he'd ever seen.

❧22❧

Raine woke slowly, reluctant to leave the cozy little hut that her dream lover had built from palm fronds at the edge of the sugar white sand. The first thing she saw when she opened her eyes was Jack, sprawled in a wing chair beside the window. He was wearing jeans and a chambray shirt he hadn't bothered to button. All it took was the sight of that broad chest to assure her that last night's passion had been neither hallucination nor dream. The warmth in his eyes only reconfirmed that fact.

"How long have you been awake?"

"A while. I ordered breakfast, but you were sleeping so soundly, I didn't want to wake you."

"Oh." She glanced over at the clock radio, amazed at the time. "I'm sorry. I can't remember ever sleeping in so late."

"You were probably worn out by all the exercise."

She felt the heat flood into her cheeks again. "Perhaps."

The friendly sensuality gleaming in his eyes had her wanting to drag him back to bed. Every nerve in her body felt wonderfully alive. She felt wonderfully alive. It was all she could do not to stretch like a lazy cat. Raine couldn't recall ever feeling so exquisite after a night of hot, unbridled sex. Actually, she couldn't recall ever experiencing a night of such hot, unbridled sex, but that wasn't the point.

"I'm not exactly at my best in the morning."

"If I remember correctly, and I do, the last time we made love was just before dawn. And you were terrific."

His grin was a wicked slash that had her imagining him as a pirate, standing, legs braced, on the deck of his ship, the Jolly Roger flying overhead in a stiff ocean breeze, cutlass in hand. Dear heavens, she really was crazy. Crazy about him, she admitted.

"I think I'll take a shower."

"Sounds like a plan." He stood up, crossed over to the bed, lifted her from the love-tangled sheets, and carried her into the bathroom, where they spent a very long time driving each other crazy.

Somehow, when he realized that they could be in danger of drowning, Jack managed to get the water turned off and Raine wrapped in a thick terry cloth robe with the gold hotel crown insignia. Since he'd always felt a little silly wearing a bathrobe—the last time had been when he'd been recovering from being shot and the nurse, who'd he'd decided had been Atilla the Hun in a previous life, insisted—he put his jeans and shirt back on.

They were drinking coffee, engaged in the type of morning-after small talk that lovers who have begun to grow comfortable with each other do, when Jack decided that the time had come just to lay his cards on the table.

He stood up, took hold of her hands, brought her to her feet as well, touched his lips to her temple, and felt her heartbeat, a stepped up rhythm that echoed his own. That's what he wanted—that unity of heart and body. Of mind and soul.

"I love you."

Jack was not surprised when she stiffened in his arms. Disappointed, but not surprised. "You can't."

"Sure I can." Despite her discomfort, he was determined to forge on. "You may have been a bit of a pain in the butt in the beginning," he said in a teasing tone designed to calm her nerves, "but you're certainly not unlovable."

"It's too soon."

"Just because it happened fast doesn't mean that it isn't right."

"Falling in love wasn't part of the deal."

"I don't remember making any deal."

"Well, perhaps we didn't state the terms out loud," Raine allowed. "But it was certainly implied that we were going to have an affair. A brief affair," she stressed. "Just while I was in Coldwater Cove. I don't want you to love me."

"Too bad. And too late."

Raine pulled away and went over to the window, where she pressed her forehead against the glass and stared out at Elliot Bay. Wishing he possessed the power to read minds, Jack folded his arms and waited. Since a cop had to learn patience or turn in his badge, Jack forced himself to let the silence spin out.

Finally, she turned back toward him. "I don't know what to say."

"You don't have to say anything."

"Yes. I do. But I've got so many thoughts going through my head right now, I can't sort them all out."

Jack was about to let her off the hook when the phone rang. Frustrated at the interruption, he scooped up the receiver.

"O'Halloran," he ground out. "Oh, hi Ida." He exchanged a look with Raine. "Sure. She's right here."

Raine took the receiver he was holding out toward her. "What's wrong? . . . Oh, no. Are you certain she's all right? Of course we'll take the first ferry back. And give her my love."

After exchanging goodbyes, she hung up.

"Lilith will be impossible to live with now," she said with a faint smile. "I know she'll insist she predicted this with those damn tarot cards."

"Maybe she did. How is the kid?"

"Fine. She's only a couple centimeters dilated, so Ida says we have plenty of time to get there."

He pulled the schedule out of the front pocket of his jeans. "Looks as if we've got a couple hours to kill before the ferry to Coldwater Cove leaves. You know what you said that first time? About fast being okay?"

"I wasn't thinking very clearly at the time, but the words do ring a bell."

"So, how serious were you?"

Momentarily putting aside all concerns about the future, Raine smiled, with her lips and with her eyes. "Fast sounds terrific."

* * *

As they packed to leave Seattle after making love one last time, neither Jack nor Raine spoke of his earlier declaration. Finally, standing on the deck of the ferry on their way home, Raine broke the silence.

"What would happen," she asked cautiously, "if, just hypothetically speaking, I were to say I loved you?"

"Why don't you try it?" he suggested mildly. "And see what happens."

When she didn't answer, he sighed. "You, of all people should know that life doesn't come with gold-plated guarantees, Harvard. Every time you go into a courtroom, you don't really have any idea how things are going to turn out. You might win. Or you might lose. Life's a gamble, darlin'. Even getting out of bed in the morning is taking a risk."

"That's a very neat analogy. But there's one thing wrong with it. When I go into a courtroom, I have *some* power over my own destiny. My client's destiny. I'm a good lawyer—"

"I never doubted that for a minute."

"Thank you. But my point is that I know how to play the legal game. I know the rules."

When her obvious vulnerability brought out his protective side, Jack was forced to wonder if a modern man of the '90s should even want the woman he loved, a woman more than capable of slaying her own dragons, to need him. *Hell yes*, he decided.

"After Peg died, I drove my family nuts because I kept turning down their efforts to set me up," he said quietly. "Because I didn't believe I'd ever be lucky enough to find another woman I could love with all my heart. Like I do you. A woman I wanted to spend the rest of my life with. Like I do you."

She drew in a deep, hitching breath. "I don't have any experience with love, Jack. I'm afraid of doing something wrong. Something that will ruin it."

Knowing how much that admission cost her only made Jack love her more. "It isn't that easy to screw up if it's meant to be. And this is."

A gust of wind coming off the water blew her hair across her cheek. Her hand trembled as she brushed it away. "Let's also say, hypothetically speaking again, that we got married. Where would we live?"

"Is that a prerequisite to you falling in love with me?"

"No. Of course not. I just like to know where I'm going."

"Sometimes it's not the destination, but the journey."

"You sound just like Lilith." she complained, the frown now carving canyons into her forehead. "You have to understand. . . . I'm not that way. I don't *think* that way." Her eyes glistened with suspicious moisture. "I've never been a person to trust fate or believe in destiny, or to just go with the flow. I need to know where I'm going to be next week. Next year. Five years from now."

"I can understand that." Given her unstable childhood, Jack could, indeed, understand her need for guideposts. But that didn't mean he was willing to stand by and let her fear of the unknown keep them apart.

"If there's one thing that Peg's death taught me it's that we never really know what's around the cor-

ner. We thought we had our life all figured out, too.
I was going to make detective, which would get me
off the streets, because she worried about me being
killed. And, to tell the truth, so did I. Just a little.

"We never talked about it, but I think that in the
back of both our minds, we figured I'd be the one
to go first. Meanwhile, since she couldn't have children, we were planning to adopt more kids—at least
one, maybe two. But then we discovered the hard
way that the old cliché about God laughing when
you make plans is all too true."

She bit her lip and turned away again, staring out
over the water that the setting sun was turning a
brilliant copper and gold. Jack waited.

"Everything I've ever wanted, everything I am, is
tied up with being a lawyer," she said in a quiet
voice that was barely audible over the hum of the
ferry's engines.

"If that were true, it'd be the most pitiful thing
I've ever heard. But as good an attorney as you are,
you're more than that, Raine. A great deal more."

"Would you move to New York?"

"Would you ask me to?"

"No." She turned back toward him and shook her
head. "I can't imagine you being happy in New York.
Though Harriet would probably be thrilled," she
added on an afterthought.

"Who's Harriet?"

"A woman in our office. She's got a thing for
alpha males."

"And you consider me an alpha male?"

"Absolutely." A faint smile shone through the
moisture brimming in her eyes. Her lovely, distressed eyes.

"Hypothetically speaking," Jack qualified, wanting to see her smile again.

"No. That's the absolute truth."

In the distance, Jack could begin to make out Coldwater Cove's green hills and decided they'd spent enough precious time on hypothetical conversations.

"I sure don't have all the answers, Raine. Hell, I don't even know all the questions. But I do know we shouldn't be wasting whatever time we have left together. So, why don't you come over here?"

She hesitated only a moment. Then went into his arms.

By the time Raine arrived at the hospital, Gwen had been settled into bed in the birthing room, a fetal monitor strapped about her belly, an IV of saline solution placed in the back of her hand, and was well into labor.

Having always felt the need for control, Raine hated feeling so helpless as she took her turn comforting Gwen. What if something went wrong? Granted, contrary to what could have happened if Ida hadn't taken her home from the ferry so many months ago, the teenager was strong and healthy. And, between Ida and the doctor, she'd had excellent prenatal care.

Still, even in modern times things could go wrong. Terrible, frightening things that hovered in Raine's mind like monsters in a night closet. In an odd twist of roles, she was a nervous wreck, while Lilith remained absolutely calm, soothing the mother-to-be with encouraging words and gentle hands. Yet more proof, Raine thought, that her formerly orderly world had turned upside down.

Since they didn't want to overwhelm Gwen, the family took turns sitting with her throughout the labor. Savannah had gone to call the Stevensons again, to update them on the situation, when Gwen went into transition. As she moistened the teenagers chapped lips with pieces of ice, and allowed fingernails to dig into the back of her hand, instead of feeling queasy, as she feared she might, Raine found herself thinking of Jack, who'd been patiently waiting, taking her downstairs to the cafeteria for coffee breaks and offering the reassurance she'd come to expect from him.

She thought about how her life had changed in such a short time, thought about how much more little things—like the sunshine glistening on a field of wildflowers, a mother's touch, a little girl's carefree laughter, and a man's warm smile—had come to mean to her. And most of all, she imagined herself in Gwen's place, carrying Jack's child. Giving birth to a brother or sister for Amy. Remarkably, rather than terrifying her, the fantasy was eminently appealing.

"The baby's crowning, Gwen." Ida's voice broke into Raine's thoughts. Although Ida wasn't officially Gwen's obstetrician, nothing could have kept her from being with the at-risk teenager she'd rescued from the streets.

"Just a little bit more, Gwen," the doctor said encouragingly. "A couple more really strong pushes should do it."

Panting harshly in a way that had Raine worrying she was on the verge of hyperventilating, Gwen pushed again. As the infant girl slid from Gwen's womb into the world, Raine suddenly knew what it was to witness a miracle. When the expected cry didn't come, she understood true terror.

The nurse quickly, deftly, suctioned the baby's nose and mouth, and an instant later the screech that escaped the rosebud lips shattered the hushed, expectant stillness. The baby was placed on Gwen's stomach while the doctor clamped the umbilical cord.

"As perfect a moment as this is, unfortunately you've still got a little bit of work left to do," the doctor told Gwen.

Assured that the new mother was in good hands, and more than a little overwhelmed by the emotional impact of what she'd witnessed, Raine escaped to the waiting room in order to regain her composure.

Jack stood up as she entered, took one look at her face, and nodded in understanding. "Nothing like it, is there? Since we had an open adoption, we were able to be there when Amy was born. I decided at the time that short of having a bush suddenly start burning in front of us, it's probably as close as any of us mortals will come to witnessing a miracle."

"That's pretty much what I was thinking."

He drew her into his arms, brushed away an errant tear that had escaped, and lowered his forehead to hers. "I love you, Raine."

"I know." Shouldn't a woman be thrilled when a man like this professed his love? Especially after she'd spent a good part of the day fantasizing about having his children? "I love you, too, Jack." She drew in a deep, shuddering breath. "So much."

He drew back, put a finger beneath her chin, and tipped her face up to his. Rather than the irritation she feared, or the frustration she knew he had a right to feel, his expression was one of infinite patience. The kind of patience a man who'd stand in the rain for hours to protect three teenage girls would need to have. "You don't sound all that happy about it."

"I think what I am is scared."

"Don't feel like the Lone Ranger." His hands were stroking her back in a soothing way that caused smoldering embers to flare.

Raine told herself that she should feel better knowing that she wasn't the only one of them who felt as if she were on the verge of leaping out of a plane without a parachute. She should. But she didn't.

"I don't know if I can give you what you want. What you need." She drew in a deep, painful breath. What you deserve, she thought but did not say.

"Now there you go, underestimating yourself again." He brushed a finger across her downturned lips. "You're everything I want, Harvard. Everything I need."

"You don't understand." Instead of backing away, she clung tighter, hating herself for giving him such mixed messages, but needing his strength. "The woman you think you love." Another breath, more painful than the first. "She isn't really me."

She felt his deep, rumbling chuckle as he rested his chin atop her head. "I've always admired your intelligence, Harvard. But that statement just flew right by me."

"I don't do things like this." Because she feared

that if she didn't let go now, she never would, she forced herself to back away. In a vain attempt to work off the nerves that were tangling inside her, she began to pace.

"Like what? Kiss in hospital waiting rooms? Because if that's the only problem, I promise we'll just stay out of hospital. How do you feel about home births?"

She'd reached the window, spun around, fisted her hands on her hips, and gave him a frustrated look. "You're not taking this seriously."

"I told you. I take everything about you seriously, Raine. Now, I understand that under normal conditions, you probably wouldn't have made love with a guy you only knew a few days—"

"Of course I wouldn't." She cut him off as she began to pace again. "Never in a million years. Unless . . ." She stopped in midstride and shut her eyes.

He was standing in front of her. She felt him. Wanted him. Oh, God, so much.

"Unless you loved him," Jack finished her statement up for her, "and were sure, not in your head, which can perform all sorts of fancy mental gymnastics, but deep down in your heart where it really counts, that he loved you, too."

She pressed her hand against his chest, unable to decide whether she wanted to push him away or pull him to her. Raine figured she'd probably suffered more episodes of indecision in the past two weeks than during her entire six years practicing law.

"Oh, dear. I'm sorry to interrupt." At the familiar voice, Raine spun toward the waiting-room doorway, never so glad to see her mother as she was at this minute. "That's all right. We were just wrapping up anyway." She ignored Jack's faint chuckle behind her. "How's Gwen doing?"

"Physically, she's fine. The baby's all cleaned up and looking like a little blue-eyed doll. The Stevensons are on their way."

"How's she doing emotionally?"

"As well as can be expected. According to Savannah, the Stevensons are floating on air."

"I can imagine." Raine sighed. "It's so wonderful. And so sad."

"It's also for the best," Lilith reminded her.

"I suppose so. . . . I'll be right there."

Lilith's gaze went from Raine to Jack and back to Raine again. "Take your time."

"Speaking of time, I need some," Raine told Jack when they were alone again. "To think."

"I suppose, under the circumstances, that's reasonable."

Before she could thank him for being so understanding, he ducked his head and kissed her—a quick, hard kiss that ended too soon and left her head spinning. "Think fast."

With that he left. But as she leaned against the wall and closed her eyes, she could hear the tap of his boots on the tile floor of the hallway. And the unmistakably cheery sound of him whistling *My Girl*.

❦ 23 ❧

The Stevensons returned to the hospital the following day, arriving at the same time the family arrived to take Gwen home. The couple's mood was appropriately subdued, but their joy radiated so brightly, Raine almost understood her mother's alleged ability to read auras.

They were exchanging slightly stilted greetings when a hospital volunteer showed up in the room with the camera. "Would you like a picture taken with your baby?" she asked with a perkiness ill-suited to the occasion. The sudden silence her question created was thick enough to be cut with a knife.

"I don't know." The desperately needy look on Gwen's face nearly broke Raine's heart. The girl was sitting on the edge of the bed, the suitcase Lilith had brought to the hospital last night at her feet.

"I think you should." Taking charge of the uncomfortable situation, Terri placed the infant girl in Gwen's arms. She was wearing a pink knitted cap that was a gift from the hospital and a pink drawstring nightgown covered with white hearts. "In fact, we should take two. One for you and one for your baby, so she'll always have a picture of the mommy whose tummy she grew in for her first nine months."

Gwen looked more than a little nervous as she held the wobbly little pink-capped head steady and managed a faint, equally wobbly smile for the camera. There was another strained silence as they all waited for the image to appear on the Polaroid film.

"Whatever you ultimately decide about keeping in touch, I'll make certain Lily gets this when we tell her about how she was adopted," Terri promised.

"Thank you." Gwen's voice was soft, but, Raine was relieved to see, surprisingly steady. "I wrote her a letter last night. So she'll know how much I loved her." She took the envelope from the pocket of her oversize denim top and, since Terri's arms were filled with the baby again, handed it to Bill.

After tearfully thanking Gwen again, Terri left with her new daughter and husband.

"Well." Gwen exhaled a long shuddering breath. "I guess that's that." Her eyes were swimming, but Raine thought she seemed at peace with her decision. "They're going to make good parents."

"Absolutely," Savannah promised.

Although the mood was not exactly festive as they drove home to Coldwater Cove, Raine could sense the burden that had been lifted from Gwen's shoulders. And when she began discussing medical schools with Ida, Raine knew that the teenager had begun to move on with her life.

Raine spent the next three days taking a long, hard look at her life. Her options. If she didn't have

her career to think of, she'd stay here in Coldwater
Cove with her family. With Jack.

But the problem was, while she might honestly
wish differently, Raine knew she needed more of a
challenge than small-town law could offer. However,
whenever she thought about returning to New York,
which, compared to Coldwater Cove, was as user-
friendly as a convertible submarine, she'd experience the twinges of a headache and was forced to
stop by the market and buy a new bottle of Maalox.

In a perfect world, she wouldn't be forced to make
these choices. Unfortunately, Raine had discovered
at a very young age that there was no such thing as
a perfect world. There had to be a solution, she kept
assuring herself as she walked in the lush spring
garden Gwen had planted and continued to tend in
Ida's backyard, rocked endless miles in the porch
swing, and paced the kitchen, as she went over and
over the options with Savannah, always ending back
at the same place. Jack and a family she'd never
dared dream she could have, or her career. Coldwater Cove or New York. She was an intelligent
woman, she kept reminding herself. There had to be
a solution. Finally, early one morning, just when she
thought she'd go crazy from wandering through her
mental maze all day and most of the nights, a possible solution occurred to her. She leaped out of bed
and made two calls. One to Oliver Choate. The second to the man who held the final piece of her
life's puzzle.

After dropping Amy off at her best friend Sarah
Young's house, where the two girls were going to
spend the day playing Barbies, Jack drove to Port

Angeles. He arrived home just as a new fire engine red Ford Expedition pulled into his driveway. He climbed out of the Suburban, folded his arms, and enjoyed the view of those long, slender legs climbing out of the driver's seat.

"Nice truck."

"Thank you. It's new."

"I figured that from the temporary tags. So, who does it belong to?"

"Me."

"Isn't four-wheel drive overkill for the city?"

"I have no idea. Since I don't intend to drive it in the city."

"I see." He was beginning to. Or at least he hoped he was.

Raine closed the distance between them. "I'm not going to be driving it in New York because I'm not going back. As it turns out, Dan has quite a few deals pending between old friends from the Silicon Valley and Seattle-area computer companies. In fact, thanks to referrals, he's got more business than he can handle alone. Which is why he jumped at the idea of taking on a partner."

"That partner being you."

"None other."

"What about your job back east? Are you saying you walked away from that?"

"Not exactly. I called Oliver Choate this morning. He's the founder of Choate, Plimpton, Wells & Sullivan. The firm has been wanting to get into Eastern Rim business, but it's been difficult from the East Coast. We worked out a deal where I'll work for them on a consulting basis. Dan thought it was a great idea."

"I'm sure he did. Sounds as if you've got every-thing figured out."

"Not quite." He watched her take a deep breath. "So, were you serious about getting married?"

"I suppose that depends on whether you want me to be serious or not." It was going to be okay, Jack thought. They were going to be okay.

"You're ducking the question, Sheriff. If you re-fuse to answer, I may have to go track down Judge Wally and have him hold you in contempt."

"Never happen. Wally's wife just happens to be my second cousin on my daddy's side."

"And you O'Hallorans stick together."

"Like glue. . . . You know what they say about a picture being worth a thousand words?"

"Yes, but you're out of order. And you still haven't answered my question."

"I'm getting there. If you're going to move home to Coldwater Cove, you're going to have to learn pa-tience, Harvard. Since we country boys tend to like to take things a little slow. Sorta heightens the antic-ipation." He took a folder from his denim-jacket pocket and handed it to her. "Here's exhibit one. I picked it up in Port Angeles this morning."

The cover of the folder featured a lush, romantic palm-tree-fringed white beach. Adding a splash of brilliant color to the travel poster scene, a shim-mering rainbow arced over an aquamarine lagoon.

"Tickets?"

"To Bora Bora. You said you've always wanted to go to some tropical island. I figured this one might not be such a bad spot for a honeymoon."

"A honeymoon implies marriage."

"Smart and sexy. That's definitely an irresistible

combination. . . . Next, I'd like the record to show that I, too, made a few calls to some old-friends-turned-small-town-police-chiefs who professed to be more than willing to hire me onto their police forces. All within commuting distance of Manhattan."

"You were willing to do that? For me?"

"For us. However, since you seemed to have come up with an equally clever solution, we may as well move on so I can put my next exhibit into evidence. The one that goes to relevance."

He dragged her up against him and kissed her so hard and so long that by the time they finally came up for air, Raine had nearly forgotten her plan to make him suffer.

"Well." She had to fight to catch her breath. "That certainly rules out reasonable doubt."

"God, I love it when you talk like a lawyer." He nipped at her ear and turned her into a puddle of need.

"I am a lawyer," she managed as he stroked his finger down her throat, lingering where her pulse was beating furiously.

"I know." His caressing touch continued downward, slipping below the neckline of her blouse. "A cop and a lawyer. The gods must be having one helluva laugh over that one." He tormented her with kisses as he unbuttoned her blouse. "So, Counselor, what would you say to playing a little stop and frisk?"

He'd pressed her against the side of her new truck, effectively trapping her as he slipped his knee between her legs and made her ache. "I'd say a change of venue is definitely in order."

"Good idea." Without taking his mouth from hers, he carried her into the house and up the stairs, where he dropped her onto the bed.

It was on her second bounce that she noticed the photograph was gone. She'd come to terms with Peg's place in Jack's life. In Amy's life. Still, this proof that she wouldn't have to live with the ghost of his wife between them caused a glorious sense of joy melded with relief.

"So," he said, as he lay down beside her and slid her blouse down her arms. "What's the verdict? Are you going to marry me?"

"Of course I am." She pressed her hands against his chest, where his heart was beating as wildly as her own. "I'll want us to have more children." She pressed her mouth against his. "One would be a nice start. Two would be even better."

He tangled his hands in her hair and tilted her head back. "Are you sure? What about your career?"

"Having a career doesn't preclude having babies. In fact, impatient city girl that I am, I was hoping we might get started on that project today."

He closed his eyes briefly. Then opened them and grinned, that cocky, masculine grin that Raine knew would still have the power to thrill her when she was ninety. "I'm sure as hell not going to argue with that."

This time their lovemaking was different. As if committing to a future together had moved it to a higher plane. When Jack braced himself on his elbows and fixed his dark gaze on hers, Raine looked up into his ruggedly handsome face and knew she'd be forever grateful that fate, and three teenage girls, had brought her to this place in time with this passionate, patient, wonderful man.

As if reading her mind, he smiled as he linked their fingers together. "Welcome home." Then he slipped into her, filling her, loving her.

Home. Having finally discovered her heart's own true place, Raine vowed to never, ever leave again.

⮜Epilogue⮞

The weddings took place in the garden. A garden that Gwen had tended with increased devotion these past two weeks, resulting in a riotous explosion of color. The day dawned bright and sunny and warm, a gift that Lilith attributed to several ancient Celtic goddesses and a complex spell involving star power that Raine didn't even try to understand.

Not wanting to ruin this perfect day, she wasn't about to challenge her mother's belief system. Besides, there was a part of her who, when she thought about all the ways her life had changed—her homecoming, her reconciliation with her mother, being blessed with a man who loved her and a daughter she already adored—couldn't help but wonder if perhaps magic had played a part.

Folding chairs had been set up on the lawn, claimed by various O'Hallorans, Lindstroms, Dottie and Doris Anderson, and so many others who'd come to the house to share the family's joy.

"Don't lock your knees," Cooper Ryan advised as the flutist who'd been at the Beltane ceremony at the Heart of the Hills began to play a traditional wedding march. The music was one of the many compromises Lilith and Raine had managed to achieve. "Or you'll pass out."

"I may anyway," Jack muttered. He put his hand against the front of his white shirtfront. "In fact, I think I might be having a heart attack. Maybe I should have had Ida check me out before the ceremony."

"Well, it's too late now," Cooper said as Amy, clad in a pink dress she'd picked out herself at The Dancing Deer and a new pair of white patent leather Mary Janes, skipped down the white satin runner, energetically throwing rose petals into the air from a white wicker basket. "Lord, she's a doll, Jack. You're a lucky man."

"I know." About this Jack's tone was firm and sure. "Okay. That's it. I can't have a heart attack in front of my own daughter. It'd scar her for life."

"You're both cops," Dan said, laughter in his low voice. "I can't believe you're this scared of getting married."

"It's not the marrying part," Cooper said. "It's all this." He motioned surreptitiously toward the lilac arbor, the puffy white satin bows on the chairs, and all the guests dressed in their Sunday best.

"Just wait until it's your turn." Jack shot him a warning sideways glance. "I'm going to remind you of this."

The best man to both grooms grinned. "I figure we'll just elope to Vegas and get hitched by some Elvis impersonator. It's easier and faster."

"Try telling that to your bride," Cooper advised sagely.

"I will," Dan agreed. "At the first opportunity." He glanced over toward Savannah, who, in her role as maid of honor to her mother and sister was standing on the other side of the aisle. Their eyes met and any guests who might have been looking at either of them would have caught the quick flash of remembered heat.

There was a strum of harp strings. "Jesus, Lilith looks gorgeous, doesn't she?" Cooper asked beneath his breath.

"Gorgeous," both men agreed as the first bride walked down the aisle behind the three teenage bridesmaids.

She was wearing a flowing gown made of some material that caught the sun and looked as if it had been spun from spiderwebs and then dipped in dew. She'd explained that the gown was cut on the bias, and although Cooper had no idea what that meant, it draped over her curvaceous body like a dream. She'd brought out the crystals, but she'd left her left hand bare, awaiting the ring he'd been carrying around in his pocket since the day after he'd arrested her in the park.

When she reached him, her smile, filled with love and a lust for life he knew she'd still possess when she was a hundred, dazzled as it always had.

Another strum of harp strings had the guests turning behind them again. There was a collective intake of breath as Raine appeared, dressed in a white lacy froth of a wedding gown that, had Jack not already discovered that his bride was a closet romantic, would have surprised the hell out of him.

"Oh, Raine looks just like a fairy princess, Daddy." Amy's voice, ringing out above the flute, caused

laughter to ring through the assembled guests.
"She's even prettier than Ariel, isn't she?"

"Absolutely," Jack said, his words directed to his
daughter, but his eyes on the stunning woman who
seemed to be floating toward him. Her eyes, shimmering with love, stayed on his as she approached.

As she walked toward Jack, Raine felt as if she
were walking on air. Listening to him repeat the
words that she'd never expected to hear, let alone
say, Raine knew how solemnly he took those vows.
He was the most loving, honorable man she'd ever
met. And now, wondrously, he was hers. For ever
and ever. Amen. When she held out her hand for
him to slip the woven gold band onto her finger, she
felt the unwavering warmth of his love flow straight
to her heart.

"You may kiss your brides," the minister announced.

"It's about time," Cooper and Jack said at the
same time.

Afraid that she might float straight up into that
clear blue June sky, Raine held on to Jack's shoulders as she lifted her face for her husband's kiss.

FAR HARBOR

To my outstanding editor,
Caroline Tolley, who, in the beginning,
knew my story better than I did

1

She was not running away. Savannah Townsend might not have a firm grasp on every little aspect of her life these days, but about this she was perfectly clear.

She may have walked away from her marriage, the career she'd worked hard to achieve, and a spectacular Malibu home with floor-to-ceiling windows that overlooked the vast blue Pacific Ocean. But what was a woman to do when her seemingly idyllic existence turned out to be little more than a pretty illusion, as ephemeral as the morning fog curling around her ankles?

"Well?" Lilith Lindstrom Ryan's smile was brimming with self-satisfaction. "Isn't it perfect?"

"For Norman Bates, perhaps," Savannah murmured as she eyed the Far Harbor lighthouse with misgiving.

Savannah remembered the lighthouse standing regally at the edge of the cliff like an empress above a forest of dark green conifers. Now it had the look of a dowager who, through no fault of her own, had somehow found herself on skid row.

Graffiti covered the graceful tower that had once gleamed like sunshine on snow; the glass of the lantern room had been broken, and the railings that had been painted to match the red top cap were not only rusted, they looked downright dangerous.

The two houses on the cliff-side property were in even worse shape. Paint was peeling off the once white clapboards, and curling red shingles suggested that the roofs would leak.

Surprisingly, the grounds hadn't been entirely ignored since the lighthouse duties had been taken over by an automated light housed in an unattractive but utilitarian concrete tower a mile away. Someone had planted the most amazing garden Savannah had ever seen. A dazzling mix of tall, stunningly beautiful lilies, irises, Shasta daisies, and spiky bright snapdragons in primary colors were bordered by snowy white clouds of baby's breath.

"It was beautiful once," Savannah's mother reminded her. "And could be again. You just need to use your imagination, darling."

"I am. I'm imagining spiders the size of my fist and the hordes of mice that are undoubtedly living in the place." Savannah really hated rodents. Especially these days, when they reminded her so much of her rat of an ex-husband. "It's a good thing we're here in the daylight, because if we'd come at night, I just might start believing in the ghost."

The lighthouse was rumored to be haunted. By whom was a matter of speculation that had kept the good citizens of Coldwater Cove, Washington, arguing for nearly a century, but the most popular notion was that the ghost was a former lighthouse keeper's pregnant wife, Lucy Hyatt.

"A ghost would be wonderful publicity," Lilith said enthusiastically. "But even without it, lighthouses are incredibly romantic. And that sweet little assistant lighthouse keeper's cottage will make a perfect honeymoon getaway."

"Good idea. Are you going to call Frankenstein and his bride for the booking, or shall I?" Savannah asked dryly.

"You were always such an optimistic little girl." The silver crescent moons hanging from Savannah's mother's ears caught the stuttering morning sunlight as she shook her head. "So open to new things. Your aura used to be as bright as a morning star. These days it's distressingly muddy. . . .

"Why, if I weren't a white witch, I'd put a spell on your horrid ex-husband for hurting you so badly. At least you had the foresight not to take his name."

"Savannah Fantana would have sounded like something from an old Gilda Radner *Saturday Night Live* skit." Savannah wished the subject hadn't come up. Talking about her unfaithful, amoral ex-husband definitely wasn't on today's to-do list.

Today was about finding a suitable bed-and-breakfast location. Having spent weeks searching Washington's Olympic Peninsula, Savannah had begun to despair of ever finding a suitable candidate for her post-divorce venture.

"Besides," she said, "as I told Raine when I first came home, I think my pride was a lot more wounded than my heart."

"That's why you spent all those days hiding in bed and the nights crying into your pillow."

"All right, perhaps I was more upset than I let on," Savannah reluctantly allowed. "But I've put my marriage behind me." Didn't she have the papers, stamped with the official seal of the state of California to prove it? "In fact, I honestly believe Kevin might have actually done me a favor."

Lilith arched a perfectly formed brow. "And I suppose his restraining order trying to prevent you from using any recipes you came up with while working at Las Casitas Resort was yet another favor?" Sarcasm was not her mother's usual tone. But when necessary, Lilith could wield it like a rapier. "Not to mention stealing half the equity in your beautiful house."

"Raine forced him to drop that restraining order." While Savannah had always been proud of her sister, she'd never imagined needing her legal skills. "As for the house, California's a community property state. Kevin was entitled to half the proceeds."

"By law, perhaps," Lilith allowed grudgingly. "Common decency is another matter altogether and something the man was definitely lacking.

I'm still tempted to turn him into a toad. The only problem is, some other witch has obviously already done it."

Savannah certainly couldn't argue with that. She wondered how many women grew up believing in Prince Charming, only to wake up one morning to discover they'd ended up with the frog instead.

"I thought you'd given up paganism in order to sell real estate."

"A person can be both Wiccan and Realtor, dear."

While she tried to be tolerant of her mother's lifelong flighty behavior, Savannah hadn't been at all pleased to learn, upon returning home to Coldwater Cove, that Lilith had been arrested for setting illegal fires and dancing nude in Olympic National Park during Beltane. With her usual flair for making the best of a bad situation, her mother had recently married the arresting officer.

"I wonder who planted the flowers," she murmured, deciding that the time had come to change the subject.

Whoever had chosen the landscape design definitely had an artist's eye. The varying hues of the flowers swirled together like ornate patterns in a priceless Oriental carpet. Unfortunately, the riot of color and lush, shiny green leaves only made the buildings look more ramshackle by comparison.

"Oh, that'd be John."

"John?"

"John Martin. He's Daniel O'Halloran's nephew.

He has a bit of a mental disability, I believe, but he's never let it get in his way. He's also the sweetest boy you'd ever want to meet and the reason Daniel came back to Coldwater Cove last year."

"Why is that?" Since her sister had become a partner in Dan O'Halloran's law practice this past spring, as well as marrying his cousin, Jack, and Dan had done some legal work for the family, Savannah had heard bits and pieces of the story. But she wasn't aware of the details.

"Oh, it's the most tragic story," Lilith said with another shake of her head. "John's parents were killed when a log truck hit their car on the coast road near Moclips. John survived the crash, but he spent months in intensive care. Worse yet, since John's grandparents on his paternal side were no longer living and the elder Mr. and Mrs. O'Halloran couldn't give up the income from their fishing charter business to care for the boy, Daniel took a leave of absence from his prosecutor's job in San Francisco and returned to Coldwater Cove so John wouldn't have to recover in some rehabilitation center among strangers.

"Needless to say, Dan's wife, who they say is from a wealthy old Bay area family, wasn't thrilled with the idea of leaving her Pacific Heights mansion to play nurse to a mentally handicapped thirteen-year-old boy in the little house in the woods, so she remained behind in California.

"By the time John was finally released from the hospital, Dan must have come to appreciate the slower-paced lifestyle of our little burg,"

Lilith wrapped up her story, "because he bought
a lovely home on the water. In fact, you can see
it from here." She pointed toward a house, constructed of native cedar logs, that overlooked
the Strait of Juan de Fuca.

"It's spectacular." The two-story glass wall
thrusting out from beneath the wood shake
roof reminded Savannah of the prow of an ancient sailing ship. All that was missing was a
painted figurehead.

"Isn't it stunning? Unfortunately, by the time
it closed escrow, his high-society wife had already divorced him."

"Seems to be a lot of that going around," Savannah said dryly.

"Sad, but true," Lilith agreed. "However, in
your case, you're right about it being for the
best. . . . Well, what do you think about refurbishing this place?"

Savannah had confidence in her ability to
run a small inn, but she'd never considered herself a miracle worker. "Didn't you say something about a Victorian in Port Townsend that's
just gone on the market?"

"Yes, but Victorian bed-and-breakfasts are so
common these days. And you couldn't ask for a
better location than this."

Good point. The lighthouse had, admittedly,
been built on one of the most stunning sites on
the peninsula. "I'm surprised a developer hasn't
bought the property for a resort."

"Oh, I can't imagine the owner allowing that.
Having grown up on the grounds, he's very sen-

timental about the lighthouse. Didn't I tell you
his name?"

"No. It didn't come up."

"He's Henry Hyatt."

"Hyatt? Surely not Lucy's son?"

"The very same. He was five years old when
Lucy drowned. In fact, there are some who insist that Lucy's spirit refused to leave the lighthouse as long as her child still lived there."

Although she'd never believed any of the
ghost stories, Savannah couldn't resist a glance
upward toward the railing surrounding the
lantern room where, according to local legend,
Lucy could often have been seen, weeping as
she stared out toward her watery grave. Although the August sun had burned off the last
of the morning fog, Savannah shivered.

After spending another three days visiting
countless houses from Port Angeles to Port
Gamble, Savannah found herself back at the
Far Harbor lighthouse. Ever since she was a little girl, she'd been drawn to this special, romantic place.

Savannah's mother had been a flower child, a
war protester, an actress usually cast as the
soon-to-be-dead bimbo in low-budget horror
films, and a singer with a frail but pretty voice
who'd managed to stay in the business mostly
because of her looks, which were still stunning.
Whenever Lilith Lindstrom Cantrell Townsend
Ryan's life had spun out of control, which it did
with an almost predictable regularity, she'd

bring her two daughters back to Coldwater Cove to live with their grandmother, Ida.

On every one of those occasions, the moment Savannah would catch sight of the tomato red cap of the lighthouse in the distance as the ferry approached the small town, she'd feel as if she was coming home. Or at least to the closest thing she'd known to a real home during her unstable childhood years.

She had to agree with Lilith that the Victorian in Port Townsend wasn't what she was looking for, yet she had seen others that had possibility.

"A lot more possibility than this place," she murmured as she walked along the path between the houses and the lighthouse. Fragrance from the remarkable garden floated on the evening breeze.

The sun was setting over the Olympic Mountains like a brilliant fan, turning the water to molten copper and gold. Savannah sat down on a bench in the garden and thought that Lilith was certainly right about one thing: this would make a perfect honeymoon location. That idea brought to mind the first bride who'd come to this lighthouse.

No one had ever known why Lucy Hyatt had been a passenger on the *Annabelle Lee,* a passenger ship bound for San Francisco that had foundered during a winter squall. There were as many stories as there were people who could still remember that so-called storm of the century, but the most popular and prevailing theory continued to be that she'd abandoned

her husband and five-year-old child and was
running away with her big-city lover, the dashing scion of a Bay area family who'd made their
fortune in imported sugar and California land
speculation.

Lucy and the sugar heir had been seen talking at the railing shortly before the ship's departure from its Seattle port, and although more
than eighty decades had passed since the
tragedy, rumors continued to persist that he'd
paid for Lucy's ticket.

Whatever the reason for her having been
aboard in the first place, survivors at the time
had all agreed that Lucy had been washed overboard by the violent, storm-tossed waves. The
following morning her broken body was found
on the rocks below her husband's lighthouse.

When that tragic tale proved depressing, Savannah rubbed her arms to ease the goosebumps, took the heavy brass key her mother
had given her from her purse, and went inside.

She strolled through the rooms, stepping
over fast-food bags and empty beer bottles she
suspected had been left behind by vagrants and
partying teenagers and imagined lace Priscilla
curtains framing sparkling windows that
looked out over the water.

"Candles in the windows would be a nice
touch," she decided out loud. Her voice echoed
in the empty, high-ceilinged room. "But electric
ones." She certainly wouldn't want to accidentally burn the historic building down.

An odd sensation teased at her mind, like the

misty-edged remnants of a dream after awakening. A warmth began to flow through her blood, easing the tensions of the past months, and while she suspected her New Age mother would ascribe her feelings to some sort of fanciful past life *déjà vu,* Savannah couldn't quite ignore the feeling that the lighthouse was once again welcoming her home.

Instead of the odor of damp wallpaper and mold that hung on the musty air, she breathed in the imagined scent of lemon oil and pictured how the scarred heart-of-pine floor would gleam once it had been sanded and stained.

"I hope the fireplace works."

She ran her fingers over stones that didn't appear to be crumbling too badly. A crackling blaze would certainly warm rainy winter evenings. She'd recently seen a pair of andirons in Granny's Attic, an antique shop on Harbor Street across from the ferry terminal, that would prove the crowning touch.

"It really is perfect," she assured herself as she tried to decide between a seascape or a mirror over the hand-carved cedar mantel.

She crossed the floor and looked up the spiral staircase leading to the lantern room.

"Are you there, Lucy?" she called out. She didn't really expect an answer, and if Henry Hyatt's mother's ghost *was* actually haunting the lighthouse, she was keeping silent. "You're not going to be alone anymore, because I'm going to buy your home and clean it up."

Her words echoed around her. "It's going to

be lovely again," she promised, undaunted by the lack of ghostly response. "A place you—and I—can be proud of."

Outside, the sun was sinking ever lower in the late summer sky; inside, dust motes danced in the slanting sunbeams like ballerinas wearing gilt tutus. Giddy with anticipation, Savannah began dancing herself, spinning across the scuffed and scarred floor in time to the swelling music playing inside her head as the shadows darkened and draped the Far Harbor lighthouse in a deep purple veil.

2

"So, what do you think, Uncle Dan?"

"I think you're terrific." Daniel O'Halloran reached over and ruffled his nephew's hair.

"That's what you always say." John Martin grinned and ducked his head. "I meant about the flowers."

"Hey, you're the designer. I'm just the manual labor guy." He turned the Tahoe onto the gravel road that led up to the Far Harbor lighthouse. "But I think using these branch berries as a groundcover is a great idea."

"They're bunchberry."

"Right. Yet another reason why you're the gardener." Dan paused, deciding that the time had come to break the news he'd been with-holding for the past week since the lighthouse had gone on the market. "There's something we need to talk about, Sport."

"What?"

Since subtlety had never been John's strong suit, Dan decided to just dive straight into the dangerous conversational waters. "Henry Hyatt's put the lighthouse up for sale."

"The lighthouse?" The color drained from John's face. "*My* lighthouse?"

"Technically it's Mr. Hyatt's," Dan reminded him carefully.

"But he doesn't care about it. He let it get all run down so that kids would write on it and throw rocks. If it wasn't for me, it'd be really ugly."

"I know." Dan sighed, thinking of all John had overcome in his life already and wishing he could spare him this. "But to be perfectly fair to Mr. Hyatt, he hasn't exactly been in the best of health the past few years."

"He moved out before that. And never came back."

"He moved out because the place was too much for him to handle after he fell and broke his hip. And we really don't know for certain that he never came back." Dan decided to try a different tack. "Besides, I have the feeling that after his wife died, it got to be a little hard emotionally on him to live there alone."

"Because of his mother. Because she drowned."

"That'd be my guess."

"But he was just a little boy when that happened. Now he's old. He should have gotten over that hurting by now."

"I'm not sure anyone can ever get over the loss of a loved one," Dan said quietly. "Not completely."

There was a moment's silence. Dan could practically hear the gears cranking away in John's head. "Now you're talking about my mom and dad."

"You, of all people, should understand that sometimes people feel a lot of stuff deep down inside that they're not real comfortable sharing with strangers."

"Yeah. Sometimes, when I think about the accident, I feel like crying. But I don't, at least not when anybody can see me, because I don't want them to think I'm a dummy."

"No one could ever think that."

"Sometimes people do," John said matter-of-factly. "But Mom always said that I just need to work harder to change their minds."

"Your mom was a wise woman."

"I know." John sighed. "Sometimes I miss her a lot."

"Me, too, Sport." It had been more than a year, and the loss of his older sister still hurt. Dan figured it always would.

After having made the decision to buy the Far Harbor lighthouse, Savannah was back on the grounds, the inspection report in hand. It wasn't as bad as she'd feared. The roofs would need replacing, there was a little dry rot in the basement of the larger of the two houses, and the wiring would have to be brought up to code in all three buildings, but at least they remained structurally sound.

Mostly all that was needed was a lot of hard

work and elbow grease. After these past months of feeling like a ship adrift at sea without a rudder, Savannah found herself looking forward to having her sights set on a new goal.

When she'd caught her husband having sex with the relentlessly ambitious, take-no-prisoners attorney from the resort's legal department, right in his office, on the glove-soft Italian leather couch she'd bought Kevin for an anniversary present, Savannah had discovered that the old saying was true—fury really did cause you to see red.

As a scarlet flame blazed before her eyes, she'd been sorely tempted to commit castration with her new filet knife. Fortunately, common sense kicked in, and after deciding that the unfaithful, lying, narcissistic husband she'd once adored wasn't worth going to prison for, she moved into the Beverly Wilshire hotel, arranged to have all her calls—except those from her adulterous spouse—forwarded, ordered a ridiculously expensive bottle of champagne from room service, and then proceeded, for the first time in her life, to get rip-roaring drunk.

The following morning the phone had jarred through her skull like a Klaxon. It had been Raine, calling with the news that their grandmother had been taken to the hospital after a fall and now the courts were demanding that an adult other than Lilith take over the care of Ida's pregnant teenage foster child.

Nursing the mother of all hangovers, bolstered with a Thermos of strong coffee and a large bottle of extra-strength pain reliever, Savannah had left California that day. As soon as she'd arrived back in Coldwater Cove, she'd immediately been swept up into a series of family emergencies. Once those crises had been taken care of, her own problems had belatedly come crashing down on her like a blow from behind.

She still wasn't certain exactly how long she'd spent curled in a fetal position beneath her covers, wrapped in an aimless lassitude. Finally, when she'd just about decided that she was destined to spend the rest of her life in bed, she'd awakened one sunny August morning feeling as if she'd survived a coma. Thinking back on those weeks, Savannah realized that she'd been behaving much the same way she had during childhood when, terrified by the violent thunderstorms that rumbled and crashed over the mountaintops, she'd cower in the closet beneath the stairs. The only difference was that this time she'd been hiding from life.

Determined to create a new identity, she'd called her mother, who'd recently gotten her Realtor's license, and began searching for the perfect property to turn a lifelong dream into reality. And now she'd found it.

Immersed in chipping away at the paint that was flaking off the window shutters like cheap fingernail polish, Savannah wasn't aware of the truck coming up the hill. It was only when she heard first one, then a second metal door close, that she realized she was not alone. A moment later a teenager in a T-shirt that read He Who Plants a Garden, Plants Hope appeared from behind the lighthouse carrying a black plastic flat of bedding plants.

"Hello." She gave him her friendliest smile. "I'm Savannah Townsend. And you must be John Martin."

"That's my name, all right." His eyes narrowed ever so slightly. "Are you the lady who's going to buy the lighthouse?"

"I'm thinking about it. But to be perfectly honest, the only thing going for it is your garden."

"How did you know I planted the flowers?" His cautious expression turned panicky.

"Well, the fact that you're carrying a flat of plants was my first clue. Also, my mother told me when we were here a few days ago. It's absolutely stunning. You're definitely an artist."

"People say that a lot," he agreed guilelessly. "They say, John Martin, you were born with the greenest thumb in the entire Pacific Northwest."

"They're probably right. So, does Mr. Hyatt pay you to do his gardening?" Savannah couldn't understand why, if Henry Hyatt cared so much about the grounds, he'd let the rest of the lighthouse fall into disrepair.

"No." The strange, edgy panic was back. He reminded her vaguely of a wild rabbit about to bolt. "Nobody's ever paid me. It was all my idea. But I didn't mean to do anything bad."

"Oh, I wasn't implying you did," Savannah said quickly. "I mean, I wasn't suggesting—"

"He understands the word *imply*," Dan, who'd appeared carrying a second flat of plants, offered.

"I do understand *imply*," John seconded his uncle. "I have a disability," he explained. "But I'm not stupid."

"Of course you're not," she agreed.

"How do you know that? Since you don't know me?" John asked.

She exchanged a brief look with Dan, who seemed to be watching her carefully. "You just told me."

"Oh." He appeared to accept that. "This is my uncle Dan. He's my best friend."

"Isn't that nice?" She turned her smile toward Dan. "Hello."

"Savannah." Little lines crinkled outward from morning glory blue eyes when he smiled, reminding her of a bittersweet secret crush she'd had on him the summer she'd turned twelve. "You're looking well—as always."

"She looks beautiful," John corrected. "Like a movie star. And the sun makes her long hair look like it's on fire."

Savannah laughed. "I can tell you've got O'Halloran genes, John." During their high school days, Dan and his cousin Jack had certainly charmed more than their share of Coldwater Cove's female population. "You must have kissed the Blarney stone."

The boy's freckled forehead furrowed. "I don't remember doing that."

"Well, perhaps I'm mistaken."

"Or I was too young to remember," he said helpfully.

"That could be."

"But usually I have a real good memory. Better than people without a disability, even. Huh, Uncle Dan?"

"Absolutely."

"Like I said, I'm just slow. When I was a little kid, my mom read me the story of the tortoise and the hare. About how the hare did things a lot faster, but in the end the tortoise finally won the race. I'm like the tortoise. Slow and steady."

"That certainly makes sense to me." Savannah exchanged another brief look with Dan. "So, if you don't work for Mr. Hyatt, how did you come to plant this garden?"

"Sometimes other kids take advantage of me. One Halloween, right after I got mainstreamed into public middle school, some boys talked me into throwing rocks to try to break the lantern room glass. I threw a lot, but only a couple hit.

"The sheriff caught us. After he explained that what we did was vandalism, I felt real bad. I thought and thought how I could make things better, but I didn't know how to fix the broken glass. And that's when I decided that I could plant some flowers and make it look prettier. So I did. And it really did look prettier, didn't it, Uncle Dan?"

"You bet." His grin was quick and warm and obviously genuine.

"The next spring I planted some more. Then some more after that. And pretty soon everyone started calling me the flower kid. I'm saving my money so some day I can start my own landscaping business. My mom used to say that everyone should have a dream. I figure a garden is about as nice a thing to dream about as anything else."

"You're right. I've always had a fantasy of starting my own inn, where people could come and relax and forget all about the outside world."

"And dream?"

"Definitely dream, and I can't think of a better place to do that than right here. But since I've been known to kill plants as easily as look at them, I hope I can hire you to keep up this magical garden."

"It's not magic. But I will keep it up, if you want."

"Then it's a deal." She held out her hand. "Partners?"

His grin was as wide as a Cheshire cat's. "Partners."

"Hey, John," Dan said after Savannah and John had shaken hands, "why don't you go get started planting and I'll be right along."

"Okay."

When he was out of earshot, Dan put the flat down on the bench. "So, you're really going to stay?"

"Absolutely."

He didn't answer for a moment. Instead, he skimmed a look over her, from the top of her head to her feet, clad in expensive designer sneakers that were one of the few reminders of her past life. Savannah had the impression that after the years she'd spent in Paris, Atlantic

City, New Orleans, and Los Angeles, he didn't think she'd still fit into Coldwater Cove.

"It isn't going to be easy."

"That's okay." She lifted her chin and did her best to pull off at least a bit of her sister Raine's Xena-the-warrior-princess impression. "I'm tougher than I look."

"You're going to have to be, if you're planning to tackle this place. Because it's definitely a wreck."

"A challenge," she corrected.

He chuckled. "You and John should get together and open a Coldwater Cove chapter of Optimists Anonymous."

His words rubbed at some still-raw wounds and had her feeling perversely annoyed. Savannah seriously doubted that he would have questioned Raine taking on such a challenge. Then again, Raine had always had the reputation of being the "smart, sassy" sister, while Savannah was known throughout Coldwater Cove as the "sweet, pretty one."

Well, she was going to change that. There was nothing she could do about pretty since she'd been gifted—or cursed, she sometimes thought—with the best of her parents' looks. Her mother might be fifty, her rock-star father five years older, yet both had remained stunningly attractive individuals. Nevertheless, when Savannah had finally quit hiding beneath the covers, she'd vowed to abandon her lifelong habit of avoiding unwanted conflict by abandoning her own wishes. No longer would she be so damn accommodating, especially when such knee-jerk submission wasn't in her best interests.

"Do you have something against optimism, counselor?" Her back stiffened along with her resolve even as she secretly wondered which of them she was trying to convince, Dan or herself.

"Not at all."

"Good. Because I'm going to make this lighthouse beautiful again, and when it's done I'm going to throw the biggest blowout grand opening party Coldwater Cove has ever seen."

"Sounds like a plan."

He made another of those long, silent assessments that made her feel as if he were evaluating her for jury duty, then, just when her nerves were on the edge of screeching like banshees, he picked up the flat of glossy-leaved, dark green plants. "Guess I'll be seeing you tomorrow, then."

"Tomorrow?"

"I handle all of Henry Hyatt's legal affairs, including property sales, and while I don't want to scare you off, if you happen to have a suit of armor in your closet, you might think about wearing it for your meeting with the guy."

Dan's tone suggested that negotiating with Henry may prove nearly as difficult as refurbishing the buildings. Before she could respond that she was certainly capable of doing business with a frail old man, he flashed a quick grin that was even more charming than it had been back in those long-ago days of her adolescent crush, then sauntered away, his cheerful, off-key whistling drifting back on the fir-scented breeze.

The following morning Savannah lay in bed, futilely chasing sleep. She'd left the shade up so the stars that she'd never been able to see while living in California could shine into the room. A full white moon floated in the center of the darkened rectangle of the dormer window. The ring around the moon meant something, but she couldn't remember exactly what. Magic, perhaps? Or trouble?

The moon drifted by, eventually slipping out of sight as she struggled with her churning thoughts. By the time a shimmering lavender predawn glow revealed the violets that blossomed on the wallpaper she and Raine had compromised on so many years ago, she surrendered to the inevitable. There'd be no more sleep tonight.

Untangling herself from the twisted sheets, she pulled on a robe, went into the adjoining bathroom, splashed cold water on her face, brushed her teeth, and clipped her unruly red-gold hair into a quick twist. Then, not wanting to wake her grandmother, who was sleeping across the hall, she crept down the stairs to the kitchen, where she made coffee in the snazzy red coffeemaker she'd sent Ida last Christmas.

Drawn by the lure of birdsong, she went out on the front porch and sat down on the swing where she'd spent so many lazy summer afternoons daydreaming. Cradling the earthenware mug in her hands, Savannah breathed in the fragrant steam. As she thought back on those days, she decided that despite her mother's marital instability and gypsy lifestyle, her own life had certainly seemed a great deal simpler back then.

A few stars still shone on the horizon. After an early sprinkle that was more mist than rain, the day was dawning a gloriously bright one. Despite the popular stereotype of gray clouds, sunny skies weren't that uncommon during late summer. Since the Puget Sound cities of Seattle, Tacoma, and Olympia were being flooded with new residents, content with their remote peninsula town just the way it was, Coldwater Cove's residents tended to pray for rain whenever tourists were in town.

Ida Lindstrom's Victorian home was set atop a hill overlooking the town that could have washed off an American primitive painting of New England. The flagpole in the grassy green town square at the end of Harbor Street was surrounded by a blaze of color Savannah guessed was another example of John Martin's green thumb.

Those same vibrant blooms encircled the clock tower, which was made of a red brick that had weathered to a dusty pink over the century and could be seen for miles. Its four sides had each told a different time for as long as Savannah could remember, which didn't prove any real hardship, since things—and people—tended to move at their own pace in Coldwater Cove.

As she watched a white ferry chug across the sound, which was as smooth as sapphire glass this morning, her mind flashed back to a long-ago evening when choppy waters had caused her to throw up the hot dog, barbecue potato chips, and Dr. Pepper Lilith had fed her for dinner shortly before they'd all boarded the ferry that would take them from Seattle to Coldwater Cove.

She couldn't remember what, exactly, her mother had been doing during the short trip, but the memory of Raine dragging her out of the glassed-in observation desk into the fresh air, pushing her onto a wooden bench, and wiping her face with a wet paper towel was as vivid as if it had occurred only yesterday.

Her four-years-older half sister had always been there for her, hovering over her like an anxious mother bird, taking on the role of surrogate mother. Fate may have given them different fathers, but love had made them sisters of the heart.

Savannah couldn't count the number of times Raine had come to her rescue, banners flying, like bold, brave Joan of Arc riding into battle. Now, despite being grateful for her sister's unwavering support, she'd begun to suspect that perhaps she'd been overprotected.

Perhaps, she thought as she sipped her cooling coffee, if she'd been forced to fight a few more of her own battles, she wouldn't have so blithely ignored marital warning signs that only a very blind—or naive—woman could have missed.

"Stupid, stupid, stupid," she said into the still air perfumed with late summer roses. The scarlet blossoms drooping with the weight of diamond-bright dew were as large as a child's fist and as velvety as the formal gown she'd worn to the Coldwater Cove high school's winter festival.

She'd made the dress herself, laboring over the rented sewing machine late into the night for two weeks, buried in a pile of velvet and white satin trim that took up the kitchen table and had all of them eating on TV trays for the duration of the project.

Listening to Ida's grumbling and giving up sleep to baste and hem had proven worth it; when Savannah entered the gym that had been decked out in white and silver crepe paper for the occasion, with the crinolines that show-cased her legs rustling seductively and her long hair, which she'd managed to tame with a curl-ing iron, bouncing on her bare shoulders, she'd felt exactly like a fairy-tale princess.

The velvet fantasy of a gown was gone, but not forgotten, turned into pieces of a memory quilt she'd hung over the tester bed a Melrose antique dealer had assured her had once be-longed to Lilian Gish. The quilt, which had also incorporated white lace squares from her high school graduation dress, a piece of shiny black silk from a negligee her mother had worn in a movie about female vampires that had opened on Savannah's tenth birthday, and ivory satin ribbons from her wedding bouquet, was cur-rently packed away with other sentimental items in a cedar trunk at Jack Conway's U-Store-It on Spruce Street.

Fat black-and-yellow bees droned lazily around the roses. Next door the neighbor's cat was returning from his nightly rounds of the town. Ignoring Savannah, the fat old tom curled up into a ball in a slanting sunbeam on his owner's front porch and began washing his marmalade fur.

A familiar car turned onto the road leading up the hill. A minute later, it pulled to a stop in front of the house; the driver's door opened, and Lilith emerged in a graceful swirl of skirt the hue of crushed blueberries. Along with the silk skirt and tunic she also wore a necklace of hand-strung crystals, a pair of lacy webbed dream-catcher earrings and a frown that made Savannah's stomach knot.

Having already pinned her hopes on her admittedly ambitious project as a means of reinventing herself, Savannah didn't know what she'd do if her mother had come bearing bad news about the lighthouse she'd already come to think of as hers.

3

"You're certainly up and about early," Savannah greeted her mother with far more aplomb than she felt. "I thought we weren't scheduled to meet with Mr. Hyatt until late this afternoon."

"Your grandmother's on the committee for this year's Sawdust Festival," Lilith divulged as she climbed the front steps, bringing with her the exotic scent of custom-blended perfume that always made Savannah think of gypsies dancing around blazing campfires.

"She roped me into helping with entertainment, so we're going to Port Angeles this morning to check out a couple bands and have our fortunes told by Raven Moonsilver. Raven's a friend of mine, and since the committee's split on whether or not to hire her to read palms, as chairman, Ida gets to cast the deciding vote."

Her mother's gaze took in Savannah's blue mug. "Thank God you've made coffee. While I try to stick to herbal teas these days, my system definitely needs a jump start at this ungodly hour of the morning." She disappeared into the house.

The thought of the always practical Ida Lindstrom having her palm read was nearly as difficult to accept as the idea of this glamorous creature, who'd periodically blazed through Raine's and Savannah's lives like a comet, turning her creative talents toward something as prosaic as a small-town logging festival.

Lilith returned with a mug of steaming coffee liberally laced with cream and sat down on the top step.

"I ran into Dan yesterday at the lighthouse," Savannah divulged. "He'd come with John Martin to plant flowers. He mentioned something that's been worrying me." She paused, hoping as she had all night that she was making too much of Dan's remarks regarding the lighthouse owner.

"What's that, darling?"

"That Henry Hyatt might prove a problem."

Lilith took a careful sip of coffee before answering. "I'm not certain *problem* is precisely the word I'd use."

Concern stirred again, along with a niggling suspicion. "What are you holding back?"

"Absolutely nothing." Lilith toyed with her necklace. "The Board of Realtors would take away my license if I failed to give full disclosure on a property."

"Okay. Perhaps you're not hiding anything about the lighthouse. What about the owner?"

"You always were my more intuitive child."

Lilith's pansy blue eyes gleamed with affection. "I believe you take after the same Celts who gifted you with all that lovely Titian hair. After all, it's common knowledge that the women from that branch of the family all possess second sight, and—"

"Mother." Savannah cut Lilith off and looked her directly in the eye. "We're not talking second sight here. It's merely the process of elimination. If there's some impediment to my buying the lighthouse, and it doesn't involve the property itself, then it would stand to reason the problem is with the owner."

Lilith slid her veiled gaze out over the sparkling bay. "I don't believe Henry really wants to sell the lighthouse."

There had been several times over the past days when Savannah had questioned the practicality of attempting to refurbish such a ramshackle property. Still, her heart sank at this news.

"Then why on earth would he list it in the first place?"

"Because he doesn't want it any longer."

"I don't understand."

Another sigh. "The problem is, he doesn't want anyone else to own it, either. Not so long as his mother's spirit is still there."

"I should have known you'd believe in the ghost."

"I've never seen her. But that doesn't mean she doesn't exist."

"Well, if she does, I certainly hope she knows

how to use a paint brush, because her former home is in definite need of a new coat of paint."

Lilith waved the comment away with a graceful, beringed hand; her recently acquired wedding band—engraved with wolves because they mate for life, she'd explained—gleamed in the morning light. "Well, whatever Henry's feelings, you shouldn't have any problem convincing him to sell. He may be getting up in years, but he's still a man."

"A bitter, dried-up old man," a voice offered from the doorway. Ida Lindstrom's head was barely visible over the huge cardboard box she was holding. "He was never all that much of a charmer, but after his wife died, he turned downright ornery."

Savannah's grandmother was a small, wiry woman known throughout the county for her seemingly endless trove of energy, her dedication to her former patients, and her strong, often controversial opinions.

In contrast to her glamorous daughter, she was wearing baggy jeans and a T-shirt that read Of Course I Believe You, But Can I Get It in Writing? The message was pure Ida, which Savannah feared didn't exactly bode well for Lilith's palm reader friend.

"It must be eight years since Ruth passed on," Lilith reminded her mother. "Which means that Henry's been without female companionship for a very long time. I can't believe that he wouldn't jump at the chance to spend the afternoon with our Savannah."

"I refuse to stoop to using feminine wiles to talk Henry Hyatt into selling me his lighthouse," Savannah insisted.

"Of course you wouldn't," Ida agreed briskly. "You're my granddaughter, after all, and everyone knows that rolling stones don't fall far from the trees." Along with her bumper-sticker T-shirts, the retired general practitioner had long been Coldwater Cove's queen of malapropisms.

Lilith rolled her expressive eyes as she rose from the step, handed Savannah her empty mug and took the box from Ida's arms. "This weighs a ton," she complained. "What do you have in it, rocks?"

"Of course not. Why would I want to be mailing rocks to anyone?" Ida was looking at the box as if seeing it for the first time. "Who's it for, anyway?"

Lilith exchanged a brief, puzzled look with Savannah. "Since it's addressed to Gwen, I assume it's for her."

"Well, of course it is." Ida's brow cleared. The momentary confusion in her eyes was replaced by the usual bright intelligence that reminded Savannah of a curious bird. "When she called last night from science camp, I could tell she was homesick, so I'm sending her a bunch of her favorite things. Wouldn't want the girl to get so upset she starts shoplifting again."

Knowing that they were the first reasonably stable family Gwen had experienced during her rocky sixteen years, Savannah could understand how hard it must be for her to be away from Coldwater Cove for any length of time, even if the teenager who dreamed of following in Ida's physician footsteps was doing something she loved—something Savannah dearly hoped would help keep her mind off the baby she'd recently given up for adoption.

"Well, the day's not getting any younger, and neither am I," Ida announced suddenly. "If we're going to get our futures told, we might as well get going."

"Please promise that you'll keep an open mind," Lilith asked her mother with a deep, exaggerated sigh.

"Does this palm reader friend of yours wear a turban?"

"No."

"How about talking to the dead?"

"That's not her field of psychic expertise."

"Then we'll probably get on well enough." The pewter bird nest of hair piled precariously atop Ida's head wobbled as she nodded with her typical decisiveness that eased any lingering concern Savannah might have had about her earlier confusion. "So long as you girls both keep your clothes on."

With that pointed reference to Lilith's nude Beltane dancing, she marched toward the car, leaving her daughter to follow.

"Wish me luck," Lilith murmured as she bent to kiss Savannah's cheek. "After this outing, the meeting with Henry this afternoon should be a piece of cake."

Eight hours later, Savannah discovered that her mother's prediction had been optimistic.

The Evergreen Care Center was a redbrick building nestled in a grove of fir trees at the far end of town. The designers had done their best to make the center appealing, with outdoor patios, a sunroom, bright colors, and framed paintings designed to stimulate both the eye and the mind. A bulletin board, covered in grass green burlap, announced a crowded activity schedule that included wheelchair bowling, a morning newspaper group, and the monthly visit of Pet Partners, an organization of dog owners who'd bring their pets to visit the residents.

"Can you imagine ever putting your grandmother in a place like this?" Lilith murmured as they entered the lobby furnished with tasteful antique reproductions.

"Not in a million years."

Savannah thought that there must be a better way than to warehouse people at the end of their lives. Not that Ida was at the end of her life. She may have edged into her late seventies during Savannah's time away from Coldwater Cove, yet except for that little unexplained dizzy spell that had landed her in the hospital a few months ago, her grandmother was as energetic and strong-willed as ever.

Despite the fact that Savannah and Lilith had arrived at the care center ten minutes early, Henry Hyatt was already waiting for them in the sunroom.

"Oh, dear," Lilith said under her breath. "That's

him, in that chair upholstered in the bright nautical-theme sailcloth."

The elderly man's back was to the glass wall, which, Savannah noted with a grudging respect for his negotiating tactics, would force her to look directly into the setting sun. The scowl on his face could have withered a less determined woman.

Refusing to be intimidated, Savannah reminded herself that getting into a power contest with this frail, elderly man was no way to achieve her goal.

"Good afternoon, Mr. Hyatt." Her brilliant smile, an unconscious replica of her mother's, revealed not an iota of her churning emotions. An emerald ring once given to her by a Saudi prince who'd hired her to cook his fiftieth birthday dinner flashed like green fire in the slanting rays of tawny light streaming into the room.

"It's a pleasure to finally meet you." When his talon-like hand stayed right where it was atop the carved wooden cane, Savannah slowly lowered hers. "I've admired the Far Harbor lighthouse for years."

"You and all those other tourists who keep coming around, pestering a man, wanting to take pictures and have themselves a tour, never once thinking that a lighthouse isn't some new attraction at Disneyland."

Acid sharpened a scornful tone that wavered ever so slightly with age. Or emotion? Savannah wondered. In either case, it was not a propitious beginning.

"Now, Henry," Lilith soothed as she gracefully settled into a chair across from him. "You know very well that Savannah's not a tourist. Why, she spent practically her entire life growing up on the peninsula."

"Because her scatterbrained gadfly of a mother didn't see fit to take care of her," he snapped querulously.

Savannah heard Lilith draw in a breath at the sharp accusation, but outwardly her mother appeared unscathed. "You're right. I'll always regret not having been a better mother, but we all make mistakes." Lilith's voice was as warm and throaty as ever, but Savannah noticed that her hands trembled ever so slightly as her fingers creased the broomstick pleats of her skirt. "Sometimes all we can do is move on."

"You've always been good at that," he grumbled. "Moving on."

Savannah had humored him enough. Henry Hyatt may hold the keys to her future in his age-spotted hands, but that didn't give him the right to intrude on her admittedly complex relationship with Lilith.

"I came here today to discuss a business proposition with you, Mr. Hyatt, not to stand by and listen to you insult my mother."

An errant thought occurred to her. Could Henry possibly be comparing Lilith's behavior to the way his own mother had abandoned him at such a tender age? Was it even possible to harbor a hurt or hold a grudge for so many years?

He tilted his head and looked up at her.

"Didn't anyone ever teach you, when you were down in California"—he spat out the name of her former home as if it had a bad taste—"that sassin' a man who has something you seem to want so damn bad is a piss-poor way of doin' business?"

"The Far Harbor lighthouse is not the only piece of property for sale on the peninsula, Mr. Hyatt." She sat down in a wing chair beside her mother and crossed her legs. Proving that Lilith wasn't the only actress in the family, she kept her smile cucumber cool and just the slightest bit condescending. "Merely the most run-down."

Before Henry could respond to that, the door opened and Dan walked in, bringing with him a distant scent of the sea. "Sorry I'm late." His face was tanned from the sun, his hair windblown. "My meeting ran late."

"Meeting, hell." Henry focused his ill humor on his attorney. "Anyone with two eyes and half a brain can see you've been out sailing."

"Got me there," Dan replied equably. "As it happens, my meeting took place on a yacht."

"Ha! That's a likely story."

"It's true. My client's a software mogul who, like so many of his breed, tends to be a bit paranoid. He prefers doing business where there's less likelihood of conversations being overheard—such as out in the middle of the sound."

"You always were quick with the excuses," Henry shot back. "Like that time you broke the window on my Olds."

"When I fouled off my cousin Caine's curveball through your windshield." Dan glanced over at Savannah and winked. "I spent the rest of the summer paying it off by painting the lighthouse."

"Wouldn't have taken you so long if you hadn't been so damn slow."

"If I was slow it was because I spent the first two weeks shaking like a leaf from my newly discovered fear of heights. I got more paint on me than I managed to get on the lighthouse."

"Mebbe I should have you paint it again." Henry waved a faintly palsied hand toward Savannah. "Since this little gal thinks it's a bit rundown."

"More than a bit," Savannah corrected.

The way she tossed up her chin and stood up to a man who'd elevated the knack of being irritating to an art form had Dan suspecting that Savannah may have toughened up a bit since having been elected Miss Congeniality of her senior class.

"Girl's got a funny way of charming me into selling the place," Henry complained. Having come to know his irascible client well, Dan realized that the old codger was actually enjoying himself.

"I'm making you an offer for the lighthouse." Savannah's clipped tone revealed her growing frustration. "I'm not asking to become your new best friend."

He cackled at that. "Gal's got spunk, O'Halloran."

"Seems to." Dan nodded. "Perhaps even

enough to save the place from a wrecking ball."

Henry's pale blue eyes narrowed. "That's your job."

"Fending off developers is my job. Replacing the wiring, reglazing the windows, sweeping spiders out of the corners, and chasing bats out of the attic is beyond the call of lawyerly duty."

"Bats?" Savannah's incredible green eyes widened. "Please tell me you're not serious."

"Now you've done it, O'Halloran," Henry spat out. "Probably caused the price to drop another ten thousand bucks. Ten thousand I should take out of your fee."

Dan refrained from responding that Henry would have to pay him first before he could go deducting anything. Old man Hyatt was not only Dan's most irascible client, he was also the most time-consuming of his pro bono cases.

"Now there's an idea," he murmured.

"Actually, bats may be a plus," Lilith offered in her usual blithe way. "Since they eat insects."

"Anyone knows about bats, it should be you," Henry barked on a laugh roughened by old age and years of tobacco smoke. "Seein' how your own mother has a few in her belfry these days."

"My grandmother served this community for fifty years," Savannah reminded Henry in a flash of very un-Savannah-like anger. Dan resisted the urge to applaud. "Which undoubtedly means that she's treated you."

"From time to time, mebbe," Henry muttered. "It's hard to recollect."

"I seem to recall Mother mentioning a case of pneumonia that nearly proved fatal because you were too stubborn to seek medical help," Lilith interjected. "Why, if Gerald Lawson hadn't stopped by that day to collect for the newspaper and called Mother, who, by the way, came out in a blizzard to care for you, you might not be here today, Henry."

Lilith's own flare of heat suggested she was on the verge of losing her temper. A woman of strong emotions, she'd advised Dan after his sister's funeral that holding in one's feelings was unhealthy for mind, spirit, and body. Months later, apparently practicing what she preached, she'd been arresting for dancing nude in Olympic National Park and ripping up Cooper Ryan's citation book.

That little display of unbridled emotion had gotten her hauled into the park jail, but displaying a seemingly lifelong ability to land on her feet, a month later she'd become Mrs. Cooper Ryan. If there was any more nude dancing going on, Lilith was staying out of public parks and restricting her audience to her new husband.

"Only God can decide whether or not a body's gonna live or die," Henry argued. He raked his fingers through snow white hair as wispy as dandelion fluff. "Though I reckon Ida may have had a hand in the outcome," he tacked on reluctantly.

Dan decided that it was time to move things along. "Well, now that we've got all that settled, what would everyone say to getting down to discussing what brought us here today?" he asked with forced enthusiasm.

"Might as well," Henry muttered in a way that suggested since neither Lindstrom woman had turned out to be a pushover, there was no point in baiting them any further. He hooked his cane over the wooden arm of his chair, folded his arms, set his face, and looked straight at Savannah. "You want the place, here's what you'd better be prepared to pay."

The price was at least twice what the property was worth.

"That's a bit more than I'd planned." Dan admired the way Savannah kept her voice calm even as the outrageously inflated price caused the color to drain from her face.

"After all," she said, obviously mustering strength, "as I mentioned before, according to the inspector who examined the property, there's a great deal of work to be done to even bring the lighthouse up to code."

She opened a manila envelope, pulled out some papers, and held them toward Henry. When he refused to take them, she placed the papers on the pine coffee table between them.

"That cost doesn't even factor in what it will take to make it livable." She countered with a price half what he'd stated.

"Some high-flying resort company from down in your old neck of the woods offered a helluva lot more than that."

"I have no doubt they did. Having worked for a number of resorts, and knowing how they operate, I also suspect that the first thing they'd do is raze the house."

Henry held his ground. "Can't see why they'd want to do that. Wouldn't be much market for a Far Harbor lighthouse resort without the keeper's house."

"It's not that large," she pointed out. "If the new owners tore it down, they could construct one of those huge redwood and cedar resorts that are springing up all along the coast."

She'd obviously done her homework; as Henry's attorney, Dan knew that International Timeshare Resorts had indeed suggested a plan to tear down both houses.

"Of course, they might decide to keep the lighthouse," she allowed. "After all, they could always use it to sell fake scrimshaw, miniature totem poles, and CDs of whale songs to tourists."

"No jackass is going to be selling fake scrimshaw made in Taiwan or Tijuana outta my lighthouse," Henry warned.

"I'd hate to see that as well," Savannah replied smoothly. "But if you sell it to ITR, it won't be your lighthouse any longer, will it?"

Henry harrumphed. "Won't be my lighthouse if I sell it to you, either."

"I was thinking about that on the drive over here." Savannah reached into the folder again and pulled out a sheet of handwritten figures. "I believe I may have a solution that would suit both our purposes."

He gave her the long, unblinking stare that

Dan had gotten used to. If she was even slightly intimidated, Savannah didn't show it.

"Well," Henry demanded crankily, "you gonna share this idea or keep it all to yourself? I'm not a damn mind reader."

"I was thinking we could become partners."

"Partners?"

Savannah nodded. "That's right."

"Why in sam hill would I want to be partners with you?"

"Perhaps because it would allow you to retain part ownership of a home that's been in your family for three generations. At the same time, you'll be making a profit from the property."

"What makes you think you can even turn a profit from that ramshackle old place?"

Dan flashed Savannah a discreet thumbs-up for having gotten Henry to agree that the property was far from livable. The only indication that she'd seen the gesture was a fleeting glint of satisfaction in her eyes—a glint that came and went so fast, Dan would have missed it if he hadn't been watching her carefully.

"I'm very good at what I do, Mr. Hyatt. I know the hospitality business and I've been preparing for this all my life." Her expression and her voice softened. "Also, quite frankly, I can't afford not to, either financially or emotionally. . . .

"There's one more thing," Savannah offered. "If we're partners, you'll always have a home at Far Harbor." She glanced around the plant-filled room that, despite the staff's attempts at cheeriness, couldn't overcome the odor of illness and despair. "You could move out of here."

Henry blinked. Once. Twice. A third time, reminding Dan of an old owl that used to live in the rafters of his grandparents' barn when he was a kid.

"Place won't be ready any time soon," Henry pointed out. His voice had lost its usual sardonic edge. It now sounded faint and frail.

"That shouldn't prove a problem." The way Lilith slipped so smoothly back into the conversation made Dan realize that she and Savannah had planned this tag-team approach ahead of time. "Mother only has one foster child living with her at the moment, and as it happens, Gwen is away at science camp. Of course I've moved out since my marriage, which means there's more than enough room for you at the house."

A three-generational female tag team, Dan thought with admiration. There was no way either Savannah or Lilith would have dared volunteer such a thing without first getting Ida's okay.

"House?" Shaggy white brows flew upward like startled pigeons. "You suggesting I stay at that crazy old woman's house?"

"I'm going to say this one more time, Henry," Lilith said with a swish of silk as she crossed her legs. "I do hope you'll listen. My mother is not crazy. She can, admittedly, be eccentric. However, since it appears that your life has settled into the doldrums these days, perhaps having it shaken up a bit might not be such a bad thing."

Henry rapped the cane on the Berber carpeting with scant, muffled effect. "My life's just dandy the way it is, damn it."

Not a single person in the room challenged the obvious lie.

"All right," he surrendered finally on a wheezing huff of breath. "Since you seem so determined to buy the place, but can't meet my asking price, I reckon I don't have much choice but to give you a break."

"Thank you, Mr. Hyatt." Her eyes swimming, Savannah stood up and took both his hands in hers. "I promise you won't regret this."

"I'm already regretting it." He tugged his hands free, pushed himself out of the chair with a mighty effort, and looked up at Dan. "It's time for *Wheel of Fortune*. You take care of the paperwork, then bring it to me to sign when it's done."

"No problem."

"Better not be." Warning stated, he shuffled away.

The three of them watched him go. Finally, Savannah sighed. "I hope I never become that dried up and bitter."

"Of course you won't." Lilith's full sleeve fluttered like a brilliant butterfly's wing as she put her arm around her daughter's shoulder. "Despite that horrid man you made the mistake of marrying, you're still my sweet, open-hearted little girl who used to bring home stray kittens."

Savannah was watching Henry make his slow, painful way down the hallway. "I seem to recall you saying something about my aura being muddy these days."

"So I did," Lilith agreed blithely. "But it seems to be glowing again." She looked at her younger daughter with approval. "It does my heart good to see things finally working out for you, darling. And now that we've got this little transaction settled, I must run."

"I thought we'd go out and celebrate," Savannah said.

"Oh, sweetheart, I'd dearly love to, but I only have an hour to get ready for the dance at the VFW."

"The VFW?" Savannah was clearly surprised. And no wonder. Dan was also having trouble envisioning this former Vietnam War protestor—who'd been arrested back in the late sixties for throwing red paint on army recruiters—doing the two-step at a hangout for former military personnel. "You do realize that those initials stand for Veterans of Foreign Wars?" she asked. "Which you're not."

"Well, of course I'm not." Lilith combed a slender hand through her long slide of silver hair. "But Cooper is. Since my behavior after he shipped out to Vietnam all those years ago was admittedly less than admirable, I feel I owe him this one."

Savannah's smile was soft and fond. "Better watch it, Mom. You're entering the danger zone. Any moment now you might discover maturity."

"Wouldn't that set tongues wagging?" Lilith's laugh reminded Dan of the silver wind chimes his mother had given him for a housewarming gift. She kissed Savannah's cheek, then Dan's. "Have fun, you two."

She left in a fragrant cloud, her skirt swirling

around her still-shapely calves and her hips
swaying in a way that caused a host of masculine eyes to watch her leave. Dan couldn't help
chuckling when one elderly man, apparently en-
thralled with this voluptuous goddess who'd suddenly appeared in their midst, actually ran his
wheelchair into the wall.

He exchanged a look with Savannah, who
burst out laughing. Enjoying the sound that was
half honey, half smoke, Dan realized that it was
the first time he'd heard her reveal an iota of
humor since she'd returned home.

Savannah Townsend had been the quintessen-
tial small-town girl most likely to cause boys to
hold their notebooks in front of their jeans:
prom queen two years in a row, pep squad all
four years, yell queen her senior year. The male
membership of the senior class had voted her
the girl they'd most like to be stranded on a deserted island with, and she'd been equally popular with the girls. The fact that her father had
been world-famous bad-boy rock guitarist Reggie Townsend hadn't hurt her reputation, either.

Dan had recently represented Savannah's
grandmother Ida's pregnant teenage foster child
in an adoption case. When he'd met the family at
the winery of the adoptive parents, he'd taken
one look at Savannah, recently returned from
LA, and decided that she was even more beautiful than he'd remembered.

With her wild clouds of fiery hair, golden California tan, and emerald eyes, she'd resembled a
member of some mythical race of women,

forged in fire by a master alchemist. Yet, although she'd grown up to be dazzling, he'd sensed a sadness in her that had nothing to do with the solemnity of the occasion.

They'd been thrown together again a few weeks later at his cousin's wedding, where Savannah, wearing a dress that shimmered like moonlight on sea foam, had provided a dazzling contrast to the bride's cooler, luminous beauty.

Watching her closely, Dan had noted that even as her lush ruby lips had curved often, befitting the joy of this family event, the smiles had never quite touched her eyes. As the wedding festivities went on into the night, she'd grown more and more emotionally distant—almost ethereal, like the ghost of Lucy Hyatt, rumored to still reside in the lighthouse.

But now, as she laughed, she reminded him of the Savannah he'd once known, the glowing girl who could make a guy renowned for his hit-and-run dating style think terrifying, forever-after thoughts.

When her floral perfume slipped beneath his skin, creating an inner tug more complex than mere sexual attraction, Dan reminded himself that after a tumultuous and exhausting eighteen months, his life was finally getting back on track. The last thing he needed right now was a romance with a woman on the rebound. Especially one who, despite her apparent whim to settle down in Coldwater Cove, would undoubtedly soon find small-town life too confining for her big-city tastes.

4

Ida Lindstrom sat at the old oak rolltop desk she'd bought when she'd first begun her medical practice, right here in this very house, and stared down at a leather-bound address book stuffed with pieces of paper. The book, along with the telephone that was now buzzing with that annoying off-the-hook sound, was a sign that she'd been about to make a call. But to whom?

"Think, damn it!" She pressed her fingers against her temple and forced her mind to focus on the clues at hand. She had, after all, become very good at following clues since her once razor-sharp mind had turned so uncooperative.

"A waist is a terrible thing to mind," she muttered, unwittingly falling back into her unconscious habit of malapropisms.

Frustrated, she pulled one of the pieces of paper from the flap on the inside front cover of the address book and read through the list she'd made the morning she'd returned home from the hospital after that stupid fall that had gotten everyone so excited.

"Number one. Does recent memory loss affect job performance? Ha! It can't affect my job performance because I'm retired."

All right, so she may have gotten a bit more absentminded, but that was only natural, especially in this hurry-up world when so many outside things demanded immediate attention, all at the same time. It was perfectly understandable that she'd occasionally forget things, such as her reason for having come into her former examining-room-turned-den in the first place.

"It'll come," she reassured herself as she rubbed her uncharacteristically icy hands together. The trick was to remain patient and not panic. *Concentrate.*

"Number two. Does patient have difficulty performing familiar tasks?"

No problem there. Relief came in such a cooling wave, she decided that boiling all the water out of the teakettle this morning didn't really count. That, after all, could happen to anyone.

She also didn't have any problems with language. Perhaps she mixed up her words from time to time, but if her family and friends were to be believed, and she had no reason to doubt them, she'd been doing that all her life. Nor had she suffered any disorientation of time and place, problems with abstract thinking, or decreased judgment.

"Does patient misplace things?" She frowned.

"Stupid question. Name me one person who doesn't lose their car keys from time to time." Hadn't Raine, whom everyone knew was smart as a tack, done the same thing when she'd dropped by to visit last Saturday? They'd practically turned the house upside down before finding them behind a sofa cushion.

Number eight regarding mood swings didn't count, nor did nine: changes in personality. She'd never been a moody person, had never suffered PMS, and had breezed through menopause with hardly a ripple even without the hormone replacement that was so readily available for women these days.

Why, she was the same person she'd been at thirty. "Better," she decided.

Ida had to laugh out loud at the final "warning sign" on her diagnostic list. If there was one thing she wasn't suffering from, it was loss of initiative. Hadn't she managed to take care of three delinquent teenagers when the entire social system of the state of Washington had given up on them?

Two of the girls were now safely placed with relatives, and while Gwen, admittedly, might have gone through a rough patch, she certainly seemed on the straight and narrow. Her therapist had assured the family that the girl was coming through the separation from her infant daughter as well as could be expected.

When she heard a car engine outside the house and saw Savannah's red convertible pulling into the driveway, Ida folded the piece of paper and slipped it back into the front of the address book, hiding it behind a checklist of things she should make certain she did before leaving the house. Not that she'd ever leave the shower running or the stove turned on, but it never hurt to be cautious.

"I'm a doctor. I've been diagnosing people's illnesses for fifty years. I should certainly know whether or not I have Alzheimer's," she muttered. "And I don't."

The front door opened. "I'm in here, darling," she called out to her younger granddaughter with feigned cheeriness. Today had been important for Savannah, she remembered, frustrated anew when she was unable to recall exactly why.

"I got it!" Savannah breezed into the den, her smile as bright and happy as it had been back when she'd cheered the Coldwater Cove High School Loggers to victory.

"That's wonderful!" *Got what?* Ida sneaked a quick glance at her checklist, hoping for some small assistance. "I'm so pleased for you."

"Of course now the work begins." Savannah crossed the room and picked up the phone receiver that was still lying on the desktop. "I'm sorry. Did I interrupt you making a call?"

"It's not important." So that's what that annoying sound was. Ida forced a smile that wobbled only slightly as Savannah replaced the receiver in its cradle. "Tell me all about your day. I want to hear everything."

"You were right, as usual." Savannah settled down on the sofa, kicked off her shoes, and tucked her legs beneath her.

"Of course. Grandmothers are always right."
In contrast to her icy hands, Ida felt a bead of
sweat form above her upper lip. Her mind
turned with the heavy, slogging effort of truck
tires stuck in a mud bog.

"Offering Henry Hyatt a chance to move in
here clinched the deal."

Henry Hyatt. . . . She'd treated him for prostate
trouble ten years ago. It had been a cold wet June
during a spring of record rains that had made it
seem as if summer would never come. Ida recalled the case, as she did that of all her other patients, with crystal clarity. But surely that wasn't
what Savannah had been concerned about?

"I've always loved that lighthouse, but I have
to admit, Gram, I'm still having a little trouble
believing that it's actually mine."

Ida latched onto the clue like a drowning
woman reaching for a piece of driftwood in a
storm-tossed sea. The lighthouse! Savannah
was buying the Far Harbor lighthouse to turn
into a bed-and-breakfast. How had she forgotten such an important thing?

"You'll make a grand success of it," she assured her granddaughter with renewed vigor
born of her relief at having finally sorted out
the puzzle. "And I'm pleased as peanuts that my
offer of hospitality to Henry helped clinch the
deal. But I have to warn you, Savannah dear, if
that cranky old man expects breakfast in bed,
like they undoubtedly do for invalids over at
Evergreen, he's going to have to sleep in the
kitchen."

When Savannah laughed richly at that suggestion, Ida's clenched shoulders relaxed and
the blood flowed warmly back into her hands.

"I'm so proud of you," she said as her mind
cleared and her heart lifted. "Not that I ever
had any doubts. In fact, anticipating your success, I bought you a little present." She reached
into a desk drawer and pulled out a tapestry
lighthouse tote bag.

"Oh, I love it!"

"There's something inside," Ida remembered.

Savannah laughed again as she pulled out
the message T-shirt. "Behind every successful
woman is herself," she read aloud.

"And don't you forget it," Ida said briskly,
pleased with the way Savannah was coming out
of her recent divorce funk. "We Lindstrom
women are tough cookies." Although she was
still furious at that shifty-eyed weasel her
granddaughter had made the mistake of marrying, at least his behavior had brought Savannah
home again, proving that every silver lining had
a cloud around it. "They may be able to chew us
up from time to time, but they can't swallow. . . .

"We'll have to call Raine right away," Ida said
decisively after grandmother and granddaughter had hugged. "And, of course, Gwen. So you
can tell them the good news."

Everything was going to be fine. Her girls
were back home again. All except Gwen, who
would soon be back from science camp in time
to start her senior year of high school. Even
Lilith, after a lifetime of rebellion, appeared to

be on the straight and narrow, happily married
to Cooper Ryan and working at something she
seemed to enjoy.

Despite those recent annoying little memory
glitches, life had never been better. Fretting
about things she couldn't control—such as getting older—was a waste of time and would ac-
complish nothing.

As she found Gwen's number in her address
book and picked up the receiver, Ida put her concerns away and decided to let sleeping ducks lie.

Five very long days later, Savannah sat on
the bench in the lighthouse garden, running
through the numbers again. She'd borrowed
Raine's laptop computer, hoping the fancy
money-management program would make her
prospects look more encouraging. It didn't.

"It doesn't help that I keep expanding the
original concept," she muttered as she glared at
the flashing cursor.

John, who rode his bike to the lighthouse
every day, was weeding nearby. His sunflower
yellow T-shirt read Cultivate the Garden Within.
Every time she'd seen Dan's nephew he'd been
wearing another message shirt, which had Savannah thinking that he and her grandmother
would undoubtedly get along like gangbusters.

"You're unhappy," he diagnosed.

"Not unhappy." Savannah sighed. "Just frustrated."

She took in the sight of the bunchberry he'd
planted as a groundcover the first day she'd met

him here at the lighthouse. The white blossoms looked like tiny umbrellas amidst the dark green foliage he'd promised would eventually spread all the way along the cliff.

"That's lovely." There was something vastly soothing about the garden, which was why she'd chosen to work here today.

"It's going to be even better," he assured her with the enviable confidence he seemed to possess regarding his horticultural work. "When summer ends, the flowers will turn to bright red berries that'll attract more birds to your lighthouse."

If it *was* her lighthouse by then. Savannah shook her head to rid it of that depressing thought. Henry had begun to waffle about signing the final sales agreement, but she refused to consider the possibility of failure.

"I like the idea of attracting birds," she said as she watched a fat red-breasted robin energetically tug a worm from the moist ground.

John rocked back on his heels. "Sometimes when I get worried and need to figure out an answer to a problem, I work in the garden and my brain works better," he offered. "Even when I don't get any answers, I don't feel so bad." He paused. "I have an extra pair of gloves."

Savannah immediately turned off the computer. "You're on." She spent the next hour attacking weeds, and while she didn't come any closer to solving her financial problems, she discovered John was right: she did feel better.

Despite her new-found garden therapy, Savannah's stress level escalated as she continued to juggle figures and go around and around with Henry, who appeared to believe that his role in life was to make people—and her in particular—as miserable as possible. Whenever she could steal a free moment, she worked off her frustration in John's garden. He seemed to enjoy her company, even after she'd mistaken a bed of newly sprouted seedlings for dandelions.

"That's okay," he assured her easily, revealing no irritation that she'd destroyed an entire day's work. "I can plant more."

She'd shown up the next morning with a Thermos of cold milk and a tin of crumbly, home-baked chocolate chunk cookies as an apology. John had taken one bite, then rolled his eyes.

"These are the very best cookies I've ever tasted." He flashed her a grin that reminded her of his uncle. "Any time you want to dig up more flowers, I won't mind—so long as you keep bringing more cookies."

Savannah laughed and promised the cookies without the destruction. But the incident did give her an idea. After checking with the charge nurse at Evergreen to make sure Henry wasn't on a restricted diet, she showed up at the nursing home with a tin of cookies still hot from the oven. It may just have been a coincidence, but that was the evening he finally agreed to her terms.

Wanting to get the deal locked up before Henry changed his mind again, Savannah was at the legal offices of O'Halloran and O'Halloran first thing the next morning.

The offices her sister shared with Dan were housed in a century-old building next to the ferry dock. The brick had been painted a soft gray-blue that reflected the water, and beneath the front windows scarlet geraniums cascaded from flower boxes she suspected were John's contribution.

A brass bell tied to the inside of the door jangled as she entered. Apparently the receptionist hadn't arrived yet, because Raine came out of her office to greet Savannah.

"Congratulations. I hear you're now a lady of property."

"I will be as soon as I sign the final papers. I thought I'd go crazy when it looked as if Henry was going to back out."

"Henry's an ornery old bird." Raine shrugged. "I think he was really just trying to make you squirm. He's an expert at that, of course. Hopefully getting out of that nursing home will give him a new lease on life."

"At least living with Gram won't be boring."

"She'll whip him into shape, all right," Raine agreed. "I'll go tell Dan you're here."

"No need." Dan appeared from the hallway around the corner. "I was on the phone, but I knew the minute Savannah walked in the door."

Since the offices faced the bay, Savannah knew he couldn't have seen her walking across the street from where she'd parked her car in front of the Dancing Deer Dress Shoppe. "I hadn't realized you were psychic."

"I'm not. I smelled the flowers and decided that either John's expanded into indoor gardens

or the most gorgeous lady in Coldwater Cove
has decided to grace me with her presence." He
glanced over at Raine. "Present company ex-
cepted, of course."

"Of course," Raine said with easy good
humor. She'd never resented her sister's beauty.
To do so would be like the cool silver moon resenting the bolder, brighter sun for rising in a
blaze of glory each morning. "Well, I've got
some partnership papers for that software firm
to write and a brief on Japanese timber sales to
polish up, so I'd best get back to the salt mines.
Congratulations, baby sister."

She hugged Savannah, then scooped up the
yellow legal pad she'd carried into the reception
area with her.

"Congratulations," Dan said. "I ran by Evergreen before breakfast this morning and got my
client's signature on the sales agreement."

"Thank you." He'd promised to expedite matters when she'd called him at home last night
with the news that his client had finally agreed
to her terms, but she'd still worried that any
delay might allow Henry to change his mind.

"That's my job," he reminded her. "I'm sorry
Henry gave you so many headaches. I tried to
hurry him along, but I think the problem was
that he was enjoying having you visit every day."

"If that's his idea of enjoyment, he undoubtedly spends the morning craft hour pulling
wings off butterflies."

"The old guy can be a bit of a challenge on
occasion."

"Spoken exactly like a lawyer. Talk about mincing words," she muttered.

"I suppose we can all be accused of attorney-speak from time to time," he admitted. "Speaking of which, do you know what you get when you cross the Godfather with a lawyer?"

"No, but I'm afraid you're going to tell me."

"An offer you can't understand."

"That's terrible."

"But true," he said good-naturedly. "Let me try another one," he suggested as they passed Raine's office. "Did you hear about the lady lawyer who dropped her briefs and became a solicitor?" He'd raised his voice just loud enough to ensure that his partner heard him.

"Better be careful, Counselor," Raine called out. "You're skating perilously close to a charge of sexual harassment in the workplace."

Dan paused and stuck his head in her open doorway. "Hey, you know very well that we're an equal opportunity law firm. Which means you're welcome to take your best shot."

Knowing her sister, Savannah was not at all surprised when Raine proved ready for him. "Okay." She folded her arms across the front of her charcoal gray blazer. "What do a male lawyer and a sperm have in common?"

Dan rubbed his square chin. "I'll bite."

A familiar competitive glint shone in Raine's hazel eyes. Her smile was smug and claimed early victory. "Both have a one-in-three-million chance of becoming a human being."

"Bull's-eye." Dan clutched his heart and stag-

gered against the wall. He glanced over at Savannah, who was beginning to enjoy herself.
"Your sister is a cruel-hearted woman. I have
no idea why my cousin seems so taken with
her."

"Because Jack has very good taste," Raine
countered. "Which, if that atrocious tie is any
example, is a great deal more than I can say for
you."

"Hey, this tie makes a statement." He turned
toward Savannah. "What do you think?"

Savannah chewed on a thumbnail lacquered
in Sunset Coral as she studied him. What did she
think? That the man was drop-dead gorgeous,
with that thick chestnut hair that seemed perpet-
ually tousled and blue eyes enlivened by dancing
flecks that flashed like mica in the sunlight. His
complexion was tanned a rich, burnished gold
from days spent sailing on the sound, his skin
taut over strong, masculine bones.

His mouth was full, but roughly sculpted in a
way that made it very much a man's. When an
errant, distant memory of long, slow, sensuous
kisses stirred in some dark corner of her mind,
Savannah's hormones spiked.

"I'm not sure I get the message," she said as
she took in the cartoon marsupials wearing
somber black judicial robes.

"I thought it'd be obvious. Maybe it's a
lawyer thing." He sighed heavily. "It's supposed
to represent a kangaroo court."

Since the ridiculous tie was just about the
single amusing thing about her life these days,

Savannah didn't censure her smile. "I think I like it."

"See?" He shot Raine a triumphant look. "Your sister approves of my sartorial taste. And she should know about style, having spent so many years in the playgrounds of the rich and famous."

"Last time I checked, money didn't buy taste," Raine argued.

"And I wasn't the one playing," Savannah pointed out.

"All the more reason to make up for lost time." He winked at Raine, then they continued down the hall. "It's a gorgeous day. After you sign the last of the papers, how about we pick up some lunch and go sailing?"

"Perhaps your life has become so laid-back you can take a day off, but I've got work to do. I was intending to wade through paint chips and wallpaper samples during lunch."

"You have to eat."

"I packed a salad in an ice chest in the back of my car before I left the house this morning." Raine wasn't the only sister who could prepare ahead.

"Rabbit food," Dan scoffed dismissively. "You need red meat to keep your strength up, Savannah. I was thinking we might stop by Oley's and pick up an order of ribs."

Savannah assured herself that it was only the mention of Oley Swenson's barbecue—not the prospect of an afternoon sailing with Dan—that was proving unreasonably tempting. "Thanks anyway, but I think I'll pass."

"Have you ever seen your lighthouse from the water?"

Her lighthouse. Those were, Savannah thought, the most beautiful words in the English language. "I've seen it from the ferry lots of times."

"That's only one view, coming across from Seattle. You really should see it from the strait as well. It gives you an entirely different perspective.

"When I was a kid, overdosing on Horatio Hornblower novels, I used to imagine how relieved sailors coming in from the sea must have felt when they saw the light flashing, guiding them safely into the shallows of the cove. I also thought how exciting—and frightening—it must have been to sail back past it toward dangerous, open waters again."

"I've thought the same thing," Savannah allowed as they entered an office papered in a cobalt blue that echoed the water outside the tall windows. The furniture was upholstered in a gray leather the color of a storm-tossed sea. "But as much as I'd enjoy seeing the lighthouse from that vantage point, I really can't take the time. At least not now."

"You've got a rain check," Dan said equably as he gestured her to a chair on the visitor's side of an antique partner's desk.

While he opened a scuffed leather barrister's bag to get the contract, Savannah took the opportunity to study the room in greater detail. One wall was taken up by bookshelves. A quick glance revealed several legal thrillers lurking among the leather-bound law books.

Calligraphically prepared diplomas displayed in simple wood frames hung on another wall, along with lithographed copies of the Declaration of Independence and the Magna Carta. Keeping company with the august legal documents was a needlepoint sampler that read Please Don't Tell My Mother I'm a Lawyer. She Thinks I Play the Piano in the Local Bordello.

"My sister made that for me when I passed the bar," he said when he saw her looking at it.

Savannah would have had to be deaf not to hear the lingering pain in his voice. "You must miss her terribly." She couldn't imagine losing Raine. It would be easier to have her heart ripped out.

"Every day." Dan sighed, picked up a pen and began switching it from hand to hand. The light was gone from his eyes, almost, she thought, as if someone had pulled down a dark shade. "When I first came back home, right after the accident, I wasn't sure I could take care of John. Not just physically, which, in the beginning, was difficult enough, but emotionally.

"Never having been a parent myself, I worried that I might not have the instincts. Fortunately, Karyn and Richard did a great job of grounding their son, so mostly all I've had to do is sort of follow along and keep an eye out for the pitfalls."

"I have a feeling that you're glossing over your efforts just a bit."

Savannah considered how, if Kevin had been in a similar situation, he would have been quick to take credit for John's obvious sense of stabil-

ity. Just as he'd taken credit for all her hard
work and innovation in each of the resorts
where they'd worked together, he in a series of
upwardly mobile managerial positions, while
she'd always been more than content to stay in
the kitchen.

"It couldn't have been easy," she said. "John's
a very intuitive, open-hearted person. If he
hadn't known he could trust you to be there for
him, he could have been devastated."

She knew, firsthand, how important it was during those tender growing-up years to have someone you could count on. Fortunately, while Lilith
had proven all too fallible, Savannah had been
doubly blessed in her sister and grandmother.

"Things were admittedly a bit rocky in the
beginning," Dan allowed with what Savannah
was beginning to realize was characteristic understatement. "But, as I said, his parents built a
strong foundation and John's a great kid. I only
wish his mom could be here to see how well
he's doing."

"I'm certain she knows."

"I sure hope so." The shutters lifted; a brief
pain flashed in his eyes.

"Well, whether he got it from his parents, or
whether it's inborn, his never-say-die mentality
is definitely contagious," Savannah said. "I
don't know what I would have done if he hadn't
let me attack weeds instead of your client this
past week."

"Ah, yes." The harsh lines bracketing either
side of Dan's mouth softened. "He mentioned

something about you having developed a real knack for gardening."

"Since I don't want to accuse your nephew of being a liar, I'll just say that he's overly optimistic. My weeding talents leave a great deal to be desired."

"Join the club. While I'm still permitted, with supervision, to do some planting, after I created a horticultural miracle last fall he took my hoe away from me."

"A miracle?"

"See these hands?" He held them up for her perusal.

"Yes." When her unruly mind threw up a quick, hot fantasy of those long dark fingers, which could have belonged to a pianist, playing over her flesh, Savannah had to remind herself to breathe.

"They single-handedly turned an entire bed of perennials into annuals."

Their shared laughter lightened the mood that had been threatening to turn gloomy. Dan exhaled another brief sigh, then, squaring his shoulders, slid the document across the desk toward her.

"You need to initial here"—he pointed toward the line accentuated with a flourescent red Post-it flag—"and here." He tapped the pen point on another line on the second page, then flipped to the last page. "Last chance to change your mind."

Undaunted by the herculean task ahead of her, Savannah ignored his warning.

This morning, when she'd been sitting at the kitchen table, fretting over a proposed construction schedule that dragged into late fall, her grandmother had briskly pointed out in her no-nonsense way that "even Rome wasn't burned in a day."

The Ida-mangled advice had reminded Savannah of what she'd suspected when she'd packed up her belongings and walked away from her former comfortable California existence. Rebuilding an entire life from scratch would undoubtedly not be easy.

Knowing she'd suffer setbacks, she wrote her name with a flourish on the final page of the contract to purchase the Far Harbor lighthouse, and for the first time in a very long while, Savannah felt blissfully, incredibly happy.

5

The Far Harbor lighthouse was draped in a soft haze. A cool curtain of fog hung low over the water, and the dense grove of Douglas fir and western hemlock behind the lighthouse loomed dark and mysterious. The dawn sky had been streaked with crimson, predicting that by afternoon thunderstorms would be rumbling their way from the sea over the mountaintops, creating rain that would hit the water like bullets. Winds would stir up whitecaps, and stuttering trees of white lightning would flash across the blackened sky. Living amidst so much nature might not be for the faint of heart, but Dan found it invigorating.

As his running shoes pounded on the wet sand near the water's edge, he thought, not for the first time, how ironic it was that after so many years spent plotting his escape from Coldwater Cove, here he was, back home again, right where he'd started.

He dodged a green tangle of kelp that had
ridden onto the pearl gray beach on a surge of
tide and decided that Savannah Townsend's recent arrival back in town was additional proof
that life tended to have more jigs and jogs than
the narrow roads twisting through the jagged
Northwest mountains.

The too-early deaths of his sister and brother-
in-law had been, hands down, the worst event of
his life. But there'd been no time for self-pity as
he'd sat vigil beside John's hospital bed, praying
for him to regain consciousness—which, thank
God, he had.

During his nephew's long recuperation, Dan's
attention had been focused on getting John back
on his feet. But other events forced him to face
the fact that his wife didn't possess the same
deep-seated sense of family that he'd been moderately surprised to discover guided his own life.

His first clue had been when Amanda had refused to even visit him in Coldwater Cove,
claiming that social obligations and her part-
time career as an interior designer to the mega-
wealthy made it impossible for her to leave San
Francisco for any extended period of time.

By the time the divorce papers had arrived,
he'd taken a long hard look at a marriage that
should have been declared dead at the altar and
vaguely wondered why Amanda had waited so
long. As soon as John was back on his feet and
had returned to school, Dan had thrown his en-
ergies into establishing a new law practice.

The tide ebbed, leaving behind a sparkling

trail of diaphanous sea foam. He pounded up the stone steps leading from the beach and compared the morning solitude with San Francisco's vibrant pulse. Once, in what now seemed like another life, before youthful illusions had been snuffed out by the cold harsh winds of reality, he'd run every morning on this very same beach and daydreamed of bright lights and big cities. The Olympic Peninsula town founded by one of his ancestors had always seemed too provincial, too confining, for someone of Dan O'Halloran's lofty talent and ambition.

The only son of a Coldwater Cove commercial fisherman and homemaker turned charter boat cook, by the time he'd entered junior high school, Dan had a very firm future in mind. The plan, laid out with all the care and precision of the Joint Chiefs preparing for invasion, was to get a prestigious law degree, work for a few years in a high-profile job—prosecution, perhaps—which would set him up for partnership in a respectable big-city law firm.

Rounding out the mental picture was a Tudor-style house like the one belonging to some Wall Street wizard he'd seen profiled in a glossy magazine while waiting for the orthodontist to tighten his braces. The house would boast acres of rolling emerald lawn someone else would mow, a blue tiled swimming pool and a tennis court—red clay, rather than the more pedestrian concrete the public courts at Founders Park were made of, because that's what the mutual fund titan had chosen.

At twelve he wasn't really interested in the family part of his dream, yet from those magazine pages he'd unconsciously absorbed the idea that living in this dream house with him would be a gorgeous, intelligent trophy wife from a good family and their equally attractive, brilliant children.

Dan's laugh was directed inward as he considered how close he'd actually come to achieving his youthful dream. Including the Tudor which had been filled to twelve-foot-high ceilings with pricey Oriental porcelain he'd always been terrified of knocking off those marble pedestals. Befitting his upwardly mobile position and his wife's lofty social status, he dutifully subscribed to the symphony, the ballet, and the opera, and doubted that any of their Pacific Heights friends would ever suspect that he secretly preferred classic Beetles to Beethoven, Willie Nelson to Wagner.

He'd nearly achieved everything he'd ever dreamed of; all that had been missing was the partnership, and if he'd caved in to Amanda's pressure to accept the extremely lucrative offer he'd received from that Montgomery Street law firm the day after his sister's fatal accident, the final piece of the plan would have fallen into place before his thirty-third birthday.

Which just went to show, Dan considered as he yanked off his damp cardinal Stanford sweatshirt and entered his house by the kitchen door, that a guy had better be careful what he wished for.

The house was silent, revealing that John

had already taken off on his summer morning gardening rounds. The aroma of freshly brewed coffee enticed; Dan filled a mug from the Mr. Coffee carafe and took it into the bathroom to drink after his shower.

Ten minutes later he was sitting out on his redwood deck, surveying his domain. The mist had already been burned away by the rising sun.

The moment he'd first seen this house perched on the edge of the cliff, Dan had found it perfect, much preferring the open floor plan and vast expanse of glass that looked out over heart-soaring views to the gloomy San Francisco mansion with its dark silk walls and windows heavily draped in antique brocade that he'd lived in with his former wife. While he still loved the place and figured nothing short of dynamite would ever get him out of it, he'd begun to sense that something was missing. But he hadn't quite gotten a handle on what, exactly, it could be.

When a sporty red BMW convertible pulled up in front of the lighthouse, Dan put the puzzle aside and decided to pay a call on his new neighbor.

Savannah was sanding the dining room chair rail when she realized she was not alone. It was not the first time she'd experienced the feeling. This time, however, when she turned around, she saw Dan standing in the open doorway.

The sunlight streamed over him, gilding the ends of his hair in a way that made her want to run her fingers through it. Heavens, he was good-looking. But having had her fill of good-looking men, Savannah was about to inform him that she was far too busy for neighborly visits when he held up a white bag bearing the ivy-covered-cottage logo of Molly's Muffins and More.

"I figured you might be able to use a little nourishment. Hopefully you haven't turned into one of those California bark eaters during your time in LaLa land."

The enticing, forbidden aromas of deep-fried dough and coffee wafted over the pungent odor of turpentine and paint stripper and nearly made her drool.

"There's something to be said for refined white sugar—in moderation." So much for sending him on his way. Besides, she reasoned, since Dan practically lived next door, she might as well get used to having their paths cross.

Deciding that a few minutes one way or the other really wouldn't make a difference in her overall schedule, she tossed down the sanding block and wiped her hands on the damp cloth she kept dust free in a sealed, oversized plastic bag.

He took two foam cups from a second bag, pulled off the plastic covers, and set them on the thick front door that was currently resting on two sawhorses, awaiting a new paint job and hardware.

She'd arrived at the lighthouse at six o'clock that morning to meet the electrician, who'd made a big deal about squeezing her into his busy schedule. The man's estimate—nearly twice what she'd anticipated and budgeted for—had left her with an aching head. Skipping breakfast, combined with two hours of hard physical labor, had her stomach rumbling.

"Chocolate!" She dove into the bag and pulled out an éclair. When she bit into the gooey cream center, she nearly wept. "Oh, God, I think I love you."

"We aim to please." He selected a bear claw for himself. "I have to admit I was a little worried when Molly didn't have a single edible flower on the menu."

Savannah assured herself that it was an instantaneous sugar high and not Dan's self-satisfied grin and close proximity that jolted her pulse. It took a moment for his words to sink in. When they did, she tilted her head and looked up at him.

"That almost sounds as if you've eaten at Las Casitas."

"I have."

"When?" Deciding that Lilith and Oscar Wilde were right about being able to avoid everything but temptation and convinced that she must have already worked off about a gazillion calories today, Savannah dipped into the bag again, this time choosing a white frosted cinnamon roll studded with fat raisins.

"A couple years ago," he answered. "I attended a prosecutors' conference in Malibu."

"A conference?" The cinnamon roll tasted every bit as sinful as it looked. Savannah feared she'd have to sand woodwork eight hours a day for a solid week to make up for the indulgence. "That implies more than one night."

"Two nights and three excruciatingly boring days spent listening to attorneys, all of whom, like most lawyers, love the sound of their own voices."

"Three days," she repeated. "Did you know I was working there?"

"That fact would have been a little hard to miss, since all the elevators had huge framed pictures of you dipping petunias into melted chocolate while looking incredibly sexy in your white apron and tall chef's hat."

"They were nasturtiums," she corrected absently. "Why didn't you let me know you were staying at the resort? I would have enjoyed seeing you."

That was mostly true. Over the years since high school, Savannah had thought of Dan on occasion, mostly in the over-romanticized, gilt-edged way she suspected most women remembered their first crush.

"I left a note for you when I checked in."

A note. One that Kevin, who, on constant lookout for celebrities, watched over the front desk with an eagle eye, had obviously kept from her. Strangely, for a man whom she'd belatedly discovered hadn't known the meaning of fidelity, her husband had always been unreasonably possessive. When they'd first been married, she'd been somewhat flattered by his jealousy. Now she'd come to understand that he'd merely considered her another trophy, like his state-of-the-art sound system or the black Porsche Targa housed in the three-car garage of their Malibu house.

"I never received any note." She began shredding her paper napkin in lieu of wringing her ex-husband's neck.

Dan didn't look all that surprised, which made her wonder what, exactly, Raine had told Jack about her marriage. And what Jack, in turn, had told his cousin.

"The place was a madhouse, with two conventions there at the same time," he said easily. "It undoubtedly got put in someone else's box."

"That must have been what happened," she agreed.

Savannah had the feeling that neither one of them really believed that explanation.

They sipped their coffee in companionable silence broken by the sound of shingles and layers of tar paper being ripped off the roof overhead. Finally Dan tossed his empty cup into a large brown cardboard box that had originally held a case of Rainier beer that she was using for a trash can, rocked back on his heels, and glanced around.

"I think it's looking better."

Savannah imagined she heard the sound of laughter, but since the voice was too light and high to belong to any of the roofers, decided that it must be the wind whistling through the now open rafters.

"Liar." There were paint cans everywhere, the walls, stripped of paper, revealed patching, and the pine floor was still deeply gouged and in desperate need of sanding and sealing. Reluctantly deciding that her coffee break had lasted long enough, she dropped her foam cup into the box with his and returned to her sanding.

"It's a disaster. But at least it's *my* disaster. Mine and Henry's," she amended.

Dan shrugged out of his leather jacket, tossed it onto the top of a stepladder, picked up an extra putty knife and went to work scraping paint off a nearby windowsill. "Speaking of Henry, I hear you're springing him today."

"This afternoon. After the doctor makes her rounds."

"Better make sure she checks out his heart."

"Why?" Savannah glanced back over her shoulder at him. "Do you know something about his health I don't?" Neither the doctor nor the nurses she'd spoken with had suggested that by moving the elderly man out of Evergreen, she might be risking his life.

He flicked a casual but decidedly masculine look over her. "You really are a fabulous creature, Savannah. Just the sight of you in that getup might set off the old guy's built-in defibrillator."

She was wearing the new T-shirt Ida had given her tucked into the waistband of her oldest jeans. Yet Savannah suddenly felt as if she'd absently run out of the house this morning in her underwear.

"You make it sound as if I'm wearing a leather miniskirt and a sequined spandex tube top," she complained between her teeth as she reattacked the chair rail.

"I've always thought sequined spandex was overkill, but I can't deny that the mental image of you in leather is definitely more than a little appealing." He put down the putty knife and picked up the wire brush she'd been using for detail work.

"I hate to disappoint you, Dan, but I don't even own any leather."

"Don't worry. That can be remedied. I know a guy in town who used to be a member of a biker gang until bad judgment landed him in prison, where, instead of engraving license plates, he learned tailoring.

"After his release six months ago he opened a shop, and business has really taken off. Even Oprah ordered a dress from him, and though I haven't seen him wear it on the air yet, word is that Dan Rather bought a jacket that reads Hard News Guy on the back. Needless to say, everyone in town's been arguing exactly how Rather meant that. . . .

"You know," he warned, "if you're not careful, you're going to sand that wood all the way down to the plaster wall."

Savannah spun back toward him, her planned retort cut off by the friendly warmth in his eyes. "I'm having a hard time picturing Dan Rather buying his clothing from a former felon in Coldwater Cove, Washington."

"My hand to God." He lifted his right hand. "The guy's a client of mine. In fact, he paid his bill with that jacket."

Of course she'd noticed the jacket the moment he'd shown up in her doorway. It was black, looked as soft as butter, and gave him a sexy James Dean rebellious appearance that she suspected hadn't been encouraged at Stanford law school.

"That's quite a step, going from prosecuting criminals to springing Hell's Angels from jail."

"He's not a Hell's Angel, just a wannabe who learned his lesson the hard way and paid for it with some hard time. Also, I didn't spring him. I wrote up his shop's lease agreement after his release and found him an accountant to handle bookkeeping and tax stuff."

The leather jacket may be a long way from Brooks Brothers, but Savannah could more easily imagine Dan arguing a case in a San Francisco federal courtroom than she could picture him doing routine paperwork for a convict biker wannabe. Even one who'd sold a jacket to Dan Rather.

"You don't have to do that," she said as she realized he appeared inclined to stay. "Surely you have work to do."

"Not at the moment. I've got to run by a print shop in Port Townsend later this morning, but until then I'm free as a bird."

Savannah pursed her lips and nodded. "Good idea. Having flyers printed up to hand out at accident scenes." She'd meant the uncharacteristically sarcastic dig as retaliation for his blatantly sexist defibrillator remark, but wasn't all that surprised when he remained unwounded.

"Speaking of accident scenes," he drawled, "do you know the difference between a lawyer and a Dalmatian?"

"I have no idea." Her tone dripped with disinterest.

"A Dalmatian knows when to stop chasing the ambulance."

"That's the lamest one yet." She squelched the bubble of answering laughter and felt her neck and shoulder muscles, which had been tied up in knots for weeks, actually relax. "I thought lawyers hated those jokes."

"Actually, there are only two lawyer jokes. The rest are all true." He smiled at her.

"Don't you take anything seriously?" It was not exactly a rhetorical question. Savannah really wanted to know.

"Sure. I'm gravely serious about plague, pestilence, wars, and anyone who hurts defenseless kids or dogs. I'm also a sucker for beautiful women in distress."

When he skimmed another appraising glance over her, Savannah tossed up her chin. That description might admittedly have fit her once, but no longer. Well, at least not as much as it had when she'd first arrived home, she amended, thinking back on how she'd given in to tears this morning after the electrician had packed up his voltage meter and left the lighthouse. But only for five minutes. Then she'd picked herself up, brushed herself off, taken out her sanding block and gone to work.

"Which brings me back to the reason for going to Port Townsend." His deep voice returned her mind to their conversation. "One of my clients is a struggling divorced mother of three who hasn't received a penny of child support in five years. Her ex took off to Montana, but I've got a line on him.

"At least I hope I do. If his pissed-off girlfriend, whose credit cards he maxed out, can be believed, he's moved back to Washington and is currently working as a printer. The shop opens at ten. Meanwhile, I have some time to kill."

"And you couldn't think of anything better to do than scrape paint?"

"Nope. I also couldn't think of anyone I'd rather spend my time with."

His smile was friendly and unthreatening. It also created that now familiar stir. Not knowing how to safely respond to his statement, Savannah returned to her sanding.

6

Savannah watched Henry Hyatt study the bedroom, which, although small, was as tidy as a nun's cell. Framed prints of old sailing ships hung on the wall, and lace curtains dappled the afternoon sunshine, creating dancing dots of light on the antique quilt.

"The girl didn't say anything about me havin' to share the facilities," he grumbled.

"I happen to have a name, Mr. Hyatt," Savannah responded mildly. She'd learned early on in her discussions with Henry that if you gave the man an inch, he'd take it and run for a mile. "It's Savannah."

"Damn fool name if you ask me."

"Nobody asked you," Ida, who'd readied the room for him, snapped. "Not that it's any of your beeswax, but Lilith named Savannah for the town where she was born."

"Good thing Lilith wasn't livin' in Pough-keepsie."

"You get up on the wrong side of the barn door this morning, Henry?" Ida lifted her eyes to the high ceiling. "I knew this was going to be a mistake."

"I didn't ask to come here."

"That's just as well, since I would've probably turned you away. I'm only doing this for Savannah," she told him what Savannah herself already had figured out. "You're damn fortunate my younger granddaughter's such a fool optimist she actually thinks she can turn that wreck of a place you foisted off onto her into something livable."

"The Far Harbor lighthouse has been standing in that same place since before you were born," he reminded her gruffly.

"Which is undoubtedly why it's falling down. Old's old. Whether you're talking people or buildings."

"It's sound enough to have withstood plenty of gales. Including the storm of ought six," he countered gruffly. "Besides, I didn't twist the girl's—"

"Savannah's," she reminded him sharply.

"Hell's bells." He raked arthritic fingers through what was left of his hair. "I'd forgotten what a hardheaded woman you can be."

"Nothing hardheaded about wanting my granddaughter referred to by name—the very same granddaughter who's invited you into her home," she reminded him pointedly.

"Where I have to share the head."

Ida crossed her arms over a scarlet T-shirt

that announced So It's Not Home Sweet
Home . . . Adjust.

"You want a private bathroom? Fine. Since
you're so set on pissin' your life away, I'll drive
you back to Evergreen." Her sneakers squeaked
on the waxed floor as she turned and strode to
the door, pausing to shoot him a dare over her
shoulder. "Well? You coming or not?"

They could have been on the main street of
nineteenth-century Dodge City at high noon.
Both individuals were incredibly strong-willed.
Savannah suspected that until he'd broken his
hip and landed in Evergreen, Henry had been
every bit as accustomed to getting his way as
her grandmother. Ida's edge, Savannah decided,
was that she held the keys to the closest thing
he'd known to a home in a very long while.

"Guess it won't be so bad." He shrugged, as if
he didn't give a damn one way or the other. "So
long as that girl—Savannah," he amended
when Ida hit him with another sharp warning
glare, "doesn't spend all day soaking in the tub
or leave makeup all over the counter."

"Don't worry, Mr. Hyatt," Savannah assured
him. "I'm going to be far too busy for long luxu-
rious bubble baths." Every muscle in her aching
body practically wept with yearning at that idea.

"Thanks to that mess you left her," Ida tacked
on. "You also won't have to worry about makeup, since Savannah's a natural beauty. Never
has needed the stuff."

"Can't argue with you there," he said gruffly.
Savannah sighed. It figured that the first

halfway nice thing he said about her would have to do with her looks. It would be nice, she thought, if just once a man was capable of looking beyond the packaging.

"Sorta reminds me of her mother," Henry continued, unaware of her faint irritation. "But not nearly as flighty."

Since she'd had a long, exhausting day and wasn't up to getting into an argument, Savannah chose not to leap to her mother's defense this time. Besides, it was the truth. Lilith *was* flighty. That had always been part of her appeal.

"I got you something," Ida announced. She marched passed him again, opened the top drawer of a pine dresser and took out a brown paper bag.

"What is it?" Henry's expression suggested he feared the bag could contain anything from rat poison to a lit stick of dynamite.

"Why don't you open it and find out?"

Obviously not quite trusting her, he took the bag and pulled out a T-shirt the deep green of a pine forest. "What's this for?"

Looking nearly as uncomfortable as Henry, Ida shrugged her shoulders, which, while narrow, had carried more than her share of burdens over the years. Savannah would have thought her grandmother was suddenly embarrassed at giving a present to a man who'd done absolutely nothing to deserve it, had it not been for something that looked remarkably like panic in Ida's eyes.

In contrast to the comfortable silence she'd

shared with Dan at the lighthouse this morning, the one settling over the guestroom had the feel of a wet wool blanket.

"I suppose it's a welcoming gift," Savannah said as she studied her grandmother intently.

"I don't need no blamed gift," Henry said.

"Maybe *you* don't need it," Ida countered. "But *I* do." Her eyes cleared. Bright color stained her cheekbones. Proving that age hadn't made her any more patient, she snatched the shirt from his hand and held it up so he could read the message: Please Be Patient. God Isn't Finished with Me Yet.

"If I'm going to be forced to live under the same roof as you, Henry Hyatt, I'm going to need all the help I can get to remind myself that as nasty as you are, you're still a work in progress."

That stated, this time she did leave. She didn't exactly slam the bedroom door behind her, but she came close.

"Damn woman sure has a helluva temper," he grumbled.

"Not that you did anything to provoke her," Savannah suggested mildly.

He cursed, then pressed a palm down onto the single mattress. "This bed is as hard as a piece of old-growth cedar."

Her grandmother wasn't the only one second-guessing the idea to bring Henry into their home. Savannah ground her teeth and tried to remind herself that all this trouble would be worth it once her Far Harbor lighthouse was restored to its gleaming white glory.

"I was informed you preferred a hard mattress for your back."

"It's not as good as the one I used to have when I was living in the lighthouse, but I guess a man could do worse."

"I'm so pleased you approve," Savannah said dryly.

"At least this place doesn't smell of piss."

He was looking out the window at the sweep of emerald lawn, the town, and beyond that, the bay. Savannah watched his scowl soften and saw something that looked like an escaped spark from a fireplace flare hot and high in his faded blue eyes.

Looking as if his bones had given out, he sank down onto the very mattress he'd just complained about, reminding her of the collapsed scarecrow in *The Wizard of Oz*. What appeared to be a staggering emotion moved across his hollowed face in waves.

Savannah had no trouble recognizing the overpowering feeling, having experienced it herself so many times recently.

It was hope.

He was late. Savannah had been pacing the floor, waiting for the past three hours for the delivery of the window treatments. She'd called the store three times in the past forty-five minutes, and each time she'd been assured that the truck was on its way and should be there at any minute.

"Your curtains will be here soon," John assured her. In what had become a daily habit, they were eating lunch together in the garden. Since beginning her dream project, she'd discovered that budgets and deadlines shifted like changing sands in this foreign world of reconstruction. John's unrelenting optimism and amazing patience were proving a balm for frazzled nerves.

"Finally!" A truck was lumbering up the hill; the yellow lettering on the side announced that it was from Linens & Lace, located in Seattle.

The driver didn't offer any excuse for his tardiness. Savannah reminded herself that it didn't really matter. The important thing was that she was finally holding the custom-made curtains she'd pictured so many times in her imagination.

"They're really pretty," John offered as she took the first froths of snowy white lace from the box.

"Didn't they turn out lovely?" She'd had to cut back on her furniture budget to pay for the outrageously expensive lace, but as she draped one of the panels over her hand, admiring what appeared to be bridal veils for windows, Savannah decided the expense had definitely been worth every penny.

Hoping to echo John's remarkable garden, she'd selected a Scottish floral pattern that dated back to the 1860s and had been woven on antique Nottingham looms. The effect worked even better than she'd imagined. The floral lace had brought the garden indoors. But there was one problem.

"I'm afraid the sidelights for the glass panels

on the assistant keeper's cottage door are going to have to go back."

The driver's ruddy face closed up. "You can't send them back." He jabbed a thick finger at the bill of lading attached to his metal clipboard. "It says right here, no returns on monogrammed items."

"But it's the wrong pattern. The rest of the order has fourteen threads per inch. These panels are eight-point, which isn't nearly as delicate."

"They look okay to me."

"They're very attractive." Savannah drew in a calming breath and reminded herself of Ida's old saying about being able to catch more bees with honey than cider. "But they don't match the others. And they're not what I paid for."

"No returns," the man repeated with the stubbornness of an ox. "The salesman should have told you that when you placed your order."

"He did." Savannah ran her fingertips over the lovely *FH* embroidered in the center of the panel. She was not going to let this stubborn, ill-tempered man ruin her lovely mood. Or take away the pleasure from the fact that the rest of the curtains had turned out even more beautiful than she'd dreamed. "I understand the policy, since ripping out a monogram would undoubtedly destroy such delicate lace.

"However," she continued when, appearing to feel he'd won this little skirmish, the driver held out his clipboard again, "the salesman also assured me that all the lace would be fourteen point. The mistake seems to be your company's, not mine."

The man scowled. "I'm not supposed to leave here without a signature. Either you accept the whole shipment or it all goes back."

"I'm not accepting these side panels." A familiar flame flickered beneath her ribs. Her parents had both been emotional, high-strung, dramatic individuals. Their fights had resembled World War III and had, on more than one occasion caused Savannah to become physically ill. They'd also left her hating confrontation of any kind.

Over the years she'd developed the ability to remain firm when it came to her kitchens in the various hotels she'd worked in. Savannah decided that this situation was no different from insisting on the freshest vegetables or the brightest-eyed fish. Still, it was her nature to seek a compromise solution.

"I'm certain, if I call the store manager and explain the situation, you'll be off the hook."

He shrugged his huge shoulders in a way that suggested he didn't really care what she did, so long as she stopped complicating his day. Less than five minutes later he was headed back down the hill, the sidelight panels in his van.

"You did real good," John complimented her.

"I did, didn't I?" Savannah was proud of the way she'd refused to buckle under. "What would you say to going into town and letting me treat you to a hot fudge sundae to celebrate?"

"With double nuts?"

"Absolutely."

"That's a great idea." John helped her pack the lace curtains away in the white tissue paper again. "Can we stop along the way? I have a favor to do for a friend, but it shouldn't take very long."

"Sure." She was already behind schedule. What could a few more minutes hurt? Besides, this was a special day. A day she'd discovered that the world wouldn't tilt off its axis simply if she stood her ground.

John gave her directions to a small, 1930s bungalow–style house near the center of town, across from Founder's Park. It was redbrick with a wide, inviting front porch. An American flag was flying from a bracket attached to one of the porch pillars.

Savannah had driven past the house occasionally since her return to Coldwater Cove and had decided that if there was an award for tacky landscaping, this place would win, hands down. What on earth would possess anyone to plant an entire yard in cheap, dime-store flowers?

Last night's storm had torn the plastic blooms out of ground and scattered many of them into the neighbor's yard. All that remained were a trio of stone ducks, an overturned white plastic birdbath, and a brightly painted wooden whirligig of a pig dressed in a red, white, and blue Uncle Sam suit riding a bicycle.

"Darn." John frowned. "I was afraid the wind would blow all the flowers over."

Savannah parked the car, then waited on the sidewalk while John took out the small box of hand gardening tools he'd placed on the back floor. They were walking side by side toward the bungalow when the front door opened and a man in a wheelchair pushed himself over the threshold.

His age appeared to make him one of Henry Hyatt's contemporaries, but where Henry was thin and wiry, this man possessed a thick chest, huge upper arms that reminded her of tree trunks, and a lined face weathered by years spent outdoors. He was wearing a black-and-red flannel shirt and denim overalls cut above his ankles. Since loggers tended to keep their pants short to prevent them from getting caught in undergrowth and chain saw blades, Savannah guessed that he'd once earned his living felling the huge trees that grew in the peninsula's forests.

"Hello, Mr. Hawthorne," John called out. "I've come to fix your wife's garden."

"You're a good boy, John Martin." A vestige of Maine reverberated in the man's voice. "The wife was fretting about that just this morning. It was all I could do to keep her from coming outside."

"Well, you don't have to worry." John held up a green-handled trowel. "I'll have things back the way they belong real quick." He knelt on the ground and began digging holes in the dark earth still damp from last night's rain. "This is Savannah Townsend. Savannah, this is Mr. Hawthorne."

Savannah nodded. "I'm pleased to meet you,

Mr. Hawthorne." The name rang a bell, but she couldn't place him.

"Same here."

"Savannah bought the Far Harbor light-house," John revealed as he began gathering up the scattered blooms.

"Seems I recollect hearin' something about that." The elderly man took a pouch of tobacco from his shirt pocket and began filling a pipe that nearly disappeared in his huge hands. When he pulled an old fashioned strike-any-where kitchen match from the same pocket and lit it with his thumbnail, Savannah no-ticed that his index finger ended at the second knuckle.

"Heard you're turnin' the place into some sort of fancy hotel."

"I'm planning a bed-and-breakfast. But it isn't going to be all that fancy." She braced her-self for a response she'd heard from local old-timers: that the Far Harbor lighthouse was a dump and she'd bitten off more than any sensi-ble person could chew.

"It's about time somebody did something useful with that place," he surprised her by say-ing. He lit the pipe and began puffing away, the smoke rising to circle his head in white, cherry-scented rings. "It went to seed when the Coast Guard pulled out. Turned into a real eyesore in the town."

Savannah thought that an ironic comment coming from a man who'd turned his front lawn into a better-living-through-plastics display.

"I'm hoping to bring it back to its former glory."

"Good for you." He puffed some more. "You'd be Ida's youngest granddaughter."

"Yes."

"Good woman, Ida. Hardworking, salt of the earth, and a dandy doctor to boot." He held up the hand that wasn't holding the pipe. "Did a real good job sewing my finger back on when I whacked it off clearing slash over by Forks." More puffs rose from the briar pipe like smoke signals. " 'Course, her meatloaf leaves a bit to be desired, but nobody's perfect."

Savannah smiled. Ida Lindstrom's meatloaf was infamous in Coldwater Cove, but as far as Savannah knew, no one had ever had the heart to tell her that her customary contribution to potluck suppers was as hard as a brick and as dry as sawdust.

"You not plannin' to serve that meatloaf at your hotel, are you?" he asked.

"No, sir, I'm not."

"Then you'll probably do well enough." That settled, he turned his attention to John. "It's startin' to look real good again."

"That's the great advantage of plastic flowers," John said cheerfully.

Knowing how much pride he took in his work, Savannah couldn't quite believe she'd heard John correctly. He tapped some dirt around an orange rose with chartreuse leaves, then rocked back and observed his handiwork as the screen door opened.

"Just in time," Mr. Hawthorne said with a huge huff of obvious relief as an elderly woman came out on the porch. She was wearing a cotton housedress emblazoned with scarlet poppies, a misbuttoned purple cardigan with frayed sleeves, a yellow straw gardening hat adorned with huge pink fabric peonies, and a pair of high green Wellingtons that made her legs look like two pale sticks.

"We've got company, Vada," Mr. Hawthorne said gently. "It's John Martin, come to work in your garden. And Savannah Townsend. You remember, she's Ida's daughter's youngest girl."

He could have been speaking to one of the stone ducks. Vada Hawthorne didn't reveal a single sign that she'd heard him. Seeming in a world of her own making, she made her way down the front steps. Then, muttering beneath her breath, began walking through the rows of replanted flowers.

"Vada's got the Alzheimer's," Mr. Hawthorne explained. "She started getting confused and lost in her mind about five years ago. At first we thought it was just old age, but then things went downhill. It was our son, Jeremy, an ER doc over to Port Angeles, who finally made us realize what was wrong with his mom.

"Even going to the library doesn't seem to spark any memories these days."

It was his mention of the library that made Savannah recognize the name. She remembered, with vivid clarity, that long-ago day she'd walked out of the big brick building with a brand-new library card and a book entitled *Tasty Treats for Young Cooks*. She'd tried out the s'mores that first night.

Over the years Mrs. Hawthorne, who'd been Olympic County librarian for as long as anyone could remember, had continued to supply Savannah with recipes, even using the interlibrary lending program to get more complex cookbooks from Seattle and Tacoma.

Besides feeding a young girl's culinary desires, Vada Hawthorne had taken generations of children on magic-carpet rides to wondrous worlds outside of Coldwater Cove. The librarian's love of books had inspired so many. It wasn't fair that she, of all people, should end her life in such a mental vacuum.

"I'm so sorry."

"Oh, it's not as bad as it was back when she first realized what was happening to her and was scared all the time. This spring she managed to get herself down to Harbor Street and told Daniel O'Halloran that she wanted to divorce me."

"Oh, I'm sure she didn't mean that," Savannah said quickly.

"She sure did mean it," he countered. "Woman got in her mind that if I was shed of her I'd be free to marry again." His voice thickened. He cleared his throat, pulled out a blue-and-white cloth handkerchief and blew his nose with a mighty honk. "We'll be married fifty-five years come Christmas, and there's never been a single day in all those years that I didn't thank the good Lord for giving me my Vada."

"That's so sweet." Savannah had no experience with such long-term commitment; even Ida had left her gambler husband in the fifth year of their marriage after he'd come home from a three-day losing streak and made the mistake of striking his wife. Claiming that if someone hits you, it's a pretty good clue that they don't like you that much—let alone love you—she'd packed her bags and moved from Portland to Coldwater Cove that same day.

"I don't know about sweet." He shrugged his shoulders and appeared self-conscious. "It's just the way things are. These days, about the only thing left from the past that Vada still connects with is her flowers. Course, she can't take care of them anymore, and now that I'm in this contraption, I can't get around the way I used to back when I was younger.

"But then Daniel got the idea for this garden. John planted it and changes it with the seasons, so Vada can believe she's still got plants blooming year-round."

Vada Hawthorne was still talking away at the rainbow plastic flowers when Savannah and John left the house. Savannah no longer found the garden tacky, but as she drove the few blocks to the Sweet Delights ice cream shop, she couldn't decide if the former librarian's garden was the loveliest or saddest thing she'd ever seen.

7

A mental image of Vada Hawthorne stayed with Savannah during her stolen time off with John at the ice cream parlor, as she drove him back to the lighthouse, so he could pick up his bike, then on the long drive to the Christmas tree farm Raine had moved to after marrying Jack. When Savannah had called the law offices earlier, she'd been told Raine was taking a home day.

Her sister answered the door wearing a gray Sheriff's Department T-shirt, jeans, and bare feet.

"You have no idea how good it is to see you," Raine said as she stepped aside and let Savannah into the farmhouse. "I've spent all morning sewing and was about ready to tear my hair out."

"I didn't realize you even knew how to sew."

"I don't, or, more precisely, I didn't. I'm starting to get the hang of it, though it's a lot more dangerous than I would have guessed." She held out her left hand, revealing a Band-aid.

"I've run over my finger three times in the past two hours."

The kitchen looked as if a hurricane had blown through it. Or it had, perhaps, been sacked by a horde of vandals. The table had disappeared beneath pieces of brown, black, and gray fabric. Tissue paper Savannah recognized as pattern pieces were all over the floor. A top-of-the-line sewing machine sat atop the table in the midst of all the chaos; the box on the floor nearby gave proof that it was brand-new.

"May I ask why you're putting yourself through all this?"

"Amy won the part of lead scary tree in her summer day camp's production of *The Wizard of Oz*. I've been sewing damn fabric bark onto a leotard all morning. Thank God it's supposed to be a bare tree. If I had to face leaves, I'd have no choice but to throw myself into the sound."

Despite the concern that had brought her here, Savannah laughed. "Do you have any idea how fortunate you are?"

Raine's scowl instantly turned to a slow, satisfied grin. "Absolutely. Would you like some coffee? It'll just take me a minute to brew it."

"No, thanks. I already inhaled about a pot while I was steaming wallpaper while waiting for the curtain delivery."

"In that outfit?"

Savannah glanced down at her khaki shorts and black, tan, and white striped bateau-neck knit shirt. "What's wrong with it?"

"It's clean. Neat." Raine skimmed a fingernail

down the crease of the shorts. "Starched." She shook her head. "You look as if you just walked off the summer fashion issue of *Vogue*. What the hell do you do, spray yourself with Teflon each morning before you leave the house?"

"I wear an apron."

"An apron," Raine repeated, looking skeptical.

"It's actually more of a smock. To keep the paint and dust off."

"Honey, in order to look half as good as you do right now, the rest of us would have to wear a hazardous waste team incubation suit."

She shook her head in amused disbelief again. "Of course I'm happy to see you, but what's so important that it brought you out to the boonies this afternoon?"

On the long drive to the farm, Savannah had tried to tell herself that she was overreacting. The problem was, she hadn't quite been able to make herself believe that.

"Where's Amy?" She belatedly realized that she hadn't been hit with a ball of blond energy the moment she walked in the front door— which just proved how distracted she was. Normally, she loved any opportunity to see her new niece.

"In Seattle with Lilith. They're having a girls' day on the town. They're shopping at Nordstrom's, having lunch at Pike Place Market, then capping the day off with a trip to the Aquarium."

"Sounds like Mom's really getting into being a grandmother."

"She adores it." Raine took a longer, more probing look at Savannah. "Whatever's bothering you can't be all that bad."

Savannah sat down on one of the kitchen chairs. "John and I took off early today and went out for ice cream and stopped by Vada Hawthorne's house on the way. You remember her, she was town librarian."

"Of course I remember Mrs. Hawthorne." Raine sat across the fabric-strewn table. "She always used to save the new Nancy Drew books for me."

"She introduced me to the *Little House* books. And *Little Women*." After reading that novel, Savannah had decided that the solidarity she and Raine shared was just like the March sisters'. Needless to say, she'd viewed Raine as the always adventurous Jo, herself as the more settled, domestic Meg. "Did you know she's got Alzheimer's?"

"I heard something about that. How's she doing?"

"Not well." Savannah told Raine about the elderly woman asking Dan for the divorce, then described the garden.

"That was a lovely idea of Dan's."

"John told me later that he'd thought of it after they'd gone to the cemetery to put flowers on Karyn and her husband's grave and they saw all the plastic flowers other people had left on family gravesites.

"I hate thinking of Gram ending up like Mrs. Hawthorne." Savannah took a deep breath. She decided that she'd stalled long enough. "Do you think Gram's got Alzheimer's?"

Instead of immediately denying the suggestion, or laughing it off, Raine folded her hands atop the brown cloth. "I don't know. The thought's occurred to me since I've been back. But I've always managed to convince myself that I'm imagining things—making mush out of a molehill, as our grandmother would say." Raine's attempt at a smile fell flat. "I told you about her outburst in court."

"During Gwen's custody hearing?" Savannah nodded. "Yes. But not the details."

"It wasn't pretty. She ended up telling the entire court the story of how she'd once prescribed birth-control pills for the presiding judge, back when the judge was a college student. At the time I was so busy trying to keep 'em both from getting tossed into Jack's jail for contempt of court, I put it down to her strong feelings for Gwen and her eccentric personality."

"How do you feel about it now?" Savannah felt a distant pain and realized that she was digging her fingernails into her palms.

"I think she should get a complete physical, but she insists that there's nothing wrong with her."

"You've discussed this with Gram? Without first talking with me?"

"You've been a little distracted," Raine reminded her. "What with your divorce, and trying to restore the lighthouse and beginning a new business. Besides," her tone turned a bit defensive, "I mentioned it to Mother back when you were depressed. We decided that the last thing you needed was one more problem to worry about."

The conversation must have taken place while she'd been hiding beneath her covers. "How nice of you both to decide what's good for me."

"We were only trying to protect you."

"I know." It was consummate Raine, watching out for her little sister. Savannah decided that nothing would be gained by sharing her thoughts that such protection had resulted in her taking too long to acquire a sense of independence. "I also appreciate your concern. But I'm an adult, Raine. From now on, I don't want to be left out of the loop."

There was an awkward moment as the sisters looked at each other. Then, instead of arguing, or behaving as if her feelings were hurt, Raine gave her a slow smile.

"Good for you," she said, her words unknowingly echoing that of Mr. Hawthorne.

"We need a plan," Savannah said.

"A battle plan," Raine agreed. She reached into a cookie jar shaped like Winnie-the-Pooh's honey pot, took out a handful of Oreos, and put them on a plate. "Do you want to confront her directly?"

"We'll undoubtedly have to, eventually." Feeling six years old again, Savannah separated the chocolate halves and scraped the white filling off with her teeth. "But perhaps we should observe her more closely, first, to gather evidence."

"In a controlled setting." Raine took a carton

of milk from the refrigerator and poured them both a tall glass.

"Like a scientific experiment," Savannah said.

"Exactly." Raine crunched a cookie and appeared thoughtful. "You know, we still haven't had a proper celebration for you having bought the lighthouse."

"I thought we'd agreed that we'd wait for the party until all the restoration was done."

"That's your party," Raine reminded her. "There's no reason why I can't throw an earlier one." She nodded again, seeming pleased with this idea. She polished off her milk in long swallows, then took a pen and magnetic pad from the refrigerator door. "We'll invite the entire family, of course. That way we can all watch for signs."

"Do you think that's wise? Gram might notice something's up if everyone's in on it."

"The reason we're doing this is because she isn't all that lucid these days," Raine reminded her. "We'll swear everyone to secrecy and be extra careful not to be too obvious. Besides," she pointed out with the unfailing logic Savannah had always admired, "this way, if one of us slips up, the others can provide backup distraction."

She sounded so confident, Savannah believed her. "What about the menu? I can fix something—"

"You will not. From what Lilith tells me, you're working nearly around the clock now. We'll order out from Oley's," Raine said decisively. "Everyone likes barbecue. And so you won't have to lower yourself to eat red meat,

I'll even split the order between ribs and chicken."

That settled, they picked a time two evenings away. While Raine began calling the other family members to inform them of the dinner, Savannah ate her way through the honey pot cookie jar and hoped with all her heart that their concerns would prove ungrounded.

Pregnant with rain, heavy clouds the color of tarnished silver hung low over Coldwater Cove when Ida awoke. There was something she needed to do. Something important. Something for the family.

"It'll come to you," she assured herself briskly as she tucked in the sheets with tight, hospital corners, straightened the bright handmade quilt, and fluffed the pillows. She had no trouble remembering that Savannah had made the Sunshine and Shadows quilt for her 4-H project the summer she'd turned twelve, so why couldn't she remember the thought that had been teasing at the edge of her mind moments earlier?

"It's not Alzheimer's," she assured herself yet again as she showered. Savannah had installed pretty little soaps that looked like colorful seashells in the bathroom. She'd said that they weren't only for looks, that they had glycerin and some sort of fancy oils in them that would make your skin smooth, but Ida figured at her age, it was a little late to worry about soft skin. "The only thing wrong with me is Old-Timers."

She dressed, pinned her hair up in its usual haphazard bun, and went downstairs to make coffee. By the time she was on her second cup, the caffeine had kicked in.

"Raine's party is tonight," she recalled in a flash of sudden awareness as bright as the lightning that had just lit up the sky outside the kitchen window. "The family will be expecting me to make my meatloaf."

She checked the freezer and wasn't surprised to discover that she didn't have a single pound of ground beef. Savannah had pretty much taken over the cooking since returning home from Los Angeles, and the girl had never been much of a fan of red meat. Ida didn't mind all the meals of fish and chicken since her granddaughter was, after all, a whiz in the kitchen. But she'd put her foot down about the sushi.

"Might as well buy some Glo-eggs down at the Hook, Line, and Sinker," she'd told Savannah at the time. "They're bound to be cheaper."

She rinsed out her mug, then hung it on the cute little hooks Savannah had put up. She made a list of ingredients she'd need, took the keys to her Jeep down from another rack that was new since her granddaughter's return, and picked up her pocketbook, which was right where it belonged on the end of the counter.

Outside, thunder rumbled and lightning flashed. The day was shaping up to be a real frog strangler. As she plucked her rain gear from the hook beside the kitchen door, Ida decided that the fact that she remembered her umbrella proved there was nothing at all wrong with her mind.

"It's going to rain," John announced when he brought the morning paper into the kitchen.

"Sure looks like it." Dan glanced out at the threatening sky. He could vaguely make out the silhouette of the lighthouse in the fog. Farther down the beach, the new Coast Guard light flashed brightly. Dan missed the old red-and-white beacon that had made the Far Harbor lighthouse unique among the others on the strait. He also hoped the guys had finished the roof on Savannah's keeper's house yesterday.

"Do you think the rain will ruin the dinner tonight?" John asked with obvious concern.

"If it's still raining tonight, they'll just move the party indoors. When Jack called yesterday, he said Raine was ordering out from Oley's, so there won't be any outdoor cooking to interfere with."

"That's good. I like Oley's barbecue a lot." John drowned the stack of silver dollar pancakes in blueberry syrup. "Savannah's coming, right?"

"Right." Dan didn't share the details of the sisters' plan to observe their grandmother's mental state in a family setting.

"Good," John said again, with a decisive nod. "I like her a lot, don't you?"

"What's not to like?" Dan chose the maple syrup. "She's gorgeous, friendly—"

"And smells like the garden after it rains," John broke in.

"That is a decided plus."

While the thunder rolled across the fog-blanketed cove, John fell silent. Dan could tell that he was mulling something over. Knowing his nephew would share his thoughts when he was ready, he turned to the sports section to check out last night's box scores.

John was cleaning off the counter ten minutes later when he looked up from putting the pancake batter bowl in the dishwasher. "Do you think you and Savannah might get married?"

"Marriage is a pretty big step," Dan said mildly. Certainly it was a bigger step than either of them was ready for. Even so, he had been thinking about her a lot lately: during the day when he was wading through legal briefs at the office, in court when he should be keeping his mind on the case he was arguing, and mostly late at night when he was lying alone in bed, watching the lights still on in the lighthouse, and wondering if, just maybe, she was thinking of him, too.

"People usually date for a while before they start thinking about making a commitment like that," he said.

"Then maybe you ought to ask her out on a date," John suggested.

"Maybe I will."

They were in the Tahoe, on the way to Nelson's Green Spot, where John had a weekend day job when his nephew shared another, less optimistic thought.

"You don't think Ida Lindstrom's going to bring her meatloaf to the dinner tonight, do you?"

Dan laughed at the expression of dread on John's face. "I'm afraid that's pretty much a given, Sport."

Ida pushed her cart around the mercantile, gathering up the ingredients for her meatloaf. Eggs, two pounds of ground chuck—because although Savannah insisted the round was less fatty, chuck had more flavor. Then, of course she needed a pound of ground pork, which she had to wait for Glen Harding to grind for her, which wasn't all that much of a hardship since they had a nice chat about the weather and his wife Betty's lumbago, which was doing much better, thanks to the ointment Ida had suggested, Glen revealed.

"I'm pleased as Punch and Judy to hear it," Ida said. It was always rewarding to know that you'd made a difference in someone's life.

She moved on to the vegetable section, where she ran into Winnie Randall pulling back the husks from ears of sweet corn.

"Good morning, Winnie." Ida bagged a fat yellow onion for her meatloaf. "How's your mother doing?" Winnie had recently gotten a nursing home in Gray's Harbor closed down after she'd visited and discovered that her aged mother, Pearl, had acquired bedsores about as dark and deep as Mount St. Helen's craters.

"A lot better." Winnie discarded three more ears of corn. "We've got her at Evergreen, and she seems more alert and coherent. That treatment you had the nurses put on her sores worked like a charm." Two fat yellow ears made the cut and ended up in the cart.

"It always does." Ida remembered the case well. After the horror of finding Pearl in conditions the county would have shut down the dog pound for, Winnie had checked out Evergreen six ways to Sunday. Although she trusted the staff, she'd still asked Ida to drop by and examine her mother. Ida had driven to the care center that same day and immediately prescribed a "baker's cure."

The mix of equal parts of granulated sugar and hydrogen peroxide might be an old remedy and not nearly as fancy as the medicines being manufactured today, but it still worked, and as far as Ida was concerned, that was all that mattered.

While she no longer kept office hours, Ida still considered herself a working physician. A person didn't retire from the medical profession the way one might from selling insurance or working for the telephone company. When you became a doctor, you signed on for life. Ida wouldn't have had it any other way.

She exchanged a bit more chitchat, sidestepping questions about Henry's recent move into her house, Savannah's divorce, and when Raine was going to make her a great grandmother. Claiming the need to hurry home to begin cooking, Ida moved on to aisle six and picked up the Quaker Oats that was her meatloaf's secret ingredient. She checked her list, satisfied that she had everything she needed.

As she pushed her cart toward the checkout

counter, where Olivia Brown was waiting behind her newly computerized cash register, a
vivid memory of Winnie's mother flashed
through Ida's mind. In her years as a doctor,
she'd witnessed a lot of tragedies, but the sight
of Pearl, who'd once been the prettiest flapper
in Coldwater Cove, wasted away to bones and
skin and looking like a death camp survivor had
been one of the worst.

Deciding that she'd rather drop dead right
here in the mercantile than spend the last years
of her life in a nursing home, even one as nice
as Evergreen admittedly seemed to be, Ida
pushed her cart straight past Olivia, who was
busy gossiping with Fred, the seventy-year-old
bag boy, about Lilith Lindstrom Cooper having
had the nerve to show up at the VFW dance.

Old biddy, Ida thought.

"Well, I guess if her war-hero husband can
overlook her behavior back in the sixties, the
town might as well," Fred was saying as Ida
continued out through the automatic doors into
the parking lot.

She was putting groceries in the back of the
Jeep when a huffing and puffing Olivia—who'd
gained fifty pounds since starting work at the
market where the Klondike ice cream bars were
all too available—finally caught up with her.

8

Savannah was taking a shower in the claw-footed bathtub when the ringing of the phone finally infiltrated through the drumming of the water and the rattle of the hundred year old house's copper pipes. She snatched a towel from the rack, shoved aside the curtain, scrambled over the tub's high rim, and, dripping water on the floor, dashed into the bedroom, managing to scoop the receiver from its cradle just as the ringing stopped.

"Damn." Water from her hair streamed off her soap-slick body in rivulets. Wrapping the towel around her, Savannah shoved her wet tangle of hair off her forehead and blinked her eyes against the sting of shampoo.

She stood beside the bed, waiting another long moment for the phone to ring again, hoping that whoever had tried to call would give it another shot. The only sounds were a rumbling warning of thunder and the muffled clang of a buoy from somewhere out in the fog-draped harbor. Even the birds refrained from singing their morning songs, apparently hiding out somewhere in the treetops, anticipating the coming rain.

A louder clap of thunder shook the house, followed by a jolt of lightning that flashed in the bedroom like a strobe light. Old fears sparked at her nerves and made all the hair on her arms and the back of her neck stand up. Reminding herself that she was no longer that fearful child who hid from storms—both natural and emotional—Savannah returned to the bathroom, hoping that the roofers who'd finally finished up yesterday had done as good a job as they'd promised when they'd accepted their hefty check.

"It's about time you got here," Raine complained when Dan arrived at the office.

"I took a little detour to drop John off at the Green Spot, since it was raining too hard for him to ride his bike." With his mind on Savannah, as it had been too often lately, he'd forgotten to turn on his cell phone.

"I figured that might be it. Warren Cunningham's been calling every five minutes for the past half hour. He's in Tokyo, shoring up some sort of Asian Rim finance deal.

"Jack picked his son up about four this morning on a complaint, and since you've taken care of the kid's problems in the past, Warren wants you on the case."

J. C. Cunningham was a sixteen-year-old who spent the school year with his mother in Dallas, and summers and holidays at one of his father's many homes here in Coldwater Cove. Dan suspected a great deal of the trouble he caused was his way of trying to get attention from parents too wrapped up in their own lives to notice that their only son was falling through the cracks.

The boy wasn't really a juvenile delinquent. In fact, he wasn't much more wild than Dan's own cousin Jack, whose teenage stunts had landed him in judicial hot water on more than one occasion during his teen years. Fortunately, Jack had outgrown his infamous reputation and matured into a respectable adult, even following in his father's footsteps as sheriff.

But these were different times and since what once might have been considered normal juvenile transgressions seemed to be leading to more dangerous adult crimes these days, Dan could understand why Jack felt the need to lay down the law.

"What did J.C. do now?"

Raine's lips twitched. "According to Mildred Zumwalt, J.C. and his pals got a little too rambunctious last night and committed a 'drive-by shouting.'"

"That's a new one."

"It's also typically Mildred."

The woman who'd terrified a classroom of eighth graders for nearly half a century appeared to have decided to liven up her golden years by filing lawsuits against everyone in the world. Just last week she'd wanted to sue God for destruction of property when a lightning bolt had struck her tree. No fan of nuisance lawsuits, Dan had been able to talk her out of the suit by patiently reminding the former middle school civics teacher that every defendant had a legal right to answer the charges against him or her in court, and until someone came up with a way to serve a subpoena on God, he doubted there was a judge in the country that would hear the case.

"Mildred is the easy part of this morning's caseload." Raine's expression sobered. "On the flip side, I think Kathi Montgomery might just be ready to file for divorce. Looking at her, I think you're going to want to file for an order of protection as well. I put her in your office."

Dan glanced down the hallway. "It's about time," he murmured.

Jason Montgomery was a former fisherman who'd lost his boat to an Olympia bank and his sense of manhood to the bottle. It was Coldwater Cove's dirty little secret that he'd begun to beat his wife; it was Dan and Jack's dual frustration that short of tossing the guy in jail whenever his behavior got bad enough to result in a 911 call from the neighbors, they'd never been able to talk his wife into testifying against him, or taking the steps necessary to save herself.

She jumped like a startled doe when he opened the office door. The last time he'd tried to talk reason into her, her nose had been slender and delicately sloped. Today it was swollen to twice its size, her top lip had an ugly split, and her flowered print cotton blouse bore rust-colored blood spatters he hoped to hell were from Jason, but suspected were from her broken nose. Bruises new enough to still be blue braceleted both upper arms and darkened the puffy flesh around her left eye. Both eyes were dulled with pain.

A cold rage shot through Dan. For her sake, he controlled it. "Hey, Kathi." They'd dated for a time, in school, when they'd been on the debate team together. It hadn't gone beyond some making out on the bus trips to various competitions around the state. After two months, she'd dumped him for Montgomery, who'd been all-state high school offensive linebacker three years in a row.

"Oh, Dan." Her split lip quivered. Her eyes swam. "I'm so sorry."

"You don't have a damn thing to be sorry for." He crouched down in front of her. When he touched his hand to her hair, she flinched and fear filled her eyes.

"Now there's where you're wrong." She sniffled. "I'm sorry for so many damn things. Especially for having chosen brawn over brain."

The words were the same ones that, suffering from wounded teenage pride, he'd thrown at her when she'd broken up with him. Her soft tone revealed a vestige of the spunk that had drawn him to her in the first place. Back then, before Montgomery had broken her spirit, she'd reminded him a lot of Jamie Lee Curtis in *Halloween*. Unfortunately, Dan thought grimly, Kathi had ended up with her own personal bogeyman.

"I've always believed that there should be a general amnesty for everything we say and do in high school." He took a Kleenex from the box on the table next to the couch and gently dabbed at her swimming eyes. She flinched again when he touched the swelling beneath her black eye.

"I tried to make things right between us. I kept thinking that if only I worked at our marriage harder, if I was more understanding of Jason's feelings, we could make it work."

Dan privately considered that Mother Teresa couldn't have made marriage to that goon work.

"I'd just graduated from school when we got married. I was looking forward to working as a speech therapist, but Jason didn't want me to work outside the home. He said I made it look as if he couldn't support me."

Once again Dan thought the real problem was that Montgomery hadn't wanted Kathi out in the real world where she could meet someone who might truly care about her. Once again he kept his thoughts to himself.

"We moved to Alaska, and we were doing okay. But the fishing wasn't what he'd hoped it would be, so we came back here." She dabbed at her eyes. "Then things got even worse. The more he was out of work, the more he drank. Which made it harder to work. It was a vicious cycle.

"After the boat was repossessed, I went back to work for a private home-care agency. That's when things really started going downhill. . . .

"Then last night he called me a lot of things

I'd just as soon not repeat." She pressed the
balled-up tissue against her mouth and struggled for calm.

"You don't have to. That's all in the past,
Kathi. What you need to concentrate on is the
terrific future that's waiting out there for you."

Dan smiled encouragingly, not because there
was anything at all humorous about her situation, but because she needed it.

An hour later, he'd prepared the divorce complaint and had arranged for Kathi to move to a
shelter for abused women at least until her husband could be picked up and put behind bars.

Ida had been the impetus behind the shelter
back in the late seventies. Bucking initial objection from those who believed that a man's
home was his castle where he was entitled to do
as he pleased, she'd gone on a statewide speaking tour, pitching her project to the Rotarians,
the Elks, the American Legion, PTA, AMA, any
group who'd listen and write out a check.

With typical Ida-like candor, she'd told of her
own abusive experience, something that wasn't
being done in those days when tidy homes
in nice neighborhoods had harbored dark secrets that weren't really secrets, and neighbors
looked the other way.

Dan would have preferred to cut the wife beater
into little pieces of shark bait, but civilization
being what it was, he figured he'd have to settle for
putting the guy away for a very long time.

That problem taken care of, as well as he
could for now, he moved on to J.C., whose situ-

ation at least offered a bit of comic relief, he thought as he entered the sheriff's office.

Any prospect of humor instantly died when he viewed Ida sitting in the office, looking like death warmed over. Her complexion was the color of cold ashes, there was a trapped animal look in her eyes, and she was gripping the scarred arms of the wooden chair as if trying to keep herself tethered to earth.

She was also doing something Dan had never seen before. Indeed, he doubted that very few people had ever witnessed the sight of Ida Lindstrom openly weeping.

Henry Hyatt was frying eggs when Savannah entered the kitchen. The aroma of bacon filled the air.

"Ida said I was welcome to help myself," he said defensively, "since I chipped in for the groceries."

"Fine." Savannah looked at the dishes already piled up in the sink and wondered if Henry was expecting her to clean up the mess. "Have you seen my grandmother this morning?"

"Isn't she in her room?"

"No." Ida's bedroom door had been open when Savannah had passed by, the bed neatly made. She wondered if the call had been from Ida and worried that her grandmother had gotten into trouble.

"I don't suppose you could have picked up the phone?"

He shrugged and flipped the eggs. "I was taking the bacon from the pan when it rang. Besides, odds are it wasn't for me."

Savannah had to practically bite her tongue to keep from setting down some house rules. It was, after all, her grandmother's house, which meant that if there was any rule setting to be done, Ida'd be the one to do it.

She went to pour herself a cup of coffee, but the carafe was empty. Deciding to pick up a cup on the way to the lighthouse, she'd taken her raincoat from the rack when she viewed Dan's Tahoe pulling up in front of the house. When she saw her grandmother sitting beside him, she flung open the door and ran out into the rain.

"What happened?" she asked as Dan helped Ida down from the high passenger seat. Her heart clenched when she realized that her grandmother had been crying.

"Nothing that important," Ida insisted. When Dan retrieved two plastic bags of groceries from the back seat, she snatched them out of his hands and marched past Savannah into the house.

"I'll wait out here," Dan offered.

On her grandmother's heels, Savannah didn't take time to respond. "Are you all right?"

"I'm fit as a fiddler." Ida's red-rimmed gaze circled the kitchen.

"Then why did Dan drive you home? Where's the Jeep?"

"At the market, and you don't have to worry, it's not wrecked or anything." She muttered something under her breath, then shot Henry a stern look. "I'm not cleaning this mess up."

"Don't get your britches in a twist, I'm planning to take care of it." Ignoring her sputtered protest, he took the bags, put them on the counter, and began putting the groceries away. "You'd better sit down." His blue eyes swept over her. "You look like hell."

"You're no Paul Newman yourself," she shot back as she grabbed the ground meat from him and yanked open the refrigerator door.

"Grandmother," Savannah repeated with dwindling patience, "what happened?"

"I told you, nothing important." Ida slammed the door shut. The look she shot her granddaughter was even harder than the one she'd used to scant avail on Henry. "Just a little mix-up at the market."

"What kind of mix-up?"

"The mixed-up kind," Ida retorted. "And that's all I'm going to say about it."

Savannah may have toughened up over the last weeks, but she suspected that even Genghis Khan would have had difficulty facing down Ida at her most resolute. Dragging her hands through her hair, she decided to get answers from another source.

Dan was waiting for her on the front porch. He was leaning back in the porch swing, his booted feet propped on the railing. The driving rain had lightened to mist.

"What happened?" she repeated. "Why was my grandmother crying?"

The expression of sympathy she viewed on his face when he looked up at her made her dread his answer. "I suppose crying is a standard reaction when you get arrested for shoplifting."

"Arrested?" His words buzzed like a swarm of wasps. Savannah latched onto the loudest one. "Jack arrested my grandmother?"

"He didn't exactly arrest her." Dan sighed, dropped his boots to the porch floor and leaned forward, his fingers linked between his knees. "He just took her down to the station for her own protection. . . . It's a little complicated."

Name one thing about her life that wasn't these days. She was living proof that trouble, like nature, seemed to abhor a vacuum.

"My grandmother wouldn't steal anything." About this Savannah was very sure.

"I know that. So does Jack. Hell, Olivia Brown knows it, too. The trouble is, the new owners of the mercantile are from the city, and they established a no-tolerance policy for shoplifters.

"Olivia was afraid she would lose her job if she didn't call the sheriff, especially since Fred Potter was there to witness Ida breezing past the checkout with a cartload of groceries."

The wicker creaked as Savannah sank onto the porch swing beside him. "Oh, God. . . . She forgot to pay for them."

"That'd be my guess. Needless to say, she was pretty shook up when Jack arrived a couple minutes after Olivia stopped her from leaving. He didn't want to let her drive home by herself."

"I can understand that. But how did you end up getting recruited?"

"I happened to walk in the door of the sheriff's office right after Jack struck out trying to get hold of you or Raine. I knew Raine was on her way to Tacoma to take a deposition and figured you were already at the lighthouse. So I volunteered to chauffeur Ida home.

"Jack's going to come by with a deputy later on today to drop off the Jeep, but you might want to hide the keys for a while, at least until your grandmother gets a clean bill of health."

She wasn't surprised he knew about Ida's problems. Undoubtedly Raine had told her husband, who'd told his cousin, about tonight's dinner plans.

"The trick, of course, is getting her to agree to a comprehensive physical in the first place—short of tying her up and dragging her into the city." Savannah's voice was as flat as her spirits.

"We'll think of something."

"It's not your problem."

"You're family, Savannah. When Jack married Raine, that made you part of the clan. And we O'Hallorans stick together."

Clan. It was a strange, old-fashioned word for a concept as foreign to Savannah as Amazonia. For years her immediate family had consisted of Ida and Raine. Lately Lilith, too, had returned home to be part of that nuclear unit, which had expanded to include Raine's husband Jack and his daughter Amy, as well as Cooper Ryan and Gwen.

Her father had sent her an invitation to his wedding in London last year, but it had taken place on Christmas, the busiest time of the year

at Las Casitas, not that Savannah was all that
sure she would have gone even if it had occurred during the off-season. Still, even if she
counted Reggie's new wife, whom she'd never
met, the number didn't begin to come close to
that of the O'Hallorans, who'd first settled on
the peninsula over a hundred years ago and had
seemed to take to heart the biblical admonition
to be fruitful and multiply.

They were sitting very close together, close
enough for her to see the change in his eyes.
Distracted and unwillingly fascinated by the
blue flame, she wasn't prepared for him to
touch his mouth to hers. For a brief moment,
her already unstable world tilted.

Because it would have been so easy—too
easy—to sink into the tender kiss, because she
could still feel the hum of it vibrating on her lips,
Savannah pulled back, seeking solid ground.

"What was that for?" Her voice sounded too
defensive even to her own ears.

"Luck." The familiar grin flashed. His hand
lifted, as if to touch her face, then merely
tugged on a curl that had fallen across her
cheek instead. "See you tonight."

Because she didn't want to let him know that
he had, in that fleeting instant, made her feel
things she'd forgotten she could feel, things she
had no business feeling, Savannah resisted the
schoolgirlish urge to stay on the porch until
he'd driven out of sight.

Instead, she went back into the house,
searching for Ida, who'd sequestered herself in

the den and tartly informed Savannah through the closed door that she was busy with household accounts and did not want to be disturbed.

There were no lingering tears in her grandmother's voice. No tremor, no confusion. She sounded as resolute as she'd been in the days when she'd served as a stabilizing rock for two little girls, who, without her, could have drifted so far astray.

Myriad memories, both good and bad, assaulted Savannah, ricocheting in her mind like gunfire as she drove to the library to research Alzheimer's before tonight's dinner. She felt the moisture on her face, realized she was crying, and swiped at the tears with the back of her hand.

Surrendering a day's work on the lighthouse wouldn't begin to make up for the personal sacrifices Ida Lindstrom had made for her granddaughters, but it was a start.

9

"Some of the symptoms are right on the mark," Savannah said to Raine when the sisters had slipped away to the back porch of the farmhouse before dinner. Afraid she might be overheard by either Henry or Ida if she called from the house, Savannah had waited until she'd arrived at the farm to tell her sister about today's research trip. "But others don't fit at all."

"I imagine each case is different," Raine mused as she skimmed through the pages Savannah had copied.

"That's what all the books say." Savannah took a sip of the red wine that had been Dan's contribution to the family dinner. "They also say the warning signs may apply to dementias other than Alzheimer's."

"Terrific." Raine sighed and looked out over the acres of conical blue-green spruce and firs.

"All the more reason to get Gram to the doctor as soon as possible."

As they silently sipped their wine and considered the difficulties involved in that challenge, it was Savannah's turn to sigh.

Displaying an ability to compartmentalize that Savannah had always admired, Raine switched conversational gears. "With all that's been happening, we haven't had a chance to talk about you. How are you doing?"

"Better than last week. The shingles are finally all replaced, so I can finally start finishing up the inside. I ran by to check on things before I drove here, and wonders of wonders, the roofs weren't leaking."

"That is good news. But I wasn't asking about the lighthouse. How are you doing now that you've put some time and distance between yourself and the weasel?"

"I've turned the corner on that, too. At least I haven't had the nightmare for two weeks." Savannah didn't mention that concerns about Ida had precluded a great deal of sleep.

"What nightmare?" Raine was looking at her in that same deep way that Dan had on more than one occasion. Savannah decided it must be a lawyer thing.

"Didn't I tell you about it?"

"No."

Savannah wished she hadn't brought the subject up. She also knew that since Raine had definitely inherited their grandmother's stubbornness, it wouldn't do any good trying to dodge the issue now. "I dream I'm getting married at the lighthouse."

"That's not such a bad start."

"For you, perhaps." Savannah was pleased her sister seemed to be basking in marital bliss, but she had no intention of ever walking down the aisle again. Better, she'd decided, to stick to things she did well. "It's a garden wedding. In the summer, I think, because the sky is wide and blue and I'm surrounded by John Martin's flowers."

"It sounds gorgeous. So what's the problem? Is this one of those naked dreams?"

"No, I'm wearing a gorgeous, traditional white satin gown, with lace and seed pearls and about a mile-long train."

"If you tell me the groom is Kevin, I'll understand why you consider it a nightmare."

"It's him. And I'm feeling as stupidly blissful as I did in Monaco—until after we exchange vows, when, instead of lifting my veil, he pulls a hedge clipper out of his tuxedo and clips off my wings."

Raine lifted a brow. "Your wings?"

"Wings," Savannah repeated. "They're even prettier than my gown, all gossamer silver and gold, as delicate as a spider's web. I begin to cry, and ask him what he's doing, and he answers that now that I'm married, I won't need them anymore."

"And what do you say?"

"I try telling him that I need to fly. That I've flown since I was a child, and that's when it happens."

"What?"

"All the guests stand up, and they're wearing white-and-black masks, like the comedy ones that are the flip side of drama?"

"Right."

"And they all say 'Silly girl, you've been fooling yourself. You never learned how to fly.' When they start to laugh, I try to run away, but they're all standing on my train, so I grab the hedge clippers from Kevin and hack it off. Then I run away, off the edge of the cliff."

"And?"

"I don't know. I remember thinking that if I look down, I'll fall, like that Roadrunner cartoon. But then I wake up."

"Well." Raine looked out over the fields of Christmas trees again. "It doesn't exactly take a shrink to figure out that you're facing big freedom issues, which is certainly expected, given your situation."

"It's true, though," Savannah insisted earnestly. "I have never really flown. You and Mother were always the ones with the wings in this family."

"Me?" Raine looked honestly surprised by that idea.

"You left here, went to Harvard, then on to New York, forged a life for yourself—"

"A life, you'll note, that I was more than happy to give up."

"Still, you were brave enough to try. And succeed. All on your own."

"Going off to cooking school in Paris took a lot of nerve," Raine pointed out.

"I was homesick for months."

"So was I when I was at Harvard. And it was even worse when I first arrived in Manhattan."

"Really? But you always used to talk about how you couldn't wait to get away from here. And how much more exciting life was in the big city."

Savannah thought that Raine was definitely proof that the world kept turning and changing. Oh, Raine still practiced law, and had kept ties to her former firm with her Asian Rim business, but she had put far behind her the eighty-hour weeks that had defined her life as a high-powered New York litigator.

Savannah was still amazed that Raine had settled down on a Christmas tree farm in this small, remote town, become a stepmother to one child, and claimed to want more of her own. Still, she thought now, she'd never seen her sister looking more radiant.

"You know what they say about not appreciating something until you don't have it anymore." Raine shrugged. "Besides, mostly I was missing you and Ida."

"But you got over that."

"Let's just say I learned to adapt."

"I don't think I ever really did, which was one of the reasons I eloped with Kevin. At the time, getting married seemed a better choice than returning home a failure."

Just as Lilith had done so many times. Raine didn't say it, but Savannah knew they were both thinking about their mother.

"No one could ever consider you a failure," Raine argued with the unwavering loyalty Savannah had always been able to count on. "Especially these days. What you're doing with the lighthouse is nothing short of a miracle. To tell you the truth, sis, I wasn't honestly sure you'd be able to pull it off."

"Neither was I," Savannah admitted. "But if luck holds, I'll be open for Christmas."

Despite having gotten behind schedule in the beginning, she still had four months to pull off her miracle. The mental picture of the restored buildings lit up with bright white lights for the holidays warmed the heart she'd feared had been shattered. She could practically hear the crackle of the logs and smell the cedar in the fireplace, welcoming guests to her lighthouse.

"Do you realize," Raine said, as if the thought had just occurred to her, "that this will be the first holiday season in years that we're all back home together?"

"With Amy beginning a new generation."

"To us." The late afternoon sun made the wine gleam like rubies as Raine raised her glass. "And all four generations of strong, soaring Lindstrom women."

Savannah lifted her own wineglass to her sister's toast, her attention momentarily drawn to her fingernails. They were chipped and torn from scraping moldy, water-stained layers of paper off walls.

Not so long ago, her French manicure had been kept flawless by weekly visits to a Beverly Hills salon. Her nails may have been perfect, but her life had been a mess. As difficult as things were now, she couldn't imagine returning to that former existence she'd managed to convince herself was everything she'd ever wanted.

She might not be soaring up there with the eagles yet, but having tested her wings, she was finally learning to fly. And despite having hit a few air pockets, it was wonderful.

"I'm glad you're fixing up the lighthouse," Amy O'Halloran said after the family had gathered around the dining room table. "I like it a lot, especially the flowers John planted, though it's sad that bad boys broke the windows."

With her long, golden curls and bright blue eyes, the six-year-old girl was the most beautiful child Savannah had ever seen. She was also precocious, unrelentingly curious about everything around her, and despite having lost her mother to cancer, amazingly well-adjusted. Savannah thought that said a lot about Raine's husband.

"Well, they've all been replaced now."

"I saw that when we were driving home from town yesterday. Mommy said you're going to make it as pretty as it used to be, before I was born."

Savannah watched the pleasure move across Raine's face when Jack's daughter called her Mommy. "That's my plan."

"Speaking of plans," Lilith trilled, "thanks to Mother's army of volunteers, this year's Sawdust Festival is going to be the best one yet. We're even having a palm reader."

"Damn foolish notion, if you ask me," Ida muttered.

"I thought you liked Raven."

"She's okay—for one of those New Age types," Ida allowed. Tonight's sweatshirt was bright purple and proclaimed Age and Treachery Will Always Overcome Youth and Skill.

"Mebbe this year you can liven things up by bein' arrested again," Henry suggested with a sly grin. When she'd discovered that Ida had invited her boarder to the family dinner, Savannah had worried he'd make an already delicate situation worse.

"That was nearly half a century ago. And every one of those years, you have to bring it up, Henry Hyatt. A gentleman would just let sleeping dogs out of the bag."

"Never been much of a gentleman," Henry said, proving himself a master of understatement. "And it's damn hard to forget the sight of a woman setting up a mobile castration clinic in the parking lot."

"If I've told you once, I've told you a thousand times, it wasn't a castration clinic!" Ida huffed. She'd yet to reveal any lack of memory this evening, which once again had Savannah hoping that she and Raine were overreacting to what were merely the normal signs of aging.

"Daddy, what's a castration clinic?" Amy asked.

Jack exchanged a resigned look with Raine. "It's sort of a medical office, honey."

"That's precisely what it was, Amy, dear," Ida concurred. She turned toward Dan. "Times were tough in the logging business that year, and people were having trouble feeding the children they already had. Seemed like a good idea to offer two-for-one pricing to help the situation."

"Vasectomies," Savannah murmured in explanation, for Dan's ears alone.

He arched a brow and looked across the table at Ida, who'd folded her arms and was daring him with a look to criticize her behavior. "Makes sense to me," he said easily.

"We Lindstrom women have a knack for stirring things up," Lilith said with a radiant smile, "which is why we're so fortunate that Coldwater Cove's sheriff is part of the family."

When Jack had the good sense not to suggest that he couldn't let his marriage keep him from doing his duty, Lilith deftly turned the conversation back to this year's festivities.

"No one's supposed to know it yet, but Becky Brennan's going to be this year's Sawdust Queen," she announced.

"Oh, goodie!" Amy jumped up and down in her chair and clapped her hands. "Becky's my baby-sitter. I like her a lot. She plays Barbie with me and reads *Lilly's Purple Plastic Purse* over and over again, just the way Gramma Lilith does."

"That's one of my favorite stories," Lilith said with her trademark dazzling smile that had once lit up the silver screen. "I'm not surprised Becky likes it, too."

Raine and Savannah exchanged a look. Savannah had no doubt they were thinking the same thing: that for a woman who'd found motherhood so difficult, Lilith seemed to be reveling in her new role as Gramma Lilith.

"Oh, Savannah, darling." Lilith turned toward her daughter. "Don't forget, the rehearsal for the queen's pageant is tomorrow afternoon."

"Pageant?"

"Didn't I tell you?"

"No."

"Oh, dear. I've been so busy lately, it must have slipped my mind." Savannah didn't trust her mother's innocent tone. Despite her B-movie acting career, Lilith had never been a convincing liar. "We've added something new this year. All the former queens are going to be on hand for Becky's coronation. Roxie Denton, at All That Jazz Dance Academy, has worked out the cutest choreography number."

"I was planning to sand floors this weekend."

"Oh, you can't do that!" Lilith pressed her hand—which had never known a chipped nail—against the front of her scarlet silk blouse. "You can work anytime. But how often do you get to dance across the stage to an orchestra playing Joe Cocker's 'You Are So Beautiful'?"

"I wasn't aware Coldwater Cove had an orchestra." Sensing that Dan was doing his best to smother his laughter, Savannah refused to look at him.

"Well, actually, it's not exactly an orchestra," Lilith admitted.

"It's the Davis twins playing trumpets, Archie McCoy on guitar, his sister Aretha on keyboard and Joe Bob Preston singing the song," Cooper

Ryan, who was sitting beside his wife, revealed. "They're not half bad."

"Heard a lot worse," Henry supplied gruffly.

"So they're not the Grateful Dead or the Eagles. It'll still be fun," Lilith continued to coax.

There had been a time, in the not so distant past, when Savannah would have caved in to her mother's coaxing. But that was in another lifetime—before she'd gotten her wings.

"It sounds like quite a show, but you'll have to do it without me. As much as I'd like to help you out, Mother, I've too much work to do."

"But, darling—"

"No." Resisting Lilith was not for the faint-hearted. Savannah managed, with an effort, to firm up her mild tone. "I'll try to drop by the park for an hour or so. But I'm not playing rural Rockettes."

"Well." Lilith's expressive eyes narrowed. An expectant silence fell over the dining room. As she submitted to her mother's long, silent look, Savannah sensed she wasn't the only one at the table holding her breath. Her nerves tangled like a ball of barbed wire in her stomach.

Finally, Lilith's lips curled in a slow, pleased, almost feline smile. "Brava, dear."

She was an adult, an adult who'd suffered, survived, and had gotten on with her life. She was no longer the child who slept with her nightlight on, who cowered in closets or had tea parties with an imaginary mother who wore cozy aprons and didn't look or smell like a movie star. Her mother's obvious approval shouldn't mean so much.

It shouldn't, but, damn it, it did.

Savannah thought back on all the missed dance recitals, birthdays, and holidays, and realized she'd been waiting to hear those words all her life.

The mood in the room lightened. There was laughter. The conversation continued, as if the little battle of feminine wills had never taken place.

Dan reached beneath the table and took hold of Savannah's hand, his fingers squeezing hers in a friendly, encouraging way. Feeling immensely pleased with herself, she glanced up at him, intending to return his gesture with a smile.

But then she found herself getting lost in his quiet, confident blue eyes, just as she'd done when they'd been sitting together on the porch earlier today. The other voices faded into the distance; it was as if the rest of the family had suddenly vanished.

"I can't wait to ride the merry-go-round," Amy was announcing. "The big white horse with the gold saddle and the pretty flowers in its mane is my favorite. I like the happy music. Do you like to ride merry-go-rounds, Aunt Savannah?"

She forced her attention back to her niece, who, she belatedly realized, was looking across the table at her expectantly. Dan released her hand. The moment, which she guessed had lasted no longer than a few seconds but had seemed like an eternity, ended.

As she assured Amy that she did, indeed, love to ride merry-go-rounds, Savannah felt a growing unease building somewhere in the region of her heart.

10

"Well, Gram certainly seemed quite lucid tonight," Savannah said as she slid pieces of apple cobbler onto plates.

"Didn't she?" Raine's face lit up with a hopeful optimism that made Savannah think how odd it was that in this case, she was turning out to be the more cautious sister.

A born lawyer, before her marriage to Jack, Raine had always been more logical, more likely to study all sides of a problem before making a decision. Savannah, on the other hand, had always followed her heart. *And look how that turned out.*

"That's what's been so troubling about this." She went to the freezer and took out a half gallon of ice cream. "The memory lapses and confusion seem to come and go. Sometimes, like tonight, she's as sharp as ever." The scent of vanilla bean mingled with the rich aroma of baked apples, brown sugar, and cinnamon, re-

minding Savannah of when she'd been nine
years old and had seen an old-fashioned ice
cream churn in the window of Granny's Attic.
She'd brought it home, and she and Raine and
Ida had spent that evening on the porch, taking
turns cranking. The handle had broken the second time they'd used it, but she'd never regretted having spent a week's allowance. Savannah
had never tasted anything as sweet as that
homemade ice cream they'd made together on
that perfect summer day.

"But there are other times, like the incident
at the market and when I bought the lighthouse, when she just seems to glitch out."

Raine glanced over at Savannah with surprise. "You didn't tell me anything about a
problem when you bought the lighthouse."

"It didn't really register at the time. I was tired
and excited, and I guess I wanted to overlook the
fact that I don't think she knew what I was talking about when I first came home. After all my
reading today, it sort of clicked into place."

She began scooping ice cream atop the cobbler. "I had a thought during dinner. What if we
do an intervention, like families do when someone they love is an alcoholic or drug addicted?"

"It wouldn't be easy, but it'd be for her own
good." Raine nodded, looking more like her Xena
the Warrior-Princess self. Her jaw was set, her
eyes clear and focused on her goal. "And that's all
that matters. Do you want to do it tonight?"

Balancing protecting Ida's pride with possibly protecting her life was proving more than a

little difficult. They were, Savannah thought sadly, caught between Ida and a hard place.

"Now that we've come up with a plan of action, we might as well get it over with while we're all here together."

"Then it's settled. I'll put Amy to bed after dessert." While Savannah returned the carton to the freezer, Raine picked up two of the plates.

Having decided on a plan of action, they returned to the dining room. As she picked at her cobbler, Savannah listened to Ida regale the family with a lively tale of another Sawdust Festival when she'd delivered Polly Lawson's twins in the pie judging tent.

"Fool girl spent all day in labor, but didn't tell anyone because she was waiting around to make sure she won the blue ribbon for her lemon meringue pie."

"Did she?" Amy asked, wide-eyed.

"No. Gladys Quincy won it, like she always did in those days, for her blueberry buckle. But Polly won the red. She also took home the grand prize—two of the cutest red-haired babies you ever saw."

Her grandmother's memory appeared as clear as the special-occasion Waterford crystal adorning the table, her vivid detail and colorful description making the story come alive.

It was going to be all right, Savannah assured herself firmly. Her grandmother Ida would be all right. She could not—would not—allow herself to think otherwise.

*   *   *

After dinner they moved to the cozy living room. Savannah was, at first, relieved when Ida didn't interrupt Raine, who, being the attorney in the family, had chosen to make the opening argument. Their grandmother didn't so much as flinch as Raine listed all the incidents of memory loss and of apparent disorientation that the family had documented.

Savannah hoped Ida was listening. The way her grandmother was staring out the front window made it difficult to tell for certain.

Finally, having lost momentum when she didn't get any feedback, Raine ran down. Savannah watched as Jack put a comforting arm around his wife and, despite her recent vow to become totally independent, envied Raine, just a little, for having someone who obviously loved and cared for her so very much in her life.

"Is that all you have to say?" Ida asked. Her small, wiry frame was practically swallowed up by the wing chair.

"For now," Raine answered.

She continued to sit there for another long minute, still as stone. Then she turned to Savannah. "I suppose you agree with your sister?"

"You haven't exactly been yourself the past few months," Savannah said carefully.

"It's called aging. I don't like to admit it, but I'm not exactly a spring chicken anymore." Her voice was as brittle as dried autumn leaves. "Besides, everyone suffers from memory lapses from time to time. You forgot to return the plumber's call yesterday."

"Savannah has a lot on her mind right now, Mother," Lilith tried to help out.

"And I don't?" Ida folded her arms across the front of her purple sweatshirt. "I never thought I'd live to see the day that my own family turned against me."

"We're not turning against you, Gram," Savannah argued. "We're trying to take care of you."

"I'm not a child, Savannah. And I can damn well take care of myself, thank you very much."

"You may not be a child," Henry entered the family conversation uninvited. "But you're a damn fool."

"Just because you sit in front of the television and watch *Jeopardy!* every day doesn't make you Alex Trebek," Ida returned grumpily. "You don't know everything, Henry Hyatt."

"Got that right enough. But I spent enough time in Evergreen to know when someone's not right in the head." He met her glare with a hard, level look of his own. "And you're not."

Ida's curse was one Savannah had never heard come out of her grandmother's mouth. "I don't have Alzheimer's."

"Then why don't you put your money where your big mouth is and prove it? Or aren't you a betting woman?"

Crimson flags of color waved high on Ida's cheeks. Her mouth pulled into a tight line, and her eyes snapped with barely restrained temper.

Savannah felt torn. Part of her thought she shouldn't let Henry talk to her grandmother that way. After all, he was only a boarder in Ida's house; he had no business even being at this dinner tonight, let alone barging into family matters.

But another, stronger part realized that just perhaps he could reach Ida on a level none of the rest of them could. They were contemporaries who'd already learned that Bette Davis wasn't kidding when she proclaimed that old age wasn't for sissies.

"My husband was a gambler," Ida said. "Being married to him taught me to bet only on myself."

"Then do it," Henry prodded. He reached into a pocket, pulled out a small wad of bills, and peeled a rumpled one from beneath the rubber band. "Here's twenty bucks that says you're too chicken to give up control long enough to let some other doc do the tests." He slapped the money onto the coffee table.

The color in her grandmother's face flared hotter and brighter. "You're on." Ida dug into her purse, retrieved a crisp bill of her own, tossed it next to his, then added another. "And ten more says I don't have Alzheimer's." She speared a look toward Savannah. "You satisfied now?"

"It's a start." Savannah refused to let her grandmother's practiced glare cower her. "I'll be more satisfied once you actually make the appointment for the tests, and happier still after you've completed them."

"Ha!" Ida dug into the black pocketbook she'd had for as long as Savannah could remember and pulled out a piece of paper that she placed with great ceremony next to the money. "I'm proud of the way you girls turned out. You're both bright and courageous, and except for screwing up your marriage, which unfortunately is pretty much run-of-the-mill for us Lindstrom women, you've made yourselves a real good life. . . .

"But you're going to have to get up a lot earlier in the morning to stay ahead of your grandmother."

Savannah leaned forward and picked up the piece of yellow paper. She skimmed the lines, then handed the paper to Raine, who arched a brow as she read it, then passed it on to Lilith.

"Mother!" Lilith shook her head, her expression filled with fondness touched with exasperation. "Why didn't you tell us you'd arranged for tests next week?"

"A woman's entitled to some secrets," Ida huffed. "Besides, ever since you girls set up this dinner, I've been looking forward to seeing how you were planning to handle the intervention."

"You knew all along," Raine guessed resignedly.

"I'm not a fool, Raine. Nor do I tolerate fools. You're both bright girls. I knew it was only a matter of time before you decided to try to lay down the law. After that little mistake in the mercantile, you really didn't have much choice.

"The way I see it, if my family's worried enough to resort to subterfuge, the least I can do is ease your minds. But not until after the Sawdust Festival," she said firmly. "This is the first year I'm in charge, and my reputation's at stake. If I'm not there to keep everyone on their toes, the whole weekend could just go to hell on a Harley."

Savannah wouldn't be able completely to put her concerns behind her until Ida's doctors presented them with test results that revealed that they'd exaggerated their fears. However, the comforting familiarity of her grandmother's malapropism and characteristically brisk, matter-of-fact attitude gave birth to a faint ray of light that brightened, ever so slightly, her dark and looming fear.

After they'd driven home, Ida went directly to bed, declaring herself exhausted from all the family intrigue. Henry looked inclined to make it a night, as well, when Savannah stopped him at the bottom of the stairs.

"Thank you."

He looked down at her hand, resting atop his on the newel post, as if wondering how it had gotten there. "For what?"

"For helping us with Grandmother. That was a very nice thing to do."

"Hasn't it sunk in yet, girl?" he asked gruffly. "I'm never nice."

"Liar." She leaned forward and brushed her lips against his cheek.

Henry flamed lobster red. "What the hell was that for?" he asked, unknowingly nearly echoing her words of this morning when Dan had kissed her.

"Because you're a fraud, Henry Hyatt." She'd seen through the gruffness to the man beneath, the man who'd lived the solitary life of a light-

house keeper not so much because he didn't
want to have any interaction with neighbors,
but because he loved the Far Harbor lighthouse
and cared about others' safety enough to make
personal sacrifices.

She smiled. "Good night."

He muttered something that could have been
"good night" in return, then made his way upstairs. Watching him, Savannah thought she de-
tected a bit of a spring in his step.

Savannah was back at the lighthouse, energetically sanding the floor of the keeper's cottage,
when Dan showed up with an electric sander of
his own, rented from the same hardware store
where she'd gotten hers. He was wearing a
sleeveless sweatshirt, ragged shorts that looked
as if he'd whacked away at a pair of jeans with a
pocket knife, and work boots. His body looked as
hard and dark as teak. She decided that it should
be against the law for any man to look so seductively male—at least this early in the morning.

"Don't you have to work?"

"It's Saturday." He didn't mention that he'd
dropped by the women's shelter to take Kathi
Montgomery some peanut butter fudge from
Coldwater Cove Confectionery before coming
here. It had always been her favorite. He'd been
glad to discover it still was.

Kathi's bruises were starting to turn an ugly
purplish green, but as they'd sat out on the deck
of the middle-class house, watching a pair of
hummingbirds spin and whirl in a noisy battle

over claim to a bright red glass feeder, she'd
seemed a bit more relaxed. Neither Jack nor the
state police had been able to locate her husband yet, but just knowing that she was no
longer having to handle her domestic problems
all alone had given her strength and taken some
of the fear from her eyes. When he'd left, she
was talking about returning to work. Dan had
taken that as a very positive sign.

"I figured you could use some help."

She looked around the enormous expanse of
flooring left to sand. "I can't deny an extra hand
would be nice, but you don't have to—"

"I know. But I want to, Savannah. Besides,
the hardware store was having a special on
sander rentals, and hey, I've never been one to
overlook a good deal."

Though it was a lousy joke, she laughed,
which made him feel as if he'd just scaled
Mount Olympus.

The work was hard, hot, and dusty. Savannah didn't even try to tell herself that she was
grateful for Dan's presence because he was cutting the work and the time it took to do it in
half. The truth was that they worked well together, passing each other with an easy rhythm,
each choosing rooms without discussion. Even
when they were working in different locations,
there was an easy camaraderie that she'd only
felt when working in a kitchen where the entire
staff had slipped into a mind sync and performed as if in a ballet.

She smiled behind her dust mask at the idea

that there was anything at all ballet-like about this particular work. Obviously, she was becoming too fanciful. If she wasn't careful, the next thing she knew she'd start seeing Lucy's ghost.

Dan was upstairs when she moved into the closet of the downstairs bedroom. One of the planks beneath her sneakers creaked, then tilted when she stepped on it. Curious, she turned off her sander, knelt, and, using the putty knife she kept in the new leather tool belt she wore on her hips, she pried up the board.

"Treasure," she murmured, looking down into a small space that contained what appeared to be personal items. She reached in and pulled out a Bull Durham tobacco bag filled, she discovered, with marbles.

She tugged down her mask. "Dan, come look," she called out over the roar of the sander's motor overhead.

He cut it off. She heard his footsteps coming down the stairs.

"Did Henry and Ruth Hyatt ever have children?" he asked as he observed her find.

"Not that I know of."

"Then they're probably Henry's." Delving deeper into the space, he retrieved a few more items: a top wound with white string, a small model of a clipper ship, complete with yellowed newspaper sails, a stuffed one-eyed brown teddy bear, and a tarnished silver–framed photo of an obviously pregnant woman and small boy.

"Oh, that must be Henry and his mother."

"That'd be my guess. He was a cute kid."

"I think he'd hate to hear you say that. But he had been cute," Savannah agreed. His nearly white blond hair had been cut like the Dutch Boy paint boy, and he was wearing a miniature sailor suit with short pants accessorized by a pair of in-congruous cowboy boots and jingly spurs. A wide Huck Finn grin wreathed his freckled face. "From the state of Lucy's pregnancy, this photo must have been taken shortly before her death."

Lucy Hyatt's smile was warmed with inti-macy and lit up her eyes in a way that revealed an unmistakable love for whoever was holding the camera. Standing in front of the mother and son was a small fox terrier.

"She looks so happy," she murmured. "Not at all like a woman who's planning to run away with her lover."

"Perhaps her lover is the one holding the camera."

Upstairs a door slammed, the sudden sound echoing in the empty rooms. The temperature in the house seemed to drop at least ten degrees.

"Must be another storm coming," Dan said, glancing up toward the ceiling.

"That must be it," Savannah agreed with a bit more assurance than she was feeling. This was not the first time she'd experienced a strange sense of . . . something . . . while work-ing on the lighthouse buildings. Something that defied her facile explanations.

Putting that fanciful thought away, she stud-ied the photograph in more detail. The Far Har-bor lighthouse was in the background. "Since I doubt if she would have risked inviting a lover here to the lighthouse, it had to have been her husband who took the picture."

"I'd guess you're right. Especially since Henry's in the picture with her. But if that's the case, from the way she's looking at him, you have to wonder why Lucy even took a lover."

"I guess we'll never know." Savannah sighed. She was about to put the board back in place—saving the personal items for Henry—when she realized that there was still one more thing in the space.

The small journal had a cover that was the same dark gray as the shadows in the room, which was what had prevented her from seeing it right away. The yellowed, fragile pages were edged in gilt, and the front page revealed, in a slanted, feminine script, that the book was *Lucy Randall Hyatt's Far Harbor Adventure. Book One.*

She looked up at Dan and saw her own excitement reflected in his eyes. "Treasure," they said together.

They took the book out to the garden bench overlooking the water. There were no workmen scheduled for today, and with John working at the nursery, they were all alone save for the seagulls.

The first entry was headed "Farmersburg, Iowa." " 'Dear Diary,' " Savannah read. " 'It's nearly time to leave for the train station. I still cannot quite believe that I've chosen to leave my family and travel halfway across the country to a place I've never been to marry a man I've never met.

" 'But Harlan Hyatt's letters make me think that he must be a nice and considerate man, and I must admit that his obvious love of his surroundings is contagious. I've always wanted to see the sea. Now, in a mere few days, I'll be living in a lighthouse.' "

Savannah glanced up from the pages. "She must have been a mail-order bride."

"Sounds like it." Dan eased back on the bench and put his arm comfortably around her shoulder in a gesture so quick and smooth she almost didn't see it coming. She went still for a moment but didn't pull away.

" 'Needless to say, Hannah's still against what she refers to as "Lucy's latest act of impulsiveness," but how could she possibly understand how badly I want to leave Farmersburg? For I know that I would surely suffocate if I were forced to spend the rest of my days living under my sister and brother-in-law's roof, teaching reading and writing to a classroom of students who'd rather be running free outdoors and playing Aunt Lucy to Hannah's children into my dotage.

" 'My older sister keeps pointing out that there's no earthly need for me to travel so far to find a husband. Indeed, I've received numerous proposals, most recently from John Hoffman. With her usual eagle eye toward security, Hannah insists a woman could do far worse than marry such a successful hog farmer, but the thought of spending my days and nights living with the smell of pig manure quite honestly makes me gag.'

"Well," Savannah said, "I can certainly identify with that."

"Hey, you have to be grateful to pig farmers. After all, a life without smothered pork chops would undoubtedly be a life not worth living."

"I like a man who knows his priorities," Savannah said dryly.

He grinned and tugged on the gilded tips of her hair. "Don't worry. You're far above pork products on my personal priority list."

"That's certainly one of my higher achievements—being ranked above pork products."

She returned to the journal. " 'As for my other prospects, I've grown up with all the men around here. I've worked in the fields with them, talked with them on market day, and even danced with many of them at the grange, but there's not a single one I'd want to put his boots next to my bed. Or his mouth and hands on my body.' "

"Sounds as if Lucy certainly had her priorities right," Dan murmured.

The warmth of his body so near hers and the crisp tang of male sweat emanating from his skin was causing her mind to create erotic pictures that were awakening needs that Savannah told herself were nothing more than hormonal aberrations. Hoping Lucy would move on to the travelogue part of the story, Savannah ignored the provocative comment and kept on reading.

" 'Of course I haven't told Hannah this last part for fear of scandalizing her. While she and Jacob may indeed have a full and love-filled marriage, outwardly they've always appeared so distant from each other, it's hard to imagine how my sister managed to conceive three children.

" 'In each of his letters, Harlan warns me that lighthouse life, with its days and sometimes months cut off from civilization, can get lonely and monotonous. Yet his rousing stories of storms and shipwrecks lead me to suppose that he doesn't begin to know the meaning of monotony. And surely the loneliness I feel surrounded by my family is far worse than any isolation due to geography.' "

"I know that feeling," Dan surprised her by saying.

Savannah looked up at him. "Me, too," she admitted. She wondered if he was talking about his marriage, then reminded herself that she wasn't interested in his relationship with other women, most of all with his ex-wife.

Liar.

" 'Besides,' " she continued, " 'the way Harlan always ends with a witty anecdote suggests he'll be an amusing companion, and if the photograph accompanying his first letter even remotely resembles his actual countenance, he's a robust, handsome man. I blush as I write these words and pray that this journal never falls into anyone else's hands, but such strong, confident features suggest that he will prove a good lover. I only hope that he will find me adequate in that respect, as well.' "

"Hey, you can't stop there," Dan complained when she closed the journal. "We were just getting to the good part."

"That's all there is."

"Of course there's more. They didn't get Henry by mail order. And she must have liked sex enough to do it at least twice because she was pregnant when she died."

"It's the end of the book. Which is just as well, since I was starting to feel like a voyeur." A hot, shockingly needy voyeur who had begun to tingle in places she hadn't even realized *could* tingle.

"If Lucy hadn't wanted us to find her journal, she wouldn't have kept it."

"She didn't exactly leave it out on the book-shelf in plain sight."

"True. But she didn't burn it, either, which would have been the more logical thing to do. Especially if she was about to abandon her husband and son."

"Leaving Henry has always been the part of the story that's bothered me," Savannah said. "I can't imagine any mother abandoning her child."

"Not every woman has your nurturing instincts."

"No." When Lilith came immediately to mind, Savannah breathed a soft sigh.

"Your mother loved you, Savannah." He drew her a little closer, so their thighs and hips were touching. A flare of heat threatened to melt her jeans to her skin. "In her own flawed way."

"We weren't talking about Lilith." She'd gotten over any resentment against her mother for not having lived up to some idealized Mother Knows Best image that had probably never existed in the real world and now was seen only on Nick at Nite. So why were there those out-of-the-blue times that it still hurt? Like now.

"But you were thinking about her."

"Now you can read my mind?" Savannah welcomed the quick flare of irritation. It took her mind off her growing desire—a desire every bit as unwise as it was unruly.

"No. But I'm getting pretty good at reading your face. A piece of advice, sweetheart." He framed the face in question between his palms. "If you decide to change careers again, I wouldn't recommend following in your maternal grandfather's gambling shoes, because you'd make a lousy poker player. That lovely face would give you away every time."

His voice was rough and deep and rumbled through her like distant thunder. Without taking his eyes from Savannah's, giving her ample time to read his intention, he slowly lowered his head.

11

Having expected power, Savannah was surprised when he skimmed his lips up her cheek with a touch that, while feathery, still caused the breath she'd been holding to shudder out. She felt his smile against her too-warm skin. Then, appearing to have all the time and patience in the world, he caught her lower lip between his teeth. His eyes, which had returned to hers, darkened as he nibbled lightly, seductively.

Oh, the man is good, Savannah thought as renewed arousal began to flow through her veins like a thick, golden river. He knew how to coax a woman, to make her want. To make her ache.

"Dan." It was a whisper, blown away by a gust of wind swirling around the lighthouse. "Kiss me."

"I am." His teeth closed tighter, not hard enough to cause pain, but enough to make her breath tangle in her throat.

"No." Lucy Hyatt's journal fell to the ground unnoticed as Savannah pressed her hands against his chest. Her fingers tangled in the material of his shirt as she strained closer, so close that a whisper of breeze from the strait couldn't have come between them. "I mean, *really* kiss me."

He smiled again. With his mouth and with his eyes. "I am." He soothed the pink mark his teeth had made with the tip of his tongue. "I will."

And he did.

But still he took his time, drawing out the pleasure, his kiss slow but exquisitely scintillating. How could such a strong, firm mouth be so blissfully tender? Savannah wondered as his lips brushed against hers with the delicacy of butterfly wings. Once, twice, then a third time, lingering in a way that caused her eyelids to drift shut and her bones to melt.

Gulls cried as they whirled and dive-bombed for fish, a buoy clanged, a ferry whistled as it pulled out of the harbor. Savannah didn't notice. Her entire world narrowed down to the feel of Dan's mouth, his dark, mysterious male taste, the strength of his hands as they slipped beneath her T-shirt, the caressing, velvety touch of his fingertips skimming up her spine, rough and soft at the same time.

Her head spun. She felt so light she could have floated right up to the sky; so warm she might have swallowed the sun.

A lone gull flew past, his shriek rending the salt-tinged air, then fading away on the wind as he flew out toward the horizon.

Dan lifted his head and drew her away just enough to allow him to look down into her face again.

"That was even better than I remembered." He brushed the pad of his thumb against her tingling lips.

"I'm surprised you remember anything," Savannah said. "After all, we only had one date." *And you never called the next day. Like you promised.* A feminine teenage pique she was surprised to discover lurking inside her uncurled like a serpent.

He didn't appear at all embarrassed. A bit chagrined, perhaps, she thought. But that didn't stop his eyes from lighting up with that easy humor she was starting to expect from him.

"After which I never called you again."

"Really? I don't recall that." She tossed her head, pretending indifference.

"Unfortunately, I do. I also remember feeling lower than a snake in a rut for a long time after that," he said against her mouth. "I was wrong. An idiot." He was punctuating his words with kisses. "Feel free to stop me any time."

"When you say something that isn't true, I will." With all the problems she'd had to face lately, it was nice to be able to find humor in something.

"My only excuse for my behavior back then is that I was too scared to think straight."

"I refuse to believe you were actually afraid of me."

"Not of you." Taking her hand, he lifted it to his lips in a gesture so natural she couldn't think of a single reason to complain. "Well, maybe just a little. You were, after all, the closest thing to a living, breathing goddess Coldwater Cove had ever seen. That's pretty intimidating for a kid who tended to stumble all over his feet whenever you got within sniffing distance."

He made her giggle by snuffling at her neck. Savannah couldn't remember the last time she'd giggled. He was also making it more and more difficult for her to remember exactly why this was a mistake.

"Speaking of which," he said against the sensitive skin behind her ear, "have I mentioned that you still smell damn good? Light and fresh and pretty. Like a garden after a summer shower."

"That sounds remarkably like a line."

Dan groaned inwardly as he heard himself say the words and figured a guy was getting pretty rusty when he had to steal seduction lines from his thirteen-year-old nephew.

"You're right. It is. And not a very original one. But that doesn't make it any less true." He touched his mouth to her chin. Her cheek. Her temple. "It's a scent all your own, Savannah. The kind that gets beneath a man's skin. It stays in his mind and has him imagining making love to you in a sun-dappled meadow of wildflowers."

She drew back. Hitched in a breath. "Dan . . . I'm not ready for this."

Because he wasn't certain that he was ready for it, either, Dan reminded himself that just because a woman smelled great and looked even better shouldn't be reason enough to drag her off to bed.

There were other, more important things . . .

like admiring her mind. Her resiliency. Her warm heart, generous nature, and deep-seated sense of family. Oh, hell.

Better watch it, O'Halloran, an inner voice of reason counseled. *You're getting dangerously close to the edge of a very steep cliff.*

"I have a feeling I'm going to regret asking, but you've piqued my curiosity," she said.

"About what?" Having been sidetracked by the thought of how easy it would be to fall headfirst off that cliff, it took Dan a moment to realize that she was talking to him.

"What it was about a teenage girl you found so frightening you had to resort to the age-old ploy of pulling a disappearing act?"

"Oh, that." He shrugged, pretending a casualness that was at odds with the way he was feeling. "I'm admittedly a little vague on all the details of that night, but I do recall a moment, somewhere between when I brought you up here to watch the submarine races and when I kissed you good night on Ida's front porch, when I actually found myself thinking of ever-afters."

"That's another line."

"Actually, that one is the truth. It was also one helluva terrifying idea for a hormone-driven kid who was about to head off to college to be contemplating."

"Oh. Well." He could tell, of all the excuses he might have offered, Savannah definitely hadn't expected that one.

A trio of fat-billed pelicans flew by as she considered his answer. A ship steamed past, carrying cargo from the Port of Seattle to far-off places.

"That was a long time ago," she decided, telling him nothing that he hadn't already been telling himself. "We're both different people now."

"If there's one thing the law has taught me, it's that people don't change, Savannah. Circumstances do. Times do. But deep down inside, where it really counts, we remain pretty much the same."

"I refuse to believe that." Her hair fanned out like a gilt banner as she firmly shook her head. Her chin rose along with a flash of pride. "I've changed."

Savannah bent down and picked up the journal. "We'd better get back to work."

"That's one idea. Or we could just stay out here and neck."

Her lips twitched, giving him the impression that she was fighting a smile. The way her eyes darkened to a deep jade suggested that Savannah was also struggling against the same unbidden desire that kept digging its unruly claws into him.

"Work," she repeated with that firmness he'd watched her develop since she'd returned to Coldwater Cove. "I have a man arriving from Gray's Harbor first thing Monday morning with a truckload of stain, and before he agreed to come all this way, I had to promise him that the floors would be ready."

Wondering how many males with blood still flowing in their veins could deny this woman anything, Dan pushed himself off the bench and followed her back down the garden path. As he watched the feminine sway of her hips in khaki shorts that amazingly still held a knife-edge crease, he decided that this place really did have the best view on the peninsula.

"Hey, Captain Bligh," he called out.

She glanced back over her shoulder, impatience replacing the earlier touch of reluctant desire on her face. "What now?"

"You're right. You have gotten tougher. And you know what?"

"What?"

"It looks damn good on you."

Savannah didn't respond, but she didn't need to. Dan read both pride and pleasure in her remarkable eyes and decided that it was enough. For now.

The Sawdust Festival was, hands down, the most important annual event to occur in Coldwater Cove, surpassing even the Fourth of July as the highpoint of the year. It was part carnival, part county fair, part logging competition, along with a lot of music and even more food—an all-around good time.

The rain that had been falling off and on all week stopped a few hours before the festival began. As a full moon rose in a clear deep purple sky over Founder's Park, not a single person challenged Lilith's assertion that ancient pagan gods had pulled off a weather miracle.

Japanese lanterns had been strung around the town square, illuminating the George Strait wannabe crooning somebody-done-somebody-wrong songs in the lacy Victorian bandstand. Smoke from Oley's portable barbecue drifted on air enlivened by the sound of guitars, the plink of horseshoes hitting iron stakes, and the wasp-like drone coming from the far end of the park, where men and women wielding souped-up chainsaws were turning huge logs into sawdust.

"Oh, look," Raine said. "There's Lilith's friend." She pointed in the direction of a fifty-something woman seated in a booth painted with gold stars and silver crescent moons. Wooden beads had been woven into jet black hair that fell straight as rain to her waist. She was wearing a flowing purple caftan embroidered with yet more moons. "Let's get our fortunes told."

Savannah looked at her sister with surprise. "I can't believe that you, of all people, are suggesting we spend ten dollars to hear someone wearing more turquoise than is probably found in the entire state of New Mexico tell us that we're going to meet tall, dark, handsome strangers who'll take us on a sea cruise."

"Lilith says she's not a fake."

"Our mother also burns bonfires to ancient goddesses and draws down the moon."

"Well, there is that," Raine agreed, glancing across the green to where Lilith and Amy were riding the carousel. Amy was astride her favorite flower-bedecked white horse; Lilith had, unsurprisingly, chosen a dragon with shiny green scales. "But it'll still be a kick. When was the last time you had any real fun?"

Because she'd almost managed to convince herself that it hadn't really meant anything, that they'd only been responding to sensual ideas stimulated by Lucy's journal, Savannah decided not to mention her little interlude with Dan on the garden bench.

"No wonder you win all your cases," she muttered as she allowed Raine to pull her by the hand toward the fortune-teller's booth. They could have been children again, with her big sister leading the way. "It's useless trying to argue with you."

"Try telling Amy that," Raine complained lightly. "She's begun questioning everything Jack or I tell her. Jack assures me that it's just a new phase, but sometimes, when I find myself arguing with a six-year-old, it's hard to remember that I once tried cases in a New York federal court."

"It could be a phase," Savannah said. "Or it could be that you're going to have another lawyer in the family."

Raine laughed at that. "Heaven help us."

They handed over their money, and after Raven had correctly pegged Raine's recent marriage and career change, she also predicted more children.

"How many more?" Raine asked.

"Two," the fortune-teller said with conviction. "A boy who will resemble his father and a little girl who'll look like the best of both of you."

The amazing thing about the prediction, Savannah thought, was that Raine actually seemed to believe it. Or perhaps, she corrected as she watched her sister's face light up, perhaps she wanted to believe it.

It was Savannah's turn next. "You've recently been badly hurt." Raven Moonsilver's fingernails were short, lacquered in a blinding amethyst metallic shade and adorned with airbrushed silver stars that matched her caftan. She trailed a purple tip across Savannah's palm. "By a man."

"Name me one woman over the age of ten who hasn't," Savannah suggested mildly.

"Ah, but it was not your heart that was so cruelly wounded, but your confidence. Along with your pride."

Savannah assured herself that again, she certainly wasn't alone in that regard. The same thing was undoubtedly happening to women all over the world at this very minute.

"You are an old soul. You have lived other lives that have touched many." Savannah rolled her eyes and waited to hear she'd been Marie Antoinette.

"I know you are skeptical." The silver replica of a Northwest tribal totem the fortune-teller was wearing in one earlobe glinted in the light of the Japanese lanterns as the woman nodded with apparent approval. "This is good. When you finally break through the wall of disbelief, you will no longer have a single doubt."

She studied Savannah's palm in greater detail. "I see someone."

"Here it comes," Savannah couldn't resist telling Raine. "My tall, dark stranger."

"I know you're joking. But this is a woman." Raven Moonsilver's eyes narrowed. Her fingers, gleaming with silver rings, tightened around Savannah's. "A woman caught between the realms."

"Surely you're not talking about a ghost?" Raine asked with interest, earning a sharp, warning look from Savannah. There was no point in encouraging the woman.

"A spirit," the fortune-teller corrected. She was crushing Savannah's hand now. "A lost soul who needs your help to free herself from the bonds that are holding her to this mortal coil."

Savannah tugged her hand free. "How am I supposed to do that?"

"It's not for me to tell you. Open your heart and the answer will come to you."

"Open your heart," Savannah was still muttering five minutes later as they followed the high-pitched, wasp-like drone toward the timed chain-saw art competition where Raine had arranged to meet Jack. "The answer will come to you.

"Gee, talk about wasting money. Even if Mother hadn't told her, which Lilith undoubtedly did, everyone in the county knows I bought the Far Harbor lighthouse. It's also no secret that the lighthouse is supposed to be haunted. The woman is obviously a fraud."

"It's not impossible that she could be in touch with Lucy."

"Then she should be the one to help her. I have enough to do trying to fix up Lucy's house."

"Are you sure you haven't sensed anything? Nothing out of the ordinary has happened there?"

Savannah decided that Dan's kiss momentarily tilting her world wasn't what Raine was re-

ferring to. "Nothing worth mentioning. Perhaps
there have been a few occasions . . ."

Her voice drifted off as she thought of the
slamming door, the times she'd been working
alone late at night and heard soft, breathy
sounds that resembled sighs but were undoubtedly only the wind in the tops of the trees.

"What kind of occasions?"

"Nothing. Just shutters banging in the wind,
rafters creaking, glass rattling. You know how
spooky old houses can be late at night."

She thought of the journal but decided that
didn't count, either. People were constantly
finding all sorts of things hidden in old houses.
Whatever her reasons for hiding her journal,
Savannah refused to believe that Lucy was attempting to send her some sort of secret message from beyond the grave.

They'd reached the sawdust ring where the
competition was to take place. Savannah stood
with Raine and Jack, watching as a man turned
a log into a wooden statue of a bear holding up
a fish, in a record time of six minutes. Deciding
that chainsaw art really wasn't her thing, Savannah wandered on, pausing to observe the
women's ax-throwing contest.

"Now there's a frightening sight," said a familiar deep voice behind her as one ax landed right
in the middle of the red bull's-eye with a loud
thud. "A female with a double-headed axe."

She turned and didn't even try to hide her
smile. "Hi."

"Hi, yourself." Dan skimmed a look over her.

"You're still the most gorgeous Sawdust Queen ever."

She glanced across the lawn to the fir-draped royal arbor where fifteen-year-old Becky Brennan stood laughing with friends and flirting with a group of star-struck teenage males. The boys were wearing jeans so new they looked as if they'd stand up by themselves, Garth Brooks–style shirts, boots, and Stetsons. The numbers pinned to the back of those colorful western-cut shirts revealed they were contestants in the battle of the country band competition.

"Becky's lovely." The memory of being impossibly young and carefree, feeling for at least one night that she'd been the most special girl on earth, was bittersweet.

"Adorable," he agreed. "But she can't hold a candle to you. You take a man's breath away."

She shrugged. "Luck of the genes."

"Perhaps that has something to do with it." He reached behind his back and pulled out a bouquet wrapped in green tissue. "But as my mom always used to remind Karyn, beauty is as beauty does. And you, sweetheart, do real well."

"Oh, they're lovely." Savannah murmured as she lifted the bouquet to her nose and breathed in its delicate scent.

A man who excelled at outward romantic gestures, Kevin had gifted her with a dozen long-stemmed roses at every holiday during their marriage. She'd finally realized that it hadn't taken any effort to have his secretary place a call to the florist.

Other men, most particularly wealthy resort guests who, arrogantly overlooking the fact that she was married, seemed to believe that she could be seduced by a gift of long-stemmed red roses. They had, of course, been wrong.

No man had ever given her wildflowers.

"They're growing all around my house," Dan said. "Whenever I look at them, I think of you. Of course, that's not unusual, since thinking about you seems to be what I've been doing most of the time lately."

When his remark reminded her of his comment about wanting to make love to her in a field of wildflowers, her mutinous hormones spiked.

"How do you feel about roller coasters?" Dan asked suddenly.

"I used to love them—until my life became one."

"The Ferris wheel, then. What would you say to coming for a ride in the sky with me, Savannah?"

Torn between prudence and pleasure, Savannah looked up at the revolving double wheel that was lit up like a gigantic Christmas tree.

"If that suggestion doesn't tickle your fancy, we've got just enough time to make the greased pole climb."

"It's a tough choice." She laughed and made her decision. "But the Ferris wheel it is."

"Terrific." Dan linked his fingers with hers as they strolled hand-in-hand beneath the fairy lights twinkling like stars amid the leaves of the huge red-leaf oaks.

*   *   *

The festival was turning out to be a grand success. As she made her way toward the pie-judging tent, Ida decided that this year's event would go down as the best on record.

"Whoever takes over next year will have a helluvan act to follow," Henry said. He munched on a hot dog loaded with the works as he and Ida watched the teams of loggers trying to climb the towering greased pole.

"I was thinking pretty much the same thing. But I didn't say it because I didn't want to sound like I was bragging on myself."

His salty curse was learned during a decade spent in the merchant marines before he'd returned home to take over the lighthouse duties from his father. "It isn't bragging if it's the truth."

Ida glanced over at him in surprise. "You keep handing out compliments like that and I'm going to think that you've been taken over by one of those pod people or something."

He shrugged. Then his eyes narrowed as he watched her dig into her pocketbook and pull out a plastic bottle of aspirin. "You okay?"

"I'm fine." She swallowed two white tablets with a sip of her iced tea. "It's just a little noisy, what with all the chainsaws whining away and those drums. Whose idea was it to have a battle of the bands, anyway?"

"Lilith said it was yours."

"Oh. Well, like I said, it's a great idea. Brought more young people in."

Strangely, the pounding behind her eyes seemed to have synchronized itself with the throbbing sound of the drums coming from the Victorian bandstand. She glanced around at the crowds of teenagers with satisfaction. There must be a third more in the park than Florence Heron had managed to pull in last year.

Of course, to give Florence her due, it had probably been thirty years since the woman had spoken with any teenager other than the boy who delivered her morning *Coldwater Cove Chronicle*. And then she was likely to scold him for tossing the paper in the rhododendron bush.

What had begun as an act of altruism—bringing foster kids into her home—had turned out to benefit her, as well. Ida had quickly discovered that being around the younger generation helped her stay young. They'd admittedly been a challenge, but she'd always thrived on challenges.

She was thinking that they were also good company when the park, and everyone in it, suddenly went all fuzzy, as if she were looking through a camera lens that had suddenly gone out of focus. Ida blinked.

"Henry." She reached out to steady herself, her fingers digging into his arm.

His brows drew together as he looked down at her. "What's wrong?"

"I don't know." She was struggling to focus when she heard someone call her name. Ida was vastly relieved when her vision cleared, allowing her to view the teenager standing at the other side of the sawdust horseshoe pit.

"Why, it's Gwen." The momentary blurriness was immediately forgotten.

Henry followed her surprised gaze. "You talking about that little girl who looks like she stuck a wet finger in a light socket?"

"That's her." The bright red Little Orphan Annie curls were longer than they'd been when Gwen had left Coldwater Cove two months ago, and even more unruly. "She wasn't due home from science camp for another three days. I guess she came early so she could attend the festival."

The problem was, Ida thought, the serious expression on the teenager's face as she approached didn't give the impression that she'd come here tonight to have a good time. Ida cast a glance upward toward the heavens and said a quick, silent prayer. *Please don't let her be in trouble with the law again.*

Never having known a stable home until she'd landed in Coldwater Cove, in the past Gwen's chosen response to unpleasant experiences—of which she'd had more than her share—had been to shoplift. Ida dearly hoped she'd put such self-destructive behavior behind her.

"Hello, darling." Tamping down her concerns, Ida hugged the foster child she'd grown so fond of.

"Hi, Mama Ida." Gwen hugged her back. Her youthful body had lost all its pregnancy weight. The jeans clinging to her hips were so baggy, Ida figured there was room for a second teenage girl inside them.

"You're home early."

"I know." She'd matured, Ida realized, looking up into the sober face that was more woman than child. Of course that wasn't very surprising. Carrying a baby for nine long months, only to give it up the day after it was born, was bound to make any girl grow up a bit faster than most.

"There's something I need to talk with you about," Gwen said. "Something I've been thinking a lot about while I was in Texas. Something that wouldn't wait three more days."

Ida felt a sharp, tension-caused twinge behind her eye. She ignored it.

"This might not be the best time or place to be talking about this," Henry warned. Ida sensed he was trying to forestall the conversation out of concern for her.

"Nonsense, Henry," she argued. "If Gwen skipped science camp graduation, it must be important." The weekly reports from the counselors had been unanimously glowing.

"What is it, dear?" Ida asked with feigned calm, even as she feared she knew exactly what Gwen was about to say.

The teenager drew in a deep breath, then slowly let it out. "It's about my baby."

Her words echoed in Ida's ears as if she were speaking from the bottom of the cove. Slender teenage hands raked through bright curls, but Ida didn't notice their tremor. Every atom of her attention was riveted on Gwen's lips, which now seemed to be moving in slow motion. Her voice had the odd, drawn-out sound of an old 45 record played at 33 1/3 speed. "I think I want her back."

12

They were riding up backwards, higher and higher, until the people on the ground resembled toy action figures.

"Oh, look," Savannah pointed out. "There's John." She was surprised to see the teenager holding hands with a tall blond girl who was wearing a plastic lei over her sweater and carrying a stuffed animal nearly as big as she was. "I didn't realize he had a girlfriend."

"They sort of tumbled into puppy love this past spring when they met at the Special Olympics," Dan said. "Cindy fell into Coldwater Cove when she was two. By the time they pulled her out, she'd already been brain-damaged."

The Ferris wheel jerked to a halt. Down below, people were getting off, others getting on. "If the scuttlebutt is to be believed, her father never quite forgave her mother for what he considered her carelessness. Plus, the burdens of taking care of a toddler are tough enough without tossing a mental handicap into the mix."

The wheel began to move again, picking up speed.

"The guy left Mrs. Kellstrom with the chore of teaching their daughter how to walk and talk and do all that other basic stuff again from scratch."

"That must have been horribly difficult."

"I suppose it may help that she's a nurse. Even so, it would have to be a helluva test of strength. But she obviously did a great job, because Cindy Kellstrom's one of the nicest, most hardworking kids I've ever met."

She sounds a lot like John, Savannah thought. "They look sweet together," she said as the wheel stopped again, leaving them at the very top, with a bird's-eye view of John buying his girlfriend a cone of fluffy pink cotton candy.

"They are kind of cute," he agreed. "Of course I'm not looking forward to dealing with his wounded heart when they break up, which they're bound to do at their age, but I suppose we all have to learn from experience."

"I suppose so." Savannah heard the laughter and shrieks from the Tilt-a-Wheel and watched as it dipped and spun, the riders pressed hard against the side by centrifugal force.

"That's exactly how I felt when my marriage broke up," she murmured, surprised when she realized she'd said the words out loud.

He followed her gaze. "Dizzy and sick to your stomach?"

"No." She watched the floor drop away. The wheel spun faster. The people shrieked louder. Savannah's hands tightened on the metal bar in front of them as the wheel began its rapid descent.

"Well, the sick-to-the-stomach description pretty much fits." Or at least it had the morning after she'd left Kevin when she'd awakened at the Beverly Wilshire with a killer hangover. "But mostly I felt as if the bottom had dropped out of my life."

"Perhaps that's not so bad." He pried her hands off the bar and held them between his as they swooshed past the ticket taker and headed back up again. "Maybe the bottom should drop out of all our lives every so often, if for no other reason than to let some fresh air in."

"That's a nice philosophy. But the next time I feel my life getting a little stuffy, I believe I'll just open a window."

She'd lost track of John and Cindy. But looking out over the park, Savannah could make out her grandmother and Henry. Miracle of miracles, they seemed to be actually getting along as they ate hot dogs and watched men trying to scale towering greased poles. Not far away, Lilith and Amy had moved on to the spinning teacup ride.

"Want to talk about it?" he asked mildly.

"Not particularly."

"He hurt you." It was not a question.

"Yes." So much for fun, Savannah thought.

"Did he hit you?"

"Of course not." She glanced at Dan in surprise. She was even more surprised to see something new in his eyes. Something dark and dangerous. "It's not that big a deal." She shrugged. "Divorce hurts. However it happens."

"Mine didn't."

"Really?"

"I suspected I was making a mistake the day I got married. I think Amanda did, too."

"Then why did you go through with it?"

"Beats me. Because five hundred of her father's closest friends were coming to dinner?"

"Don't joke. Since you brought it up, I'd really like to know." Surely he couldn't take what was supposed to be a lifetime commitment so casually?

"Okay." His expression turned pensive. Unreadable. "I suppose the simplest way to put it is that Amanda and I were unlucky enough to meet at a time when we were both asking ourselves that old song lyric, 'Is that all there is?' There was a brief chemical flash, but we were adults who'd admittedly been around the block a few times. Neither of us would have gotten married just for lust."

Savannah worried when the idea of Dan lusting after some society blond named Amanda caused a stir of something that felt uncomfortably like jealousy.

"The bottom line was that she thought I had something she wanted. And I thought she had something I wanted. By the time we finally called it quits, the only thing either of us wanted from the other was freedom."

"That's sad."

"I'm certainly not a proponent of divorce.

But in some cases, like ours, where both parties are financially independent, with no kids, and seemingly unable to do anything but make each other miserable, it might be the best solution all around."

"I suppose I can understand that." But she couldn't really identify. "I was never miserable."

They'd reached the bottom again. When the ticket taker leaned forward to open the bar, Dan shoved a bill into his hand.

"We'll be staying a bit longer." The man looked inclined to argue. He glanced over at the ticket booth, then back toward Dan again. Massive shoulders that appeared to have been carved from oak shrugged. He jammed the money into the pocket of his black T-shirt. "Suit yourself."

"Now then." Dan put his arm around Savannah and drew her closer as they slowly climbed back up to the top of the double wheel. "You were saying? About not being miserable?"

"I wasn't. Really," she insisted, meeting his openly skeptical look. "In fact, for a long time, I thought I was blissfully happy."

"Women who are blissful in their marriages don't usually get divorced."

"True." She sighed and wondered how she could possibly explain her behavior to Dan since she was just beginning to understand it herself. "You'd have to know Kevin to understand."

Dan decided that it would probably be best if he never met the weasel.

Neither of them said anything for an entire revolution. Dan was a patient man. Years of in-

terrogating individuals on the witness stand
had taught him to use silence well.

"I met him right after I'd graduated from
culinary school. I'd gotten a job as an assistant
to the assistant pastry chef at the Whitfield
Palace hotel in Paris."

Dan whistled softly. "When deluxe will no
longer do," he murmured the slogan of the
worldwide luxury hotel. "I'm impressed." He
didn't mention that he and Amanda had stayed
at that same hotel on their honeymoon. *Had Savannah been working there then?* he wondered.

"Kevin had just been hired as assistant manager of customer services. Before that he'd been
night manager at the Hôtel de Paris in Monaco.
The day he arrived, I ran into him at the end of
my shift. He was sitting at a corner table, all
alone in the deserted dining room, poring over
a tourist guide of popular Paris sights, trying to
figure out the way to the Eiffel Tower."

"Which you promptly offered to show him."

She looked surprised. "Yes. How did you
know that?"

"Lucky guess," he said dryly.

"Well, anyway," she forged on, "it was Paris
in the spring, I was horribly homesick and lonely, and he was just enough years older to seem
so much more worldly than most of the boys I
knew. He was also suave and sophisticated and
looked incredibly handsome in his Italian
suits."

"If you don't mind, I'd just as soon skip the
roll call of attributes."

"But that's just my point," Savannah said earnestly. "He seemed like every young girl's romantic fantasy. Like Prince Charming. He even shared my dream of someday owning a little inn together, and he made it seem so wonderfully romantic. . . .

"Even after we eloped, whenever I thought I sensed cracks in the facade of what I wanted to believe was our perfect marriage, he convinced me that I was only imagining things. The hotel business gets a lot of women—about-to-be-divorced women, lonely women, career women on business trips who want a fling away from home. He told me that some of those women may occasionally come on to him, but I didn't need to worry because I was the special one. I was the only woman he could ever want."

She managed a sad smile. "Unfortunately, I discovered that I wasn't the only woman he was telling all those pretty words to.

"My ex-husband was manipulative, seductive, and unfortunately without any moral core. After I came home, Ida described his charm as being the oily kind that washes off in the shower."

"That's probably one of the few things your grandmother has ever said that I understand." Dan skimmed his fingers over her shoulder to toy with the ends of her hair. "I'm sorry."

He honestly *was* sorry she'd been hurt. But Dan couldn't really regret her marriage breaking up, because if the husband had been the paragon she'd mistaken him for, Savannah would still be happily whipping up soufflés in Malibu instead of sitting here at the top of Coldwater Cove with him.

"So was I. I was sorry, hurt, and angry, and I've recently realized exactly how much of my self-confidence and self-respect he stole while I wasn't looking." She fell silent and looked out over the midnight-dark waters of the cove.

The carousel's cheery calliope drifted up from the midway. The twangy sounds of a country guitar and fiddle band rode on air scented with popcorn, peanuts, fir, and sawdust. Once again Dan waited.

"You know about Lilith," she said, turning back toward him. "About her life before Cooper. Her marriages."

"I've heard a few stories."

"I love my mother. . . . Really," she insisted when he didn't immediately respond.

"I believe you."

"I've always loved her. And I was never as angry about her behavior as Raine seemed to be."

"Perhaps you were too busy bottling your anger up."

That suggestion hit a little too close for comfort. "All right. I have to admit to wondering recently, now that we're all home again, if in my need to avoid confrontation, I'd managed to convince myself that Lilith's behavior didn't disturb me as much as it did Raine.

"Maybe one of these days I'll work that out. But what I have realized, since I discovered Kevin making love—"

"Not love."

"What?" His quiet comment sidetracked her.

"I've never met the guy, but from the little you've said, and what I've inferred from Jack and Raine, I'm guessing the weasel doesn't know the first thing about love."

She wondered if becoming an attorney had made him so perceptive, or if he'd chosen the law because of what appeared to be a natural talent for reading people.

"It's difficult to love someone else when you're so enamored with yourself," she responded dryly. "When I discovered he'd been having an affair with the head of the resort's legal department, I think what really hurt, more than his infidelity, was that deep down inside, I'd known it all along.

"It was as if we had this secret, unspoken contract. Kevin screwed around, and I knew it, and he knew that I knew it. So by overlooking his lapses in monogamy, on some level, so long as he remained discreet and we could both continue to lie about his behavior, I believed that I was keeping my marriage intact."

"Then he breached the contract by bringing the affair out into the open," Dan suggested.

"I think I was the last person at Las Casitas to know." She shook her head. "No, that's not exactly right. I was the last person to *acknowledge* it."

Except for a few general comments to her family, and telling Raine whatever details her sister needed to handle the legal aspects of her divorce, Savannah really hadn't talked about the breakup of her marriage.

She'd been too embarrassed. Too ashamed. Now she realized that Kevin was the one who should be ashamed.

"The entire time I was growing up, I swore that I wouldn't make the same mistakes regarding men that Lilith did. I promised myself that when I got married it would be for keeps."

"Given Lilith's marital history, I suppose it makes a certain cockeyed sense that you'd stick out a bad relationship longer than you should have. But I still can't understand why you married a jerk like that in the first place."

"Neither can I, now. I suppose I read too many fairy tales growing up. I was waiting to get swept off my feet, so when Kevin proposed eloping to Monte Carlo a week after we met, I thought it was what love was supposed to feel like."

She was looking out over the park again in a way that had Dan suspecting that she was seeing that long-ago day she'd exchanged vows with a guy that was so very wrong for her. Even though he could see how she'd gotten herself in such an impossible situation, he was still surprised that a girl who'd always seemed like the princess of Coldwater Cove could have ended up playing the role of Cinderella.

"Sometimes it's mutual. Guys can get swept off their feet, too. My folks only knew each other a week when they got married."

"Really?"

"Really. Dad had just graduated from college, and since the Air Force had paid for his education, he was about to ship out to Vietnam, which, I suppose, admittedly helped move the timetable up a little.

"Mom was the nurse who gave him his inoculations, and he insists that he fell head over heels. Literally. He fainted right after she stuck the needle in."

A silvery laugh bubbled from between Savannah's lips. Luscious lips Dan could still taste. Lips he wanted to taste again. "That's a wonderful story."

"I've always thought so. Dad hates Mom to tell it because he says it makes him sound like a wuss. They'll celebrate their thirty-seventh anniversary next spring.

"My grandparents didn't even take that long to get married. Gramps was in the navy. He met Gram when she was handing out doughnuts at a USO during World War II, and they eloped that same night, had eight kids, and are still crazy about each other. In fact, the way they slow dance at family reunions is downright embarrassing."

She smiled. "It sounds as if war has been very good for your family."

"They would have all gotten together, anyway," he said with a shrug. "As Gramps always says, you can't fight destiny."

Savannah looked skeptical, but she didn't argue.

They fell silent. Enjoying the night. Enjoying each other. Music from far below played on. The Ferris wheel continued its revolutions. When they stopped at the top again, Dan cupped her cheek in the hand that had been playing with her hair and turned her face toward him.

"Advance warning, Savannah. I'm going to kiss you. If you don't want me to, you'd better say so now."

She didn't say a word. She didn't need to. Her eyes, two limpid pools of need, gave Dan the answer he needed.

All it took was the taste of her to make him hard. Dan wasn't gentle this time. Unable to get enough of her, his mouth turned hot and hungry. Needing more, he used his thumb to coax her lips open.

The kiss grew more and more ravenous as he swallowed her soft moans and throaty whimpers.

Dan wanted to touch her. To taste her. Everywhere. He imagined his mouth on her flesh, following the lush curves while his hands played hot licks on her body—that incredible body that he was literally aching to be inside.

"If we're not careful, we're going to end up falling into the cove." He wondered if that would cool them off and decided they'd just set the water to boiling instead.

She drew her head back and blinked slowly. Sometime during the heated kiss, her hand had landed in his lap. Dan ground his teeth as she absently stroked him. "It just might be worth it."

Because he was on the verge of exploding, he took hold of her hand to keep them both out of trouble. "You keep touching me that way, sweetheart, and you may just end up getting us both arrested for disorderly conduct when I rip off your clothes and ravish you atop a amusement ride in a public park."

"Ravishing sounds pretty good," she admitted as the wheel jolted again.

"Maybe later." With his gaze still on hers, he kissed her again, lightly this time, and watched a mingling of pleasure and need rise in her eyes. "When we both have our feet on the ground again."

Before she could respond, they'd reached the end of Dan's money. "Time's up," the ticket taker said firmly.

Wanting to be alone with Savannah, this time Dan didn't argue. They'd no sooner started back across the park when John came running up to them.

"I've been looking all over for you, Savannah," he said. He was obviously agitated and out of breath.

Her fingers tightened on Dan's. He felt her hand turn cold. "Did something happen to my grandmother?"

"No. Dr. Lindstrom's fine. But she sent me to get you. She said it's an urgent family problem and you all need to go back to the house right away. She and Henry and Gwen are waiting for you at the car. With Raine and Jack."

"Gwen's here?"

John nodded earnestly. "I think she's what the problem is about."

Savannah's gaze cut from John to Dan.

"Perhaps it's not as bad as it sounds," he said encouragingly.

"We can always hope." She did not sound encouraged.

As they headed toward the parking lot, Dan reminded himself that Savannah had made a substantial financial and emotional commitment here in Coldwater Cove. She wouldn't be going anywhere.

There would be plenty of time to pick up where they'd left off. Hopefully sooner rather than later.

13

"I didn't say for certain that I wanted her back," Gwen insisted after they'd gathered in the front parlor of Ida's home.

To keep Amy out of the discussion, Henry, Jack, and John had taken her upstairs to watch a National Geographic video about whales on Ida's bedroom television. Since he was the attorney who'd written up the initial adoption agreement, Dan had stayed downstairs with the Lindstrom women and Gwen.

"I said I was *thinking* about it." The teenager's bottom lip thrust out as she turned to Raine. "When I signed the adoption contract, you told me I could change my mind."

"There's a window of opportunity," Raine agreed. "But just like adoption, it's not a decision to be made lightly, Gwen."

"Which is why you need to be very, very sure about this, darling," Lilith added.

"I know. That's why I need to go see her," Gwen insisted, her eyes glistening. "So I can make up my mind."

Savannah exchanged a worried glance with her sister, then with her mother, then finally directed her gaze toward Ida, whose complexion appeared oddly putty colored.

"Are you all right?" she asked her grandmother.

"I wish everyone would stop asking me that," Ida snapped. "Besides, how can anyone be all right? This is a mess."

"I-I-I'm s-s-sorry." The tears began to fall. Gwen's hands were clasped together so tightly her knuckles were white. "I've really tried not to think about her. But I do. And I know you'll all think I'm behaving irresponsibly, but I have this h-h-huge empty feeling in me that won't go away."

She scrubbed at the free-falling moisture, appearing so like a child herself that Savannah felt like crying too. Gwen closed her eyes. Her lashes looked like thin threads of copper silk against her splotchy, freckled cheeks.

"I can't stop wondering what she looks like now. If she's got h-h-hair. If she's h-h-happy."

Savannah didn't think she'd ever seen anyone look so wretched. Gwen hadn't even been this distraught the day at the hospital when she'd handed her infant daughter over to Terri and Bill Stevenson. She knelt beside the chair the teen was slumped in and took her in her arms.

"It'll be all right," she said reassuringly. Somehow, whatever Gwen's decision, the family would find a way to work the problem out, as they had so many others over the years.

"I just need to see her, Savannah," Gwen repeated through her tears. Her voice was shaky, but determined. "To m-m-make sure."

After a great deal of discussion, and a decidedly uncomfortable telephone call to the Stevensons, it was decided that Savannah would drive Gwen to Sequim first thing in the morning.

Both Dan and Raine objected when the parties involved opted against bringing attorneys into the meeting at this point, but after a great deal of argument—which became heated for a few moments—they were overruled.

"I'll keep my cell phone on," Dan promised as Savannah walked with him out to the Tahoe. His voice was resigned, but she could tell he still wasn't happy with the arrangement for the private meeting she'd worked out with the Stevensons.

"If you or Gwen need any legal advice, or if you just need a friend to talk to, all you have to do is call. I can be there in thirty minutes."

And he'd come, Savannah thought. Without hesitation, without question. Because he cared. She tried to think how long it had been since she'd been able to count on anyone but her grandmother or sister.

Too long, she realized. Perhaps even forever. It was nice knowing that she could count on Dan O'Halloran. Nicer still knowing that she could count on herself.

Savannah was beginning to view her divorce not as something she'd suffered through and survived—like mumps or a tax audit—but as a born-again experience. She'd been gifted with a new beginning, a chance to reinvent Savannah Townsend. And so far, she thought with a burst of pride, she was doing a pretty damn good job of it.

"We'll be fine."

"Oh, you're a lot better than fine, sweet-heart." They'd reached the truck. Ignoring the interested side glances from the others, he drew her into his arms. Ignoring the looks from her family, Savannah went.

He didn't kiss her. Just held her, offering comfort and strength. Allowing herself to accept both, just for a minute, Savannah circled her arms around his waist and rested her head against his shoulder.

She watched him leave and felt a sudden, cowardly urge to go with him. Despite how far she'd come in a few short months, as she got ready for bed, Savannah couldn't help dreading tomorrow. She washed her face in the old pedestal sink in the bathroom she shared with Henry and thought how, if given the choice, she would rather have discovered Kevin sleeping with the entire LA Lakers cheerleader squad in their custom-made king-sized bed that looked out over the sea than watch Gwen suffering such emotional pain.

While she brushed her teeth, she decided that it would be easier to go through a dozen divorces than risk shattering the fragile new family bonds of her longtime friends, whose

idea to adopt this particular baby had been hers
in the first place.

Even with all those unpleasant prospects
tumbling around in her mind, as she crawled
between the sheets that smelled of the Mrs.
Stewart's bluing Ida used in the wash, Savannah thought back to the kiss she'd shared with
Dan. Had it been only a few hours ago? It
seemed much, much longer.

But even the distance of time hadn't stopped
the moment from being permanently etched in
her mind. She knew that years from now, when
she was Ida's age, looking back on the fortunes
and follies of her life, she'd recall in vivid detail
sitting atop the world with Daniel O'Halloran
and feeling as if she could have reached out and
grabbed a handful of the glittering stars that
had been stitched against the night sky like bril-
liants on velvet.

Unfortunately, Gwen's return home had sent
her crashing back to earth.

A rose bush climbed a white lattice trellis outside the window, its fragrance perfuming the
room. The late summer roses were overblown, as
if to put on one last spectacular display before autumn frost would curl their serrated green leaves
and turn the blossoms from wine red velvet to a
sad dead brown that would crush between your
fingers, then blow away like dust. Like her old life.

The house was dark and mostly quiet. If she
was very still, she could hear the faint night-
time rustling of bird wings in the monkey puzzle tree on the front lawn, the distant bark of a

dog, Henry's muffled snores from beyond the violet papered wall. She could not hear anything from Gwen's room. But Savannah sensed the teen's silent weeping and knew that she wasn't the only person in the house finding sleep difficult tonight.

The lady or the tiger? Savannah worried as she spent the long night staring up at the shadows moving across the swirled plaster ceiling. Each door held potential heartbreak.

The day dawned pastel pink and silver. A veil of soft, hazy mist lay low over the cove. The mood in the kitchen was strained, cautious, as if a wrong word could set off a deadly chain reaction. Ida remained uncharacteristically silent, as though determined not to influence what Savannah knew could be the most important decision Gwen would ever make. Henry had chosen to stay upstairs, displaying either surprising sensitivity or, more likely, a desire to avoid any more emotional storms.

The morning sun flashed buttery yellow bars on the asphalt as Savannah drove along the narrow, twisting road that ran along the coastline to Sequim. Gwen didn't say a word. But the brittle metallic tension surrounding her was so palatable, Savannah imagined she could taste it.

Bill and Terri Stevenson were refugees from California who'd bought a house built in the late 1800s as a summer estate for a wealthy Seattle lumber baron. A former wine master at a world-renowned Napa Valley vineyard who'd grown weary of fighting the accountants who seemed to be running the larger wineries lately, Bill had opted out of the rat race. These days he was focusing on the work he loved, turning his carefully tended grapes into award-winning wines while his wife Terri, a graphic artist, designed labels featuring the century-old stone castle-like building that harkened back to the original owner's German roots. Terri also handled the equally successful advertising and marketing end of the business.

It was a modern-day cottage industry, one that allowed the couple to work at home and lavish attention on their newly adopted daughter.

Since the day was bright blue, they all sat outside, as they had that first day, on a little patio overlooking the duck pond and the sweep of vineyards set in dark soil that stretched nearly to the strait. Only a few months ago, the vines had been bright and spring green with promise; now they were dark, their limbs bending with ripening, deep purple grapes approaching harvest.

Baby Lily, dressed in a frilly dress the color of lilacs and pink ruffled socks, was strapped into an infant swing beneath a blue and white fringed awning. The day the infant had been born, Savannah thought her face had resembled a sweet, round pink pumpkin. She'd changed considerably since then. Her satiny skin was the peachy cream of a true redhead, like her birth mother, and a fuzz had sprouted on her formerly bald head like coppery thistledown. The sweet scent of Johnson's baby powder suggested she'd been bathed shortly before Gwen and Savannah's arrival.

Oblivious to her surroundings or the tension in the air, she was cooing happily to herself, sounding a bit like the doves that gathered beneath Savannah's bedroom window each morning. It would have been obvious to anyone that this was a contented child, a baby who was well and truly loved.

For the first time in her life, as they exchanged small talk, Savannah understood the old saying about the elephant in the living room. It hovered there, huge and menacing as they discussed the prospect of a good harvest despite the need for more rain in what was known as the Olympic Sunbelt, Gwen's summer at science camp, and Savannah's ongoing restoration of the light-house. It was as if all the participants at the possibly life-altering meeting were avoiding the subject they'd all come together to discuss.

Finally Bill, after sharing his hopes for this year's merlot, broke the conversational ice.

"We've been worried about you," he told Gwen.

She tossed up her chin. Insecurity radiated from her slender body that had lost all its baby weight. "Worried that I'd change my mind?"

The girl who, not so long ago, had dared Jack, Raine, and an Olympic County judge to throw her back into the revolving door of the state's foster care system, had returned. Which only revealed, Savannah thought, how frightened she really was beneath that truculent exterior.

"No," he said in the quiet, thoughtful way

that was such a contrast to his wife's more ebullient personality. "We've been worried about how you've been dealing with your decision. For your sake."

"You've had a great deal to overcome already in your young life, Gwen," Terri said gently. "We hated thinking that giving up your baby may have caused you any more pain."

"Not that we regret adopting Lily." Bill's tone was calm; the emotion swirling in his normally calm brown eyes was not.

"She's the best thing that could ever happen to us." Terri's voice choked up. Her eyes swam. "The answer to all our prayers." She reached blindly for her husband, who linked his fingers with hers.

His hands were rough and dark, his knuckles scraped, and Savannah either saw, or imagined she saw, dirt around his ragged cuticles. They were not the hands of some San Francisco yuppie who one spring day awakened with a whim to make a nice little wine to serve at small gatherings of the kind of attractive, articulate friends so often depicted in wine advertising.

They were the hands of a working man, a man more comfortable laboring in soil than pushing a pen behind a desk.

But she'd also seen how gentle those very same hands could be when he'd placed his daughter into her swing.

"We told you that we're proponents of open adoption," he reminded Gwen. "We haven't changed our minds. We adore Lily, which is why we can understand how much you must love her, too. The way we see it, a child can't have too much love."

Savannah could tell from Gwen's expression that his response was not what she'd expected. She'd come here today to fight; by offering to share their lives, they may have managed to disarm her.

When the tears the teenager had so stubbornly held back on the drive from Coldwater Cove began to trail silently down her face, Savannah realized that they were right back where they'd been three months ago. Once again her grandmother was right. It was a mess.

"You realize that if you keep it up, you're going to wear a damn hole in the rug," Henry told Ida.

Her nerves about as jumpy as a frog in a French restaurant, Ida spun back toward him, her hands on her narrow hips. "It's my house."

"It's also your blood pressure." He pointed the remote at the TV he'd been watching and hit the mute. "Speaking of which, when was the last time you had it checked?"

"I'm a doctor. I can check it myself."

"So?"

"So what?" Just when she was beginning to think that having this man living under her roof might be tolerable, he'd begun to irritate her all over again.

"So when did you check it? At your age, you can't be too careful."

"I'm younger than you."

"Mebbe. By a few years. But like you said, old's old."

If there was one thing Ida hated worse than having someone try to tell her what to do, it was having her own words tossed back in her face. Especially when she couldn't quite remember them. Though it sounded like something she might have said, she allowed.

They stared at each other.

She might not be as young as she once was, but her will was still strong as cold forged steel. Unfortunately, it was beginning to look as if she'd met her match in Henry Hyatt.

He finally shrugged. "Stubborn as a Missouri mule."

He turned the sound back on, the noise of the Seahawks game grating on her nerves.

Ida left the parlor and began pacing the wide planks of the front porch. What was keeping them? She'd never been patient. A change-of-life surprise baby, she'd come barreling into her parents' life just at the time they'd begun looking forward to slowing down and perhaps bouncing a grandchild or two on their knees. Looking back on it now, her mind on babies anyway because of Gwen's pickle, Ida realized that trying to keep up with a child who didn't know the meaning of the word *slow* would have been a challenge.

Her weary mother had, on more than one occasion, accused Ida of possessing the attention span of a hummingbird. Which, now that she thought about it, was much the same thing she'd always said about her own daughter. It was the first time in fifty years that it had ever occurred to her that she and Lilith might have anything in common. It was a thought that merited some consideration.

Once she'd quit worrying about Gwen.

She stared toward the direction of Sequim, as if she could will Savannah's little red car to appear. But the only car on the road was Melvin Baxter's old clunker of a Buick he insisted on calling a classic, when what it really was was a wreck. The sky between the mountains and the cove was a clear robin's egg blue, marred only by the puffy white contrail of a jet flying high overhead, the plane's body glinting like quicksilver.

Quicksilver. That had been the word her mother had used to describe her mind, which had admittedly hopped from subject to subject, never seeming to find a topic worthy of interest. Her grades had been mediocre at best, which, since she was a girl and not expected to have a career, wouldn't have worried her parents overmuch had it not been for their concern that her unfortunate habit of speaking her mind would greatly diminish her marriage potential.

Then, on a Christmas Eve she'd never forget, two weeks before her fifteenth birthday, Ida's life had drastically and inexorably changed. As she'd been doing since she was old enough to ride along on the wooden sled, she'd gone out into the New Hampshire woods with her father to cut down their Christmas tree. A typical taciturn New Englander, John Lindstrom had not mentioned the pain that had been lurking beneath his ribcage when he'd awakened that morning.

Indeed, there'd been scant time for conversation as Ida had been downstairs impatiently waiting for him, already bundled up in woolens and boots.

Her mother had always been a perfectionist when it came to the family's annual tree, and it had taken a great deal of trekking through knee-deep snow to find a spruce Ingrid Lindstom wouldn't be able to find fault with.

They'd been returning down the mountain with their lush blue-green prize when her father's knees had suddenly buckled and he'd come crashing to the snowy ground in the same way the tree had fallen to the ax.

The next few hours of terror passed in a mind-numbing blur, but, frightened as she'd been, the instant Ida rushed into the emergency room behind her father's stretcher, she felt suddenly whisked from her boring, black-and-white world into a Technicolor wonderland. She could have been Dorothy, landing in Oz.

The bustling, foreign world of medicine that caused her mother to fret so was the most fascinating thing Ida had ever seen. She was fascinated by the nurses, whose starched white uniforms rustled like dry leaves and whose crepe-soled shoes made not a sound as they moved through the halls in a brisk, efficient manner. Even today, Ida could recall in vivid detail the little boy who had fallen through the ice while skating and had miraculously escaped anything worse than a probable head cold.

Another man had been sitting on a gurney, his long legs dangling over the side. He was pressing his hand against a blood-soaked white towel as he'd awaited stitches for a nasty cut on his forehead. Ida overheard his wife telling the nurse that he'd received the wound when he'd leaned too far forward to put the star on the top of the tree and had fallen off the ladder.

There were more people crowded into the emergency room, more than she would have expected for such a small population, all of them dependent on the larger-than-life white-jacketed individuals who moved among them like gods who'd strolled down from Mount Olympus to play with the mortals.

It was only years later, when she was in medical school, that it would dawn on Ida that the doctors had all been men. Not that it would have mattered if she *had* realized that the only women in the emergency room had been wives, mothers, or nurses. She'd discovered her true calling on that memorable Christmas Eve, the one thing in all the world that could capture and hold her attention.

The god attending her father informed the family that John Lindstrom would live. He would, however, have to remain in the hospital for the next six weeks. "To allow his heart to rest," the doctor had explained to his relieved wife and spellbound daughter.

Ida visited her father every day. She drank in

the always changing sights and sounds and scents like a girl who'd spent years crawling across parched desert sands and had finally stumbled across a sparkling oasis. And she was never, ever bored.

Nor had she ever suffered a moment's boredom during all the years she'd served as Coldwater Cove's general practitioner, caring for entire families in a way that made her an intricate part of the community.

She'd kept up with the times, attending seminars and spending her nights reading medical journals to learn new techniques, new methods of healing.

But the one thing Ida had never been able to learn was patience.

14

"Can I hold her?" Gwen asked.

"Of course," Terri and Bill said together.

They exchanged a quick look, then Terri rose, lifted Lily from the swing, and carefully placed her, one mother to the other, into Gwen's arms. It escaped no one's attention that this was a reversal of the gesture of that morning in the hospital when Gwen had surrendered her child to the Stevensons' for safekeeping.

Lily stopped cooing. Her brow furrowed beneath the pink elastic headband. Eyes as wide and blue as a china plate observed this newcomer with sober intensity. On some deeper level, Savannah realized that all three adults on the patio were holding their breaths. Watching the turbulent emotions move across Gwen's face, she feared the teenage mother had forgotten how to breathe. Gwen's yearning was painful to watch.

It was as if they'd all been turned to stone—

or wood, like the life-size tableau of the crèche and the wise men Ida put out on the front yard every Christmas.

Then it happened.

"She smiled at me!" Gwen exclaimed.

Terri beamed through unshed tears. "She's been doing that more and more lately. It's like looking into the sun, isn't it?"

"Yes." Gwen's voice was filled with an awe that, Savannah belatedly realized, she hadn't been allowed to experience the day she'd given birth to Lily.

Concerned for Gwen's feelings, attempting to help smooth over the wrenching pain of loss, the family had inadvertently stolen any sense of maternity from her. Only Terri, who'd insisted that the baby be photographed with her birth mother, had begun to understand the complex emotions the teenager might be experiencing on that unforgettable day.

"She's grown so much," Gwen said softly.

"Like a weed," Bill said.

"A beautiful, one-of-a-kind weed," Terri said. "She looks like you, Gwen."

"Do you think so?" Hope and an unmistakable maternal pride warred on the freckled face.

"Absolutely," Terri and Bill said in unison.

Gwen ran her finger down her daughter's cheek. "I decided to give her up for adoption in the first place because she needed a better mother, a better family than I could be right now."

None of them challenged that truthful appraisal.

"Until that day I was panhandling on the ferry and Mama Ida took me home with her, I never felt as if I belonged anywhere. It's hard to fit in when you're being dragged from home to home, always changing schools."

She smoothed the frilly organdy skirt. Lily cooed and kicked her plump, stocking-clad feet. "I want Lily to know where she belongs. To know who her family is."

Gwen bit her bottom lip as she dragged her gaze from her daughter, out across the rolling vineyard, then back to the Stevensons.

"You're her family. I love her with my whole heart. I always will." She sighed, a sad little shimmer of sound. "But she belongs with you."

Bill and Terri exchanged another look. If the subject hadn't been so serious, if so much hadn't been at stake, Savannah might have envied their silent marital conversation. She couldn't remember ever sharing such obvious telepathy with Kevin.

"We want you to be very, very sure about this, Gwen," Bill said. Again, his voice was gentle, but firmer than Savannah had ever heard it. "We're willing to make accommodations for your feelings and whatever need you have to be included in Lily's life. Within reason," he tacked on.

"But you can't go changing your mind every few months. It'd be too hard on all of us—you, Terri, and me, and most of all it would be too hard on Lily."

"I know." Gwen hugged her daughter closer. Her expression was hidden by her cap of red hair as she brushed her lips against the top of the baby's head.

"I didn't really want to take her away from you. On the way home from science camp, I was thinking that maybe we could share her. Not just on special days, like her birthdays, or Christmas. But all the time."

She turned to Terri. "It must be hard being a working mother."

"It takes some juggling," Terri allowed. "But she's a remarkably easy child, and at this age, I can keep her with me while I'm working."

Gwen considered that. "My mother always said I ruined her life."

Savannah couldn't let that hurtful statement go unchallenged. "I never knew your mother, Gwen." But she'd heard the stories from Raine and Ida, horrific stories of drugs and prostitution and child abuse. "But since we're all ultimately responsible for our own behavior, I have to point out that your mother ruined her own life."

"Yeah. That's what the counselor said."

The only thing that had worried Savannah about Gwen going to off to science camp was that her court-appointed weekly therapy would be interrupted. She was moderately relieved at this indication that at least some of the self-esteem Gwen had developed while living with Ida had stuck during her time away from home.

"It'd be confusing for Lily to have two mothers." Gwen sighed again with obvious sadness and resignation. "But I want her to grow up knowing that *she* never ruined my life. That I loved her." She hitched in a shaky breath. "More than anything."

"Absolutely," Terri said.

"I'm going to register with one of those bureaus that let adopted kids find their natural parents when they're adults. That way, if she ever wants to m-m-meet me"—she struggled against renewed tears—"she can."

Terri nodded. "I believe that's a very wise, very mature decision. And you can trust us to support Lily if—and when—she wants to discover what a brave, special woman her birth mother is."

In contrast to the first time they'd all sat together out here on the patio, sheltered from a spring rain, as Gwen gave Lily back to Terri and good-byes were said and hugs exchanged, there were no tears. Savannah suspected the teenager was cried out.

"I understand how hard it is to lose a child." Savannah said as they drove back home.

Gwen glanced over at her with surprise. "Did you have to give away a baby?"

"No. I had a miscarriage early in my pregnancy. It was the same day I brought home a new crib."

It had been painted in a gleaming white enamel that shone like sunshine on new snow and had been topped with a ridiculously feminine, peony-hued ruffled canopy made for a princess.

The crib had still been in the nursery, a vivid pink and white reminder of her loss, when Savannah had returned from the hospital. Despite her doctor's instructions to rest, she'd spent the entire afternoon with screwdrivers and wrenches, taking it apart and putting it away. She'd hoped that if she didn't have to look at the symbol of so much hope and happiness, she'd feel better. Of course she hadn't.

"That must have been awful."

"I thought my heart would break."

"But it didn't break," Gwen said, with obvious hope.

"It was pretty much shattered," Savannah contradicted, deciding that she owed Gwen the absolute truth.

Savannah had never told anyone but Raine about her miscarriage. Not even her grandmother, partly because she hadn't wanted Ida to worry, partly because she hadn't wanted to think about it herself. She decided the fact that she could talk about it with Gwen now, without that horrid, wrenching pain, was yet more proof of personal growth.

"It's gotten better. But I can't imagine that I'll ever put it entirely out of my mind."

"I'll never forget Lily," Gwen said with a sad little sigh.

"No. You won't."

"When I was a little kid, the only thing I ever wanted was a mom who loved me and who'd take care of me."

"I felt the same way a lot of times."

"Yeah. I guess Lilith wasn't a very good mom."

"I think she was just too young to take care of two children." But not once had she ever accused her daughters of causing the turmoil her life had been for so many years, as Gwen's mother had done.

"Yeah," Gwen repeated. "She was probably too young to be a mother. Like me."

A thoughtful little silence filled the car. Wanting to leave Gwen to her thoughts, Savannah didn't speak until they were nearing the lighthouse.

"How are you with a paintbrush? I'm finishing up the trim on the inside of the lantern room today and could really use some help."

"You're just trying to get my mind off Lily."

"Partly," Savannah agreed. "But mostly, I honestly could use another hand. John also said something about planting mums today." She knew that Gwen loved to garden; indeed, the garden she'd created in Ida's back yard had proven a beautiful place for Lilith's and Raine's weddings.

"Okay. If you and John Martin really need help, I guess I could pitch in." She hitched in an audible breath. "Thank you. For coming with me today. For letting me make my own decision."

"It was your decision to make," Savannah said mildly.

"I know." Gwen stared out the passenger window, pretending grave interest in the trees flashing by, then turned back toward Savannah. "Thank you for being my family."

Savannah smiled. "That's the easy part."

That crisis dealt with, Savannah found herself embroiled in yet another problem when it came time for her grandmother's visit to the doctor. Independent to the bone, Ida, whose shirt informed them all that I May Have Many Faults, But Being Wrong Isn't One of Them, was not at all pleased when she came downstairs and found her daughter and both her granddaughters waiting. Even though Gwen had professed a desire to go with them, she had reluctantly headed off to the high school to get her books and confirm her schedule for her upcoming senior year.

"It's just a routine physical," Ida grumbled. "I don't need an entourage."

Raine folded her arms and met her grandmother's stubborn glare straight on. "Tough."

The grandfather clock in the front hall announced the half hour with a peal of Westminster chimes. Ida checked the time on her own watch—the one she'd worn for as long as Savannah could remember, with a wide leather band, round white face, and red sweep hand that ticked off the seconds.

Then she shot a look at Henry, who was sitting at the table, drinking coffee and pretending to read the morning paper. Savannah had known he was pretending when ten minutes had gone by without his turning the page.

"I left you a cold meatloaf sandwich for lunch," Ida told him. "It's wrapped in waxed paper in the fridge."

"Sounds real good." Savannah gave him points for lying with a straight face. "Thanks."

"You're a guest," Ida reminded him briskly. She turned toward the others. "Well, since I seem to be stuck with you three, we might as well get going."

It was, Savannah thought as she followed her grandmother out the kitchen door, one of the few times she'd ever seen Ida Lindstrom surrender without a prolonged fight.

The day seemed a month long. While Ida may have always found medicine fascinating, Savannah, forced to wait with her mother and sister while her grandmother—clad in a white cotton hospital gown that hung past her knees—was moved from room to room, cubicle to cubicle, found it bewildering and frightening.

Armed with informational brochures found in the waiting room, she, Raine, and Lilith learned more detail about tests they'd mostly only seen on *ER* or *Chicago Hope*. There were tests to determine how long it took for Ida's blood to clot, tests to measure her glucose level, and the amount of fat and cholesterol in her blood. There were chest x-rays, a CAT scan, and an EKG, which a friendly, chatty technician had explained was necessary to check heart function, since clots could often be thrown off from the heart and enter the arteries of the brain.

Exhausted herself when the battery of tests were finally concluded, Savannah couldn't imagine how Ida was feeling.

When the neurologist, Dr. Burke, finally brought the family into his office, Ida was already there. Despite the grueling day, she looked a great deal more chipper than Savannah felt, and if appearances were anything to go by, Raine and Lilith were also wrung out.

Lilith looked especially drawn. Her normally smooth forehead had been furrowed for hours, her midnight blue eyes lacked their usual sparkle, and concern carved deep brackets along both sides of her mouth, drawing her lips down. For the first time in memory, Savannah's mother looked not just her age, but older.

"I've already heard the verdict." Ida stood up when they entered, pocketbook clutched in her hands. "Since I can't see any point in sitting here while you all rehash it, I'll wait down in the cafeteria. Those fool tests cost me breakfast and lunch and I'm starving."

Savannah decided that the fact that the doctor was letting Ida walk out of his office instead of admitting her immediately was a good thing. Then again, she considered, from her reading, she knew that Alzheimer's patients could live with the disease for years before hospitalization became necessary.

She was vastly relieved when the doctor skipped the getting-to-know you small talk and went straight to the point.

"Dr. Lindstrom tells me that you've been concerned about recent memory lapses she's been experiencing."

"We've been worried she may have Alzheimer's," Raine, equally to the point, answered.

"Alzheimer's is admittedly something we all worry about, especially on those days we can't find our car keys." When he folded his hands on his desk, Savannah found herself studying them, as she had Bill's yesterday. They were capable hands, she decided, in their own way as reassuring as the plethora of framed diplomas covering the walls.

"But I don't believe that's Dr. Lindstrom's problem."

"Is that good news? Or bad news?" Savannah asked.

"Obviously, in the case of dementia, all diagnoses are relative."

"Excuse me if I don't find any diagnosis of dementia very comforting," Lilith interjected.

"I understand." The look he gave her suggested he just might. "It's one of those words that doesn't come with any positive connotations. Still, if we were talking about my grandmother—"

"Which we're not," Raine broke in.

"Actually, we could be," he countered mildly. "My maternal grandmother was diagnosed with multi-infarct dementia five years ago. MID is the second leading cause of progressive mental deterioration, or, in layman's terms, tissue death in the brain."

Savannah heard her sister let out a breath. "What causes it?"

"MID is caused by damage or death to brain cells due to a deprivation of oxygen and nutrients."

"That sounds like a stroke." Savannah felt the blood leave her face.

She'd secretly worried about this, but had

been afraid to let herself even consider the possibility. A friend—a pastry chef at the resort she'd worked at in Atlantic City—had suffered a stroke that had left the thirty-seven-year-old woman unable to speak and completely paralyzed on one side. When she had finally gotten her voice back months later, she'd sounded like a slow-minded toddler, and when Savannah had left, she'd only been able to get around with a walker.

"Surely we would have noticed if Mother had suffered a stroke," Lilith insisted.

"Not necessarily. Transient ischemic attacks, or TIA—which are essentially ministrokes—aren't that easy to spot, especially in the elderly, since the symptoms—dizziness, clumsiness, fainting, numbness, forgetfulness—are brief, usually lasting less than five minutes, and they tend to get dismissed as a normal process of aging."

"She fell off a kitchen stool this past spring," Raine said flatly. "She was hospitalized, but no one ever diagnosed a stroke."

"I've only been on staff for three weeks, so I don't have any personal knowledge of the incident. But looking at her chart, I can understand why the admitting physician wasn't overly concerned, especially since she didn't reveal any other symptoms at the time."

"I don't know anything about strokes," Lilith murmured.

"That's not surprising. In this information age, you can't turn on your television without hearing about the dramatic new techniques in preventing or treating cardiovascular problems or cancer. But while approximately half a million people a year have strokes, they don't garner the same press. I suppose part of the reason is that strokes are harder to pin down. Most people, when they have a heart attack, suffer much the same damage.

"But strokes are different. Unique. Our brains consume the largest percentage of our body's energy—about twenty-five percent," he said, slipping into a pedantic mode that made him sound like a medical school professor, which, Savannah noted from one of the diplomas, he'd once been. "There are twenty billion neurons in the brain and each of those makes, on average, ten thousand connections. Our brains are the miracle of our human frames, the supercomputers of the universe, so to speak. They're also our greatest human mystery.

"In fact, it was only about three hundred years ago that physicians first started noticing that some people without any signs of head injuries would suddenly complain of head pain and collapse. Since the condition seemed to appear from out of the blue, a stroke of bad luck, so to speak, they started calling it a stroke. And the name stuck."

"That's an interesting bit of medical history," Raine said dryly. She was clearly impatient, as was Savannah. But of the two of them, Raine had always had the greater need for controlling her environment and everyone in it. "But what's my grandmother's prognosis?"

"These things are very individual." Savannah

suspected the doctor's vague answer only irritated Raine further. "But TIAs *are* the most predictive risk factor for a more serious cerebral-thrombosis stroke."

Lilith, sitting between Raine and Savannah, moaned softly. Raine took hold of her left hand, Savannah her right.

"Thrombosis is caused by narrowing of the arteries to the brain, right?" That was what Savannah's friend had suffered.

"Exactly." Dr. Burke nodded in a way that reminded her of the gold stars her third-grade teacher used to put on her spelling tests. "In fact, it's the same type of atherosclerosis that results in heart attacks.

"Unfortunately, not only do TIAs multiply the risk for cerebral thrombosis tenfold, approximately a third of patients who experience them suffer a stroke within five years. Half within a year."

"Well, I asked for a prognosis," Raine muttered grimly.

"It's not as bad as it sounds," the doctor said. "In many cases, MID is not only preventable, it's treatable. Daily low-dose aspirin can help prevent the internal blood clots that cause TIAs. It also appears to stabilize mental decline. Some test study subjects also show improved cognition."

"I don't believe this." Lilith's face was also now a study in frustration. "That sounds remarkably like a neurologist's version of 'take two aspirin and call me in the morning.' "

"I realize it sounds simplistic," Dr. Burke

countered. "But aspirin has been proven to be an extremely effective preventative. Of course, in the case of a cerebral hemorrhage, it can increase bleeding, but that's definitely not what we're dealing with in Dr. Lindstrom's case.

"In her favor is the fact that she doesn't have additional risk factors. She's not overweight, her cholesterol is within the acceptable range, she's never smoked, only drinks occasionally and exercises regularly, and she has a positive, forward-thinking attitude that helps her deal with stress. Those are all very encouraging factors."

Savannah desperately wished she could be encouraged.

They continued to question him for another half hour, during which he impressed Savannah by neither retreating behind a wall of medical jargon nor appearing offended when Raine fell back into her cross-examination mode, grilling him as if he were a hostile witness she had on the stand.

Afterwards, they found Ida sitting at a cafeteria table with a trio of women in scrubs. Savannah smiled when she heard her grandmother advising one of the women on the best way to treat colic.

But as they left the hospital, Savannah heard the doctor's words replaying inside her head and suddenly felt the same way she had when she'd let go of Ida's hand during a shopping trip she'd taken with her grandmother—just the two of them, which had made the day extra special—to buy birthday presents for Raine at Nordstrom's in Seattle.

She couldn't recall how old she'd been, but she must have been very young because she remembered, with absolute clarity, feeling like Hansel and Gretel in the forest, right before they'd found the wicked witch's house. Right before they were put in the cage to be fattened up for eating.

As she remembered the rush of relief she'd felt when she'd been lifted out of that teeming sea of adult legs, Savannah desperately wished that there was something she could do to save her grandmother, the same way Ida had rescued her.

15

It was late afternoon, almost evening. Raine had returned to the farm, Ida was up in her room, napping, Savannah hoped. After hearing the less than encouraging diagnosis from the others, Gwen had also gone upstairs, ostensibly to get a start on this year's reading list for her honor's English class. Savannah suspected she was doing what the rest of them were doing—worrying.

Henry was nowhere to be found, but a note on the refrigerator said that he'd be back in time for dinner, which he'd pick up from Papa Joe's on the way home. Savannah found that little act of charity the sole positive note in a miserable day.

Feeling too cooped up and edgy to stay in the house, she went out on the porch and was surprised to find Lilith still there.

"I thought you'd gone home."

"I'm not in any hurry, since it's Cooper's monthly poker night and my den will be full of cops."

"I'll bet you never thought you'd be married to a policeman." Savannah sat down on the steps.

"I never thought I'd be married again, period." Lilith opened her purse, then seeming to remember she'd quit smoking on her wedding day, closed it again. "But then again, Cooper's special."

"He is that."

"And you know what they say about second marriages being a prime example of the triumph of hope over experience. Of course in my case, my third marriage was proof of love triumphing over experience."

"I think I've had enough experience for one lifetime."

"That's what you say now," Lilith said. "But you'll get over it."

"That's just the point. I don't *want* to get over it. I can't think of a single reason to get married. Except to have children," she said in afterthought, thinking of how Amy seemed to have made such a difference in Raine's life.

"I'm glad I had you and Raine. But it undoubtedly would have been easier on all of us if I'd married Cooper the first time."

As much as she honestly loved her father, Savannah couldn't argue with that.

They fell into a companionable silence, watching as dusk draped long purple shadows over the town. The old-fashioned gaslights on Harbor Street flickered on; the pink and blue neon bordering the Orca Theater's marquee, which had seemed terribly old-fashioned when Savannah had been a teenager, had come back into vogue.

"Do you think she's going to be okay?" Lilith asked.

"She has to be." Savannah would not allow herself to think otherwise.

Lilith nodded. "I honestly can't imagine life without Mother. She's always seemed as strong as the trees surrounding the town. It was always so good to know that whatever trouble I got into, she would be here, whenever I needed her."

"When any of us needed her."

They sighed.

"I wonder how old you have to be before you stop being your mother's daughter," Lilith murmured.

Savannah had been wondering that same thing herself lately. "I don't think you ever do." She paused, then decided that since burying her feelings deep inside her to keep the peace had definitely proven harmful, she'd be straight with her mother now.

"When I first came home, I think there was a part of me, a part I was afraid to admit even to myself, who blamed you for everything that had gone wrong in my life."

"Well, of course you did."

"You knew?"

"You don't have to look so surprised. My own life may have been a disaster for years, but that doesn't mean that I couldn't recognize when my daughters were making mistakes. It was obvious that in your own individual ways, both you and Raine were struggling to be the opposite of me."

Her faint smile seemed to be directed inward. "Raine, of course, is the most like me. I was five when your grandmother divorced my father. That hurt me more than I think Ida realized at the time, but I've recently come to the conclusion that I wasted a great many years desperate for men to find me attractive, to make up for the loss of my father."

"You *are* attractive," Savannah pointed out. "And Raine has never depended on her looks."

But she could have. The funny thing was, her sister had never realized how lovely she was. Determined to be admired for her mind, Raine had set her feet firmly on her legal career path and hadn't allowed herself so much as a sideways glance until she'd come home to Coldwater Cove and fallen in love with Jack.

"Owen Cantrell was the most brilliant, egocentric, ruthless man I've ever met," Lilith revealed. "I've no doubt that his being an attorney is one of the reasons Raine chose law as a profession. As she grew older, it was obvious that she was trying to win her absent father's approval—and love—by being equally ruthless."

As much as she loved her sister, Savannah decided that that unflattering observation made some sense. "But Reggie isn't anything like Owen Cantrell. I've never doubted that my father loves me. In his own way."

The same way a two-year-old loves a shiny new toy. When it came to penning lyrics that the rebels and wannabe rebels of the world could identify with, Savannah suspected that Reggie Townsend was as brilliant as Raine's famous defense attorney father. But Reggie's attention span was incredibly short, and he'd never demonstrated an ability for long-term commitment.

She had not a single doubt that if there ever came a moment when performing in front of adoring crowds no longer gave him a rush, a moment when music wasn't fun anymore, her father would hang up his electric guitar without a backward glance.

"Reggie's my favorite ex-husband, but he's certainly been no model of stability for you, darling. Why, he's been married more times than I have. It's only understandable that you were trying so hard not to repeat your parents' serial marriages, you willingly blinded yourself to your own husband's lack of decency."

It was the same conclusion Savannah had come to. The same one she'd shared with Dan atop the Ferris wheel. But accustomed to her beautiful, willful mother's life-long disregard for the consequences of her actions, she was surprised by Lilith's uncharacteristic insight.

"When did you get so smart?"

Lilith laughed the trademark crystal laugh that had been as popular with movie-going fans as her screams. "What a polite, Savannah-like way of asking when I started to grow up." She lifted a fond hand and smoothed Savannah's hair back over her shoulder. "I've discovered that wisdom—the little I've acquired at any rate—is one of the few advantages of turning fifty."

How strange, Savannah thought, that such a light maternal touch could cause an easing of

the tension that had practically twisted her
into knots during the long stressful day at the
hospital.

"I love you," she said on a burst of heartfelt
emotion.

"I love you, too, darling." Lilith's voice turned
husky. "And I do so want for you to be happy.
As happy as I am. As your sister is."

They were sharing a mother-daughter hug
when Dan's Tahoe pulled up in front of the
house. He and Henry emerged, the older man
carrying two red-and-white pizza boxes.

"How did things go?" Dan asked.

Once again, as she had with Gwen, Savannah shared the condensed version of the doctor's diagnosis.

"Could have been worse," Henry volunteered.
"I know lots of folks who've had TIAs and never
had a major stroke."

Savannah wanted to find comfort in his words,
yet couldn't help thinking that a great many of
those people could well be patients at Evergreen.

"It's tough." Dan sat down beside her, untan-
gled her hands, which she was unconsciously
twisting together in her lap, and linked his fingers with hers. "But Ida's a tough old bird. My
money's on her."

"Mine, too." Lilith, who had been watching
them with open maternal interest, stood up.
"I've been meaning to talk with Gwen about a
new school wardrobe. Obviously she can't wear
last year's maternity clothes."

Gracing both Savannah and Dan with a satis-

fied, almost feline smile, she deftly shepherded
Henry into the house.

"My mother," Savannah said wryly, as she retrieved her hand, "has never been known for
her subtlety."

"I can't imagine her any other way. She's one
of a kind. Like her daughter." He leaned over
and sniffed at her neck. "Thank you."

She pulled back just far enough to look up at
him. "For what?"

"For smelling so damn good." He combed his
fingers through the long waves Lilith had
smoothed earlier. "Do you know, it's gotten so I
wake up imagining your perfume on my pillow?"

So he'd been dreaming of her, too. "It's undoubtedly pollen," she said mildly. "Perhaps
you should start closing your window at night."

Dan reluctantly decided against suggesting
that perhaps she ought to just start spending
the night in his bed so he could wake up with
the real thing instead of some lingering remnants of the dreams that had him starting each
morning with a cold shower.

"Now there's an idea."

Because it had been too long since he'd
kissed her, because he'd been thinking of little
else all day, he touched his mouth to hers, encouraged when her arms lifted and wrapped
around his neck.

Her lips heated. Clung. Then parted to allow
him to deepen the kiss. Which he did.

A nagging voice in the back of his mind was
trying to send a warning to his body that the

house behind them was full of people who could, at any minute, decide to come out on the porch.

As a woman of the world who could undoubtedly recognize sexual undercurrents, Lilith wouldn't. But Gwen was a teenager, so impulsiveness was a given, and while Henry had actually been behaving like a human being lately, it was not unthinkable that he'd come outside just for the sheer pleasure of screwing up the moment.

As for Ida, she'd managed to put the fear of God into the entire male population of Coldwater Cove High. Every boy in school had known that getting caught going beyond first base with either Raine or Savannah was a sure-fire way to make your life a misery.

Obviously she wouldn't expect her divorced granddaughter to still be a virgin, but Dan suspected the contrary female wouldn't hesitate to make her displeasure known if she thought for a moment that he might be taking advantage of the recent upheavals in Savannah's life.

Which he wasn't. But damn, how he wanted her. Dan knew he was in deep, deep trouble when even the prospect of Ida Lindstrom's ire didn't do a thing to lesson the hunger that had him in a vice grip.

Reluctantly relinquishing her lips, he settled for skimming his mouth along the fragrant skin just beneath her slender jaw. "Lord, you taste good." Down the line of her throat. "Even better than you smell."

Dan might be a little uncertain about all his feelings where this woman was concerned, but he knew damn well that he was too old to be making out on Savannah Townsend's front porch.

"Come home with me, Savannah." She hitched in a breath as he touched his mouth to the hollow of her throat and felt her pulse leap. "I want you."

"I know." She briefly closed her eyes. When she opened them again, they gleamed with arousal in the gloaming. "I want you, too." Dan watched as that arousal was slowly replaced by regret and knew that she wasn't ready. Not yet.

"But?"

"It's too soon. While I admittedly haven't gone out with a man for years, I have the feeling that I'm not the kind of woman who goes to bed on the first date."

She smiled, a slight, tentative smile that still had enough warmth to knock him back on his heels if he hadn't already been sitting down. "Which we haven't even had yet."

"Objection sustained." He ran his hand over her shoulder, which today was clad in a black silk that brought out the fire in her hair. As soft as the silk was, Dan suspected that her skin would be a great deal softer.

"I've been remiss."

His hand continued down her bare arm. The night was getting cool. If she wasn't going to allow him to take her somewhere private and warm her all over, he was going to have to let her go into the house.

"How about coming sailing with me tomorrow evening?" he asked. "It'll give me something to look forward to while I'm in court all

day battling for my client's custody of a batch
of frozen bull sperm."

"You are kidding."

"Hey, it's not exactly on a par with fighting
for truth, justice and the American Way. But the
sperm in question just happens to belong to a
champion rodeo bull owned by a syndicate that
went bust when the members decided to
branch out and invest in Thoroughbreds. A
couple test tubes of that stuff would probably
have paid for your new roof."

"What an appealing thought," she murmured. "But I'll be wallpapering the kitchen of
the assistant keeper's house tomorrow evening."

Still drawn by her scent, he leaned closer again
and nibbled on her earlobe. "No, you won't."

She stiffened in his arms. Then drew back.
"Excuse me?"

The fire had turned to ice. Dan had already
discovered enough of what pleasured Savannah
to know he could melt it. "You're not wallpapering the kitchen because it's already done."

She folded her arms and gave him an accusing look that wasn't quite the display of gratitude he'd been hoping for. "Are you telling me
that you hung my wallpaper?"

Hell. She definitely was not pleased.

"I knew your schedule was tight enough that
losing today would cost you, so I thought I'd
give you a hand."

"Didn't you have any law work to do?"

"The nice thing about being your own boss is
you can give yourself an afternoon off from

time to time. Besides, I had help, so it didn't take that long."

He watched the awareness dawn. "That's where Henry was?"

"The guy's got a real talent with a paste brush, which was fortunate since, left to my own devices, I would undoubtedly still be there, turning the air blue with my curses.

"Hanging wallpaper," he said dryly, "is not quite the snap they make it out to be on that video at Olson's hardware store."

"I appreciate the help," she allowed. A bit reluctantly, Dan thought. "But I don't need it."

"There's such a thing as being too independent, sweetheart." He took hold of her hand. When she'd first returned home, her palms had been smooth. The row of calluses were mute evidence of how hard she'd been working all these weeks. Yet as much as he admired her determination to toughen up and handle everything by herself, there were limits. "All of us can use a little help from time to time."

She seemed to be processing that suggestion as she looked out over the town. Warm yellow lights curved around the cove, reminding Dan of the train layout he'd earned a Boy Scout merit badge for building back in the sixth grade. The breeze from the water was rustling the leaves in the trees.

"Besides," he reminded her quietly, "Henry's part owner of the lighthouse. He jumped at the chance to work on his old home."

"Oh. Of course he would want to be involved. I should have thought of that."

"You've had a lot on your mind lately."

Her soft sigh confirmed that statement.

"I apologize if I overstepped my bounds, Savannah." He brushed a kiss against her knuckles. "If I promise to never lift a hand to help you again, will you come sailing with me?"

She laughed lightly, as he'd meant her to, then turned back to him, her eyes meeting his. "I may have overreacted, just a bit. . . . Thank you."

"It was my pleasure. So, is that a yes?"

This time her sigh was one of surrender. But the warmth that had returned to her eyes revealed that it wasn't a reluctant one. "Yes."

Having been born in Coldwater Cove, Dan had grown up on the water. But he couldn't remember ever enjoying an afternoon more than this one. Just the sight of Savannah—her face lifted to the sun, her hair blowing in the breeze like a gold and bronze flag—was enough to take his breath away.

But it was more than the fact that she reminded him of some mythical mermaid. It was the ease with which she laughed and talked with him. They'd stopped at the house so she could check on her grandmother, who'd complained about the way everyone was fussing over her lately. During the brief stop, Savannah had run upstairs to admire the new clothes Lilith and Gwen had brought home from the Dancing Deer Dress Shoppe, leaving him to dodge some pointed questions about his intentions that had Dan thinking that Ida would have made one helluva prosecutor.

He was in his thirties, successful, and, he liked to think, a pretty good catch for the right woman. Yet Savannah's grandmother had managed to send the clock reeling backwards in a way that had him feeling like a hormone-driven, sweaty-palmed seventeen-year-old promising to bring Savannah straight home after their date. And no speeding.

Now, as he maneuvered the skiff over the water, enjoying the sound of her laughter, the way the wind and sun brought color into her high cheekbones, Dan decided that the brief discomfort spent undergoing Ida's cross-examination had been worth it.

He was also considering sailing away with Savannah to some faraway island where they could spend their days basking in the sunshine on spun-sugar beaches and their nights making mad, passionate love.

Jack and Raine had gone to Bora Bora for their honeymoon, and both had waxed so enthusiastic about the South Seas island, he was tempted to try it out for himself.

"Something funny?" she asked, making him realize that he'd laughed out loud at the fanciful idea of the two of them sailing off into the sunset.

"I was just wondering how far it is to Tahiti."

"I have no idea. But I suspect it's a bit far for a first date."

"Next time, then."

Rather than point out that the idea was ridiculously impractical, Savannah smiled. "Perhaps."

It was, Dan told himself, enough for now.

16

As the air became crisper and the leaves began to turn colors, Savannah's days fell into a predictable, yet enjoyable routine.

She'd get up early every morning so she could cook breakfast for the family. Cold cereal might be fine for summer vacation, but she was determined to send Gwen off to school properly fortified. She also took the time to observe Ida closely, watching for any additional signs of TIAs, but other than her usual malapropisms, her grandmother seemed as mentally sharp as ever. What she insisted on referring to as her "spells" when she would discuss them, which was hardly ever, seemed to have passed.

Days were spent at the lighthouse, which, thanks to part-time help from Dan, Henry, and John—who'd constructed a greenhouse on the grounds to supply her with fresh flowers—was coming closer to being completed with each passing day. Optimistic enough to believe that she would actually make her scheduled holiday opening, she'd placed ads in a few magazines and had brochures printed up which she'd sent out to travel agencies.

Things were definitely looking up.

Savannah was determined to never again define herself by a relationship, but she couldn't deny that she'd be hard pressed to find a better relationship than the one she had with Dan.

He was smart, funny, sexy, and, best of all, he thought she was all those things, too. He didn't expect her to be some starry-eyed young girl afraid to speak her mind. He didn't even seem to expect her to look like a model all the time, which was a good thing since her nails were a disaster, her hair was in dire need of a trim, and there had been more than one occasion when, pressed for time, she'd actually taken jeans straight from the dryer and put them on without bothering to first starch and iron them.

Just last week Raine, who'd dropped by the lighthouse to see the progress, had marveled that even after a day spent cleaning sticky labels off acres of new window glass, her little sister was still fashion magazine material. Savannah, of course, knew otherwise. In what she'd come to realize was her own version of her sister's attempt to be the perfect New York attorney, she'd spent a great many years *looking* perfect. It had always been an important part of her image. Her identity. It had also been exhausting.

She may be all too aware of her loosening

standards, but amazingly, Dan seemed to believe she was beautiful however she looked.
Even that day she'd forgotten to wear a cap
while painting the ceiling and ended up with
Glacier White paint spatters in her hair.

Not only did he spend every weekend working on the lighthouse with her, as her project
progressed Savannah discovered she could talk
with him about anything. And everything.

He didn't think she was whining when she
complained that the new flashing those outrageously expensive roofers had installed around
one of the chimneys had ripped off during an
early autumn storm, causing rain damage inside
the house. She'd ended up having to restain a section of floor, which wasn't as bad as it might have
been, since they did it together on a Saturday.

He assured her that she wasn't being overly
critical when the faucets for the assistant keeper's bathroom arrived in chrome, rather than
the antique brass she'd ordered. And when the
plumber did not show up as promised to install
the Jacuzzi tub in the bathroom she'd built beneath the stairs leading to the lantern room—
which she'd turned into a bedroom with a
stunning 360-degree view—he'd written a terse
legal letter that had encouraged the man to
quickly finish the job.

They continued to spend nearly every
evening together, at easy outings for which she
didn't even have to dress up: barbecue at Oley's,
sails on the sound, eating ice cream cones while
they watched the ferry dock and the tourists—

not as many now that Labor Day had come and gone—disembark.

While not a professional chef, he had, on more than one occasion, fixed dinner. She'd never had a man cook for her before, but that first night, as she'd sipped a crisp Blue Mountain chardonnay while he whipped up a platter of Dungeness crab cakes, grilled corn, and crisp green salad, Savannah decided that the experience came pretty close to heaven.

Since the chemistry between them was as strong as ever, stronger since they'd been practicing such strict self-denial, their relationship wasn't totally platonic. Savannah loved to kiss him, adored the flex of his back muscles beneath her fingertips and reveled in the way he touched her in return.

She knew he wanted her. He told her that again and again with his lips, his hands, the rigid power of his erection that would press against her stomach as they made out like two frustrated teenagers on his wide suede couch. With each day that passed, she wanted Dan more, too.

But she had discovered that there was a difference between attraction and commitment. Having grown up watching marriage promises get ripped to pieces, Savannah had vowed that when she got married, it would be forever. Of course it hadn't been, or she wouldn't even be thinking about making love with Dan O'Halloran—which was something she thought about too much lately.

Since her divorce she'd made a new vow:

there would be no more broken promises. To get naked with Dan could risk new cracks in a heart that had only recently mended.

Not that she believed he'd hurt her deliberately. He was the most natural, genuinely caring man she'd ever met. Dan O'Halloran was probably as close as she'd ever find to the perfect man. The kind of man a woman could imagine spending the rest of her life with.

If she were looking for a man to spend the rest of her life with. Which, of course, she wasn't.

"I've made a decision," Ida said.

Savannah was working on her menu plan. Thanksgiving was three weeks away, and she was sitting at the kitchen table, planning the menu. Raine had offered to have the family dinner at the farm, but since her sister's culinary talents generally involved nuking meals in the microwave or heating up takeout, despite her desire to move into the lighthouse before the holiday weekend, Savannah had insisted on preparing the meal here at the house.

She did, after all, have a great deal to be thankful for this year.

"What decision is that, Gram?" she asked absently, trying to decide between chestnut and oyster dressing.

On the other hand, perhaps Amy would prefer sausage or cornbread. Maybe she could make all four, baking them in separate pans. The problem with that idea was that Ida's old oven was definitely not as spacious as the state-of-the-art commercial one she'd installed in the lighthouse.

"I want to adopt Gwen."

That got Savannah's attention. She put her pen down and looked up at her grandmother. "What?"

"I said, I want to adopt Gwen."

"Why?"

"To make her part of the family, of course."

"She's already part of the family."

"Not legally." Ignoring Dr. Burke's warning about caffeine intake, Ida poured herself her third cup of coffee of the day and sat down at the table. "She's still underage. There's not a single thing to keep Old Fussbudget from showing up at the house and taking her away from us."

Old Fussbudget, Savannah knew, was Gwen's probation officer.

"Gwen's behavior has been exemplary. She's back at the top of her class, and unless something drastic happens, she looks to be a shoo-in for valedictorian."

"The girl's always gotten good grades, which is amazing when you consider what she's been through."

"Perhaps school was a refuge."

"That's the way I always saw it," Ida agreed. "But you know how screwed up Social Services can be. They don't seem to care about grades, or the fact that she's always made honor roll, even the semester she had the baby. They've still put her in more foster homes than Carters has Pilgrims."

Her eyes were flint, her jaw jutted out in a

way Savannah recognized all too well. When
her grandmother set her mind to something,
you had three choices: give in, get out of the
way, or get run over.

"Have you discussed this with Raine?"

"Not yet. But Raine's family. I figured it'd
look better if we had some other lawyer take
care of it for us."

Savannah knew exactly what other lawyer
she was referring to. "Have you mentioned this
adoption plan to Gwen?"

"Of course not. I didn't want to get the girl's
hopes up. I figured I'd let Dan get all the initial
paperwork done, then I'll surprise her with the
news on Thanksgiving Day."

Savannah had no doubt that the teenager
would be thrilled. There was, however, one possible major stumbling block to the plan. "I hate
to bring this up, but what about your age?"

"What about it?"

She could have been trying to cross a minefield. "Well, you're a bit older than most adoptive parents," she said carefully.

"You surprise me, Savannah. Of all my family, I never thought you'd be one to throw cold
water on my parade."

"I wasn't—"

"Fine." Ida stood up. "Then you'll ask Dan to
get started with the necessary paperwork."

"Why can't you do that?"

"Because he'll probably have a whole laundry
list of reasons why it's impractical and why Social Services is going to balk at the idea and

why I might want to consider slowing down instead of taking on the responsibility of a teenager in my early seventies."

Make that her *late* seventies. "There's nothing wrong with slowing down a bit." Savannah would dearly love to do exactly that. For just one day.

"Some old ladies might be content spending all their time knitting or playing bingo. But I'm like a salamander. If I don't keep going forward, I die.

"So," Ida finished up, "since I have no intention of wasting time arguing with a man whose butt I spanked when I brought him into this world, I figure you can be the one to ask him. Seems he'll do just about anything for you these days."

That stated, Ida left the room on a step that was, Savannah had to admit, pretty lively for a woman pushing eighty.

"Ida's age might not be a problem to her," Dan said two days later. They were at his house, where he was cooking dinner again. "But unfortunately, from what I could determine from my conversation with Old Fussbudget today, it is to Social Services. If Gwen were only older—"

"If she were older, she'd legally be an adult and wouldn't need to be adopted to protect her interests in the first place," Savannah pointed out.

"If the law were logical, the world wouldn't need lawyers." He poured two glasses of wine and handed one to her.

"I know. But there must be something we can do."

"I checked over the guardianship papers. They're pretty tightly written. There would have to be an extremely compelling reason for Old Fussbudget and her minions to pull Gwen from Ida's home, especially since she's only got a few months to go until she turns eighteen."

"Six," Savannah said. "A lot can happen in six months." Wasn't she living proof of that?

"An alternative idea occurred to me while I was shaving this morning. We could get her declared an emancipated minor."

"Can you do that?"

He grinned. "Piece of cake. As long as she keeps out of trouble," he qualified.

"If she dares shoplift again, I'll personally kill her for upsetting Gram."

"Well, that would certainly take care of the custody issue. Though I have to admit, sweetheart, the idea of trying to kiss you through a set of prison bars isn't all that appealing."

She laughed, then moved over to the glass wall and looked out at the rising harvest moon that was splashing a coppery sheen over the wine-dark water.

"Every time I come here, I feel as if I've just stepped onto the bridge of the starship *Enterprise*," she murmured. As magnificent as Dan's house was from outside, the inside was even more stunning. The ceiling soared at least fifteen feet overhead, and a two-story stone fireplace took up nearly an entire wall. "Or the *Millennium Falcon*. Just before it went into warp speed."

He came up behind her. "Believe me, sweetheart, when I finally talk you into my bed, I'm going to do my best to keep the pace a bit slower than that."

"Promises, promises," she laughed lightly as she leaned back against him.

"So, what's my surprise?" He nuzzled her neck.

"Surprise?" The touch of his mouth on her skin was enough to wipe her mind as clear as the glass window.

"When I came by the lighthouse to pick you up this evening, you told me you had a surprise for me."

"Oh. I do." The brief discussion about Ida had made her forget. He murmured a protest when she slipped out of his light embrace and retrieved her purse.

" 'Lucy Hyatt's Far Harbor Adventure, Volume Two,' " he read aloud from the cover of the small notebook. "Where did you find this?"

"In the attic of the keeper's house. I was putting some storage boxes up there when I noticed that the chimney looked strange. I pulled out a couple loose bricks, and there it was."

"The lady certainly did work hard at hiding her journals," he mused. "So, are there any juicy parts in it?"

"I don't know. I wanted to save it to read with you."

His wineglass paused on the way to his mouth. Something flickered in his eyes. "I think I'll take that as a compliment."

"It was meant as one," she said as they settled down on the couch.

" 'The journey to Washington was even more thrilling than I could possibly have imagined,' " Savannah began to read, trying to keep her mind off the fact that they were in the very same spot where they'd driven each other to distraction only last night.

" 'The snow-capped Rocky Mountains were spectacular. When the train reached the top of its climb before going down the other side, the clouds cleared, revealing meadows ablaze with wildflowers as far as the eye could see, and crystal streams flowing from ancient glaciers. I felt as though I'd been granted a glimpse of Paradise. Indeed, had not I not been so eager to meet my husband-to-be, I would have been more than happy to spend eternity in that heavenly place.' "

"The Rockies have their appeal. But I'll still take the Olympics any day," Dan decided.

"Me, too." It crossed Savannah's mind that of all the places she'd lived over the world, this was the only one that had ever felt like home.

" 'Coldwater Cove, while not as breathtaking as the Rockies, proved every bit as charming as Harlan had described it,' " she continued. " 'While his letters had suggested that he was not a man prone to embellishment or untruths, as Hannah had reminded me on a daily basis, it's not unusual for a man to prevaricate.' "

"I wonder if Hannah's speaking from personal experience."

"She's a woman. My guess would be yes."

Dan didn't comment, but instead picked up reading the story.

" 'During the trip westward, the train passed through a number of small towns—some barely more than rough outposts—and in truth, there were times I feared that my destination may turn out to be equally rustic. But when I viewed the town, I was momentarily confused and wondered if the train had changed direction during the night and somehow ended up in New England.

" 'The buildings on the main street—Harbor Street, I was later to learn—are of substantial red brick that gives the impression that this town will not soon blow away, like the eerie, sad ghost towns I'd seen throughout Colorado and eastern Oregon and Washington. If buildings could make a statement, these are saying that Coldwater Cove is here to stay.' "

"She was right," Savannah said, thinking of her lighthouse.

"Absolutely. 'Wooden sidewalks line Harbor Street, which, despite being dirt, is remarkably unrutted. Huge houses, suggesting prosperity, line the top of the cliff which overlooks the Cove.' She's talking about your grandmother's house."

"I think so." Savannah had never thought of her grandmother's Victorian as a symbol of prosperity. To her it had always represented a haven.

" 'A grassy green square is the centerpiece of the town, the new bright red brick tower rising like a beacon; the clock face on each of the compass points can be seen for miles.

" 'Standing guard over all is the Far Harbor Lighthouse. *Harlan's lighthouse,* I thought to myself as I viewed the glorious white structure gleaming like marble in the midday sun. *My lighthouse.'* "

Dan smiled down at Savannah. "Your lighthouse now."

She smiled back. Their eyes met. And held.

"Savannah . . ."

He pulled her close and fastened his mouth on hers, the kiss so mindblinding that Savannah nearly dropped her glass.

"If you keep that up," she said after they'd come up for air, "you're going to have wine all over your clothes."

"I was hoping, if I keep it up a bit longer, we'll both end up naked and it won't matter." He skimmed a finger along her shoulder.

"Think about it, Savannah." The treacherous touch continued downward, causing a giddy pleasure to bloom beneath her hand-painted sweatshirt depicting a row of Coldwater Cove's famous Victorians. "You spill your wine on me." Needs she'd been fighting for weeks coiled inside her as his fingertip swirled around her nipple.

"Then I'll spill mine on you." His stroking hand moved to her other breast, treating it to a torture every bit as sublime. Her head reeled. "Then I'll lick it off." Her body throbbed. "Every last drop."

"I knew I should have taken time for lunch." Her complaint was wrenched on a husky, ragged moan she could barely recognize as her own

voice. "One glass of wine and my head's spinning."

"That's a start."

His bold grin promised wicked delights. He
put his glass on the pine coffee table with delib-
erate slowness, giving her time to back away, as
she had on past nights. When she didn't move,
he took her glass from her nerveless fingers and
placed it beside his.

"Let's see if we can make the rest of you
spin."

Since he was already doing a pretty good job
of that, Savannah didn't, couldn't, respond. But
her eyes gave him her answer.

Dan exhaled a deep breath. Then stood up,
scooped her off the couch, and carried her
across the room and up the stairs to the loft.

17

Dan put her down beside the bed, then paused to light the fire he'd set in the stone fireplace before leaving for work.

And then he was back, standing in front of her.

"I want to do this right." He brushed her hair back from her face, his touch as hot as his eyes. "Tell me what you want me to do to you. . . . With you."

"Anything." Her breath was ragged. Savannah didn't even attempt to control it. "Everything."

It was as if her words had opened a dam, releasing a torrent of passion too long denied. He dragged her down onto the bed. Savannah went willingly. Eagerly.

Her sweatshirt was ripped over her head and sent flying across the room. Her jeans were dragged down her legs. Her own hands were no less urgent. She tore at his shirt; buttons scattered across the wood floor as she yanked it off him, exposing a rock-hard chest that gleamed like polished teak in the flickering light.

He turned her in his arms, braceleted her wrists in one hand and held them over her head. Having invited this, having dreamed of it, hot erotic dreams that had her waking up unfulfilled amid tangled sheets, Savannah closed her eyes, hung on tightly and followed him into the flames.

His mouth was everywhere, relentlessly nipping and licking and sucking. Savaging her. Thrilling her. His teeth scraped against first one taut nipple, then the other, creating tremors of delicious excitement to ripple beneath her hot skin. His tongue stroked a trail of sparks up the moist flesh of her inner thigh, drawing a primal sound from deep in her throat.

Springs creaked. The fire hissed and crackled. The air grew as thick and steamy as the Olympic rain forest in summer.

His fingers tangled in the downy curls between her thighs. When his warm breath ruffled them, Savannah went hot and cold at the same time, like a woman in the grip of a fever. He parted the swollen pink flesh.

More physically needy that she'd ever been in her life, Savannah drew in a deep, shuddering breath and bent her leg.

He lifted his head. "Open your eyes, Savannah."

She forced open lids that had turned unreasonably heavy and found herself looking up into eyes that gleamed like molten cobalt in the flickering glow. There was a warrior's fierceness to his face that might have frightened her had she not already experienced his tenderness.

He smiled and the warrior turned to rogue. "Beautiful."

Then he was kissing her hard and deep, the same way he'd kissed her mouth, but then he'd merely stolen her breath. Now he was stealing her sanity.

Coherent thought disintegrated as his greedy tongue invaded the giving folds of her body, seeking intimate secrets while his teeth toyed with the ultrasensitive nub, creating a need so sharp Savannah feared she'd surely shatter.

Her stomach grew taut, her thighs tensed, a flush spread over her breasts. A final flick of his tongue caused her body to explode in a violent, dizzying release.

But still he wouldn't stop.

"I can't," she gasped as he began to drive her up again.

"You can." His clever, wicked touch was making her mad. "*We* can."

And they did. Again and again, until her body hummed from a thousand erratic pulses and his lips were wet with her orgasms.

And still it wasn't enough. Needing to touch him as he'd touched her, wanting to make him feel that same need that had escalated to a pleasure just this side of pain, Savannah pulled her hands free.

They fretted over him. Her ragged fingernails dug into his skin. It was hot and slick and moist.

"I want you." She returned her mouth to his. "All of you." She tasted herself on his lips. Desire flared. Hotter, higher. "Inside of me."

"Thank God." His voice was rough and tortured. He cursed beneath his breath as he drew away long enough to yank open the drawer of the bedside table and retrieve a condom. "Remind me to plan this better next time."

Then he was kneeling between her thighs. With his gaze on hers, he lifted her hips and slid smoothly, gloriously into her.

Breathing a shimmering sigh of pleasure, Savannah wrapped her legs tighter around his hips and began to move with him, instinctively knowing his rhythm as if they'd made love a hundred, a thousand times before.

She would not have thought it possible, but soon, amazingly, it was coming again, that hot, sharp, spiraling pressure, the wetness, the shattering spasm of release.

Outside, a swift autumn squall had raced in over the mountain tops from the sea. The wind moaned. A hard rain pelted the windows like a shower of stones. The crimson moon rose. Inside, lost in a storm of their own making, Dan and Savannah surrendered to the darkness.

Afterwards, they lay together, in a tangle of arms and legs, cocooned as the rain streaked down the windows.

"Are we alive?" Savannah asked finally.

"I don't know." He touched his mouth to her breast, his lips warm against her cooling flesh. "Your heart's beating."

"That's a relief." She cuddled closer and did the same to him. "So's yours."

"Yeah." Dan skimmed a hand down her damp hair, all the way to her hip, then back up again. "I figure it should be back to a normal rate sometime in the next century. . . . Christ, you're unbelievable," he managed with what little breath he had left.

"I'm having a little trouble believing it myself."

He rolled over to face her, taking her with him, viewed the wonder in her still slightly un-focused gaze and felt a surge of chauvinistic male satisfaction for having put it there.

"I never felt that way before. I never realized it was possible to feel that way." She lifted a hand to his cheek.

"It's us," he said as he curled his fingers around her wrist and brought her hand to his lips. "You and I together."

He kissed each fingertip, one at a time, and watched the renewed desire warm those incred-ible green eyes. Dan was considering the possi-bilities of going for a personal best when his stomach growled, reminding him of other phys-ical hungers.

"As much as I'd like to keep you in bed for-ever, I did promise you dinner."

"I suppose we should keep our strength up. Since I have a vested interest in your stamina."

"Sweetheart, the day you have to worry about my stamina where you're concerned is the day they stick me in the ground." He kissed her hard, savoring her taste in a way that almost had him deciding to forgo food.

He was given a tantalizing view of a sweetly curved bottom when she leaned down and retrieved her sweatshirt. "You won't be needing this." He plucked it from her hand and tossed it aside.

"Daniel!" she complained as the sweatshirt hit a chair across the room and slid back to the floor. "You can't expect me to eat dinner naked."

"Sure I do." He yanked on his jeans and a chambray shirt he didn't bother to button. "As a chef yourself, you undoubtedly know that dazzling scenery can improve any meal."

"I can't do it." He nearly laughed when she actually crossed her arms over her breasts. It was a little late for modesty, since he'd already seen—and tasted—just about every fragrant inch of that lush body. "I *won't* do it."

Dan had not a single doubt that if he pulled out his persuasive powers, he could change her mind, but reluctantly decided that the fantasy of Savannah perched naked across the table from him, looking like some mermaid who'd washed up on his beach, was yet one more thing to look forward to.

Which was why, minutes later, clad in the sweatshirt and a piece of lace too skimpy to be properly considered underwear, she was sitting on a kitchen stool, long legs crossed, sipping on the wine as she resumed reading Lucy's journal where they'd left off.

" 'Even after all this time, and all these miles,

the idea of what I'd done still seemed incredible,' " she read while Dan started a pot of rice steaming. " 'It was almost as if I'd been dreaming. But if I were, as I drank in the welcoming sight of the town that appeared to be as neat and tidy as a Swedish kitchen, I never wanted to awaken.

" 'Harlan was waiting on the platform, as promised. His photograph, while portraying a handsome man, had not begun to do him justice. He is tall, with shoulders the breadth of ax handles, and possesses a thick shock of dark hair. His jaw is firm, and the strong planes of his face appear to have been chiseled from granite. His size and strong features would give him a forbidding appearance were it not for his smile and his incredible eyes.' "

"I think she likes him," Dan said as he retrieved a white waxed-paper bundle of shrimp from the refrigerator.

"It seems so," Savannah agreed. "Which is fortunate, since it doesn't sound like turning around and going back home was an option." She turned the page and continued.

" 'How shall I even attempt to describe Harlan Hyatt's eyes? They reminded me of hot chocolate—warm and dark and smooth. As I stared up at him, two thoughts crossed my mind simultaneously. How could this man still be unmarried at the age of thirty? And what had I done right in my life to be gifted with such a husband?

" 'I know I'm no beauty. Hannah, who was gifted with our mother's looks and our father's

manner of plain speaking, has certainly pointed
out that unpalatable fact on more than one occasion. Yet, amazingly, Harlan seemed as mesmerized by my appearance, as rumpled and
road weary as it admittedly was.

" 'For a long, suspended moment he stared
down at me, his expressive dark eyes looking
hard and deep, as if he could see all the way
into my soul, and perhaps my heart, which was
now pounding as furiously as a drum.' "

"Bingo." Dan began chopping mushrooms,
scallions, and red bell pepper with a dexterity
that, having firsthand experience of his clever
hands, no longer surprised her. "Looks as if it's
mutual."

"Yet just a few years later, she was supposedly
running away on the day that she drowned." Savannah frowned as she took a sip of wine. "I
wonder what happened."

"Keep reading and maybe we'll find out."

Savannah shook her head and sighed as she
thought about lost dreams. " 'His first words
were not poetic. Indeed, they were more than a
little prosaic. "Welcome to Coldwater Cove," he
said in a smooth, deep voice that wrapped
around me like a velvet cape, embracing me in
its warmth. On the spot, I decided that this
man didn't need pretty words.

" ' "I'm pleased to finally be here," I responded
with equal formality.

" 'We fell silent, studying each other. Finally,
when my nerves were stretched as taut as a
piano wire, I glanced down at the wildflowers

he was holding in one huge fist and asked if they were for me.' "

Dan grinned over his shoulder at Savannah as he dumped the vegetables into a copper-bottomed pan with some grated ginger. "A man of excellent tastes."

Savannah smiled back, remembering the wildflowers he'd given her the night of the Sawdust Festival, then returned to Lucy's journal.

" 'He practically shoved them into my hand. I found the embarrassed flush rising from his collar immensely endearing and assured him that no bride could ever wish for a more beautiful bouquet.

" 'For some reason my words made him frown. "I'd hoped to marry you the moment you stepped off the train, but it seems that there's a problem," he said. The heavy regret in his tone caused my heart to take a steep and perilous dip.'

"Uh oh," Savannah murmured.

Dan topped off her wineglass. "Don't stop now."

Even knowing that they had married, Savannah was suddenly as tense as Lucy must have been at that moment.

" 'My mind spun with reasons for the frown darkening his face. I knew I'd never return home. There was no way I'd endure listening to Hannah saying "I told you so" for the rest of my life.' "

"Hannah sounds like a real gem." Dan tossed the shrimp into the pan and splashed in soy sauce.

"Not everyone is fortunate to have a sister like Raine." Savannah turned another page.

" ' "Unfortunately," he revealed, "the good citizens of Coldwater Cove won't allow it."

" ' "Oh?" I asked with very real trepidation.
My heart had now sunk down to my toes.

" ' "We're a small, close community," he explained. "A wedding is a very special occasion,
and the townspeople are not going to be denied
their chance to give you a party." As if they'd
been actors, awaiting their cue, the people who
were gathered on the platform came forward.

" 'As Harlan introduced his many friends, I
was greeted with such great enthusiasm that I
found myself looking forward to the festivities
and the wedding Harlan informed me would
take place the following day at the lighthouse.
But most of all, I looked forward to the rest of
my life with my husband.'

"Damn," Savannah murmured as she turned
the final page. "That's all there is."

"There's got to be at least another diary
somewhere." The shrimp had turned pink. He
stirred in some pineapple chunks, then spooned
the mixture atop a mound of rice.

"Unless she stopped keeping a journal once
she got married."

"I'm going to be really disappointed if she
did. It's like a cliffhanger without the final reel."

They moved to the nearby table.

"I wonder, if Lucy had known how tragically
her romance—and her life—would end, if she
would have gotten on that train in Farmersburg," Savannah considered.

"From what we've read so far, I'd guess that

she wouldn't have hesitated. Love is always a gamble," Dan said. "Sometimes you get lucky and the reward turns out to be worth the risk."

From the way his expression had turned serious, Savannah had the uneasy feeling that Dan was no longer talking about Lucy and Harlan.

After dinner, Dan lit another fire in the downstairs grate and they settled back on the sofa.

"This truly is the most stunning place," she murmured.

The swift storm had already moved on toward Seattle. The rain had stopped, washing the star-spangled sky outside the glass wall as clear as crystal.

Savannah drew in a breath as a falling star crashed down to earth in a shimmering silver trail. "I think I could just stay here, like this, forever."

"Why don't you?" Dan's tone was casual; his question was not.

She looked up at him, her eyes wide and, he thought, more than a little wary in the firelight. "I didn't mean . . . just because we had sex—"

"We made love." Strange how saying the words out loud made Dan realize they were absolutely true. "It may not have been in the plans, but you can't deny that's what happened."

"It's not that easy."

She did not, he noticed, argue the major point—that they'd shared a helluva lot more than their bodies. "Perhaps you're making it more difficult than it is," he suggested mildly.

"I explained to you how I've spent a lifetime

watching my mother jump in and out of relationships. I've seen the harm it can cause to everyone."

"Granted. And while this isn't about Lilith, I can't see her leaving Cooper."

"No," Savannah allowed. She stared out into the well of darkness. "I believe her when she says that Cooper's her soul mate."

"So, extrapolating from that, a reasonable person might suggest that when a person finds the right partner—her soul mate—she ought to just grab her chance at happiness. Carpe diem, go for the gusto, so to speak."

"Now you sound just like a lawyer," she complained. "Quibbling every little point."

"I *am* a lawyer," Dan reminded her. "Arguing and negotiating—"

"Quibbling."

He gave her a mock stern look. *"Negotiating,"* he repeated, "is in our blood."

She stared back out the window for a long, silent time. Dan had always thought of himself as an even-tempered, patient man. Indeed, his prosecutorial work had demanded it. The law was seldom tidy. Nor was it swift.

But he'd discovered another side to his personality, an impulsive side that had him wanting to drag her upstairs, tie her to his bed, and make mad, passionate love to her until she finally acquiesced to stay here with him where she belonged.

"I rushed into love with Kevin," she murmured. "And that turned out to be a disaster."

"I don't think you were in love. Oh, I know you believed you were at the time," he said when she shot him an accusing look. "But you were a young, romantic girl far away from home who had the bad luck to run into a charming louse who knows how to pick his victims, Savannah. You weren't in love with the man; you were in love with being in love."

The same thing had occurred to her. "You may be right. But if I'd only taken the time to get to know him better—"

"We've spent more time together than either my parents or my grandparents before they got married," he cut her off with an impatient wave of his hand. "Besides, for the record, I'm not the weasel."

"No, You're definitely not, and I was wrong to make the comparison. But everything's so unsettled in my life right now, Dan. Whenever I think I'm beginning to get things under control, some new crisis pops up."

"Did you know that the Chinese use the same word for crisis and opportunity?"

"Perhaps I should have bought a damn lighthouse in China." She sighed again. "I'm sorry. I didn't mean to snap at you. It's just that I need to stay focused," she tried to explain. "If I'm going to open by Christmas, I can't afford any distractions."

Dan decided that he'd pushed enough. He'd planted the seed. Now, as John was always pointing out, he'd have to be patient while waiting for it to bloom.

"It's only because I'm wild about you that I'm going to overlook the fact that the woman I've fallen in love with just referred to me as a distraction."

He ran a slow fingertip along the ridge of her collarbone. "Since you seem to find this discussion not to your liking, I'll even change the subject." He drew her closer. "Do you realize how long it's been since I kissed you?"

"Fifteen minutes?"

"At least." His lips skimmed up her cheek. "Which is, in my book, about fourteen minutes and thirty seconds too long."

"At least," she agreed breathlessly as she placed her palms on either side of his face and brought his mouth to hers.

18

The call came just before dawn, the phone shattering the darkness. Dragged from an erotic dream in which he'd spent a long, pleasurable time spreading warmed honey all over Savannah's body and had just begun to lick it off, Dan extricated himself from her arms and snatched up the receiver.

"Yeah?"

"Dan, it's Raine. I need to talk to Savannah."

"Dan?" Savannah turned on the lamp. She sat up in bed, the tangled sheet down around her waist, her hair a wild mass of sleep and love-tousled curls. "What's wrong?"

"I don't know. It's your sister." Dan handed her the phone.

"Raine?" He watched her face go unnaturally pale, then twist with pain, as if someone had just shoved a sharp blade into her heart.

"Oh, no." She closed her eyes and sagged

against him. "How bad . . . I see. . . . Of course."
Her exhaled breath was a ragged, tortured
sound. "We'll be right there."

She looked up at him, her eyes bleak and terrified at the same time. "It's Ida. Henry found
her in the bathroom. She's had a stroke."

If Savannah had disliked the hospital the day
she'd spent waiting for Ida to have her tests, she
hated it now. At least in the examination areas
the mood had been orderly, and if impersonal,
at least efficient.

She prayed the emergency department was
equally efficient, but it was difficult to tell, with
all the people in white coats and different color
scrubs running around. They all had an air of
purpose, as if they knew where they were going,
she observed.

She, on the other hand, was lost the minute
she raced through the sliding doors beneath the
lighted red sign.

They were headed to the window where a
woman with impossibly red hair was seated at
a computer, when Raine appeared.

"We're in here," she said, taking Savannah's
arm and leading her across the central waiting
room. It crossed Savannah's numb mind that
there were a surprising number of people here
for this ungodly time in the morning. "Fortunately, Gram's name still pulls some weight. Mrs.
Kellstrom—she's the charge nurse—arranged for
us to have this private waiting room."

The walls of the small room had been covered in a blinding yellow burlap, which Savannah decided had been chosen in an attempt to lift spirits. It didn't.

"It's not much, but at least it has its own coffee maker, so we won't have to drink that toxic waste from the vending machine."

Trust Raine, even in the midst of a medical emergency, to have tracked down the person in charge and found coffee.

Lilith was sitting as stiff as a statue in a plastic avocado chair with chrome legs. Cooper was hovering over her and Jack was standing by the window, arms crossed, his face grim.

"How is Gram?" Savannah asked.

"The last we heard she's holding her own. They've still got her in the examining room."

"Can't we be with her?" Savannah shot a look at Jack. "You're the sheriff. Surely you can go wherever you want."

"We were with her for a few minutes," Raine revealed. "But when we seemed to be causing Gram more stress, Mrs. Kellstrom suggested it would be better if we waited in here."

"They've got her stabilized, and they're doing tests to determine how much damage the stroke has done," Cooper informed her.

"Oh, God." Torn between relief that her grandmother was still alive and fear for what state she might be in, Savannah sank into a pumpkin orange chair beside her mother and buried her face in her hands. She was vaguely aware, on some level, of Dan's comforting hand on her shoulder.

She'd get through this, she assured herself. It was just one more hurdle in what seemed to be a year of emotional Olympic trials. The important thing was that she stay strong. For Ida. And her mother.

She glanced over at Lilith. "How are *you*?" Her mother looked terrible, pale as glass and hollow faced.

"A bit like Mother." She managed a weak, feigned smile. "Holding my own." When she dragged a trembling hand through her silver hair, her husband caught it and held it tightly, reassuringly, between his. "Thank heavens Henry found her."

It should have been her, Savannah thought miserably.

"It's not even five o'clock," Raine argued when Savannah admitted to her guilty thought out loud. "Even if you *had* been at the house, you would have been sleeping."

"She didn't cry out or anything?"

"Actually, Henry said that she seemed irritated that he'd found her, which is much the same thing the paramedics said. It seems she was determined to just brush it off and get back to bed." Her laugh was flat and devoid of any humor. "That was pretty much impossible, since Henry said she was as weak as a kitten."

"Oh God," Savannah repeated. She glanced around the small room. "Where is Henry?"

"At home with Gwen and Amy. We couldn't leave Amy all alone out at the farm, and we didn't want to wait for a sitter to show up, so we just scooped her out of bed in her night-gown, wrapped her in a quilt, and drove her to the house. She never woke up."

"I never thought I'd be grateful Henry was staying there."

She also had never thought that she would have been grateful for the construction delays. Thank goodness the room she'd promised Henry at the keeper's house hadn't been ready.

Savannah sat there with the others, trying to remember everything the doctor had told them about strokes. She struggled to recall some-thing—anything—positive about her friend's ex-perience. But her mind was fogged with worry, fear, and, as the clock on the bright yellow wall slowly ticked off the passing time, fatigue.

There was nothing for any of them to do but to wait. Savannah had never felt more helpless.

And wasn't this just a fine kettle of cossacks? Ida lay on the gurney, growing more and more frustrated as the doctor kept asking her the same questions.

What was her name? Did she know where she was? Did she know what day of the week it was? Who was president? Over and over again. She answered him correctly every time—admit-tedly having to stop and think a minute before she realized that it must be early Wednesday morning—but for some reason she couldn't make the answers sink into his stubborn head.

What was wrong with him? Ida scowled up at the face that was swimming in and out of focus.

Was the idiot man deaf? She was tempted to just get up and walk out of here. The only problem with that idea was that she was strangely too exhausted to move. There was also the little matter of her right arm and leg feeling as if they'd turned to lead.

She'd just rest a bit, Ida decided. Since they seemed so damn determined to poke and prod at her, she'd let them have their fun. Then she'd leave.

"What are they doing in there?" Savannah leaned her forehead against the window, trying to keep herself from screaming. Beneath her initial fear, resentment began to rear its ugly head.

Dr. Ida Lindstrom had put herself through medical school, receiving her degree before the doctors and nurses working in the ER had even been born. She'd served the community of Coldwater Cove for more than five decades. She was a colleague of those very same people bustling around with a purpose they didn't seem inclined to share.

Her grandmother was lying somewhere out there in one of those dark blue curtained cubicles, perhaps hovering on the brink of death, and not a single person in this entire damn building cared enough to let her family know her condition.

Outside the hospital, the weather was as bleak as Savannah's mood. Another storm front had moved in over the mountains. A sky the color of bruises hung low over the town. A dreary drizzle streamed down the glass.

"She's going to be all right," Raine, who'd come to stand beside her, insisted for the umpteenth time since Savannah had arrived with Dan. Her nerves all in a tangle, Savannah turned to inform her sister that there were some things that even Xena the Warrior Lawyer couldn't control, when a distressed look came over Raine's face.

As she ran out of the room, Savannah shot a look toward Jack. His expression appeared sympathetic, but not overly concerned. The fact that he wasn't immediately on his wife's heels was explanation enough.

Savannah followed Raine down the hall to the restrooms and handed her a wet paper towel when she came out of the stall.

"Thank you." Raine wiped her face, balled the towel and tossed it into the waste bin, then washed her mouth out in the sink. "Christ, my timing stinks."

Savannah almost smiled at the self-reproach in her sister's voice. Trust Raine to believe that morning sickness was yet another event she could schedule into her Day-Timer.

"Actually, the news will undoubtedly be just the medicine Gram needs." She hugged Raine. "I'm so happy for you."

"I'm happy for me, too. Or at least I was before Gram decided to scare us all to death." Raine leaned back and gave Savannah a searching look. "Is this going to be a problem? After last fall?"

She'd gone to New York shortly after her miscarriage, seeking her big sister's comfort.

"Of course not. My miscarriage and your pregnancy have nothing to do with each other."

"That's a relief. I've been putting off telling you all week because I felt a little guilty. Since you're the one who always wanted a large family."

"I think it's fabulous," Savannah insisted. "Especially since I've recently discovered that I love being an aunt."

"Then you should really love being a godmother." Raine began digging around in her purse. "I hate morning sickness," she complained as she popped a breath mint into her mouth.

"It'll be gone by the second trimester. Meanwhile, the trick is to keep something in your stomach all the time and carry crackers with you."

"That's what all the books say." Raine pressed her palm against her still flat stomach. "Can I tell you something? Just between us?"

"Of course." Savannah was surprised she even had to ask.

"Ever since Henry called the farm with the bad news, I've been worried that this is my fault."

"Your fault?"

"You know, one of those life cycle things."

"Life cycle things?" Savannah stared at her. "Surely you don't believe that Gram might die because you're pregnant?" The ever practical, feet-on-the-ground Raine was the last person she would have expected to even come up with such an idea.

"Do you remember when Lilith was a Buddhist?"

"After she came back from filming that slasher movie in Hong Kong," Savannah remembered.

It had been a short-lived religious infatuation, triggered, she'd always secretly believed, by her mother's very public affair with her costar. Savannah had not been able to go into a supermarket for six weeks without seeing Lilith and her Chinese martial arts champion lover looking back at her from the covers of the tabloids at the checkout stand.

"She visited me for a few days during that time."

"She did?" Savannah was surprised. Until recently, Raine and their mother had not been close. In fact, their relationship could have been described as just short of estranged.

"She was in town for a publicity event." Raine shrugged. "I couldn't exactly refuse to see her. . . . Anyway, she was positive she'd found the key to the secret of life. Quite honestly, she was chattering away—you know how she does when she's in love—and I didn't listen to much she said. But something has stuck in my mind all these years. She told me that every breath we take stirs the universe and creates a reaction. That nothing happens in a vacuum."

"Are you talking about sort of a universal quid pro quo?"

"You're laughing at me." Which was, Savannah knew from childhood experience, something a person dared only at their own peril.

"No. I'm not laughing. Not really," she in-

sisted when her sister looked on the verge of
arguing. "I just think that perhaps these are
runaway hormones talking. Because, no offense
to the Buddhists, who I'm sure are very lovely
people, but I don't believe life works that way.

"I also don't think that you would have believed it either, before this morning."

It seemed a little strange comforting her big
sister. Strange, but nice, Savannah decided.

"Besides, knowing Mother, she probably got
the concept wrong, anyway."

Raine managed a reluctant, self-conscious
laugh just as the restroom door opened.

"The doctor's finally seen fit to talk to us,"
Lilith informed them. "He's in the waiting room."

Raine and Savannah exchanged a look. Then
they followed their mother back down the hall.

Ida did not like being on the other end of the
physician-patient relationship. She'd always
known that there was no privacy in a hospital,
but this was the first time she'd been the one
lying naked beneath the impossibly thin pink
blanket.

The ICU was annoyingly bright and as frigid
as a meat locker. Someone should tell them to
turn the heat up. Machines hummed, quietly
monitoring vital signs. An IV bottle hung overhead, fluids dripping down the clear tube into
the back of her hand.

"Let's check your reflexes and see how we're
doing, dear," a chirpy voice said. A moment
later Ida was blinded by a bright penlight. She

knew the nurse only wanted to see how her pupils dilated, but Ida instinctively tried to close her eyes against the glare. Stubborn fingers held her lids open.

"Good girl," the voice said. "We're doing just dandy, Ida, dear."

As the nurse instructed her to push against her hand, Ida shoved as hard as she could—which, unfortunately, wasn't very hard when it came to her right hand—and struggled to read the woman's name tag. She wanted to tell this annoying female that she should give a person fair warning before she went shining lights into their eyes. She also had no right using a patient's first name unless invited to do so.

Unfortunately, her vision, made worse by the bright light, was still blurry. The nurse's pink face continued to fade in and out of focus.

She felt the pressure on her feet. Both feet, Ida realized. She knew that was a good thing, but couldn't remember why.

Still struggling with the answer that was hovering just out of reach in the foggy mists of her mind, Ida drifted back to sleep.

Just as when they'd first met with him, Dr. Burke didn't beat around the bush. "As you've all undoubtedly surmised, Dr. Lindstrom has had a stroke."

Somehow, hearing the diagnosis out loud from this white-coated man who was supposed to make things better, to make Ida better, hit Savannah as hard as Raine's original call. She struggled to focus on what the doctor was saying, but seemed only able to pick up the significant words. The frightening words.

"She suffered left brain damage, blah, blah, blah ... hemiplegia, blah ... weakness in her right side, blah, blah ... aphasia, blah ... apraxia, blah, blah, blah ... some relaxation of the muscles on the right side of her face, blah blah—"

"Wait a minute." Savannah held up a hand. "Would you mind going back to aphasia? And apraxia?"

"Of course. Apraxia is the inability to use the mouth and tongue muscles to formulate words."

"And Gram doesn't have that?"

"No. She's actually quite talkative for someone who's just suffered a brain insult."

He made it sound as if someone had hammered Ida with a sarcastic remark. Savannah glanced over at Raine, who rolled her eyes. Her expression also revealed that she was also thinking how difficult it was to keep Ida Lindstrom quiet when she had a point to make.

"The problem," he said, "is that her aphasia, which is the inability to express oneself in either spoken or written words, makes it somewhat difficult to diagnose whether she merely has expressive aphasia, or receptive aphasia as well."

"Which would be her ability to understand language?" Raine inquired.

"Exactly. For example, when she was first brought in, the admitting doctor asked her name, and she answered, 'Blood.'"

"Maybe she was trying to say something

about her blood pressure," Lilith said hopefully. "Perhaps she was afraid that's what had caused her stroke and she was telling them to check it."

"Her vital signs were being monitored at the time," the doctor said. "I understand that it's only natural to try to attribute some normalcy to what is, admittedly, an unnatural situation, but when Dr. Lindstrom was asked if she knew where she was, she responded with 'Brick' the first time."

"That's close," Savannah pointed out, like her mother, grasping at any straw she could reach. "This building is constructed of brick."

"The second time her response was, 'Dog.' The third time, 'Piano.'"

Language had always been so important to her grandmother. Her opinionated manner admittedly grated from time to time, but Savannah had always admired the way she'd never hesitated to speak her mind—a mind that now sounded hopelessly jumbled.

"When we tried some yes-or-no questions that she could nod to, she got most of them right," he said encouragingly. "This suggests she's able to understand a lot of what she's hearing."

"Yes-or-no questions couldn't be very complex," Raine pointed out.

"They are, by necessity, fairly simplistic," he allowed. "But it also indicates a stronger chance that she'll regain more of her comprehension and speech skills."

"Could you give us any sort of timetable for when this recovery might take place?" Lilith asked.

"Unfortunately, I can't. Every stroke is unique." He appeared to want to leave the room. "Well, if there are no more questions . . ." He was definitely inching toward the door. "The hospital Social Worker will want to meet with you regarding Dr. Lindstrom's rehabilitation team—"

"Team?" Savannah asked.

"Your grandmother will be assigned a number of specialists to help her achieve the best possible recovery. A physical therapist will determine the extent of the dysfunction in her weakened right side and help her work her muscles to allow maximum mobility."

"Will Mother be able to walk?" Lilith asked.

He frowned. "Again, every stroke victim is unique, but your mother's hemiplegia seems fairly mild. My educated guess is that her prognosis for walking—perhaps with the assistance of a cane—is quite good."

"That's very encouraging, Doctor." Lilith's faint smile was only a shadow of her usual dazzling one. "But I'm afraid you've made one grave error in treating my mother."

"Oh?" He lifted a brow.

"My mother may have had a stroke. But the one thing she's never been, and will never be, is a *victim*." At that moment, Savannah could actually see Ida in Lilith's dark blue eyes.

"Point taken, Mrs. Ryan," he murmured with a nod. "Getting back to the concept of your mother's team . . . unless anyone else has a question?" he asked.

"Fine," he said, outwardly relieved when

none of them spoke up. "Along with her physical therapist, Dr. Lindstrom will also be given speech and occupational therapists."

"My grandmother's retired, Doctor," Raine pointed out.

"I'm aware of that." There was a faint edge to his tone that suggested the Lindstrom women's continual questions were beginning to annoy him.

Tough, Savannah thought.

"An occupational therapist teaches stroke victims—"

"Patients," Lilith corrected.

"Patients," he agreed tightly. "As I was saying, this therapist will help Dr. Lindstrom with daily living skills, dressing, bathing, teaching her to feed herself, get around the house, relearn basic skills such as cooking—"

"We could probably skip that one," Savannah murmured. She'd meant to keep her comment to herself, but it had come out during a second of silence in the doctor's presentation and she knew she hadn't made points when the family all laughed.

The back and forth motion of his jaw suggested that he was grinding his teeth. "Of course, the family is one of the most important members of the team," he doggedly forged on even as he continued to move backwards. He was now standing in the open doorway.

"I'll arrange for you to see Dr. Lindstrom. She's been moved upstairs to ICU. At this time, I would suggest that you keep your visit down to ten minutes. And only the immediate family."

With that final instruction, he escaped.

"I think we're in trouble," Lilith said.

"What was your first clue, Mother?" Raine asked dryly.

"When the doctor brought up the team."

Savannah caught her mother's meaning right away. "You're right. Gram never has been a team player."

Although it wasn't very funny, they all shared another laugh because they needed one. And because, Savannah feared, what they were all facing wasn't going to offer many opportunities for humor.

19

Ida looked so small. So frail. It was all Savannah could do not to burst into tears as she stood beside her grandmother's bed, holding her hand.

"The doctor says you're going to be fine, Mother," Lilith soothed. She leaned over the bed railing and stroked damp strands of gray hair from Ida's forehead. Since her grandmother had worn her hair up in that untidy bun for as long as Savannah could remember, she'd never realized how long it was. If it had been brushed properly, it would have come nearly to her waist. "You just need a little rest."

Ida's eyes snapped. "Gorilla."

"I'm sorry." Obviously shaken by the terse non sequitur, Lilith bit her lip, avoiding her daughters' eyes, then squared her shoulders and tried again. "Are you trying to tell us something about Doctor Burke?"

Ida nodded.

"He has a very good reputation, Gram," Raine said reassuringly. "I did a background check on him when you had your first appointment," she revealed, surprising Savannah not at all. It was precisely what Raine would do. "His credentials are remarkable and he's worked at some of the top-flight research hospitals in the world, which, of course, made me wonder what he was doing here in Coldwater Cove."

"Not that you can't be a good doctor and a small-town doctor, too," Savannah said quickly.

Raine visibly cringed when she realized what she'd said. "Of course you can. You're proof of that, Gram."

Three of the four women in the room smiled brightly at that. Ida did not. Savannah couldn't tell if that was because she was insulted, or because she couldn't. The muscles on the right side of her face were lax, which caused that side of her lips to droop slightly.

"Anyway," Raine said briskly, as if wanting to move on to a safer topic, "it turns out that he's also an amateur mountain climber. Having conquered all of Colorado's major peaks, he's moved on to Washington. He's already done Baker and Rainier. Next spring he's doing Olympus. Then I suppose we'll be losing him, but of course, you'll be fully recovered by then, so it won't really matter."

Ida shook her head.

"Of course you will be, Gram," Savannah insisted. "We're all going to help you. And you're going to have a team of experts, as well, made up of all sorts of trained therapists. Which, of course, you already know about, being a doctor yourself."

Ida shook her head.

"Maybe she's forgotten," Lilith suggested quietly. "Dr. Burke says that you'll have a speech therapist." She raised her voice as if an increase in volume could facilitate understanding. "Along with a physical therapist, and—"

"Plane," Ida interrupted abruptly. She pointed her left hand toward the rain-streaked window.

"Rain," Savannah guessed.

Ida nodded. "Plane," she repeated.

"You want to go on a plane?" Raine asked.

Ida's head bobbed up and down.

"But you hate air travel," Lilith reminded her.

"Plane!" Ida slammed her hand on the bed. The angry pink hue darkening her ashen complexion would have been reassuring, were it not for a very real concern that she could work herself into a second stroke.

It took some more questioning to figure out that whatever distinguished between head shakes and nods had gone haywire in Ida's injured brain.

"You'd think that the doctor would have mentioned that a nod means *no*," Raine muttered.

They tried again, everyone, including Ida—especially Ida, Savannah thought—becoming more and more frustrated with these early futile attempts at communication.

She jabbed the index finger of her good left hand toward the window again and again. "Plane," she kept repeating.

Realizing that the word itself was useless, Savannah focused instead on the message.

She went over to the glass and looked out over the town. Then she saw it. The house, overlooking the cove.

"Home!" she said. She spun back toward her grandmother. "You want to go home."

Ida energetically shook her head back and forth on the pillow. *Yes.* Tears streamed down her face.

"Of course you'll be coming home." Lilith took a tissue from the box beside the bed and began dabbing at the uncontrolled moisture. "As soon as you're just a little bit better."

"Dr. Burke says you should be released in ten days." Raine's words revealed that she'd absorbed more of what the doctor had been saying than Savannah had. "And then, of course you'll be coming home, Gram."

Ida seemed to accept that promise. She sank deeper into the sheets and closed her eyes. Tears continued to fall at a furious pace from beneath her lids, yet her lips—even the injured side—pulled into a lopsided smile.

Hers were not the only damp eyes in the room.

Determined to make the most of the time they were allowed, by mutual unspoken agreement Lilith, Raine, and Savannah remained beside Ida's bed, surreptitiously watching the monitor overhead. A line continued to move across a green screen in reassuring peaks and valleys.

Eventually a nurse wearing bright pink scrubs appeared in the doorway. "I'm sorry, but you'll have to leave. The speech therapist is here, and she needs to do some tests on Dr. Lindstrom."

"Dr. Lindstrom is sleeping," Raine hissed. "Can't she come back later?"

"She's here now," the nurse said in a stern, no-nonsense tone that brooked no argument. "The sooner she can determine your grand-mother's condition, the faster Dr. Lindstrom can begin her recovery."

Those were, of course, the magic words. They left the room, pausing briefly to speak with the therapist, an attractive brunette in her early to mid thirties. Her hair was cut in a sleek bob she'd tucked behind both ears, and she was dressed in black jeans and black jacket bright-ened by a scarlet sweater.

"Dr. Lindstrom delivered both my parents," Kathi Montgomery informed the family. "Me, too. And she saved my social life when she treated my acne when I was fourteen."

That reference made Savannah recognize her. "You were Kathi Clifton." She'd been on the debating club, Savannah recalled. She'd also dated Dan O'Halloran.

"That was my maiden name. I'm thinking about going back to it now that I'm getting a di-vorce, but at this point, I'm just taking one step at a time. Your grandmother's my first client since I've come back to work."

"Oh?" Savannah worried about that.

Kathi smiled again. "You don't have to worry. I may have been sidetracked for a while, but

I'm very good at my job. I'll take good care of
your grandmother."

"She looks so weak," Lilith worried.

"So would you, if you were in her shoes. She's
had a rough few hours. But I was reading the ad-
mittance report, and I think she got off real lucky.
Strokes are scary, foreign territory to most people." She assured them that they were not alone
in their fears. "But no matter how bad things are
in the beginning, they can get a lot better."

"Back to the way they were before the
stroke?" Raine asked.

"Not always." Savannah admired Kathi Montgomery's honesty. "In fact, just about everyone
will have some residual effects after a stroke.
But people have amazing adjustment skills.

"We all want to believe that we can control
our lives," she said. Since she was looking
straight at Raine, Savannah added perception
to the therapist's growing list of attributes. "But
it's impossible not to run into surprises. Or de-
tours.

"Right now, even though she's a doctor, all
this is foreign territory to Dr. Lindstrom. Especially with her aphasia making it difficult to
communicate. It's a bit as if she woke up this
morning and discovered she was in Tibet."

Lilith sighed heavily. "Mother has always
hated to travel."

At least feeling they were leaving Ida in good
hands, they headed back to the ICU waiting
room the family had moved to after Ida had
been transferred from ER.

"Well, one thing's for certain," Savannah said as they walked past the nursing station.

Lilith glanced over at her. Savannah was relieved when she noticed that a little color had come back to her mother's cheeks. "What's that, dear?"

"Whatever her condition in ten days, she is definitely coming home. I don't care if she has another stroke after this one—a hundred strokes—she's not going to end up propped up in front of a television at Evergreen."

About this, they were in total agreement.

After Raine assured Jack that she'd be fine without him, and yes, she'd keep the saltines he'd brought her from the cafeteria close at hand, Jack left the hospital to check on Amy and reassure the little girl that her great-grandmother was going to be coming home soon.

The others stayed. All day, then long into the evening, going in to sit with Ida whenever the nurses allowed. As the hours passed, as the sun rose high above the cove, then set over the mountaintops, it began to sink in that this wasn't the type of life event that would be resolved any time soon.

Obviously, Savannah's planned holiday opening of the bed-and-breakfast would have to be put off. Despite having dedicated so many hours to the project, she didn't suffer so much as a twinge of ambivalence. She thought of what Dan had said about the Chinese word for crisis being the same as the word for opportunity. Her grandmother had always been there for her.

Now she was being given the opportunity to repay that debt.

In the grand scheme of things, Savannah supposed that her lighthouse, as much as it had come to mean to her, wasn't really all that important. Neither was Raine's Harvard law degree, Lilith's former theatrical career, or even Ida's medical practice.

Family was what mattered. Mother, grandmother, sisters. Amy, whom Raine adopted upon marrying Jack, and the unborn child they'd made together. Cooper and Jack, who'd married into the family but were no less a part of it, and Gwen, who had been welcomed in. Even, perhaps, baby Lily someday, if she chose.

That left Dan. He was, of course, technically family, since he was Jack's cousin. Savannah wasn't even going to begin to try to figure out the logistics, but that would make him her cousin-in-law. Or something like that.

But whenever she returned from the ICU and found him still in the waiting room, hour after hour, offering comfort, support, encouragement, and a tenderness she'd never known from any man, Savannah could no longer hide from the truth.

Despite her vow to hold her heart close, to avoid the risk of having it be wounded again, her feelings for Dan O'Halloran had gone far past cousinly.

Like most of the doctors she'd met over the years, Ida had never expected any of the illnesses she'd treated to ever happen to her. Logically, she knew that a medical degree didn't come with some invisible shield, but the simple fact was that she quite honestly had been of the belief that things like heart attacks, burst appendixes, cancer, and strokes happened to other people. They wouldn't happen to her.

Well, so much for that theory, she considered as she looked out the window at her little piece of sky and the small rectangular view that had been her entire world for the past eight days.

She knew she was fortunate that her motor skills weren't terribly impeded. The physical therapist, a huge black woman who could made Genghis Khan seem warm and fuzzy by comparison, but who Ida knew was sincerely dedicated to getting her back on her feet, had assured her that If she kept up the hard work she'd be out of her wheelchair in a month.

That prospect had been enough to keep Ida from slugging her this morning when it felt as if she'd jerked her shoulder out of its socket during her range-of-motion exercises.

She *was* getting damn frustrated at not being able to get her thoughts across. She'd tried communicating by writing on one of the yellow legal pads with a fat rollerball pen Raine had brought her, but while she thought she'd been forming the words just fine, all that the others could see was a squiggly black line that Ida reluctantly admitted looked as if it had been scribbled by a baboon.

Her speech therapist was a sweet little girl,

patient as a saint. Kathi Montgomery had suggested that she try to draw pictures, which, while she didn't have to worry about being acclaimed the next Grandma Moses anytime soon, did help get simple points across some of the time.

But Ida didn't like using the drawings because it was like admitting she might never speak again.

That wasn't an option.

That very first day, when the fog had cleared long enough for her to have figured out exactly what was happening to her, Ida had realized that she had two choices. She could just lie here, thinking that her life was over, that she was already a goner, so she might as well just die and free up the bed.

Or she could fight like hell.

This meant that there was really only one choice.

She was dozing when she became aware of someone else in the room, which wasn't all that surprising. This place was like Grand Central Station with the bright lights, people coming and going at all hours of the day and night, always poking and prodding and asking detailed questions about personal bodily functions that she'd always preferred to keep private.

She opened one eye, ready to snarl at that obnoxious nurse who continued to call her by her first name and talked baby talk to her, as if she were some drooling infant who couldn't understand proper English. After the penlight incident, Ida had vowed that she would not die.

She was going to get better. She was going to get strong.

Then she was going to kill that nurse.

But it wasn't her nemesis. It was Henry, standing there with a sunshine yellow plant in his hands, looking about as uncomfortable as she'd ever seen him.

"Didn't mean to wake you," he said gruffly. "I'll just leave this and go."

She shook her head. Once they'd explained to her that she had the head shaking and nodding mixed up, things had begun to get a bit easier. She lifted her hand—her right hand, which took an effort, but still felt more natural than her left—and waved him in.

"You're looking real good, Ida."

She pulled her lips tight, letting him know that her brain might have gotten a little scrambled, but she could still spot a lie when she heard one.

"Oh, you might not think you're looking quite up to snuff," he said when she shook her head. "But considering that you could have been lying on a slab down at Murphy's funeral home, you're looking damn fine."

Ida frowned. She'd never liked thinking about her own mortality. Recent events hadn't changed that.

He plunked the clay pot down on the table beside her bed.

She managed to lift her right brow. Or at least she thought she did. Sometimes it was hard to tell just how things were working.

"I figured it's past time I got you a thank you gift for letting me stay in your house."

She shook her head, pointing from herself to him. If it hadn't been for Henry finding her and his quick response in calling 911, she might have been a lot worse off.

He read her meaning and shrugged. "Guess we're even."

She nodded.

"Hope you like mums."

She nodded again. Emphatically this time.

"I was gonna get you some cut flowers, but the kid down at the Green Spot, that John Martin, said these would be better. They'll last longer."

Another nod. Ida was beginning to get a headache. Lord, it would be nice when she could talk again!

"I thought the color might sort of brighten the place up a bit. . . . You can quit shaking your head up and down," he suggested. "No point in rattlin' your brains more than they've already been rattled."

Vastly relieved, she drew a smiley face in the air. Ida had always hated smiley faces, but sometimes a woman had to make do.

He smiled back. Ida realized that her memory hadn't been all that good the past few months, but she was certain that she hadn't seen the man smile since he'd moved into her house.

"There's been some changes at the house," he revealed. "The family wanted to surprise you, and I don't want to ruin their fun when you come home tomorrow, but I've been thinkin' that perhaps you've had enough surprises lately and mebbe I ought to fill you in on the details."

She gestured again. This time toward the chair.

It was Henry's turn to nod. "I figured as much." He sat down and began to let her know what her daughter and granddaughters had been up to in her absence.

20

All the hours she'd spent working on the remodeling seemed almost like a vacation as Savannah ran back and forth between the hospital and the house, visiting Ida and preparing for her homecoming. Despite her grandmother's abbreviated vocabulary, Ida had made it clear that she didn't want either Raine or Savannah to sacrifice their own busy lives for her. They tried to convince her that taking care of her wasn't any sacrifice, but she'd been typically Ida-insistent.

Savannah called every rent-a-nurse agency in the phone book, but soon discovered that they weren't set up to provide the services her grandmother would need: driving her to therapy sessions, running errands, taking her out to lunch, shopping, anything to keep her from spending all day, every day, in the house. She'd always been an active woman; it was important that that not change.

Savannah had been at her wits' end when Lilith, who'd established a Coldwater Cove community theater group, had suggested a friend of hers. Martha Taylor was a widow who'd recently moved to town. Better yet, she was a former registered nurse, which, Lilith pointed out, could prove helpful. The fact that she'd won the Bette Davis part in the current production of *Whatever Happened to Baby Jane?* had worried Savannah just a bit until they'd met.

Martha seemed to be blessed with an unrelentingly optimistic attitude. She was cheery enough to lift Ida's spirits when they drooped, which they understandably did on occasion, and, having spent a two-year stint as a nurse in the King County jail, she had acquired enough toughness not to let Savannah's headstrong grandmother steamroller over her.

The two women had hit it off right away, and Martha, who'd confessed to having joined the theater group in the first place because she'd been so lonely after her husband's death, readily accepted Ida's invitation to move into the house.

Savannah felt her presence also helped provide a somewhat stable home for Gwen, who, thanks to Dan, was declared an emancipated minor, which effectively took her out of the clutches of Social Services. Despite all the recent stress, Savannah felt that the teenager seemed much less tense. More secure.

She only wished she could say the same for herself. Savannah couldn't remember when she'd been juggling so many balls. All of them breakable.

Fortunately, Raine was taking care of dealing with all the financial details. Accustomed to handling cases worth millions of dollars, even here in Coldwater Cove, since her software clients and businesses dealing in Asian Rim trade didn't care where her office was located, she found a mere insurance company and hospital billing department to be no match at all for her.

If her own grandmother hadn't been the subject of these turf wars, Savannah would almost have felt sorry for the clerk who'd tried—unsuccessfully—to deny Ida out-patient rehabilitation services.

During Ida's hospitalization, what seemed like the entire population of Coldwater Cove dropped by the house bearing casseroles, which Gwen and Henry were especially grateful for, since there were soon enough Pyrex dishes in the freezer to save them from meatloaf, in the event the occupational therapist managed to get Ida cooking again anytime soon.

The day before her grandmother was to be discharged, Savannah was in the front parlor, marking things off her checklist as activity hummed around her. For the past week the house had resembled a beehive: volunteer carpenters built ramps to the front porch and outside kitchen door, and removed moldings and widened doorways to accommodate the wheelchair Savannah hoped Ida would not need for very long.

Thresholds had been beveled, a safety rail was installed in the shower, and a second handrail had been put on the wall side of the stairs in anticipation of the day that her grandmother would be walking again.

Even the plumber who'd taken so long to install the Jacuzzi at her lighthouse showed up, accompanied by his wife, who was bearing a "Southwestern taco surprise" casserole. He took one look at the faucets in Ida's bathroom, went out to his truck, and returned with a single lever, which, he explained, would require less wrist and finger motion than the current round knobs.

"Put the same in my dad's bathroom when he had his stroke," the man informed Savannah cheerfully, as if he'd never received that stern lawyer letter Dan had written for her. "He said it made a world of difference."

He'd no sooner left when Dottie and Doris Anderson, twin owners of the Dancing Deer Dress Shoppe, showed up at the door.

"We know how Ida loves her jeans," Doris said as she took the lid off a box and revealed an olive green jogging outfit. "But this will be easier for her to get on and off."

"That's very thoughtful of you. Thank you."

"Mother Anderson had a stroke five years ago." Dottie pulled a scarlet garment from a shopping bag bearing the store's dancing deer logo. While the elderly twins dressed alike, Doris, the elder by ten minutes, preferred earth tones while her sister opted for brighter colors. "We found that putting on a terry cloth robe after her shower was often easier than toweling dry."

"I wouldn't have thought of that."

"It's a difficult time," Dottie said sympathetically. "But the important thing is that you're not alone, dear."

"That's nice to know." Savannah also knew from experience how difficult it was to break off a conversation with the Anderson twins, most notably the loquacious Dottie.

"You haven't been in the shop lately," Doris noted.

"I've been a little busy."

"Well, that's certainly understandable." Dottie patted Savannah's hand. "But you must steal a little time to drop in some day soon. We've opened up a bridal boutique since the last time you were in." Her round pink cheeks dimpled. "Our slogan is You Bring the Groom, We've Got the Gown."

"That's certainly catchy," Savannah said with a quick glance toward Raine, who'd just come from upstairs, where she'd been supervising the installation of the rented stair glide.

At first the plan had been to move Ida into the sunroom, which was on the first floor and was the cheeriest room in the house. But knowing how she valued her privacy, and wanting to keep things as normal as possible during this transitional time, the family had finally decided to put in the chairlift that would allow Ida to return to the bedroom she'd slept in for the past forty-five years.

"It was Doris who thought the slogan up,"

Dottie allowed. "Of course we don't really need any advertising these days, since your mother's and sister's wedding has gotten us business from all over the peninsula."

She skimmed a quick, professional gaze over Savannah that suggested she was taking mental measurements. "We've several models that would look lovely on you."

"I'm not really in the market for a wedding dress," Savannah murmured.

"Not yet, perhaps." Doris shot a pointed look out the front window toward Dan, who was walking up the front sidewalk.

Savannah was getting much too accustomed to seeing him at the end of the day. It wasn't just that the sight of him caused that little jolt to her heart. It was that it was beginning to feel so right.

"Do keep us in mind, dear," Dottie chirped.

The sisters left, pausing to exchange a few words with Dan.

The problem with a small town was, of course, that everyone knew everyone else's business. Then again, Savannah thought, as she watched Henry rubbing paste wax into the furniture and Martha washing the windows with vinegar and crumpled newspapers, people truly cared for one another.

Ida Lindstrom had always taken care of the people of Coldwater Cove. Now it was their turn to take care of her.

Dan knew every inch of Savannah's body intimately. He'd touched it, tasted it, dreamed of it. He could also tell, yesterday afternoon during a hurried coupling between her morning visit to the hospital and the afternoon courthouse appearance for Gwen, that there was less of it than when they'd first made love. Along with her obvious weight loss, there were deep shadows beneath her eyes and she was too pale. Dan still thought her beautiful.

"Good evening, Mrs. Ryan," he greeted Lilith cheerfully. "I've come to steal your lovely daughter."

Lilith glanced up from arranging issues of the AMA journal on a table next to her mother's favorite chair. "I do hope you mean Savannah, since I don't believe Jack would take well to his pregnant wife being kidnapped."

"If you kidnapped my mommy, Daddy would put you in jail, Uncle Dan," Amy said. She was sitting on the floor with a box of crayons, coloring a picture for her great-grandmother.

"Good point. Then it's a lucky thing for me that I've come for your aunt Savannah."

"Oh, Dan." Savannah's face fell. He recognized the look. He'd seen it a lot since she'd come back to town. More since Ida's stroke. "I'm sorry, but I've still got so much left to do."

"Oh, go with the man, darling," Lilith said. "We've got everything under control."

Knowing that he was taking unfair advantage, Dan drew Savannah into his arms. "I had this sudden yearning for fried chicken and potato salad. But it's no fun to go on a picnic alone."

"A picnic?" He could feel her softening, fitting her curves to his body.

"I have it on good authority that the Lindstrom women are suckers for picnics." He shot a grin over the top of Savannah's head toward Raine, who, amazingly for a woman who entered a courtroom looking as if she had ice water in her veins, actually blushed.

"My husband and I are going to have to have a little chat about sharing when I get home," she murmured.

"Jack never said a thing," Dan assured her. But he remembered the look on his cousin's face the day after his spring picnic with Raine in the woods. It was the first time Dan had realized that it was possible for a guy to look poleaxed and smug at the same time.

He turned his attention back to Savannah. "So, how about it? I also happen to have picked up a Bordeaux at the mercantile, which Olivia Brown assures me is voluptuous without being too bold, and nicely complex while remaining user friendly." He grinned. "Sort of like someone I know."

When he felt her wavering, he coaxed her out the front door onto the porch to escape their audience. "I just want to steal a little time alone with you, sweetheart. Before Ida comes home and things get really hectic."

"We were alone yesterday."

"I enjoyed every minute of our little tryst parked out on the skid road," he assured her. "But I have to admit that I'd just as soon tumble you without having to keep an eye out for logging trucks."

"I'm disappointed." He watched a bit of laughter spark beneath the fatigue in her eyes. "Here I thought you were a man who enjoyed adventure."

"You're all the adventure I need." It was the absolute truth. He rubbed his palms over her shoulders, soothing muscles that were as rigid as boulders. "Have pity on me, Savannah. I've spent all day thinking about you." He moved his stroking fingers up her neck.

"I've thought about you, too." She practically purred as the tension slowly slid away.

"Then come with me." He touched his mouth to hers and felt her lips soften. Yield.

She lifted her arms and linked her fingers behind his neck. "How can we have a picnic? It's going to be dark soon. And cold."

"I'll keep you warm," he promised.

"You keep me hot," she corrected as she brushed a kiss against his jaw. "All I have to do is think about you and it's as if I'm burning up with fever." He felt her soft sigh against his cheek and was encouraged again when she didn't pull away.

"I know the feeling. Very well." He touched a fingertip to her chin and brought her lips to his. The kiss was light and brief, but still, as always, packed a helluva punch. "As for the dark part, I've got that covered. You just have to trust me."

She leaned her head back and looked up at him, her eyes more sober than he'd ever seen them. Even more sober than that night on the Ferris wheel when she'd told him about her failed marriage.

"I do."

"That's a good start." Deluged by feelings, by her, he pulled her tight. "We can work from there."

Dan had known women who made him ache. Women who'd made him burn. Even women who could, on a particularly satisfying occasion, make him tremble. But Savannah was the first woman who had him willing to crawl.

If he thought that might do the trick, if there was even a chance that it would tear down that last defensive barrier she'd constructed around her heart, he'd do just that, without a second thought, on his hands and knees across shattered glass. Through burning flames. Through hell.

Through no fault of her own, Ida had thrown a monkey wrench into all their lives. Into his plans. Understandably, the aftermath of her stroke was taking up a great deal of Savannah's attention. He'd just have to be patient a while longer.

As she walked with him back down the sidewalk to the SUV, he decided to have John order some greenery. A holiday wedding at the lighthouse would be a nice touch. Christmas was a little more than a month away. Plenty of time, Dan decided with a renewed burst of optimism.

"When did you do all this?" Savannah stared around the lantern room.

"I got some of it done this morning before I went into the office."

He'd unearthed the blue and white blanket spread over the hardwood floor at the bottom of the linen closet his mother had filled when he'd first come back to town. She had been appalled to find her only son living, in her words, "like a hobo." He'd tried to tell her that he'd bought the house for the view and that the sleeping bag he'd thrown on the bed was sufficient for the time being, but that hadn't stopped her from showing up at his door with more sheets and towels than he'd figured he'd use in this lifetime.

"A little more during lunch."

The clay pots of buttery yellow flowers surrounding the blanket had been John's suggestion, as had the blue spruce, which had been a bitch to haul up the stairs. But his nephew had assured him that they could decorate it for Christmas, then plant it outside in the spring. Dan liked the idea of planting a tree with Savannah, watching it grow each year, along with their kids.

"And I did the shopping after court recessed this afternoon, before I dropped by your grandmother's house."

When she'd begun ringing up the mercantile's entire stock of candles, Olivia had asked him if he was expecting a power outage. Then she'd gotten to the wine and Johnny Mathis CD. From the knowing look she'd given him while they waited for Fred to do a price check on the wine, Dan had realized that by tomorrow everyone in Coldwater Cove would know he'd been setting up a romantic tryst with Ida Lindstrom's granddaughter.

It might have been worse, he'd thought at the time. Fortunately, he'd planned ahead and

stocked up on condoms at the busy, impersonal
Walgreen in Port Angeles.

"It's wonderful for you to have gone to so much
trouble." She toed her sneakers off and sat down
on the blanket. "I'm already starting to relax."

"That's the idea." He hit the remote for the
stereo he'd hidden behind the tree.

"All this and Johnny Mathis, too?" she asked
with a smile as the seductive light baritone
sounds of Mathis getting "Misty" drifted from
the hidden speakers.

"Hey, my dad swears by him." Dan decided it
might blow the mood if he shared the fact that
according to his mother, who should know, he'd
been conceived to Mathis.

"Better we use your father's music than
mine," she decided.

Since, from what he'd always been able to
tell, Reggie Townsend screamed his lyrics
rather than sing them, Dan concurred.

Using Mathis to set the mood might be a
cliché, but as he'd told himself while standing
in line at the mercantile, the entire picnic idea
was pretty much a cliché. But maybe that's because it worked. Because it was romantic.

The funny thing was, he considered as he
went around the room lighting the candles that
had seemed to so amuse Olivia Brown, he'd
never been the sort of guy who went in for
grand gestures. Of course, he'd never met a
woman who made him want to go that extra
distance. Until Savannah.

He suspected she could have cooked the

chicken a lot better than the extra crispy pieces he'd picked up at the mercantile deli, but she seemed to enjoy it, which was all that mattered. The potato salad and cole slaw were pretty much standard deli fare, but this evening wasn't about food. They both agreed that the wine, as promised, was excellent.

During dinner they talked about the additions to the house, about Henry's surprising decision not to move out until Ida was back on her feet, about Gwen's new independence and the fact that she was trying for early admission at Dan's alma mater. The Stanford recruiter had been encouraging and had assured her that scholarships and work-study programs should cover her costs.

Life wasn't perfect.

"But it's getting better," Savannah said. With obvious satisfaction, she glanced around the room that was lacking only furniture. "Now that Lilith's found Martha, I'm still hoping to move in here before Thanksgiving, even though I probably won't be able to open for business until after the first of the year."

"Some things are worth waiting for."

She looked into his eyes. "True."

Dan placed a hand against the small of her back, drawing her closer. He did his best to show Savannah, with every kiss, every touch, how much he loved her. Emotions he'd never felt, never realized he possessed until recently, came pouring forth from him into her. Until Savannah, Dan hadn't known that it was possible to feel so much, so deeply, and still want more.

He undressed her slowly, tenderly. With trembling hands she did the same to him. Then they looked at each other and found each other wonderful.

Skin dampened, hearts thundered, bodies entwined. She moved under him without inhibition, touched him in all the secret places he was touching her without hesitation.

Dan breathed in the scent of her—soft talc, the peach shampoo she'd used that morning, the floral perfume that lingered in his mind all day—all night—long.

He tasted her, the sweet, intoxicating flavor of her lips, the hot, tangy essence of her skin. She tasted like sex and sin and temptation. He could have drunk from her succulent lips forever.

He watched her, the mysterious, seductive darkening of her eyes, the way her hair spread over her bare shoulders and breasts like tongues of flame. Looking at her bathed in the flickering warm candlelight, her flesh gleaming like molten gold, Dan fully understood why ancient man had made sacrifices to pagan goddesses.

"Oh God," she moaned on a ragged laugh as they rolled over the blanket, "I have this terrible problem."

"Let me fix it."

"That's the problem." Her mouth, wild and willful, clung to his. "I think I've become a sex addict."

"So, what's the problem?" The taste of her flooded into him, through him.

"All day long, while I was dealing with plumbers and Dottie and Doris and a thousand other people and problems, I kept thinking about how much I love the way you make me feel. How you can drive me mad."

She rubbed her breasts against his chest in a way designed to create sparks. "And how I wanted to do the same thing to you." She sprawled over him, her firm tanned thighs draped over his legs.

"So far, you're succeeding." When she began to move against him, the blood surged from his brain to other, more vital organs. "Now that," he muttered on a breath as sharp and ragged as broken glass, "is definitely overachieving."

"Trust me, I've just begun." Savannah went up onto her knees, straddling his burning body, rubbing against him like a provocative cat as her mouth blazed a hot, wet trail down his chest. "Have I mentioned how much I absolutely adore your body?"

"It's all yours." Somewhere Mathis was singing about a thousand violins playing. "At least until you kill me." And that, Dan considered, would not be such a bad way to go.

Her hair draped over his thighs while her tongue swirled sensually around him, pulling him into a deep, swirling maelstrom. Like a drowning man, he struggled to fill his lungs with air.

Dan had thought he'd experienced passion. Believed he'd experienced pain. But Savannah was proving him vastly wrong on both counts.

On the brink of losing what minuscule control he still possessed, he grasped her waist, lifted her up and lowered her body onto his.

"Now," he panted.

Her knees were pressed against his thighs, her soft, yielding body a hot sheathe for his power.

"Now," she agreed on a breath as labored as his.

Dan surged upward. She met him thrust for thrust, hot flesh against hot flesh. All the time Dan never took his eyes from hers.

He watched them darken, then widen, as they rode up the tumultuous peak, watched her lips part in passion and stunned pleasure as they came crashing down the other side.

Their bodies were slick with perspiration. Savannah was sprawled atop his chest and Dan was still inside her, loathe to leave when the sky outside the lantern room lit up with a flare of red, white, and blue fireworks. A booming sound like cannon fire rattled the glass while Mathis declared everything wonderful, wonderful.

"Oh, my God." He felt her laughter. "We'll *never* be able to top this."

"It's Friday night. The Coldwater Cove Loggers are playing the Richland Bombers at the high school." He rolled them over, draping one leg over her hip so he could keep her close. "Obviously the Loggers just scored."

"They're not the only ones."

He chuckled at that. He dipped his head, circled the rosy tip of her breast with his tongue and felt her heart, which had begun to slow to something resembling a normal beat, quicken again. "Want to see if we can make the earth move next?"

"On one condition." She bucked when his teeth tugged on her nipple, then trembled as his hand slipped between their bodies to cup her.

"Name it." She was slick, hot, and his.

"Before you take me back to the house, we try for a tidal wave."

"A hat trick," he said approvingly as he began to move his hips in a slow, deep rhythm she immediately met. "I like it."

21

"Good morning, Ida." The nurse she'd come to dislike more with each passing day breezed into the hospital room. The family was already two minutes late picking her up, and Ida was already not in the best of moods. "So, today's the big day, isn't it, dear? I'll bet we're so-o-o excited to be going home."

"If you're coming with me, I'll just throw myself out of this wheelchair in front of an ambulance on the way out of this place. Dear." Ida answered mentally. Since she knew she wouldn't be able to string all those words together just yet, she shot the woman her most blistering scowl instead.

Blithely ignoring it, the nurse began pushing the chair toward the door. If she could have dragged her feet to stop the forward progress, Ida would have. As it was, the most she could do was make a futile grab for the door frame with her good left hand as she was wheeled through it.

"Where?" Thanks to Kathi Montgomery, she now had a vocabulary of about twenty-five words. Unfortunately, none of them were curse words, which she could have used about now.

"Oh, it's a surprise." They were headed down the hall. Ida looked around, frustrated further when she saw no sight of her daughter or granddaughters.

She could understand Lilith not being there. While her daughter seemed to have become much more responsible since her marriage, Ida supposed a little backsliding was inevitable. Savannah was usually more dependable, but it was possible she'd had to drive out to the lighthouse for some reason and had gotten sidetracked with more construction problems.

But that didn't explain why Raine wasn't here. Her elder granddaughter was as punctual as a Swiss clock. It wasn't like her to be late for anything. That thought had Ida's irritation turning to fear. What if there'd been an accident? What if something had happened to them on the drive here? What if Gwen had borrowed Savannah's little red car and skidded out of control on the rain-slick road and driven into the cove? Or perhaps Amy had fallen out of that swing Jack had hung in the tree behind the farmhouse and broken her arm? Or worse.

Perhaps that sweet child was in the ER right now, barely hanging on to life, while she was fussing because they were a few minutes late.

Ida had never been a worrier. But that was before experiencing the mental and physical equivalents of a car wreck. As a doctor, she understood that her uncharacteristic dread of the unknown was attributable to normal post-stroke depression. But that medical knowledge didn't keep her rebellious, damaged mind from spinning up the bloodiest, most unlikely scenarios, most of which starred members of her family.

Perhaps, she thought as she cast a hopeful glance toward the bank of elevators they were racing by, once she was totally recovered, she'd try her hand at writing horror stories.

A mental image of the baby-talking nurse being eaten alive by a land shark who'd crawled out of Coldwater Cove almost made Ida smile.

"Surprise!" The cheers greeted her as she was wheeled into the solarium. Bright, helium-filled balloons hugged a ceiling draped with streamers of autumn-hued crepe paper. On the wall, next to a cardboard cutout of a turkey that had gone up a few days earlier, was a huge, hand-painted sign that read Good Luck Dr. Lindstrom. It seemed to Ida that the entire hospital staff had crowded into the room, even Dr. Burke, who'd made himself as scarce as hen's feet lately.

Ida didn't begrudge the neurologist his obvious discomfort with her condition. She understood professional pride; stroke patients tended to burst the little fantasy bubble of physician omnipotence. It was, after all, difficult to pretend to be God when you couldn't heal a medical problem with either drugs or surgery. She had the feeling he would have been much happier if she'd had a brain tumor he could have carved out of her head.

"Surprise!" The way everyone was shouting didn't help the headache Ida had awoken with, but the outpouring of goodwill more than made up for it.

She felt a rush of relief when she saw Lilith, Raine, and Savannah standing beside a table that held a sheet cake with Good Luck written in red icing. As her eyes filled, Ida decided that just maybe she'd let her baby-talking nemesis live after all.

Thanksgiving morning dawned bright and clear. Having given Gwen and Henry instructions on how to start roasting the turkey, Savannah, who'd moved into the lighthouse two days earlier, was driving to her grandmother's house with a trio of pumpkin pies when one of her father's songs came on the car radio.

Reggie Townsend was a rock legend. Born in Great Britain, he had attended Liverpool's Quarry Bank High School—the very same school that had given the world Beatles Paul McCartney and John Lennon. Although the singer-songwriter had just celebrated his fifty-second birthday, his glittering star continued to rise after three decades in the music business. Savannah's father had been described by critics and fans alike as cheeky, irreverent, outrageously sexy, irresistible, and brilliant.

Right before his sixth marriage, he'd appeared on the cover of the December *Rolling*

Stone magazine, looking like a biker Peter Pan in a pair of sprayed-on black leather pants, studded vest, and silver-toed cowboy boots. It had been his wedding suit, Savannah had read.

In a masterful bit of cross-promotion, Reggie's new bride, Britta, had had her own centerfold layout the same month in *Playboy*. She'd been dressed—or mostly undressed—in the froths of satin and lace intended for her honeymoon.

"That was *Unholy Matrimony*," the DJ announced after the heavy-metal sound screeched to an end, "the song Townsend ended his Portland concert with last night. According to Portland police, the teens arrested during the short-lived melee have all been released into their parents' custody and there were no serious injuries.

"One baby was reported born during the excitement; her parents, students at OSU, announced that they've named the little girl Regina. We're told that Reggie dropped by the hospital after the concert disguised in scrubs, visited with the family, and had his photograph taken with his namesake."

Savannah smiled at the idea of her father donning surgical scrubs to sneak into a hospital. A perpetual child himself, he'd always liked kids, which, she supposed, was one of the reasons his fans ranged from teenagers who admired his rebellious reputation to older baby boomers who'd grown up with him.

While she had no intention of following in her father's marital footsteps, the one important lesson Reggie had taught Savannah was to follow her dreams, using his own brilliant career as proof that any goal could be accomplished if you only worked hard enough. Cared enough. While work might not be the first thing people thought of when they heard the name Reggie Townsend, Savannah knew he expended vast amounts of his seemingly endless trove of energy on his career.

A ticket to one of his live concerts was not inexpensive, but even his most vocal critics couldn't say that his fans didn't get their money's worth.

Even though she was accustomed to sharing her larger-than-life father with his adoring fans, Savannah was not ready for the crowd that had gathered in front of her grandmother's house.

They were uniformly clad in black Dark Dreams—The Danger Tour T-shirts. Reggie's road crew traveled with hundreds, perhaps thousands of these shirts, which he'd throw into the crowds during performances.

She parked behind a stretch limo that looked as if it could easily house a family of ten.

The crowd, for some reason that escaped her, began screaming when she got out of her car. Savannah was never as glad to see Dan as she was when his Tahoe pulled up behind her and he and John shepherded her past the fans.

"Can you believe this?" Raine greeted her sister with a hug as Dan practically shoved her in the front door and closed and locked it behind them. "I used to wish my father would at least want to meet me. I even had a fantasy of us someday practicing law together. Whenever

Reggie shows up, I remember that sometimes *not* having a father can be a good thing."

Savannah grinned. "Dad may be a bit over the top—"

"A bit?"

"Okay. He's Rock's Bad Boy. But he can be a lot of fun. In small doses."

She recalled a wonderful trip to New York when she'd been twelve. He'd taken her to a grown-up lunch at the Plaza's Pool Room, a matinee of *Cats*, and afterwards a Knicks game. Savannah wasn't much of a basketball fan, but she had been excited about being with her father, even if they were constantly interrupted by autograph seekers. And to top off a perfect day, the Knicks had won in overtime.

Of course, afterwards, while she'd been upstairs sleeping in their gilded suite, Reggie had gotten busted by security for frolicking in the Pulitzer fountain outside the hotel with two of the Knicks cheerleaders.

"Is that my luv?" the signature deep, gravelly voice called out from the living room. "Come in here and give your old man a kiss."

She hugged the man dressed in black jeans and a ribbed black shirt that hugged a washboard stomach she knew came from working out on the tour bus. "What a surprise."

"We just did a gig in Portland last night, and since we were so close, we wanted to come see how Ida's doing."

Savannah could remember a lot of things

Reggie had said about Ida over the years, none of them flattering.

He laughed at her openly skeptical look. "I know I wasn't exactly head of your grandmother's fan club. But I've always admired her spunk. Besides, it's time you met your new stepmother. She was a little nervous about crashing a family party, but I told her that it wasn't right for her to be eating her first American Thanksgiving dinner in a restaurant. Not when the best chef in the country, who just happens to be my own daughter, is doing the cooking."

As he introduced the tall blond woman towering over him, Savannah fully understood the term *supermodel*. Britta Townsend was a good six inches taller than her husband, even before you added the platform sneakers. The canary yellow diamond ring on her left hand was Texas size. Having never quite gotten over the poverty of his youth, Reggie liked surrounding himself with the trappings of wealth.

They definitely had a full house. Not only had the entire family gathered for the holiday dinner, along with Henry and Martha, but as soon as Lilith had discovered that Kathi Montgomery was going to spend Thanksgiving alone, she'd insisted Ida's speech therapist join them as well.

Amy was sitting on the living room floor beside Ida's wheelchair. They were watching the Macy's parade—a departure from *Sesame Street*, which Savannah's grandmother watched every morning, afternoon, and evening. Kathi had explained that since the stroke had wiped out the

part of Ida's brain that knew how to turn letters
into words, she'd have to relearn her alphabet.
With that end in mind, Kathi had recorded
hours of the PBS program.

The parade segued to a football game, which
had Savannah wishing for Big Bird. There was a
bit of muttering when she turned the television
off during the third quarter for dinner, but she
ignored it and soon everyone had squeezed into
the dining room, which John had decorated
with copper and gold mums and garlands of autumn leaves.

Conversation flowed easily. Savannah was a
little surprised by Reggie's new wife. She may
be young enough to be his daughter, yet she
seemed far more self-possessed than most people of her years, which Savannah thought may
be due to the fact that she'd gotten her first
modeling job—for a disposable diaper company—when she'd been six months old.

"I fell in love with Britta when she showed
up at the studio to star in one of my videos,"
Reggie announced with a cocky grin toward the
blond who, even seated, towered over him.
"Asked her to marry me that first day."

"Now why doesn't that surprise me?" Lilith
murmured.

"I've always been impulsive," he agreed easily.
"But this is different. Britta keeps me in line."

"Really?" Lilith skimmed her gaze over the
tight jeans and sweater. "Where on earth do you
hide your whip and your chair in that outfit,
dear?"

Britta looked a bit confused by the question, but Reggie just laughed. "She has her own ways of persuasion, luv. My darlin' wife's into positive reinforcement."

"Well, I'm truly happy for you," Lilith said, sounding as if she meant it.

"I'm happy for me, too. I'm even happy for you, Lilith, luv." Reggie grinned over at Cooper. "You've got yourself a fine woman, Coop, old man. Just practice your ducking skills. Lilith has lethal aim with the Waterford."

"Cooper doesn't give me any reason to throw vases at him," Lilith said with a toss of her head.

"Good for him. Man must have the patience of Job, since you're not exactly the easiest of women to get along with, luv."

"I've been thinking about something," Savannah said quickly as temper flared in Lilith's eyes.

"What's that?" Raine asked just as quickly, obviously appreciating her sister's sidetracking what could well be the beginning of World War III.

"You know how difficult it was, running back and forth between the hospital and work—not that we minded, of course, Gram."

Ida, sitting at the end of the long table in her wheelchair, just waved Savannah's words away with an impatient hand. "Go on," she said.

Savannah was suddenly a little nervous at the way everyone at the table was looking at her so expectantly, waiting to hear what had seemed like a good idea while she was driving back to the lighthouse last night after stopping by the house to have supper with her grandmother and watch a tribute to the letter *E*.

She'd been planning to discuss it with Dan, after she'd finished making the pies, but then he'd started kissing her and she'd decided the subject could wait until the entire family was gathered together today.

"I was talking to these people I met in the cafeteria, the Simpsons—"

"They're that nice couple from outside Forks," Raine remembered.

"Doesn't Mr. Simpson own a hardware store?" Lilith asked. "And they both work in it?"

"That's them. Mrs. Simpson's mother's was an oncology patient, in the late stages of lung cancer. They were telling me how difficult it was to afford a motel room every time she had to be hospitalized. This last bout, the nurses managed to find a bed for Mrs. Simpson, but whenever her husband visited, he had to sleep on either the floor or the waiting room couch."

"I saw him there one night." Lilith frowned. "Poor man looked exhausted. I was almost wishing I could just take him home with me."

"That's my idea." Savannah smiled, pleased that someone else had thought the same thing. Of course, that someone was Lilith, who'd never been known for her practicality. "That's what I want to do."

"Bring more people into this house?" Raine asked.

"No, of course not," Savannah said, shooting a reassuring gaze at Ida who'd furrowed her brow. Her grandmother had always been a generous person, but there were limits. Especially these days. "But *I* have the room."

"Which you intend to use for a bed-and-breakfast after the new year," Lilith reminded her.

"I'm still going to do that. But *I'm* living in the lighthouse and the keeper's house has a lot of bedrooms, since it was designed for a large family. . . ." Her voice dropped off as she recalled the reason Lucy's house hadn't been filled with children.

"It's okay," Henry said gruffly. "It's no secret how my mother died. I'm just glad to know my folks had some good years." Savannah had given him the journals and was pleased when they seemed to have brought him some comfort.

"My point is that in the event all the rooms in the keeper's cottage get booked, and I go ahead with my plan of adding a dinner menu, as well, I'll probably have about as much business as I can handle without having to hire more people, which I don't really want to do at this point. And that makes the assistant keeper's house superfluous."

"But it was going to be the honeymoon cottage," Lilith said.

"It would have made a lovely one," Savannah agreed. "But it should also make a lovely cottage for out-of-town guests whose families are stuck in the hospital."

"Are you thinking along the lines of the Ronald McDonald houses?" Dan asked.

"Exactly." Dan's ability to understand precisely

what she was thinking may have made her a little uneasy in the beginning, but she'd come to be pleased at how easy it was to share ideas with him. "Since the whole idea is to give the families someplace to relax and get away from the hospital atmosphere without putting themselves in debt with motel bills, I'd want them to be able to stay free. Unfortunately, even with your generosity in agreeing to carry back some of the mortgage, Henry," she said with a smile his way, "I can't afford to just give the cottage away."

"You'll need to set up a nonprofit foundation," Dan said.

"I was hoping you and Raine could take care of that."

He exchanged a look across the table with Savannah's sister, who nodded thoughtfully. "Sure. The paperwork won't be difficult to set up at all. But you're still going to need some funds to administer."

"I had a thought about that, too." Savannah turned to her mother. "I was hoping perhaps we could have a film festival of all your old slasher movies at the Orca Theater."

"Really?" Lilith's smile flashed like a newborn star. "Do you think anyone would actually want to come to a Lilith Lindstrom film festival?"

"False modesty doesn't suit you, luv," Reggie said. "Your films have reached cult status. I'll bet you'd fill all the ferries in Seattle with fans flocking to see them. Especially when they found out we were going to get together on stage for old times' sake."

"You?" Savannah stared at him. "Are you talking about giving a benefit concert?"

Reggie's grin was as bright as his former wife's. "Now, you didn't think I was going to let your mother have all the fun?"

Tears of gratitude and love burned at the back of her lids. Savannah couldn't recall the last time her mother and father had been together in a room without vases and curses flying, and she thought back to what Raine had suggested about every breath stirring the universe.

Their grandmother's stroke had been a terrible thing. Yet it hadn't happened in a vacuum. Henry had definitely become more thoughtful; Coldwater Cove had lived up to its slogan as The Friendliest Town on the Peninsula; thanks to her parents' cooperation, families with ill loved ones would be helped; and wonder of wonders, Lilith and Reggie actually seemed to be burying old hatchets. And not in each other.

That made Savannah wonder if perhaps the Buddhists might just be on to something, after all.

22

After the last touchdown had been scored and pie served, after Ida had ridden her glider upstairs for her evening nap and a drowsy Amy had been tucked into the same bed her mother had once slept in, Reggie took Dan aside and suggested they go out on to the back porch where they could have a little private chat.

The evening was cool but clear. A few resolute fans still waited in front of the house for Reggie's departure, but so far there'd been no problems. Dan suspected that one reason for their good behavior was Jack's Olympic County Sheriff's Department Suburban parked in Ida's driveway.

Reggie pulled a gold case from one of the zippered pockets of his metal-studded black leather jacket, offered a cigarette to Dan, who refused, then lit one for himself.

"Britta doesn't like me to smoke," he revealed

conversationally on a plume of blue smoke. "She's a health fanatic."

If tobacco was the only thing Reggie was smoking these days, Dan figured Britta may already have moderated her husband's behavior.

Reggie tugged on an earlobe, where a diamond stud glittered in the moonlight. "So, what are your intentions concerning my baby girl?"

"I like a man who comes straight to the point," Dan murmured.

"There's not much I haven't done, some of it I've regretted, most I haven't. But every so often, I actually learn from my mistakes," Reggie said. "Not saying anything when Savannah showed up in London with her new husband is one of the few I regret."

"She was already married. What could you have done, realistically?"

"What I should have done. Ripped out the bugger's heart and had one of my roadies toss him into the Thames."

From the dangerous edge to his tone, Dan had the feeling that Reggie wasn't kidding. Or exaggerating.

"That sounds like a warning."

"You're a perceptive bloke. I'll give you that."

"I'm also in love with your daughter."

"Loving Savannah's not hard to do." The tip of the cigarette glowed red as he inhaled. "It's what you're planning to do about it that interests me."

Dan knew he could end this conversation by telling Reggie that his relationship with Savannah was none of his business. Especially, since from what Dan had heard, Reggie had never been in the running for Father of the Year. But having been thinking a lot about family and children lately, he could understand Savannah's father's concern. He could also understand Jack's often stated desire to lock Amy in a convent closet until she turned thirty.

"I'm going to marry her."

"Does she know this?"

"I haven't said anything, but I suspect she's picked up on the signs. I'm also not certain she's real thrilled with the idea. Yet."

"Wouldn't think she would be," Reggie agreed as he looked out into the deep shadows of evergreens at the edge of the yard. "Her mum and I didn't set a real good example."

Dan wasn't about to argue with that.

"Never met anyone who could drive in a point like a barrister, though. Most of them are stubborn blokes." He slanted Dan a look. "Guess you are, too."

"When it's something—someone—I want."

"And you want my Savannah."

"Absolutely. Forever." The idea had admittedly come as a surprise. The more Dan had thought about it these past months, the more he couldn't imagine how he'd ever thought of a future without Savannah in it.

"Now there's an idea," Reggie murmured. "I envy a man who can feel that commitment for one woman. You might be almost good enough for Savannah. . . .

"I wasn't the best dad," he volunteered, proving again that Reggie Townsend also had a major talent for understatement. "But I like the idea of being a grandfather."

The wide grin that had graced the cover of *Rolling Stone* innumerable times over the past three decades flashed brilliantly in the spreading yellow glow of the porch light.

"I'll get the little nipper a set of drums. He can come on the road with his old gramps during school holidays. Another generation of Townsends makin' his mark."

"Another generation of O'Hallorans," Dan corrected mildly as he imagined a miniature Reggie, clad in black leather, hammering away at a snare drum in the living room. When the mental image made him smile instead of cringe, Dan decided that just went to show how flat-out nuts he was about Savannah.

"What were you and Reggie talking about earlier?"

They were at the lighthouse, in the lantern room Savannah had turned into a bedroom, sprawled in the lacy white iron fairy-tale bed she'd found at an estate sale in Gray's Harbor. She was playing with his hair while Dan nuzzled his face between her breasts.

"Just guy stuff." He frowned as he viewed the bruise, touched his lips against marred, fragrant flesh. "I was too rough with you."

She lifted her head from the pillow and looked down at the bluish brand. "You could never be too rough. Besides, it was mutual."

Her smile reminded him of a satisfied Siamese as she skimmed her fingertips over his cooling skin. "Wait until you see your back."

Ruled by the ravenous hunger that had been building all day during the family Thanksgiving dinner, they'd fallen on each other the moment they'd entered the lighthouse, hands bruising, mouths feasting, hearts pounding. He'd taken her like a conqueror; she'd ridden him like a witch.

They'd left clothes scattered across the floor, and he was going to have to go shopping to replace the skimpy scarlet-as-sin silk and lace that she'd been wearing beneath her sweater and that was now lying torn somewhere on the stairs.

The idea of wandering around like a bull elk lost in a frou-frou potpourri-scented lingerie shop wasn't exactly his idea of a fun time. Maybe he could just make a quick sweep through the place, buy one of everything, then bring the haul back here for her to try on. Dan imagined Savannah putting on a private fashion show for him right here in the lantern room. Now that would be a great time.

"What kind of guy stuff?" she asked.

His lips moved lazily, lingeringly down her torso. "You know. Football—"

"Reggie doesn't believe Americans play football," she reminded him.

"Basketball, then. Baseball. Fishing."

"I cannot imagine my father drowning nightcrawlers."

He felt her chuckle against his mouth as he

tasted his way down her stomach. "Okay. We mostly talked about you."

"I was afraid of that." She sighed. "When he called last month, I made the mistake of mentioning your name. Just in passing, but he latched onto it and started drilling me like he was some Victorian earl determined to keep his daughter chaste until he could marry her off."

"I think that's undoubtedly a universal feeling among fathers of daughters."

"I hope he didn't come on too strong."

"Nah. He just wanted to be certain that I was planning to make an honest woman of you."

"What?" She bucked as he dipped his tongue into her navel.

"We got along like gangbusters once I assured him that I'm not just amusing myself with your luscious body. That I intend to marry you."

Dan had decided, somewhere between the pumpkin pie and ripping her clothes off, that there was no point in wasting any more time. The lighthouse was nearly ready for its grand opening, Ida was recovering by leaps and bounds, and except for the new little detail of the charitable foundation Savannah wanted to establish, which should be a snap to set up, there really wasn't anything keeping them from making this arrangement permanent.

"Marry?" A chill raced over her skin. She stiffened beneath him.

"I guess that wasn't tonight's secret word." He sighed heavily as she pulled away. "You can't

tell me that it comes as a surprise, Savannah.
I've been up front all along about how I feel."

"I knew you wanted me."

"Wanting's easy. I want my bank statement to
balance, a cold beer when I'm fishing, and to
decimate my opponent in court.

"I *love* you." In contrast to his earlier passion-
driven caresses, he trailed a feather-light touch
over her breast. Splayed his fingers over her heart.

"Maybe you just love the sex."

"There's no maybe about it. I'm wild about
the sex. It's world class, triple-A blow-your-
brains-out sex, and if we could figure out a way
to bottle it, we'd make a fortune.

"However, whatever crazy ideas you might
have picked up from the weasel, great sex and
marriage are not necessarily an oxymoron."

Dan knew things were going downhill when
she pushed away his hand and pulled the rumpled sheet that carried the scent of their lovemaking up over her bare breasts, nearly to her chin.

"Know that from personal experience with
Amanda, do you?"

"No." He heard the edge to her tone and assured himself that a jealous woman was not an
indifferent one. "I know that from personal experience with *you*. With us together. If you
weren't so focused on the past, you'd realize
that you know it, too."

An anger born of frustration began to claw at
him; Dan ruthlessly banked it. "What we've got
going here isn't any short-term, no-strings, convenient affair that satisfies a temporary physi-

cal itch. I'm still going to want to rip your clothes off when I'm ninety. I'm still going to get hard as a boulder when I think about doing this."

He caught her chin between his fingers and kissed her, hard and deep and long until he'd drawn a ragged moan from her throat.

"And this." She was already going lax, her bones turning to water as he reached beneath the sheet with his other hand and stabbed his fingers into her. Her hips moved with him, the hot, slick moisture making a sucking sound as he unrelentingly drove her to yet another shuddering climax.

"Tell me you won't still want me sixty years from now, Savannah. Try telling me that you won't want me to want you."

"You know I can't tell you that." Her swollen, ravished lips trembled. "Of course I want you. I need you. But I don't *want* to need you, damn it."

It was the despair in her voice that slashed at him. Made him back away when he knew that if he pressed his case, he could win. But at what cost?

"I know you don't." He ran a hand down her tousled hair, feeling as if she'd taken a dagger to his heart when she visibly flinched. "But we can deal with it. Together."

"I have to deal with it on my own." Her eyes glistened, but her mouth had firmed. Along with, he sensed, her resolve. "I have to be clear, in my own mind, that I'm not just using you."

"Darlin', you're welcome to use me any time your sweet little heart desires."

His attempt at humor fell as flat as a heavy stone thrown into the cove. "This isn't funny."

"On that we agree." He reluctantly pushed himself out of her bed. "Not that I want to put any pressure on you, but how much longer do you think this journey of self-discovery might take?"

"I don't know." She was looking down at the sheet she was smoothing with nervous hands. "If we could just keep things the way they are, perhaps—"

"Nope. That's not an option."

"Why not? We're doing so well. Why risk ruining what we have?"

He'd watched the color drain from her face, turning her complexion as white as the cold sickle of moon hanging in the sky outside the windows. Then he admired the way she gathered up the composure that had momentarily scattered.

Her back stiffened; he resisted, just barely, the urge to stroke it. Part of him wanted to shake her, to make her see what was so clear to him; another, stronger part wanted to kiss her silly.

"I've reached a point in my life where I'm not all that interested in an affair. There's just no challenge in it. It's too easy to find someone to sleep with you, someone who doesn't want to hang around and try to make morning conversation afterwards when all you really have in common is lust.

"I want the whole ball of wax. And I want it

with you. Marriage, kids, even some furry mutt that'll chew up our shoes and dig up all John's carefully planted tulip bulbs. How about a golden retriever? They seem sort of like a family-type dog, don't you think?"

She blew out a breath. "I think you've gone crazy."

"Crazy about you," he said agreeably. Since the warm, fuzzy mental family image was pleasing him when their discussion was not, he decided to concentrate on it as he yanked on the briefs that had been dropped on the floor halfway between the door and the bed.

"I can't be a mother right now. I have a career."

"So does Terri Stevenson," he reminded her. "And Raine. But I understand that a new enterprise takes more time. So, I'm willing to wait a while for the kids."

"Crazy," she muttered because she couldn't argue against the two examples of working mothers he'd presented.

He tried again. "I can understand how, after all the storms you survived growing up, you'd be tempted to find a nice, pretty little harbor, drop anchor, and stay safe and sound. But sometimes those harbors aren't as safe or pretty as you might originally believe.

"Change is always a little scary, Savannah. But it's also good. Dumping the weasel and escaping your bad marriage was good. Moving home was very good. What you've done with this place is spectacularly good.

"And, at the risk of sounding immodest,

falling in love with me was one of the best and smartest changes you've ever made."

"I don't . . ." She slammed her mouth shut before the lie could come out.

The fact that she couldn't tell him that she didn't love him was enough, Dan decided. For now. He'd let her stew for a while, then he'd marry her.

"Tell you what, why don't you spend some time thinking the situation over and give me a call when you've made up your mind."

"Give you a call?" A temper she didn't show often snapped in her eyes.

"You said you wanted to sort things out on your own. So, I'll just leave and give you the space you need." He could tell this was not what she'd expected.

"Jack gave Raine all the time she needed to make up *her* mind," she reminded him on a flare of frustrated heat he enjoyed a helluva lot more than her earlier chill.

"I'm not Jack," he reminded her back. "Besides, their situation was different. She had to choose between Coldwater Cove and New York and the clock was ticking. Right now, where we're concerned, you're anchored in that safe little harbor bobbing contentedly on calm waters. There's nothing to prevent you from toying with my affections until doomsday."

"Toying with your affections?" She dragged her hands through her hair. The frustrated gesture caused her breasts to bounce in a way that had him almost reconsidering this strategy. The trouble with ultimatums was that they didn't leave you a lot of wiggle room.

"Hey, contrary to popular belief, we guys have feelings, too."

He scooped his shirt from the lacy iron pillar of the bed. "Let me know when you've made up your mind."

Dan dropped a kiss on her tightly set lips, flashed her the boyish grin that had, over the years, worked on females of all ages. Then, though it was one of the hardest things he'd ever done in his life, nearly as hard as coming home to bury his sister and claim her son, Dan walked out of the lantern room, leaving Savannah alone in bed.

With his resolve hanging by a thread, he did not allow himself to look back.

Savannah hadn't really believed Dan. Oh, she knew he loved her. But she didn't really believe that he intended to break things off entirely. Until he disappeared.

"I can't believe he didn't tell you where he was going," she complained to Raine. They were in their grandmother's kitchen drinking tea. Martha had taken the ferry to Seattle to do some Christmas shopping, so they'd spent the morning taking turns reading to Ida.

She'd always loved murder mysteries, the bloodier the better. She might not be able to tackle them herself quite yet, but Kathi, who Savannah had decided was an angel masquerading as a speech therapist, had predicted it would be only a few more weeks.

"I'm truly sorry," Raine said. "But he refused to tell me."

"He must have told Jack where he was going, since John's staying with you. What if something happened to him?"

"Jack probably does know. But he's not talking. You know how those O'Hallorans stick together."

"It's emotional blackmail," Savannah muttered darkly.

"Is it working?"

"Of course it is. Which is ironic, since he told me that he was leaving to let me make up my own mind." Savannah glared into her teacup as if she could read the answer to her dilemma in the swirl of black leaves at the bottom. "As if he isn't trying to manipulate things with this Houdini act. I'm surprised he hasn't rented one of those planes that make smoke messages to fly over town and write 'Surrender Savannah' in the sky."

"I used to think of marriage as a form of surrender, too," Raine revealed. "I spent so many years working hard for my independence, if I hadn't been so madly in love, I might have ended up resenting any man who'd ask me to give it up. But Jack never asked."

"Neither has Dan," Savannah admitted.

"I wouldn't think he would. He's confident enough that a strong woman isn't going to intimidate him, or prick his male ego."

"Do you think I'm too complacent?" she asked.

Raine didn't immediately respond. "I believe," she said, choosing her words carefully, "that we both developed our own defense mechanisms. Our coping skills. My instinct is to fight like a tiger when I feel threatened."

"While I dive for the foxhole," Savannah said with self-disgust.

"You're being too hard on yourself. You've just always preferred to find a compromise."

"I compromised in my marriage, and look how that turned out." She threw up her hands. "Don't say it. I know. There's no comparison between Dan and Kevin."

"From what I can tell, sitting on the sidelines, Dan has never asked you to compromise yourself or your dreams or goals. All he wants is for you to love him, the way he loves you."

"I do."

"Then surely you, of all people, can find a compromise between your desire for autonomy and his desire to spend the rest of his life with you."

Raine leaned forward and covered Savannah's hand with hers. Her woven gold wedding band gleamed like a promise in the light from the copper lamp that hung over the table.

"While you're making your decision, you might want to keep in mind that since my marriage, my life is fuller than I ever could have imagined possible."

"You're lucky."

"Blessed," Raine corrected with a slow smile. "I suspect you could have that with Dan."

Savannah absorbed Raine's statement. "It's not that easy."

Raine sighed. Her eyes filled with sympathy. "I wonder if it ever is."

He'd made his point.

By the time he'd been gone a week, Savannah couldn't think. How was she supposed to think about booking reservations and what flowers to put in what room when all she could do was wonder where the hell he was? And if he was thinking about her.

She couldn't eat. The rest of the family had jumped at the chance to try out possible menu items and assured her that her praline butter Belgian waffles were a gastronomical delight and her braided blueberry loaf topped with vanilla icing was a taste of paradise. But she could have been eating dried ashes. Her own taste of frustration spiced with regret was too strong.

Worst of all, she couldn't sleep. The lacy white iron Victorian wonder of a bed, which she'd fallen in love with at first sight, the bed that she'd actually seen in her dreams since childhood, now seemed to be as wide and desolate as the Sahara Desert.

She didn't need him. Not really, she told herself over and over again. She was a strong woman with her own budding career and a loving, supportive family. She didn't need a man to make her feel complete. She didn't need him to make her world complete. The little corner of the universe she'd created for herself was still safe. Still secure. And lonely.

23

"Savannah?"

Savannah glanced up from the computer, which she'd been using to pay bills, and saw John standing in the doorway.

"Hi." She was tempted, as she had been each day this past week, to ask him if he knew where his uncle was. But knowing how it felt to have your openness taken advantage of, she'd managed to restrain herself. "I'm glad you're here. I couldn't believe it when I came home last night and saw all the greenery you'd hung. I wanted to thank you for all the trouble you obviously went to."

"I'm glad you like it. The boughs in the lantern room were Uncle Dan's idea."

"Well. Isn't that nice." She wondered if he'd mentioned it to John before leaving, or if the two of them had been in contact.

She had to stop this, Savannah instructed

herself. She was not going to let him make her
crazy.

"I was just putting the poinsettias from the
greenhouse in all the rooms, like you asked,
and I thought you might want me to take a couple over to your grandmother."

"That's a wonderful idea." She shut down the
computer. "Give me two minutes to button
things up here and I'll drive you."

"You don't have to do that. It's a nice day and
I've got the baskets on the back of my bike."

Savannah looked out the windows at the
clouds stippled with the last light of the day.
"It'll be getting dark soon."

"I've got a bike light. Uncle Dan lets me ride
at night," he reminded her. "As long as it isn't
raining and the streets aren't slick."

Just because his heart was as open as a
child's was no reason to treat him like one. He
was, she reminded herself, on the Special
Olympics bicycle team. Still, she worried.

"Ida loves poinsettias. Why don't I drive by in
a while and pick you up so you don't have to
ride all the way to the farm?"

"I'm not going to the farm tonight."

Okay. She had to ask. "You're not?"

"No. Uncle Dan called Jack. He's coming
back home tonight because he has to be in
court in the morning."

"I see." So how long would he have stayed
away if he hadn't had a court case scheduled,
she wondered.

"Oh. I forgot something." He reached into an

inside pocket of his parka and pulled out a small book she recognized right away. It was another of Lucy's journals.

"Where did you find it?"

"I was putting the wheelbarrow away in the crawlspace and I had to move some stuff to fit it in."

While she didn't spend any more time than necessary down there, she'd inspected the crawlspace when she'd bought the property. It ran nearly the entire length of the keeper's house, had a packed dirt floor and a ceiling about six feet high, which made it large enough to use for outdoor storage.

"There was this old, rusted box beneath a broken wagon wheel," he revealed. "The book was inside it."

When he handed it to her, a spark of electricity arced from his fingers to hers. Savannah told herself that it was only static electricity. And that was strange, because they were both wearing sneakers planted firmly on the wood floor. Seeming not to notice, John wished her a nice evening, then left.

Savannah stood at the window and watched him pedal away with a cardboard box in each of the wire baskets on either side of his rear wheel. She looked out toward Dan's house and wondered if he was home yet.

Then she shook her head with self-disgust, sat down on the Victorian lady's fainting couch she'd had recovered, and studied the embossed leather cover of the journal. There'd been a time when she would have tried to convince herself that she was only imagining the warmth emanating from the slender volume. But there had been enough odd moments that defined explanation to convince Savannah that the stories were true. Lucy's spirit did live on in this lighthouse.

She opened to the first page and began to read.

The letter came by mail packet this morning. I was, at the same time, both shocked and saddened to learn that Hannah, of all people, could have been hiding such a secret for so long. To think that her husband would have taken to beating her these past years that I've been away is unimaginable. I do remember his temper, on those occasions when he'd overindulge in liquor, as being exceedingly hot. But it always flared out quickly, and afterwards, while a palpable tension might linger for a time, outwardly things returned to normal and such lapses were never spoken of. At least within my hearing.

I'd always believed such strains and occasional storms were part of being married. Now, of course, after nearly seven years with Harlan, I know differently. My husband is as incredibly passionate as I'd always dreamed. Indeed, I believe my darling Henry was conceived that first time we made love, on our wedding night here at the Far Harbor lighthouse.

Yet he's also a gentle man. A caring man. Having watched the way he shows his love for our son, I can as easily picture him holding this new child I'm carrying beneath my heart as I can imagine him rowing his dory out into storm-tossed seas to rescue some poor sailor who's fallen overboard.

One thing Harlan did not exaggerate was this piece of water's reputation as a "ship killer." I could not count the number of ships that have nearly wrecked on the rocks below the cliff and shudder to think what might have happened if this light, and Harlan, had not been here.

I do find myself on the horns of a dilemma. Hannah writes that she ran out of her escape funds upon reaching San Francisco. My first thought was to send her the necessary money immediately, but she then writes, in a hand so shaky that she could not be exaggerating, that she's taken ill. If I don't come to rescue her, she and the children could well be thrown out in the street.

I know I should discuss this with my husband, but Harlan is in Portland, receiving training on new shipwreck rescue techniques, and I don't expect him back for another five days. The schedule he keeps in his desk reveals that the Annabelle Lee is sailing out of Seattle tomorrow morning.

After much thought, I've decided to leave Henry in the care of the assistant lighthouse keeper's wife, take the ferry to Seattle, and book passage to San Francisco. Clouds are gathering in the western sky, which disturbs me since I've never been a good sailor. But Harlan, who points out the new ships as they pass our lighthouse, has told me the Annabelle Lee *is one of the most stable ships in the passenger fleet. I only hope that turns out to be true, since I won't be much help to my sister if I arrive in San Francisco as ill as she.*

I plan to write Harlan a letter explaining my unexpected departure. Then I will find hiding places for my journals. As much as I love my sister, I have never welcomed her unfortunate habit of invading my privacy in her apparent need to know the most minuscule details of my life. Now that I know the secret life she's been forced to live, I suppose I can understand her need for control.

There is little I would not do for my older sister. But I refuse to share the intimate secrets of my love for Harlan, and his for me. That is not only secret, it is sacred.

As she closed the journal, Savannah once again compared her situation to Lucy's. Both had left behind a former life to come to Coldwater Cove. Both women had found the lighthouse a source of comfort and fulfillment. Both had found men they loved. Men who loved them. Men who wanted to have families with them.

The difference was that Lucy had been brave enough to risk everything for Harlan Hyatt. Tragically, their time together had been cut short, but the journal entries assured Savannah that even if Lucy had been able to look into a crystal ball and see what lay in store for them, she still would have chosen those seven happy years over a life without him.

"This is what you wanted me to know, isn't it, Lucy?" Savannah murmured into the silence. "You weren't running away. You didn't desert your husband and son."

She felt a zephyr waft over her, stirring her hair. That was, of course, impossible, since it was December, and no windows were open.

Savannah reminded herself that the lighthouse was a hundred years old. It was bound to be drafty.

She almost had herself believing that logical explanation—until the electric candles she'd placed in the windows suddenly turned on.

A week after he'd left Savannah in bed at the lighthouse, Dan walked into his cousin's office.

"Hey, the prodigal returns." Jack was sitting back in his chair, his feet up on the scarred desk that had belonged to his father, working his way through one of Oley's Timberburgers with all the trimmings and an order of French fries.

"I've got a court date tomorrow." Dan snagged a fry and sat down on the other side of the desk. "Kathi Montgomery's divorce."

"How's she doing?" Jack shoved half the burger on its yellow waxed-paper wrapper across the desk.

"A lot better." Dan bit into the juicy flame-broiled burger. "As you know, she's gone back to work—"

"Yeah, Raine says Ida gets better every day."

"That's undoubtedly partly due to Ida's un-sinkable spirit," Dan allowed. "Anyway, Kathi's moved out of the shelter into an apartment, and by this time tomorrow she should be a free woman."

"I'm a little surprised her husband hasn't caused any more problems."

Me, too. Maybe the idea that he can't keep her married to him by force finally sank in."

"Maybe." Jack didn't sound as hopeful. Then again, Dan considered, if he had spent all those years as a big-city cop, he'd probably expect domestic violence cases to go from bad to worse, too.

He leaned over the desk to grab some more fries and was amused by the title of the book next to Jack's boots: *Everything the Expectant Father Should Know, But Is Afraid to Ask.*

"How does it feel to be facing fatherhood for the second time?"

"Terrific." Jack took a drink of root beer. "And terrifying. I'd also forgotten that pregnant women tend to go insane from time to time.

Raine actually cried at a tire commercial last night. You know, the one with the babies?"

"That sounds a bit extreme. But she seems pretty sane at the office. Or at least she was when I left."

Jack mumbled something around a mouthful of fries that Dan couldn't quite make out.

"Besides, it could be worse," he suggested. *"You* could be pregnant."

"That's what Raine keeps reminding me. She also suggested that it's easy for me to stay calm since I'm not the one who's going to have to pass something the size of a basketball through a small opening in my body."

Dan grimaced. "Good point."

"She's also got me reading all these damn books." He nudged the thick book with the toe of his boot.

"Never hurts to be informed."

"Yeah. But you know Raine when she sets her mind to something." He took another noisy slurp of root beer. "Christ, I keep expecting to come home to a pop quiz."

"Sorry pal, you're not going to get any sympathy from me."

During the week he'd forced himself to stay away, far from temptation at his cousin Caine's fishing cabin in British Columbia, Dan had not stopped thinking about Savannah. One of the more appealing fantasies, after the hot sex ones that had him waking up as horny as a two-peckered billy goat, was the image of her ripe and round with his child.

"You're damn lucky."

"I know." Jack glanced over at the framed photograph of his wife and daughter. "I could put up with the tears and the stacks of books she keeps bringing home. I could even handle the Mexican food we've been having every night for dinner for the past two weeks because she has a craving for hot sauce. But you want to know the kicker?"

"I'm not sure."

"You may have noticed that the Boob Fairy has paid us a visit."

"This may come as a surprise, but I don't spend a lot of time checking out your wife's breasts."

"Well, if you did, you'd have noticed that they're suddenly spectacular. Playmate quality."

"Congratulations," Dan said dryly.

"The trouble is"—Jack plowed his hand through his hair—"I'm not allowed to touch."

Dan laughed at the exasperation on his cousin's face. "That *is* a bummer."

"It's not funny." Jack took a huge bite of burger, as if attempting to crave his sexual hunger with ground beef. "She told me they're for the baby. For Christ's sake, we're talking another five months before the kid's born. . . . Remember back when we were in high school, all we could think about was how to score with a girl?"

"Sure."

"Well, second base has never looked so good."

Dan laughed as the intercom from the outer office buzzed. Still muttering about injustice, Jack scooped up the receiver.

"What's up?" Something hard Dan had never seen before moved across his face. "Goddamn it." It was fury, Dan realized. Ruthlessly, rigidly controlled. "Any word on injuries? What about people inside the house? Did you call it in to the State Police? Okay. I'm on my way. . . . Montgomery just went ape-shit and shot his wife when she came out of Ida's."

Dan shot to his feet. "How is she? Is anyone else hurt?" Had Savannah been at the house? The possibility sent a chill racing through his blood.

"Kathi's still alive, but I don't know her condition. According to Gwen, who called it in, the bastard was hiding in the bushes, shot her once, then took off. The family's shaken but, thank God, safe."

He grabbed his Stetson from its wall hook and was out the office door, Dan right behind him.

"Wait." Iris Johansson held up a hand as they passed her desk. "Another call's coming in. . . . There's been an accident. The subject hit a bicyclist while fleeing the scene of the shooting. . . . The hit-and-run victim is reported to be John Martin."

"What?" Dan spun back toward her.

"Just a minute." She tilted her head, obviously listening to the voice in her headset earphone. Her eyes, as they slid from Jack to Dan, darkened with sympathy. "The suspect is in State Police custody after running off the road on the old highway and hitting a tree. . . . The deputy on the first accident scene is reporting that the victim doesn't show any vital signs."

"Tell him to look harder," Dan shot back.

"The paramedics have arrived at the scene," she continued passing on what was coming into her ear. But the information was directed at Dan's back as he and Jack tore out of the office.

Jack hit the siren before they'd slammed the doors on the Suburban. "Fasten your seat belt," he barked at his cousin. "The one thing we don't need is another O'Halloran landing in the ER."

There'd been a mistake, Dan told himself over and over again as they raced down Harbor street. They had the wrong victim. Or the deputy didn't know how to check for a pulse.

John couldn't die now. Not like this. Not after all he'd already survived in his young life. Dan wouldn't let him.

"He isn't dead, damn it," Dan repeated again and again. His words were half curse, half prayer.

Savannah found Dan pacing the floor of the same small room where they'd all spent too many hours waiting for news of Ida.

"Raine called me." She wrapped her arms around him, held him tight.

"Thank God." He buried his face in her hair. "I need you."

"I need you, too." Strange how those words had ceased to cause that knee-jerk fear. Savannah realized that when your world went spin-

ning out of control, it was a relief—and, as
Raine had pointed out, a blessing—to have
someone to hold on to. "But we can talk about
all that later."

Dan was trembling. It broke her heart. "What
have they told you?" she asked gently.

He took a huge breath and lifted his head so
he could meet her gaze. His handsome face was
haggard and gray. His flat blue eyes had that
thousand-yard stare that a soldier's might acquire after a horrendous battle.

"Not much. The cop couldn't find any vitals,
but the EMTs brought him back on the way,
then lost him again." He dragged in another
gulp of air on a ragged moan. "Since no one's
come in to tell me any different, I'm going to assume he's alive."

"Of course he is." She couldn't imagine otherwise. "You need to sit down." She urged him
toward one of the orange chairs. "Before you
fall down and break that pretty face." She
framed the face, which was anything but pretty
at the moment, between her palms.

"I hate this," he muttered. But as docile as a
lamb, he sank onto the chair.

Savannah sat down beside him, his cold
hand tight between both of hers. "I know."

"Christ. If forcing people to wait for news
was an Olympic sport, this place would win a
goddamn gold medal."

"I know," she repeated. "But as you said, in
this case, no news is probably good news." She
looked up as Jack came into the room. "Hi."

"Hi." His tone was as flat as hers. "They've still got John in the crash room. I managed to get a look at him surrounded by people, but one of the nurses kicked me out before I could get a handle on how he was doing. I was thinking about using my badge to pull rank, then decided that if I hung around, I'd just be in the way."

"That's good news that they're still working on him," Savannah said, her positive tone meant to assure them all. Especially Dan, who was looking like death warmed over himself.

"That's what I figured," Jack said.

Dan merely grunted. Then dragged the hand Savannah wasn't holding down his face.

"Kathi's going to be all right," Jack volunteered into the silence that had settled over the room like thick, dreary winter fog. "Fortunately Montgomery was a lousy shot. There was a lot of blood on the scene, but the wound turned out to be superficial. They're going to keep her overnight, then probably release her in the morning."

"That's something," Dan said. "What about Montgomery?"

"He was thrown out of the car. Broke his neck on impact and was DOA."

Dan nodded, satisfied at least about this. "Good."

No one spoke for another long time. Finally, a nurse appeared in the doorway. Dan jerked when he viewed Mrs. Kellstrom's blood-stained scrubs. Knowing that it was John's blood made

Savannah want to burst into tears. But she was determined to remain strong for Dan.

"The doctor asked that I talk with you, since he's on the way to surgery. He wanted you to know that we've got John stabilized." Her steady brown eyes didn't reveal a thing. "It was touch and go when he first came in. We almost lost him twice, but Dr. Hawthorne refused to let him go. The entire time he was doing CPR, he kept muttering about plastic flowers."

The name, coupled with the mention of plastic flowers, rang a bell. "His mother has Alzheimer's," Savannah said. "John planted a plastic garden for her so she'll always have flowers."

"That's what Dr. Hawthorne said," the nurse agreed. "I wasn't surprised, knowing how good John's been to my Cindy." She smiled encouragingly at Dan. "He's a wonderful boy. He's bound to have built up a lot of credits in heaven."

"Just so long as he doesn't end up there anytime soon," Dan countered. "Why's he going to surgery?"

"Dr. Hawthorne believes his blood pressure crash was due to internal bleeding. John has multisystem injuries—a broken arm and nose and several fractured ribs. There was no sign of it on the x-ray, but the doctors were worried about a torn lung, so we put in a chest tube.

"Since John kept lapsing in and out of consciousness, Dr. Burke was called for a consult, but the CAT scan didn't reveal any brain damage, other than some swelling that's fairly routine in traumas like this."

"Nothing about this is routine."

"Of course it's not to you," Mrs. Kellstrom agreed with Dan's gritty assessment. "Dr. Hawthorne suspects that the internal bleeding may be coming from a ruptured spleen," she continued her report.

"Jesus." Dan turned from gray to green.

"I wish I had better news. But the doctor's an excellent surgeon," she assured them all. "So long as he can stop the bleeding, John's chances of a full recovery are excellent."

She skimmed a professional look over Dan's face, apparently not liking what she saw. "John will probably be in surgery well into the night. Why don't you go home and get some rest and—"

"No." Dan shook his head. "I'm not going anywhere."

"Neither am I," Savannah said.

Jack folded his arms. "Me neither."

The nurse didn't look at all surprised. "I'll have the cafeteria send up three dinner trays."

Savannah suspected that neither Dan nor Jack had any more appetite than she did. But it seemed easier not to argue.

With nothing to do but wait, they hunkered down for the duration.

24

They were still there in the morning when Dr. Hawthorne finally showed up in the waiting room. His scrubs bore dark blood stains, just as Mrs. Kellstrom's had last night. His face and eyes looked weary, but not, Dan determined, defeated.

"It was touch and go for a while," he told them. "But, barring complications, John's going to be fine. We didn't have to remove his spleen, his lungs are fine, and at his age, bones heal fast."

The breath came out of Dan in a slow, relieved whoosh.

"When can I see him?"

"He's in recovery now. Give him some time to come around, then you'll probably be able to visit him in the ICU in"—he glanced at his watch—"about an hour."

"Thank you." Dan could have kissed him, then decided against embarrassing the man who'd literally brought his nephew back from the dead.

"It was my pleasure." The doctor, who looked as if he needed sleep as much as the rest of them, managed a smile. "I owed the kid a huge favor for what he did for my mother. I was grateful for the opportunity to pay him back."

"You sure did that," Dan said. "In spades."

"Well," Jack unfolded himself from the hard plastic chair and stretched. "Now that we've survived this latest crisis, I think I'll go home to my wife and daughter."

"Good idea." He hadn't kissed the doctor, but Dan hugged his cousin. "Thanks for sticking around."

"John's family," Jack said simply, as if that explained everything. Which, Dan thought, it did. "So are you." Jack bent and kissed Savannah's cheek. Then left them alone.

Savannah turned toward Dan. "I missed you."

"I missed you, too."

His eyes were exhausted, but the life, the warmth, was back. So was his color. The stubble of beard was sexy, Savannah decided. Actually, everything about Dan was sexy. That was only one of the many reasons she'd fallen in love with him.

"*You're* the one who went away." Now that things were looking up, Savannah allowed herself a slight sulk about that.

"And thought of you every damn minute. Besides, you're the one who said you needed some time alone," he reminded her. "The one who equated loving me with weakness."

"I was wrong." It irked a little. But she'd get over it. They'd get over it together. "So sue me."

"I'd rather kiss you."

He skimmed his palms over her shoulders, down her arms. When his fingers encircled her wrists she viewed the flash of male satisfaction in his eyes and suspected he'd felt her pulse rate jump.

"I'd rather you kiss me, too."

The kiss was long and sweet and satisfying.

"That was nice." She rubbed her cheek against his roughened jaw.

"I can do better," he promised. "Later."

"I'm going to hold you to it." She tilted her head back and smiled. "Later."

Savannah wanted to tell him all about Lucy, about the journal and the candles, but that could wait. After all, they were going to have a lifetime together.

"My grandmother's always had a saying I've been thinking a lot about lately," she revealed. "Carpe diem. . . . Seize the carp."

He smiled back. "Wise woman, your grandmother."

"I've always thought so. I've also come to realize how there are no guarantees in life. That we can lose the ones we love in the blink of an eye."

"I've noticed the same thing."

"So, in the interest of not wasting any more time, do you still want to marry me?"

His smile widened to that bold, buccaneer's grin Savannah knew would always have the power to thrill her. "Sweetheart, I thought you'd never ask."

The Far Harbor lighthouse stood atop the cliff, looking like a dowager dressed in her best jewels. A rare snow had fallen the night before, spreading a white cloak over the ground that sparkled like diamond-studded velvet in the winter sunshine.

The fragrant evergreen boughs John had draped across the top of the lantern room windows added an even more festive note to this special day.

They'd decided that since Dan's house was larger and had more room for the growing family they planned, they'd live there. Savannah would continue to use the first floor of the lighthouse as her office. They'd also agreed that the lantern room she'd loved from the first would be a perfect romantic hideaway.

Dan had grumbled a bit, but had helped her temporarily move the bed out to allow for the gathering of O'Hallorans and Lindstroms who'd come together to celebrate the forging of another link between the families.

John, his grin broad in his still bruised face, seemed to revel in his role as his uncle's best man. Despite having been released from the hospital only two days earlier, he'd insisted on creating Savannah's bouquet. The arrangement of white roses and holly was more precious to her than emeralds.

Ida had arrived on Henry's arm, leaning on her Christmas gift—a polished wooden cane on which he'd carved the universal symbol of her profession, the coiled snakes of a caduceus.

As she exchanged vows with Dan, Savannah thought how Lucy had pledged the same promise right here in the Far Harbor lighthouse. She hadn't felt the ghost's presence since the day she'd read the last journal entry; she and Dan had decided that, having succeeded in revealing the truth about her death, Lucy's spirit had finally been freed to join with that of her beloved husband's.

Savannah had also been relieved when Doris Anderson, president of the Coldwater Cove historical society, had contacted a fellow history buff in San Francisco who'd unearthed a newspaper article revealing that Hannah had remarried a prosperous local banker. She had more children and lived a long and apparently happy life.

Proving again, Savannah had thought, the power of hope over experience.

The words they'd chosen were simple. Traditional. Timeless.

To love. To honor. To cherish.

When her lips touched Dan's in their first kiss as man and wife, Savannah knew that her heart—and the Far Harbor lighthouse—had led her to exactly where she belonged.

Here, among her family, with the man she would love until the end of forever, Savannah was finally home.

POCKET BOOKS
PROUDLY PRESENTS

BLAZE

JoAnn Ross

Coming soon in paperback
from Pocket Books

Turn the page for a preview of
Blaze. . . .

THE FLAMEMASTER HAD BEEN WATCHING the building for weeks, studying her, learning all her secret quirks. Even in her youth she hadn't been all that attractive, and despite the recent face-lift, the passing of years still showed. She reminded him of a dowager who'd fallen on hard times, then gotten an extreme makeover from a quack plastic surgeon.

A couple approached his vehicle, the woman's stiletto heels clattering on the crumbling cobblestone sidewalk.

The Flamemaster scrunched down in the driver's seat so they wouldn't see him. Not that he was in danger of being discovered; they were so blissfully oblivious to anything or anyone around them, they could have been strolling in the peaceful, moss-draped environs of Admiral's Park on a Sunday morning, rather than risking this industrial waterfront neighborhood.

The man leaned down and murmured a soft something in the woman's ear; she laughed silkily in response.

They paused, staring into each other's eyes, like some love-struck couple in a diamond commercial.

As their lips met and clung, The Flamemaster imagined a formally dressed couple in a gilded hotel room. The man opens a black velvet box, revealing an iceberg-size diamond glittering like ice on black satin. The woman instantly falls to her knees and attacks her companion's zipper.

Two carats or more, the deep voice-over advises as violins soar. And she'll damn well have to.

He chuckled at his little joke.

A purple cloud drifted over the sliver of moon, casting the couple in deep shadow. The only light was from the faint yellow flicker of old-fashioned gas lamps edging the pier. Music drifted from a dinner cruise ship somewhere out on the fog-draped harbor, fading in and out on the soft March air.

The guy's hands lifted her butt; she moaned and twined like a python around him. Just when The Flamemaster was looking forward to them doing it up against the brick wall, they came up for air.

The man tucked his shirt back in. She wiggled her dress, which had crawled nearly to her waist, back down to midthigh. They shared another laugh as they entered the centuries-old pink brick building.

The warehouse, abandoned for decades, had been on the brink of condemnation when some hotshot chef from New York City bought the building for a song and turned the top floor into a members-only harbor-view restaurant and dance club.

Tonight a throng of ultra-hip *Friends* clones with Gucci chips on their shoulders had packed into the loft on the warehouse's eighth floor to celebrate St. Patrick's Day with Guinness, overpriced shots of Jameson Gold, and lethal cocktails with names like the Dirty Mick, the Belfast Bomb, and the Blarney Stone Sour.

Paddy's Pig might be the hottest nightspot in town, but all the money the Yankee had poured into the project hadn't transformed the sow's ear of a building into anything resembling a silk purse.

The trendy pink and green neon lights and the floor-to-ceiling glass windows that had replaced the eroding brick was like dressing a bag lady in a designer gown; it couldn't change the fact that she was still as ugly as homemade sin.

He'd be doing the city a favor by getting rid of it.

Hell, the mayor should present him with a good citizen's award. A medal for beautifying Somersett.

The Flamemaster flipped open his cell phone and keyed in 625.

When he hit Send, the call triggered a remote-control device deep inside the building's wine cellar. There was a burst of white light and a faint popping sound, like a lightbulb bursting.

The retro-eighties heavy metal band rocking the building drowned out the sound. A waiter ran in and pulled a bottle of champagne from its slot. With his station full, and more people jammed into the bar waiting for a table, he'd been on the run all evening.

Which was why he didn't notice the tiny orange flame flickering behind a row of fruit brandies.

The fledgling fire fed lazily, climbing up the wooden wine racks, twining around the studs, licking at the rafters.

Outside, observing from a public parking lot a safe block away, The Flamemaster's pulse picked up a beat.

An orange glow flickered, changing to bluish white as the heat soared.

Bottles began to expand and break, like fireworks over the harbor during Buccaneer Days; missiles of heavy green glass slammed into pine studs that were weeping dark, flammable pitch.

The Flamemaster took his eyes off the building just long enough to glance down at the sweep hand on his watch. It wouldn't be long now.

Expectation rippled up his spine.

The neon-lit walls shattered; deadly shards of window glass rained down like guillotine blades. Debris fell from the smoke-filled sky. A black lacquer table hit the sidewalk, sounding like a rifle retort before shattering into pieces; a trio of chairs followed, their metal frames twisted like pretzels.

Sirens wailed in the distance as a woman, her long hair on fire, her skirt blown up over her face, landed on the sidewalk with a deadly thud, bounced into the gutter, then lay still. Screams rent the night as others followed, tumbling through the gaping hole where the glass walls had once stood, legs pumping wildly, arms windmilling on the way down to the pavement.

A red ladder truck, followed by an engine, had just careened around the corner, emergency lights flashing, air horn blasting, when the explosion ripped through the block.

The Flamemaster's vehicle rocked from side to side as a tidal wave–like force rolled beneath the tires. The night sky brightened, as if lit by a thousand suns. An instant later a dense cloud of acrid black smoke rolled down the street, engulfing everything, including the responding vehicles.

As the rigs' Jake brakes squealed, The Flamemaster drove off in the opposite direction, away from the hell-like conflagration that had turned the warehouse into a pile of stone and twisted metal.

This had definitely gone better than last week's rehearsal, which had been aborted when sprinklers drowned the flames as soon as the temperature hit 165 degrees. (Who'd have guessed a damn strip joint would've been built to code?)

Unfortunately, tonight the firefighters hadn't even arrived at the scene, let alone set up an interior attack line, before the charges he'd so meticulously set throughout the building triggered.

He'd have to work on his timing.

Oh well. The Flamemaster shrugged. Practice makes perfect.

If it was true that the third time was the charm, his next fire would be perfect.

TESS GANNON HAD KNOWN DANIEL MCGEE all of her life. She also intended to spend the rest of her life with him.

If she survived getting married.

"Planning Desert Storm had to have been easier than this," she muttered, as she flipped through the latest stack of magazine articles on theme weddings her mother had insisted she read.

"We could just say the hell with the bells and whistles and caterers and bands and elope," Danny suggested.

Tess didn't need a wedding ring to confirm their love, but her biological clock had begun ticking louder this past year and they were both old-fashioned enough to want to be married when they became parents.

"There's nothing I'd like better."

She frowned at one of the beautifully staged photographs. Would anyone really want a wedding cake made to look like a sandcastle? And wasn't decorating it with real seashells just inviting a guest to break a tooth?

"But I also don't want to break Mom's heart."

Bad enough that she'd followed in her dad's big black boots and become a firefighter against her parents' wishes. After earning a degree in fire and safety engineering technology from Eastern Kentucky University, she'd returned home to South Carolina, promptly aced both the civil service and physical firefighting exams, then fulfilled a lifelong dream of joining the Somersett Fire Department.

Having had a quickie "shotgun" marriage of her own, Mary Gannon had been fantasizing about her only daughter's wedding ceremony since Tess was in the cradle. As much as Tess hated all the hoopla, she didn't have the heart to deprive her mother of that longtime Cinderella dream.

"I thought it was supposed to be the bride's day," Danny said, proving himself to be as clueless as most males when it came to female rites of passage.

"Ha-ha-ha. That just goes to show how much you know about weddings."

Not that she was completely caving in.

Instead of the traditional formally dressed couple, the miniature bride and groom who'd be topping the tiered white wonder of a cake would be wearing firefighting gear, right down to their shiny yellow helmets. Having found the pair on eBay, Tess had opted to wait until the last minute to spring it on her mother.

"I know a helluva lot more than I did six months ago."

And a lot more than he undoubtedly wanted to. "And you've been a wonderful sport."

Better than she'd been. Tess couldn't count the times he'd leaped in to play referee when she and her mother were about to be gored on the horns of a serious disagreement.

And hadn't he addressed half of the two hundred and fifty invitations? Though secretly Tess was a little concerned the post office might not have been able to decode Danny's scrawling handwriting enough to actually deliver them.

Feeling a burst of fondness, she leaned over the table and gave him a quick, friendly kiss. He tasted of coffee and Big Red gum.

"I've gotta run. See you tomorrow morning."

"Just about the time I'm leaving," he said without rancor.

"I know." She sighed. Somersett firefighters worked twenty-four-hour shifts with a day on the job, a day off, a day on, then four days off. Assigned to different stations as they were—with Tess working the A shift and Danny working the C—their individual rotations had them both off at the same time only a handful of days a month.

"I'm going to work on getting my schedule changed," she promised. Right after she decided whether she was going to have the reception band play "I'll Be Your Everything" or the old Nat King Cole standard "Unforgettable" for their first dance as man and wife.

She'd wanted Kenny Chesney's "The Good Stuff,"

but her mother had put her foot down, insisting that it'd be unlucky to have a song about a wife dying for a bride and groom's first dance. With the wedding a mere four days away, she was running out of time.

Suspecting that actually being married was going to be a snap compared to this wedding planning stuff, Tess scooped up her car keys.

"Don't forget, you're supposed to choose the groomsmen's gifts."

He rolled his Bambi-brown eyes and groaned.

Ha! "It's a lot easier to be blasé about decisions when you're not the one stuck with making them, isn't it?"

So far just about the only thing her mother had made Danny do was select the groom's cake. Having already figured out it was easier to go with the flow, he'd instantly accepted his future mother-in-law's suggestion of chocolate. Then had it frosted in the University of South Carolina's team colors of garnet red and black.

Which, while not the least bit flattering to her attendants' sea-foam green dresses, at least wasn't nearly as bad as the groom's cake shaped like a retriever her aunt Dixie's duck-hunting third husband had chosen for their wedding last month.

"How about I give the guys gift certificates for lap dances at that new place that opened across the county line last week?"

"How about not. And it's interesting that you'd know about it so soon."

"We got called to a fire opening night, but the sprinklers had pretty much taken care of things before we arrived." Another waggle of brows. "Guess those girls are really hot."

Tess shook her head and refused to return that sexy, rakish grin. "I doubt either of our mothers would approve of strippers as gifts. Mom made up a list of suggestions."

She retrieved the three-by-five card from her purse and handed it to him.

"Money clips?" he asked. "Pocket watches? Silver flasks engraved with our wedding date? Who thinks up this stuff?"

"Mom says they're traditional."

"They also sound like something a girly groom would buy. When was the last time you saw a firefighter with an engraved sterling silver flask?"

How about never? "Do you have a better idea?"

"Sure. I'll get each of the guys a box of cigars."

He wadded up the paper and tossed it into the wastepaper basket across the room, showing that seven years after graduation, he still had the moves that had made him the top-scoring high school forward in South Carolina.

"Problem solved." He touched a finger to his tongue and made a mark in the air. "You can cross one more item off your to-do list, sugarplum."

"Cigars are okay," Tess decided. "So long as no one smokes them inside at the reception."

She might have been dragging her feet about all

this wedding stuff, but there was no way she was going to let a bunch of drunk firefighters light up stink sticks anywhere around her lovely tulle, pearl-studded Vera Wang knockoff wedding dress.

As she drove to the firehouse, Tess decided that wedding hassles aside, she was a lucky woman. She was in love with a fabulous guy who loved her back, she had the exciting career she'd always dreamed of, and by this time next year, if everything went according to plan, she'd be a mother.

Life couldn't get much better than that.

Two great books—
one great price!

Each book features two classics
by your favorite authors together
in one collectible volume!

Coast Road • Three Wishes
Barbara Delinsky

The Taming • The Conquest
Jude Deveraux

Twin of Ice • Twin of Fire
Jude Deveraux

Velvet Song • Velvet Angel
Jude Deveraux

Angel Creek • A Lady of the West
Linda Howard

Shades of Twilight • Son of the Morning
Linda Howard

Guardian Angel • The Gift
Julie Garwood

Castles • The Lion's Lady
Julie Garwood

Honey Moon • Hot Shot
Susan Elizabeth Phillips

Scandalous • Irresistible
Karen Robards

Homeplace • Far Harbor
JoAnn Ross

The Callahan Brothers Trilogy
JoAnn Ross